Noelle Stevenson • Grace Ellis • Shannon Watters • Brooklyn Allen

LUMBERJANES™

TO THE MAX EDITION

VOLUME ONE

BOOM! BOX™

LUMBERJANES TO THE MAX EDITION Volume One, September 2018. Published by BOOM! Box, a division of Boom Entertainment, Inc. Lumberjanes is ™ & © 2018 Shannon Watters, Grace Ellis, Noelle Stevenson & Brooklyn Allen. Originally published in single magazine form as LUMBERJANES No. 1-8. ™ & © 2014 Shannon Watters, Grace Ellis, Noelle Stevenson & Brooklyn Allen. All rights reserved. BOOM! Box™ and the BOOM! Box logo are trademarks of Boom Entertainment, Inc., registered in various countries and categories. All characters, events, and institutions depicted herein are fictional. Any similarity between any of the names, characters, persons, events, and/or institutions in this publication to actual names, characters, and persons, whether living or dead, events, and/or institutions is unintended and purely coincidental. BOOM! Box does not read or accept unsolicited submissions of ideas, stories, or artwork.

BOOM! Studios, 5670 Wilshire Boulevard, Suite 400, Los Angeles, CA 90036-5679. Printed in China. Second Printing.

ISBN: 978-1-60886-809-4, eISBN: 978-1-61398-480-2

THIS LUMBERJANES FIELD MANUAL BELONGS TO:

NAME:_____

TROOP:_____

DATE INVESTED:_____

FIELD MANUAL TABLE OF CONTENTS

LUMBERJANES
FIELD MANUAL

For the Advanced Program

Tenth Edition • February 1984

Prepared for the

**Miss Qiunzella Thiskwin
Penniquiqul Thistle Crumpet's**
CAMP FOR  HARDCORE
LADY-TYPES

"Friendship to the Max!"

A MESSAGE FROM THE LUMBERJANES HIGH COUNCIL

Miss Qiunzella Thiskwin
Penniquiqul Thistle Crumpet's
Camp for
HARDCORE LADY TYPES
FRIENDSHIP to the MAX!

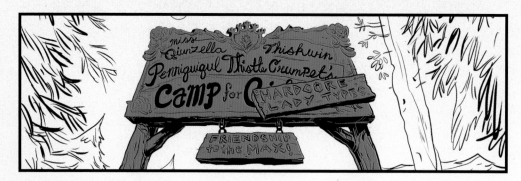

"Life is full of surprises." It's a saying that is repeated often enough that most don't give it a second thought as they move forward on their path. The Lumberjanes was a surprise, the best sort, but a surprise nonetheless.

It started out as an idea between close friends, sisters, who traveled many roads together and even more separate. It was the smallest flicker of an idea, of a hope, to create something that would not only unite young ladies but would teach the upcoming generations lessons that they would carry with them for the rest of their lives. How were they to know that it would grow into something so much bigger than themselves?

At this Lumberjane camp, we strive to push each young lady to the fullest. To give her the tools and training so that when she has an idea, no matter how small, she'll be able to find the courage she already has inside herself to share it with the world. In this advanced program you will have the opportunity to not only see many strange and new things, but to experience a whole new world, maybe even literally. This handbook will guide you, but at the end of the day it will be up to you and the amazing gifts that you already possess.

No matter what happens, no matter how the world changes, always know that you can do anything. If a group of girls can take their small idea and turn it into something to inspire even just one more person, then you have the ability to do the same, if not more. It is your hard work that will guide you, your consciousness that will keep you clear, and your strength that will keep one foot in front of the other. It will be you who watches the sun rise and set on your journey, with your closest friends with you as support in either body or mind. We look forward to seeing where this journey takes you, and we can't wait to see you on the other side.

THE LUMBERJANES PLEDGE

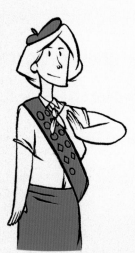

I solemnly swear to do my best
Every day, and in all that I do,
To be brave and strong,
To be truthful and compassionate,
To be interesting and interested,
To pay attention and question
The world around me,
To think of others first,
To always help and protect my friends,
[redacted]
And to make the world a better place
For Lumberjane scouts
And for everyone else.

THEN THERE'S A LINE ABOUT GOD, OR WHATEVER

LUMBERJANES™
TO THE MAX EDITION

Created by **Shannon Watters, Grace Ellis, Noelle Stevenson & Brooklyn Allen**

Written by
Noelle Stevenson & Grace Ellis

Illustrated by
Brooklyn Allen

Colors by
Maarta Laiho

Letters by
Aubrey Aiese

Design by
Scott Newman

"A Girl And Her Raptor"
Written by
Noelle Stevenson & Shannon Watters
Illustrated by
Carey Pietsch

Character Designs by
Noelle Stevenson & Brooklyn Allen

Badge Designs by
Kate Leth & Scott Newman

Associate Editor
Whitney Leopard

Editor
Dafna Pleban

Special thanks to **Kelsey Pate** *for giving the Lumberjanes their name.*

FRIENDSHIP TO THE MAX!

LUMBERJANES FIELD MANUAL
FOREWORD

I joined the Girl Scouts when I was nine. Other than the cool green outfit (including a sweet beret!!), I was excited for camaraderie, badges, and most importantly, camping.

In San Francisco, "summer camp" was a strange experience: there were the usual bonfires, s'mores, latrine duty, and singing of Taps as the flag came down at the end of the day. But we did it all in the cold. July afternoons usually topped out at about 57 degrees on the wooded hillsides of Camp Ida Smith, just a few miles inland from perpetually foggy Ocean Beach. We huddled up against the wind in our parkas. We slept under the "stars," which meant waking up to our sleeping bags covered in moisture from the low cloudy sky. The counselors served us hot cocoa at high noon. We really needed those bonfires.

And yet, the camaraderie was there. Throw a group of adolescent girls together for a week in the summer, and anything was possible. Friendships and alliances were fought for and won, territory was claimed and defended, and we made a lot of lanyards along the way. Years later, I'd find myself post-college, laughing over dinner with my old Girl Scout camp friends and their own sons and daughters. We never fought a yeti or played tag with a Greek goddess, but the bonds between my fellow campers and I were just as real as the ones forged between Mal, Jo, Molly, April, and Ripley. And Joan…Jane…Jamie? Jen, it's Jen.

Shannon, Noelle, Grace, and Brooklyn have dreamed up an incredible ensemble of characters, and whether or not the cast is all female isn't even a thing. It just is. The girls play every role, and serve every story need, just as girls do together in real life. Mal and Molly make me swoon. Jo makes me think. April makes me want to get up and fight for my friends. And Ripley makes me want to be the coolest, spazzed out, butt-kicking girl at camp. If Friendship to the Max is what summer camp is all about, the Lumberjanes have maxed it out in spades.

It's cool to live in a world where young girls are lining up to meet the creators of their favorite books at comic conventions, and making sure that those books land on bestseller lists, win major awards, and get shelved face-out at bookstores. It's awesome to live in a time where a kid can get sucked into a series, finish it, and demand something more—and there's more to recommend. It's a great time to be making and reading comics, period, and I think these hard-core lady types (by which I am referring to both the creators, and the Lumberjanes themselves) will go down in history as paving the way for many more cartoonists in generations to come.

So grab your parka and your finest marshmallow-roasting stick, turn your back to the wind, and dig in. With the Lumberjanes, anything is possible.

RAINA TELGEMEIER
#1 New York Times bestselling author of
Smile, Sisters, and *Drama*

LUMBERJANES FIELD MANUAL

CHAPTER ONE

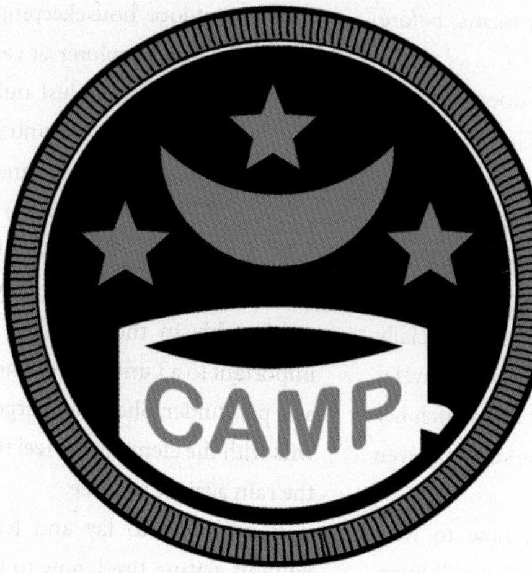
CAMP

Lumberjanes "Out-of-Doors" Program Field

UP ALL NIGHT BADGE

"Learn what goes bump in the night."

While nature is a great experience in the light of the sun, when the majority of living creatures are out and about, a true Lumberjane knows that there is even more to experience when the sun goes down. Curiosity and courage are especially important to a Lumberjane, she has an urge to get out and match her wits and fervor with the elements, to feel the cool crisp night air or possibly the rain on her face. To witness the hyper-natural power of lightning with the true darkness that a night with no moon can provide.

A Lumberjane knows about the experience and possible truths that can be found when the rest of the world is asleep. It is the urge to learn how to lay and follow trails, identify the healing abilities of the local fauna, how to walk great distances and run even farther, and how to work around the unnatural and supernatural forces that a Lumberjane is bound to confront. The *Up All Night* badge is for the Lumberjane who has already conquered the unknown in the daylight and is ready to explore the adventure of the night, ready to discover how to use all the ways of getting from one place to another. A Lumberjane is able to enjoy all of the known and unknown things that can be found in their world.

To obtain the *Up All Night* badge a Lumberjane must have enjoyed the sunset on a cool crisp afternoon with a group of cherished friends. She must have walked under the canvas of the stars and enjoyed their beauty while going where her curiosity takes her. She must have enjoyed the first wind of a new day with the moon above her head and without sleep, energetically exploring the new possibility of viewing the world under a moon. And her final step to obtaining this particular badge, is she must have enjoyed the sunset of the new day surrounded by her friends and ready to start

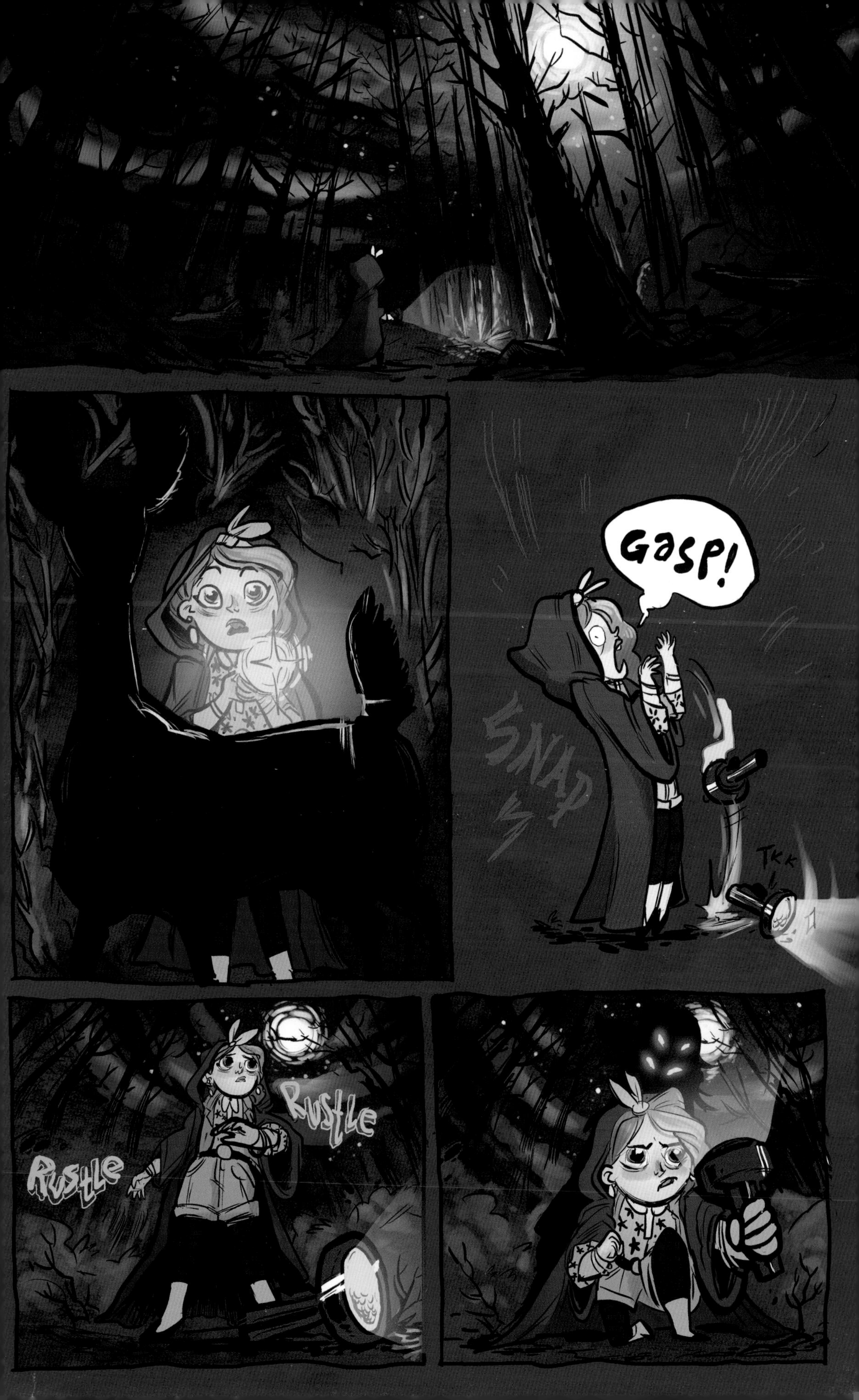
Gasp!
SNAP
TKK
Rustle
Rustle

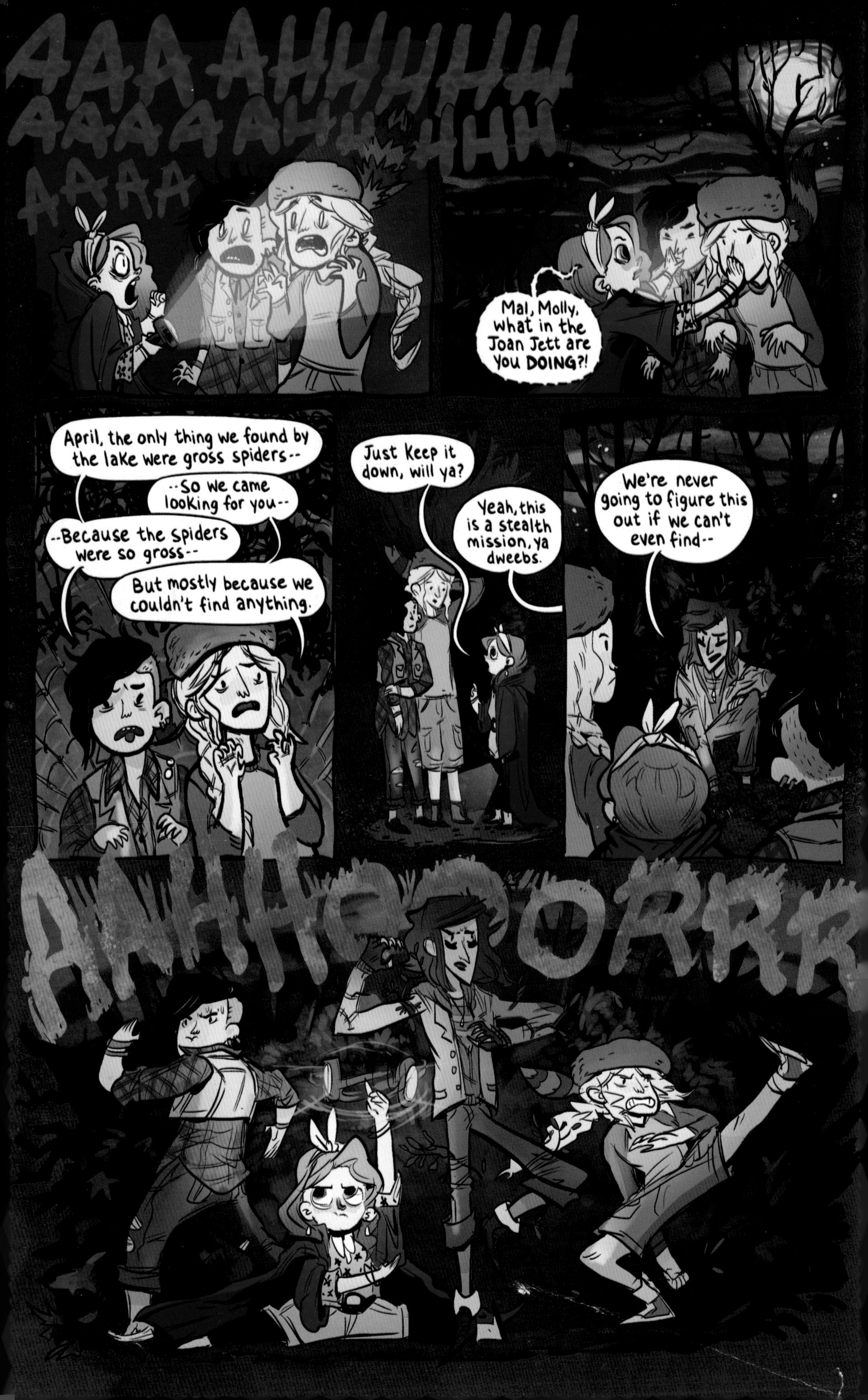

AAAAHHHHHH
AAAAAHHHHHH
AAAA
Mal, Molly, what in the Joan Jett are you DOING?!
April, the only thing we found by the lake were gross spiders--
--So we came looking for you--
--Because the spiders were so gross--
But mostly because we couldn't find anything.
Just keep it down, will ya?
Yeah, this is a stealth mission, ya dweebs.
We're never going to figure this out if we can't even find--
AAHHOOORRR

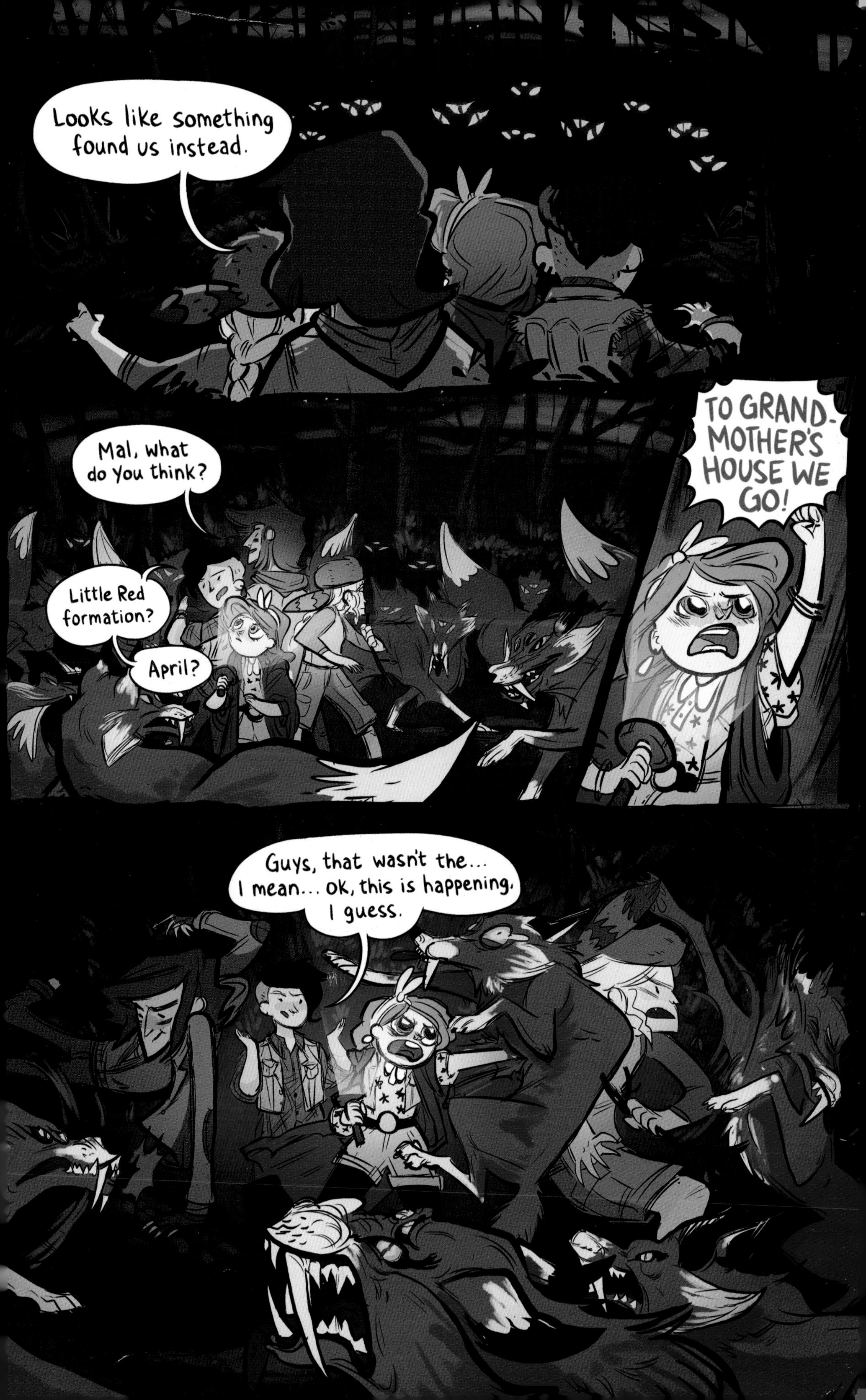
Looks like something found us instead.
Mal, what do you think?
Little Red formation?
April?
TO GRAND-MOTHER'S HOUSE WE GO!
Guys, that wasn't the... I mean... ok, this is happening, I guess.

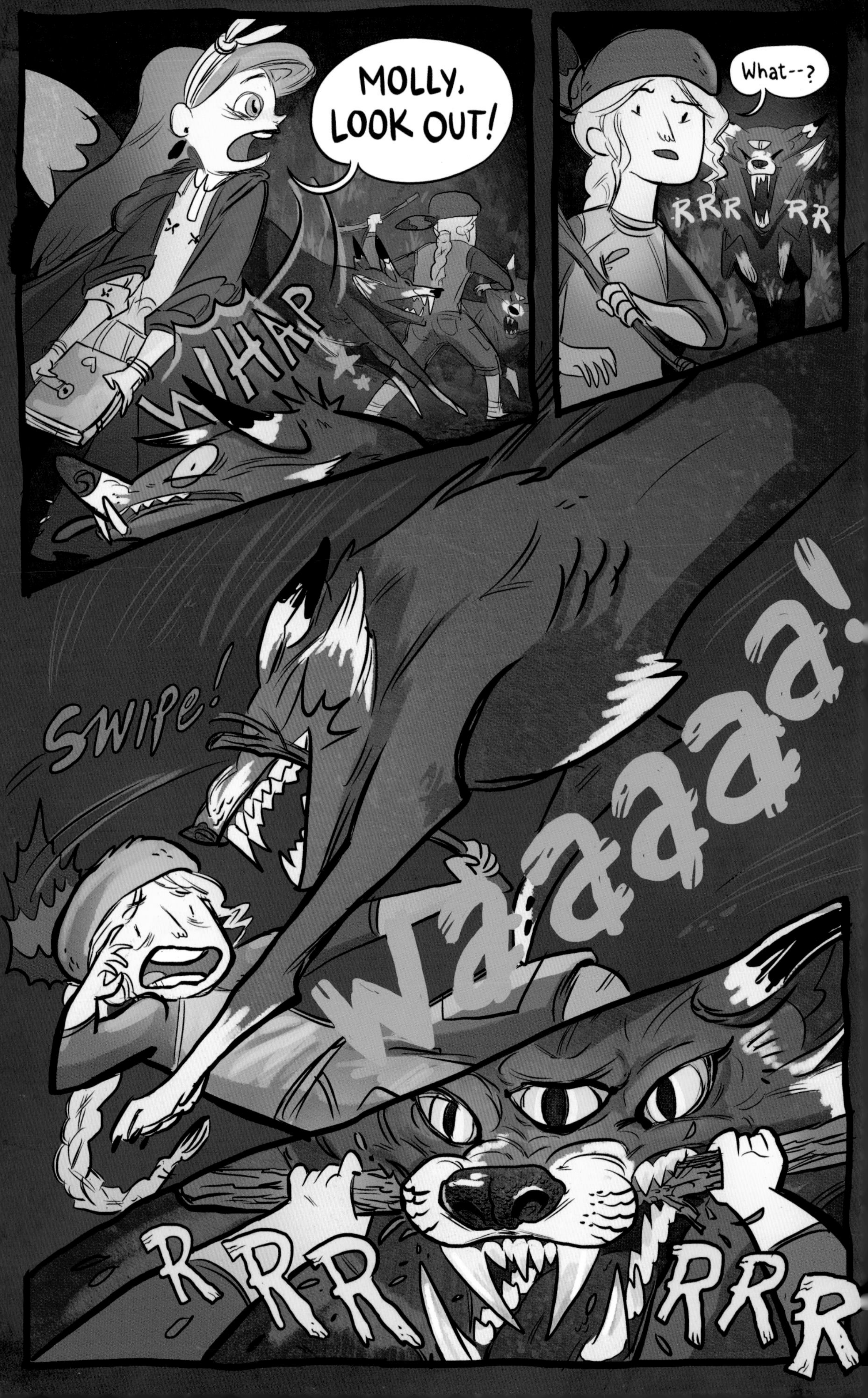
MOLLY, LOOK OUT!
WHAP
What--?
RRR RR
SWIPE!
Waaaaa!
RRR RRRR

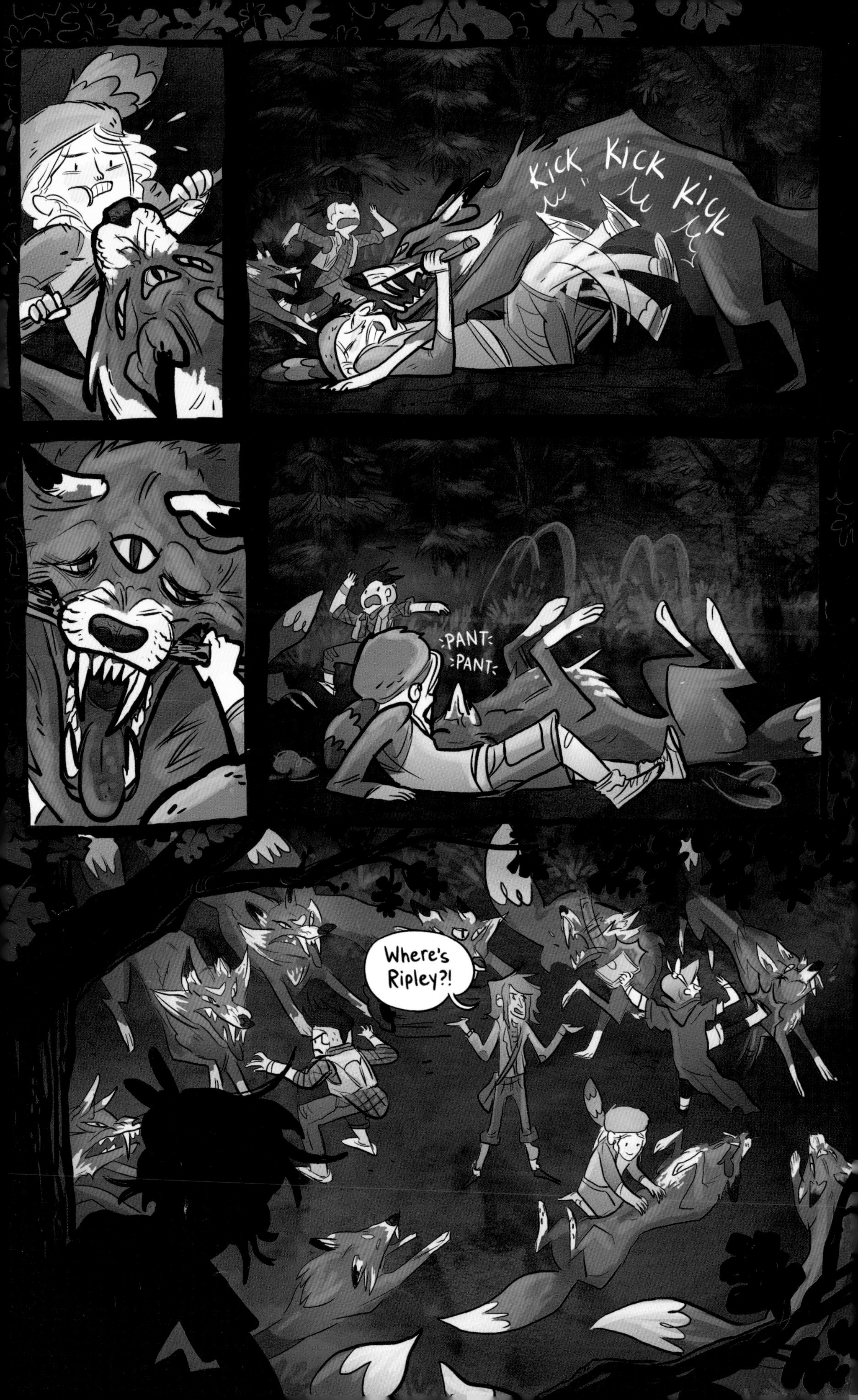
KICK KICK KICK
PANT
PANT
Where's Ripley?!

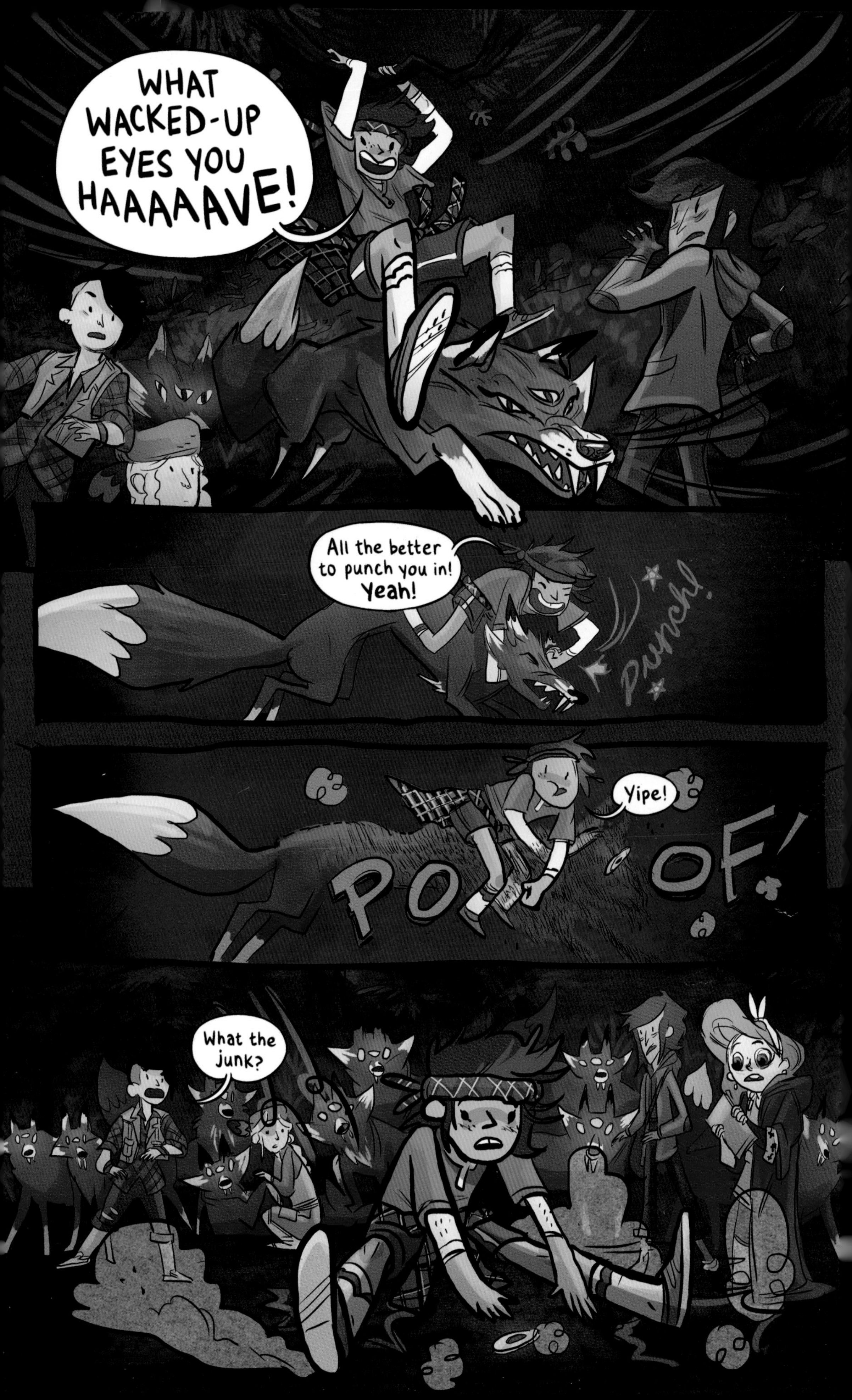
WHAT WACKED-UP EYES YOU HAAAAAVE!
All the better to punch you in! Yeah!
Punch!
Yipe!
POOF!
What the junk?

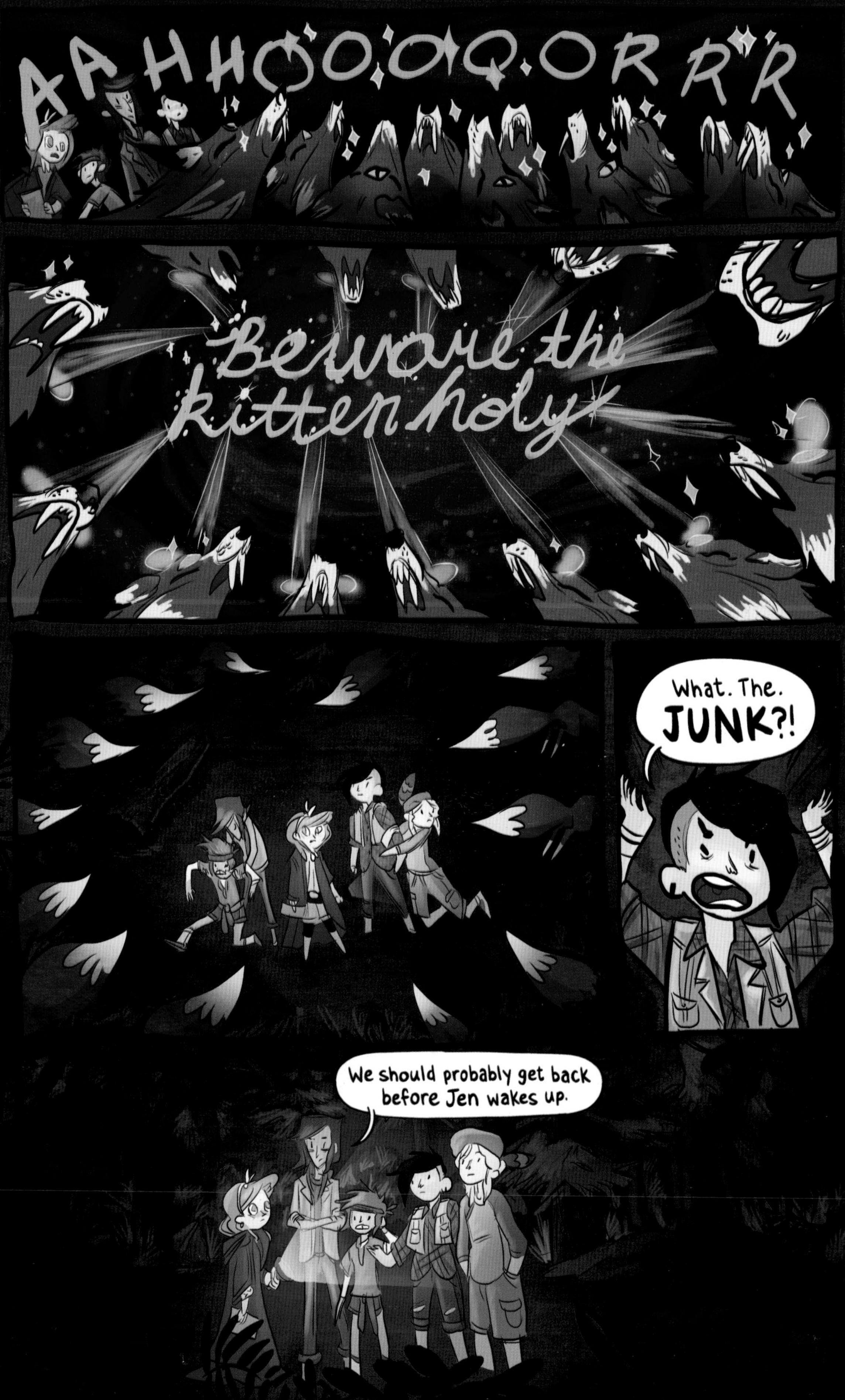
AAHHOOOOORRR
Beware the kitten holy
What. The. JUNK?!
We should probably get back before Jen wakes up.

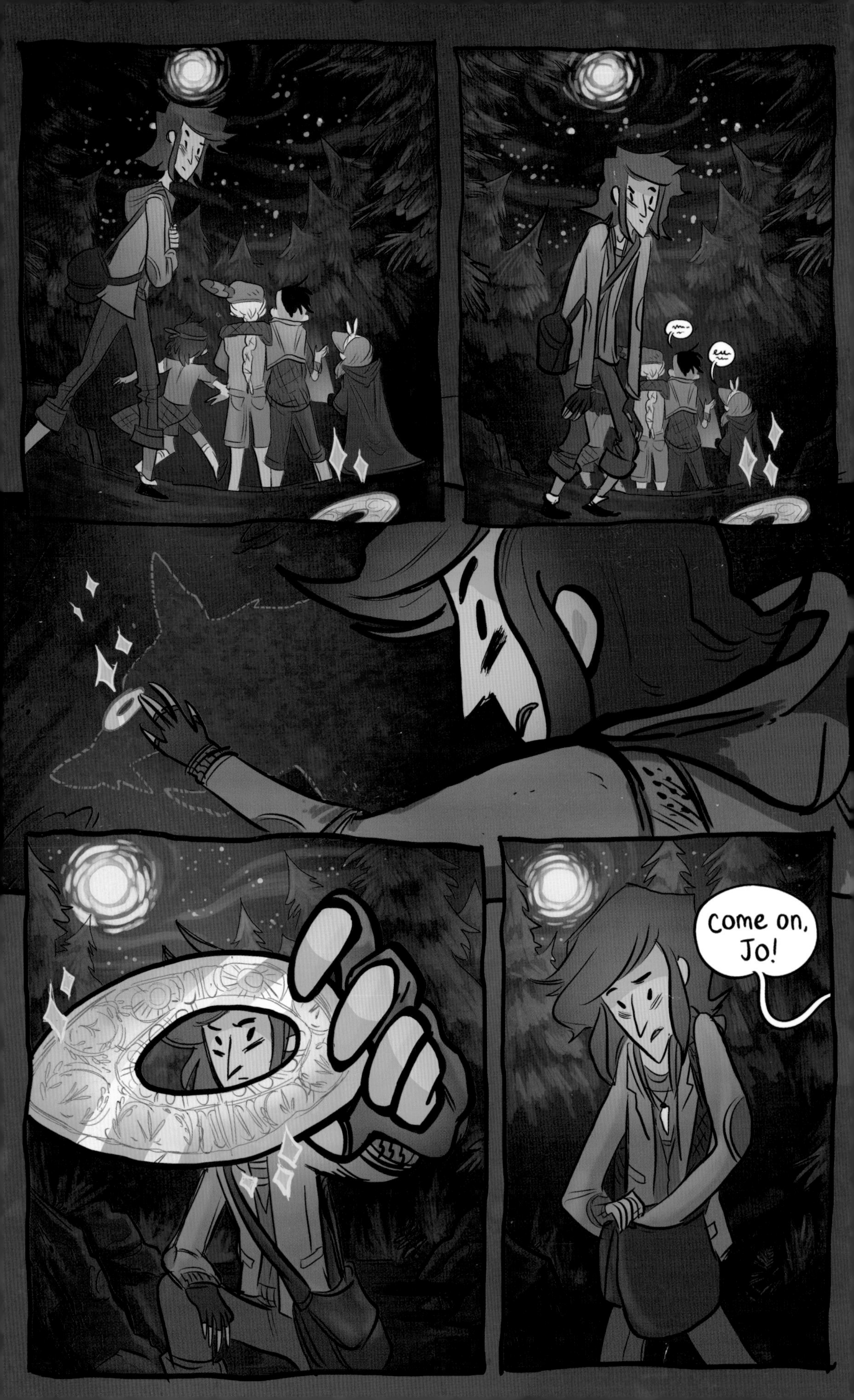
Come on, Jo!

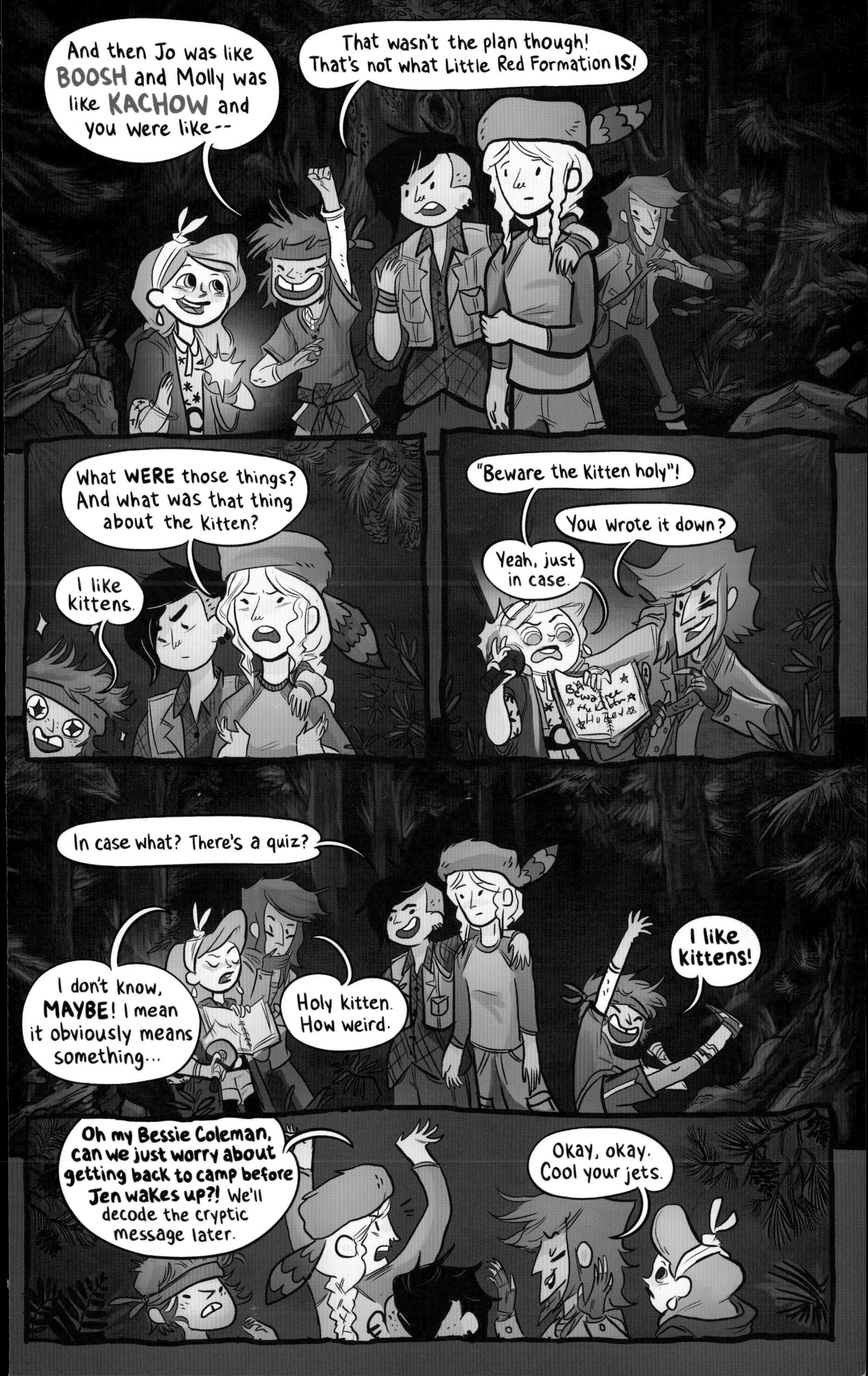
And then Jo was like BOOSH and Molly was like KACHOW and you were like--
That wasn't the plan though! That's not what Little Red Formation IS!
What WERE those things? And what was that thing about the kitten?
I like kittens.
"Beware the kitten holy"!
You wrote it down?
Yeah, just in case.
In case what? There's a quiz?
I don't know, MAYBE! I mean it obviously means something...
Holy kitten. How weird.
I like kittens!
Oh my Bessie Coleman, can we just worry about getting back to camp before Jen wakes up?! We'll decode the cryptic message later.
Okay, okay. Cool your jets.

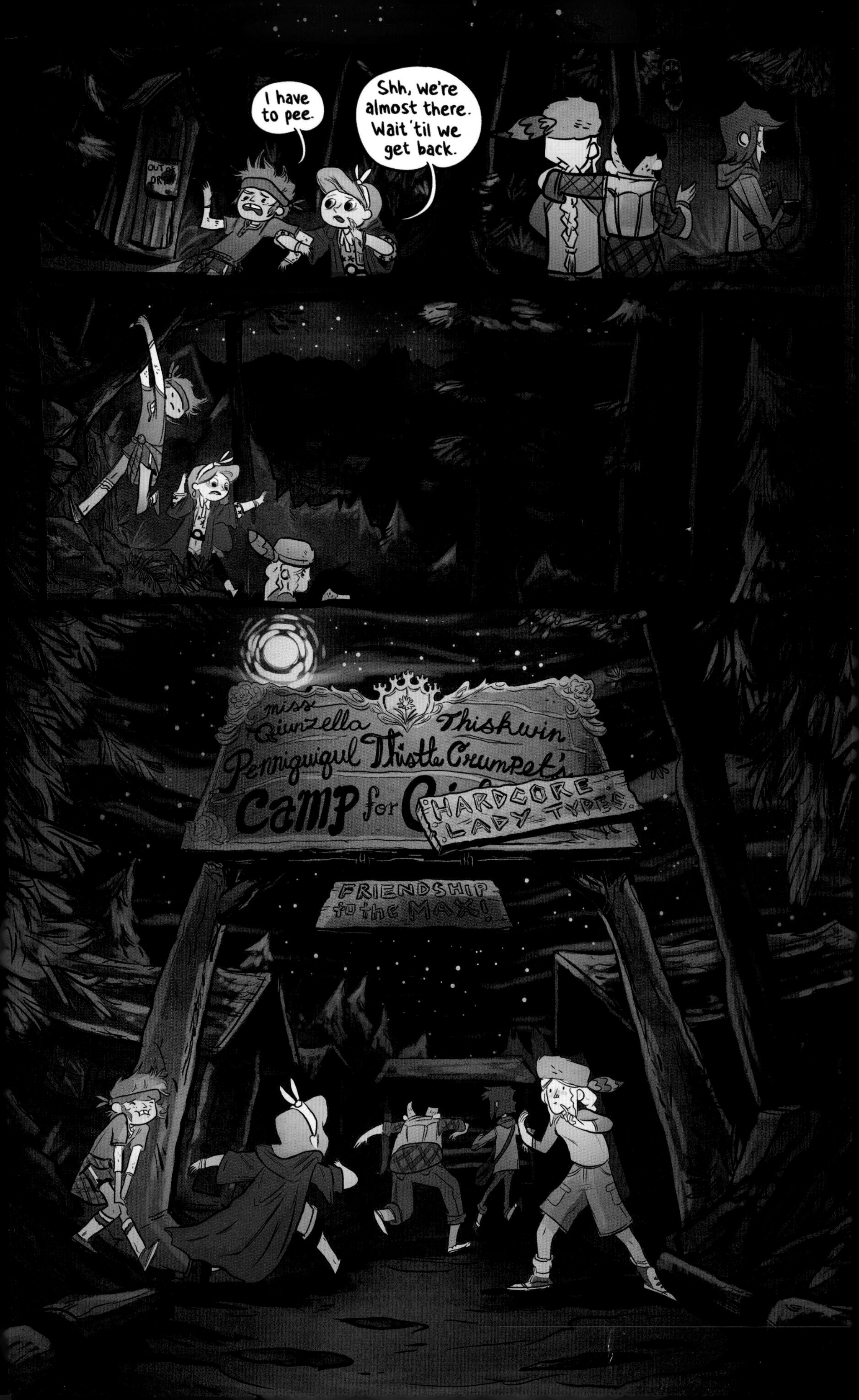
I have to pee.
Shh, we're almost there. Wait 'til we get back.
miss Quinzella Thiskwin Penniquiqul Thistle Crumpet's Camp for
HARDCORE LADY TYPES
FRIENDSHIP to the MAX!

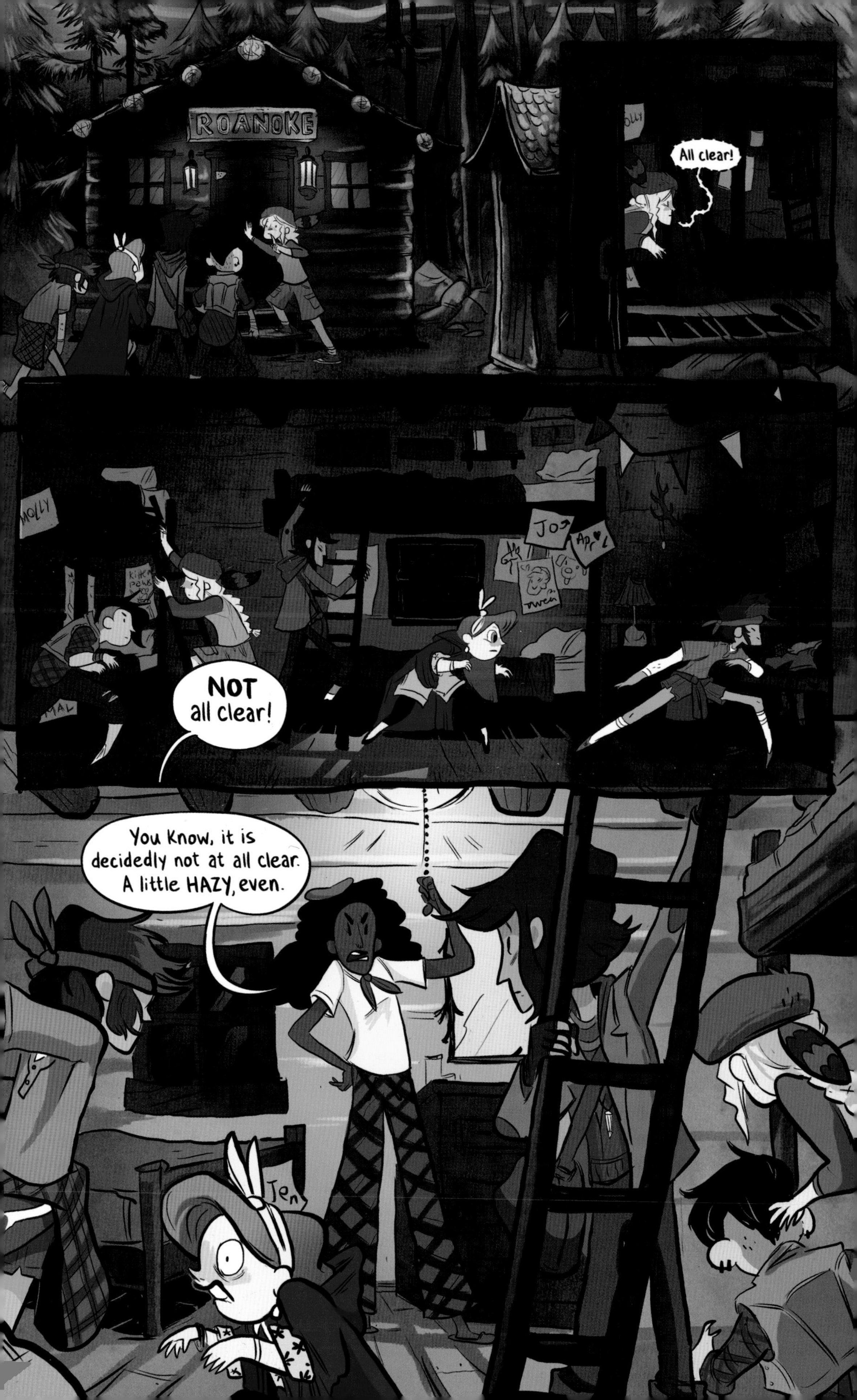
ROANOKE
All clear!
MOLLY
JO
April
kitten pews
TWEEN
MAL
NOT all clear!
You know, it is decidedly not at all clear. A little HAZY, even.
Jen

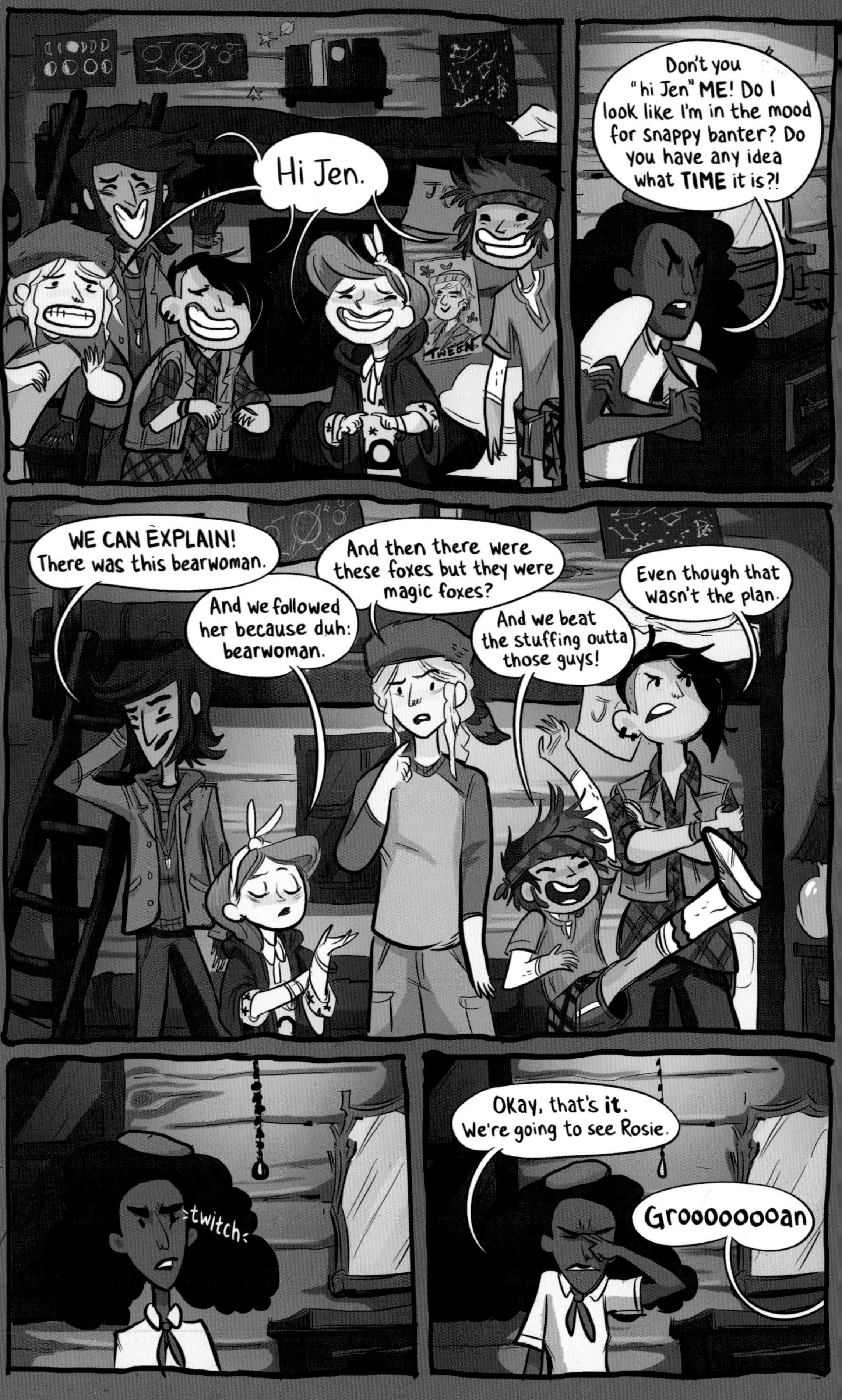
Hi Jen.
Don't you "hi Jen" ME! Do I look like I'm in the mood for snappy banter? Do you have any idea what TIME it is?!
TWEEN
WE CAN EXPLAIN! There was this bearwoman.
And we followed her because duh: bearwoman.
And then there were these foxes but they were magic foxes?
And we beat the stuffing outta those guys!
Even though that wasn't the plan.
twitch
Okay, that's it. We're going to see Rosie.
Groooooooan

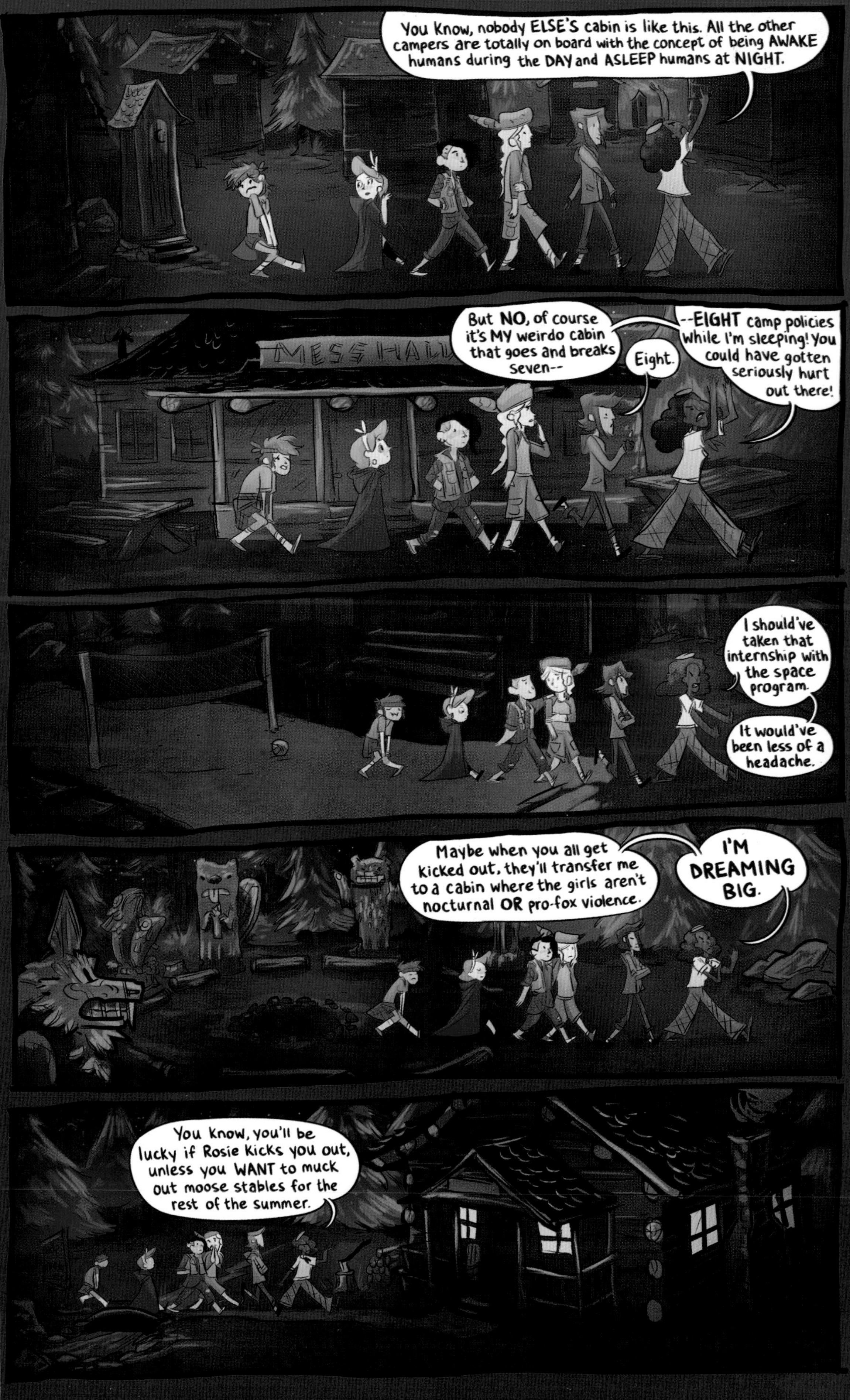
You know, nobody ELSE'S cabin is like this. All the other campers are totally on board with the concept of being AWAKE humans during the DAY and ASLEEP humans at NIGHT.
MESS HALL
But NO, of course it's MY weirdo cabin that goes and breaks seven--
Eight.
--EIGHT camp policies while I'm sleeping! You could have gotten seriously hurt out there!
I should've taken that internship with the space program.
It would've been less of a headache.
Maybe when you all get kicked out, they'll transfer me to a cabin where the girls aren't nocturnal OR pro-fox violence.
I'M DREAMING BIG.
You know, you'll be lucky if Rosie kicks you out, unless you WANT to muck out moose stables for the rest of the summer.

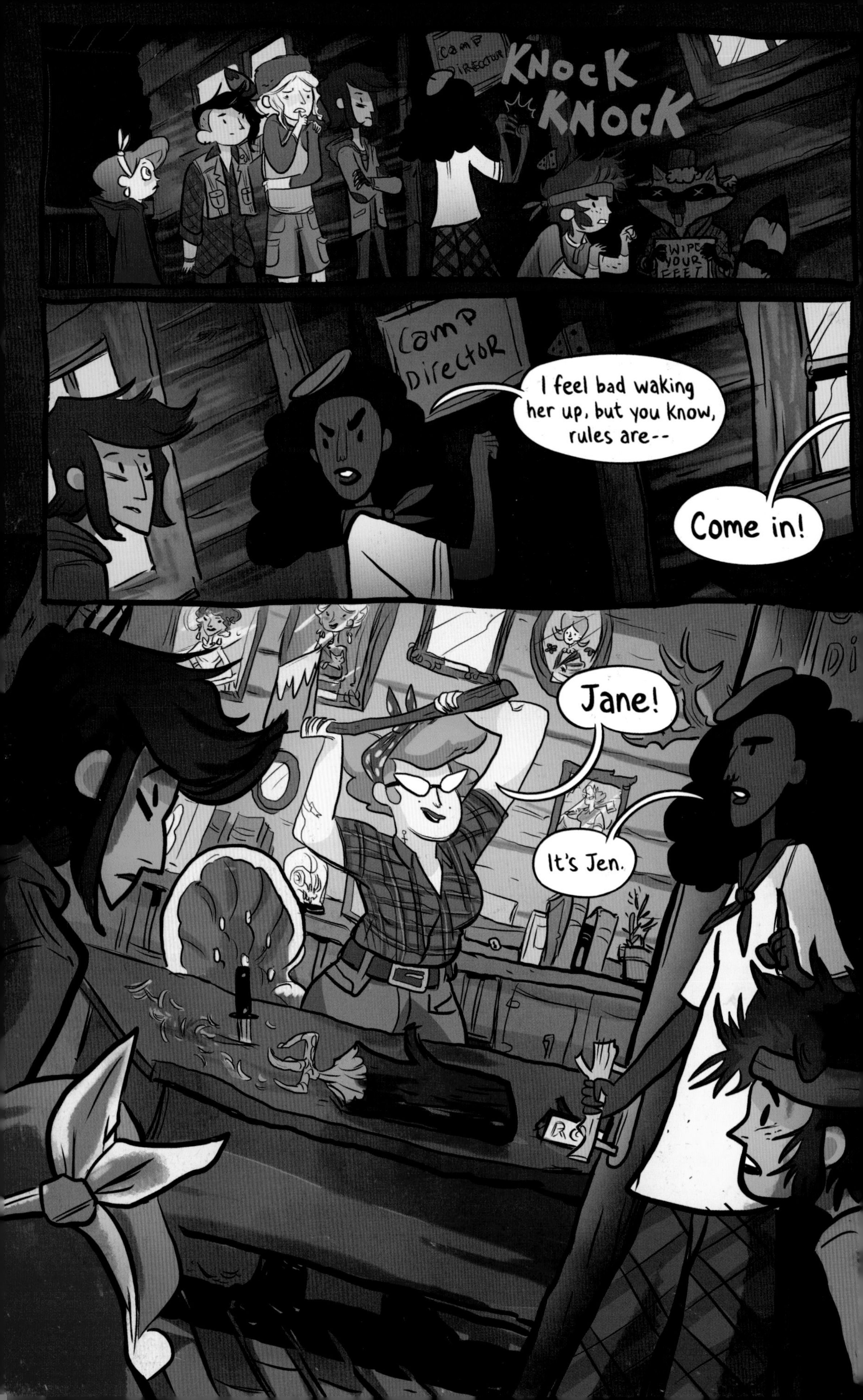
KNOCK KNOCK
CAMP DIRECTOR
WIPE YOUR FEET
CAMP DIRECTOR
I feel bad waking her up, but you know, rules are--
Come in!
Jane!
It's Jen.

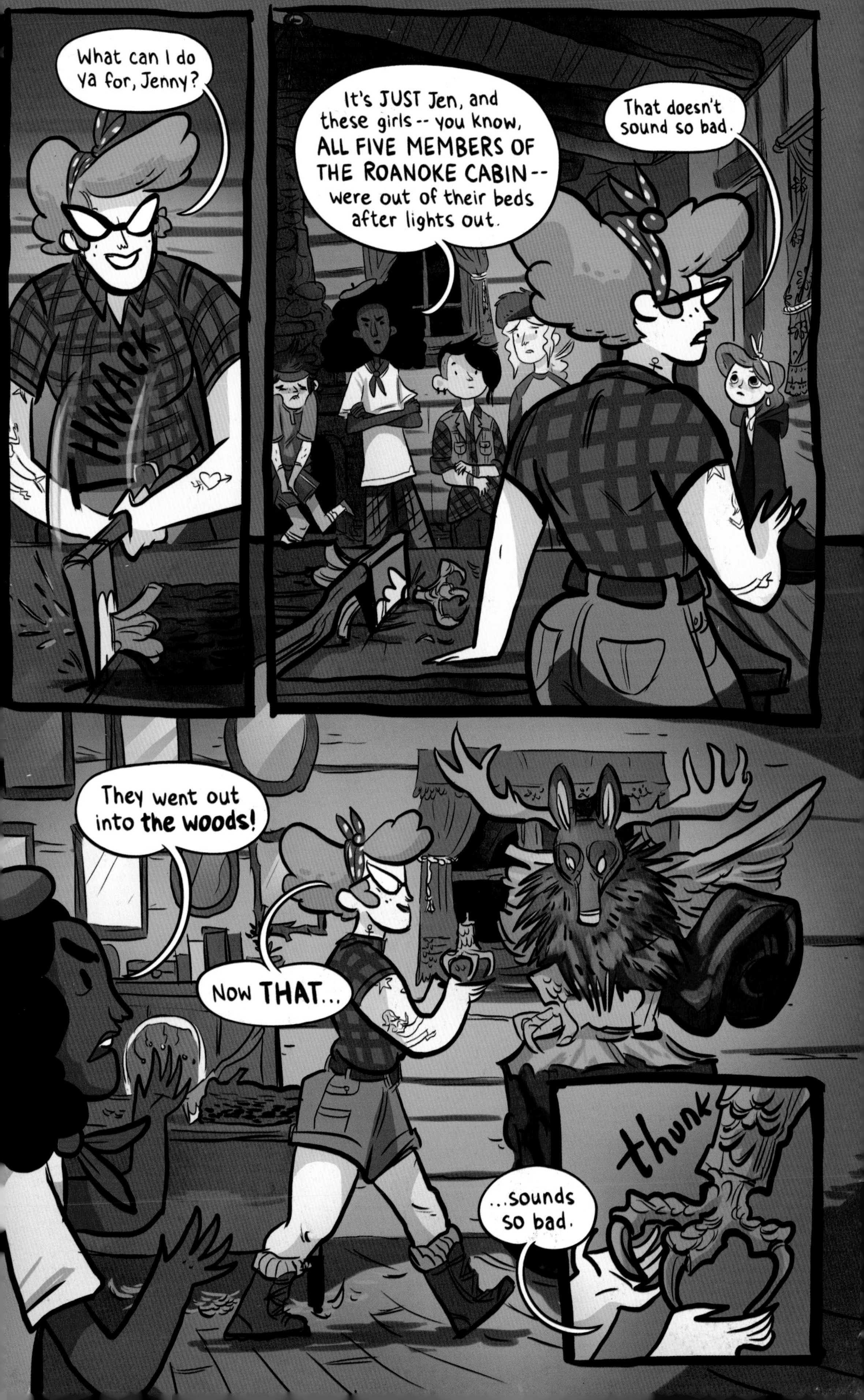
What can I do ya for, Jenny?
HWACK
It's JUST Jen, and these girls -- you know, ALL FIVE MEMBERS OF THE ROANOKE CABIN -- were out of their beds after lights out.
That doesn't sound so bad.
They went out into the woods!
Now THAT...
thunk
...sounds so bad.

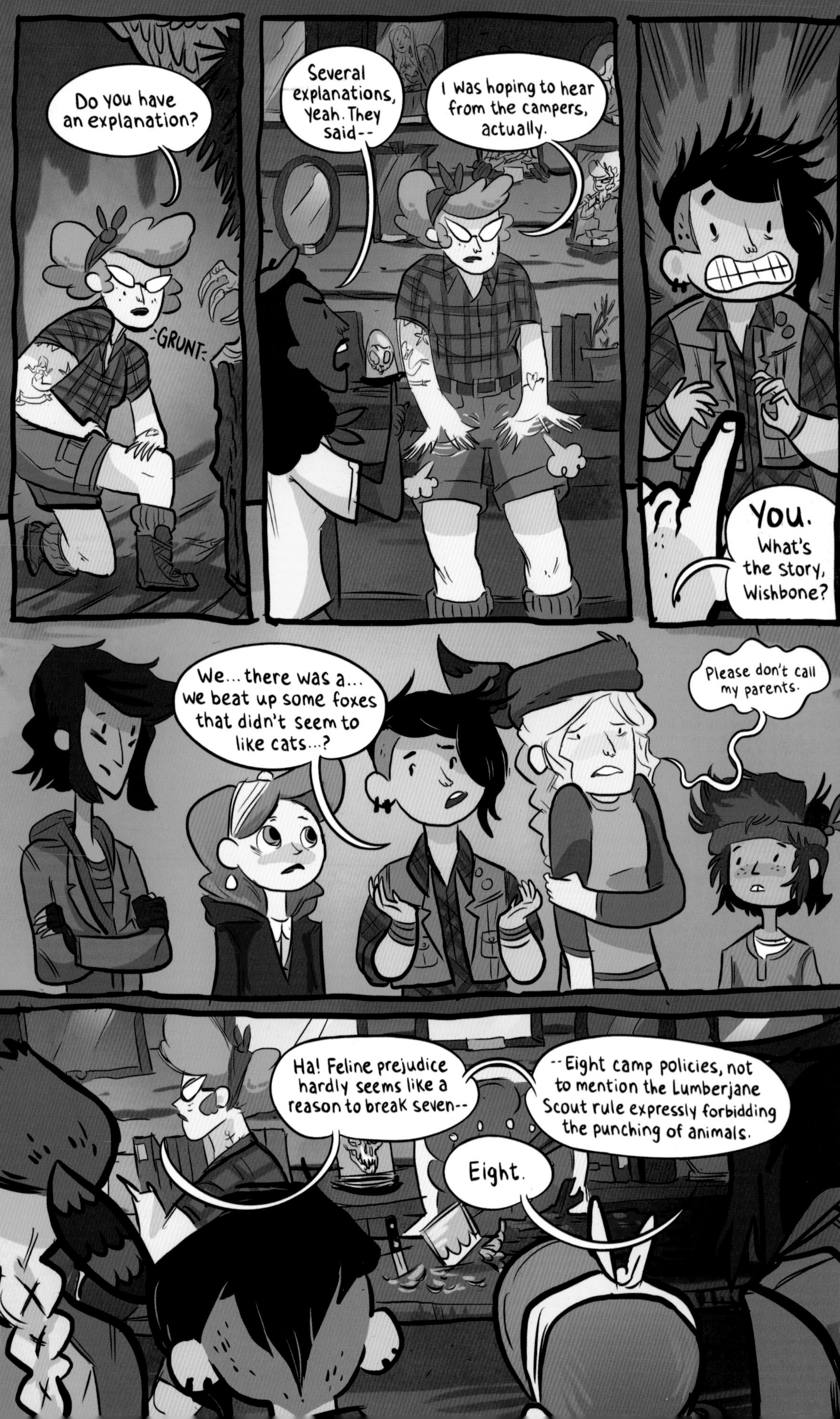
Do you have an explanation?
-GRUNT-
Several explanations, Yeah. They said--
I was hoping to hear from the campers, actually.
YOU. What's the story, Wishbone?
We... there was a... we beat up some foxes that didn't seem to like cats...?
Please don't call my parents.
Ha! Feline prejudice hardly seems like a reason to break seven--
Eight.
--Eight camp policies, not to mention the Lumberjane Scout rule expressly forbidding the punching of animals.

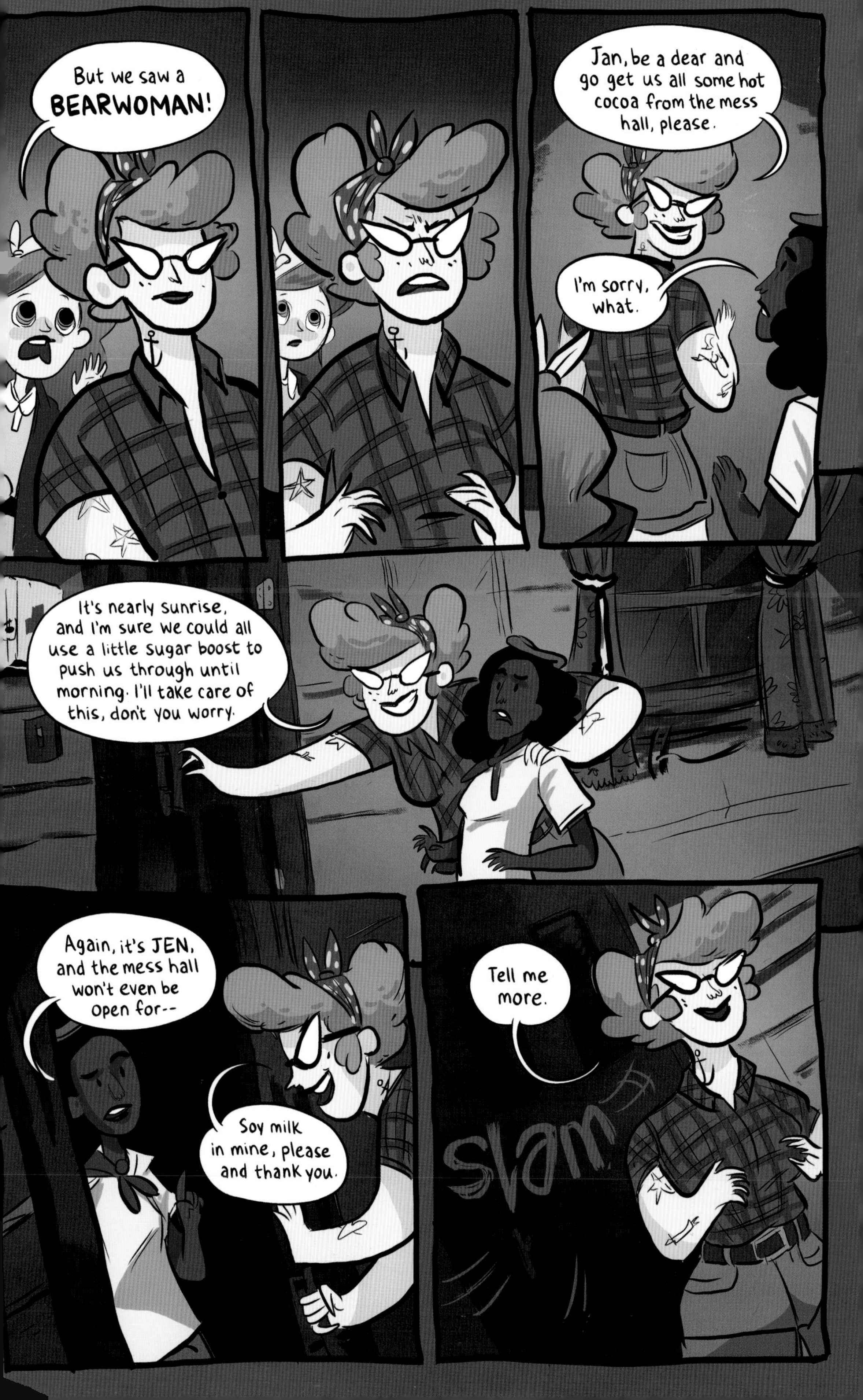
But we saw a BEARWOMAN!
Jan, be a dear and go get us all some hot cocoa from the mess hall, please.
I'm sorry, what.
It's nearly sunrise, and I'm sure we could all use a little sugar boost to push us through until morning. I'll take care of this, don't you worry.
Again, it's JEN, and the mess hall won't even be open for--
Soy milk in mine, please and thank you.
Tell me more.
SLAM

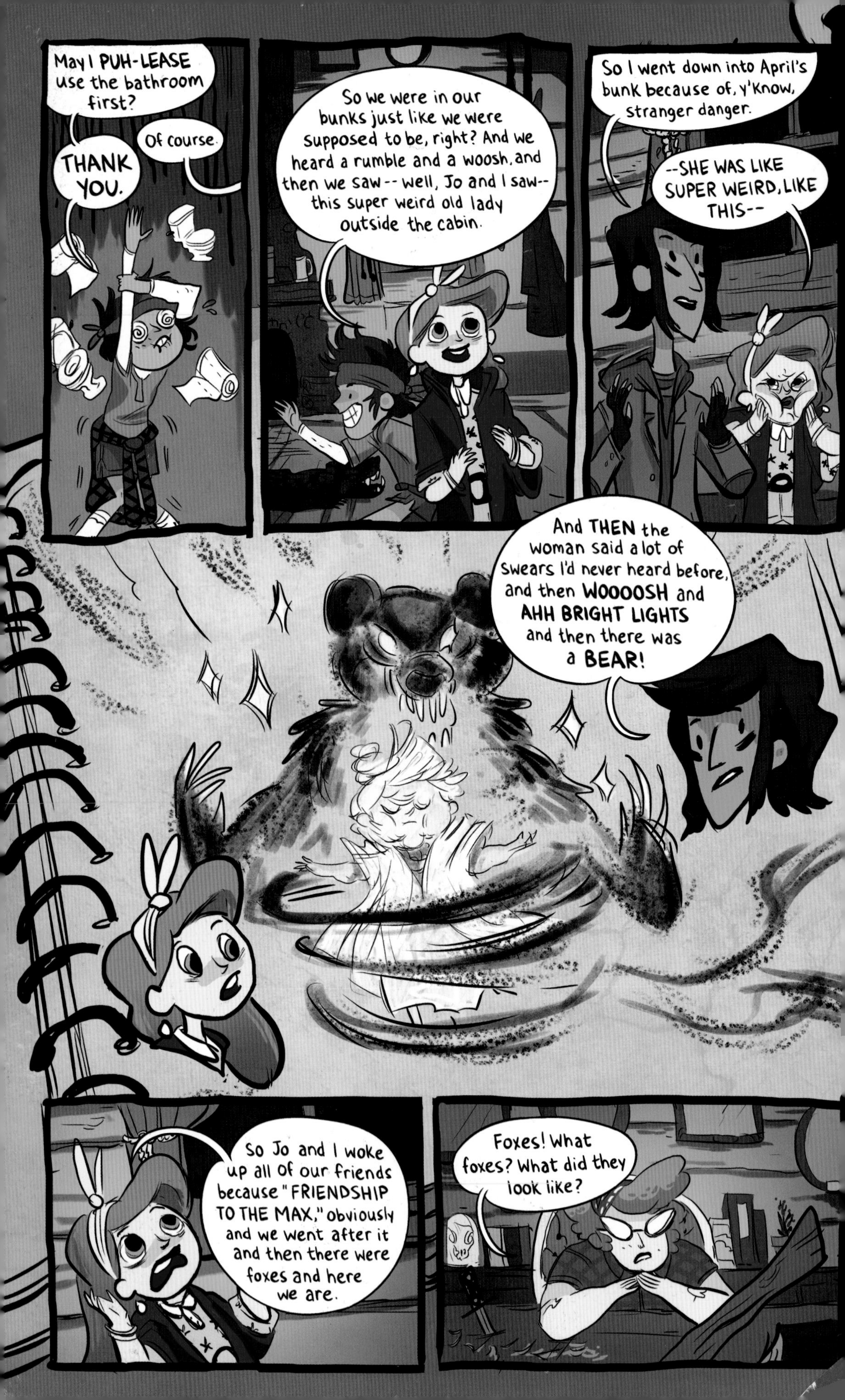
May I PUH-LEASE use the bathroom first?
Of course.
THANK YOU.
So we were in our bunks just like we were supposed to be, right? And we heard a rumble and a woosh, and then we saw -- well, Jo and I saw -- this super weird old lady outside the cabin.
So I went down into April's bunk because of, y'know, stranger danger.
--SHE WAS LIKE SUPER WEIRD, LIKE THIS--
And THEN the woman said a lot of swears I'd never heard before, and then WOOOOSH and AHH BRIGHT LIGHTS and then there was a BEAR!
So Jo and I woke up all of our friends because "FRIENDSHIP TO THE MAX," obviously and we went after it and then there were foxes and here we are.
Foxes! What foxes? What did they look like?

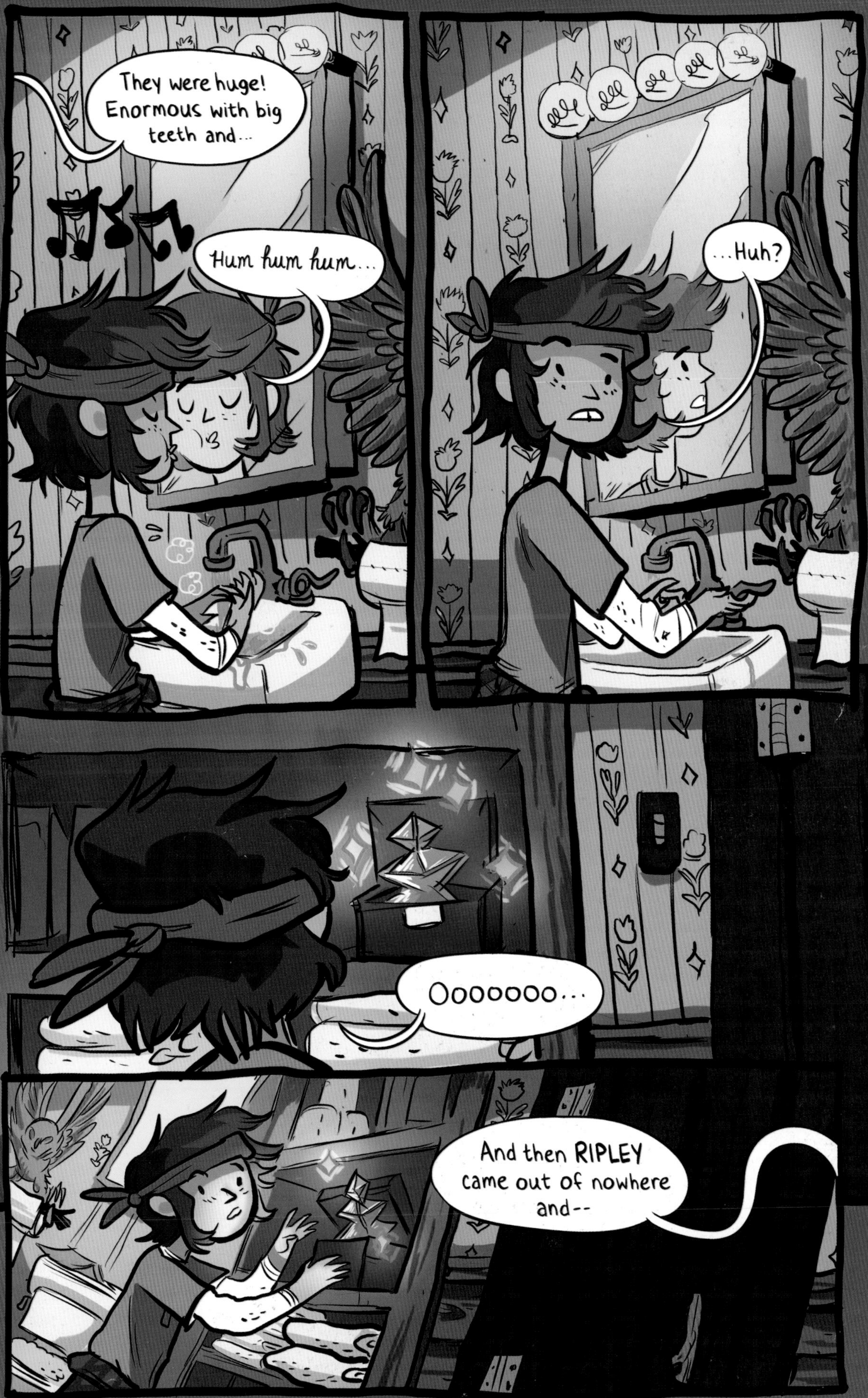
They were huge! Enormous with big teeth and...
Hum hum hum...
...Huh?
Ooooooo...
And then RIPLEY came out of nowhere and--

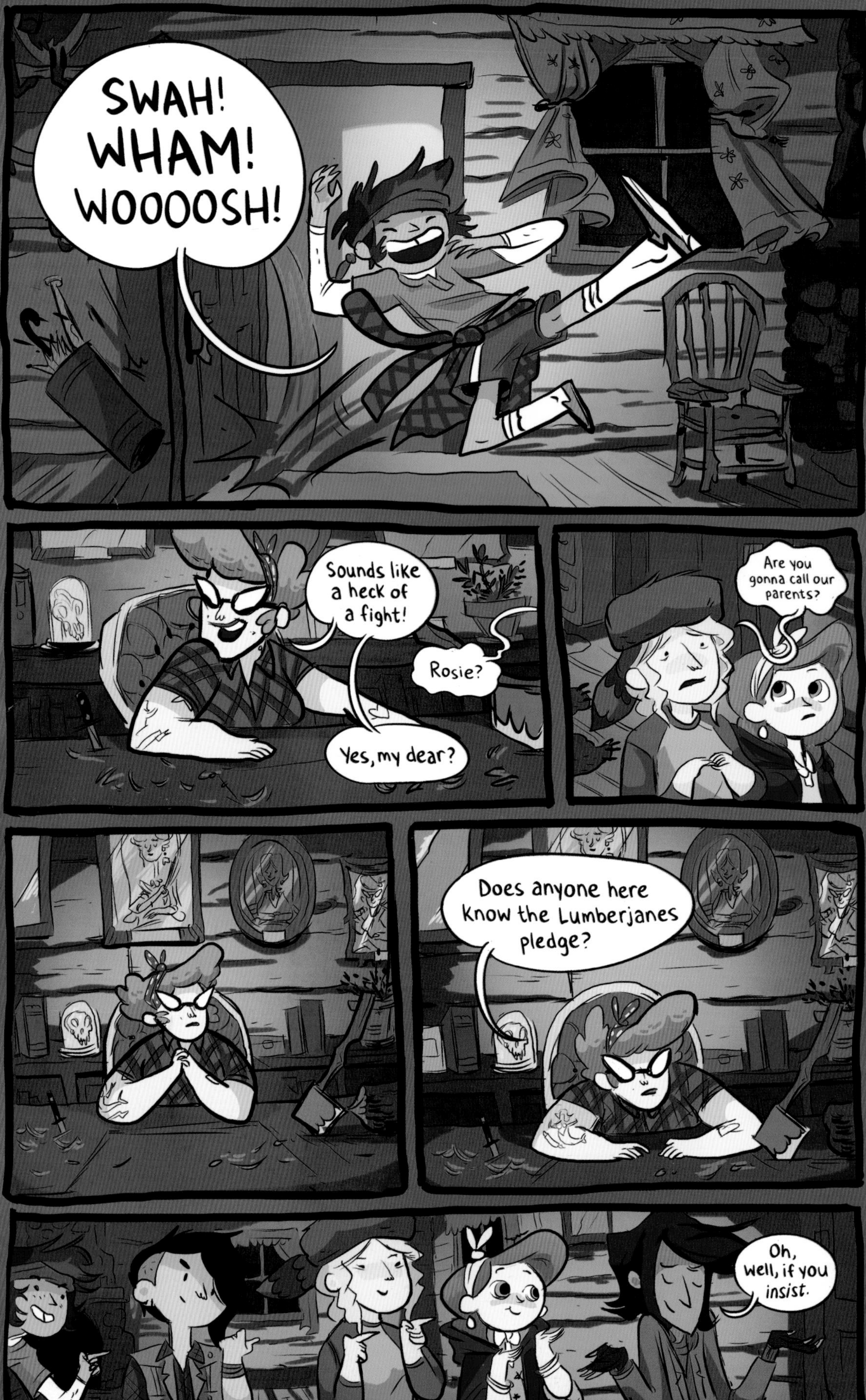
SWAH! WHAM! WOOOOSH!
Sounds like a heck of a fight!
Yes, my dear?
Rosie?
Are you gonna call our parents?
Does anyone here know the Lumberjanes pledge?
Oh, well, if you insist.

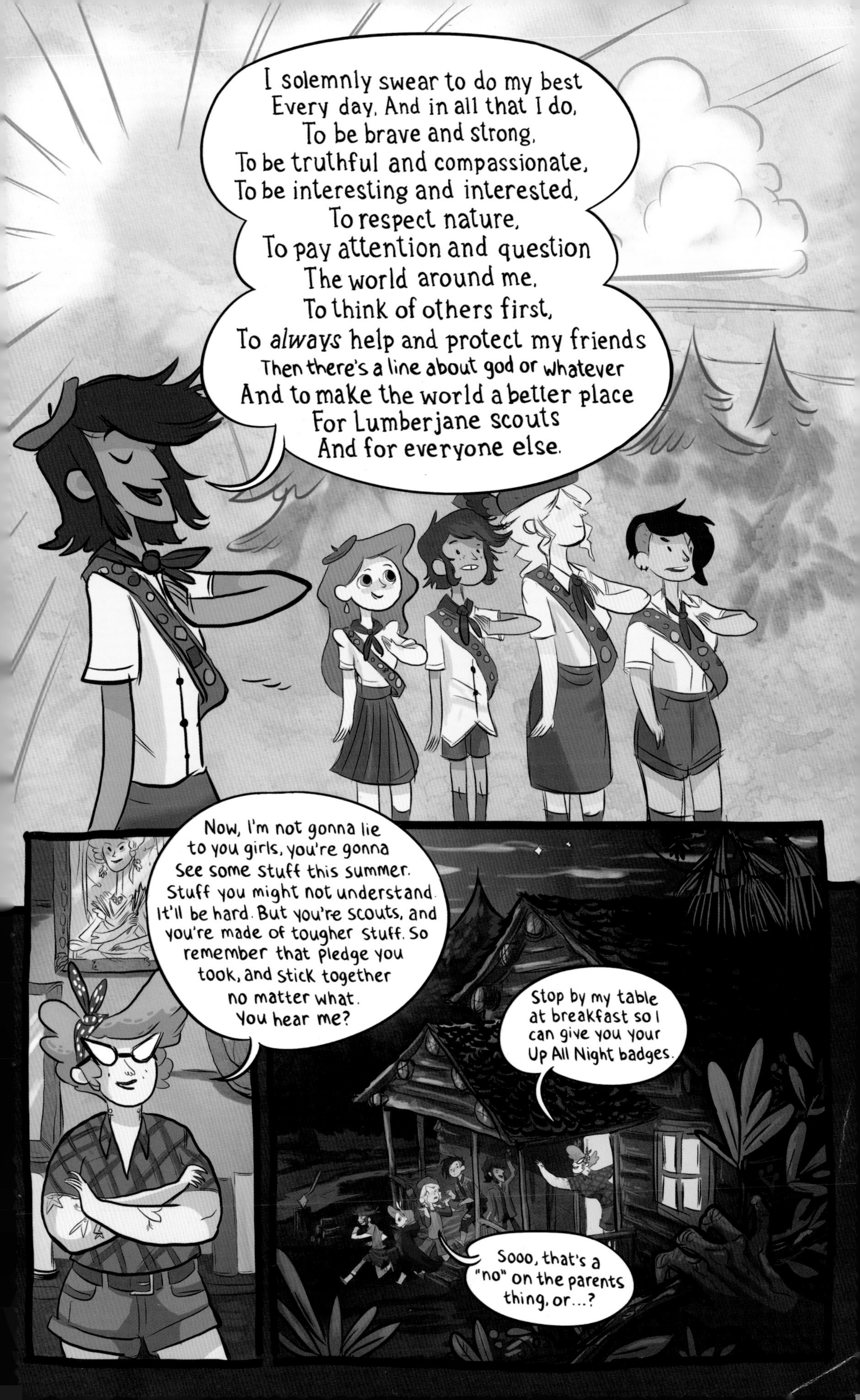
I solemnly swear to do my best
Every day, And in all that I do,
To be brave and strong,
To be truthful and compassionate,
To be interesting and interested,
To respect nature,
To pay attention and question
The world around me,
To think of others first,
To *always* help and protect my friends
Then there's a line about god or whatever
And to make the world a better place
For Lumberjane scouts
And for everyone else.
Now, I'm not gonna lie to you girls, you're gonna see some stuff this summer. Stuff you might not understand. It'll be hard. But you're scouts, and you're made of tougher stuff. So remember that pledge you took, and stick together no matter what. You hear me?
Stop by my table at breakfast so I can give you your Up All Night badges.
Sooo, that's a "no" on the parents thing, or...?

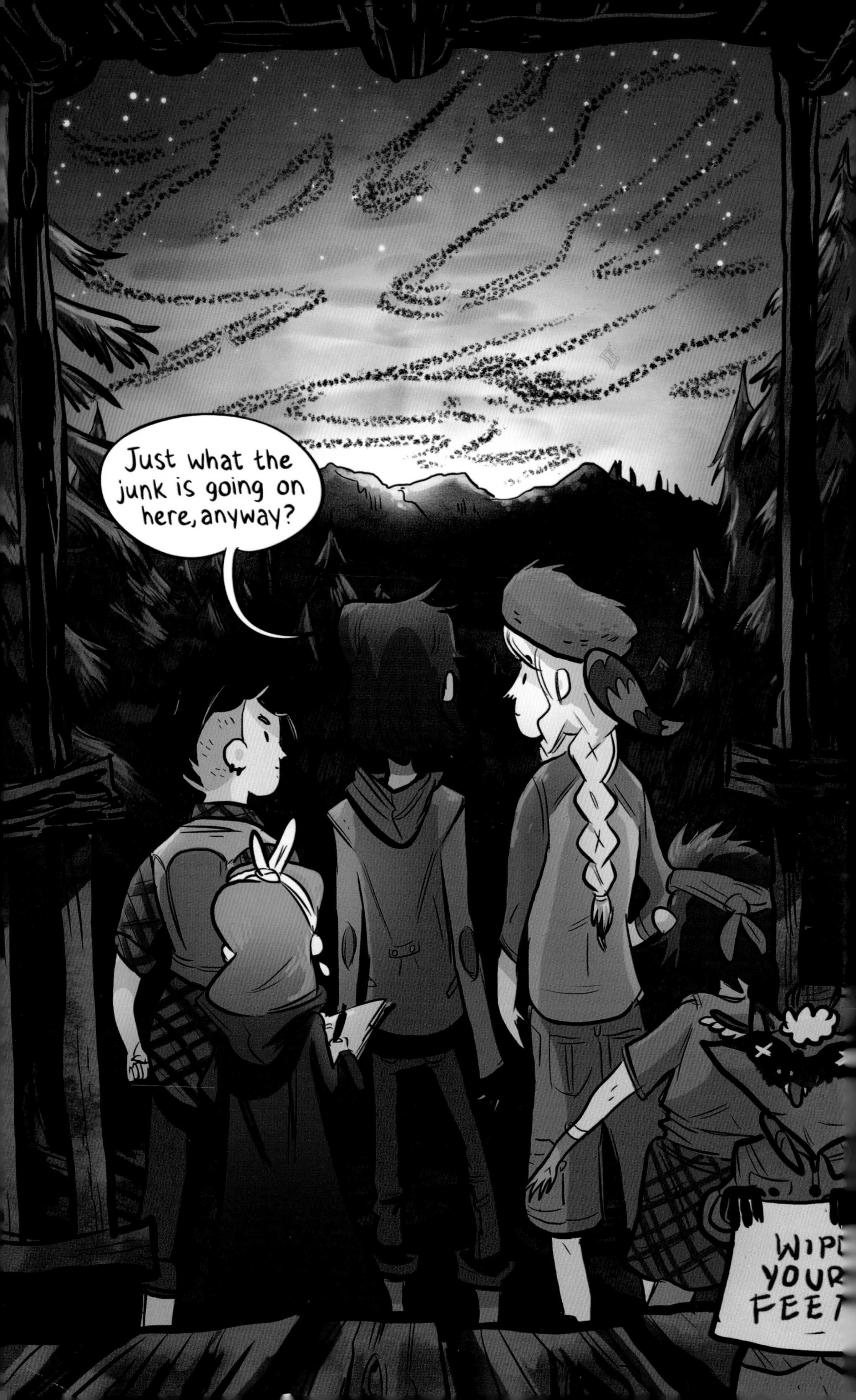
Just what the junk is going on here, anyway?
WIPE YOUR FEET

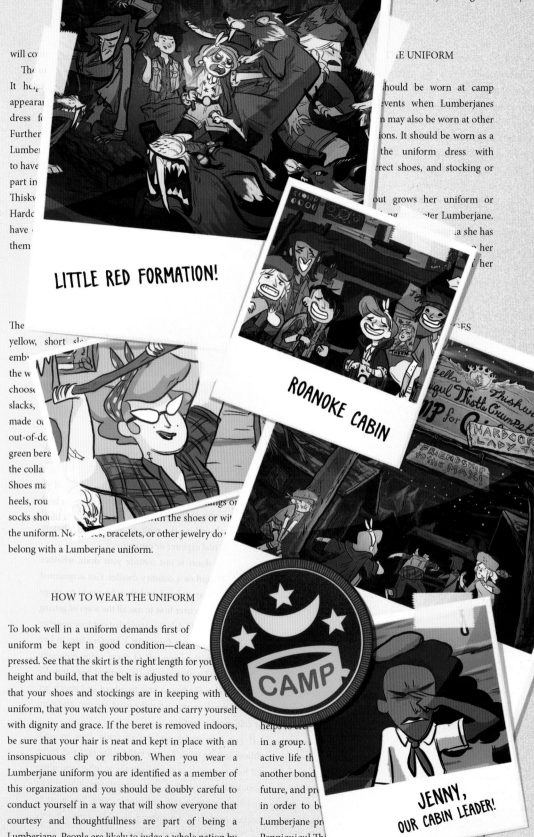

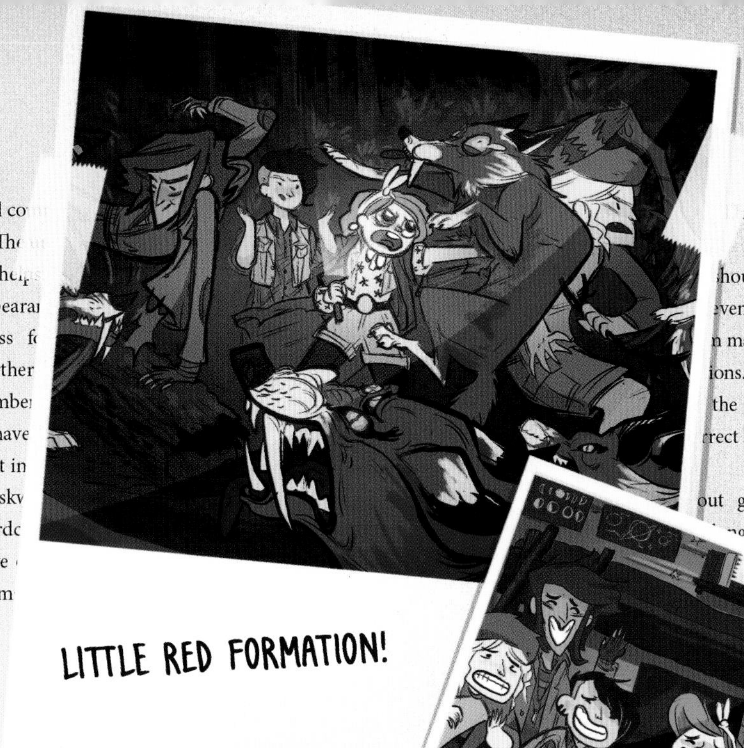
LITTLE RED FORMATION!

will co

The u

It helps

appearan

dress fo

Further

Lumber

to have

part in

Thiskw

Hardc

have

them

HE UNIFORM

should be worn at camp events when Lumberjanes n may also be worn at other ions. It should be worn as a the uniform dress with rrect shoes, and stocking or

out grows her uniform or ter Lumberjane. a she has her f her

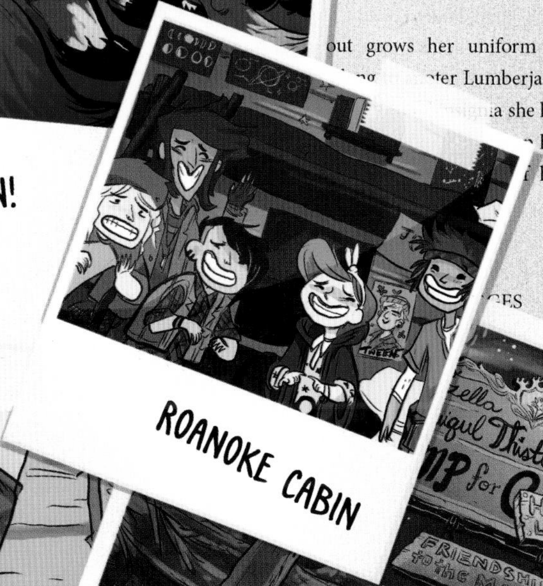
ROANOKE CABIN

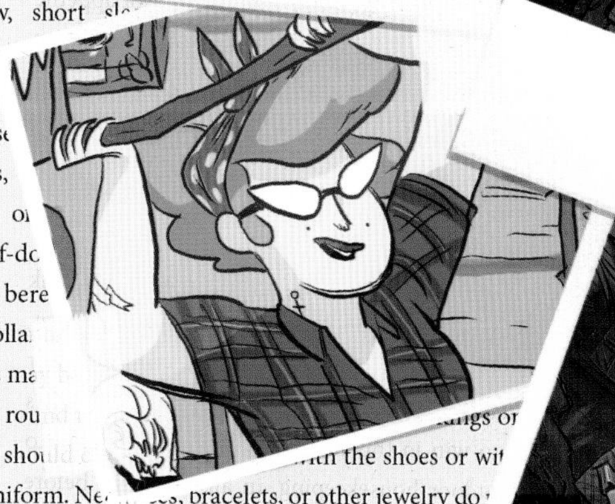

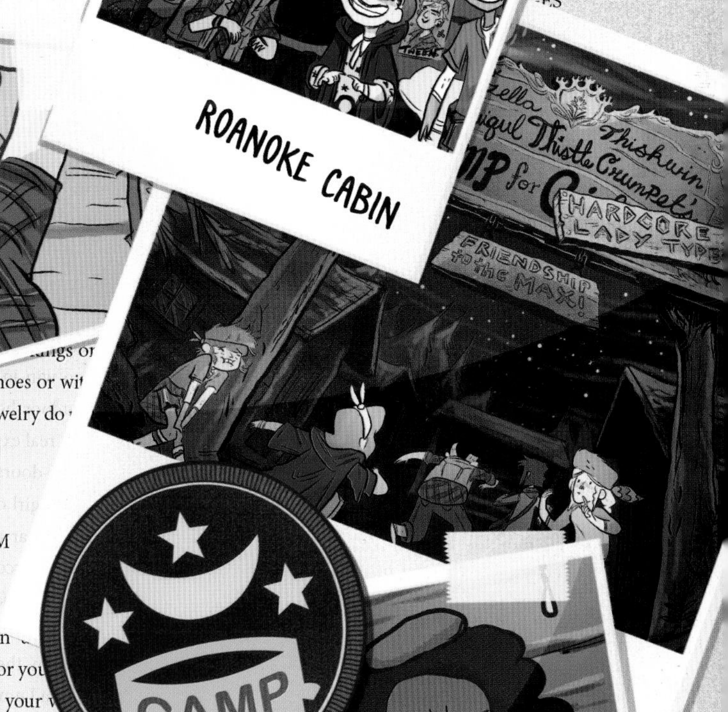
Thiskwin
Crumpet's
HARDCORE LADY TYPE
FRIENDSHIP to the MAX!
CAMP

The

yellow, short sl

emb

the w

choose

slacks,

made o

out-of-do

green bere

the colla

Shoes ma

heels, rou ings or

socks shou with the shoes or wi

the uniform. Ne es, bracelets, or other jewelry do

belong with a Lumberjane uniform.

GES

HOW TO WEAR THE UNIFORM

To look well in a uniform demands first of uniform be kept in good condition—clean pressed. See that the skirt is the right length for you height and build, that the belt is adjusted to your that your shoes and stockings are in keeping with uniform, that you watch your posture and carry yourself with dignity and grace. If the beret is removed indoors, be sure that your hair is neat and kept in place with an insonspicuous clip or ribbon. When you wear a Lumberjane uniform you are identified as a member of this organization and you should be doubly careful to conduct yourself in a way that will show everyone that courtesy and thoughtfullness are part of being a Lumberjane. People are likely to judge a whole nation by the selfishness of a few individuals, to criticize a whole family because of the misconduct of one member, and to feel unkindly toward and organization because of the

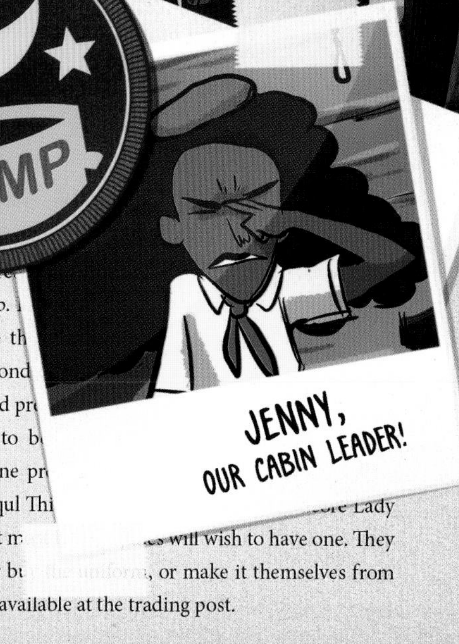
JENNY,
OUR CABIN LEADER!

helps to cre

in a group. I

active life th

another bond

future, and pr

in order to b

Lumberjane pr

Penniquiqul Thi core Lady

Types, but m es will wish to have one. They

can either bu uniform, or make it themselves from

materials available at the trading post.

LUMBERJANES FIELD MANUAL

CHAPTER TWO

Lumberjanes "Sports and Games" Program Field

NAVAL GAUGING BADGE

"Because drowning is a scary way to go."

Lumberjanes are considered to be girls who can find their way around any situation, whether it be an unsuspecting adventure in the great outdoors to the problem solving of everyday matters. As a modern Lumberjane, you will be able to recognize the importance of naval abilities and how to navigate any stream. A Lumberjane will be able to find her way through any rapid, fall, or even quiet wilderness. Will understand the importance of safety and always be wary of the false sense of security that the wilderness can lull any unsuspecting person into, a Lumberjane will remain ready and able to adapt to whatever is thrown at her.

The *Naval Gauging* badge is a sense of pride for any Lumberjane, as she continues her journey through the daily trials that every Lumberjane must face. Not only will a Lumberjane learn how to forage in the wild, learning how to care for herself and her friends on

the trail, she will learn how to explore with a seeing and vigilant eye. She will make herself at home in the woods, and any future place she finds fitting for herself.

To obtain the *Naval Gauging* badge a Lumberjane must be able to tie rapidly six different knots. She will find herself well versed in rope work as it can be extremely important in her future adventure, she must know how to splice ropes, use a palm and needle, and fling a rope coil. A Lumberjane must be able to row, pole, scull, and steer a boat; also bring a boat properly alongside and make fast. She must know how to box the compass, read a chart, and show use of parallel rules and dividers. She must be able to state direction by the stars and sun, and be capable of swimming fifty yards with shoes and clothes on. She will know the importance of a life preserver, CPR, and the basic understanding of how to respond in emergency situations. She must understand

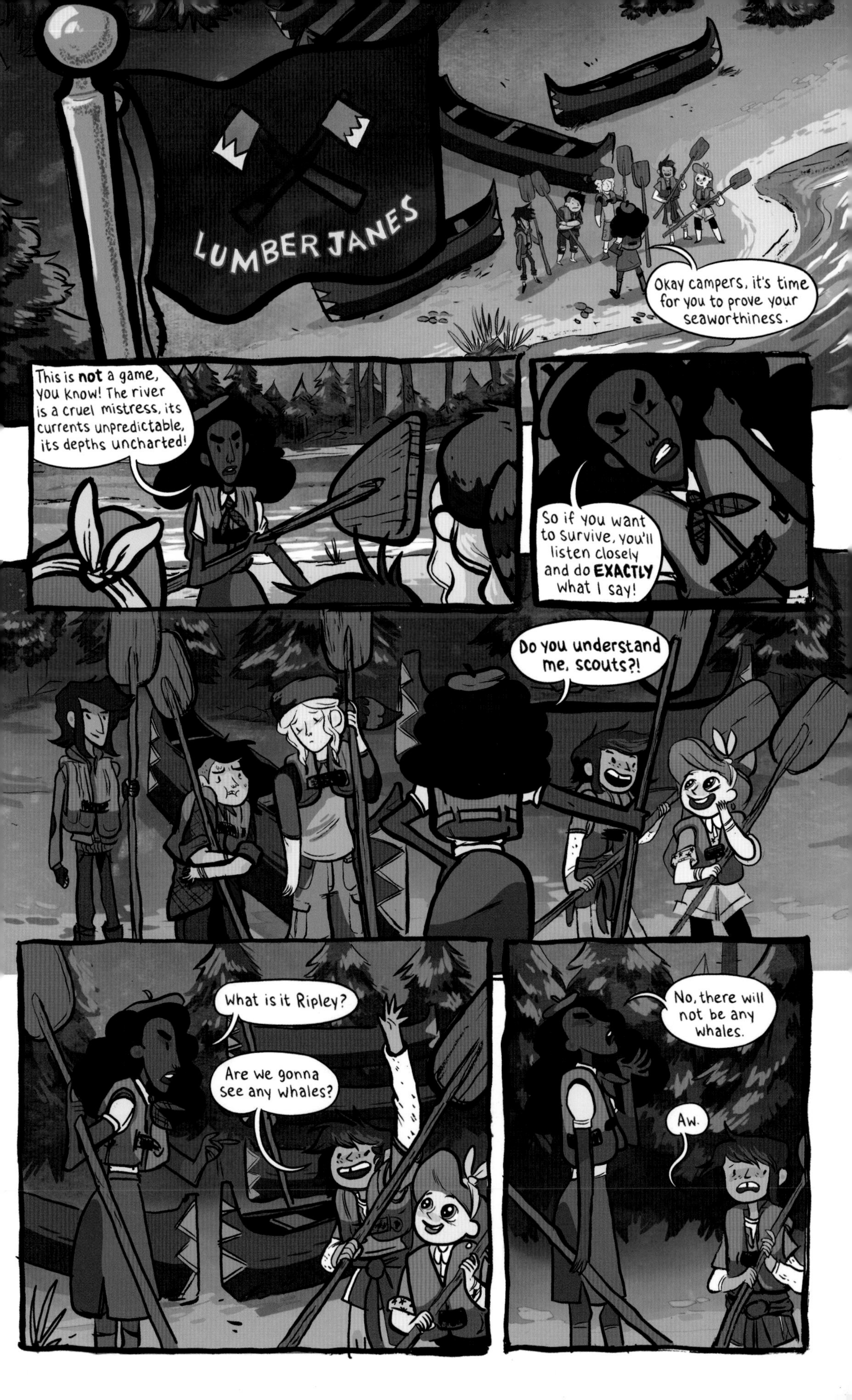
LUMBER JANES
Okay campers, it's time for you to prove your seaworthiness.
This is **not** a game, you know! The river is a cruel mistress, its currents unpredictable, its depths uncharted!
So if you want to survive, you'll listen closely and do **EXACTLY** what I say!
Do you understand me, scouts?!
What is it Ripley?
Are we gonna see any whales?
No, there will not be any whales.
Aw.

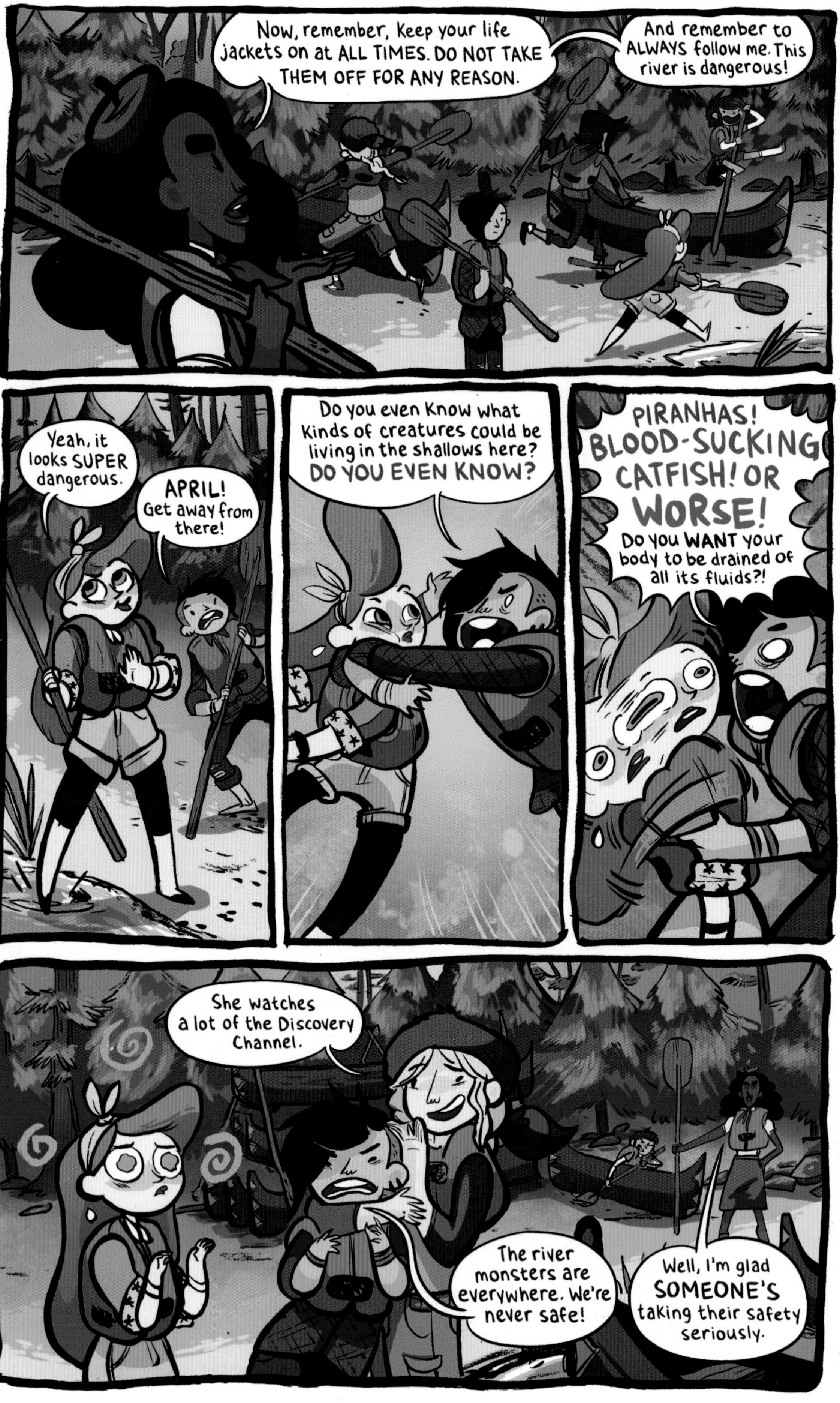
Now, remember, Keep your life jackets on at ALL TIMES. DO NOT TAKE THEM OFF FOR ANY REASON.
And remember to ALWAYS follow me. This river is dangerous!
Yeah, it looks SUPER dangerous.
APRIL! Get away from there!
Do you even Know what Kinds of creatures could be living in the shallows here? DO YOU EVEN KNOW?
PIRANHAS! BLOOD-SUCKING CATFISH! OR WORSE!
Do you WANT your body to be drained of all its fluids?!
She watches a lot of the Discovery Channel.
The river monsters are everywhere. We're never safe!
Well, I'm glad SOMEONE'S taking their safety seriously.

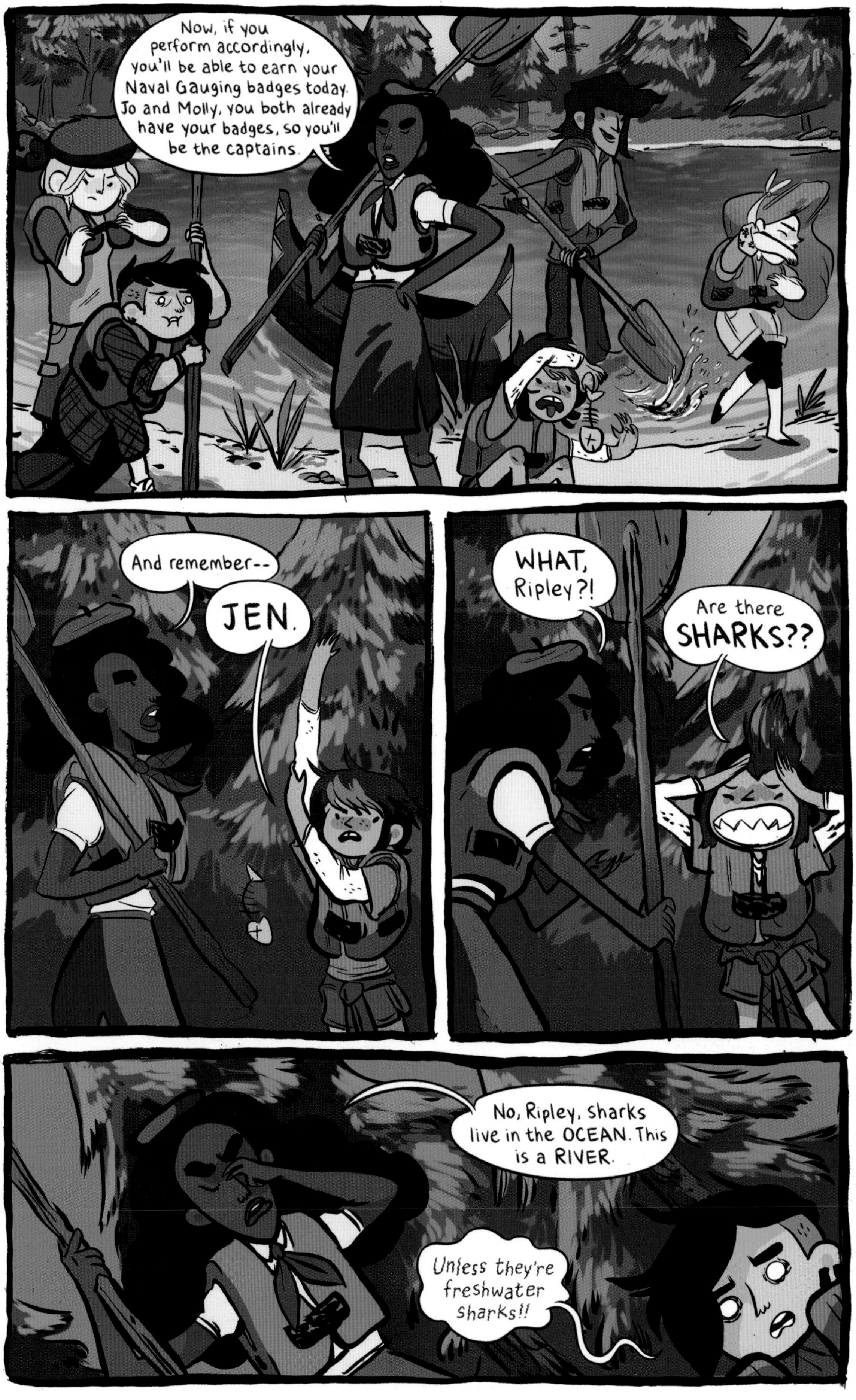
Now, if you perform accordingly, you'll be able to earn your Naval Gauging badges today. Jo and Molly, you both already have your badges, so you'll be the captains.
And remember--
JEN.
WHAT, Ripley?!
Are there SHARKS??
No, Ripley, sharks live in the OCEAN. This is a RIVER.
Unless they're freshwater sharks!!

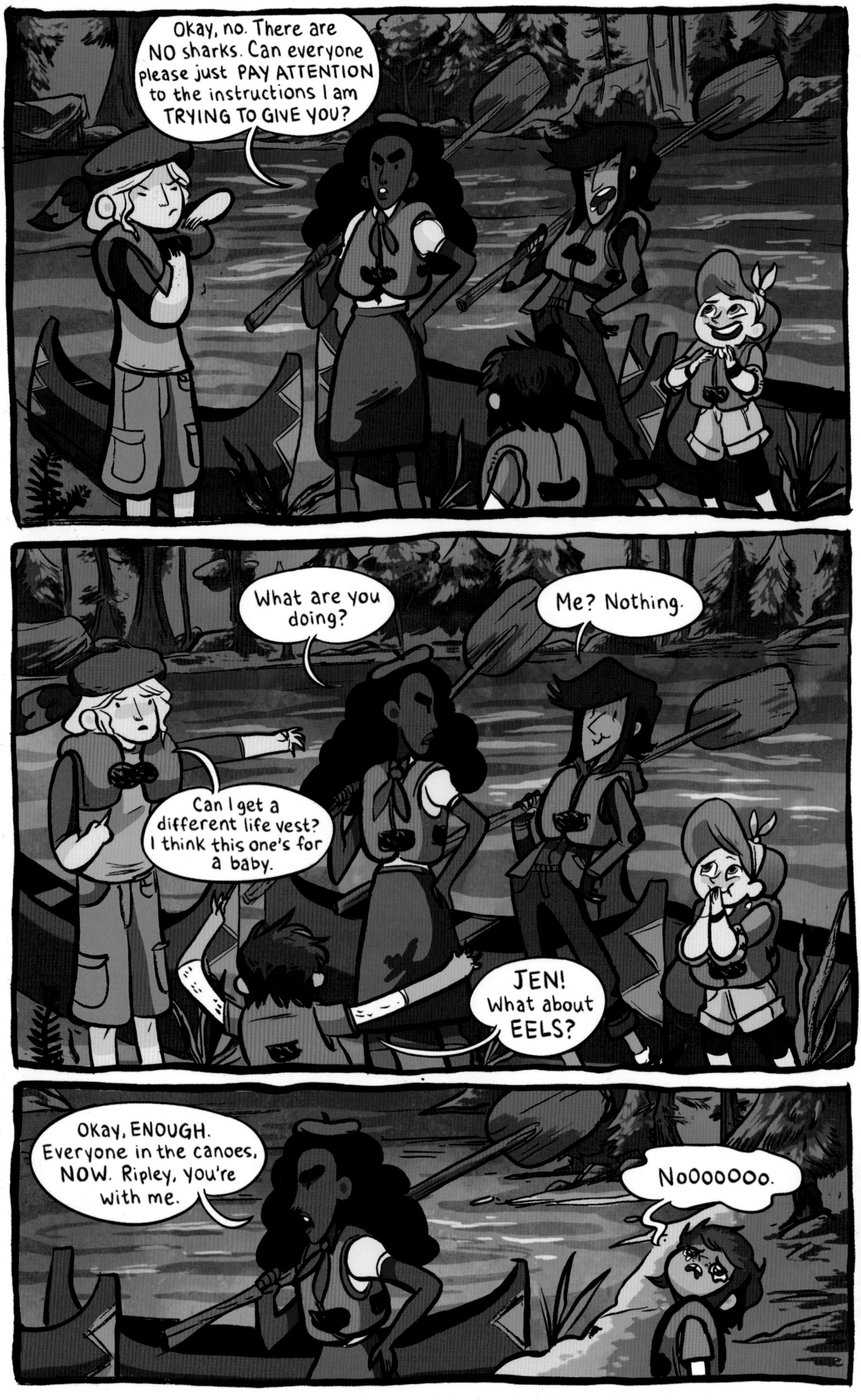
Okay, no. There are NO sharks. Can everyone please just PAY ATTENTION to the instructions I am TRYING TO GIVE YOU?
What are you doing?
Me? Nothing.
Can I get a different life vest? I think this one's for a baby.
JEN! What about EELS?
Okay, ENOUGH. Everyone in the canoes, NOW. Ripley, you're with me.
NoOooOOo.

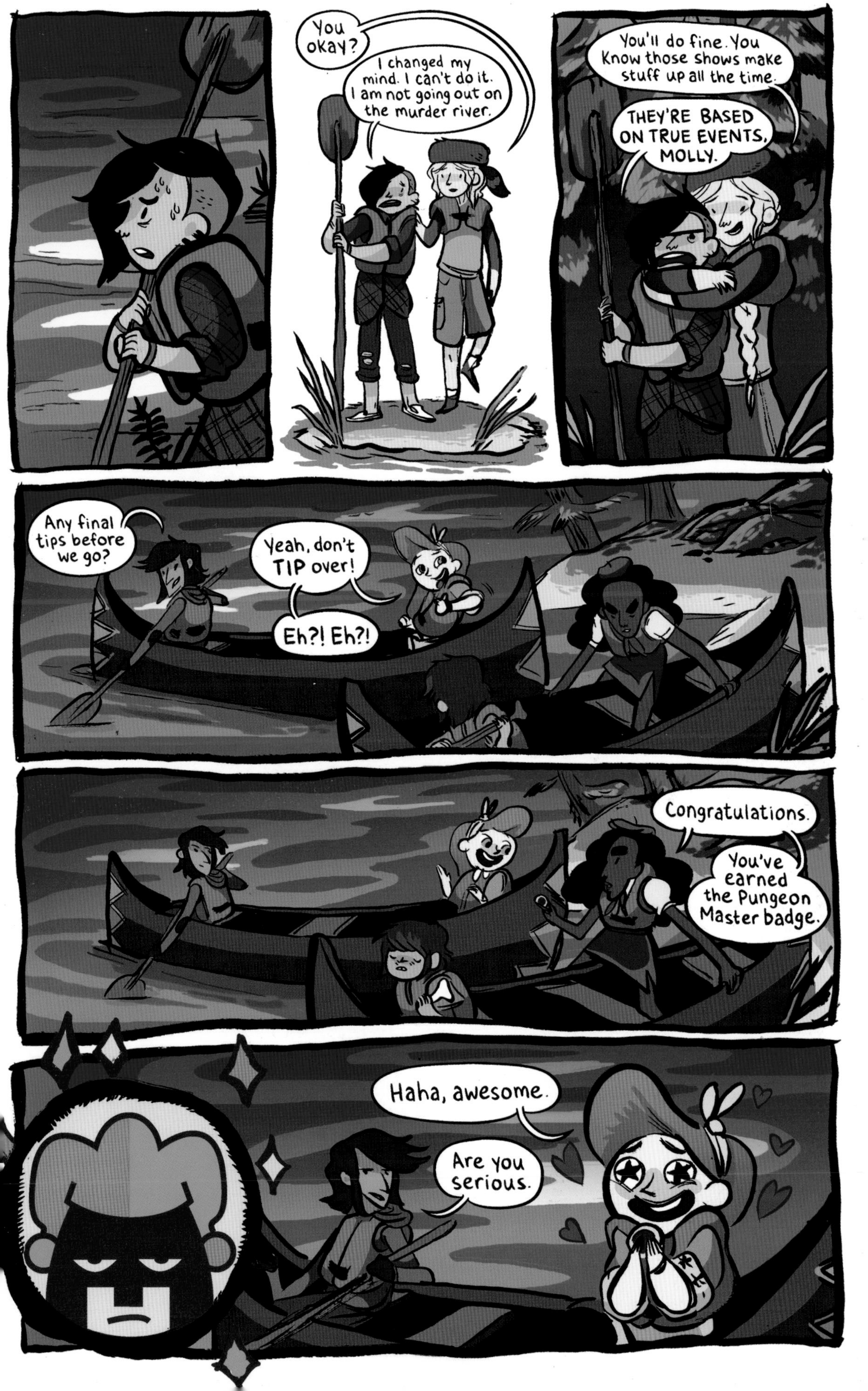
You okay?
I changed my mind. I can't do it. I am not going out on the murder river.
You'll do fine. You Know those shows make stuff up all the time.
THEY'RE BASED ON TRUE EVENTS, MOLLY.
Any final tips before we go?
Yeah, don't TIP over!
Eh?! Eh?!
Congratulations.
You've earned the Pungeon Master badge.
Haha, awesome.
Are you serious.

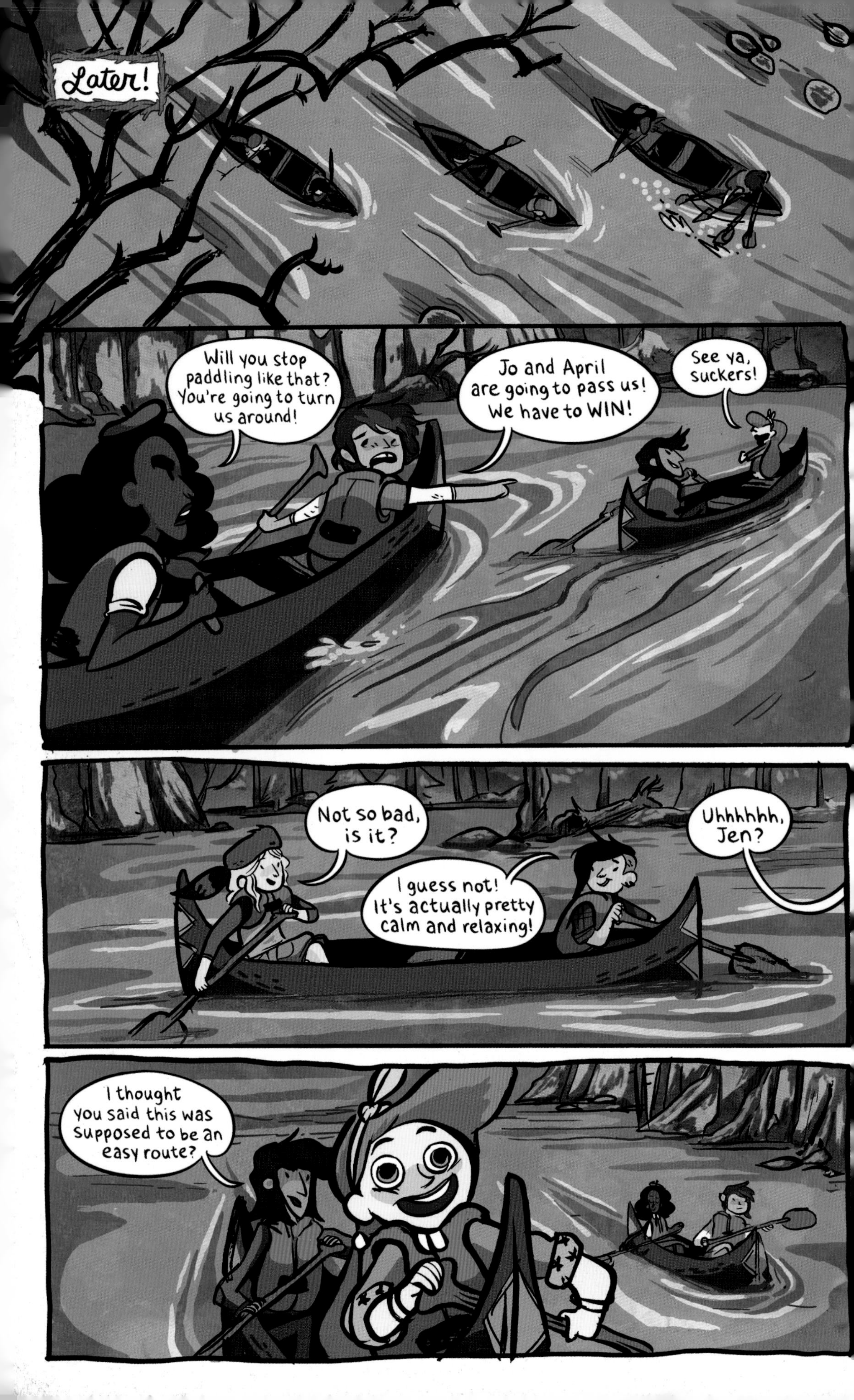
Later!
Will you stop paddling like that? You're going to turn us around!
Jo and April are going to pass us! We have to WIN!
See ya, suckers!
Not so bad, is it?
I guess not! It's actually pretty calm and relaxing!
Uhhhhhh, Jen?
I thought you said this was supposed to be an easy route?

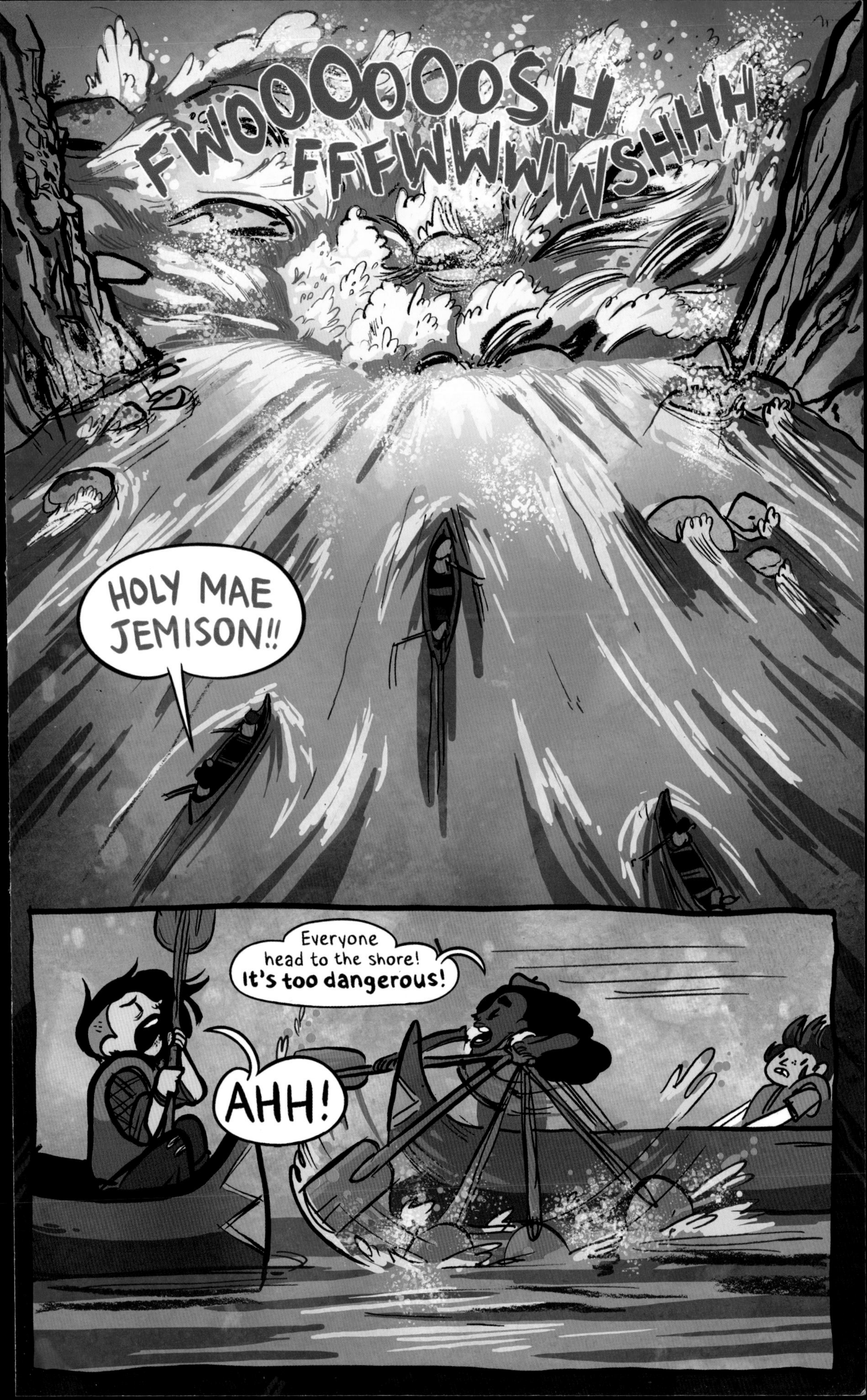
FWOOOOOOSH
FFFWWWWWSHHH
HOLY MAE JEMISON!!
Everyone head to the shore! It's too dangerous!
AHH!

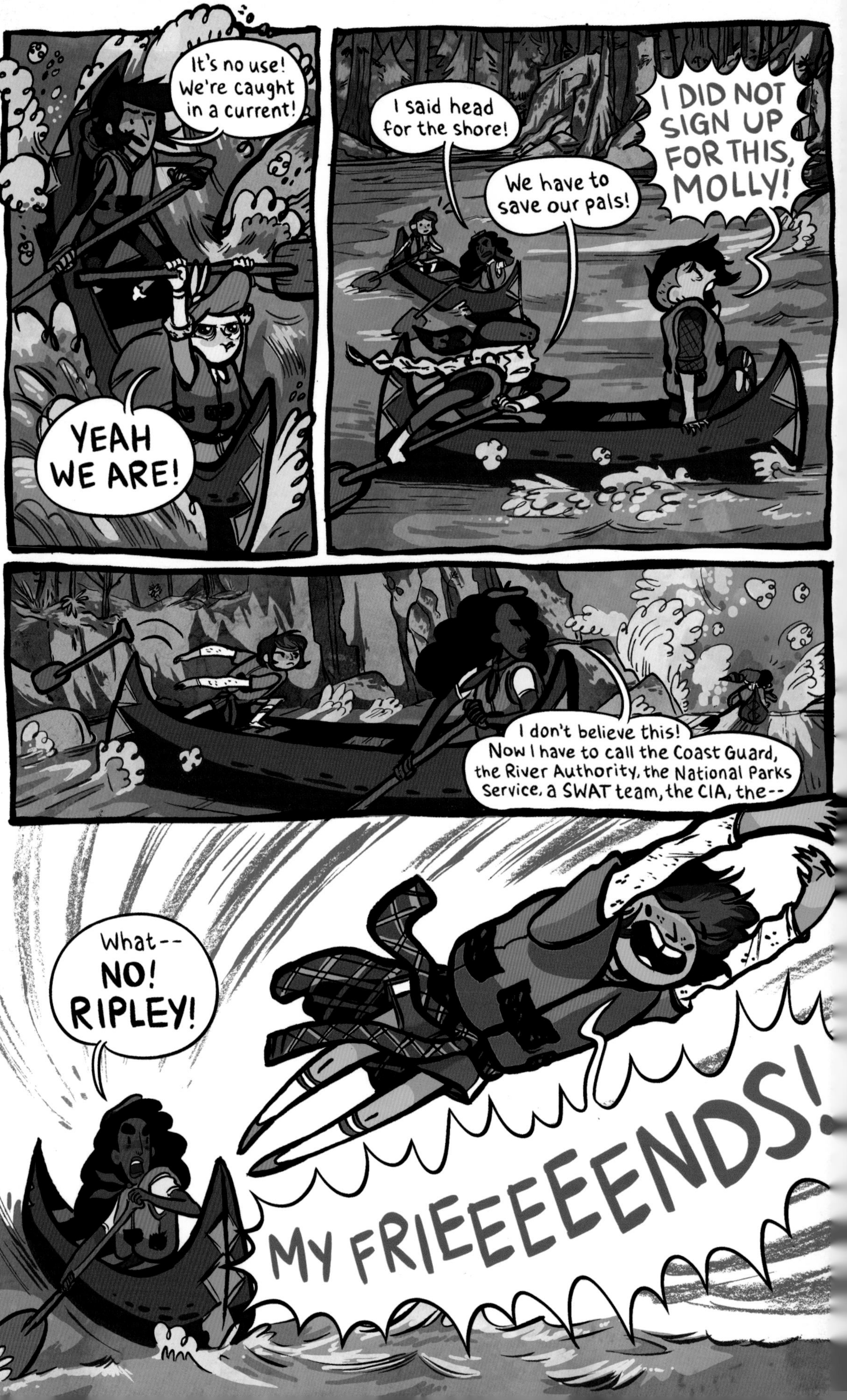
It's no use! We're caught in a current!
YEAH WE ARE!
I said head for the shore!
We have to save our pals!
I DID NOT SIGN UP FOR THIS, MOLLY!
I don't believe this! Now I have to call the Coast Guard, the River Authority, the National Parks Service, a SWAT team, the CIA, the--
What-- NO! RIPLEY!
MY FRIEEEEEENDS!

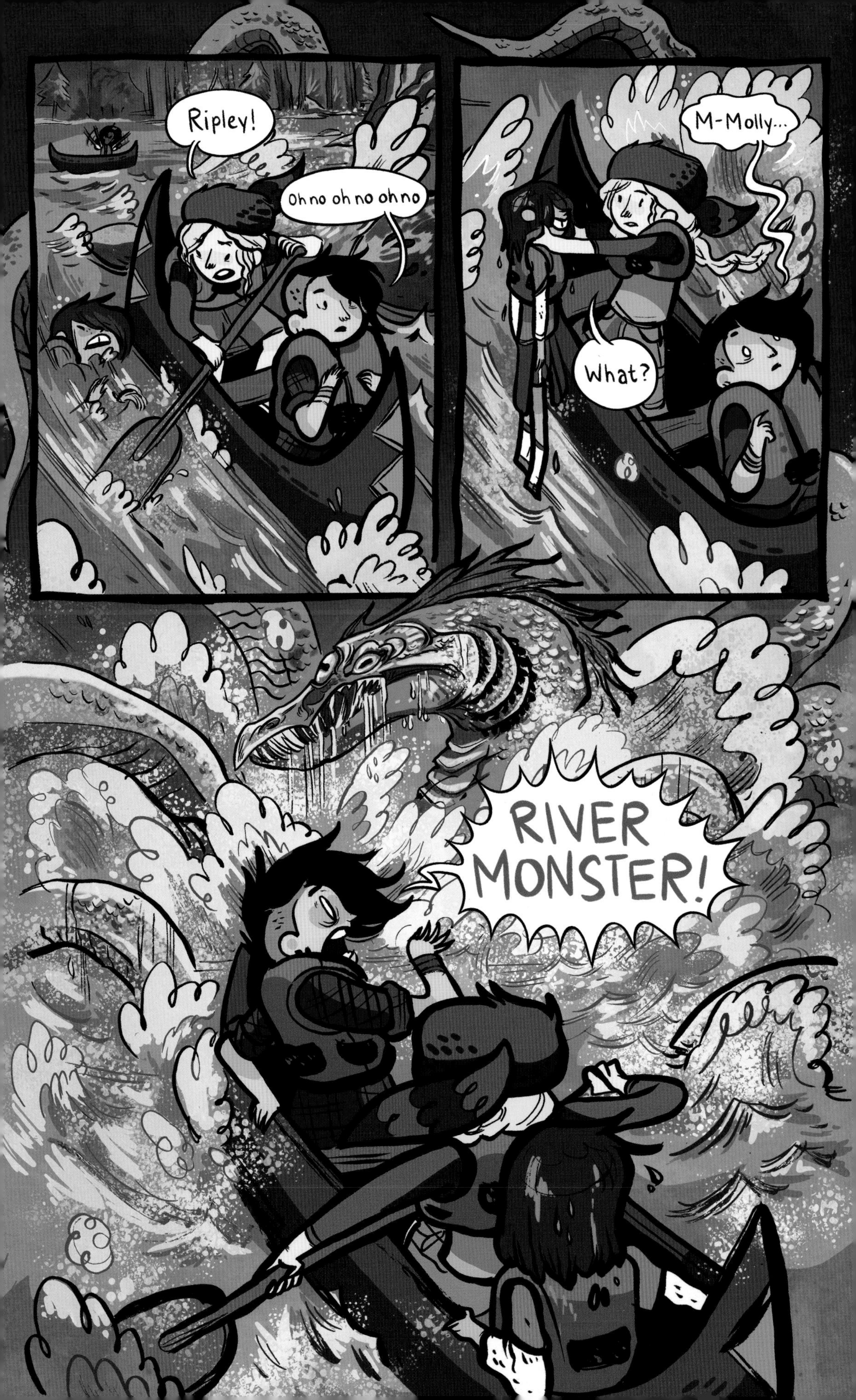
Ripley!
Oh no oh no oh no
M-Molly...
What?
RIVER MONSTER!

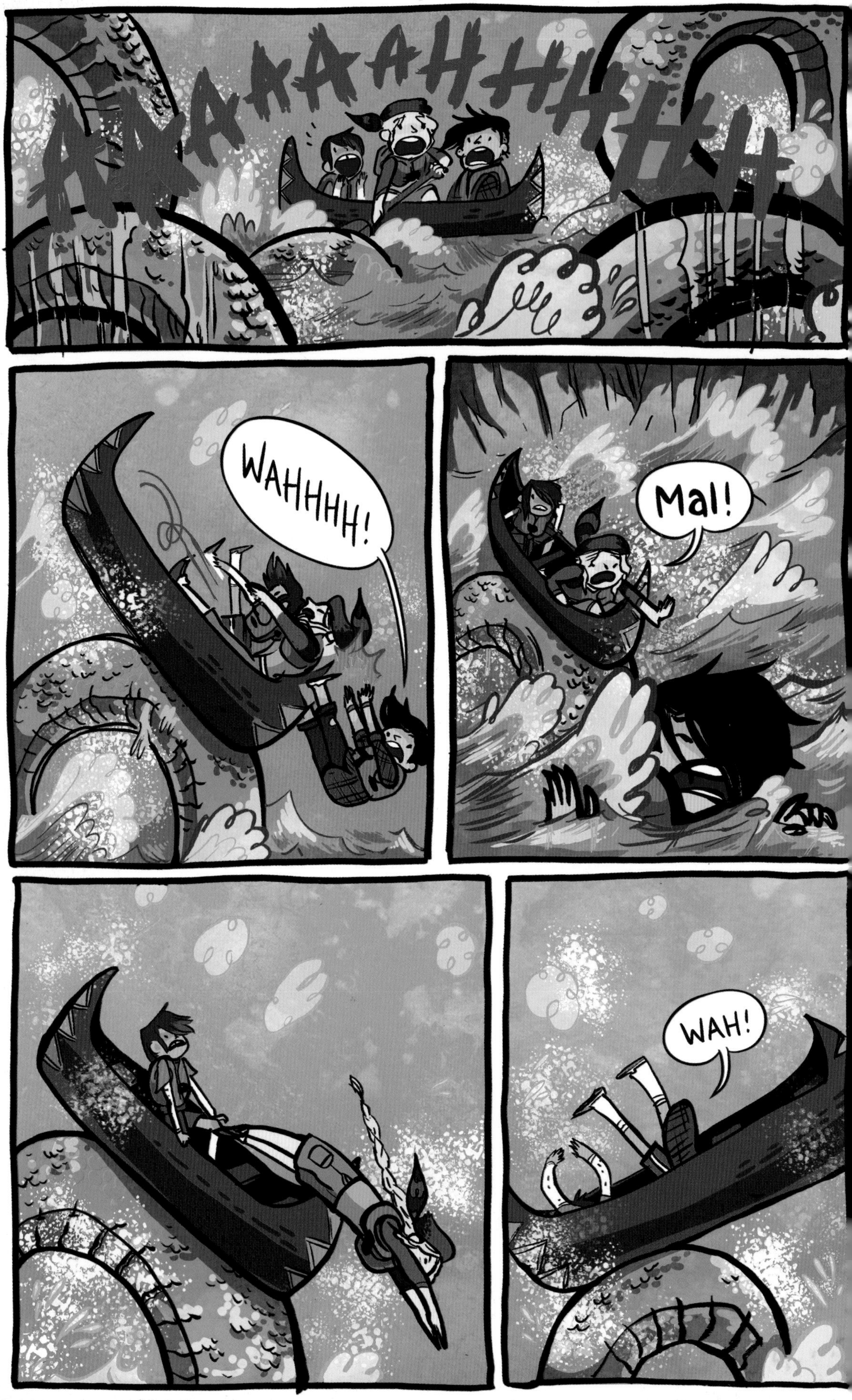
AAAAAAAHHHHHH
WAHHHHH!
Mal!
WAH!

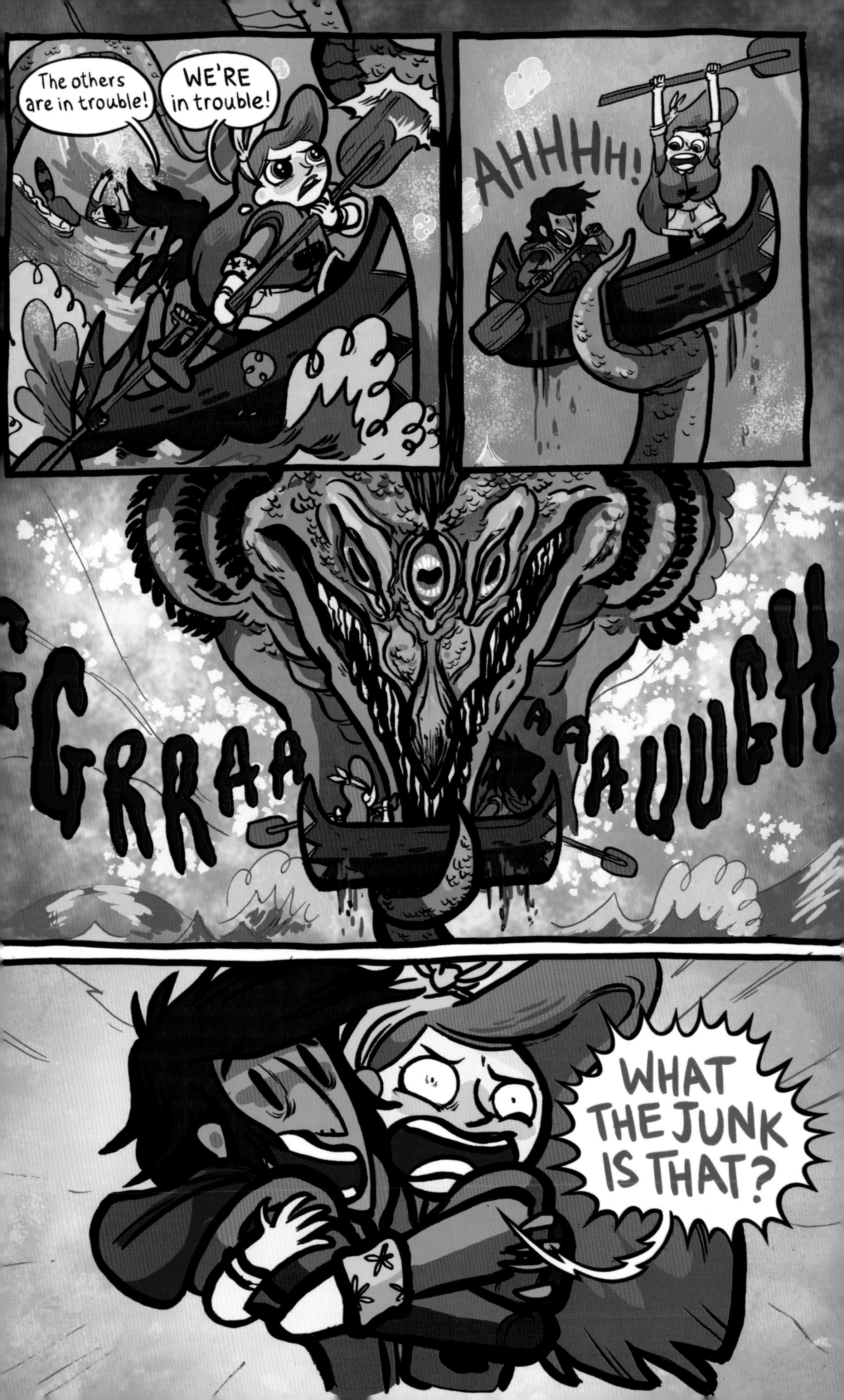
The others are in trouble!
WE'RE in trouble!
AHHHH!
GRRAAAAAAUUGH
WHAT THE JUNK IS THAT?

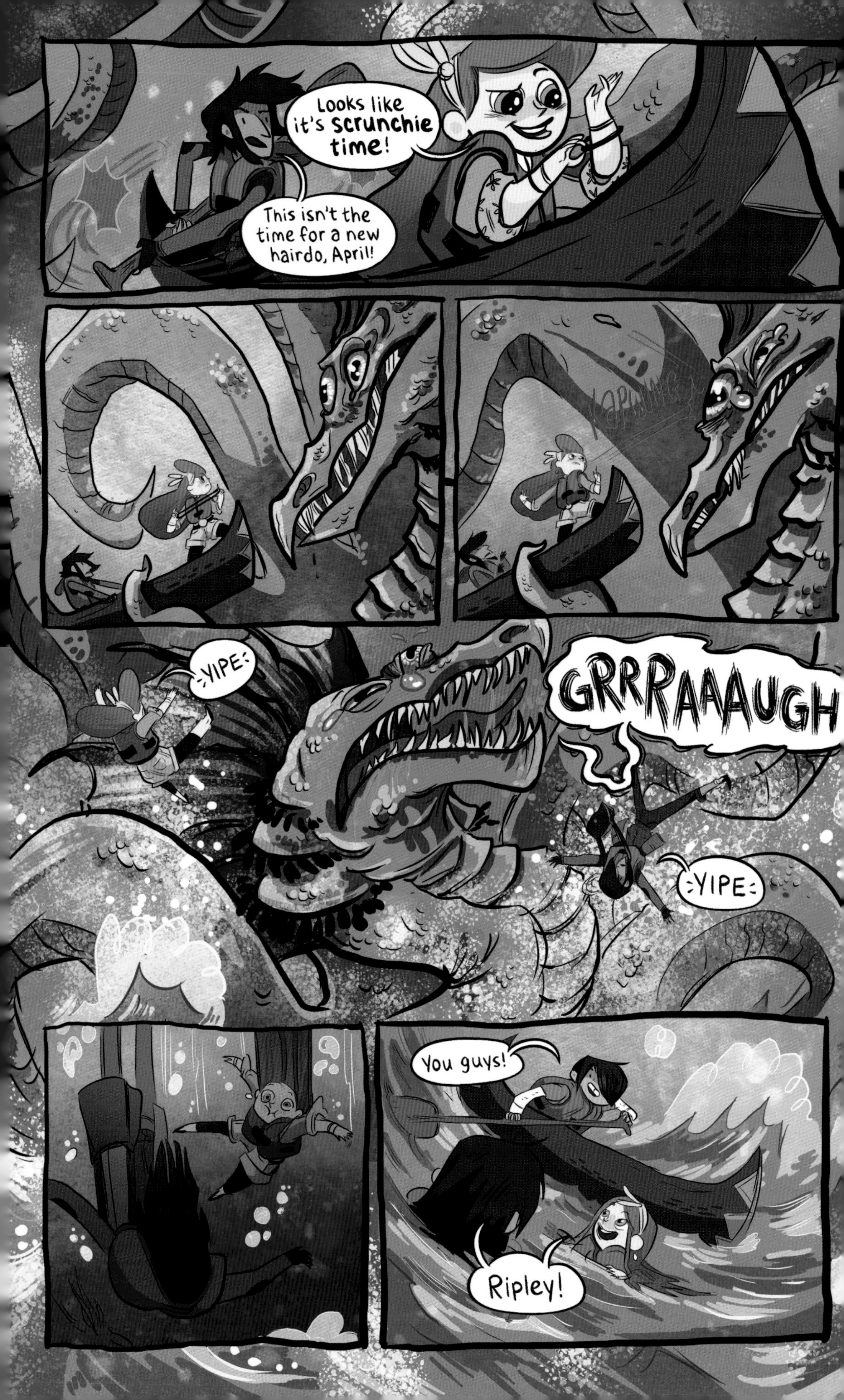
Looks like it's **scrunchie** time!
This isn't the time for a new hairdo, April!
YIPE
GRRRAAAUGH
YIPE
You guys!
Ripley!

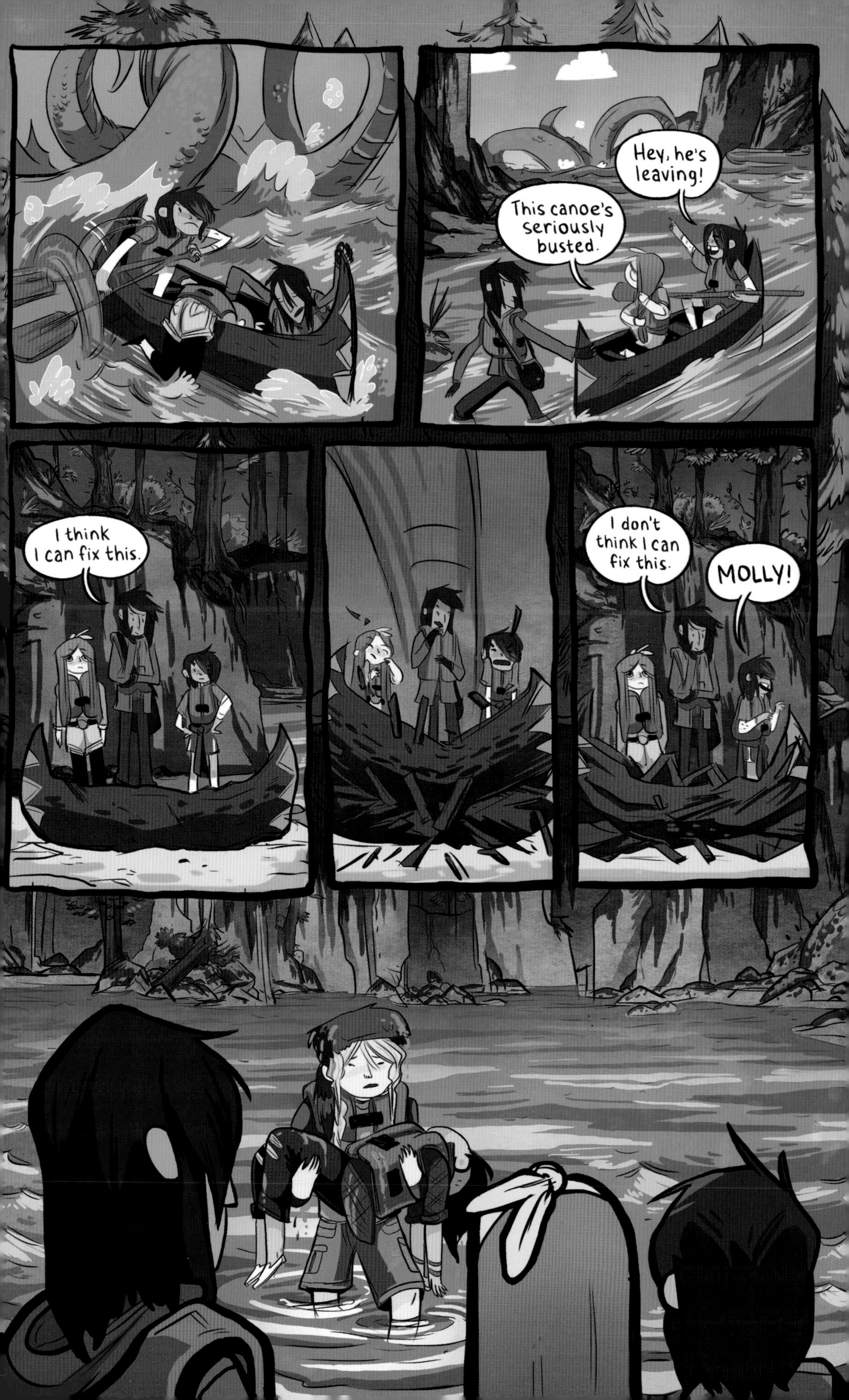
This canoe's seriously busted.
Hey, he's leaving!
I think I can fix this.
I don't think I can fix this.
MOLLY!

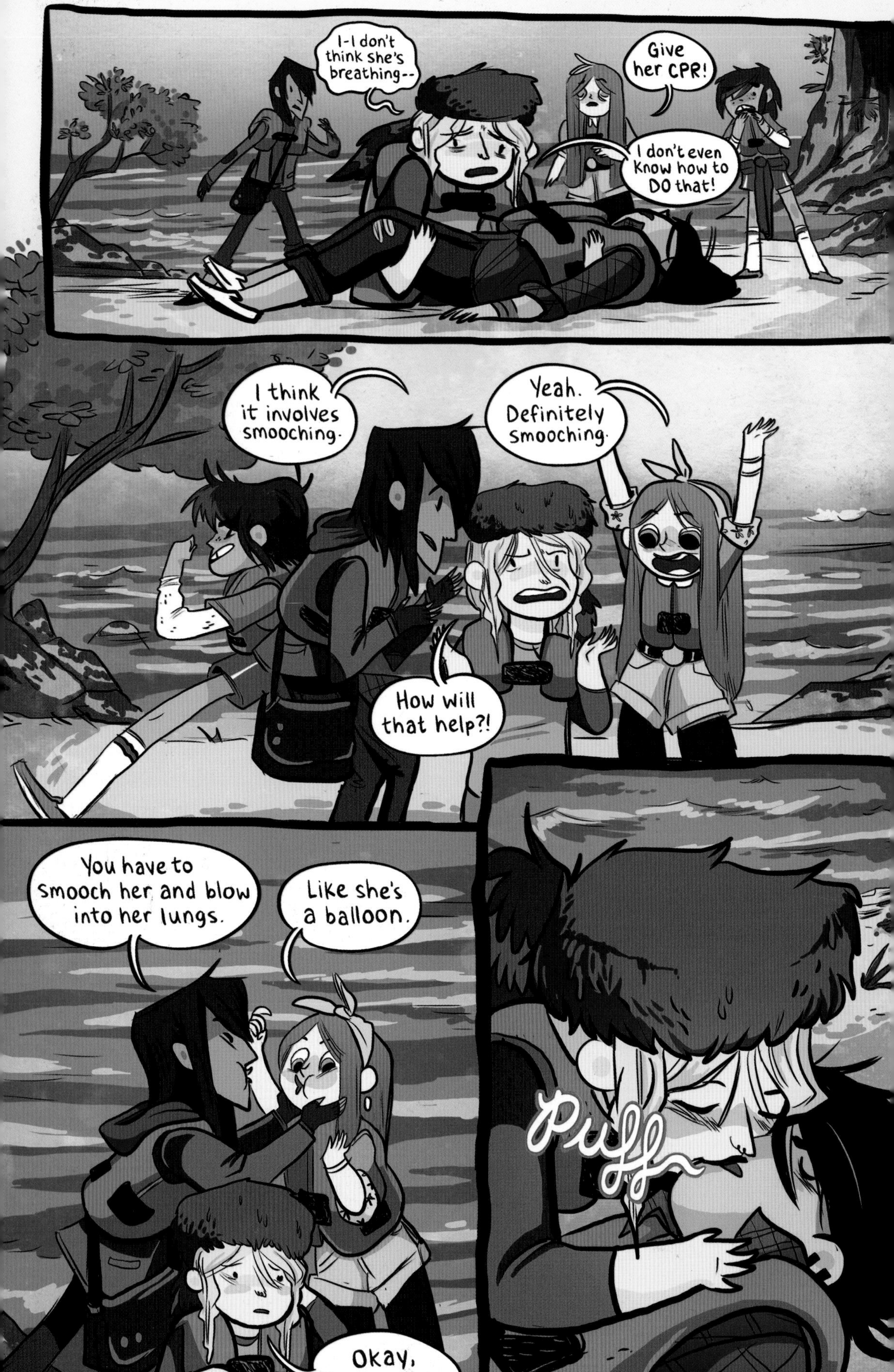
I-I don't think she's breathing--
Give her CPR!
I don't even know how to DO that!
I think it involves smooching.
Yeah. Definitely smooching.
How will that help?!
You have to smooch her and blow into her lungs.
Like she's a balloon.
Okay, if you say so.
PUFF

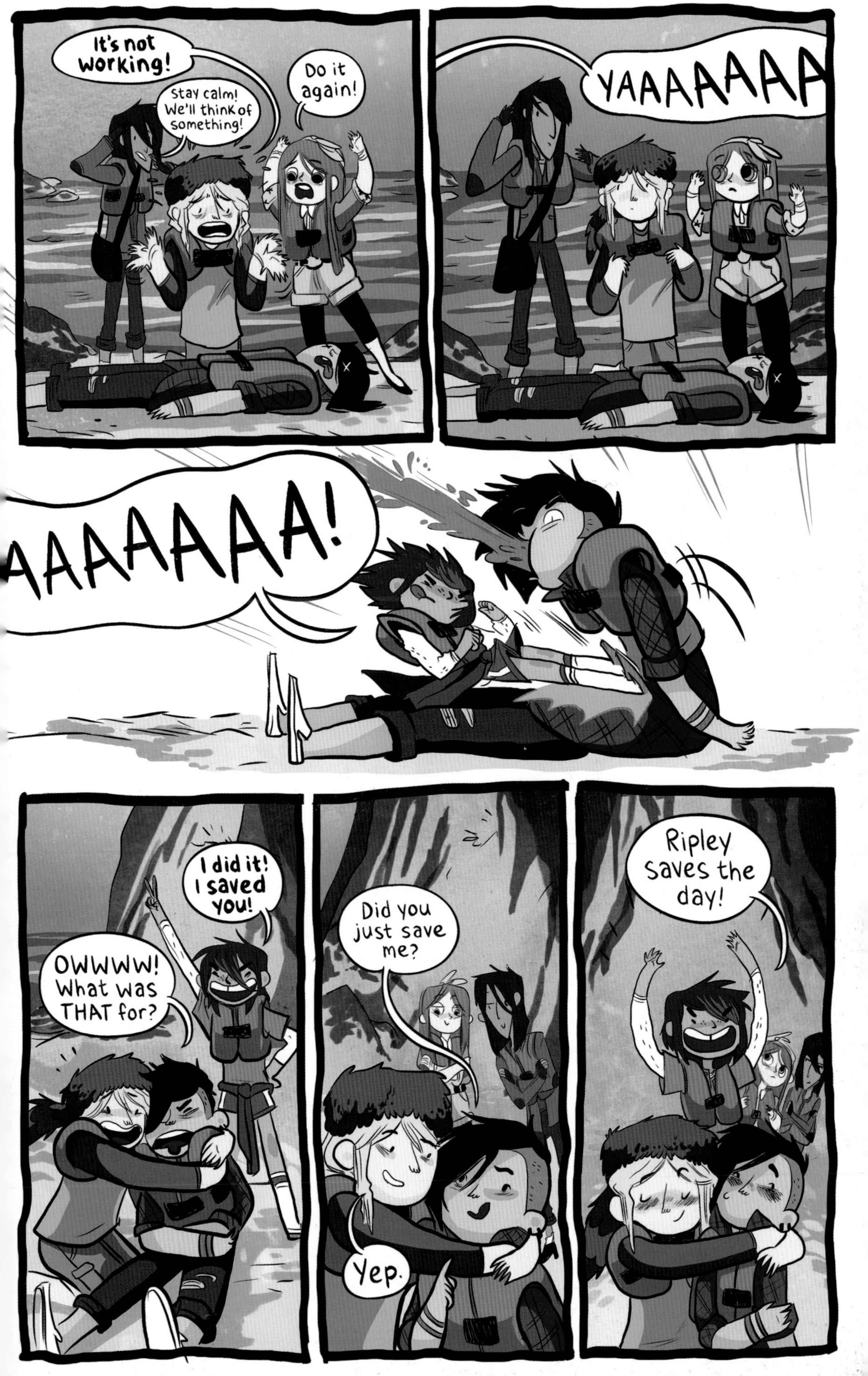
It's not working!
Stay calm! We'll think of something!
Do it again!
YAAAAAAA
AAAAAAA!
I did it! I saved you!
OWWWW! What was THAT for?
Did you just save me?
Yep.
Ripley saves the day!

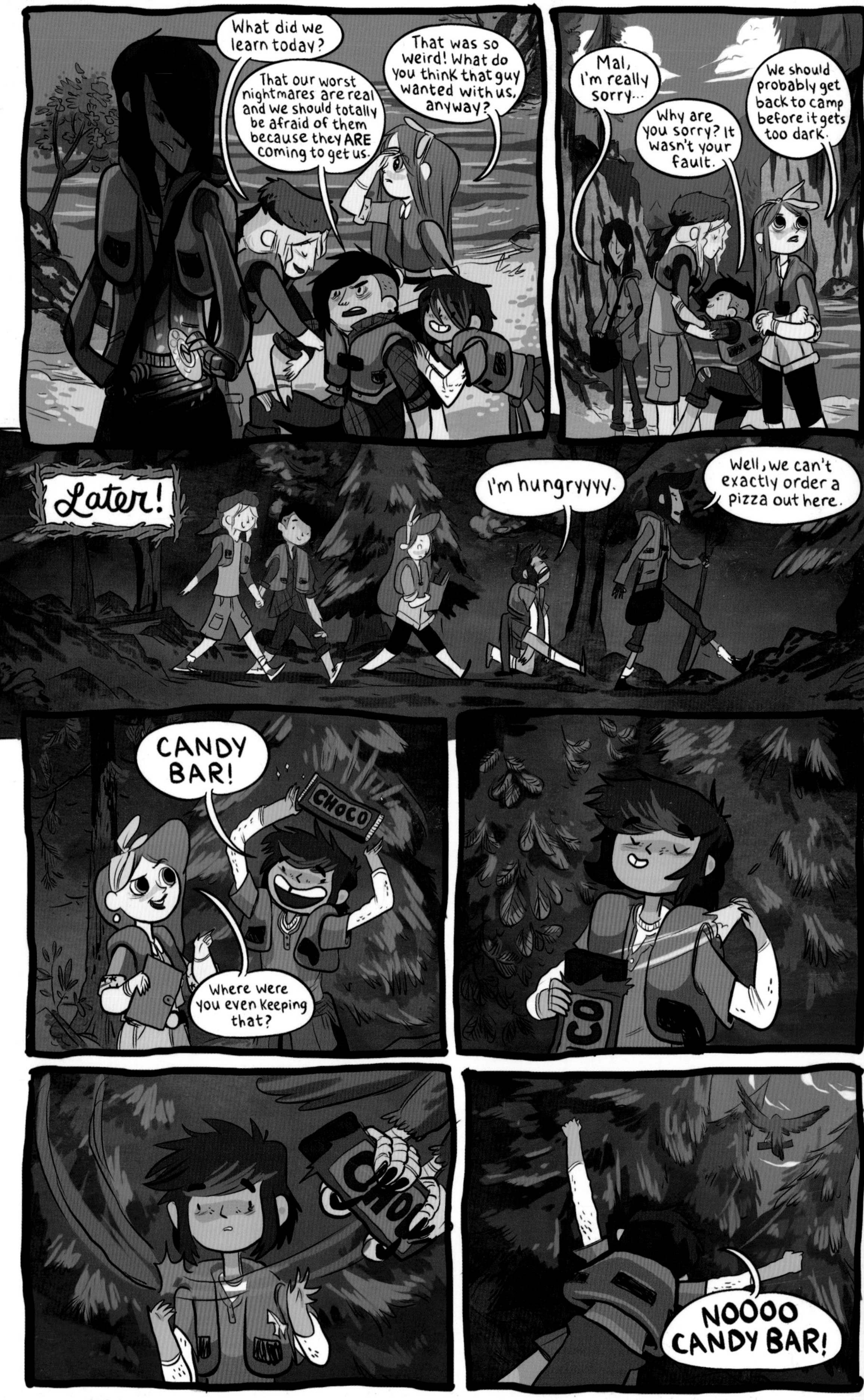
What did we learn today?
That our worst nightmares are real and we should totally be afraid of them because they ARE coming to get us.
That was so weird! What do you think that guy wanted with us, anyway?
Mal, I'm really sorry...
Why are you sorry? It wasn't your fault.
We should probably get back to camp before it gets too dark.
Later!
I'm hungryyyy.
Well, we can't exactly order a pizza out here.
CANDY BAR!
CHOCO
Where were you even keeping that?
NOOOO CANDY BAR!

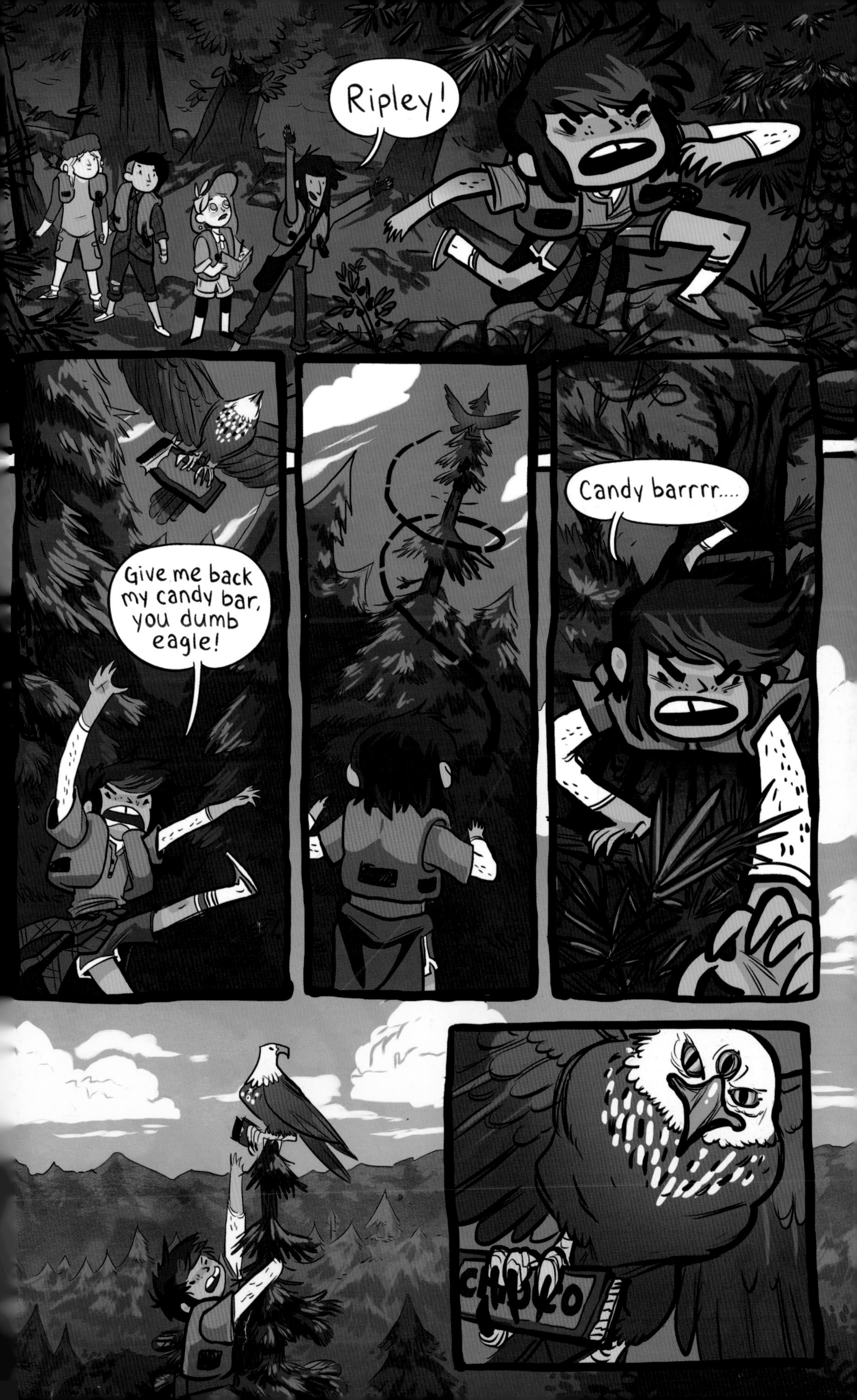
Ripley!
Give me back my candy bar, you dumb eagle!
Candy barrrr....

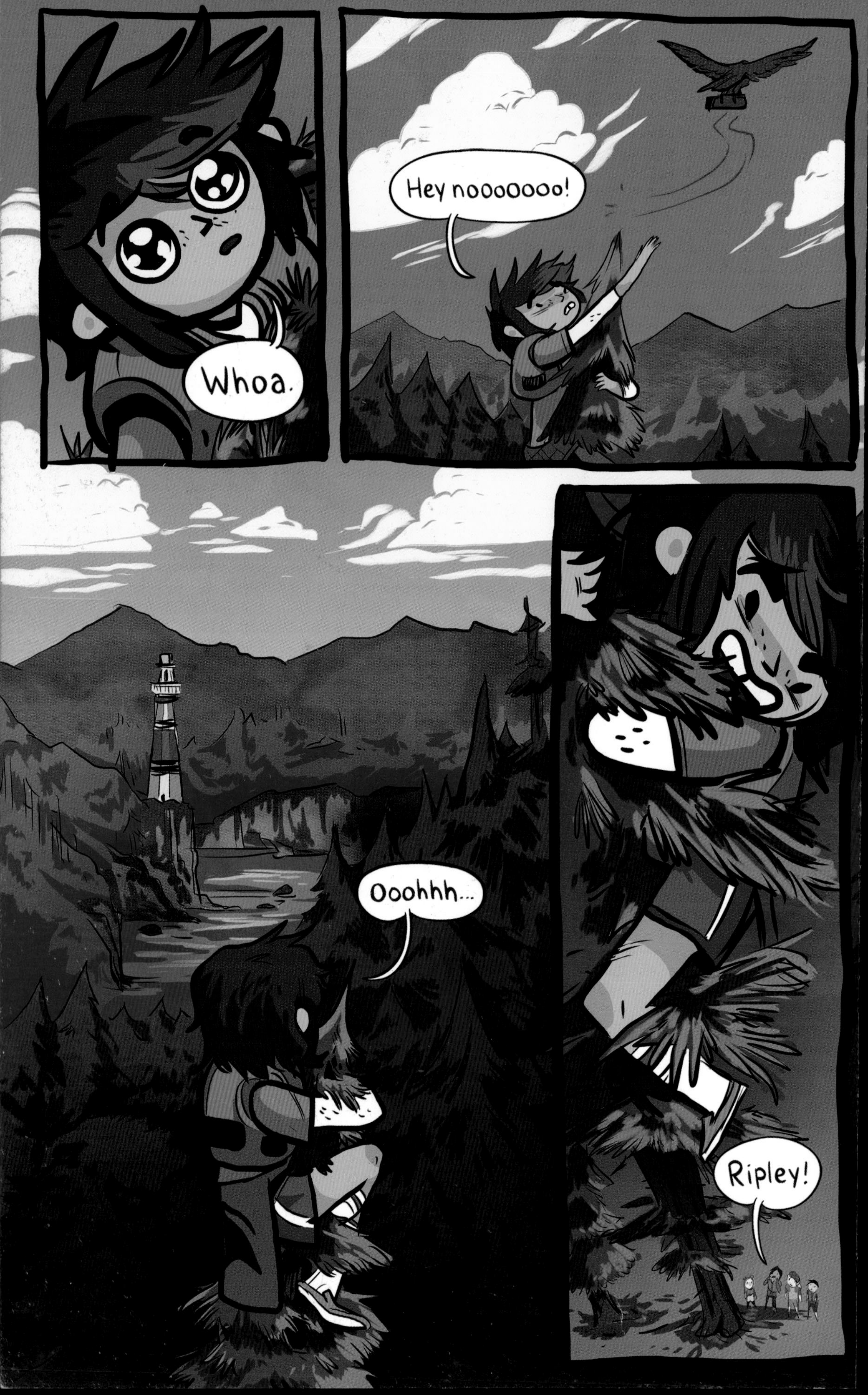
Whoa.
Hey nooooooo!
Ooohhh...
Ripley!

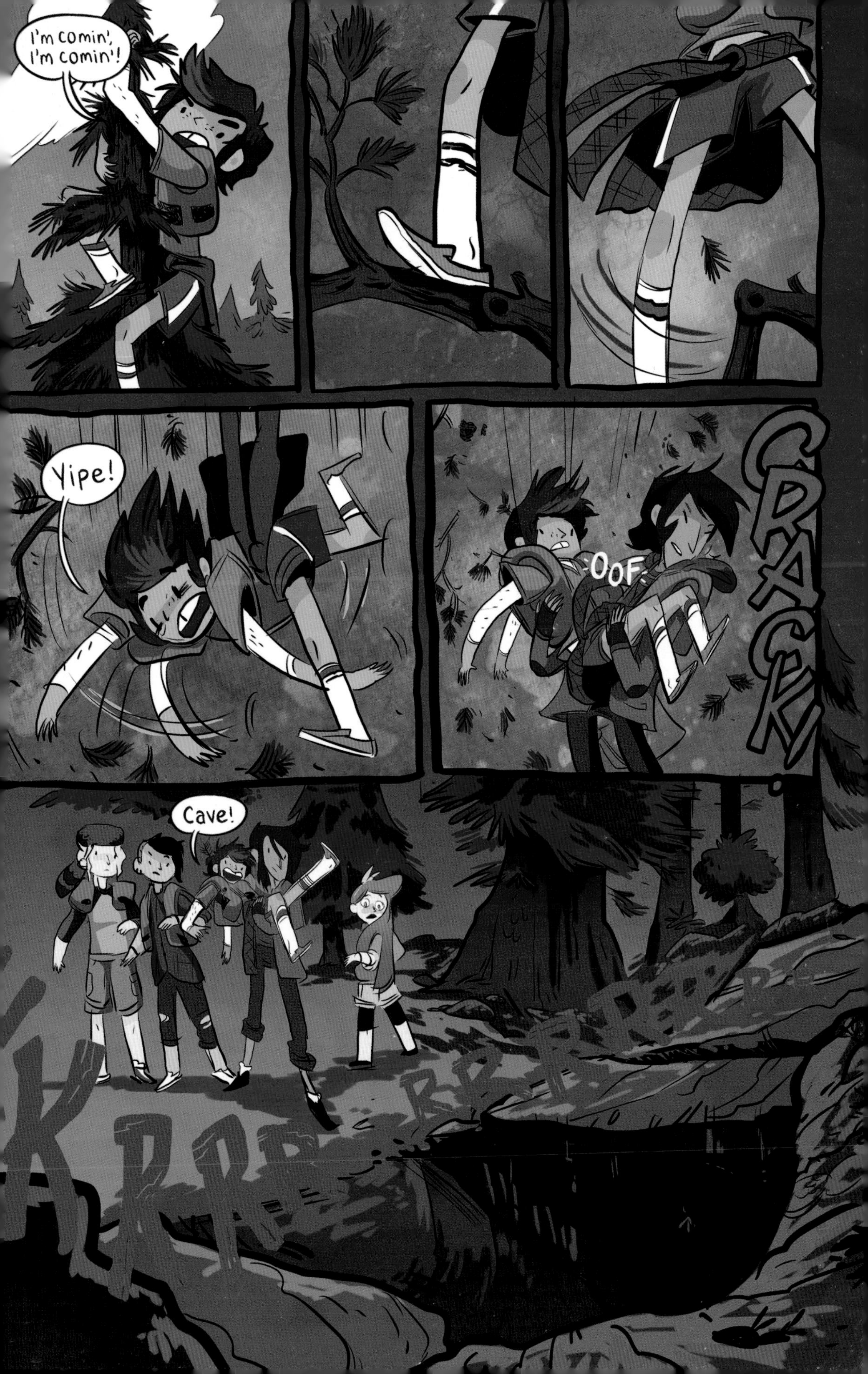
I'm comin',
I'm comin'!
Yipe!
OOF
CRACK!
Cave!
KRRR

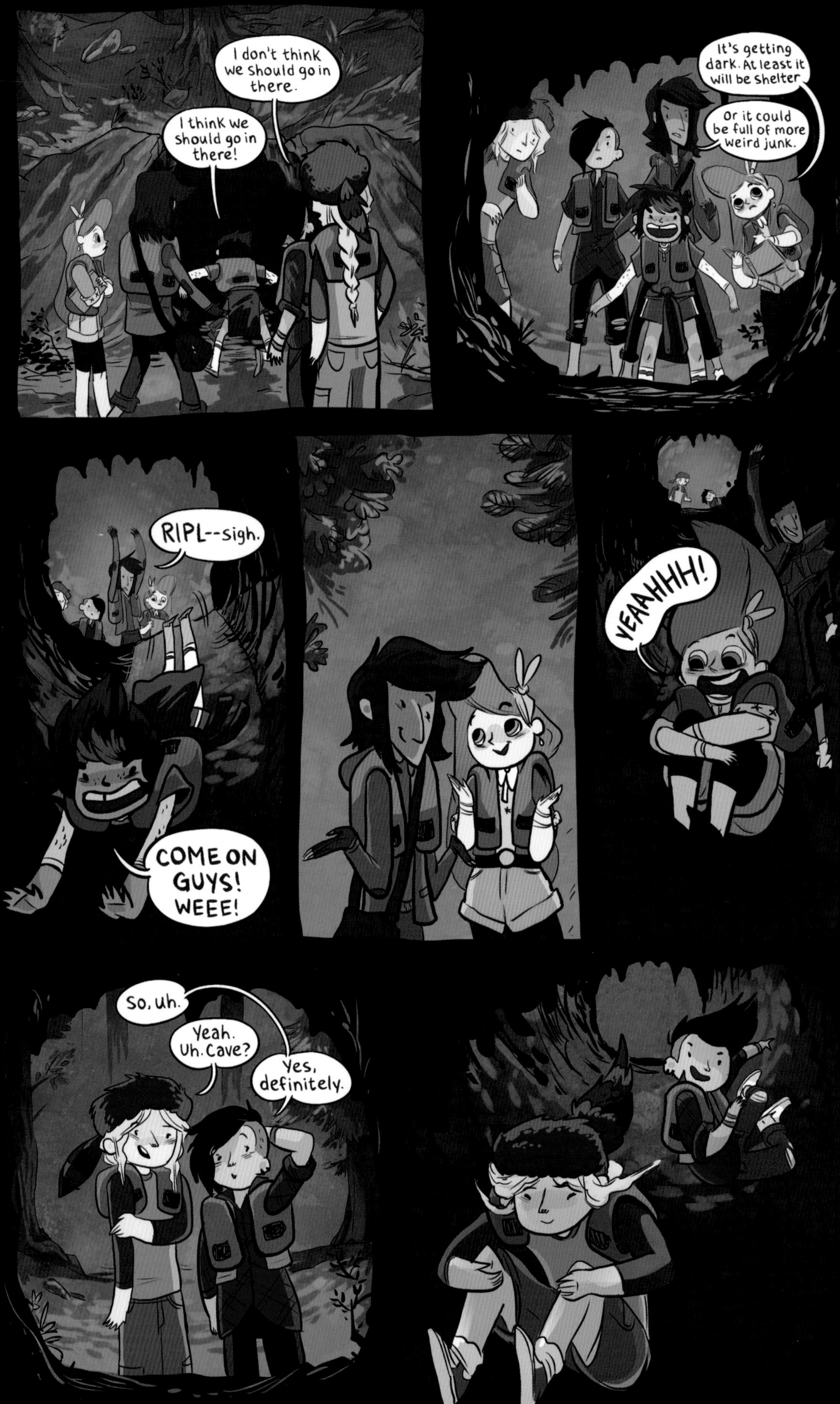
I don't think we should go in there.
I think we should go in there!
It's getting dark. At least it will be shelter.
Or it could be full of more weird junk.
RIPL--sigh.
COME ON GUYS! WEEE!
YEAAHHH!
So, uh.
Yeah. Uh. Cave?
Yes, definitely.

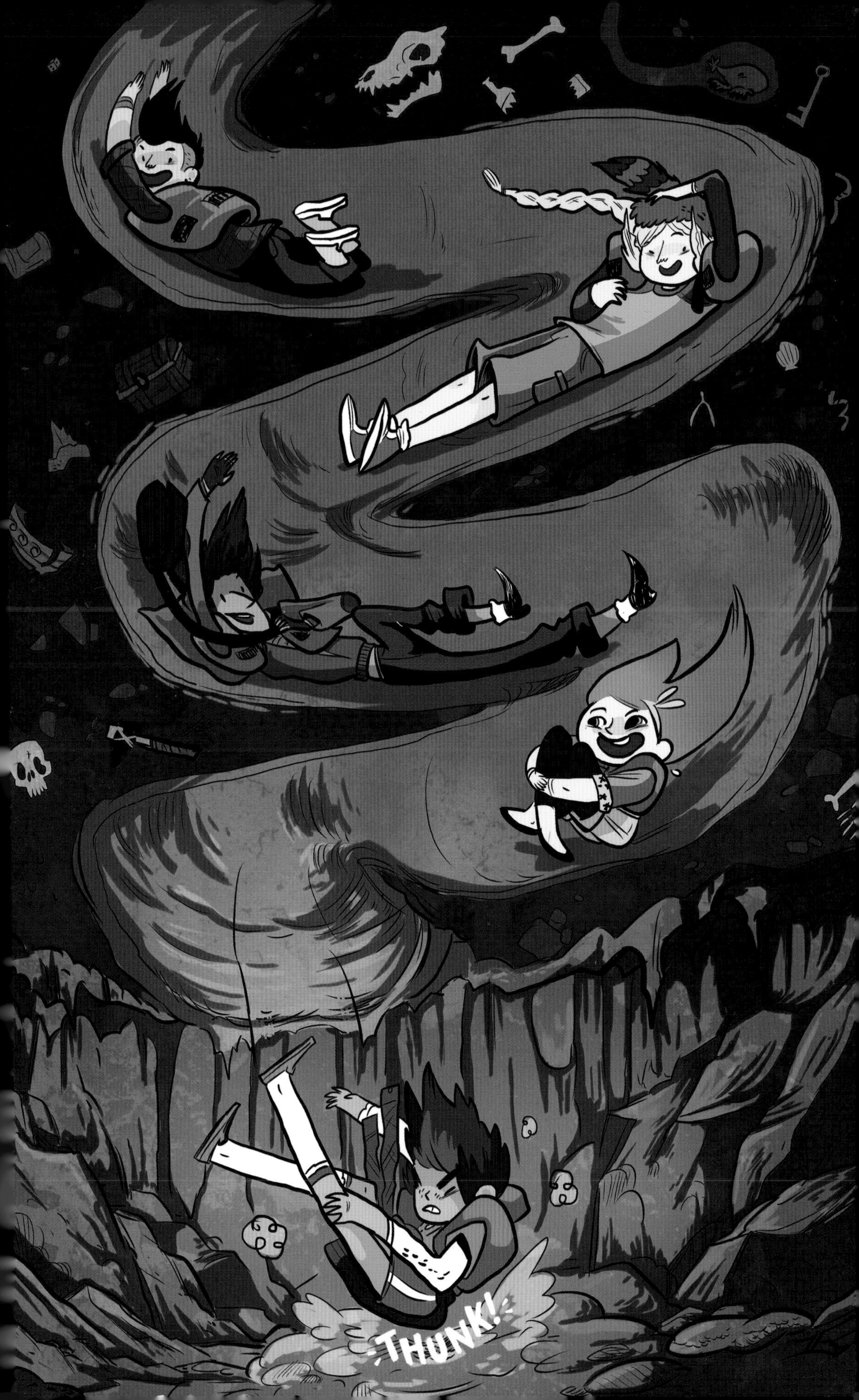
THUNK!

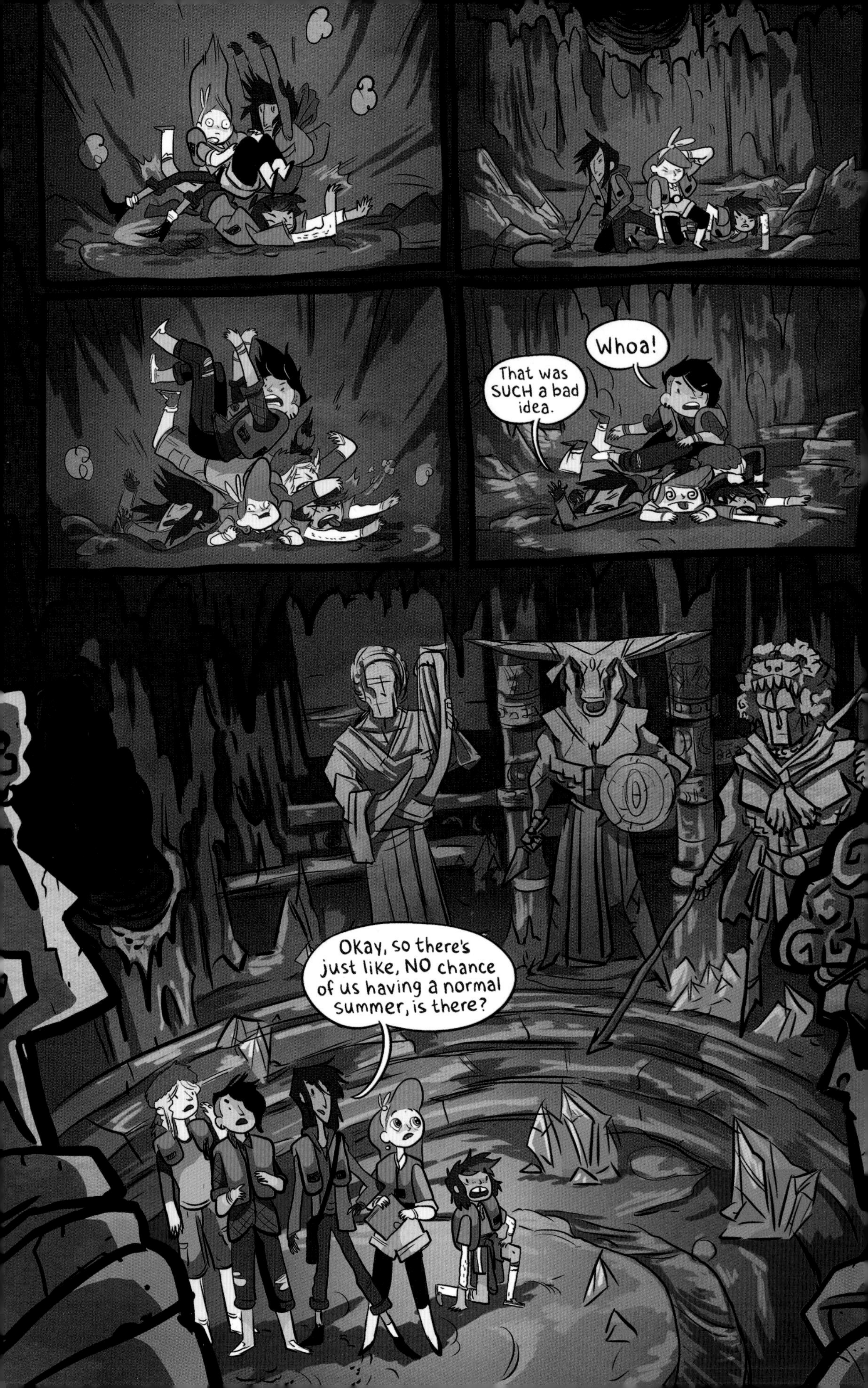
Whoa!
That was SUCH a bad idea.
Okay, so there's just like, NO chance of us having a normal summer, is there?

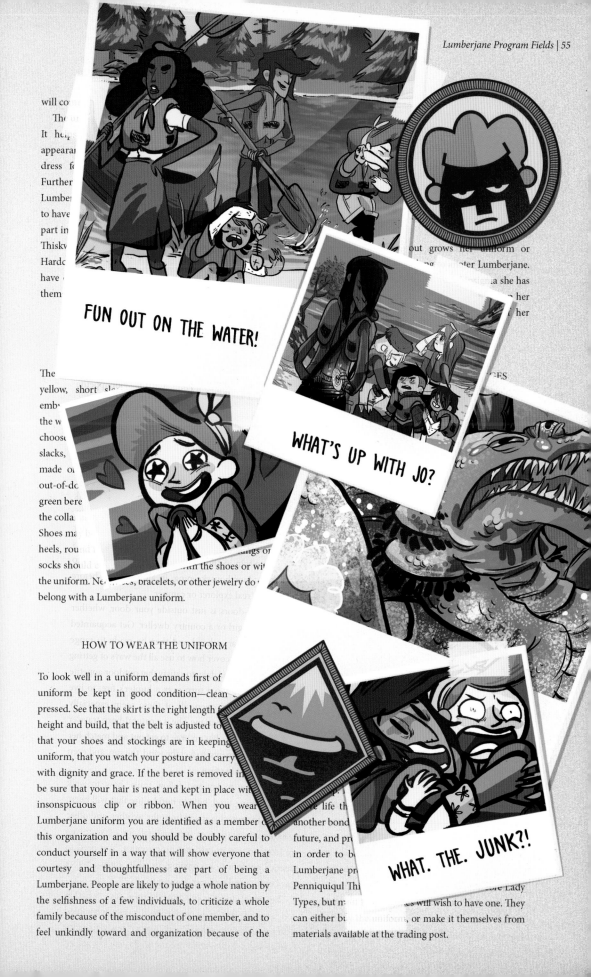

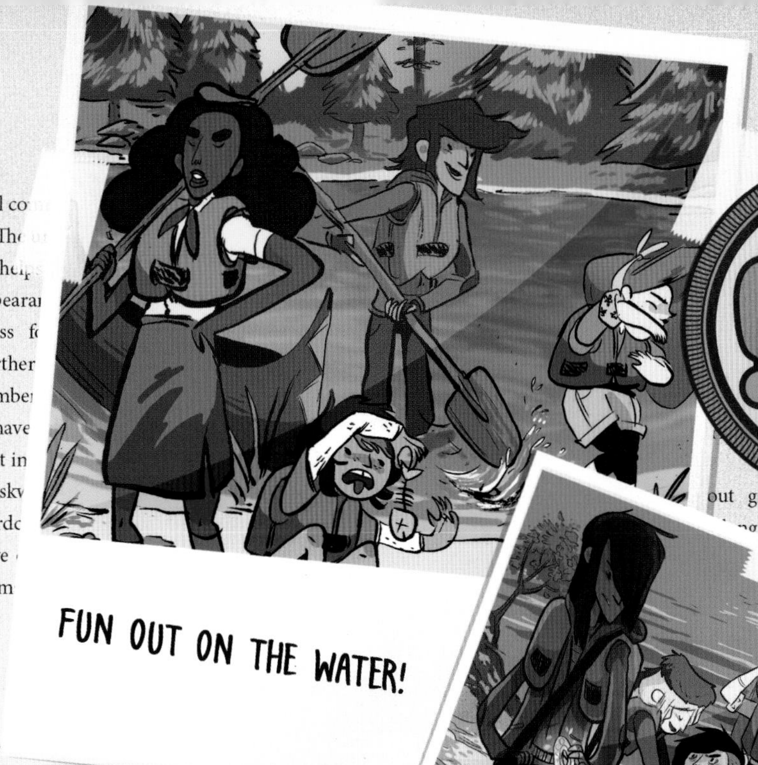
FUN OUT ON THE WATER!

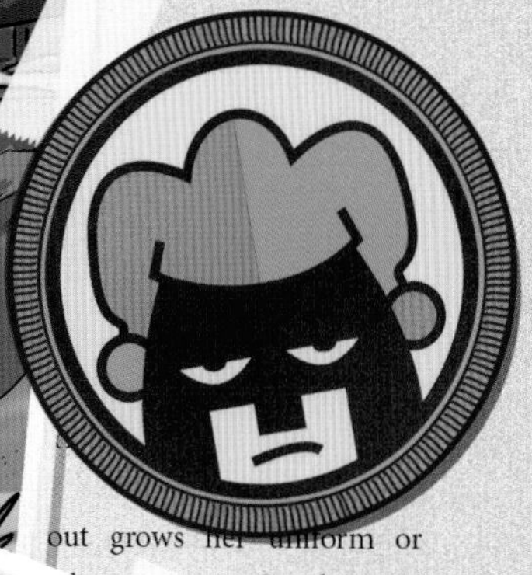

will co
The
It he
appeara
dress f
Further
Lumbe
to have
part in
Thiskv
Hardc
have
them

out grows her uniform or
...ter Lumberjane.
...a she has
... her
... her

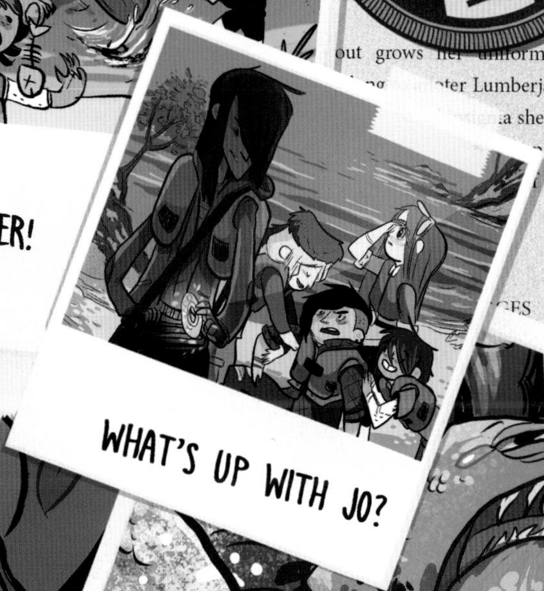
WHAT'S UP WITH JO?

The
yellow, short sl
emb
the w
choos
slacks,
made o
out-of-dc
green bere
the colla
Shoes ma
heels, rou ... ings or
socks shou ... with the shoes or wi
the uniform. Ne... bracelets, or other jewelry do
belong with a Lumberjane uniform.

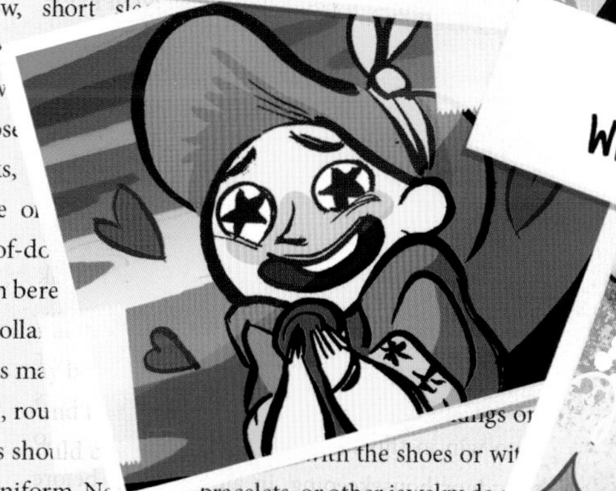

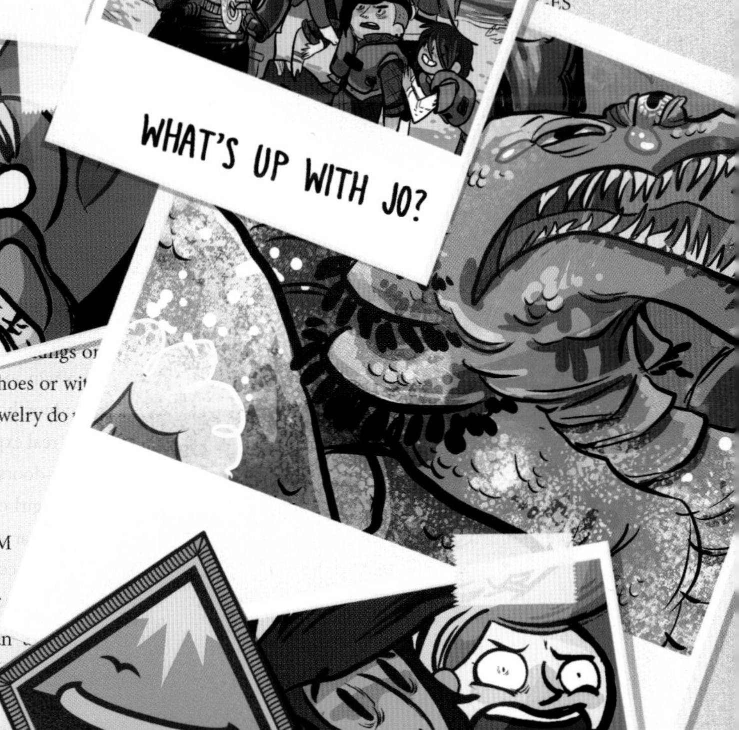

HOW TO WEAR THE UNIFORM

To look well in a uniform demands first of
uniform be kept in good condition—clean
pressed. See that the skirt is the right length
height and build, that the belt is adjusted to
that your shoes and stockings are in keeping
uniform, that you watch your posture and carry
with dignity and grace. If the beret is removed in
be sure that your hair is neat and kept in place wit
insonspicuous clip or ribbon. When you wear
Lumberjane uniform you are identified as a member o
this organization and you should be doubly careful to conduct yourself in a way that will show everyone that courtesy and thoughtfullness are part of being a Lumberjane. People are likely to judge a whole nation by the selfishness of a few individuals, to criticize a whole family because of the misconduct of one member, and to feel unkindly toward and organization because of the

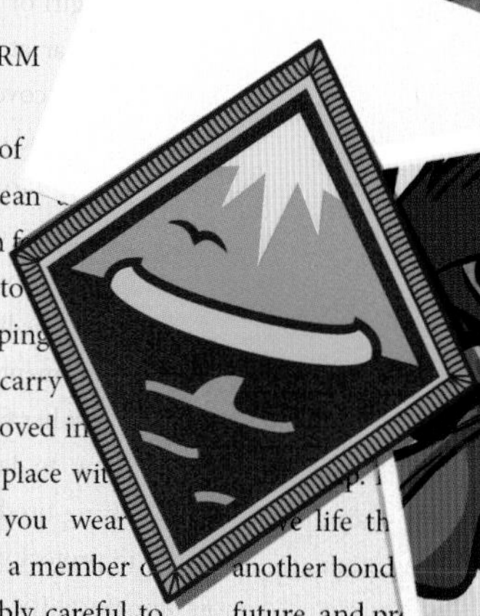

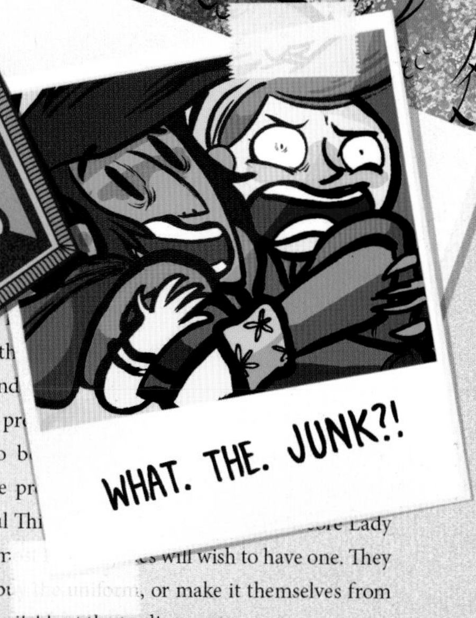
WHAT. THE. JUNK?!

...e life th
another bond
future, and pr
in order to b
Lumberjane pr
Penniquiqul Thi ... ore Lady
Types, but m ... es will wish to have one. They
can either bu ... the uniform, or make it themselves from
materials available at the trading post.

LUMBERJANES FIELD MANUAL

CHAPTER THREE

Lumberjanes "Mathematics and Science" Program Field

EVERYTHING UNDER THE SUM BADGE

"Math leads to a basic understanding of life."

While math is an important subject in schooling, a Lumberjane will learn the commonplace use in everyday situations from knowing the proper amount of kindling needed for a variety of fires to know the velocity needed to run in order to leap across a cliff and make it to the other side. A Lumberjane recognizes how basic understanding of equations can not only make the trials of the wilderness simpler but how furthering that knowledge will help them establish a firmer foothold in the adventure of their lifetime. The human experience can be boiled down to patterns and it is with this understanding that a Lumberjane sees her importance not only in the lives that she directly influences but those outside her circle.

To obtain the *Everything Under the Sum* badge, a Lumberjane must be able to map accurately and correctly from the country itself the main features of half a mile of road, with 440 yards each side to a scale of two feet to the mile, and afterward draw the same map from memory. A Lumberjane must be able to measure the height of a tree, telegraph pole, and church steeple, describing method adopted. She must be able to measure the width of a river, and estimate distance apart of two objects a known distance away and unapproachable. With this skill she will not only be able to fully prepare for her adventure or task, but be able to set her friends up for success as they go on their journey together.

With an *Everything Under the Sum* badge, a Lumberjane will be able to measure a gradient, have a basic understanding of theoretical mathematics and the of laws of physics, this will help give her a sure footing in her future career whether it be teaching the future generations or answering their patriotic call and going into the service of their country. While this badge may take some time to earn, every Lumberjane will be able to understand its importance and, while working

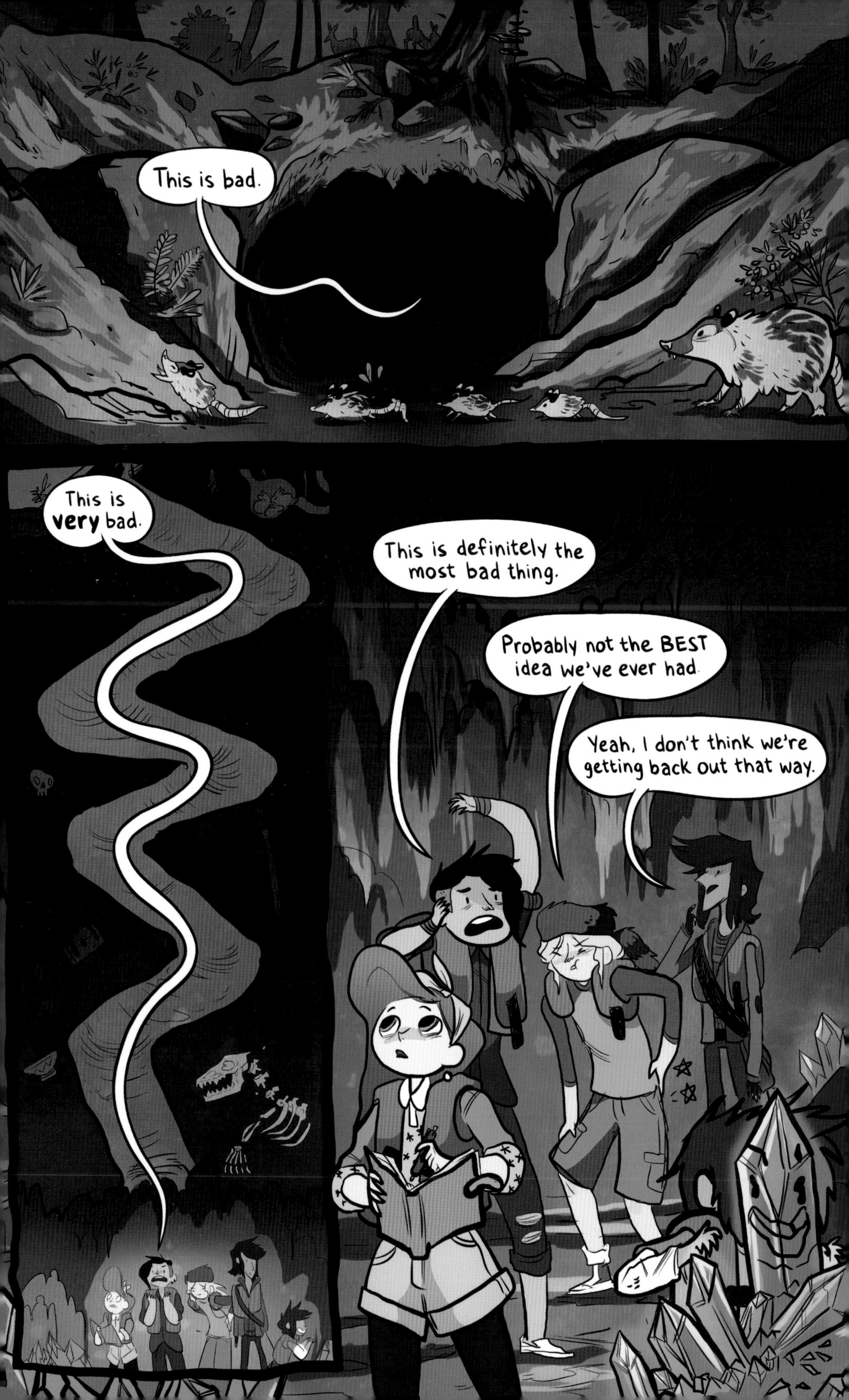
This is bad.
This is **very** bad.
This is definitely the most bad thing.
Probably not the BEST idea we've ever had.
Yeah, I don't think we're getting back out that way.

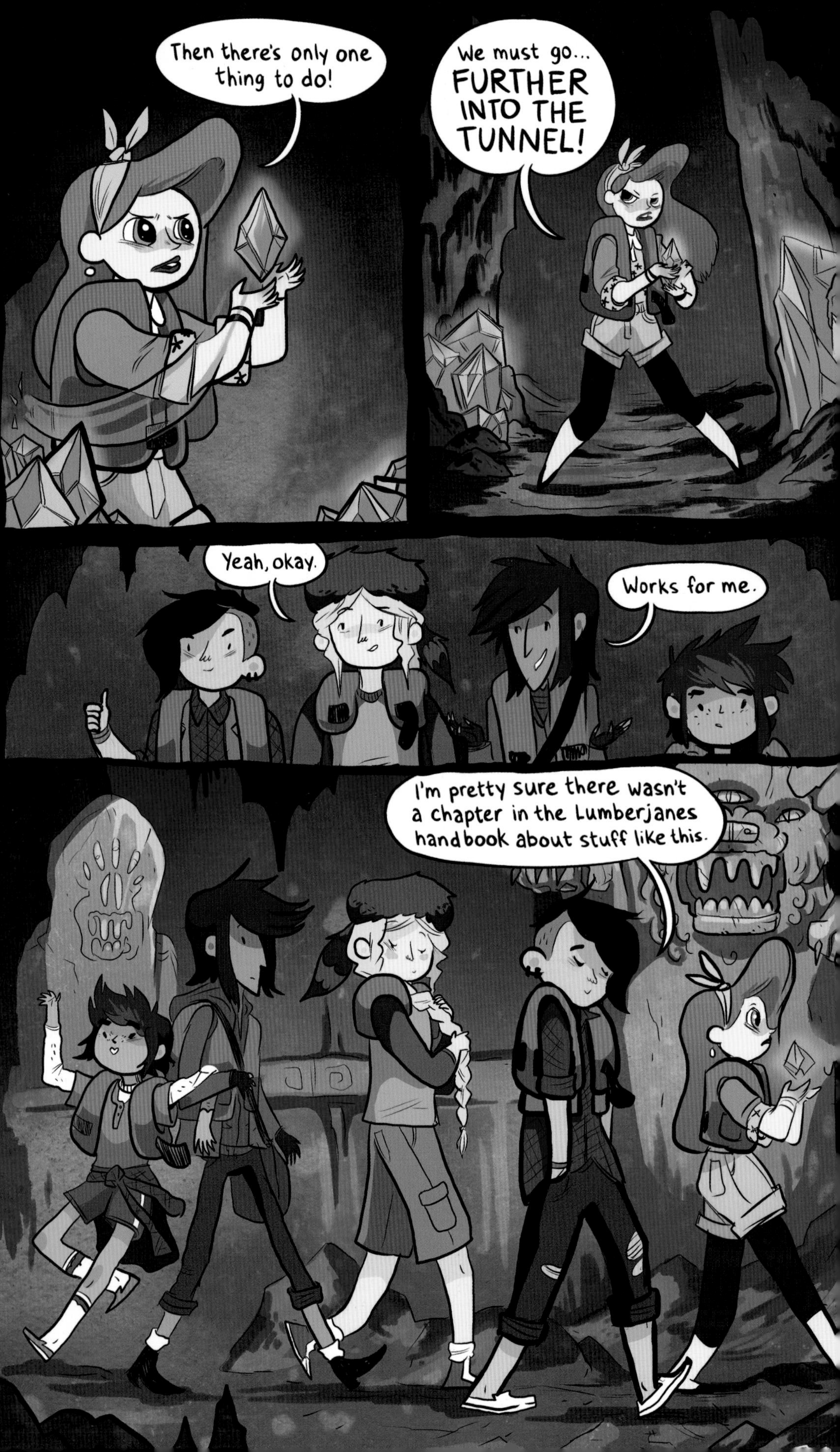
Then there's only one thing to do!
We must go... FURTHER INTO THE TUNNEL!
Yeah, okay.
Works for me.
I'm pretty sure there wasn't a chapter in the Lumberjanes handbook about stuff like this.

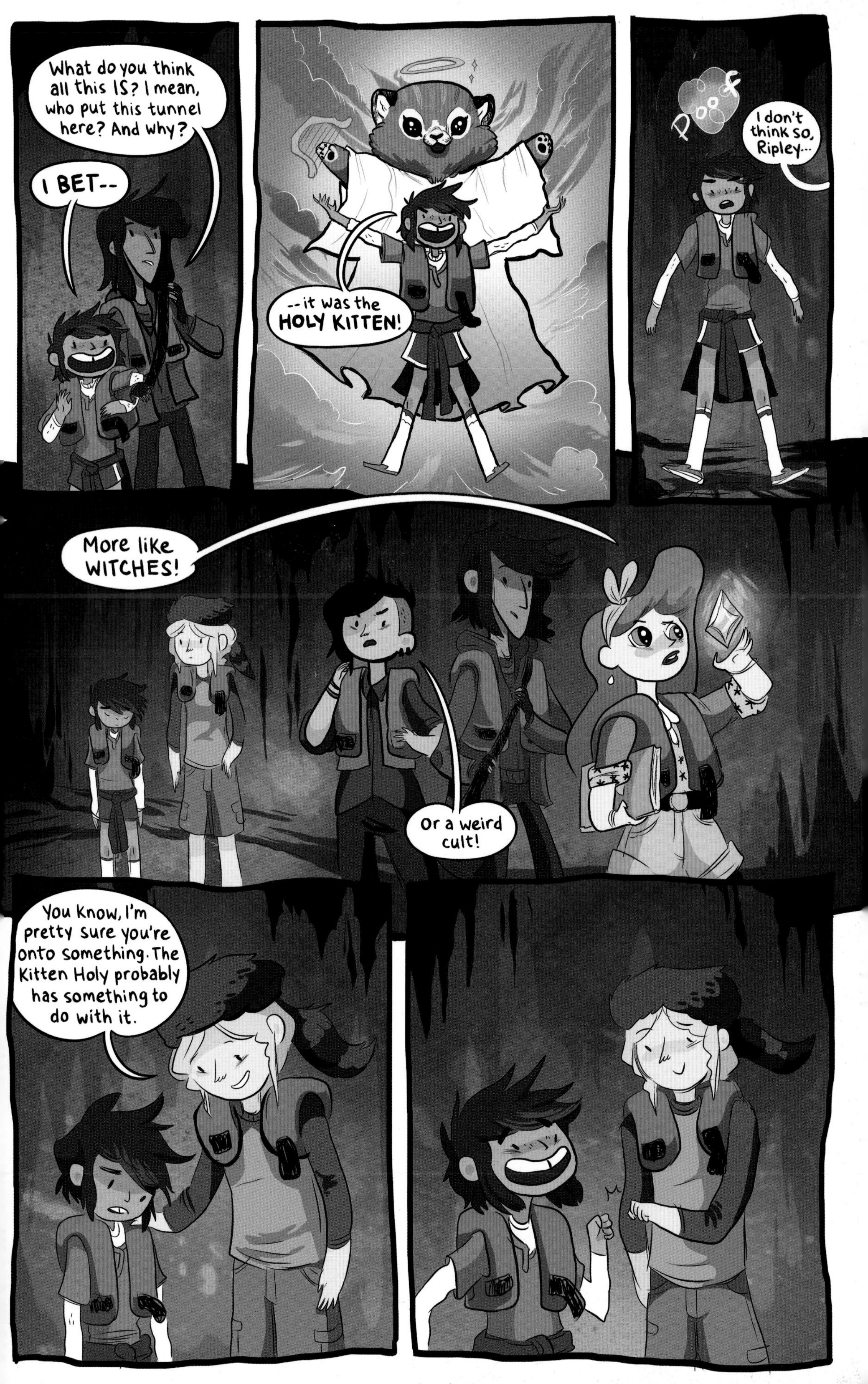
What do you think all this IS? I mean, who put this tunnel here? And why?
I BET--
--it was the HOLY KITTEN!
Poof
I don't think so, Ripley...
More like WITCHES!
Or a weird cult!
You know, I'm pretty sure you're onto something. The Kitten Holy probably has something to do with it.

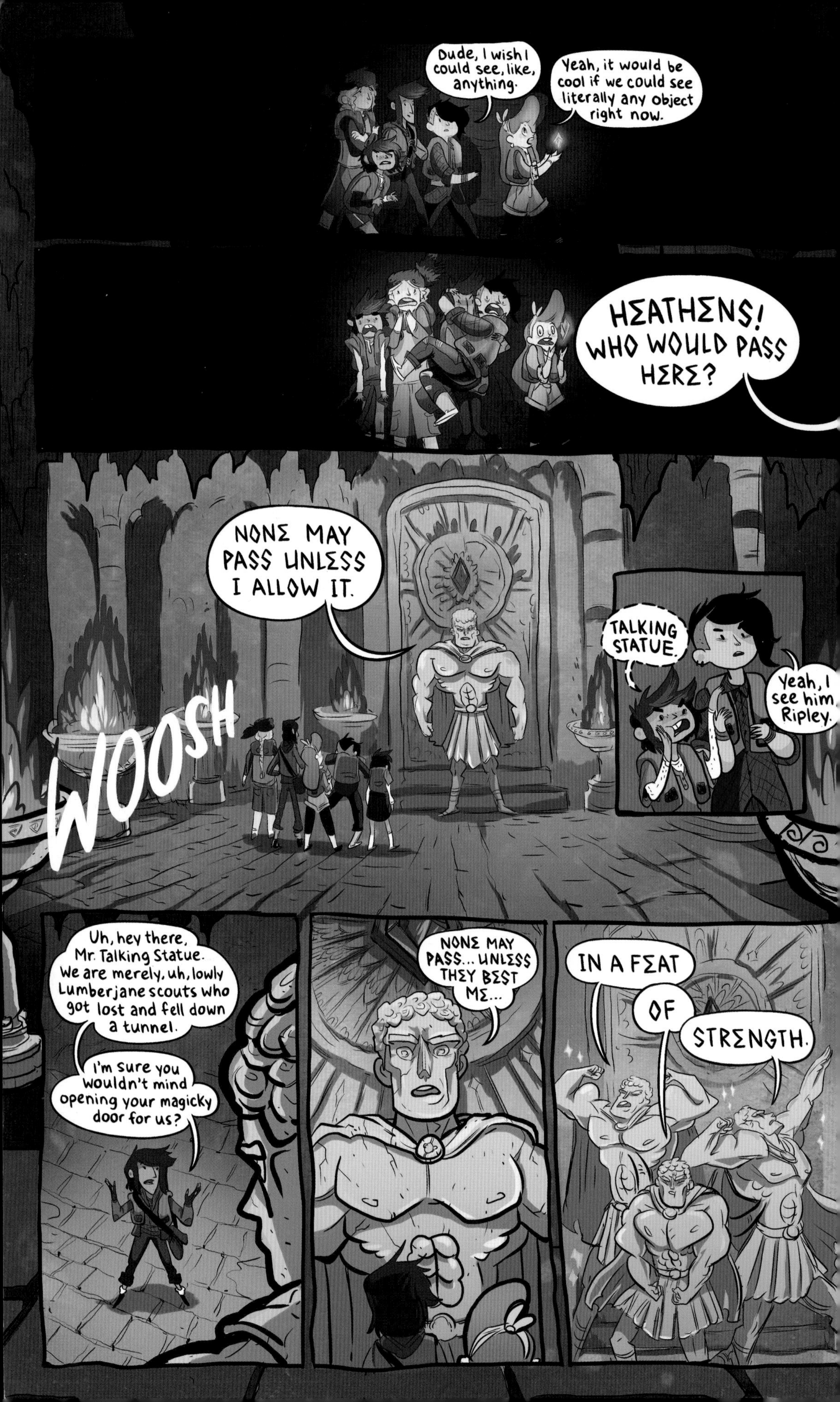
Dude, I wish I could see, like, anything.
Yeah, it would be cool if we could see literally any object right now.
HEATHENS! WHO WOULD PASS HERE?
WOOSH
NONE MAY PASS UNLESS I ALLOW IT.
TALKING STATUE.
Yeah, I see him, Ripley.
Uh, hey there, Mr. Talking Statue. We are merely, uh, lowly Lumberjane scouts who got lost and fell down a tunnel.
I'm sure you wouldn't mind opening your magicky door for us?
NONE MAY PASS... UNLESS THEY BEST ME...
IN A FEAT
OF
STRENGTH.

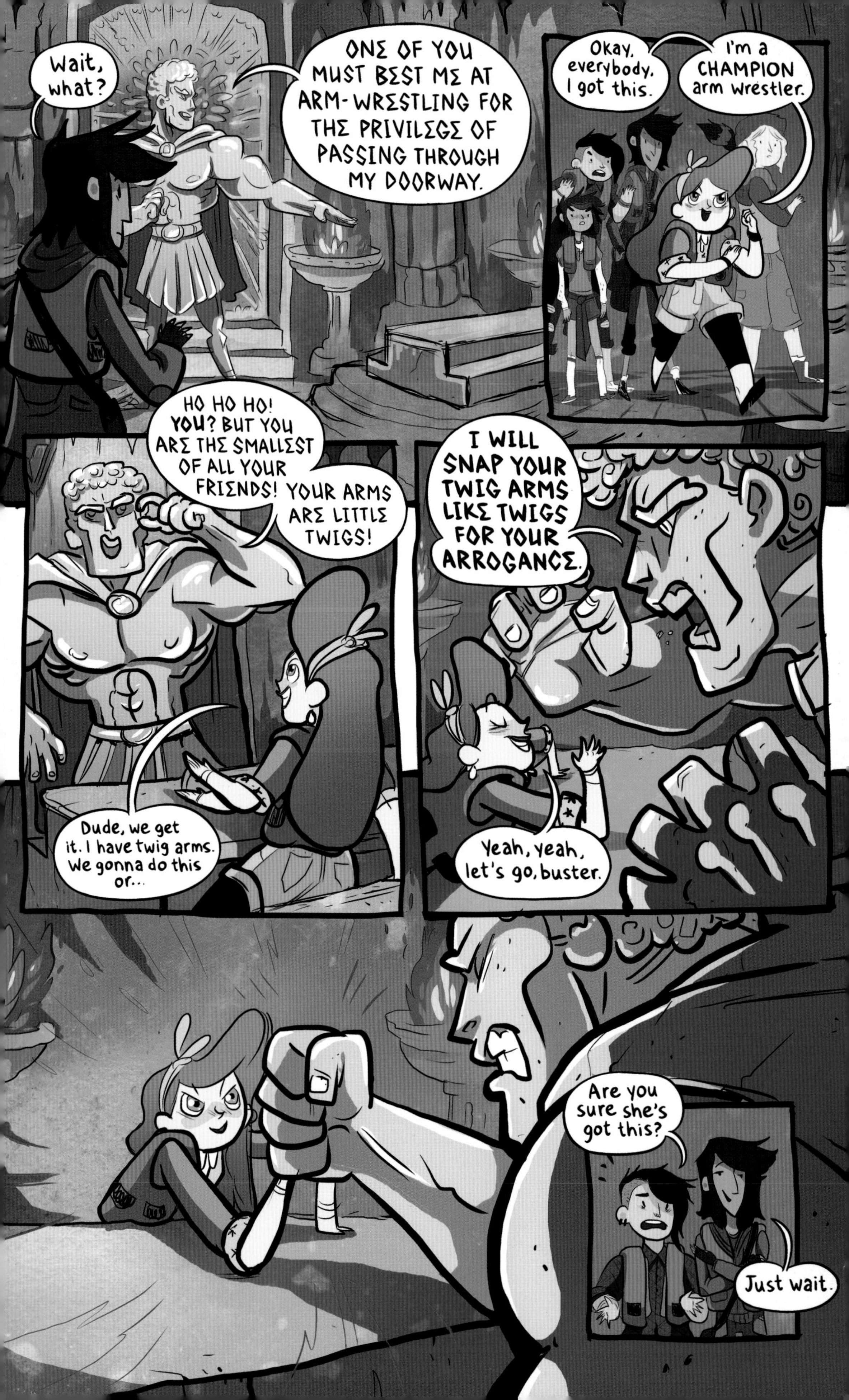
Wait, what?
ONE OF YOU MUST BEST ME AT ARM-WRESTLING FOR THE PRIVILEGE OF PASSING THROUGH MY DOORWAY.
Okay, everybody, I got this.
I'm a CHAMPION arm wrestler.
HO HO HO! YOU? BUT YOU ARE THE SMALLEST OF ALL YOUR FRIENDS!
YOUR ARMS ARE LITTLE TWIGS!
Dude, we get it. I have twig arms. We gonna do this or...
I WILL SNAP YOUR TWIG ARMS LIKE TWIGS FOR YOUR ARROGANCE.
Yeah, yeah, let's go, buster.
Are you sure she's got this?
Just wait.

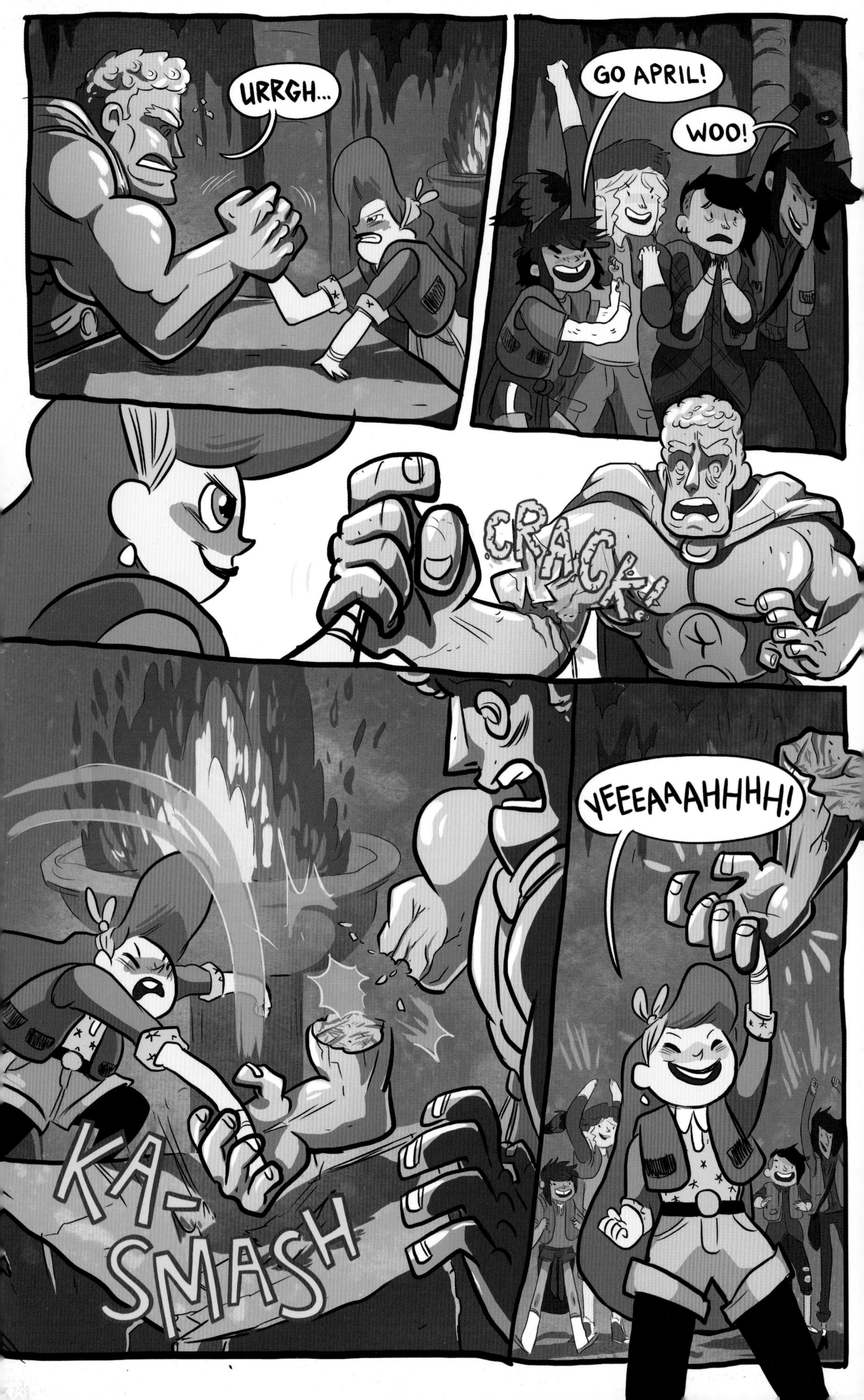
URRGH...
GO APRIL!
WOO!
CRACK!!
KA-SMASH
YEEEAAAHHHH!

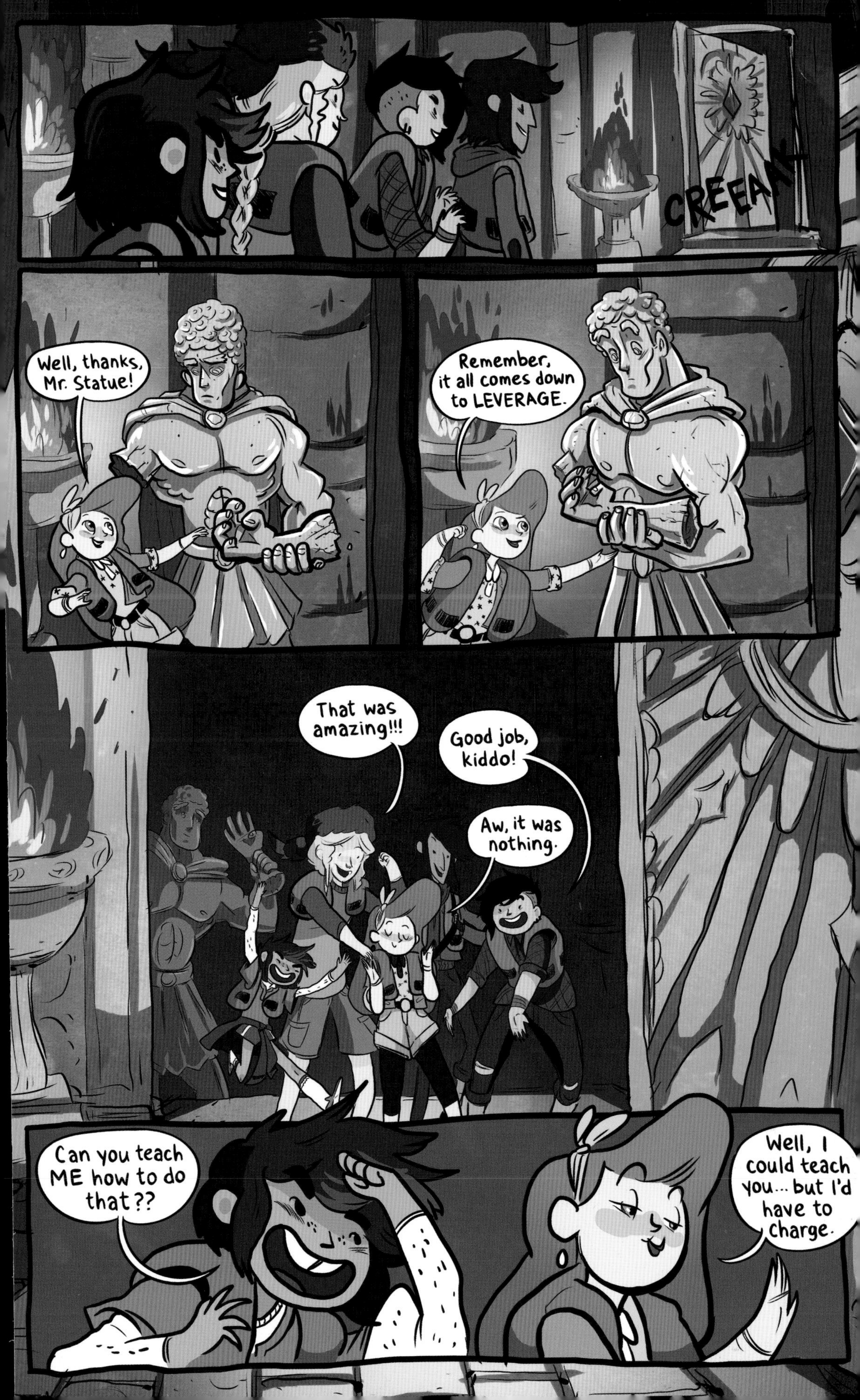
CREEAAK
Well, thanks, Mr. Statue!
Remember, it all comes down to LEVERAGE.
That was amazing!!!
Good job, kiddo!
Aw, it was nothing.
Can you teach ME how to do that??
Well, I could teach you... but I'd have to charge.

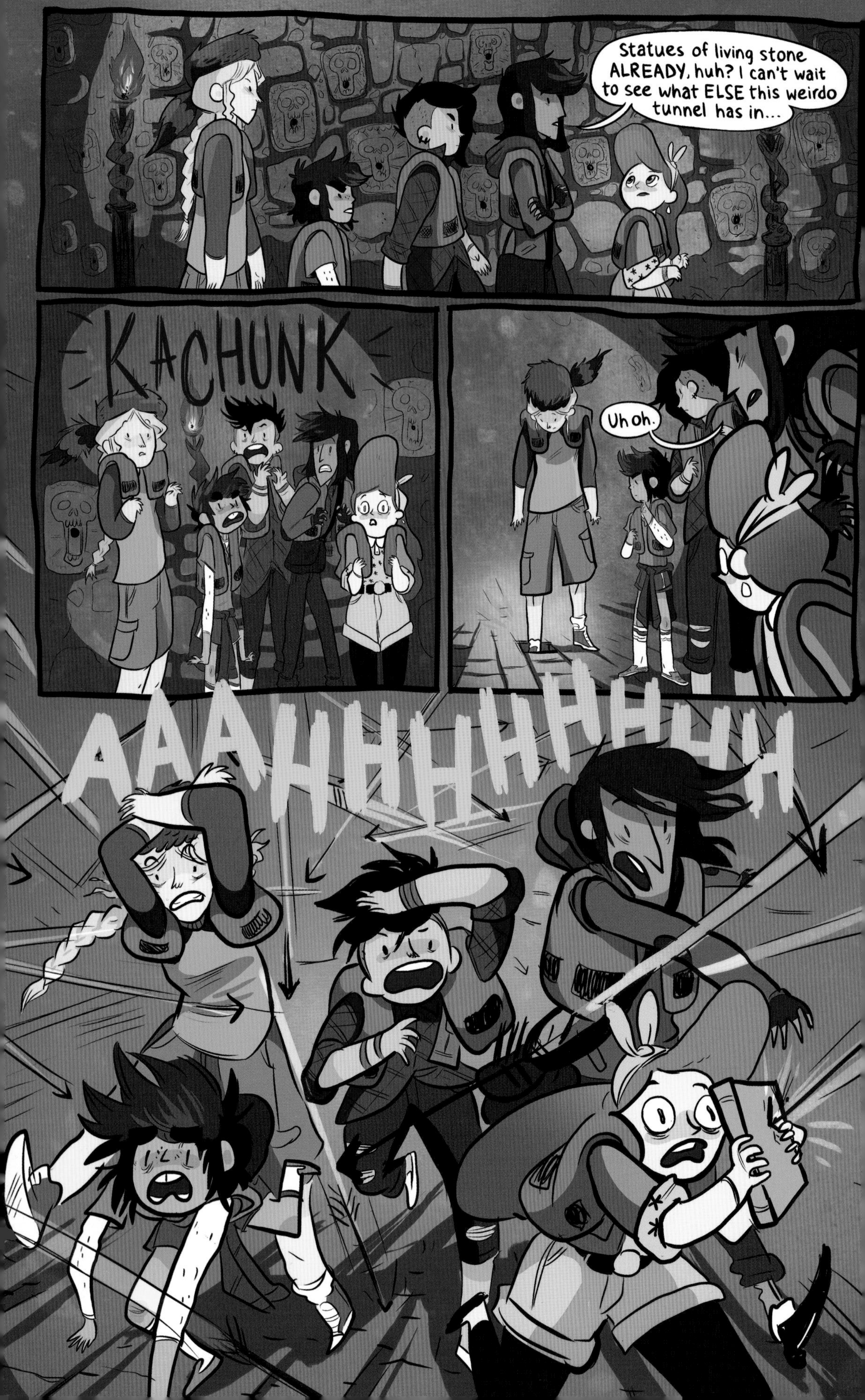
Statues of living stone ALREADY, huh? I can't wait to see what ELSE this weirdo tunnel has in...
KACHUNK
Uh oh.
AAHHHHHHHH

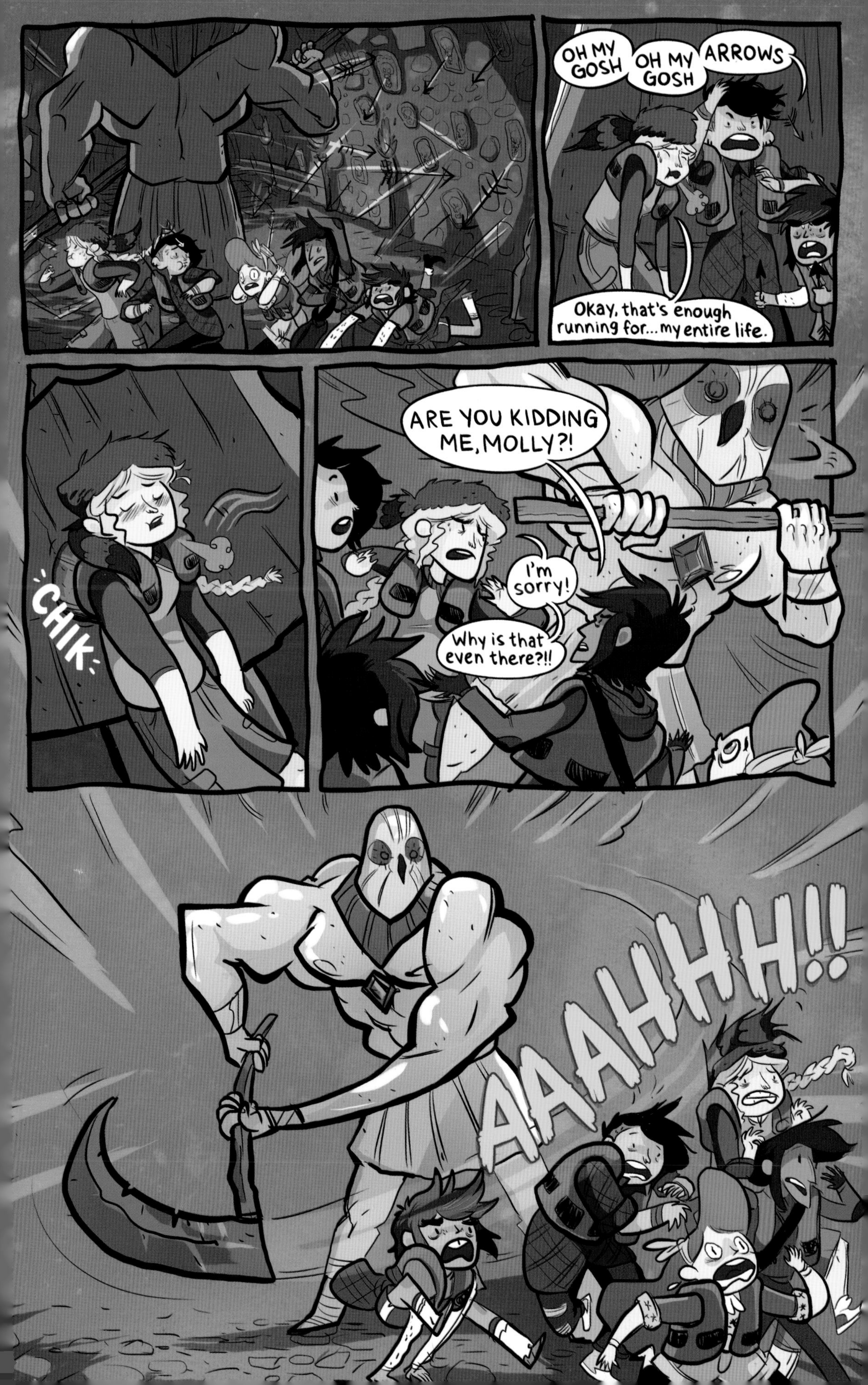
OH MY GOSH
OH MY GOSH
ARROWS
Okay, that's enough running for... my entire life.
CHIK
ARE YOU KIDDING ME, MOLLY?!
I'm sorry!
Why is that even there?!!
AAAHHH!!

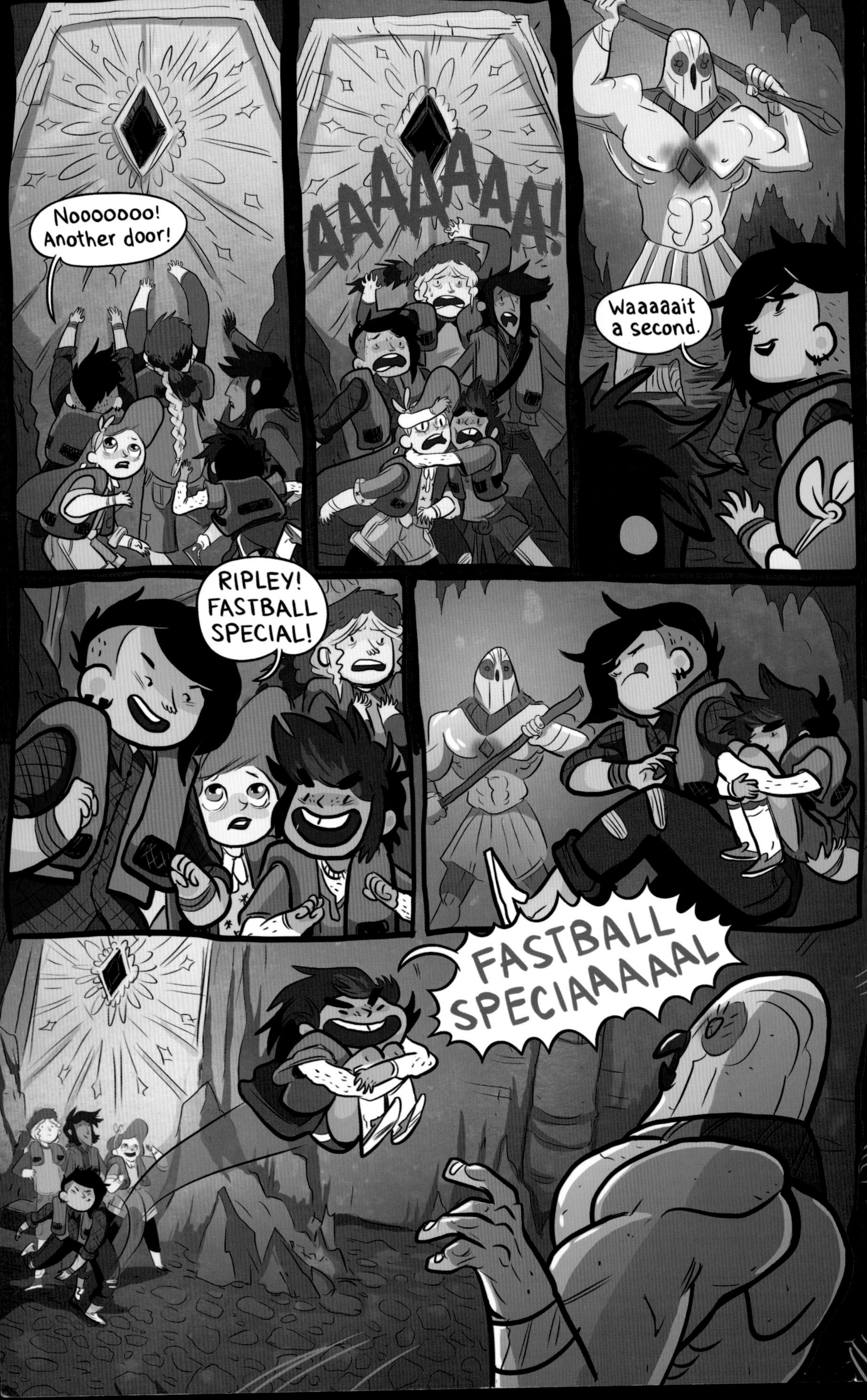
Noooooooo! Another door!
AAAAAAAA!
Waaaaait a second.
RIPLEY! FASTBALL SPECIAL!
FASTBALL SPECIAAAAAL

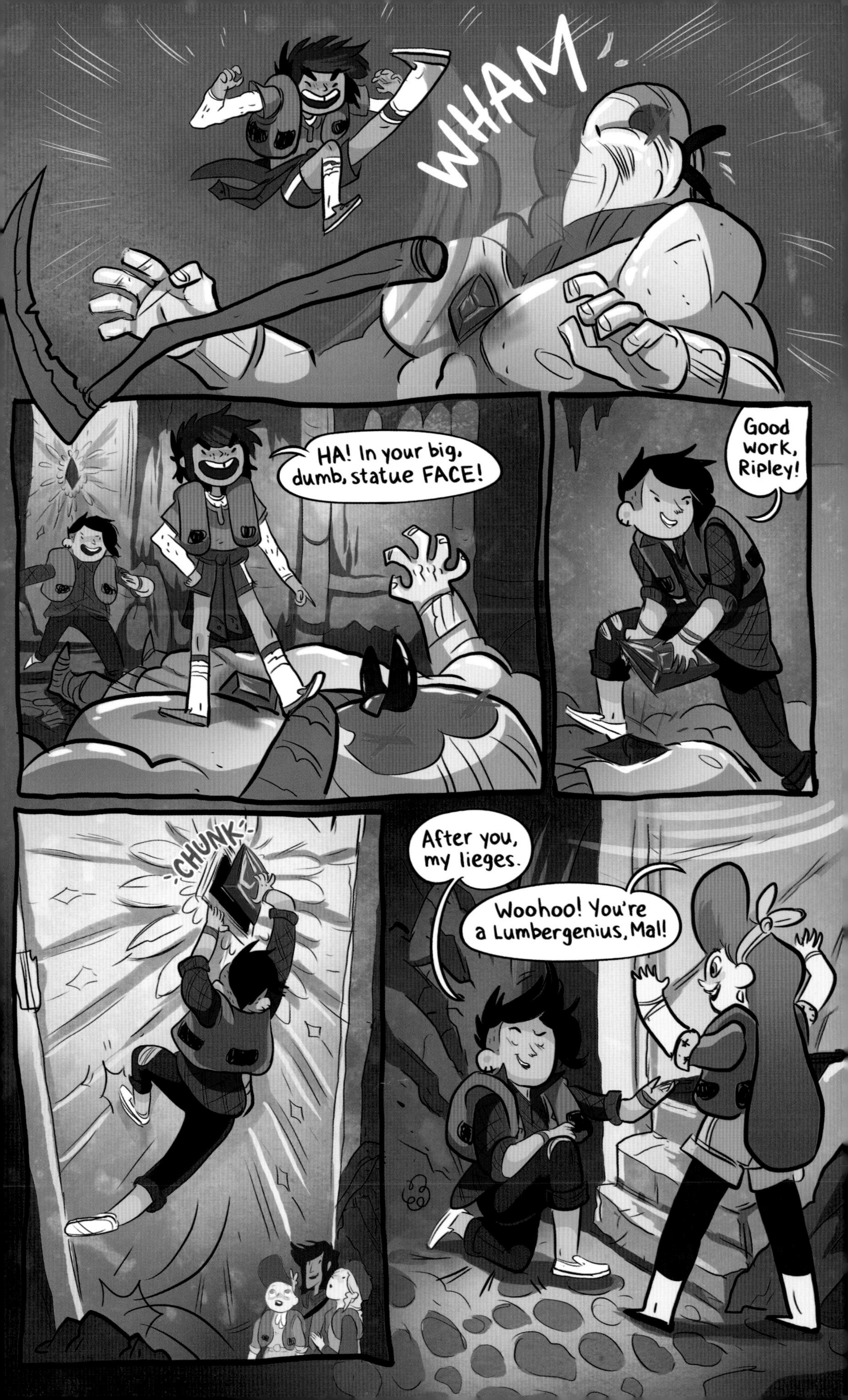
WHAM
HA! In your big, dumb, statue FACE!
Good work, Ripley!
CHUNK
After you, my lieges.
Woohoo! You're a Lumbergenius, Mal!

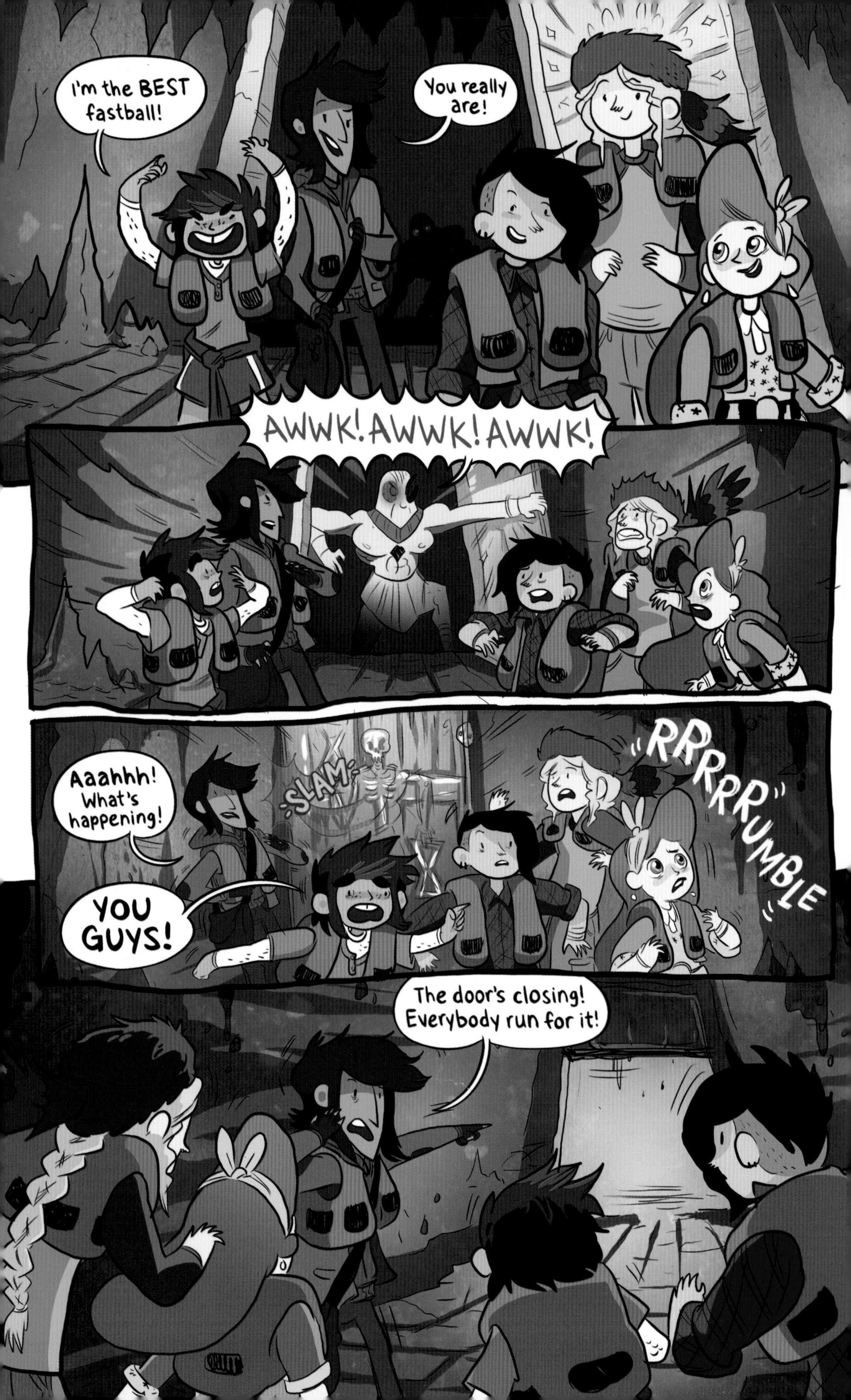

I'm the BEST fastball!
You really are!
AWWK! AWWK! AWWK!
Aaahhh! What's happening!
SLAM
RRRRRRUMBLE
YOU GUYS!
The door's closing! Everybody run for it!

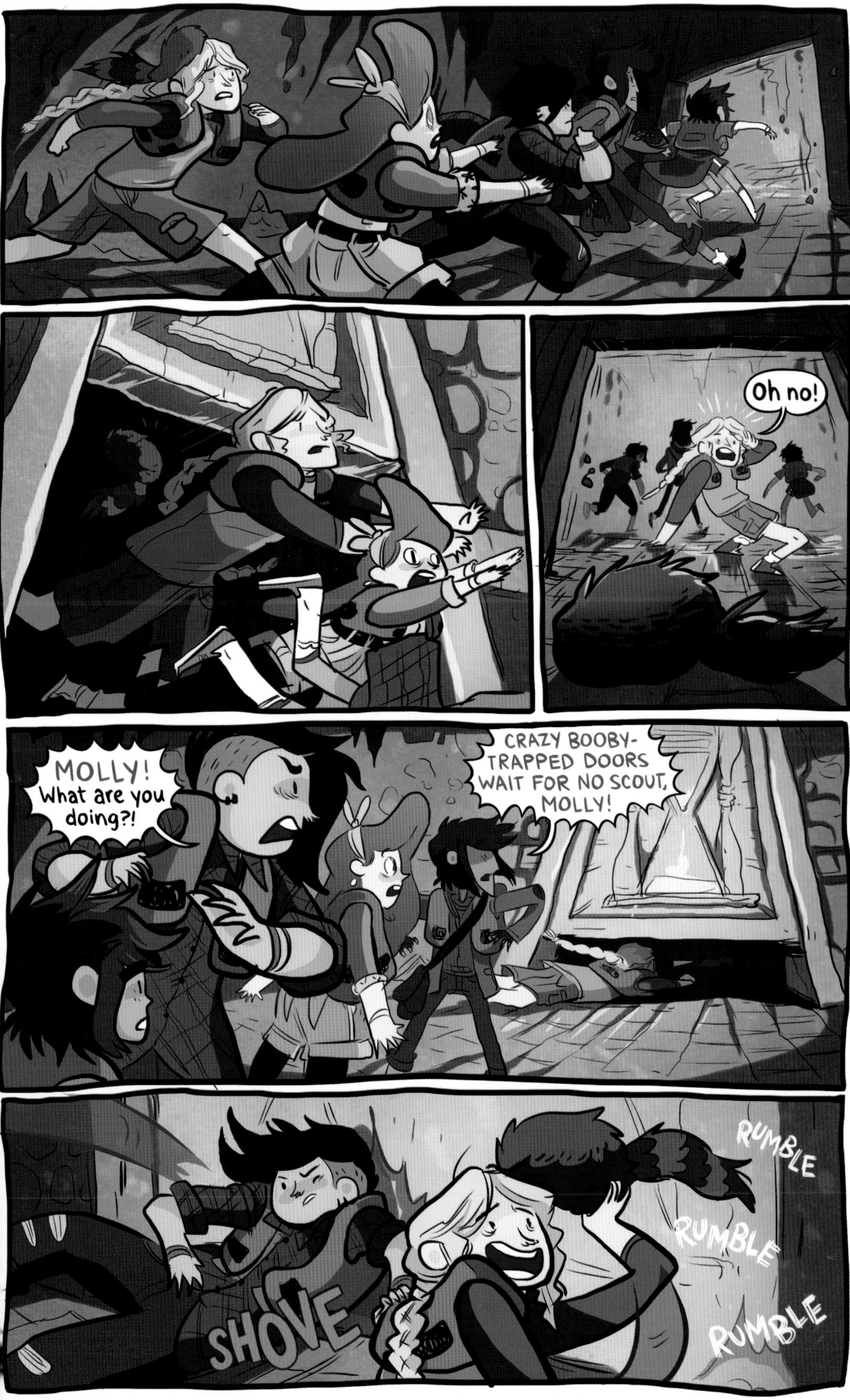

Oh no!
MOLLY! What are you doing?!
CRAZY BOOBY-TRAPPED DOORS WAIT FOR NO SCOUT, MOLLY!
RUMBLE
RUMBLE
RUMBLE
SHOVE

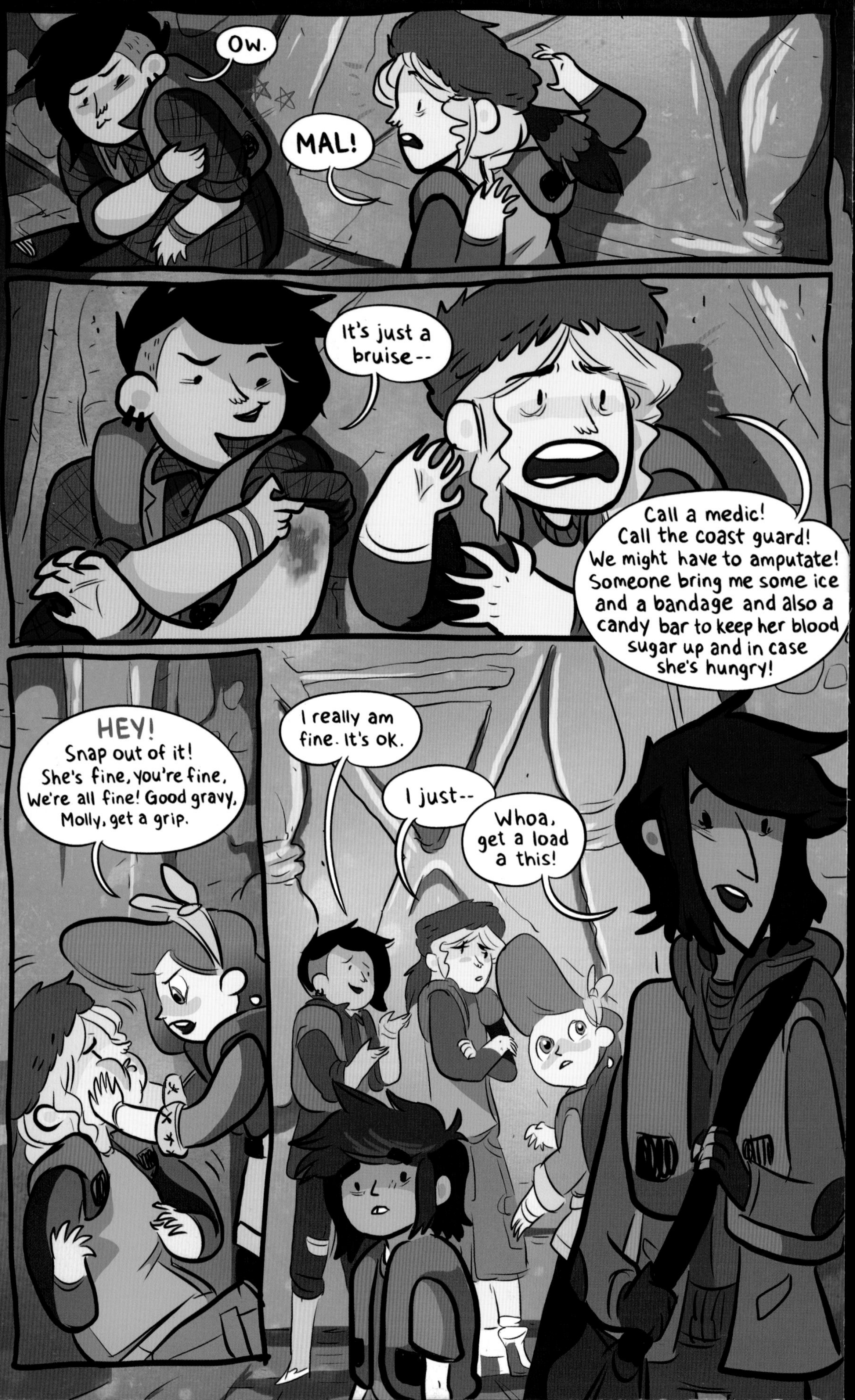
Ow.
MAL!
It's just a bruise--
Call a medic! Call the coast guard! We might have to amputate! Someone bring me some ice and a bandage and also a candy bar to keep her blood sugar up and in case she's hungry!
HEY! Snap out of it! She's fine, you're fine, We're all fine! Good gravy, Molly, get a grip.
I really am fine. It's ok.
I just--
Whoa, get a load a this!

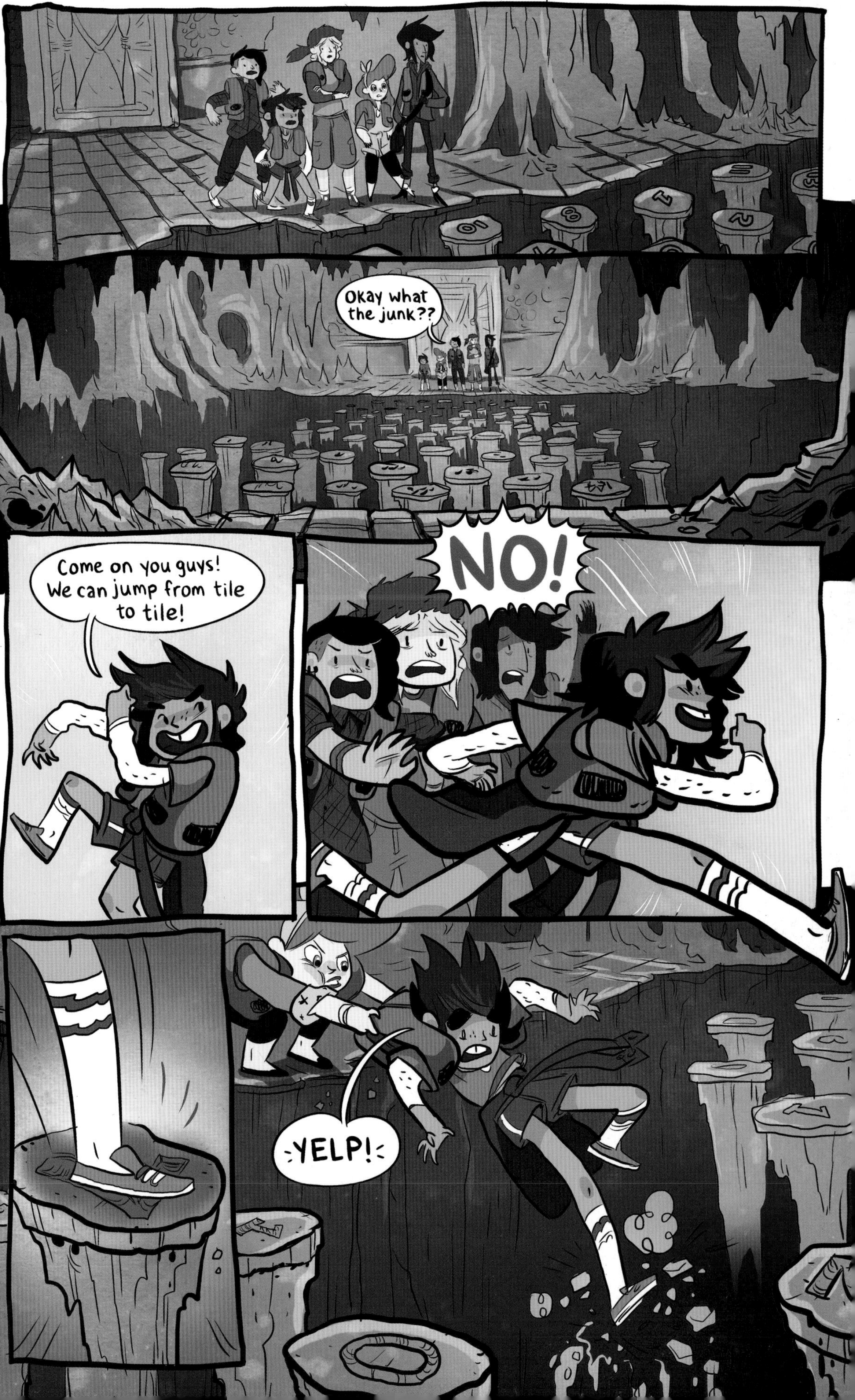
Okay what the junk??
Come on you guys! We can jump from tile to tile!
NO!
YELP!

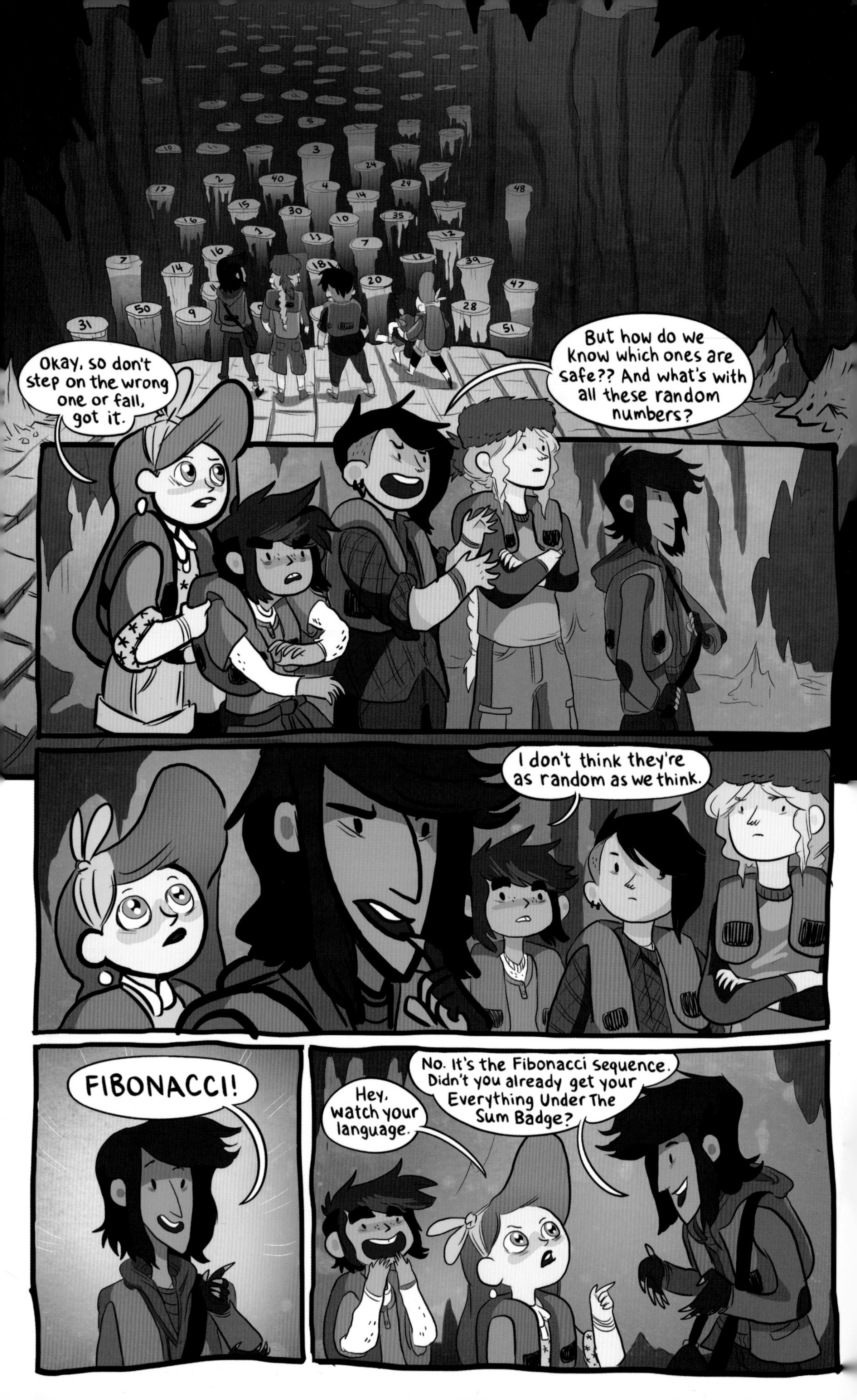
Okay, so don't step on the wrong one or fall, got it.
But how do we know which ones are safe?? And what's with all these random numbers?
I don't think they're as random as we think.
FIBONACCI!
Hey, watch your language.
No. It's the Fibonacci sequence. Didn't you already get your Everything Under The Sum Badge?

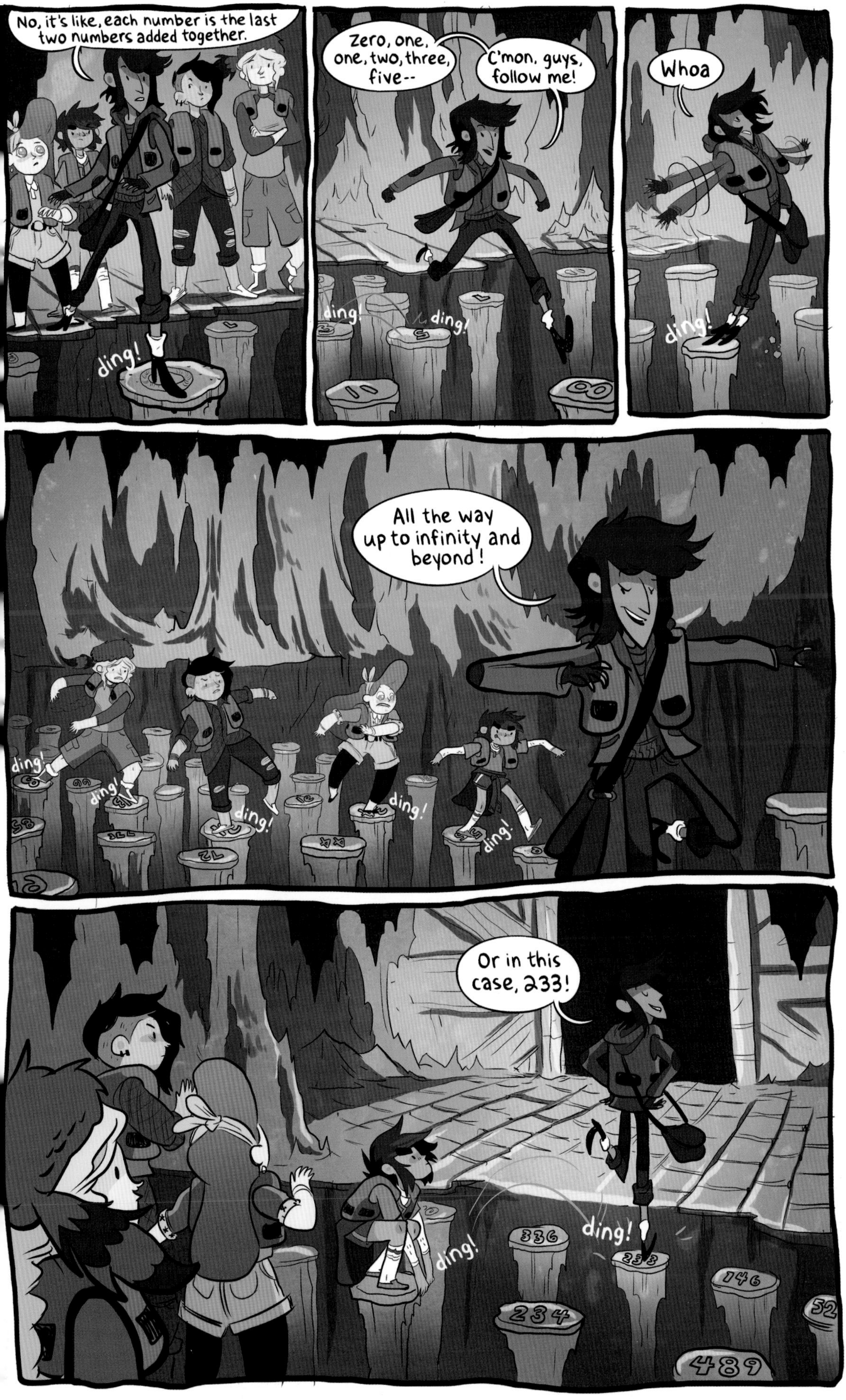
No, it's like, each number is the last two numbers added together.
ding!
Zero, one, one, two, three, five--
C'mon, guys, follow me!
ding!
ding!
Whoa
ding!
All the way up to infinity and beyond!
ding!
ding!
ding!
ding!
ding!
Or in this case, 233!
ding!
ding!
336
233
146
234
52
489

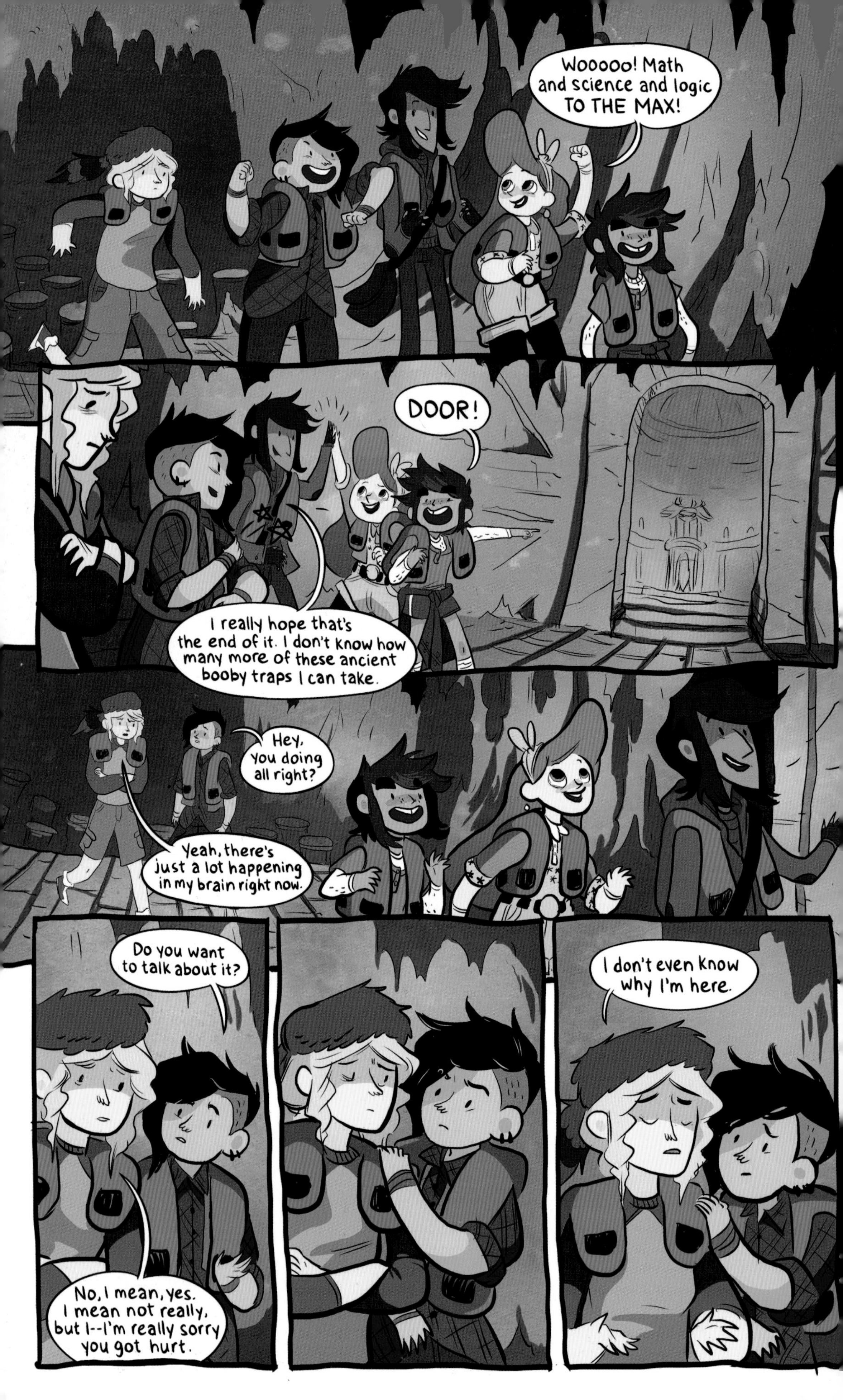
Wooooo! Math and science and logic TO THE MAX!
DOOR!
I really hope that's the end of it. I don't know how many more of these ancient booby traps I can take.
Hey, you doing all right?
Yeah, there's just a lot happening in my brain right now.
Do you want to talk about it?
No, I mean, yes. I mean not really, but I--I'm really sorry you got hurt.
I don't even know why I'm here.

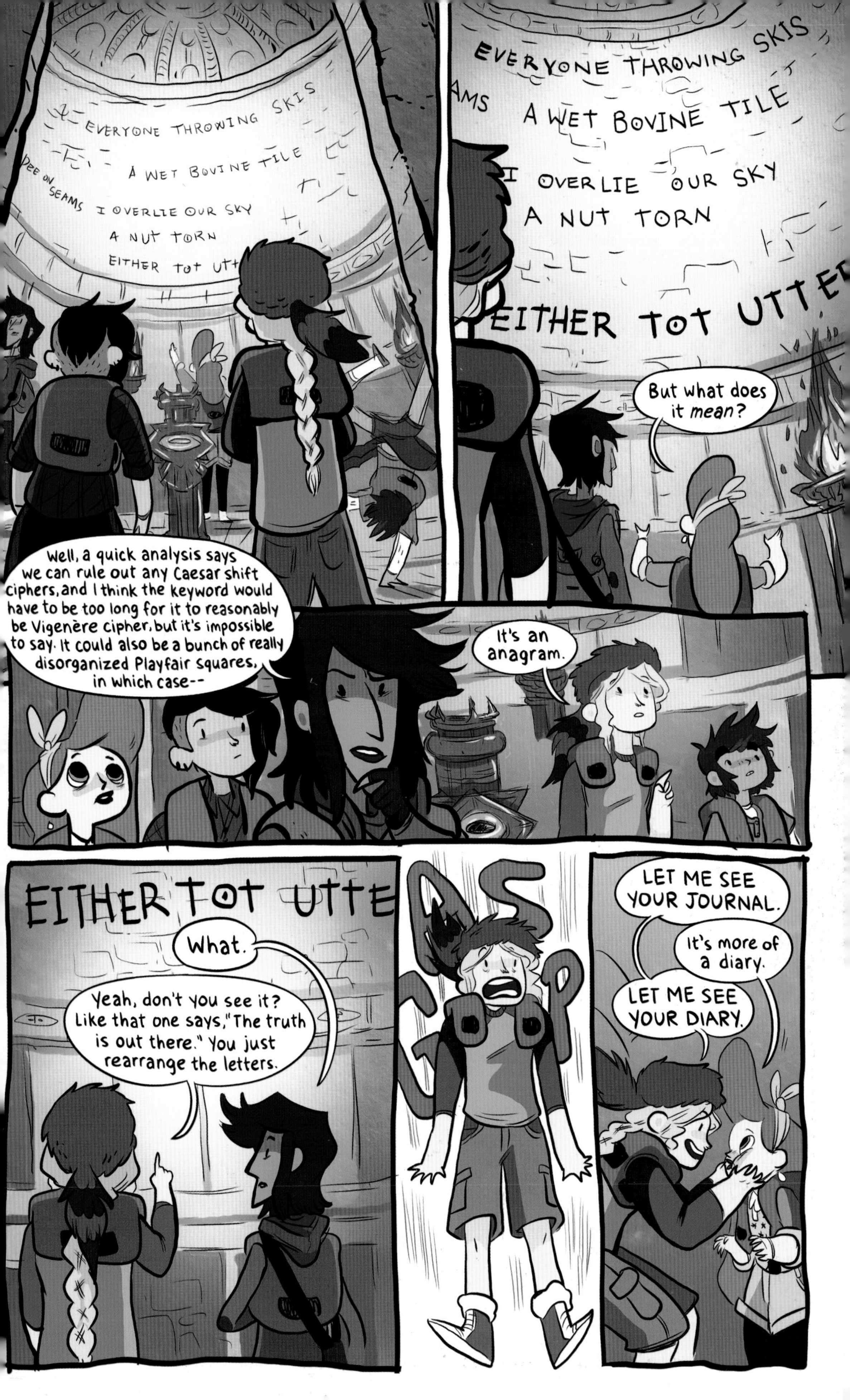
EVERYONE THROWING SKIS
A WET BOVINE TILE
DEE ON SEAMS I OVERLIE OUR SKY
A NUT TORN
EITHER TOT UTT
EVERYONE THROWING SKIS
AMS A WET BOVINE TILE
I OVERLIE OUR SKY
A NUT TORN
EITHER TOT UTTE
But what does it *mean*?
Well, a quick analysis says we can rule out any Caesar shift ciphers, and I think the keyword would have to be too long for it to reasonably be Vigenère cipher, but it's impossible to say. It could also be a bunch of really disorganized Playfair squares, in which case--
It's an anagram.
EITHER TOT UTTE
What.
Yeah, don't you see it? Like that one says, "The truth is out there." You just rearrange the letters.
GASP
LET ME SEE YOUR JOURNAL.
It's more of a diary.
LET ME SEE YOUR DIARY.

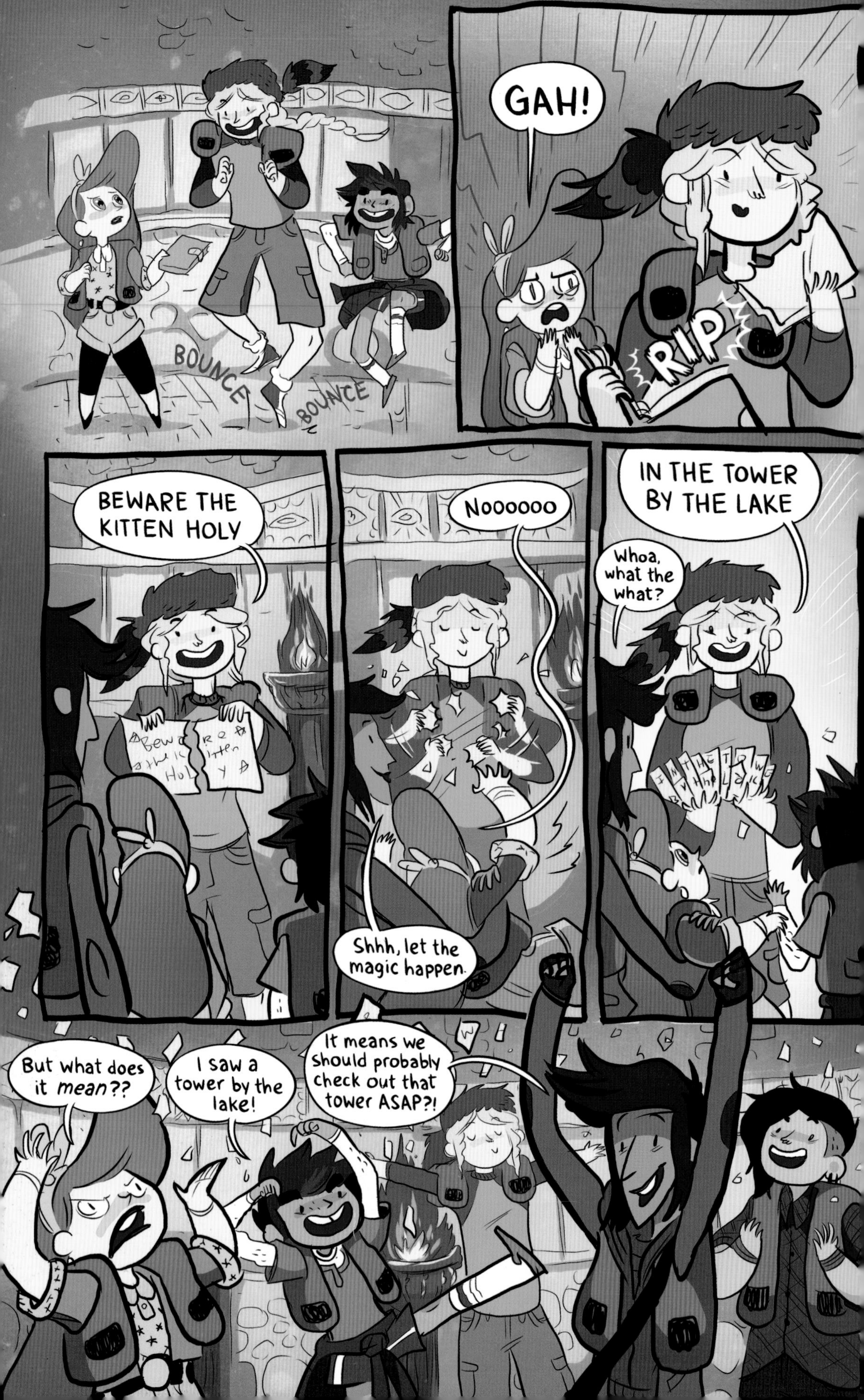
BOUNCE
BOUNCE
GAH!
RIP
BEWARE THE KITTEN HOLY
Nooooooo
Shhh, let the magic happen.
IN THE TOWER BY THE LAKE
Whoa, what the what?
But what does it *mean*??
I saw a tower by the lake!
It means we should probably check out that tower ASAP?!

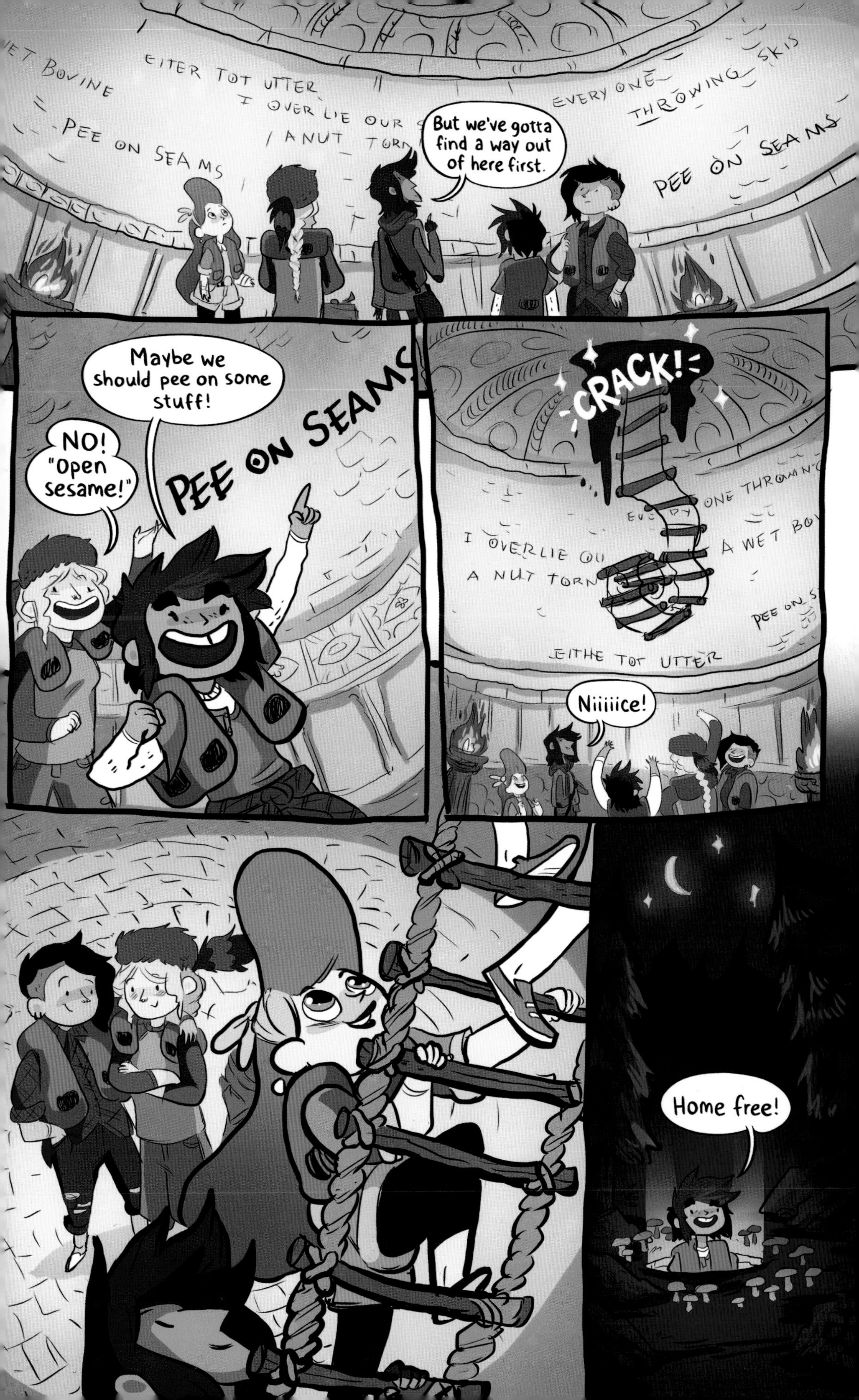
WET BOVINE
EITER TOT UTTER
I OVER LIE OUR
A NUT TORN
EVERY ONE
THROWING SKIS
PEE ON SEAMS
PEE ON SEAMS
But we've gotta find a way out of here first.
Maybe we should pee on some stuff!
NO! "Open sesame!"
PEE ON SEAMS
CRACK!
ONE THROWIN
I OVERLIE OU
A WET BO
A NUT TORN
PEE ON S
EITHE TOT UTTER
Niiiiice!
Home free!

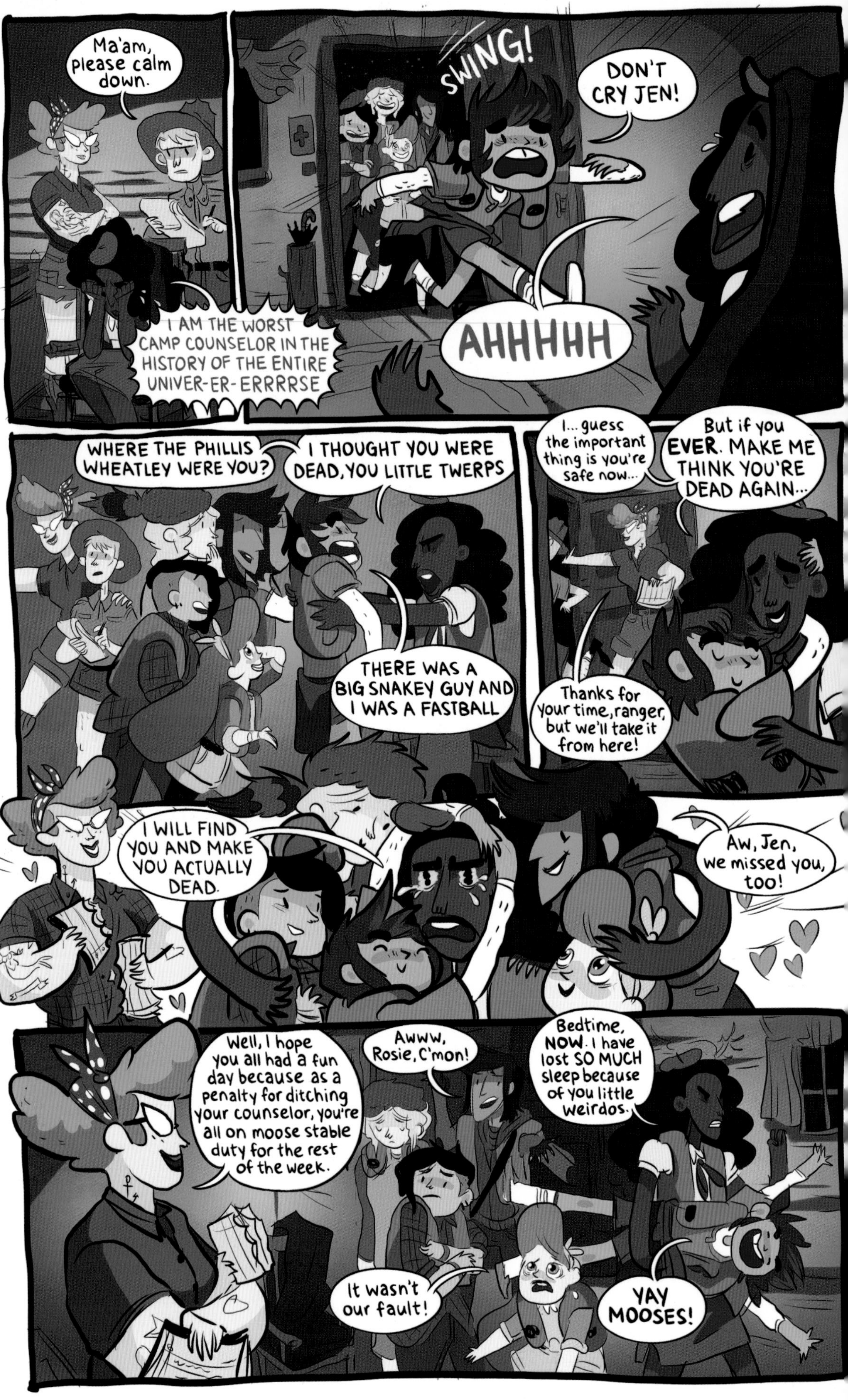
Ma'am, please calm down.
I AM THE WORST CAMP COUNSELOR IN THE HISTORY OF THE ENTIRE UNIVER-ER-ERRRRSE
SWING!
DON'T CRY JEN!
AHHHHH
WHERE THE PHILLIS WHEATLEY WERE YOU?
I THOUGHT YOU WERE DEAD, YOU LITTLE TWERPS
THERE WAS A BIG SNAKEY GUY AND I WAS A FASTBALL
I... guess the important thing is you're safe now...
But if you EVER. MAKE ME THINK YOU'RE DEAD AGAIN...
Thanks for your time, ranger, but we'll take it from here!
I WILL FIND YOU AND MAKE YOU ACTUALLY DEAD.
Aw, Jen, we missed you, too!
Well, I hope you all had a fun day because as a penalty for ditching your counselor, you're all on moose stable duty for the rest of the week.
Awww, Rosie, C'mon!
Bedtime, NOW. I have lost SO MUCH sleep because of you little weirdos.
It wasn't our fault!
YAY MOOSES!

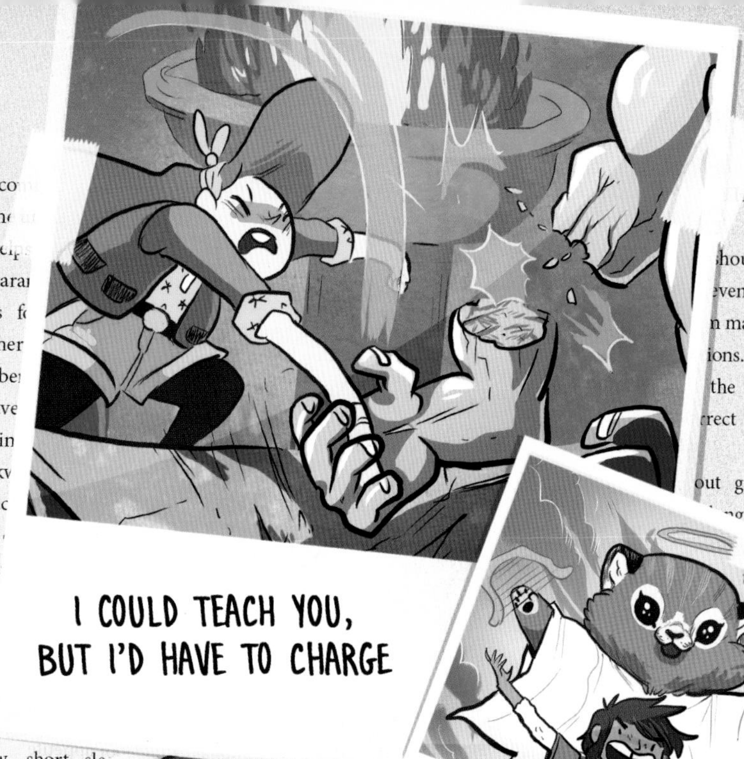
I COULD TEACH YOU,
BUT I'D HAVE TO CHARGE

will co…
Th… It help… appeara… dress f… Further… Lumbe… to have… part in… Thiskv… Hardc… have… them…

…HE UNIFORM

…should be worn at camp …events when Lumberjanes …n may also be worn at other …ions. It should be worn as a … the uniform dress with …rect shoes, and stocking or …

…out grows her uniform or …ter Lumberjane. …a she has … her … her

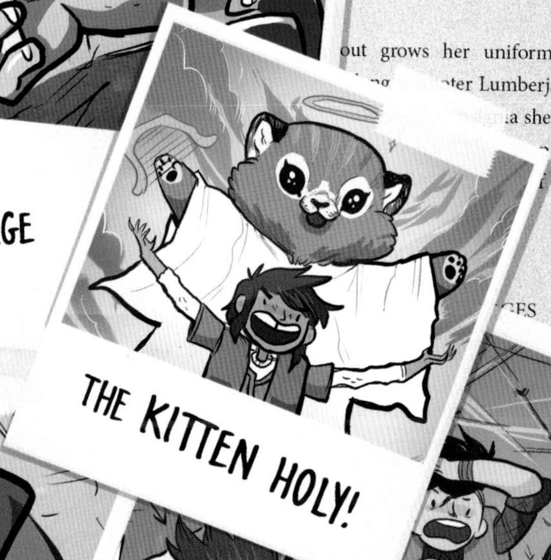
THE KITTEN HOLY!

The… yellow, short sl… emb… the w… choose… slacks, … made o… out-of-do… green bere… the colla… Shoes ma… heels, rou… …kings or socks shou… …with the shoes or wit… the uniform. Ne… …, bracelets, or other jewelry do… belong with a Lumberjane uniform.

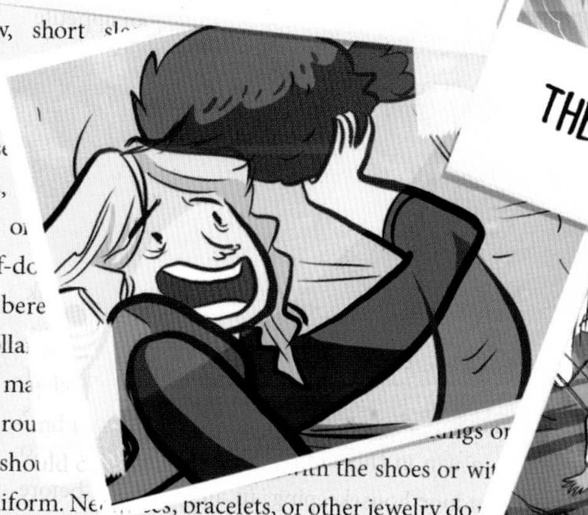

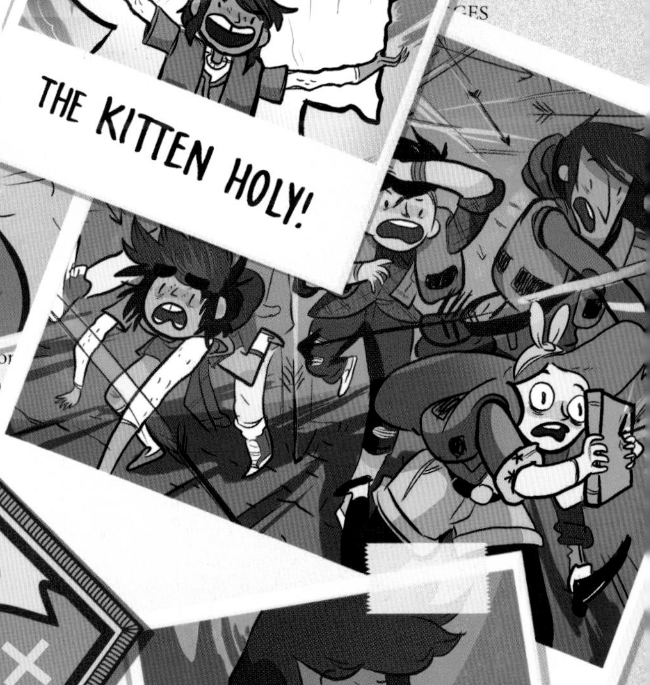

HOW TO WEAR THE UNIFO…

To look well in a uniform demand… uniform be kept in good con… pressed. See that the skirt is the rig… height and build, that the belt is adju… that your shoes and stockings are in kee… uniform, that you watch your posture and ca… with dignity and grace. If the beret is removed i… be sure that your hair is neat and kept in place with …n insonspicuous clip or ribbon. When you wear a Lumberjane uniform you are identified as a member of this organization and you should be doubly careful to conduct yourself in a way that will show everyone that courtesy and thoughtfullness are part of being a Lumberjane. People are likely to judge a whole nation by the selfishness of a few individuals, to criticize a whole family because of the misconduct of one member, and to feel unkindly toward and organization because of the

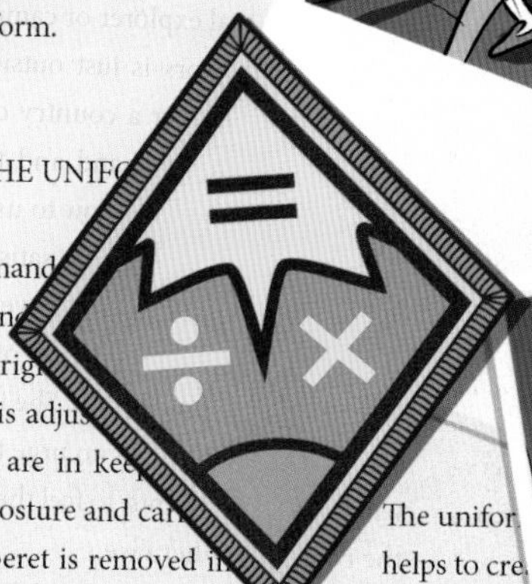

The unifor… helps to cre… in a group. … active life th… another bond… future, and pr… in order to b… Lumberjane pr… Penniquiql Thi… …core Lady Types, but m… …s will wish to have one. They can either bu… …uniform, or make it themselves from materials available at the trading post.

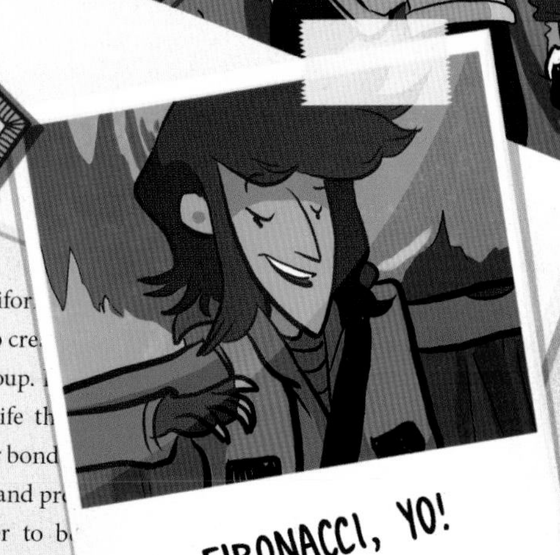
FIBONACCI, YO!

LUMBERJANES FIELD MANUAL
CHAPTER FOUR

Lumberjanes "Sports and Games" Program Field

ROBYN HOOD BADGE

"A sharp eye shows sharp wit."

Hand and eye coordination is not only important for day-to-day activities, but can be instrumental in a Lumberjane's experience with nature. In these modern times, the basic performance of what was once a standard practice is seen more as a sport, but the Lumberjanes recognize the importance of not only the respect and care for their tools, but of training with their fellow Lumberjanes. Through this, they will learn to trust in not only each other, but in themselves and the skills the they already possess. It is important for a Lumberjane to know that she can rely upon herself in the great vastness of nature and that she will not be reliant upon the machine manufactured tools of modern day. With her own two hands she will be able to step forward into whatever life throws at her.

The skill of archery teaches every Lumberjane the importance of good posture, the finesse needed when handling delicate instruments, the necessary upper arm strength and the poise of being able to take down prey from a great distance. Before a Lumberjane can earn her *Robyn Hood* badge, it is important for her to learn within the safety of the camp's archery range. She will be given the tools that she needs to succeed and with the support of her friends she will be able to hone her ability and gain the confidence she needs to send the arrow to its target.

To obtain the *Robyn Hood* badge, a Lumberjane must first make a bow and arrow which will shoot a distance of one hundred feet with fair precision. It is an essential task that will let her learn about the benefits of putting time into a job to do it right. She must prove her knowledge of basic archery safety both in the range and outside. She must make a total score of 350 with 60 shots in one or two meets, using a standard four-foot target at forty yards or three-

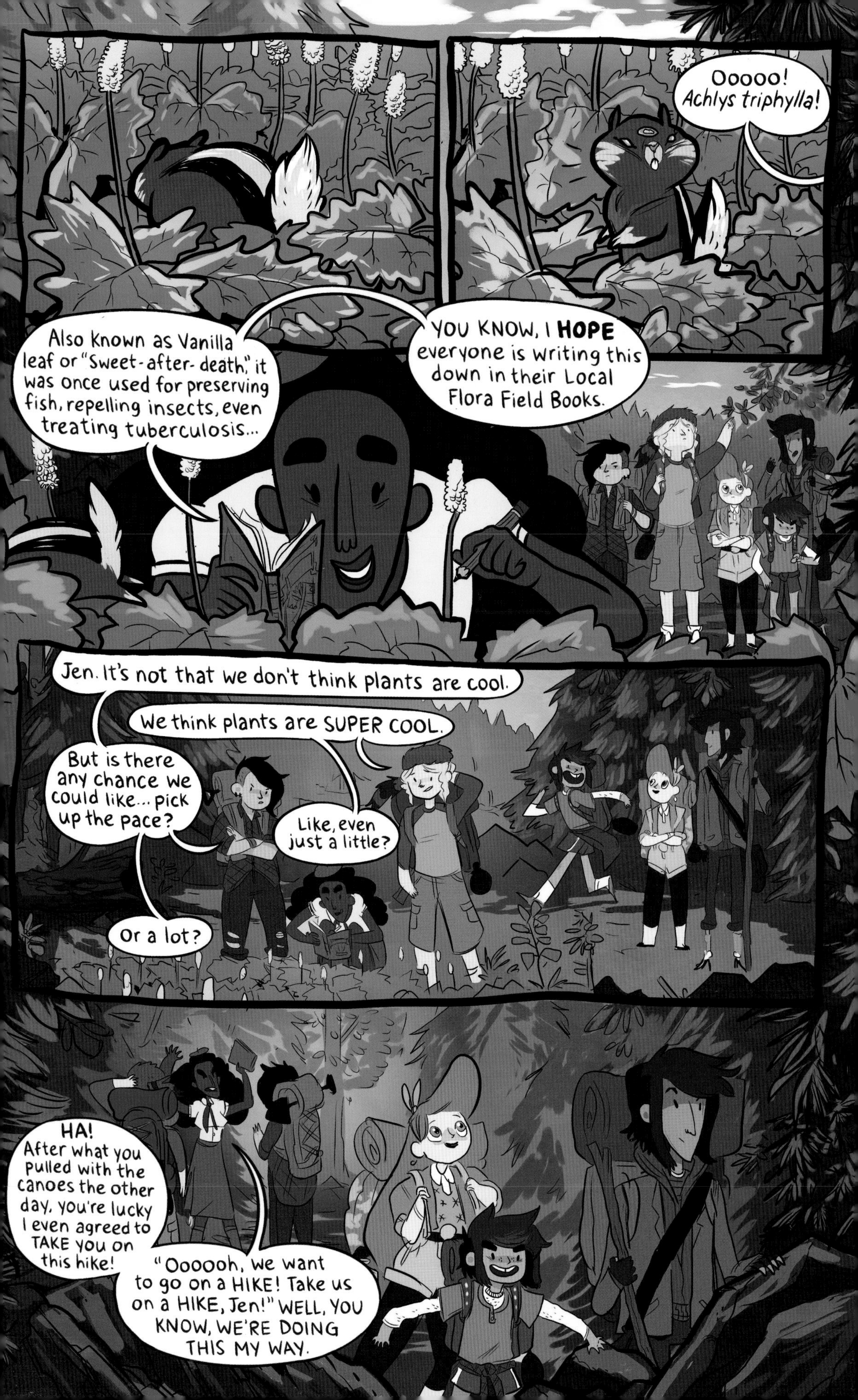
Ooooo! Achlys triphylla!
Also known as Vanilla leaf or "Sweet-after-death," it was once used for preserving fish, repelling insects, even treating tuberculosis...
YOU KNOW, I **HOPE** everyone is writing this down in their Local Flora Field Books.
Jen. It's not that we don't think plants are cool.
We think plants are SUPER COOL.
But is there any chance we could like... pick up the pace?
Like, even just a little?
Or a lot?
HA! After what you pulled with the canoes the other day, you're lucky I even agreed to TAKE you on this hike!
"Oooooh, we want to go on a HIKE! Take us on a HIKE, Jen!" WELL, YOU KNOW, WE'RE DOING THIS MY WAY.

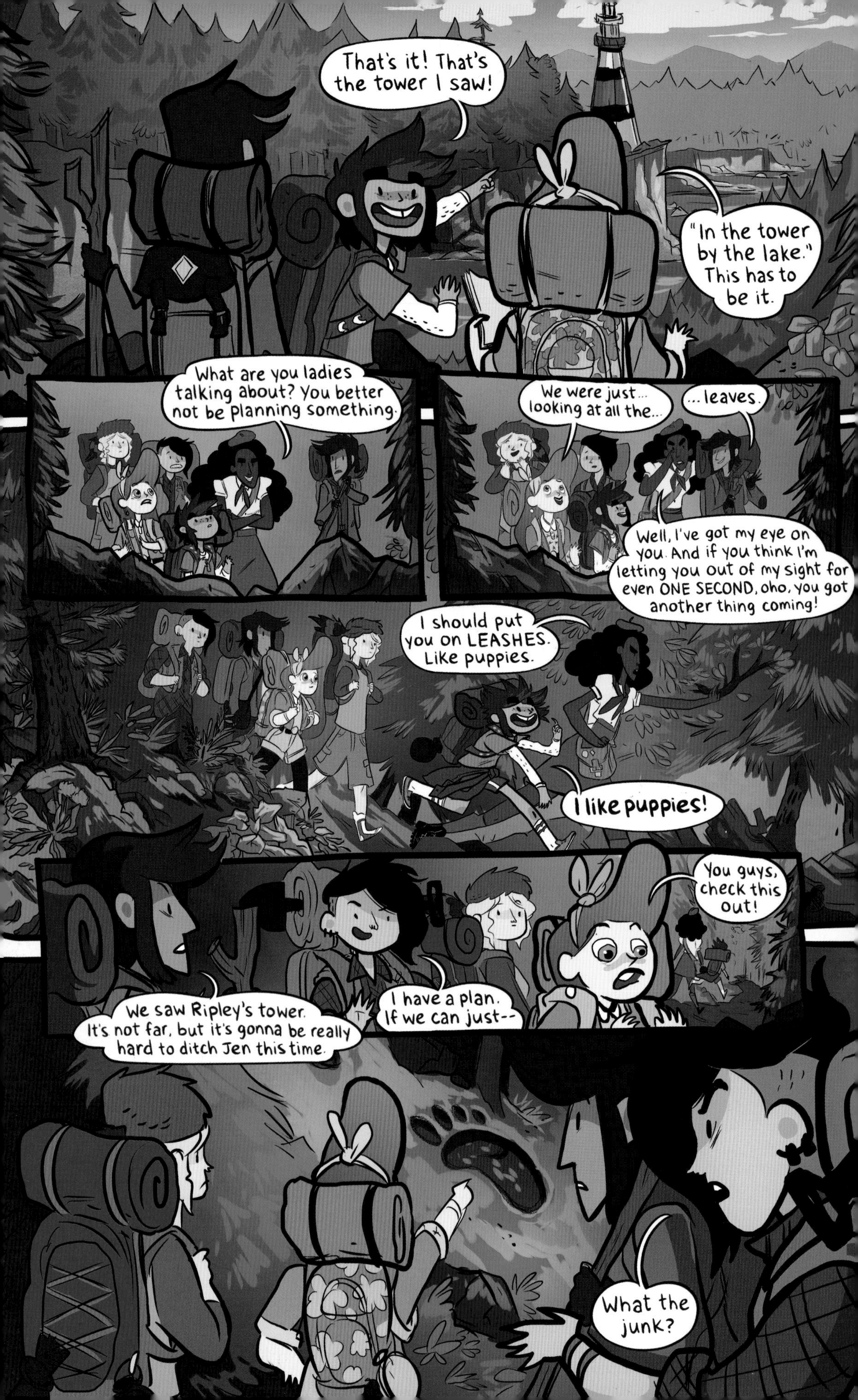
That's it! That's the tower I saw!
"In the tower by the lake." This has to be it.
What are you ladies talking about? You better not be planning something.
We were just... looking at all the...
...leaves.
Well, I've got my eye on you. And if you think I'm letting you out of my sight for even ONE SECOND, oho, you got another thing coming!
I should put you on LEASHES. Like puppies.
I like puppies!
We saw Ripley's tower. It's not far, but it's gonna be really hard to ditch Jen this time.
I have a plan. If we can just--
You guys, check this out!
What the junk?

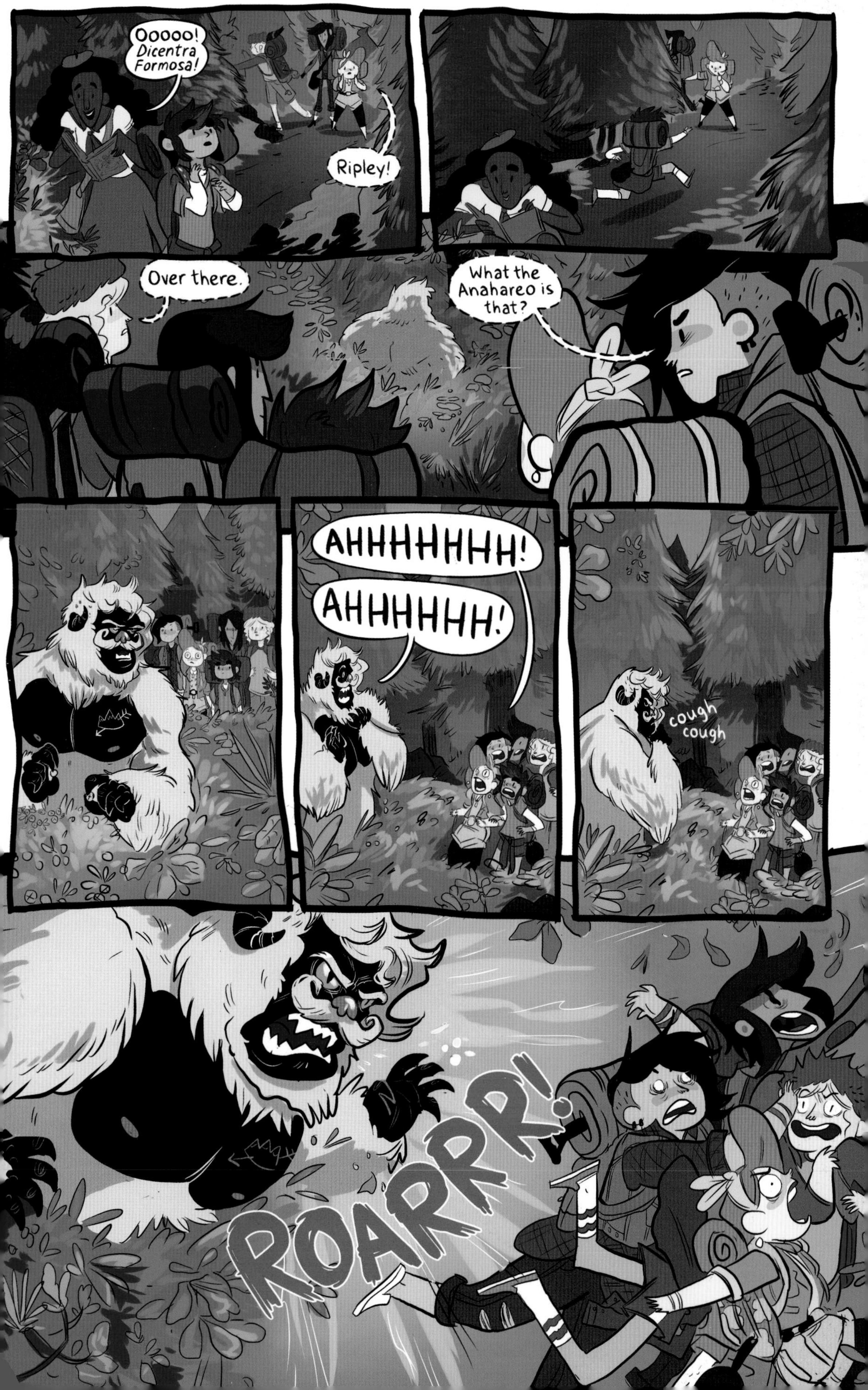
Ooooo! Dicentra Formosa!
Ripley!
Over there.
What the Anahareo is that?
AHHHHHHH!
AHHHHHH!
cough cough
ROARRR!

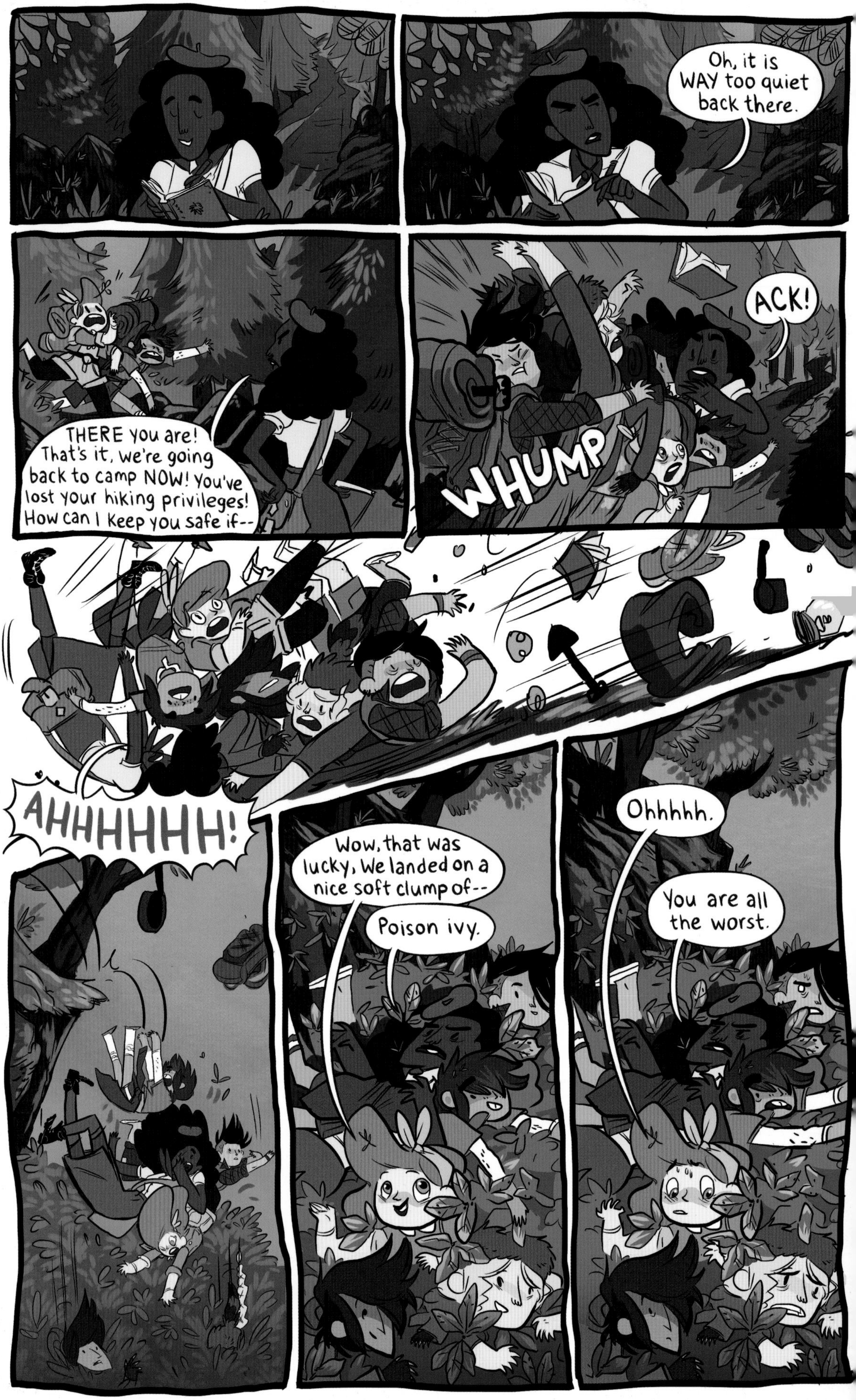

Oh, it is WAY too quiet back there.
THERE you are! That's it, we're going back to camp NOW! You've lost your hiking privileges! How can I keep you safe if--
ACK!
WHUMP
AHHHHHH!
Wow, that was lucky, We landed on a nice soft clump of--
Poison ivy.
Ohhhhh.
You are all the worst.

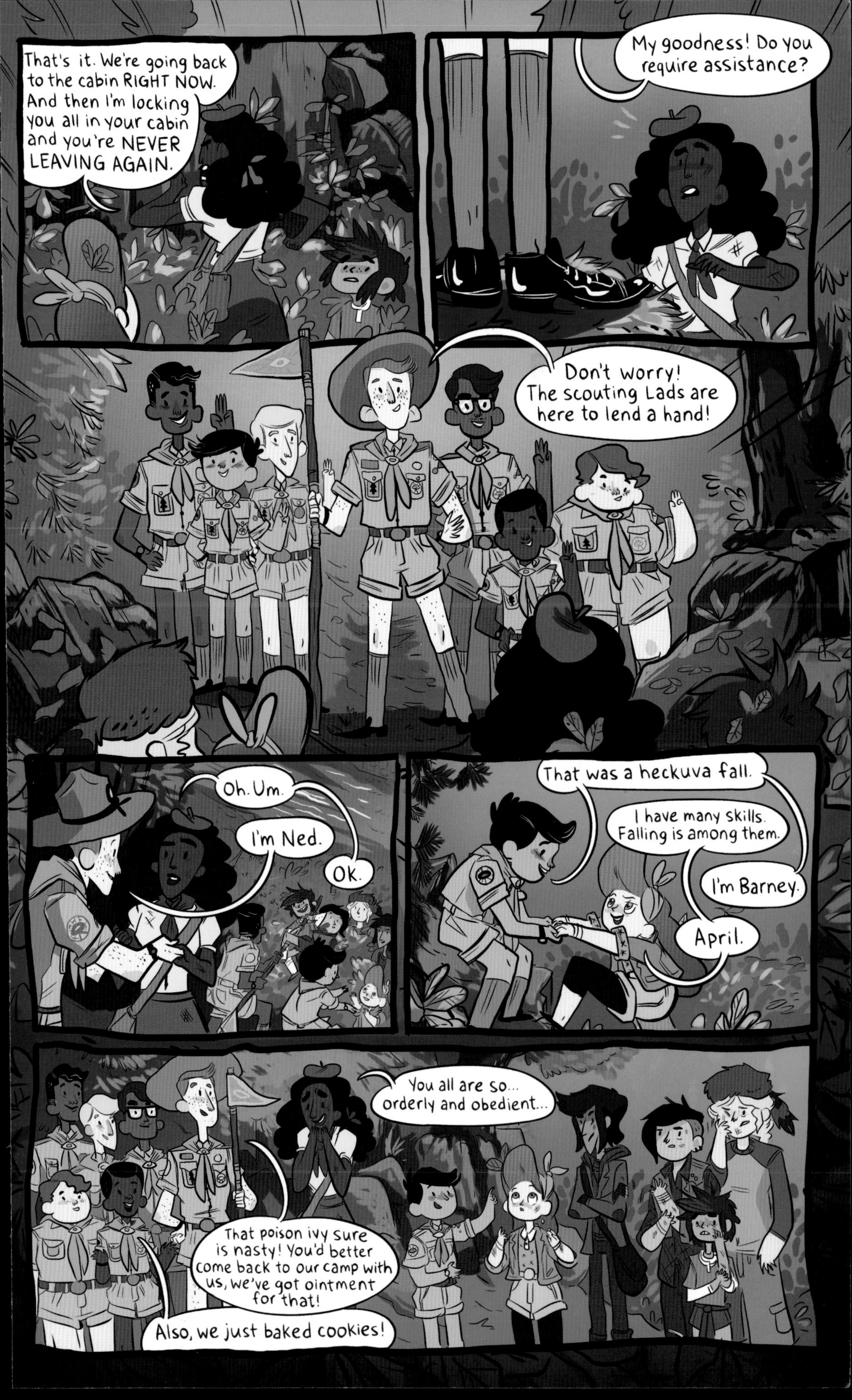
That's it. We're going back to the cabin RIGHT NOW. And then I'm locking you all in your cabin and you're NEVER LEAVING AGAIN.
My goodness! Do you require assistance?
Don't worry! The scouting Lads are here to lend a hand!
Oh. Um.
I'm Ned.
OK.
That was a heckuva fall.
I have many skills. Falling is among them.
I'm Barney.
April.
You all are so... orderly and obedient...
That poison ivy sure is nasty! You'd better come back to our camp with us, we've got ointment for that!
Also, we just baked cookies!

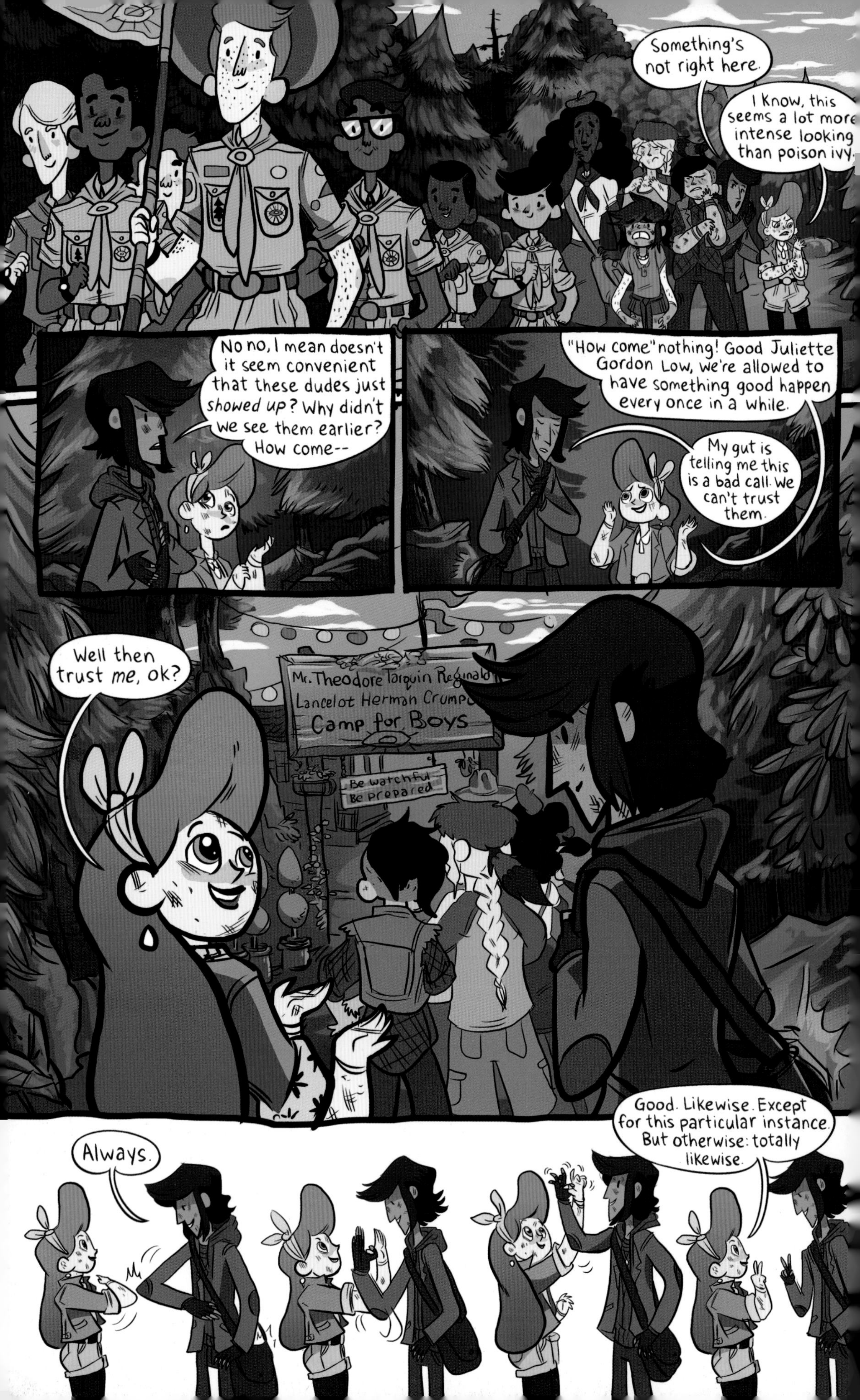

Something's not right here.
I know, this seems a lot more intense looking than poison ivy.
No no, I mean doesn't it seem convenient that these dudes just *showed up*? Why didn't we see them earlier? How come--
"How come" nothing! Good Juliette Gordon Low, we're allowed to have something good happen every once in a while.
My gut is telling me this is a bad call. We can't trust them.
Well then trust *me*, ok?
Mr. Theodore Tarquin Reginald Lancelot Herman Crump Camp for Boys
Be watchful Be prepared
Always.
Good. Likewise. Except for this particular instance. But otherwise: totally likewise.

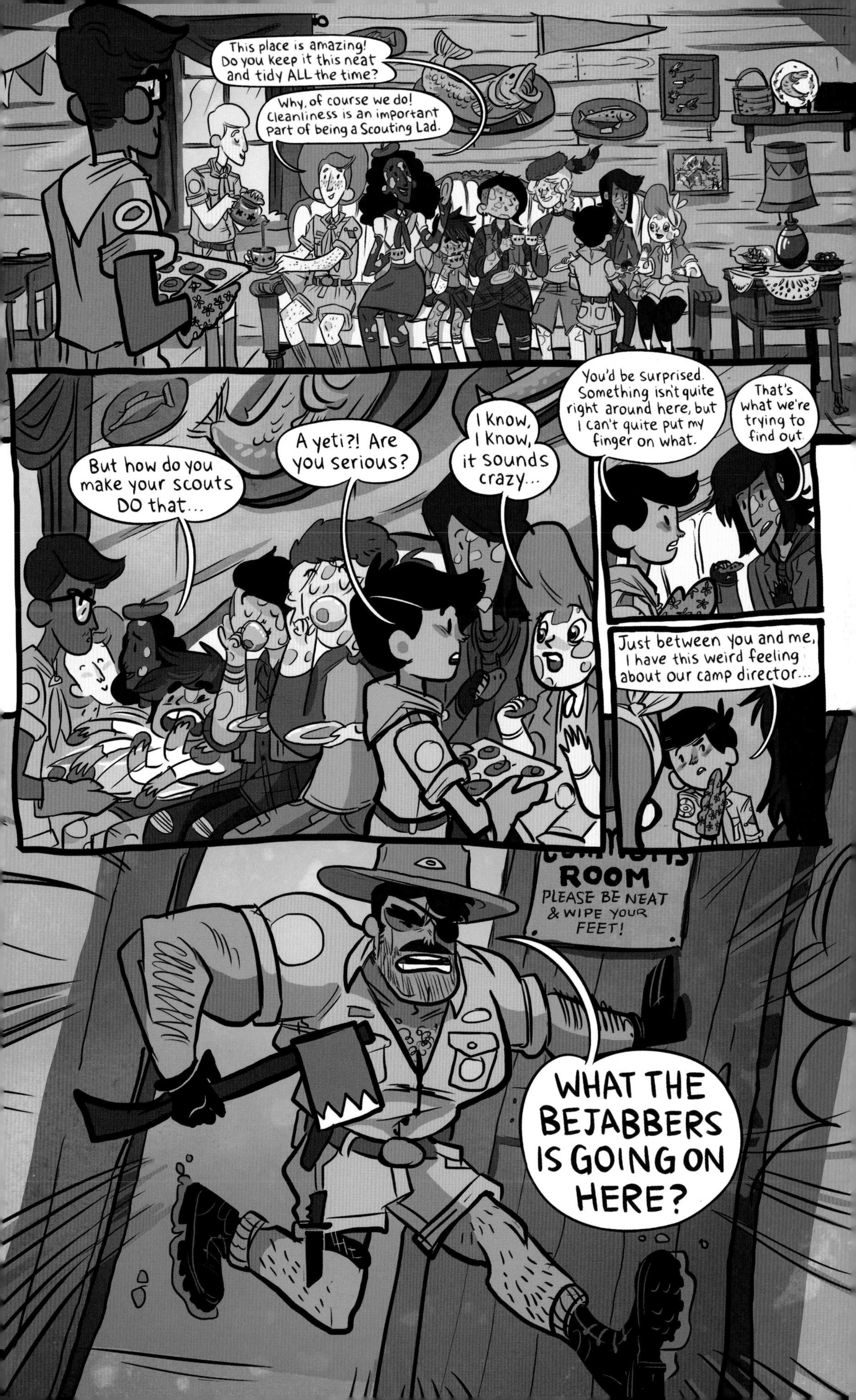
This place is amazing! Do you keep it this neat and tidy ALL the time?
Why, of course we do! Cleanliness is an important part of being a Scouting Lad.
But how do you make your scouts DO that...
A yeti?! Are you serious?
I know, I know, it sounds crazy...
You'd be surprised. Something isn't quite right around here, but I can't quite put my finger on what.
That's what we're trying to find out.
Just between you and me, I have this weird feeling about our camp director...
ROOM
PLEASE BE NEAT & WIPE YOUR FEET!
WHAT THE BEJABBERS IS GOING ON HERE?

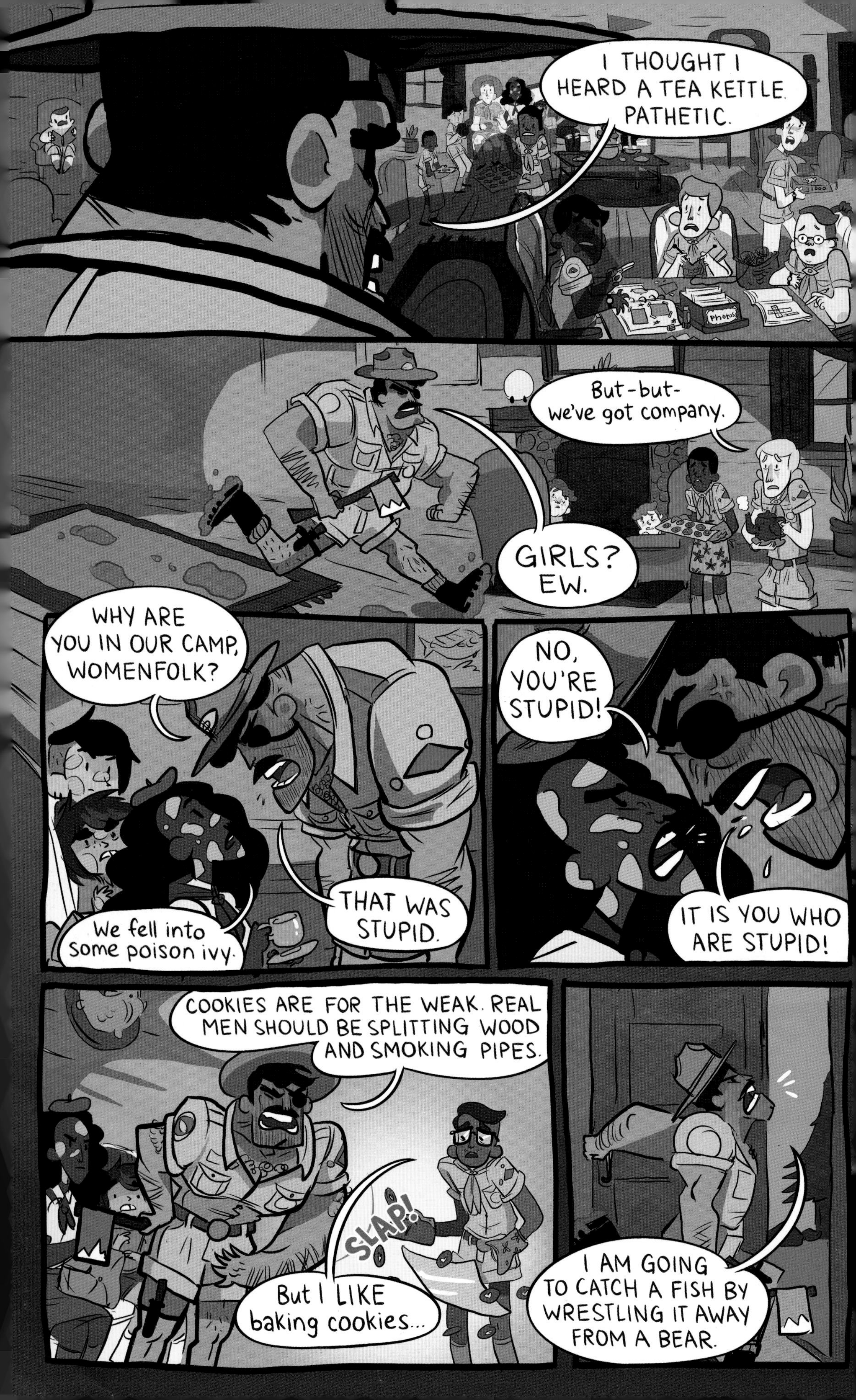
I THOUGHT I HEARD A TEA KETTLE. PATHETIC.
Photos
But-but- we've got company.
GIRLS? EW.
WHY ARE YOU IN OUR CAMP, WOMENFOLK?
We fell into some poison ivy.
THAT WAS STUPID.
NO, YOU'RE STUPID!
IT IS YOU WHO ARE STUPID!
COOKIES ARE FOR THE WEAK. REAL MEN SHOULD BE SPLITTING WOOD AND SMOKING PIPES.
SLAP!
But I LIKE baking cookies...
I AM GOING TO CATCH A FISH BY WRESTLING IT AWAY FROM A BEAR.

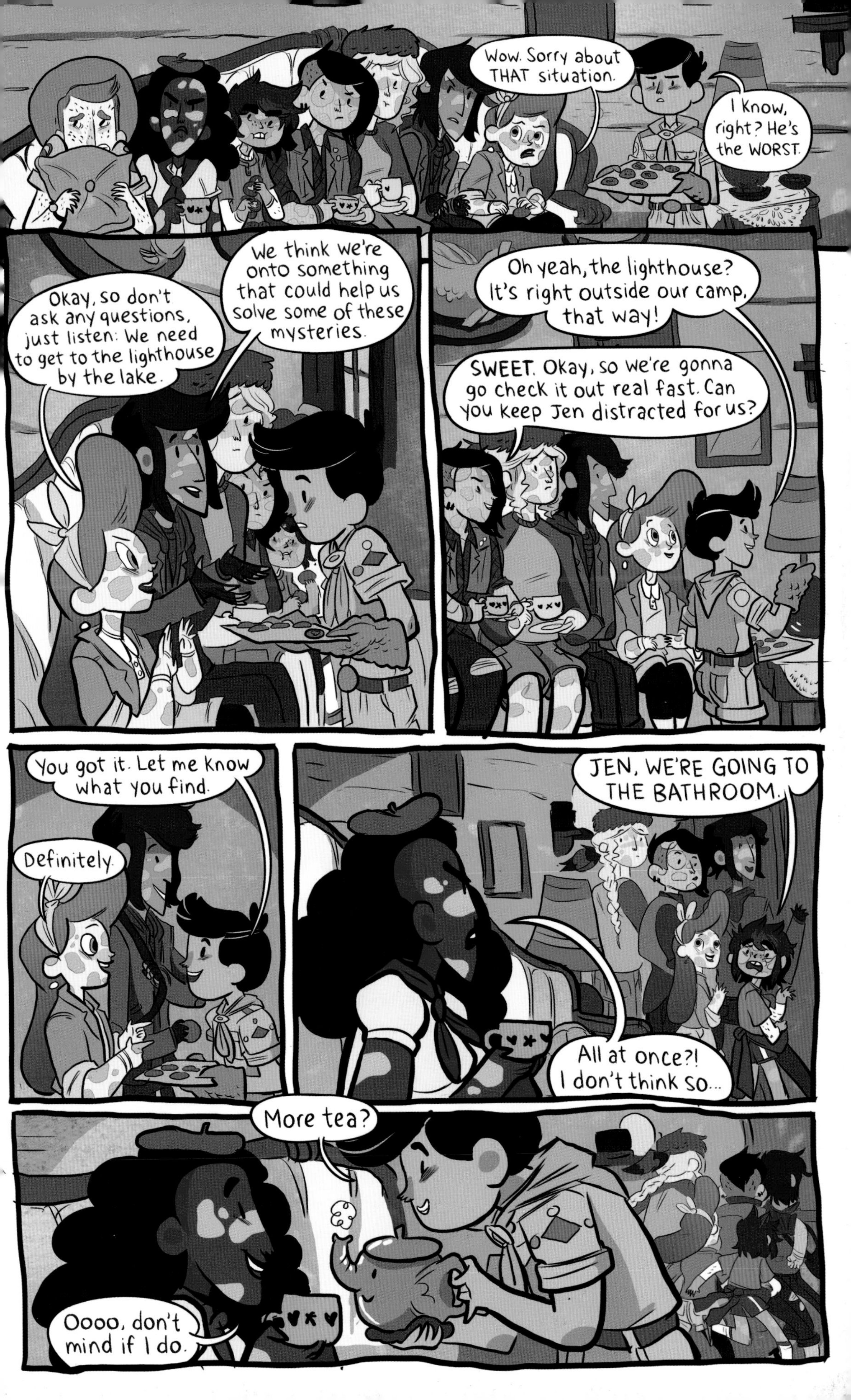
Wow. Sorry about THAT situation.
I know, right? He's the WORST.
Okay, so don't ask any questions, just listen: We need to get to the lighthouse by the lake.
We think we're onto something that could help us solve some of these mysteries.
Oh yeah, the lighthouse? It's right outside our camp, that way!
SWEET. Okay, so we're gonna go check it out real fast. Can you keep Jen distracted for us?
You got it. Let me know what you find.
Definitely.
JEN, WE'RE GOING TO THE BATHROOM.
All at once?! I don't think so...
More tea?
Oooo, don't mind if I do.

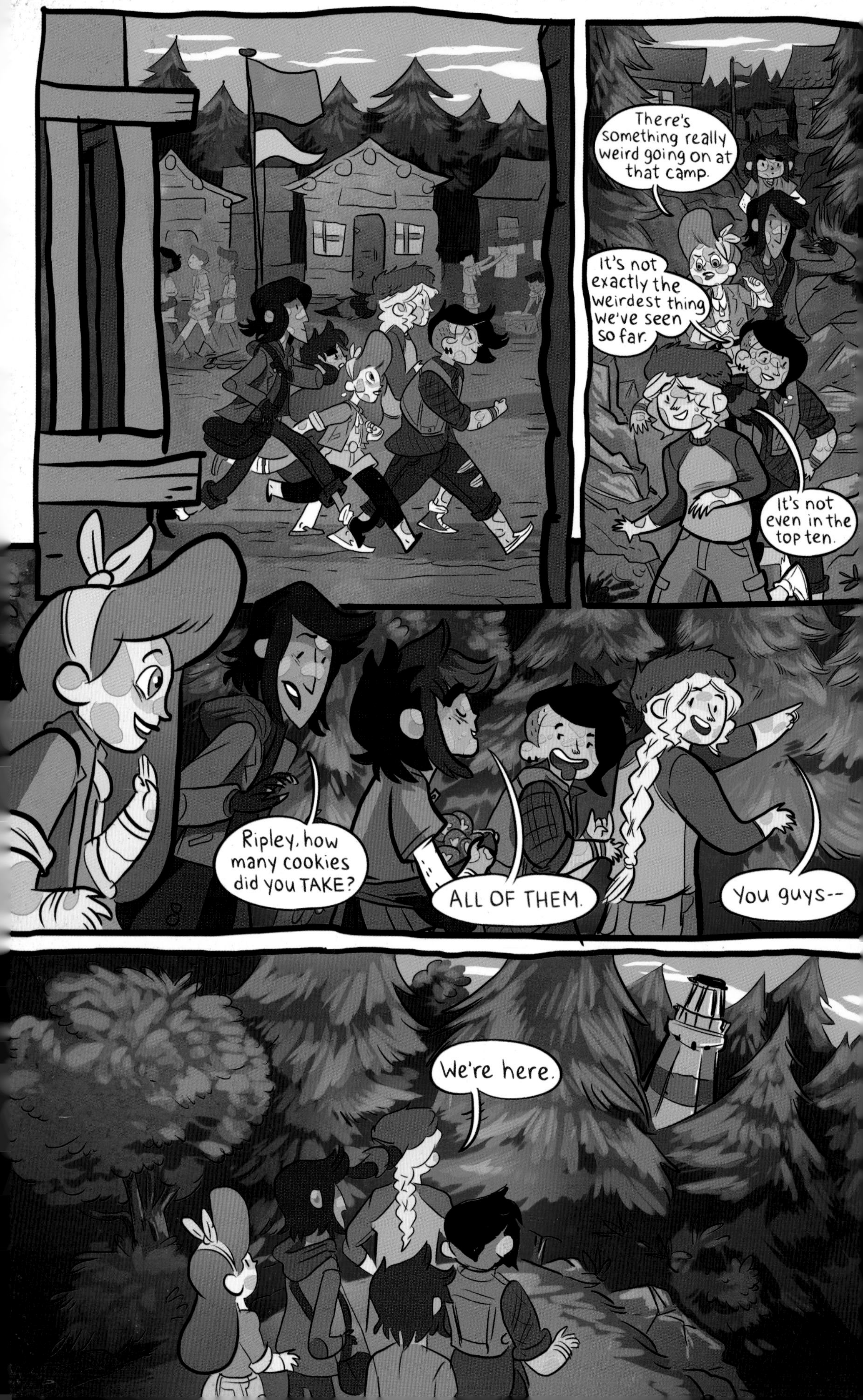
There's something really weird going on at that camp.
It's not exactly the weirdest thing we've seen so far.
It's not even in the top ten.
Ripley, how many cookies did you TAKE?
ALL OF THEM.
You guys--
We're here.

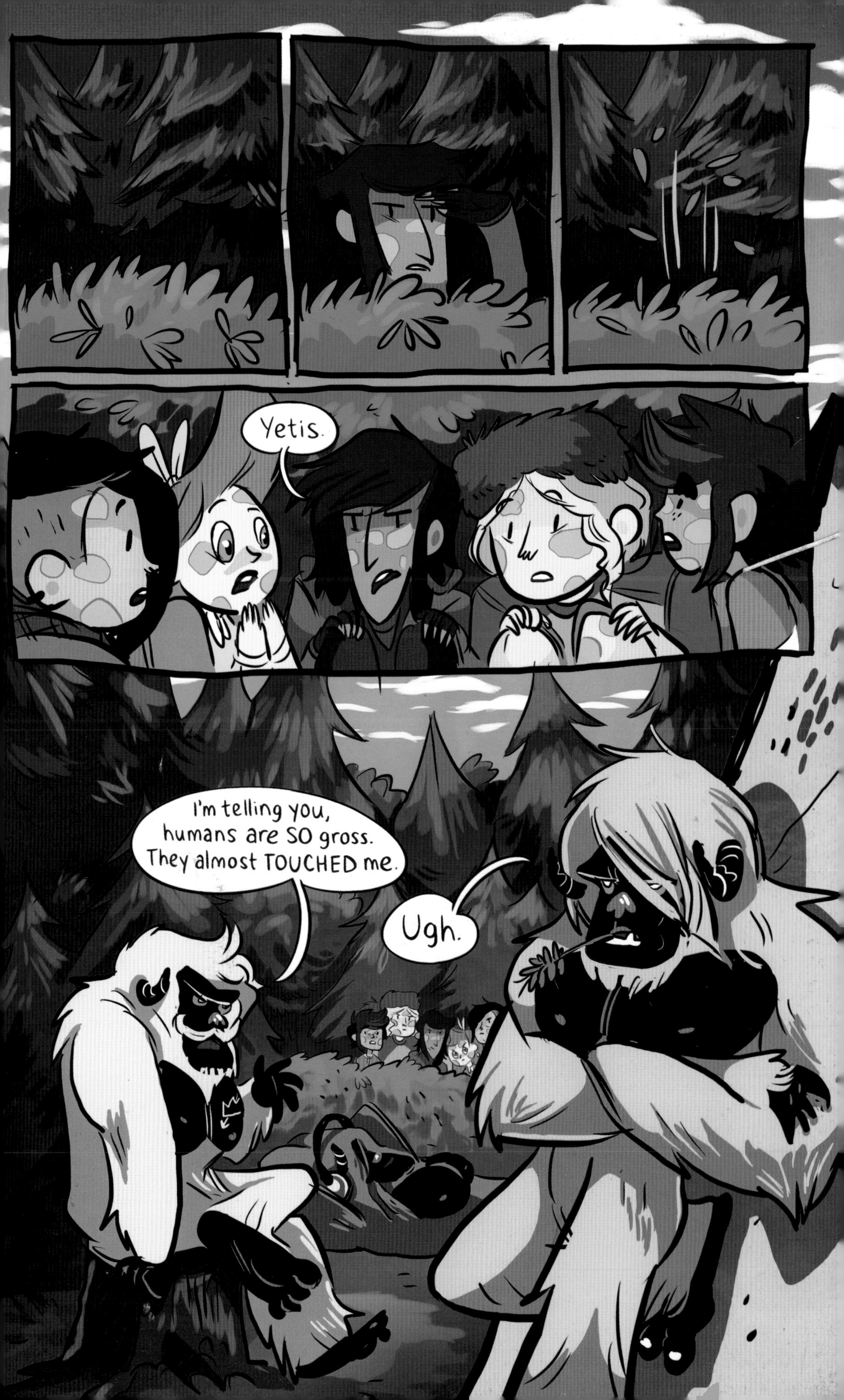
Yetis.
I'm telling you, humans are SO gross. They almost TOUCHED me.
Ugh.

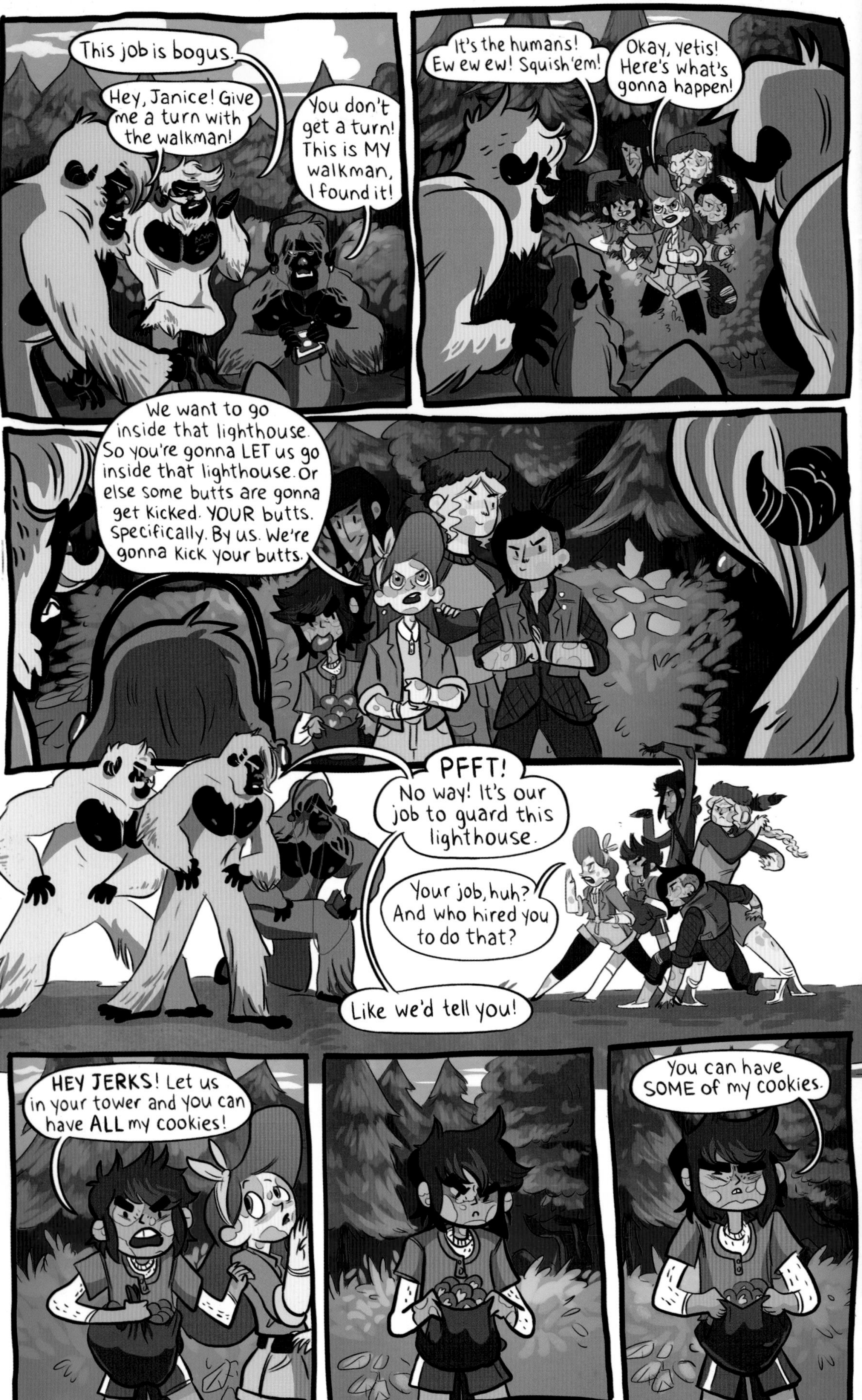
This job is bogus.
Hey, Janice! Give me a turn with the walkman!
You don't get a turn! This is MY walkman, I found it!
It's the humans! Ew ew ew! Squish'em!
Okay, yetis! Here's what's gonna happen!
We want to go inside that lighthouse. So you're gonna LET us go inside that lighthouse. Or else some butts are gonna get kicked. YOUR butts. Specifically. By us. We're gonna kick your butts.
PFFT! No way! It's our job to guard this lighthouse.
Your job, huh? And who hired you to do that?
Like we'd tell you!
HEY JERKS! Let us in your tower and you can have ALL my cookies!
You can have SOME of my cookies.

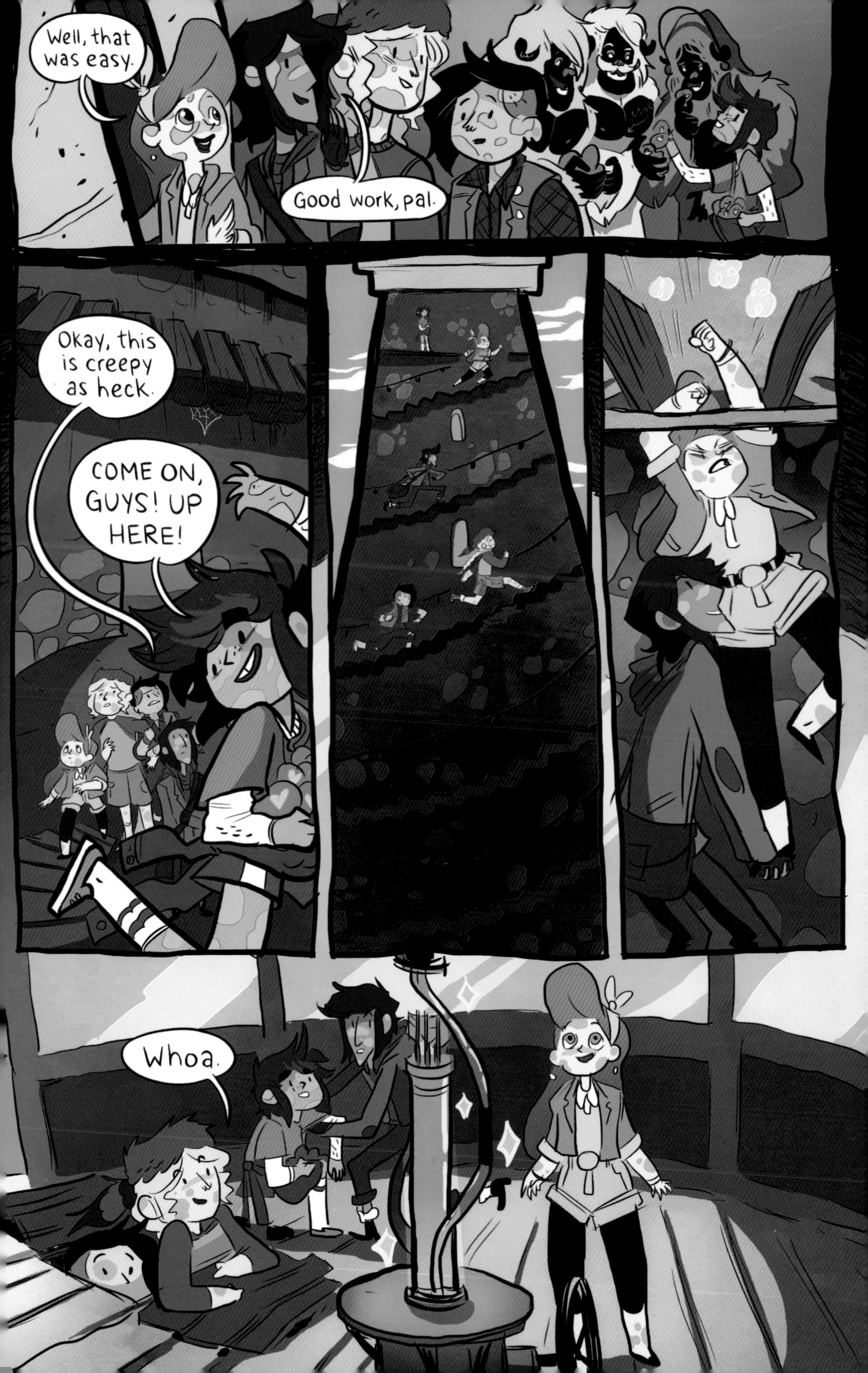
Well, that was easy.
Good work, pal.
Okay, this is creepy as heck.
COME ON, GUYS! UP HERE!
Whoa.

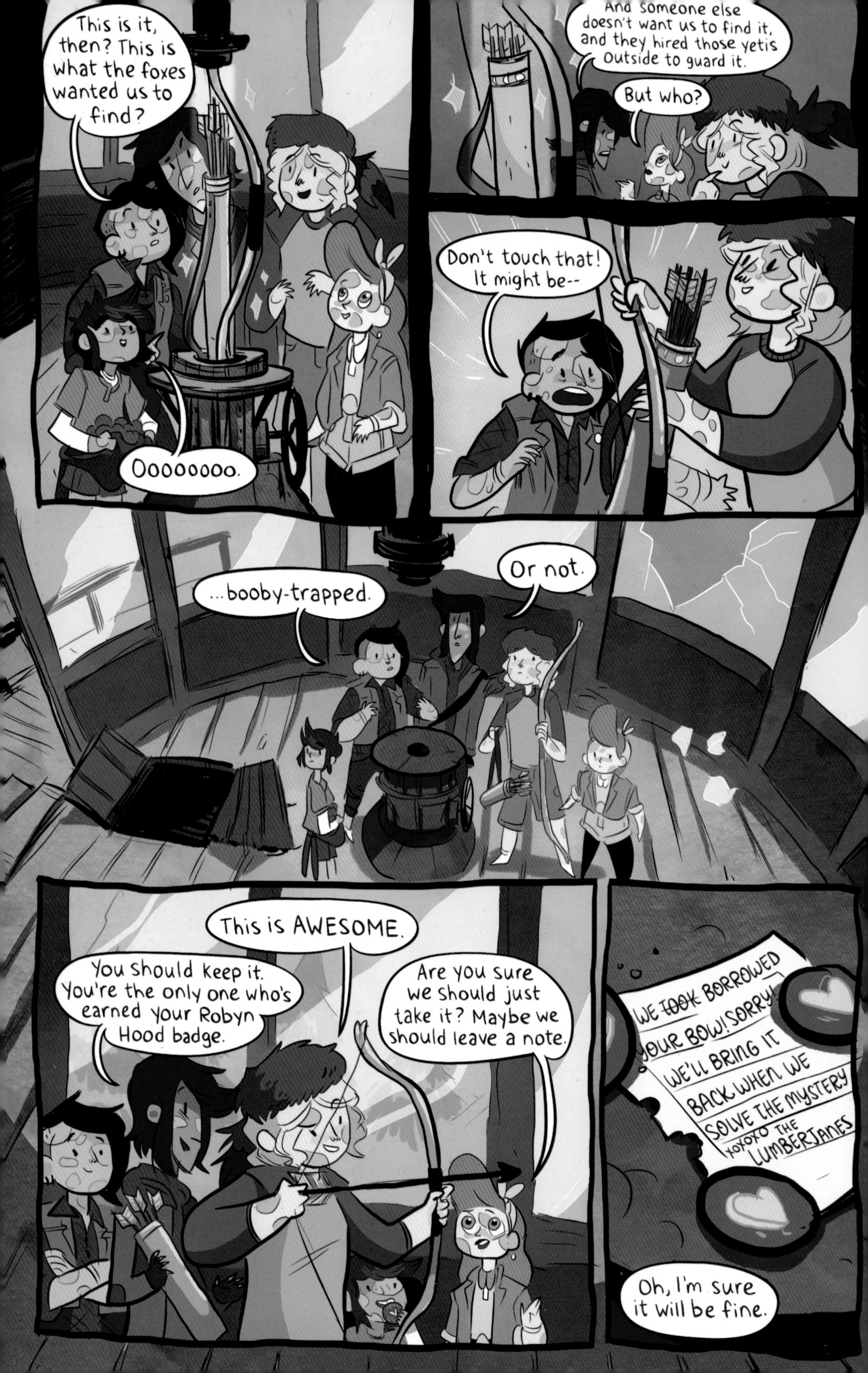
This is it, then? This is what the foxes wanted us to find?
Ooooooo.
And someone else doesn't want us to find it, and they hired those yetis outside to guard it.
But who?
Don't touch that! It might be--
...booby-trapped.
Or not.
This is AWESOME.
You should keep it. You're the only one who's earned your Robyn Hood badge.
Are you sure we should just take it? Maybe we should leave a note.
WE TOOK BORROWED YOUR BOW! SORRY! WE'LL BRING IT BACK WHEN WE SOLVE THE MYSTERY XOXOXO THE LUMBERJANES
Oh, I'm sure it will be fine.

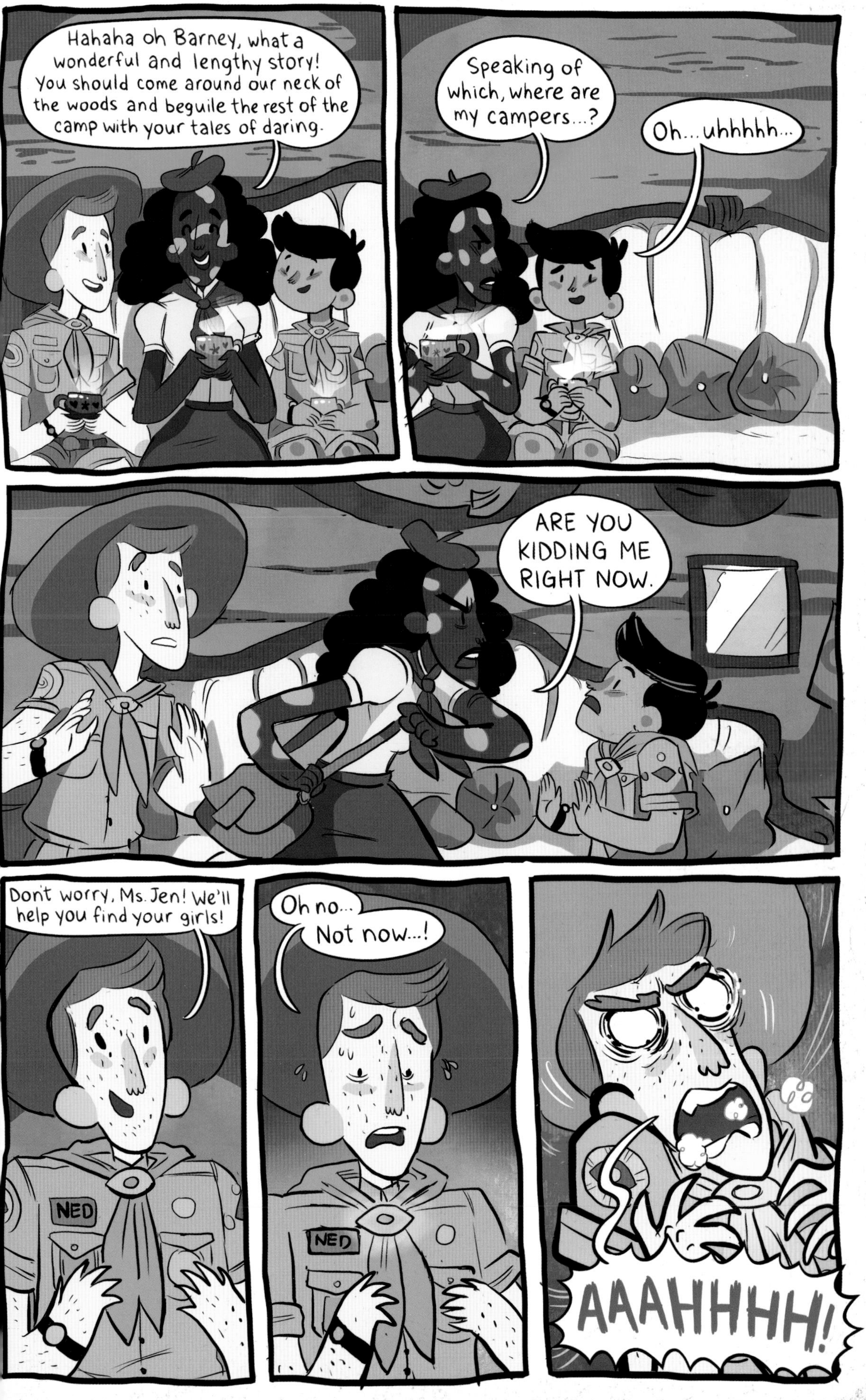

Hahaha oh Barney, what a wonderful and lengthy story! You should come around our neck of the woods and beguile the rest of the camp with your tales of daring.
Speaking of which, where are my campers...?
Oh... uhhhhh...
ARE YOU KIDDING ME RIGHT NOW.
Don't worry, Ms. Jen! We'll help you find your girls!
NED
Oh no...
Not now...!
NED
AAAHHHH!

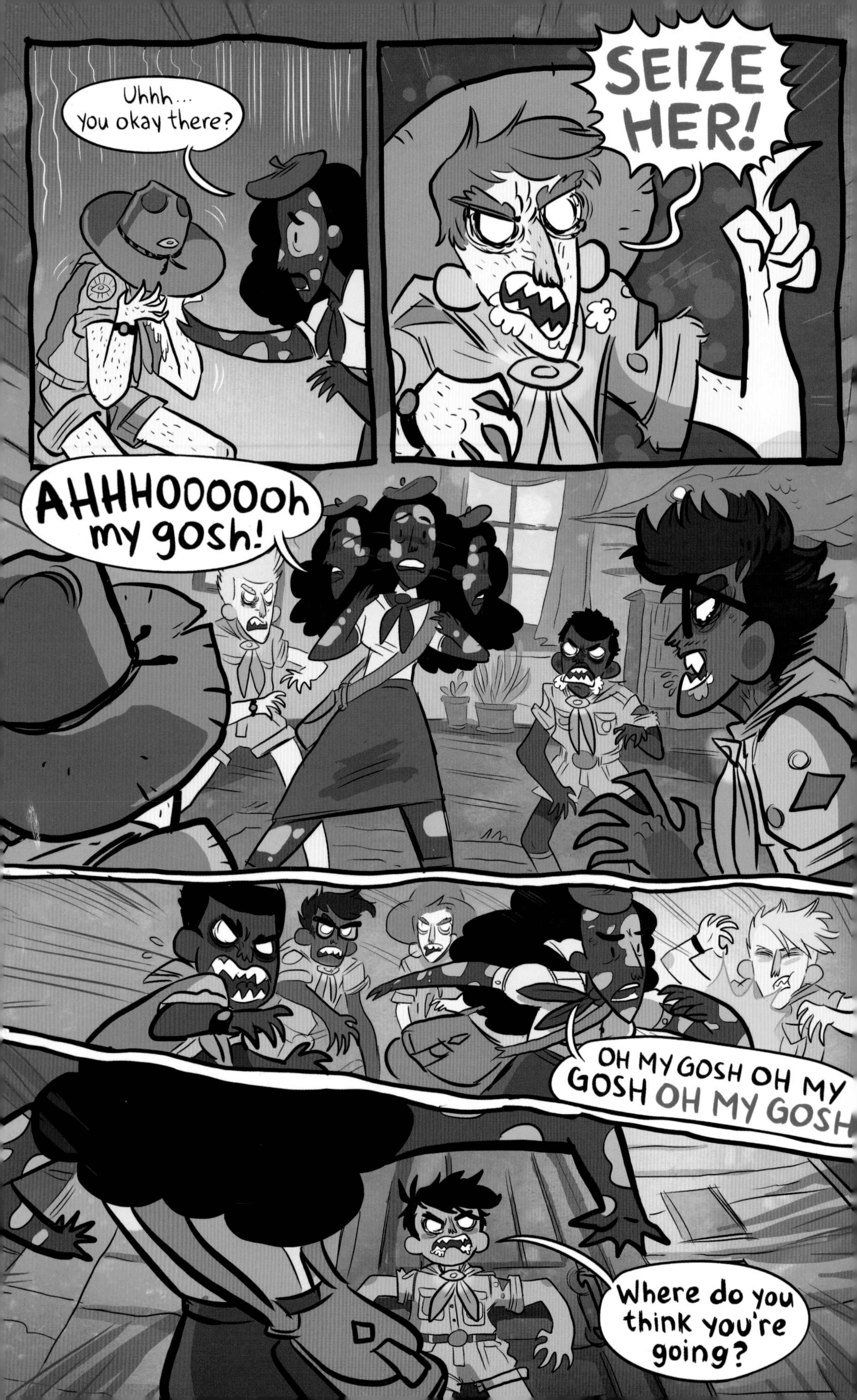
Uhhh...
you okay there?
SEIZE HER!
AHHHOOOOOh my gosh!
OH MY GOSH OH MY GOSH OH MY GOSH
Where do you think you're going?

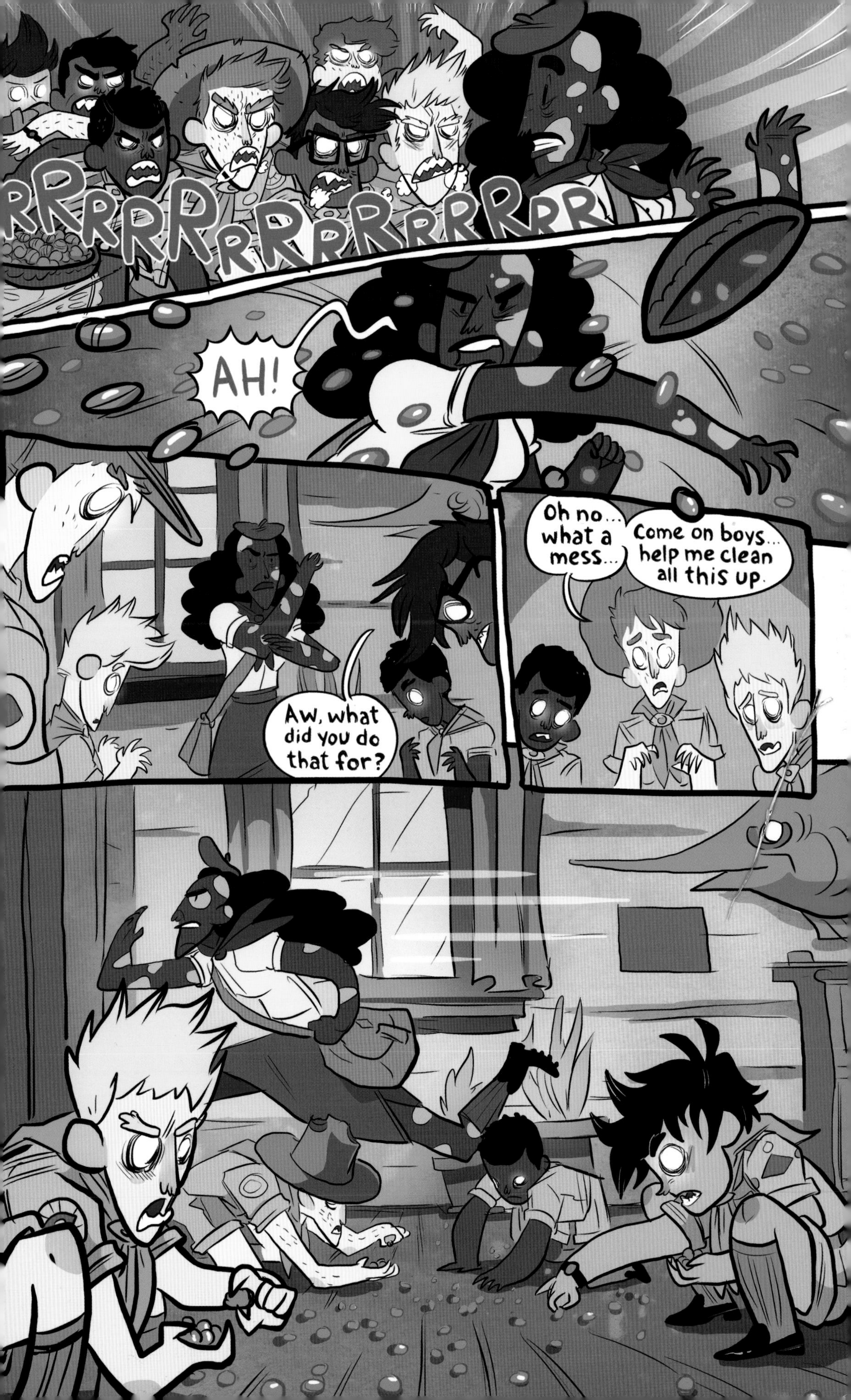
RRRRRRRRRRRRRRR
AH!
Aw, what did you do that for?
Oh no... what a mess...
Come on boys... help me clean all this up.

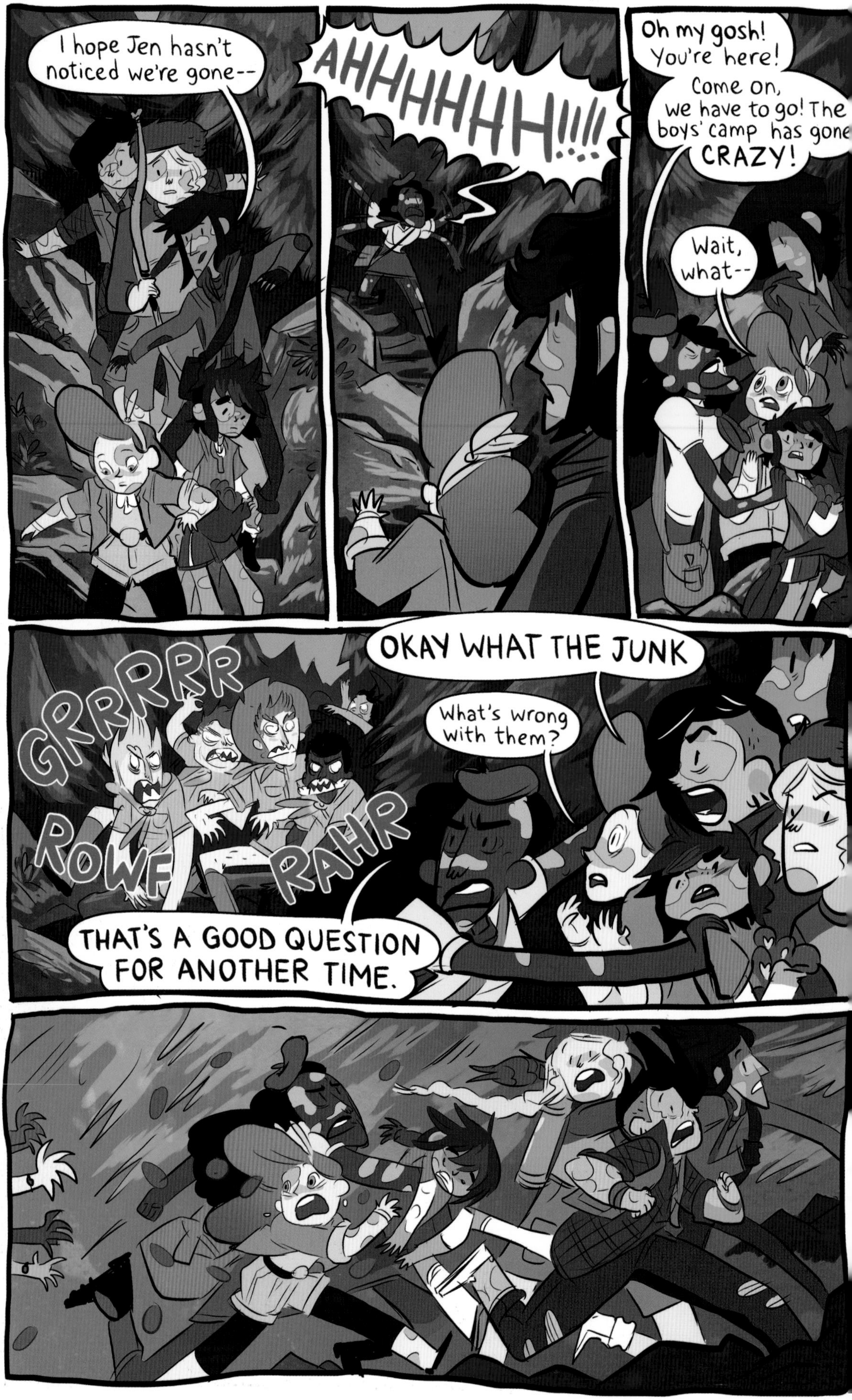
I hope Jen hasn't noticed we're gone--
AHHHHHHH!!!!!
Oh my gosh! You're here!
Come on, we have to go! The boys' camp has gone CRAZY!
Wait, what--
GRRRRR
ROWF
RAHR
OKAY WHAT THE JUNK
What's wrong with them?
THAT'S A GOOD QUESTION FOR ANOTHER TIME.

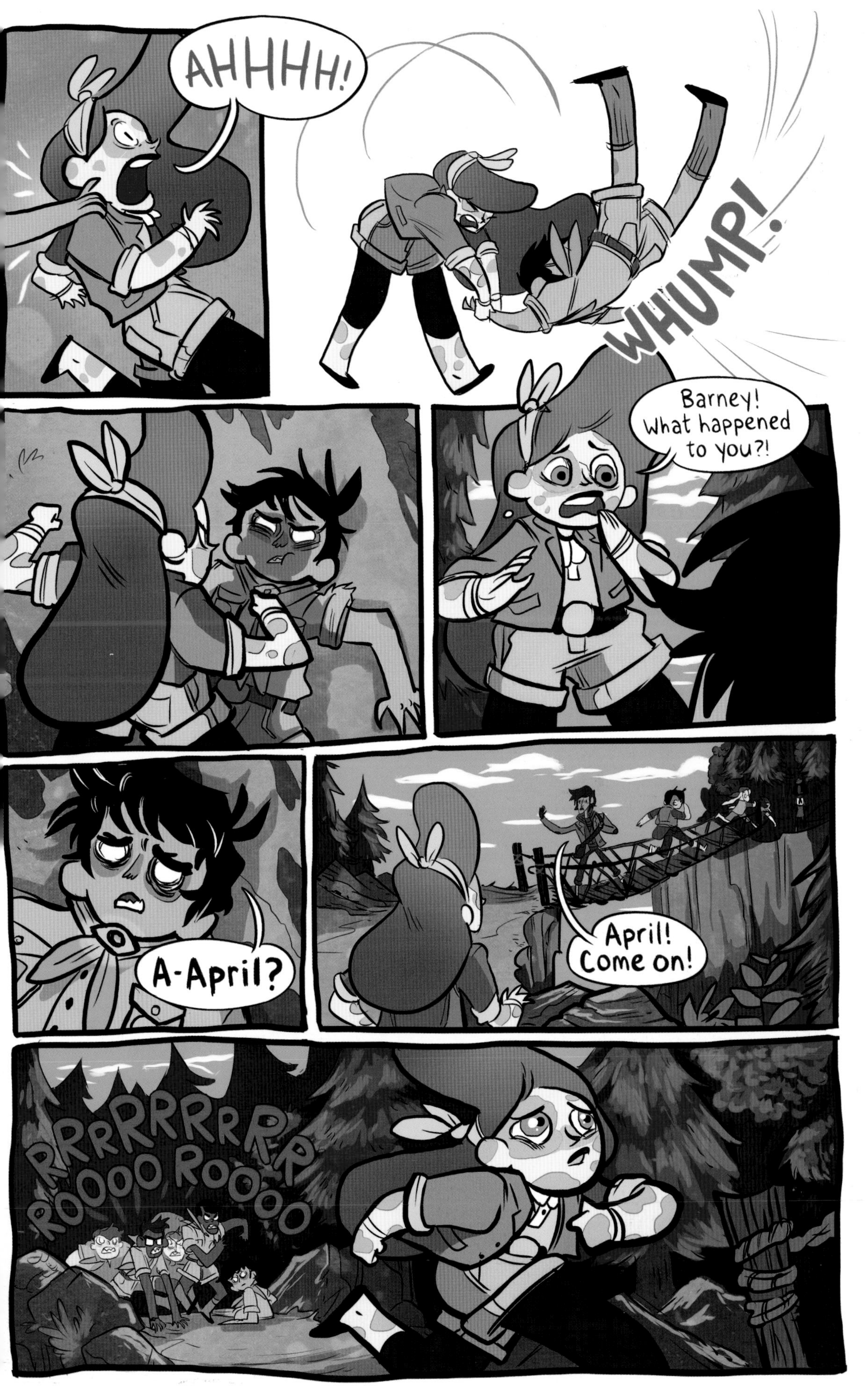
AHHHH!
WHUMP!
Barney! What happened to you?!
A-April?
April! Come on!
RRRRRRRRRR ROOOO ROOOO

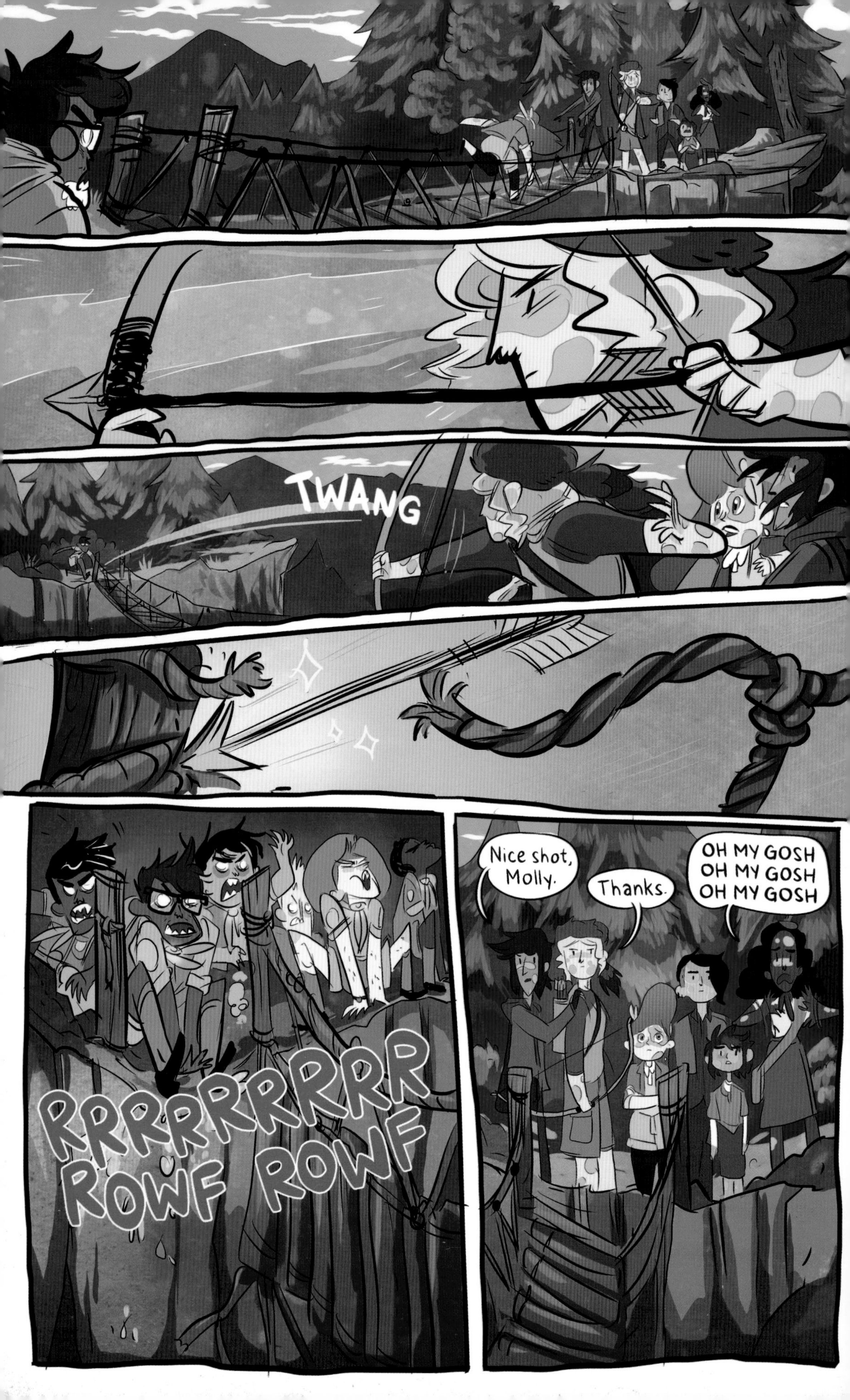
TWANG
RRRRRRRRR
ROWF ROWF
Nice shot, Molly.
Thanks.
OH MY GOSH
OH MY GOSH
OH MY GOSH

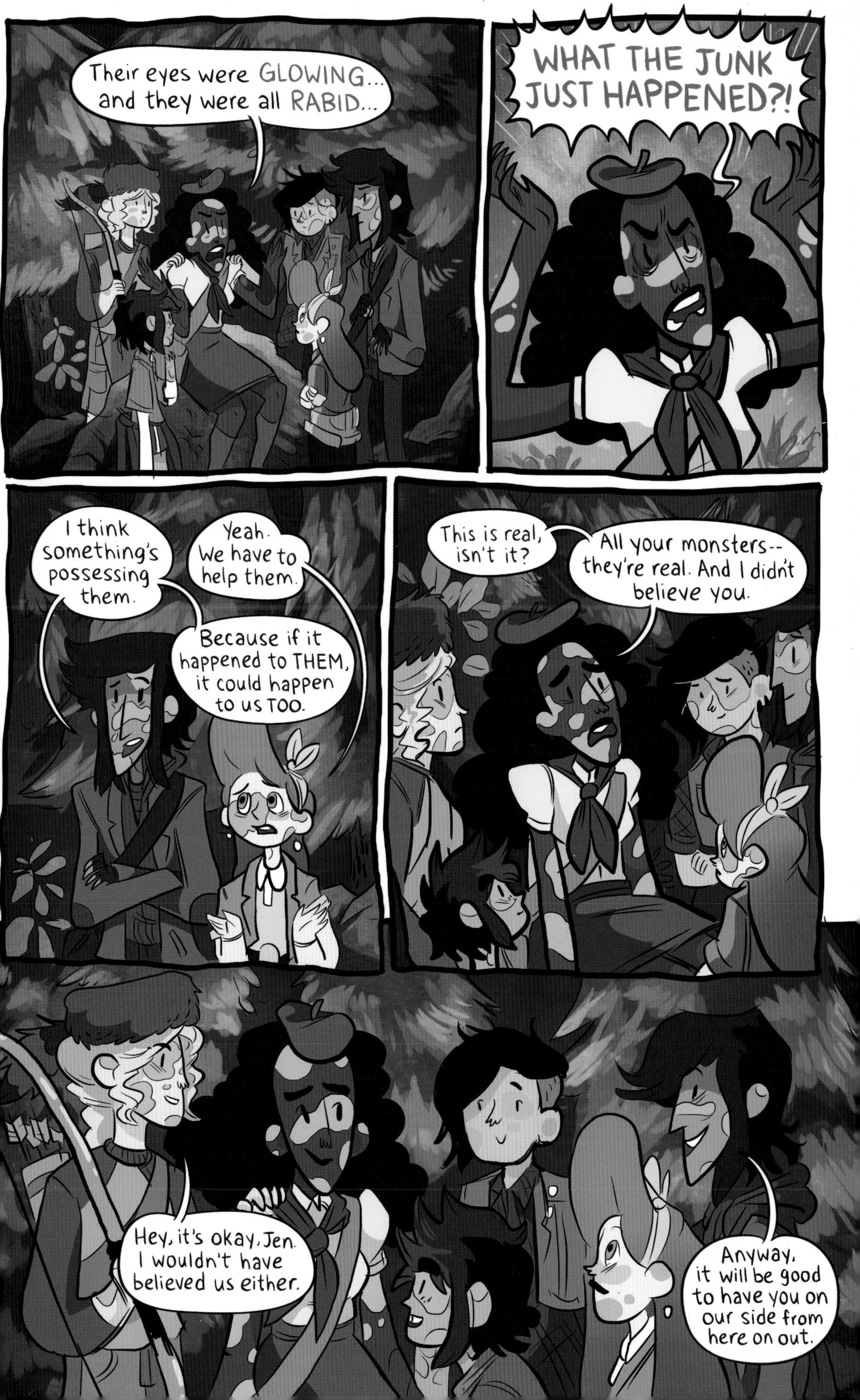
Their eyes were GLOWING... and they were all RABID...
WHAT THE JUNK JUST HAPPENED?!
I think something's possessing them.
Yeah. We have to help them.
Because if it happened to THEM, it could happen to us TOO.
This is real, isn't it?
All your monsters-- they're real. And I didn't believe you.
Hey, it's okay, Jen. I wouldn't have believed us either.
Anyway, it will be good to have you on our side from here on out.

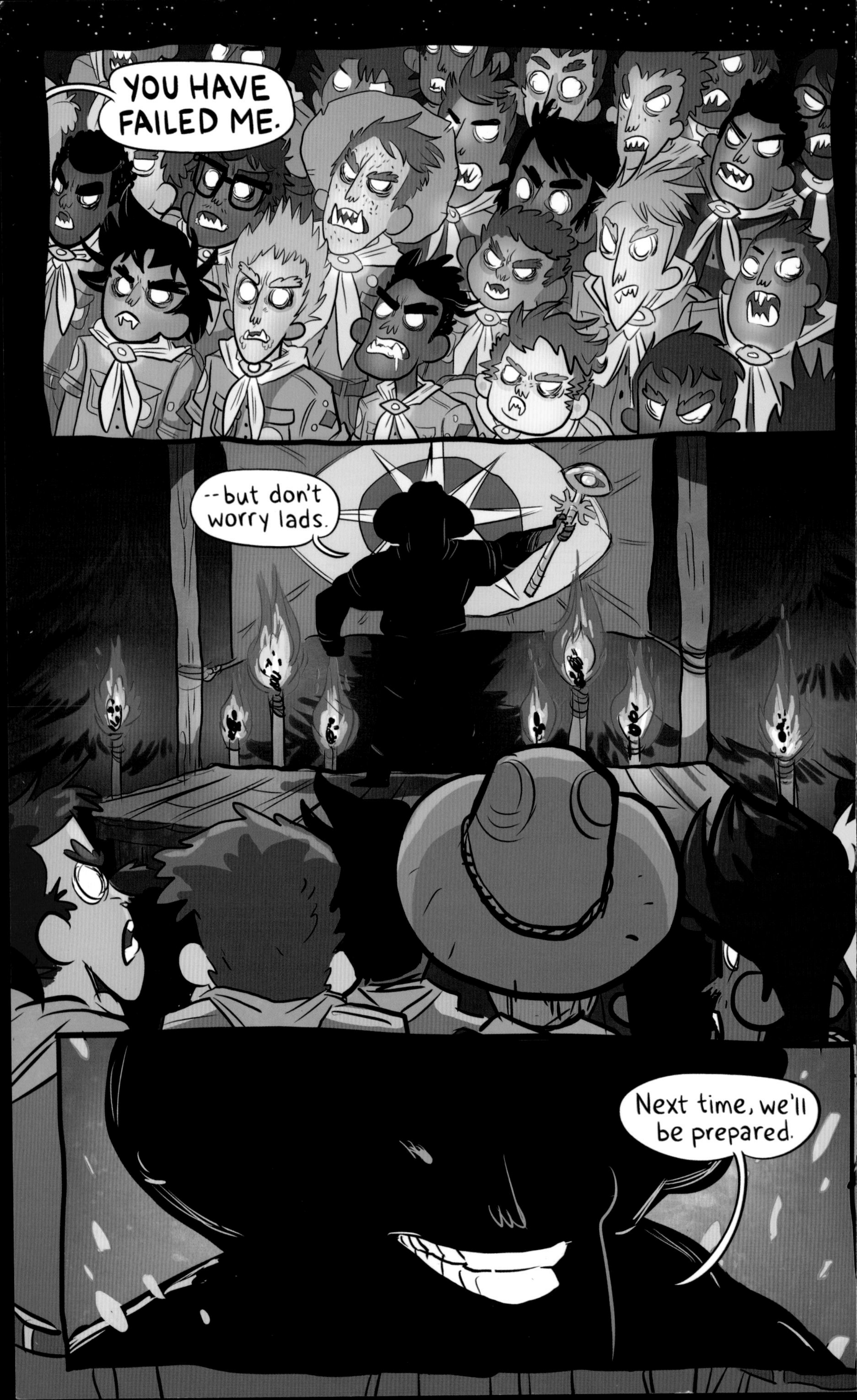
YOU HAVE FAILED ME.
--but don't worry lads.
Next time, we'll be prepared.

will co

The
It help
appearai
dress fo
Further
Lumber
to have
part in
Thiskw
Harde
have
them

The
yellow, short sl
emb
the w
choose
slacks,
made o
out-of-do
green bere
the colla
Shoes ma
heels, roun
socks should e
the uniform. Ne
belong with a Lumberjane uniform.

WHY ARE HIPSTER YETIS SO ODD? BECAUSE THEY CAN'T EVEN.

FRIENDSHIP TO THE MAX!

SERIOUSLY?

HOW TO WEAR THE UNIFORM

To look well in a uniform demands first of
uniform be kept in good condition—clean
pressed. See that the skirt is the right length for your own
height and build, that the belt is adjusted to your waist
that your shoes and stockings are in keeping with
uniform, that you watch your posture and carry
with dignity and grace. If the beret is remov
be sure that your hair is neat and kept in pla
insconspicuous clip or ribbon. When you
Lumberjane uniform you are identified as a mem
this organization and you should be doubly carefu
conduct yourself in a way that will show everyone tha
courtesy and thoughtfullness are part of being a
Lumberjane. People are likely to judge a whole nation by
the selfishness of a few individuals, to criticize a whole
family because of the misconduct of one member, and to
feel unkindly toward and organization because of the

pr
to b
mberjane pr
Penniquiqul Thi
Types, but m
can either bu
materials available at the trading post.
ore Lady
s will wish to have one. They
e uniform, or make it themselves from

LUMBERJANES FIELD MANUAL

CHAPTER FIVE

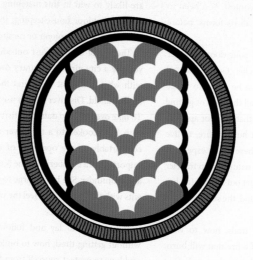

Lumberjanes "Arts and Crafts" Program Field

FRIENDSHIP TO THE CRAFT BADGE

"I get by with a little help from my yarn."

Being a scout requires more than what most might think. While Lumberjanes do the typical nature hikes and wood cutting competitions that are essential to every scout's growth, she will also do more. Every Lumberjane should leave camp with the basic understanding of problem solving, as she will encounter many problems through life. One of the many goals of the Lumberjanes is to make sure every young lady leaves with the tools to succeed. As a Lumberjane, it is vital to have a deep focus on friendship in every one of the courses offered. It should come as no surprise that both friendship and problem solving are combined in the *Friendship to the Craft* badge.

Crafting is a fine art that contains a multitude of mediums ranging from fibers to sculpting. It is the tendency of a Lumberjane to want to work with her hands and her mind that makes this badge one of the camp favorites. Each scout will be divided into groups and then given a task to complete within a limited amount of time. Some of these tasks will be easy to complete individually and will be an opportunity for the more advanced scouts to help out the less experienced. Other tasks will be so advanced that they will most likely never be completed. As every scout eventually learns, some things are bigger than us.

To obtain the *Friendship to the Craft* badge a Lumberjane must have already mastered the art of glue, and shown great promise in her creative thinking skills. She must enjoy color theory as well as be able to explain how the theory of colors works in nature and in the modern world. She must have shown that not only is she a natural leader, but is able to take a step back and allow others to guide on their journey as well. The importance of this badge is the lesson of teamwork. In learning how to make a friendship bracelet.

huff huff huff huff
JO! WHERE ARE YOU?
I'm over here! Where are you?
Jo, HURRY!
I'm coming! Hold on!!
Ripley! What's going on?
There you are.
We've been waiting for you.
AHHHHHHH!

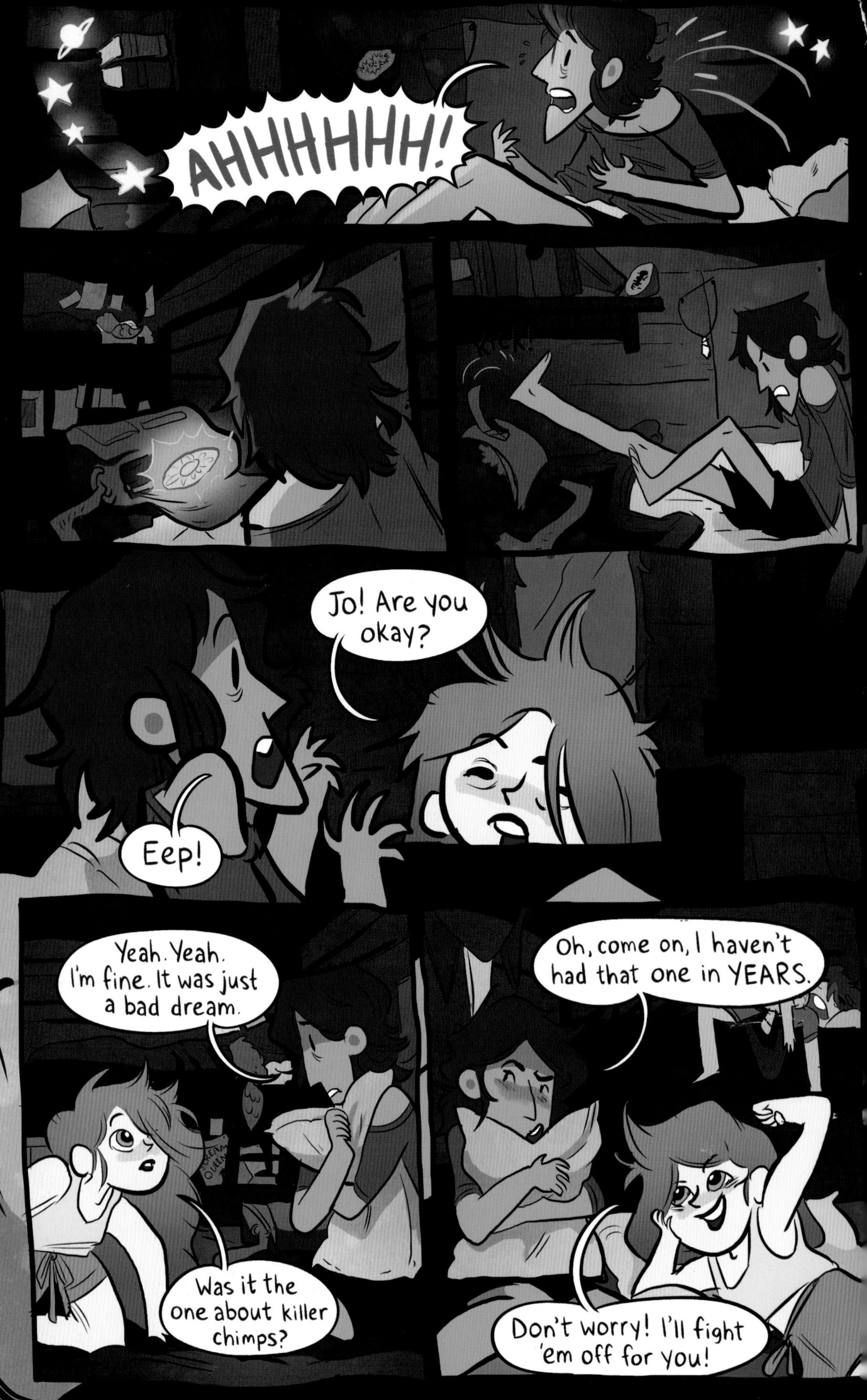
AHHHHHH!
Jo! Are you okay?
Eep!
Yeah. Yeah. I'm fine. It was just a bad dream.
Was it the one about killer chimps?
Oh, come on, I haven't had that one in YEARS.
Don't worry! I'll fight 'em off for you!

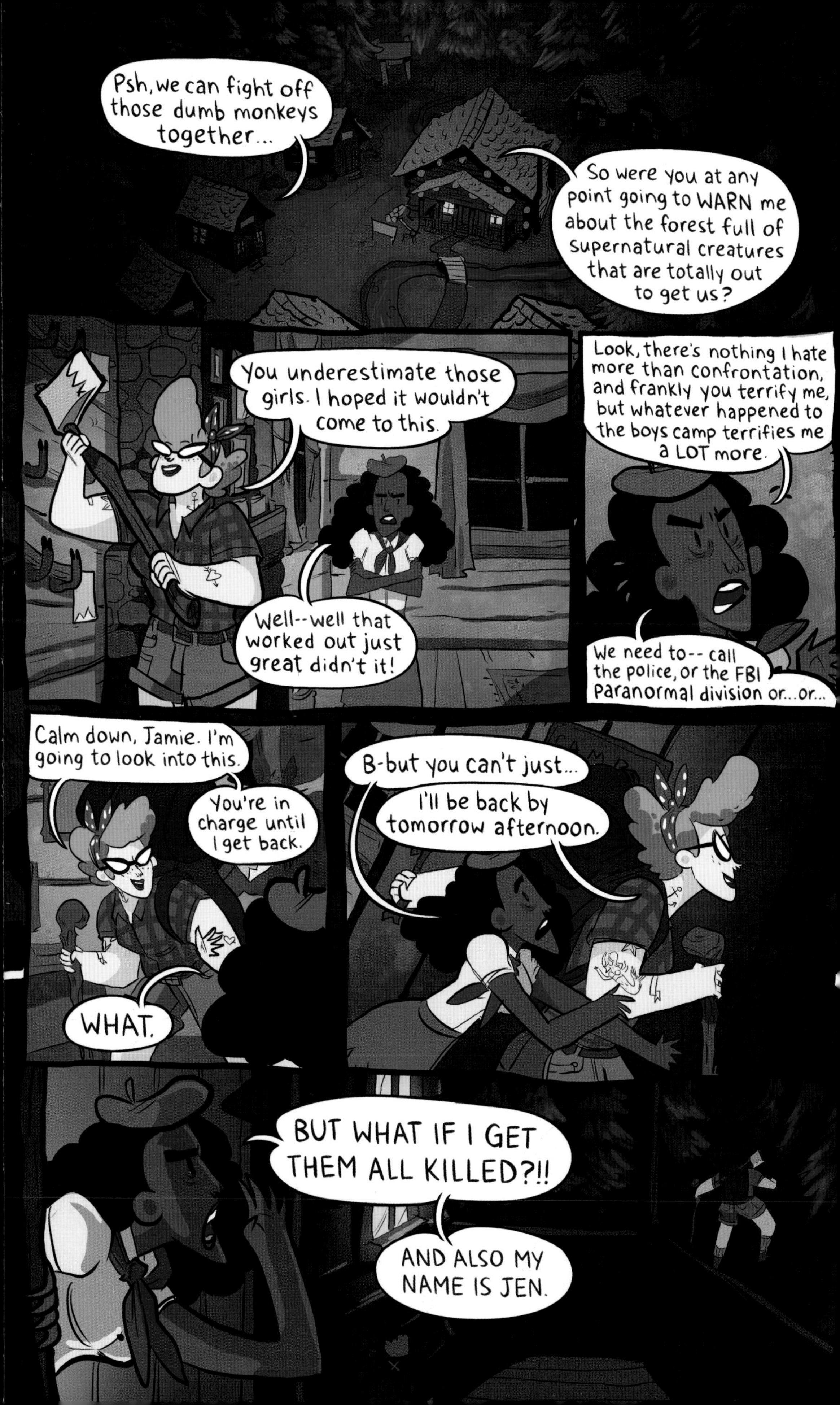
Psh, we can fight off those dumb monkeys together...
So were you at any point going to WARN me about the forest full of supernatural creatures that are totally out to get us?
You underestimate those girls. I hoped it wouldn't come to this.
Well--well that worked out just great didn't it!
Look, there's nothing I hate more than confrontation, and frankly you terrify me, but whatever happened to the boys camp terrifies me a LOT more.
We need to-- call the police, or the FBI paranormal division or...or...
Calm down, Jamie. I'm going to look into this.
You're in charge until I get back.
WHAT.
B-but you can't just...
I'll be back by tomorrow afternoon.
BUT WHAT IF I GET THEM ALL KILLED?!!
AND ALSO MY NAME IS JEN.

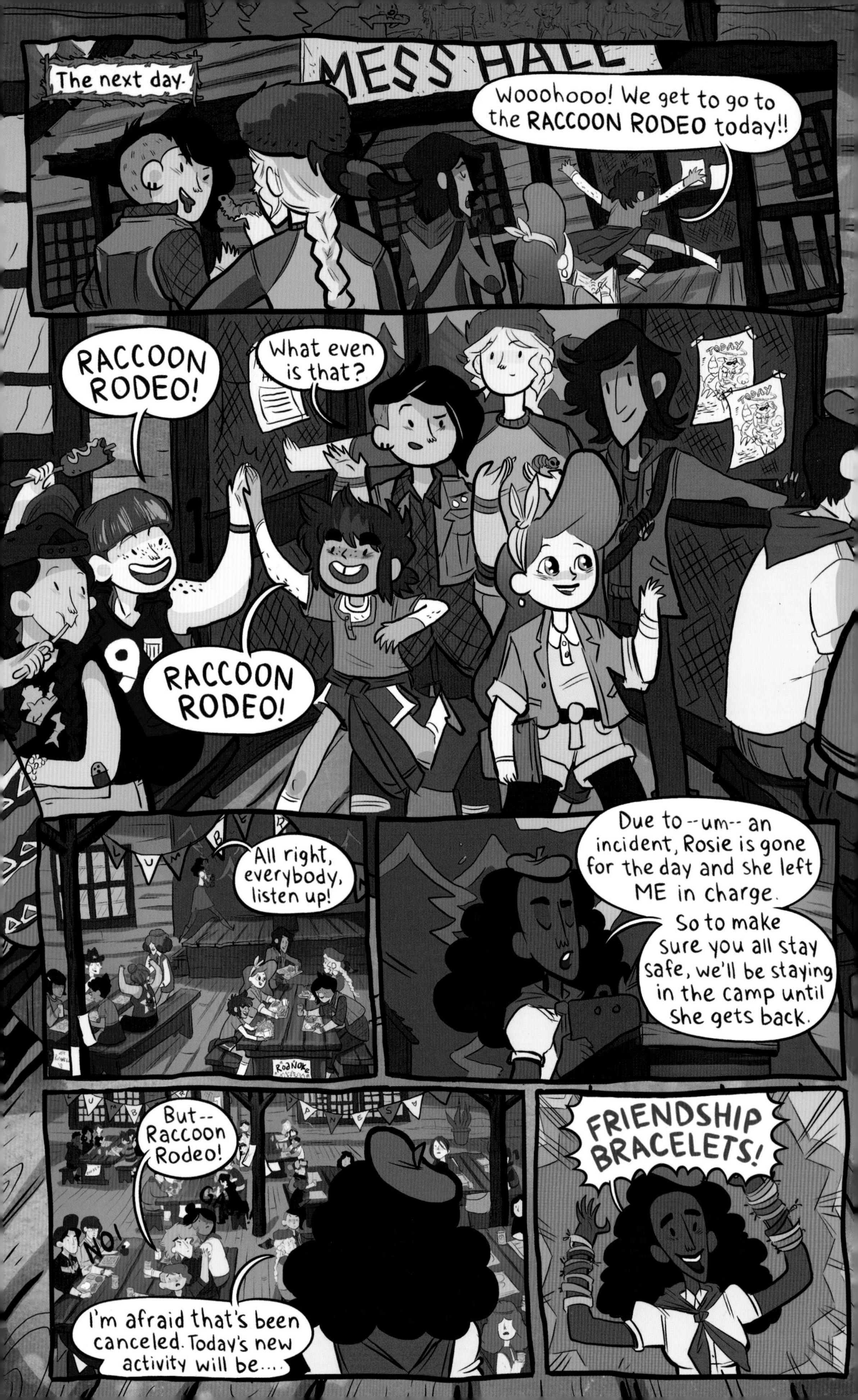
MESS HALL
The next day.
Wooohooo! We get to go to the RACCOON RODEO today!!
RACCOON RODEO!
What even is that?
TODAY
TODAY
RACCOON RODEO!
All right, everybody, listen up!
ROANOKE
Due to--um-- an incident, Rosie is gone for the day and she left ME in charge.
So to make sure you all stay safe, we'll be staying in the camp until she gets back.
But--Raccoon Rodeo!
NO!
I'm afraid that's been canceled. Today's new activity will be....
FRIENDSHIP BRACELETS!

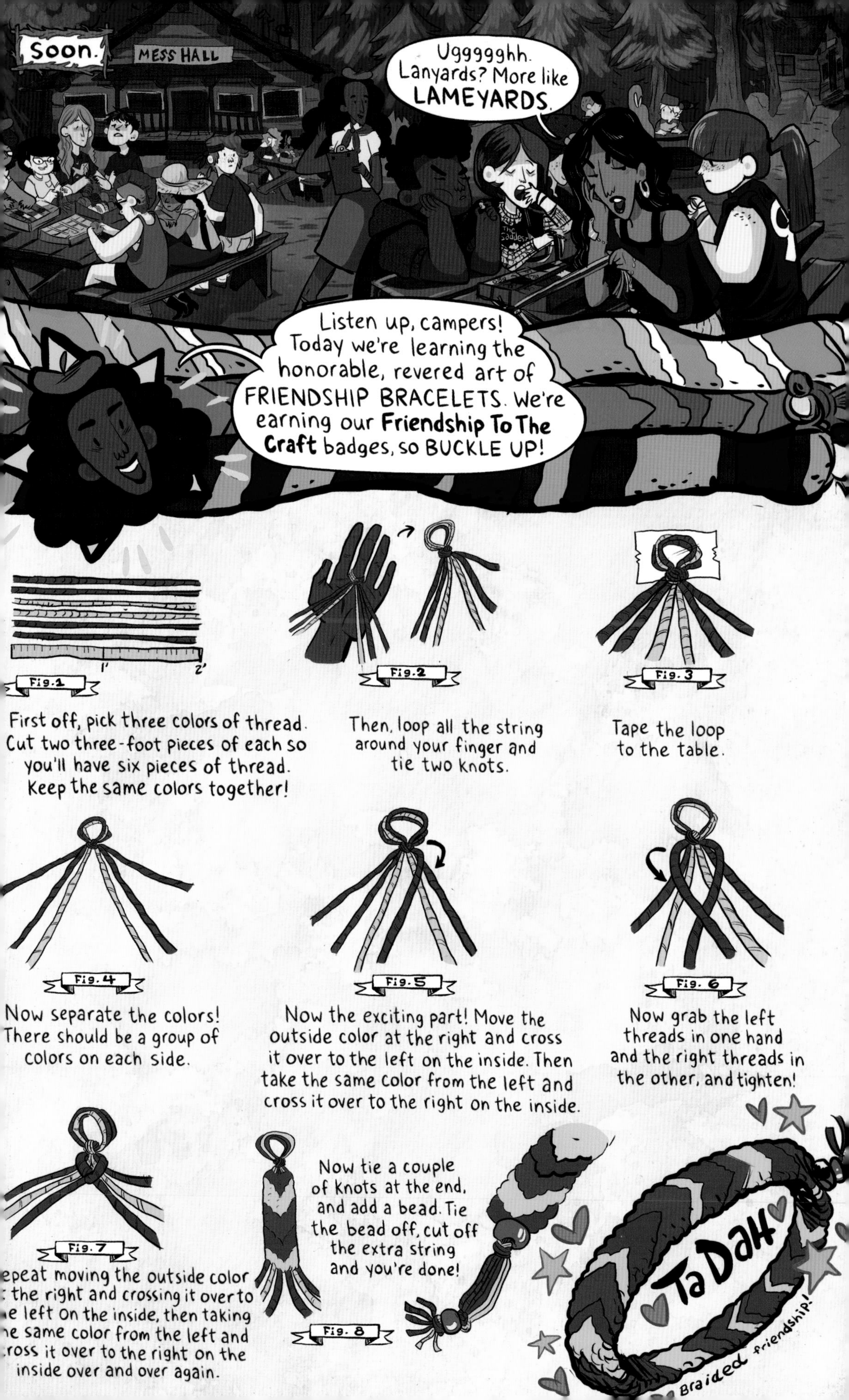
Soon.
MESS HALL
Uggggghh. Lanyards? More like LAMEYARDS.
The Saddest
Listen up, campers! Today we're learning the honorable, revered art of FRIENDSHIP BRACELETS. We're earning our **Friendship To The Craft** badges, so BUCKLE UP!
1'
2'
Fig. 1
First off, pick three colors of thread. Cut two three-foot pieces of each so you'll have six pieces of thread. Keep the same colors together!
Fig. 2
Then, loop all the string around your finger and tie two knots.
Fig. 3
Tape the loop to the table.
Fig. 4
Now separate the colors! There should be a group of colors on each side.
Fig. 5
Now the exciting part! Move the outside color at the right and cross it over to the left on the inside. Then take the same color from the left and cross it over to the right on the inside.
Fig. 6
Now grab the left threads in one hand and the right threads in the other, and tighten!
Fig. 7
epeat moving the outside color
: the right and crossing it over to
e left on the inside, then taking
e same color from the left and
ross it over to the right on the
inside over and over again.
Now tie a couple of knots at the end, and add a bead. Tie the bead off, cut off the extra string and you're done!
Fig. 8
Ta DaH
Braided friendship!

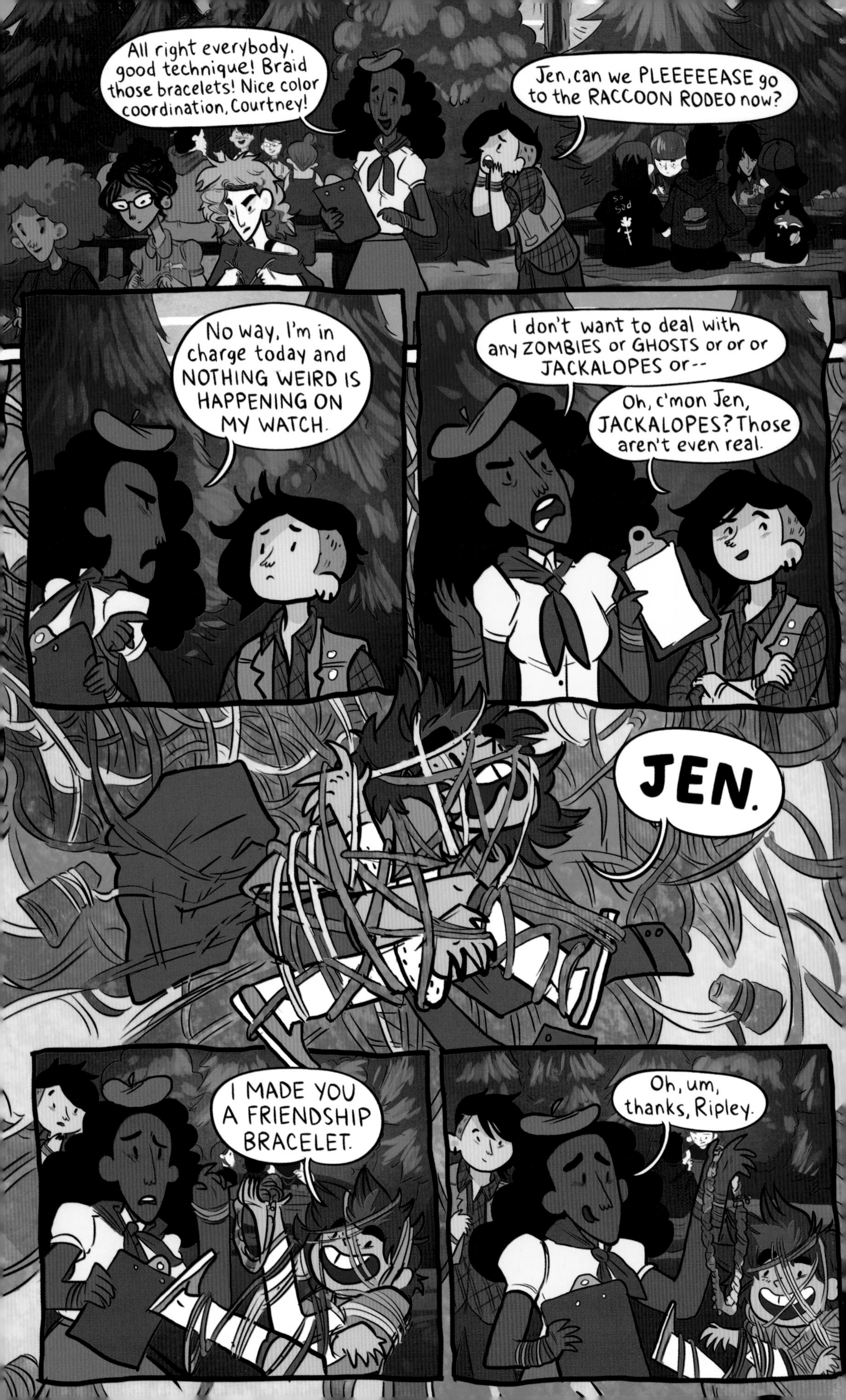
All right everybody, good technique! Braid those bracelets! Nice color coordination, Courtney!
Jen, can we PLEEEEEASE go to the RACCOON RODEO now?
No way, I'm in charge today and NOTHING WEIRD IS HAPPENING ON MY WATCH.
I don't want to deal with any ZOMBIES or GHOSTS or or or JACKALOPES or--
Oh, c'mon Jen, JACKALOPES? Those aren't even real.
JEN.
I MADE YOU A FRIENDSHIP BRACELET.
Oh, um, thanks, Ripley.

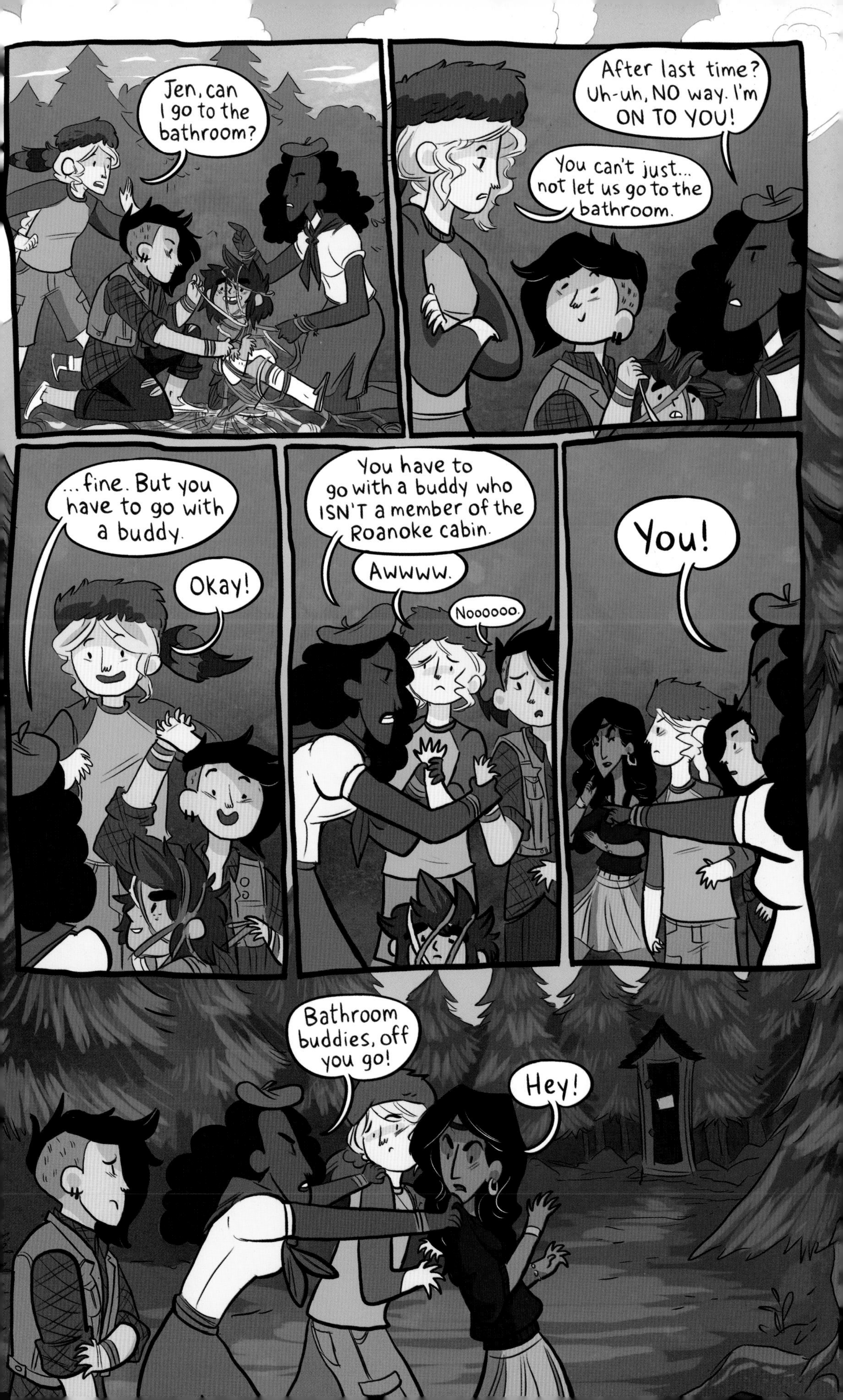
Jen, can I go to the bathroom?
After last time? Uh-uh, NO way. I'm ON TO YOU!
You can't just... not let us go to the bathroom.
...fine. But you have to go with a buddy.
Okay!
You have to go with a buddy who ISN'T a member of the Roanoke cabin.
AWWWW.
Noooooo.
You!
Bathroom buddies, off you go!
Hey!

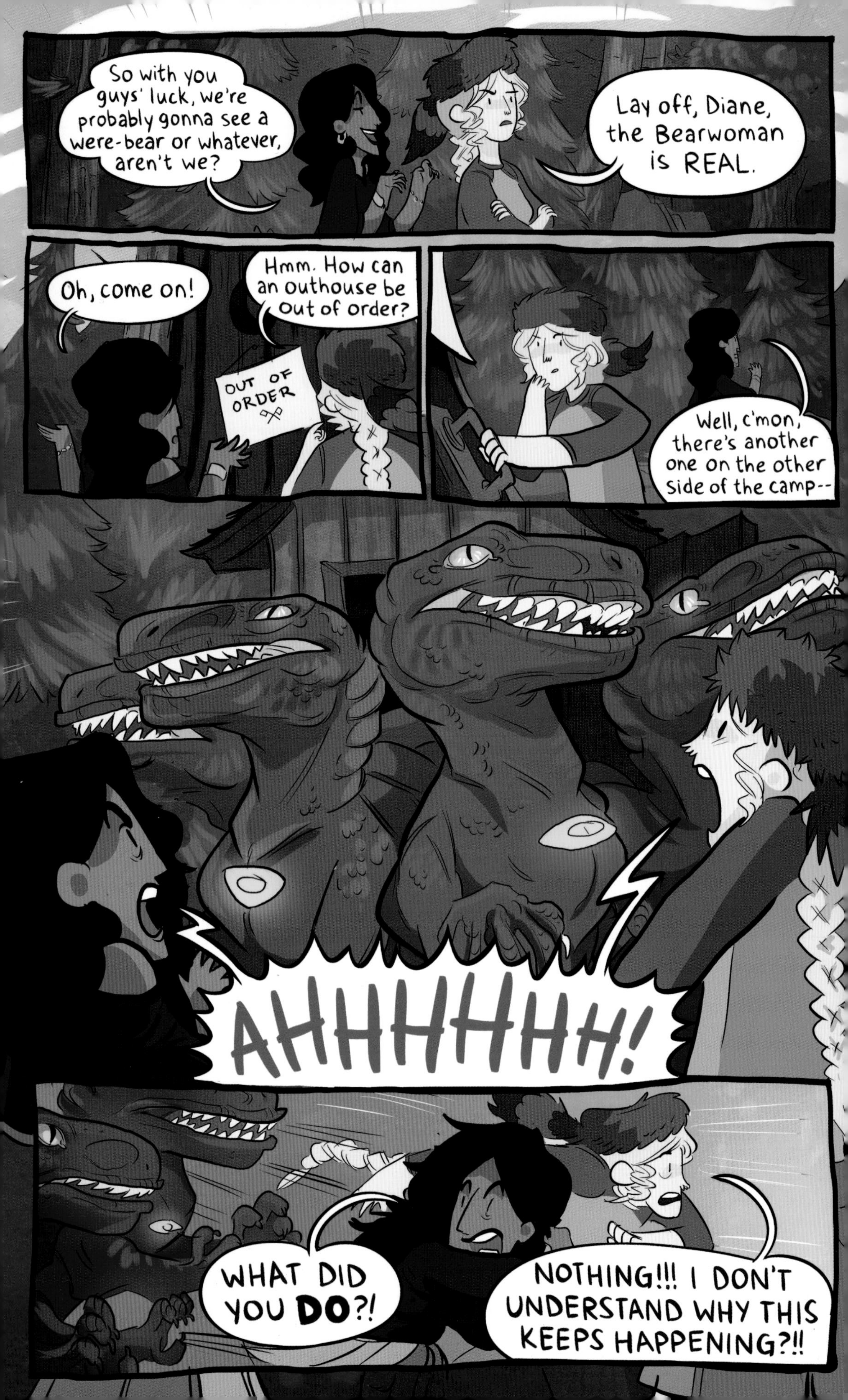
So with you guys' luck, we're probably gonna see a were-bear or whatever, aren't we?
Lay off, Diane, the Bearwoman is REAL.
Oh, come on!
Hmm. How can an outhouse be out of order?
OUT OF ORDER
Well, c'mon, there's another one on the other side of the camp--
AHHHHHH!
WHAT DID YOU **DO**?!
NOTHING!!! I DON'T UNDERSTAND WHY THIS KEEPS HAPPENING?!!

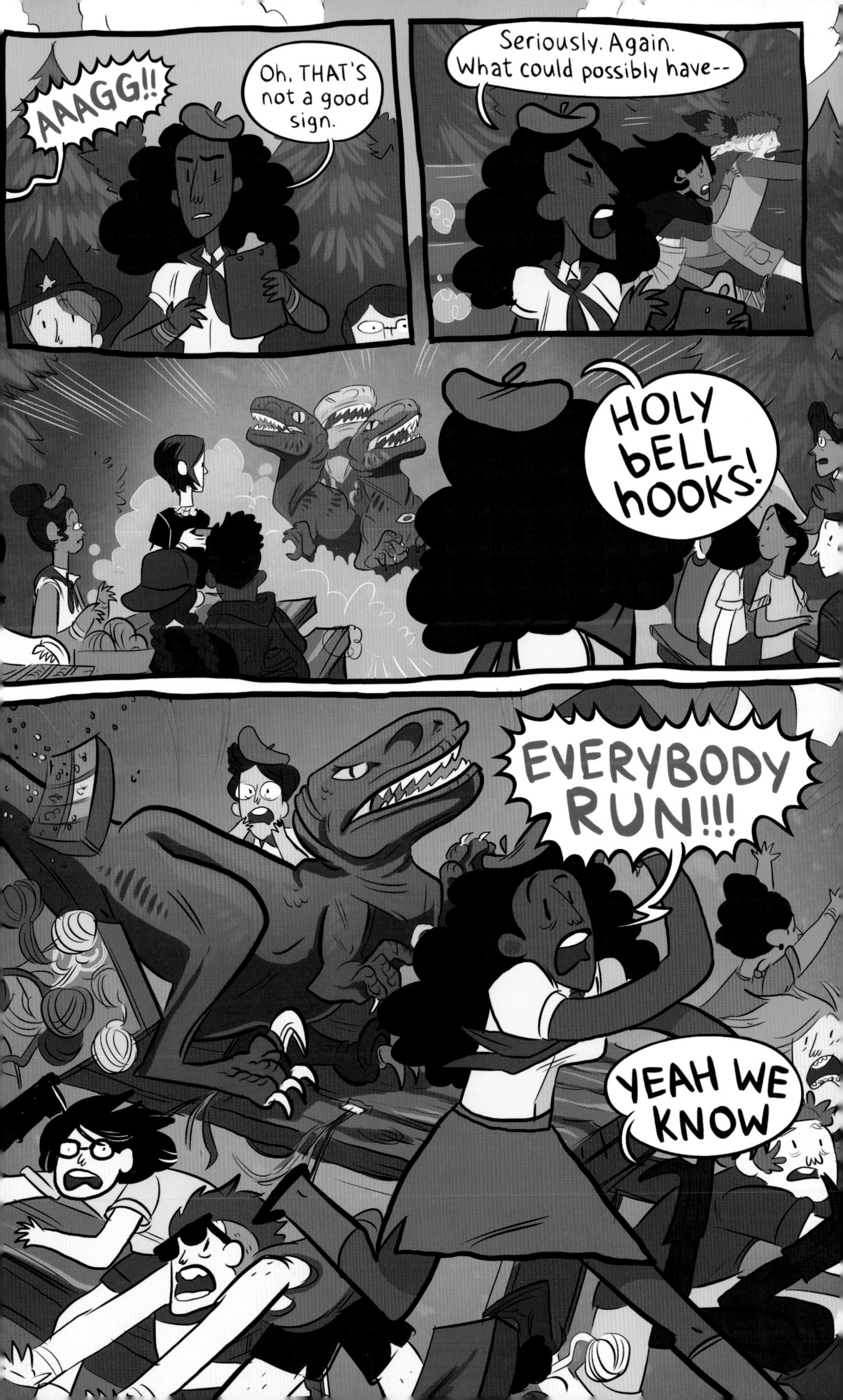
AAAGG!!
Oh, THAT'S not a good sign.
Seriously. Again. What could possibly have--
HOLY bELL hOOKS!
EVERYBODY RUN!!!
YEAH WE KNOW

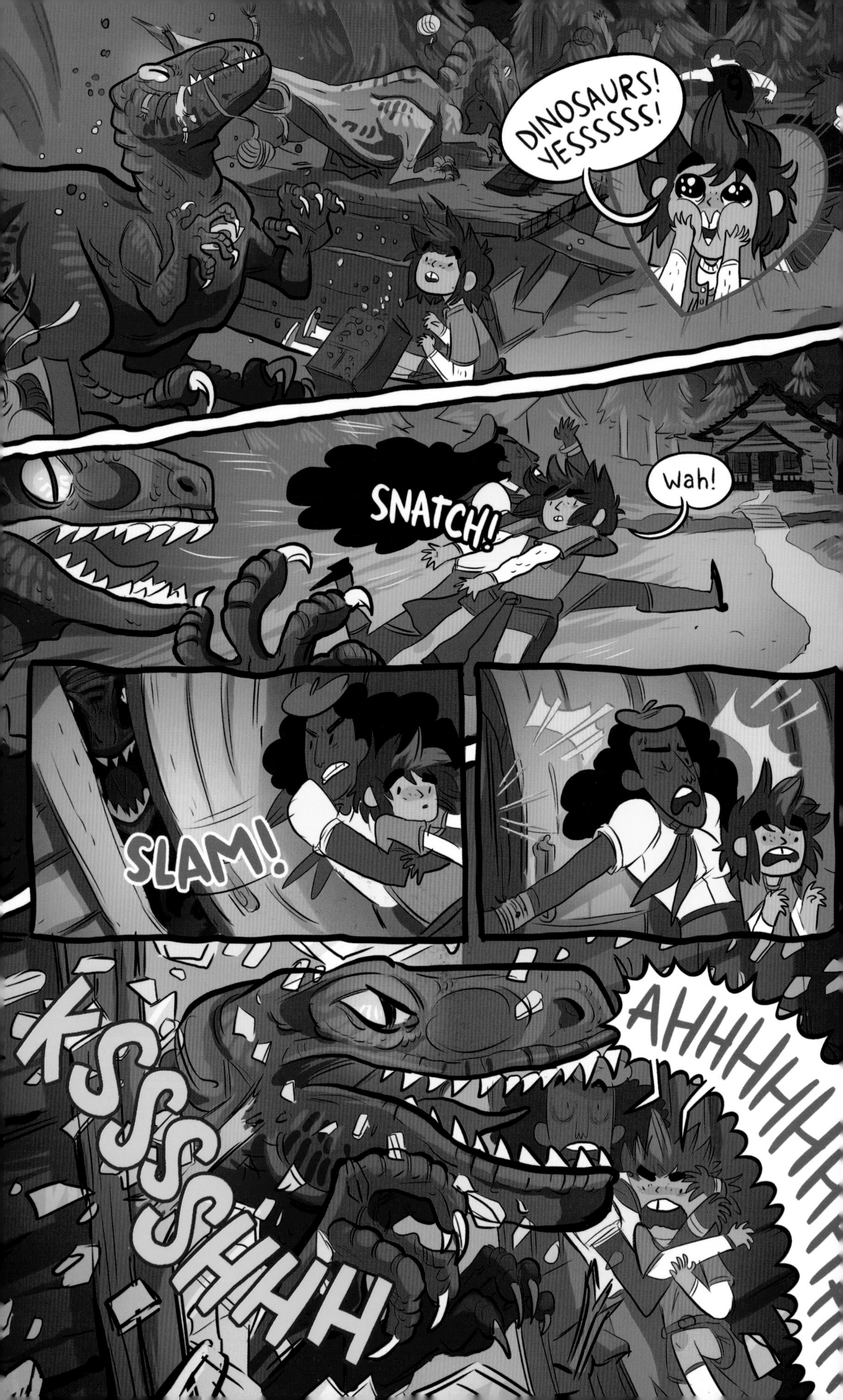
DINOSAURS! YESSSSSS!
SNATCH!
Wah!
SLAM!
KSSSSHHH
AHHHHHHH!!!

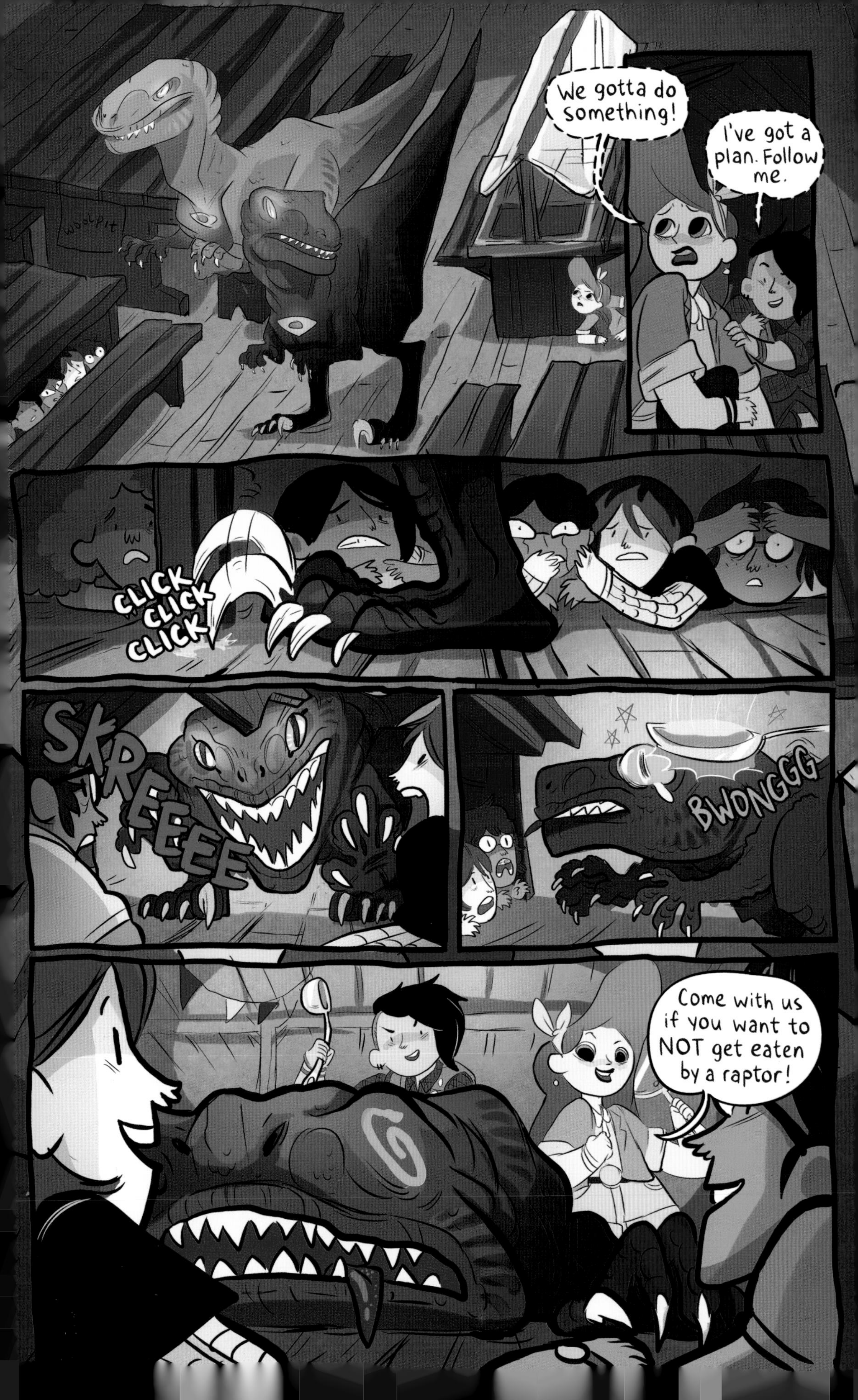
WOOLPIT
We gotta do something!
I've got a plan. Follow me.
CLICK
CLICK
CLICK
SKREEEEE
BWONGGG
Come with us if you want to NOT get eaten by a raptor!

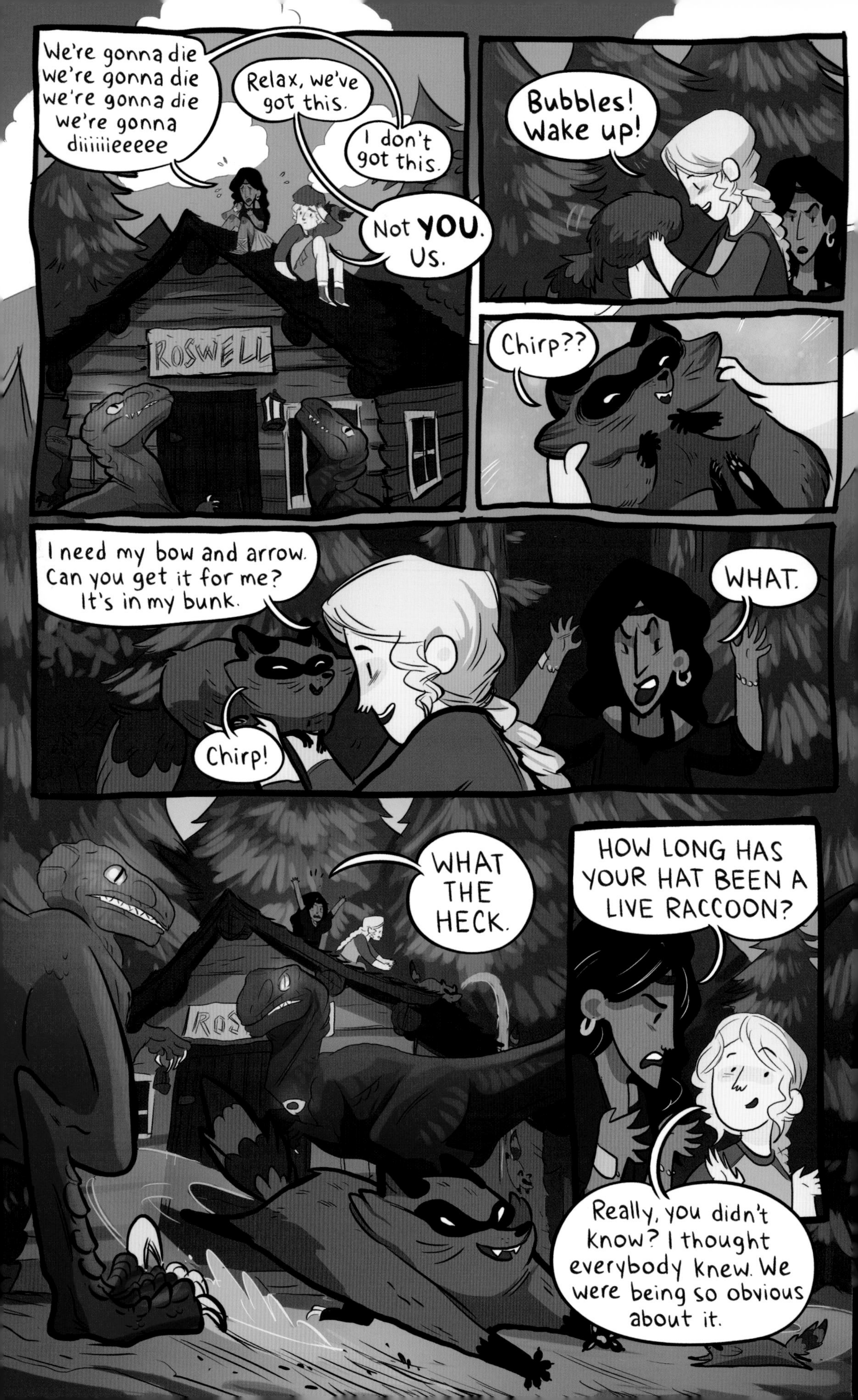
We're gonna die we're gonna die we're gonna die we're gonna diiiiiieeeee
Relax, we've got this.
I don't got this.
Not YOU. Us.
ROSWELL
Bubbles! Wake up!
Chirp??
I need my bow and arrow. Can you get it for me? It's in my bunk.
Chirp!
WHAT.
WHAT THE HECK.
HOW LONG HAS YOUR HAT BEEN A LIVE RACCOON?
Really, you didn't know? I thought everybody knew. We were being so obvious about it.

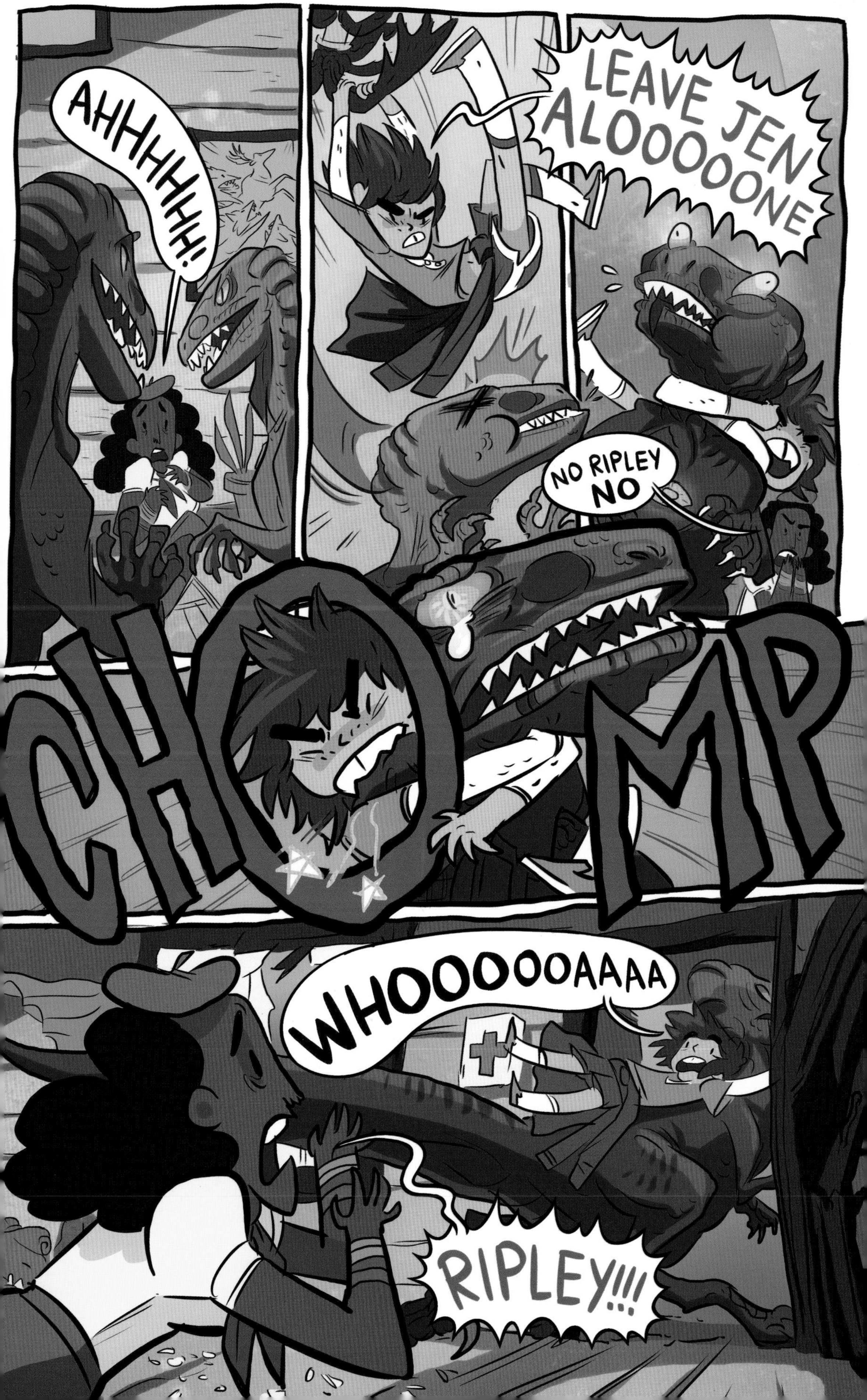
AHHHHHH!
LEAVE JEN ALOOOOONE
NO RIPLEY NO
CHOMP
WHOOOOOAAAA
RIPLEY!!!

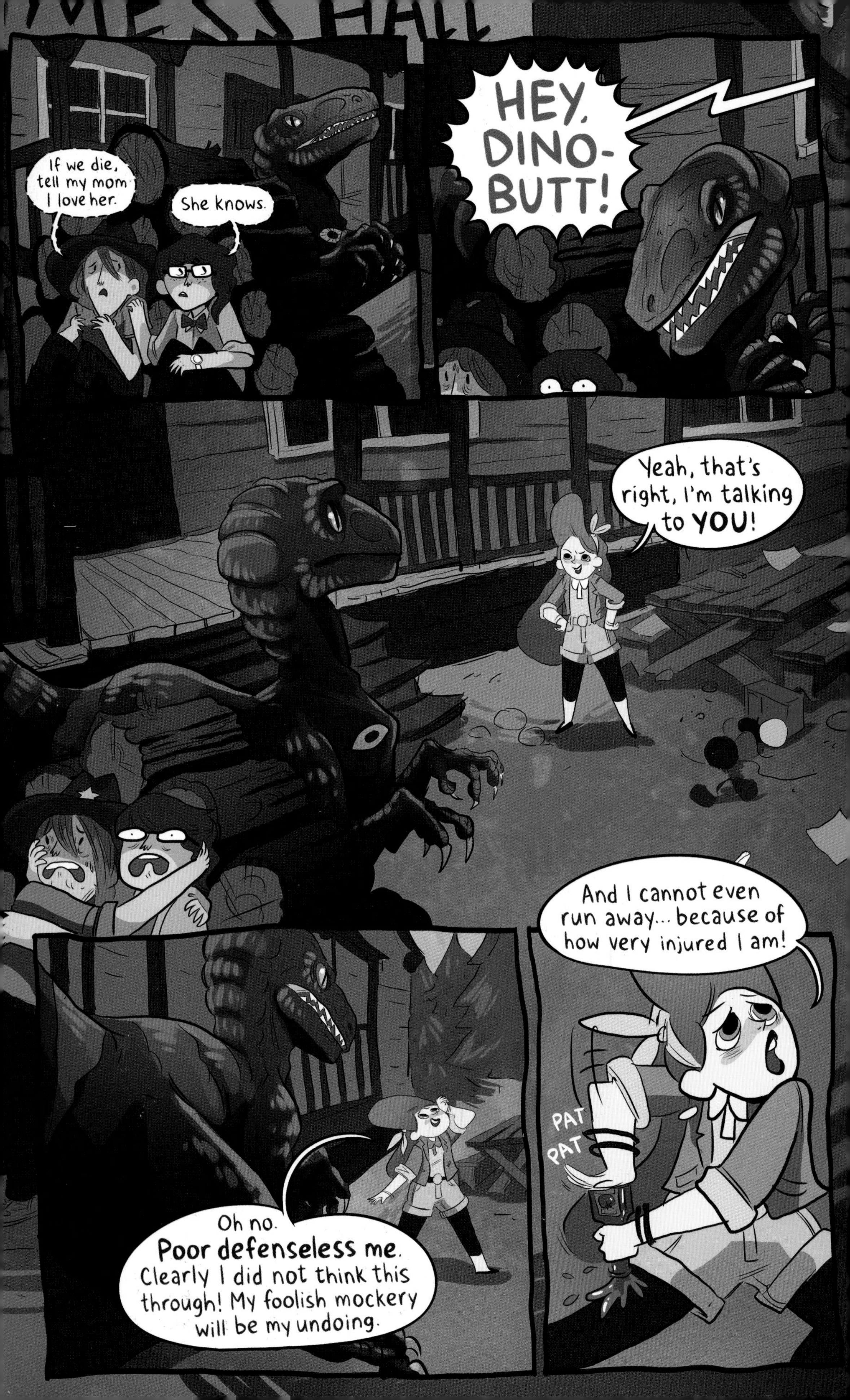
MESS HALL
If we die, tell my mom I love her.
She knows.
HEY, DINO-BUTT!
Yeah, that's right, I'm talking to YOU!
Oh no. Poor defenseless me. Clearly I did not think this through! My foolish mockery will be my undoing.
And I cannot even run away... because of how very injured I am!
PAT PAT

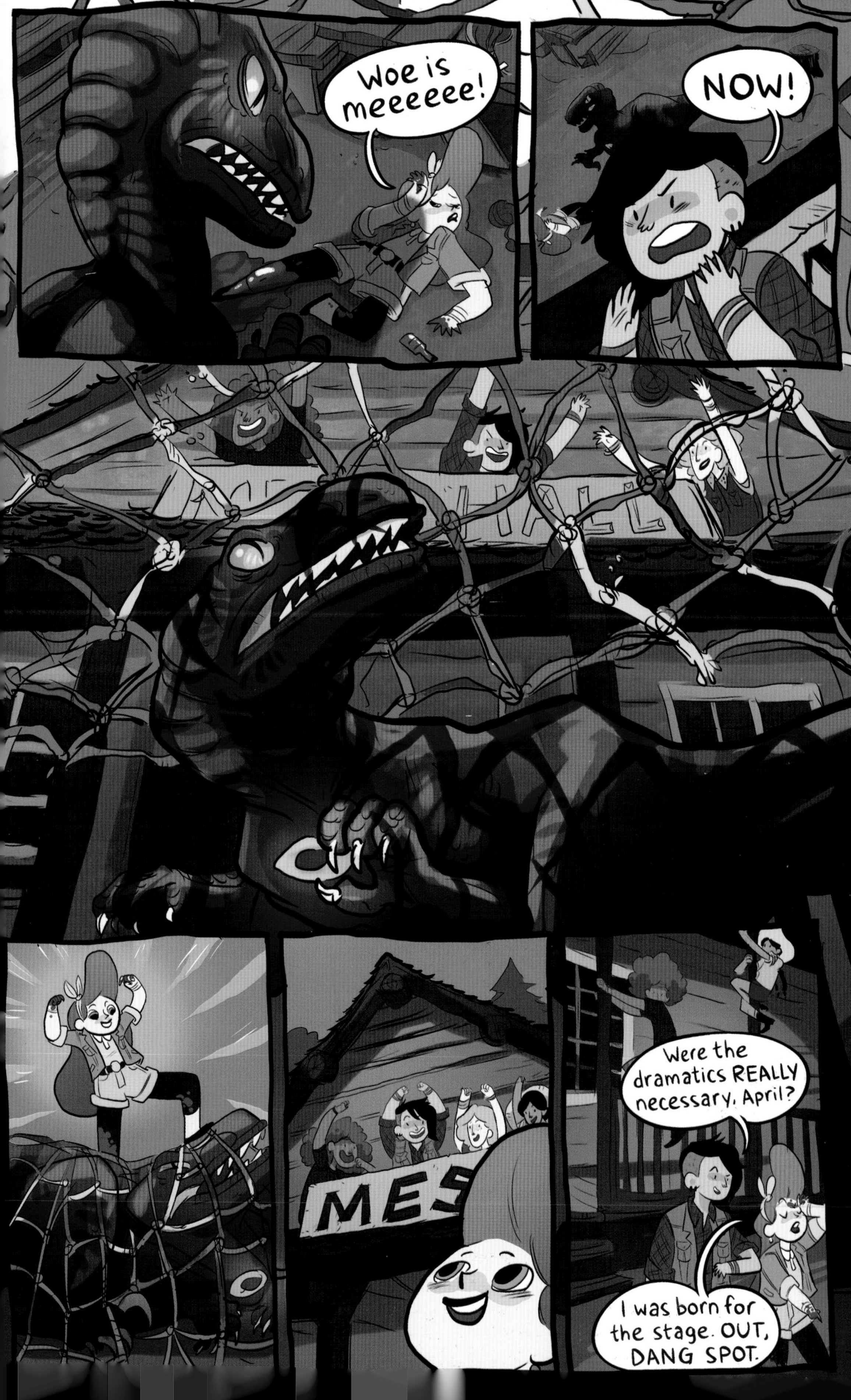
Woe is meeeeee!
NOW!
Were the dramatics REALLY necessary, April?
I was born for the stage. OUT, DANG SPOT.
MES

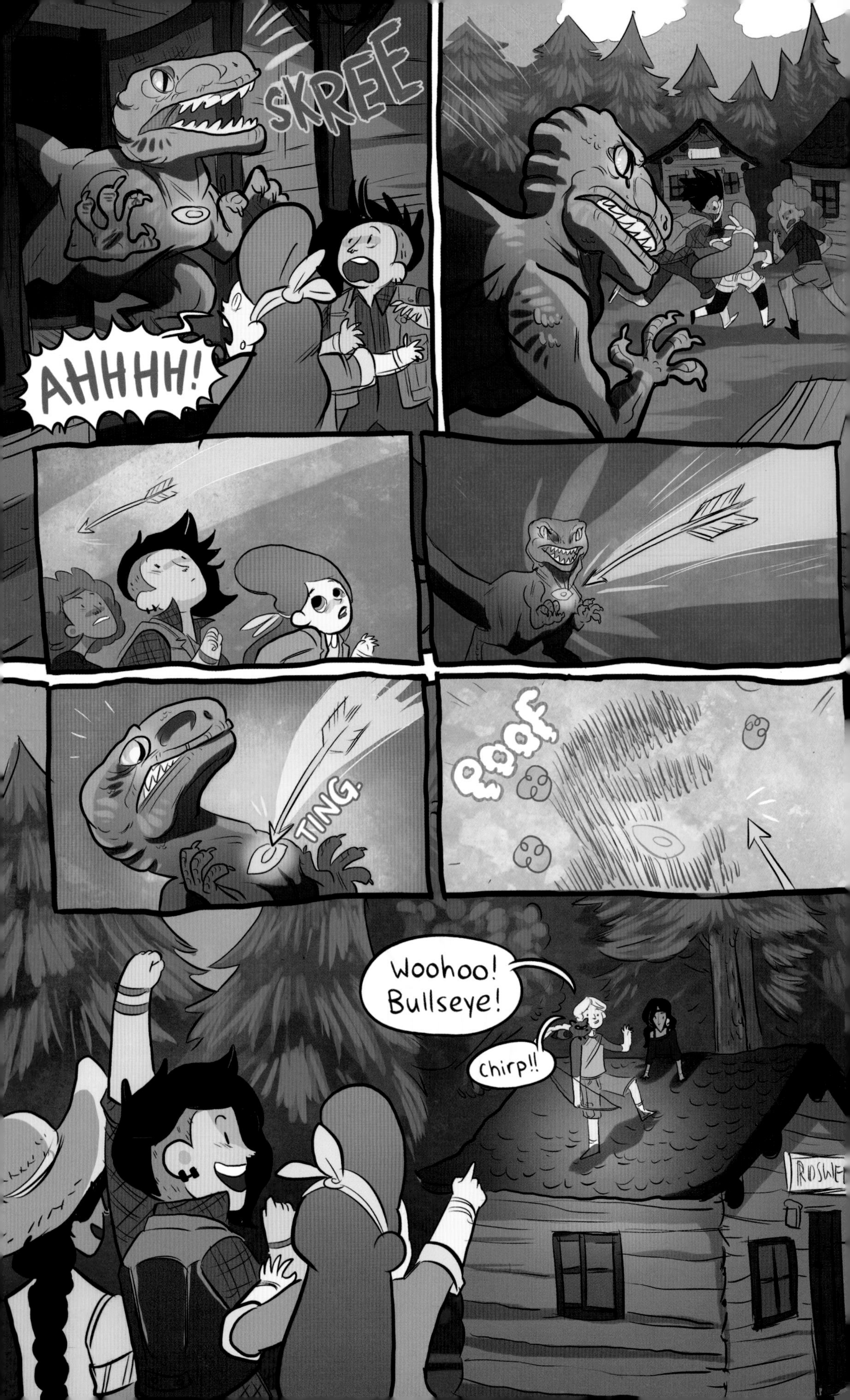
SKREE
AHHHH!
TING.
Poof
Woohoo! Bullseye!
Chirp!!

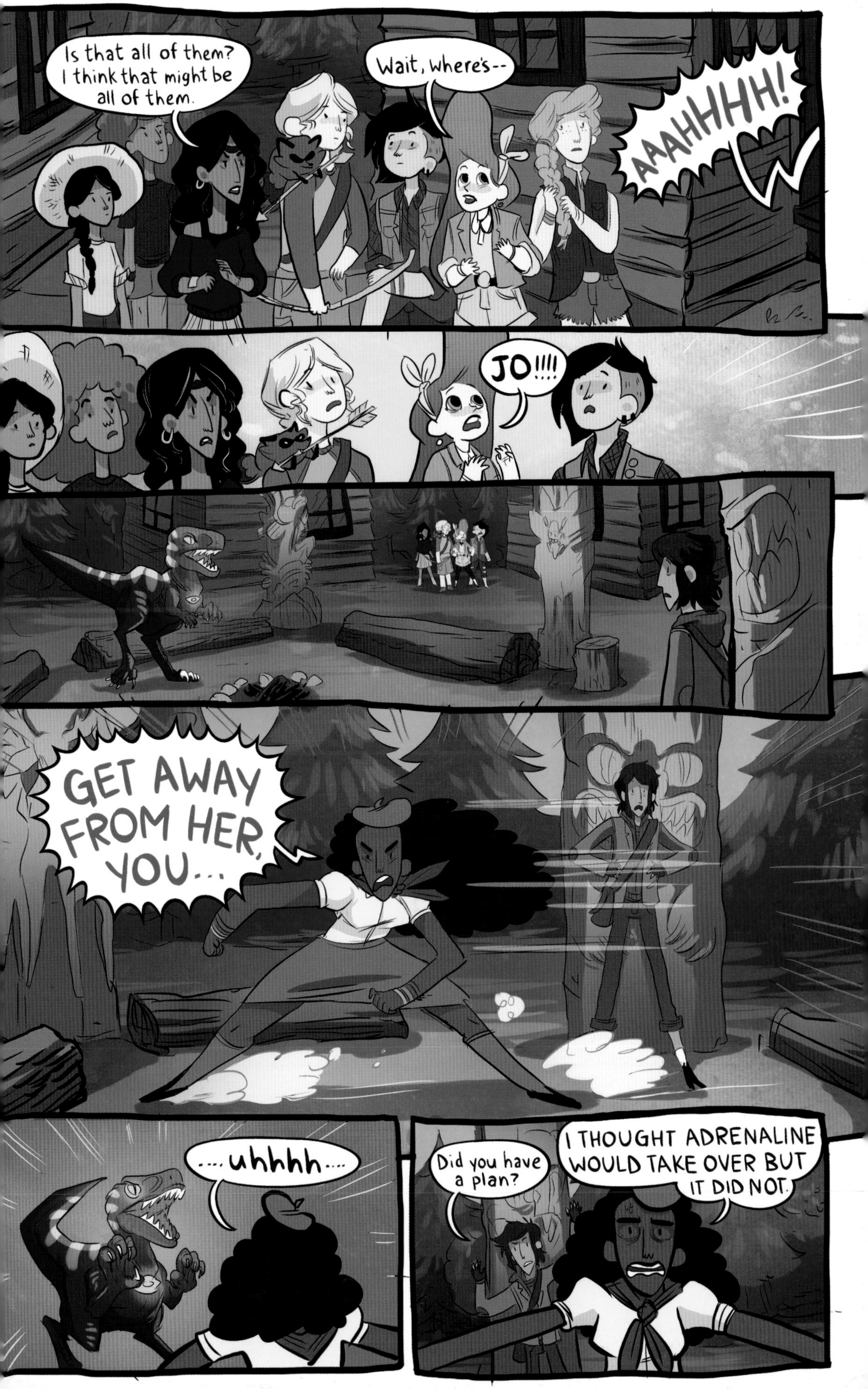
Is that all of them? I think that might be all of them.
Wait, where's--
AAAHHHH!
JO!!!!
GET AWAY FROM HER, YOU...
....uhhhh....
Did you have a plan?
I THOUGHT ADRENALINE WOULD TAKE OVER BUT IT DID NOT.

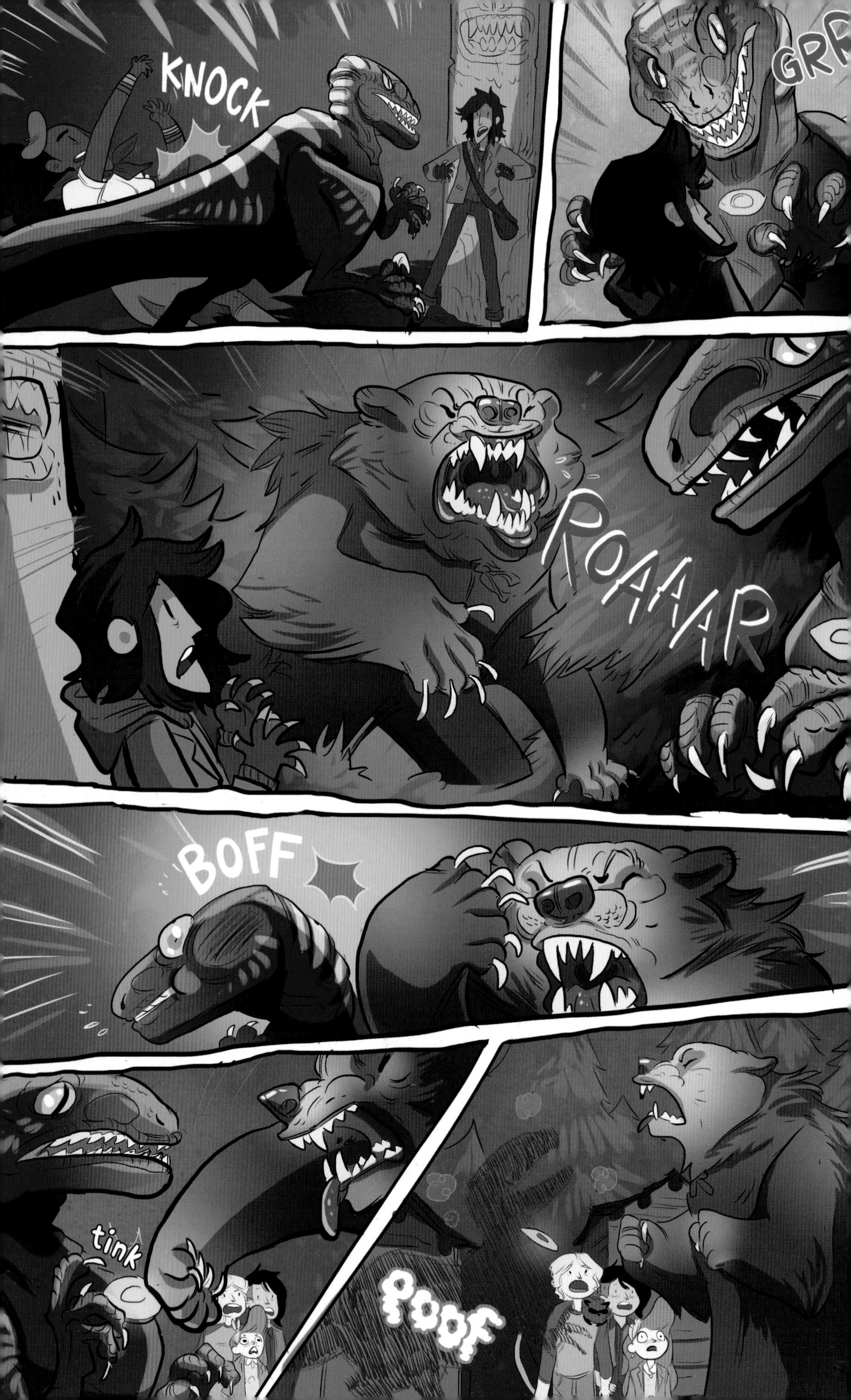
KNOCK
GRR
ROAAAR
BOFF
tink
POOF

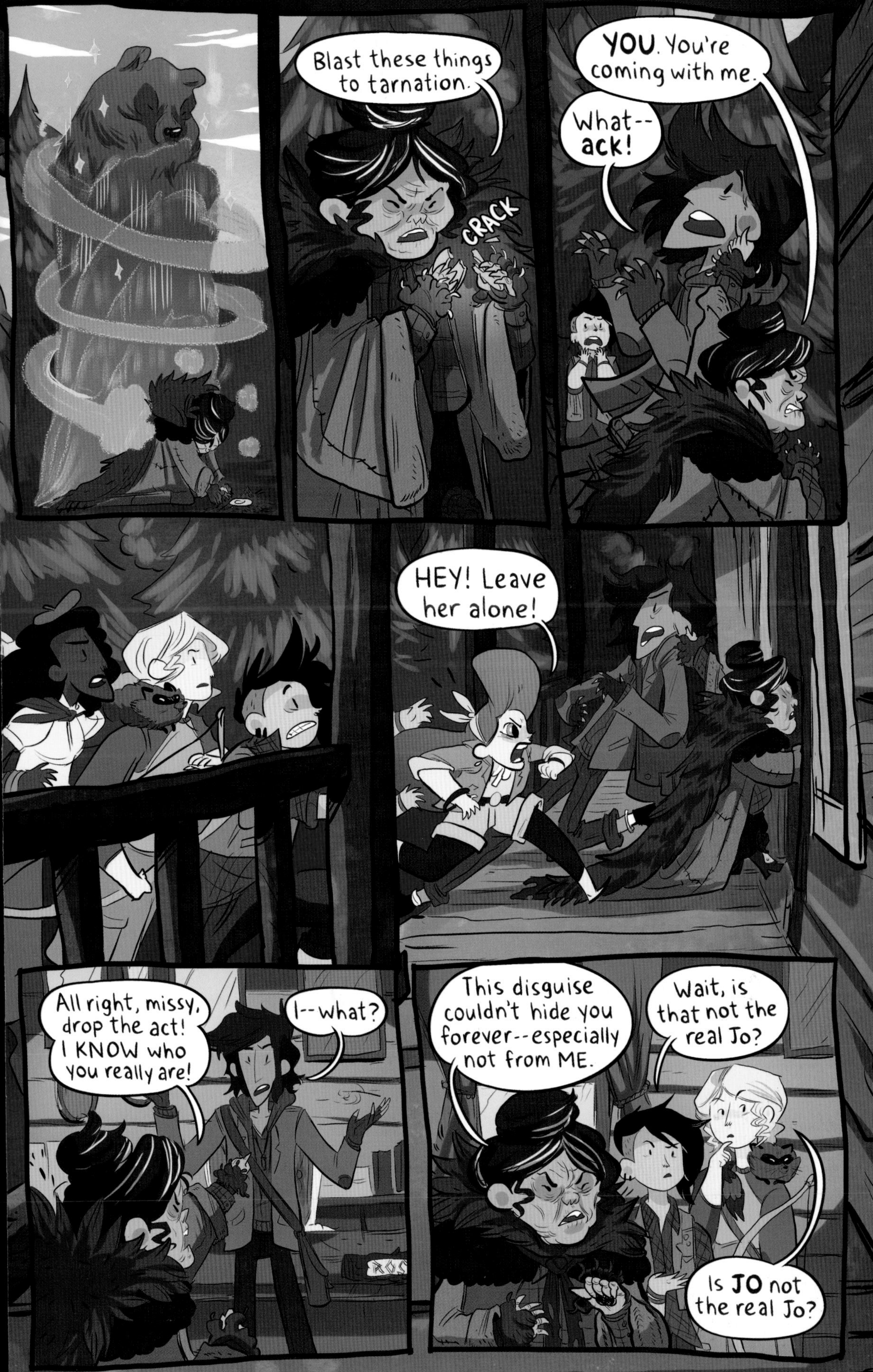
Blast these things to tarnation.
CRACK
YOU. You're coming with me.
What-- ack!
HEY! Leave her alone!
All right, missy, drop the act! I KNOW who you really are!
I--what?
This disguise couldn't hide you forever--especially not from ME.
Wait, is that not the real Jo?
Is JO not the real Jo?

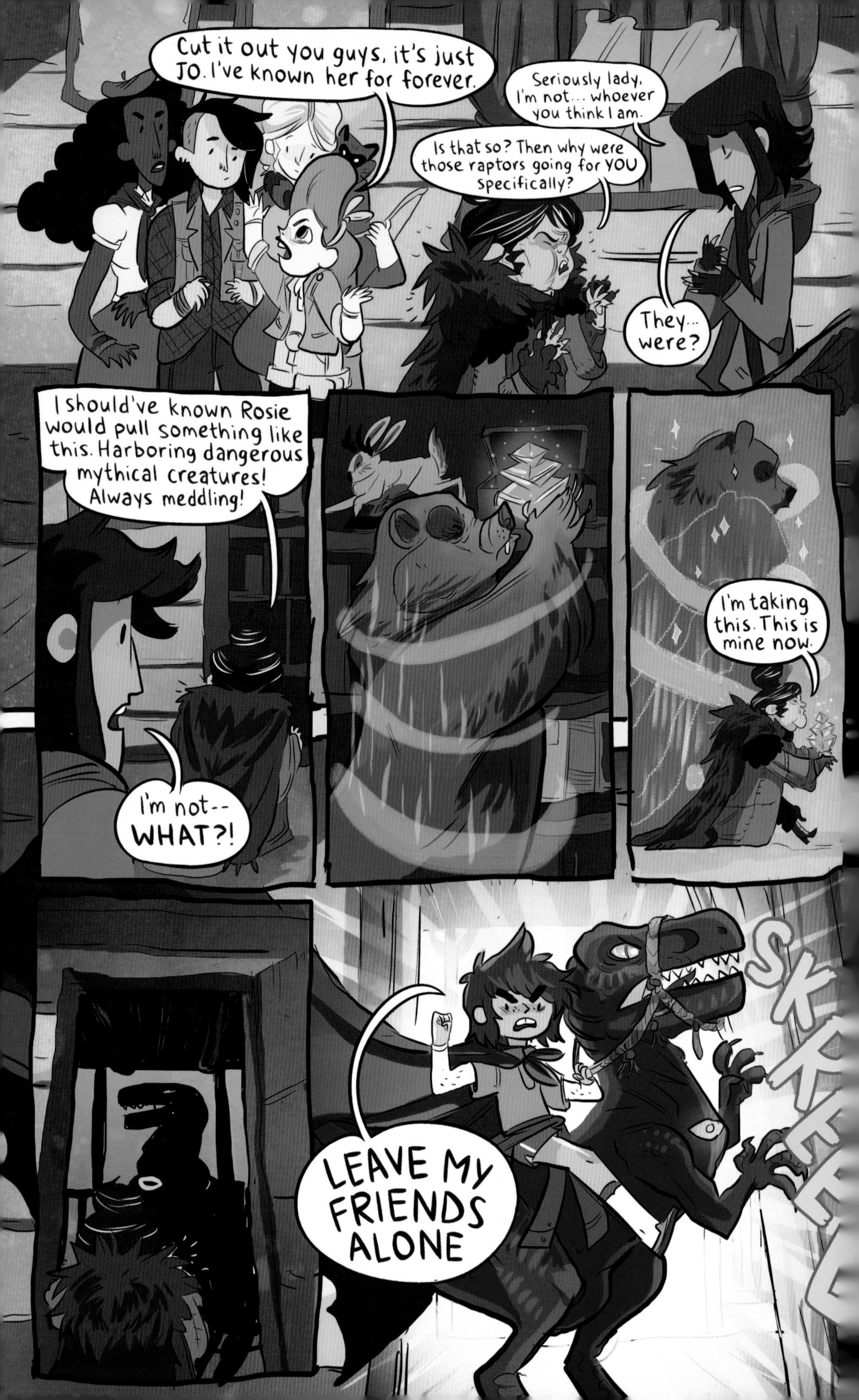
Cut it out you guys, it's just JO. I've known her for forever.
Seriously lady, I'm not... whoever you think I am.
Is that so? Then why were those raptors going for YOU specifically?
They... were?
I should've known Rosie would pull something like this. Harboring dangerous mythical creatures! Always meddling!
I'm not-- WHAT?!
I'm taking this. This is mine now.
LEAVE MY FRIENDS ALONE
SKREE

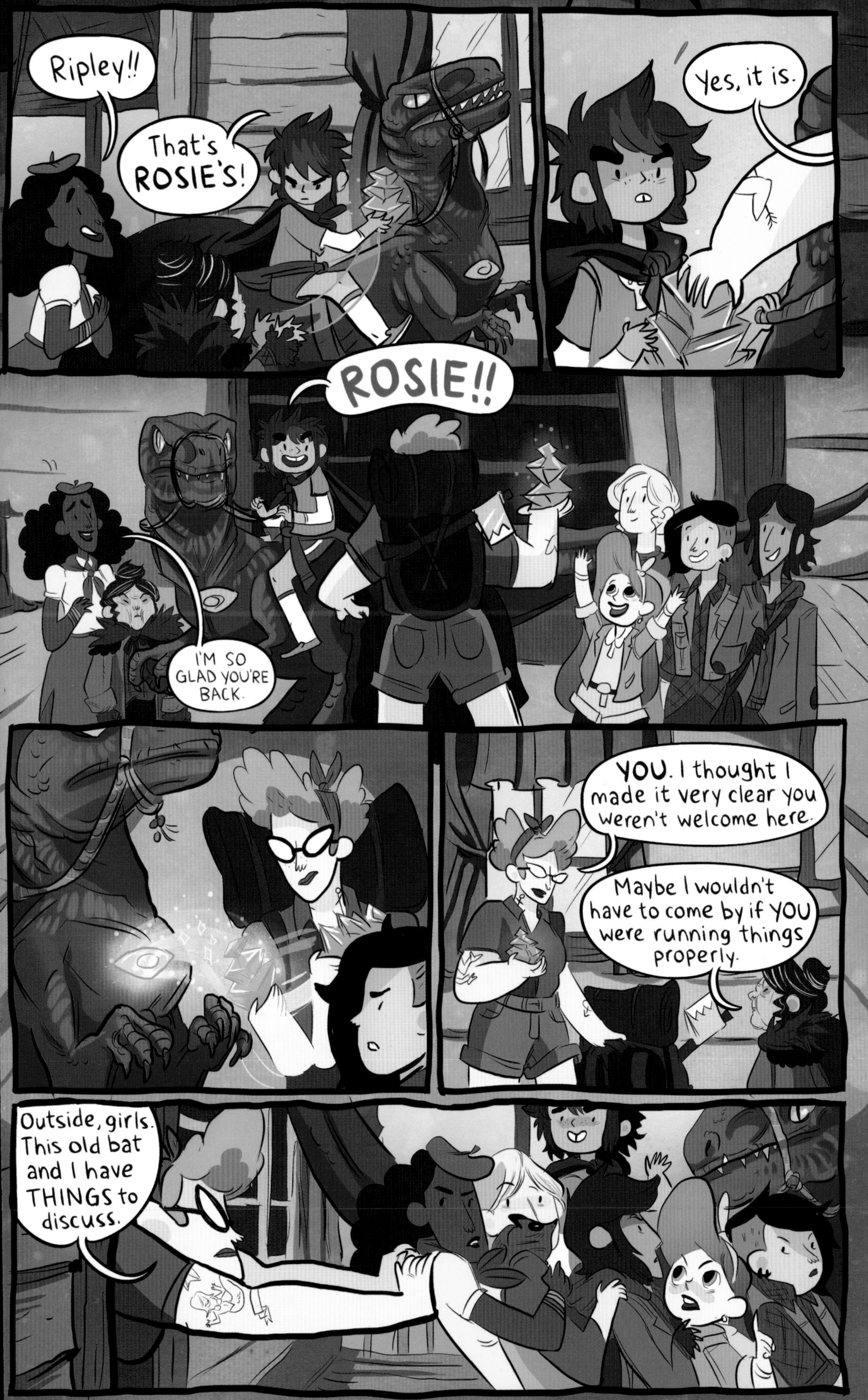
Ripley!!
That's ROSIE'S!
Yes, it is.
ROSIE!!
I'M SO GLAD YOU'RE BACK.
YOU. I thought I made it very clear you weren't welcome here.
Maybe I wouldn't have to come by if YOU were running things properly.
Outside, girls. This old bat and I have THINGS to discuss.

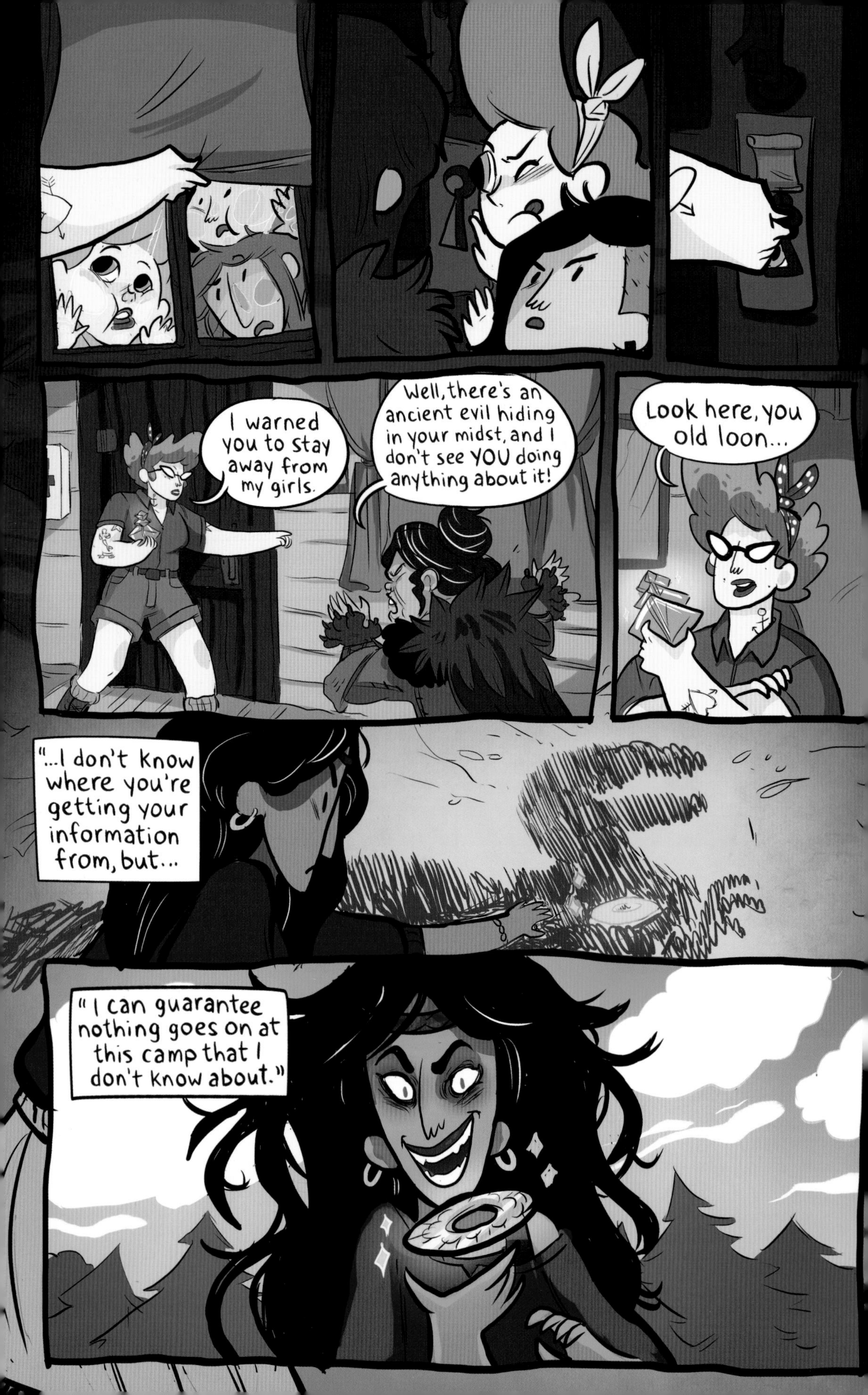
I warned you to stay away from my girls.
Well, there's an ancient evil hiding in your midst, and I don't see YOU doing anything about it!
Look here, you old loon...
"...I don't know where you're getting your information from, but...
"I can guarantee nothing goes on at this camp that I don't know about."

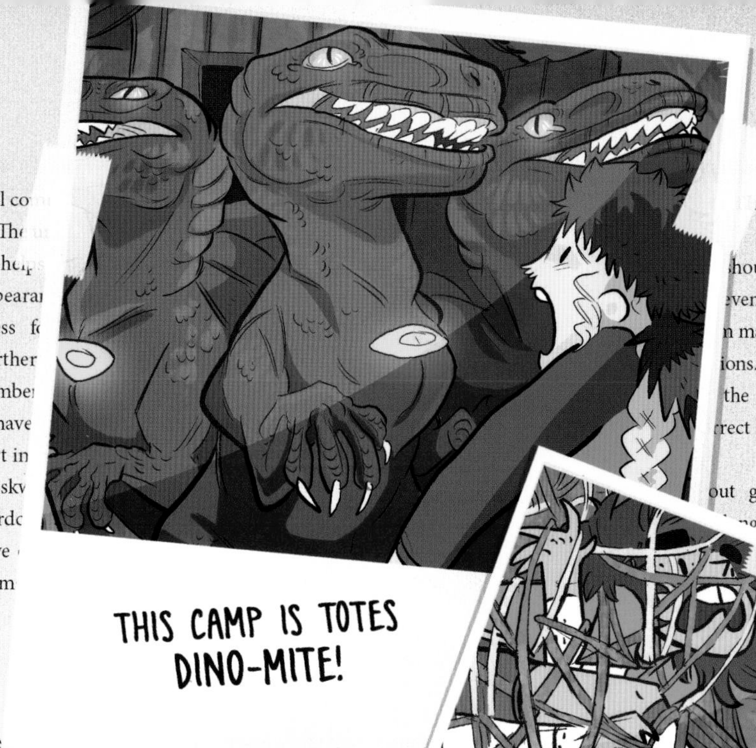
THIS CAMP IS TOTES
DINO-MITE!

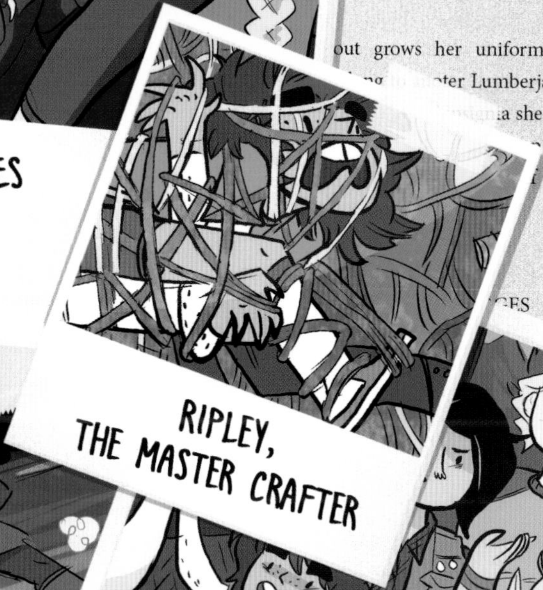
RIPLEY,
THE MASTER CRAFTER

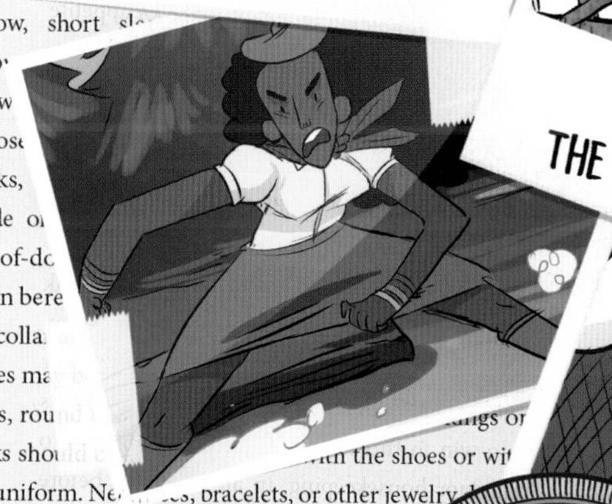

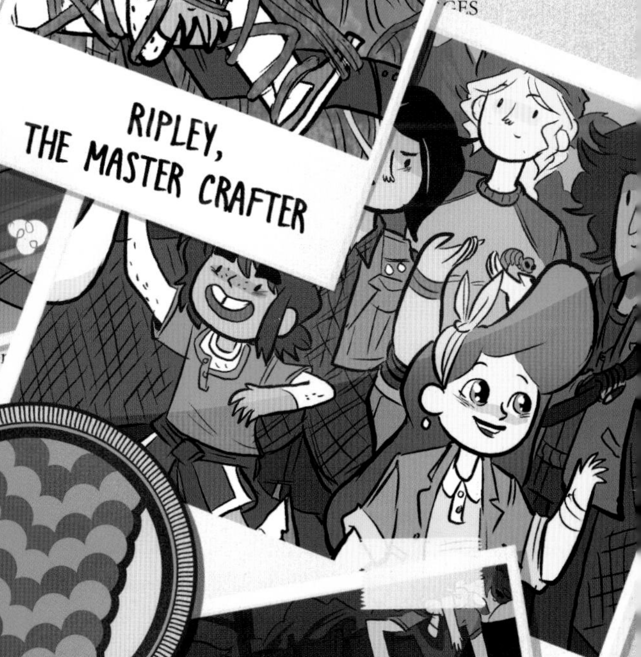

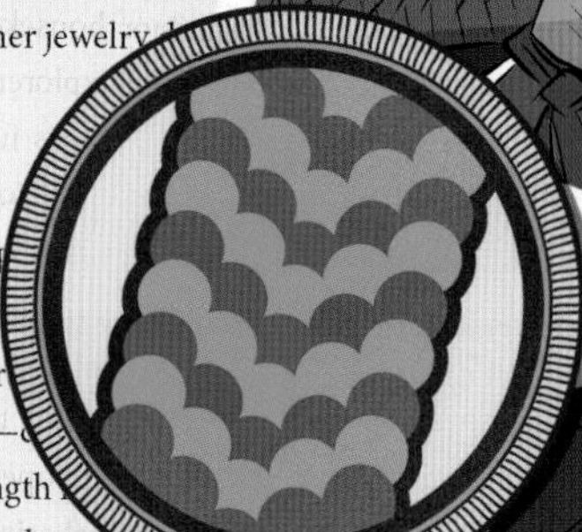

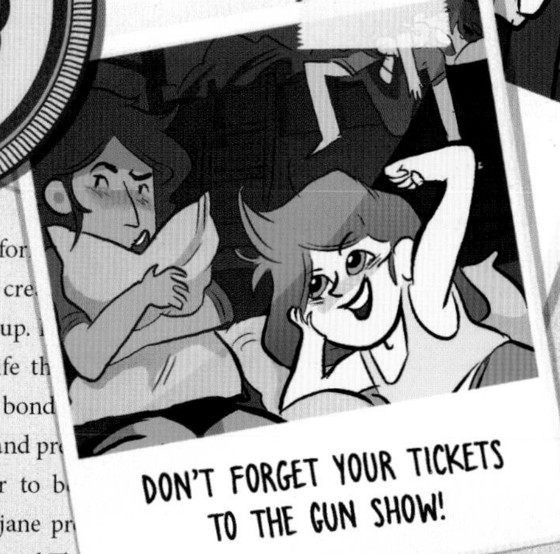
DON'T FORGET YOUR TICKETS
TO THE GUN SHOW!

will co…

The u… It helps… appearan… dress fo… Further… Lumbe… to have… part in… Thiskv… Hardc… have… them…

…HE UNIFORM

…should be worn at camp …events when Lumberjanes …n may also be worn at other …ions. It should be worn as a … the uniform dress with …rrect shoes, and stocking or …

…out grows her uniform or …ter Lumberjane. …a she has … her … her

The … yellow, short sl… emb… the w… choose… slacks, … made o… out-of-do… green bere… the colla… Shoes ma… heels, rou… …ings or socks shou… …with the shoes or wit… the uniform. Ne… …ces, bracelets, or other jewelry … belong with a Lumberjane uniform.

HOW TO WEAR THE UNI…

To look well in a uniform demands fir… uniform be kept in good condition—… pressed. See that the skirt is the right length … height and build, that the belt is adjusted to yo… that your shoes and stockings are in keeping with the uniform, that you watch your posture and carry yourself with dignity and grace. If the beret is removed indoors, be sure that your hair is neat and kept in place with an insonspicuous clip or ribbon. When you wear a Lumberjane uniform you are identified as a member of this organization and you should be doubly careful to conduct yourself in a way that will show everyone that courtesy and thoughtfullness are part of being a Lumberjane. People are likely to judge a whole nation by the selfishness of a few individuals, to criticize a whole family because of the misconduct of one member, and to feel unkindly toward and organization because of the

The unifor… helps to cre… in a group. … active life th… another bond… future, and pr… in order to b… Lumberjane pr… Penniquiqul Thi… …ore Lady Types, but m… …es will wish to have one. They can either bu… …, or make it themselves from materials available at the trading post.

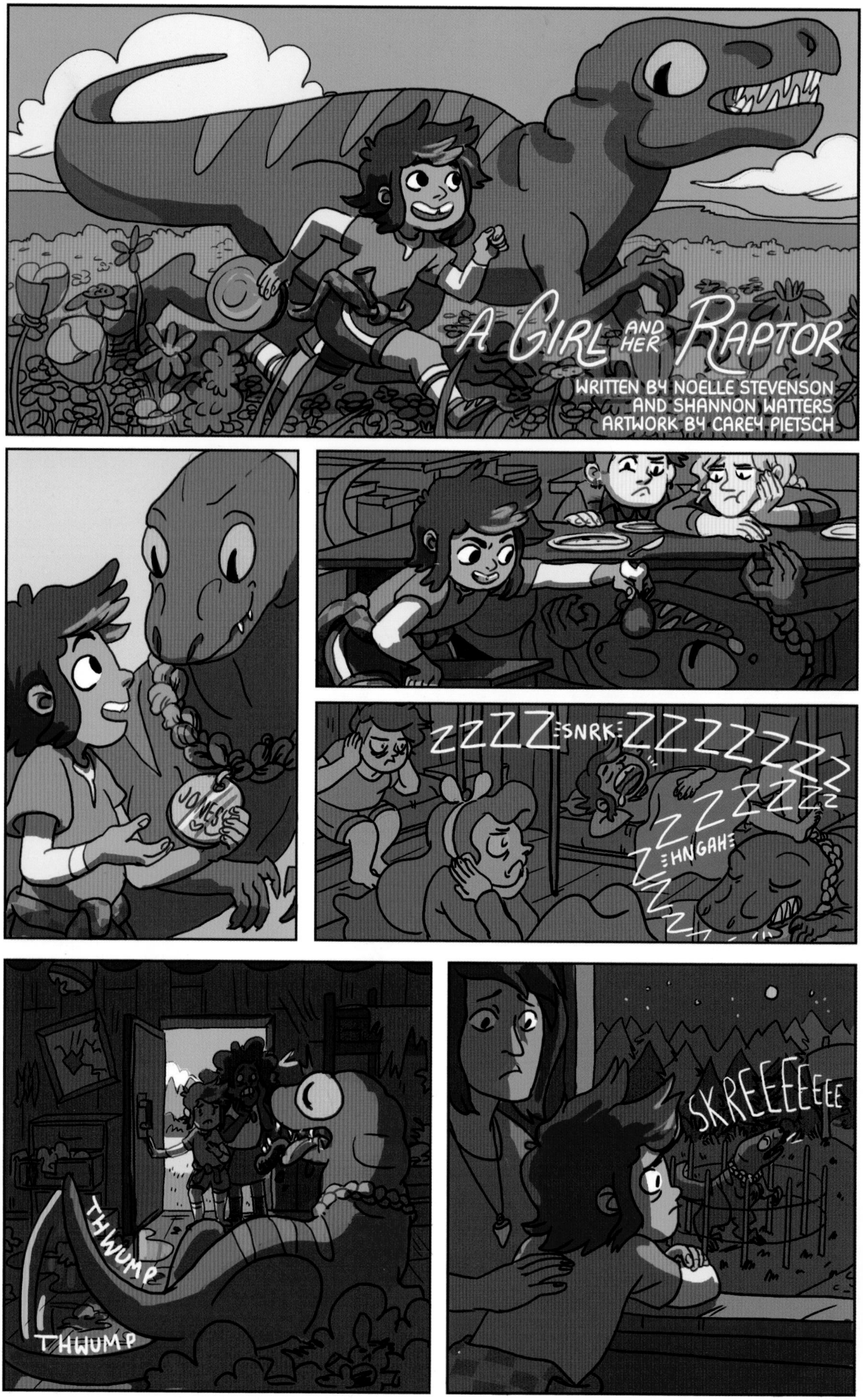
A GIRL AND HER RAPTOR
WRITTEN BY NOELLE STEVENSON
AND SHANNON WATTERS
ARTWORK BY CAREY PIETSCH
JONES
ZZZZ SNRK ZZZZZZZ
ZZZZZZZ
HNGAH
THWUMP
THWUMP
SKREEEEEEE

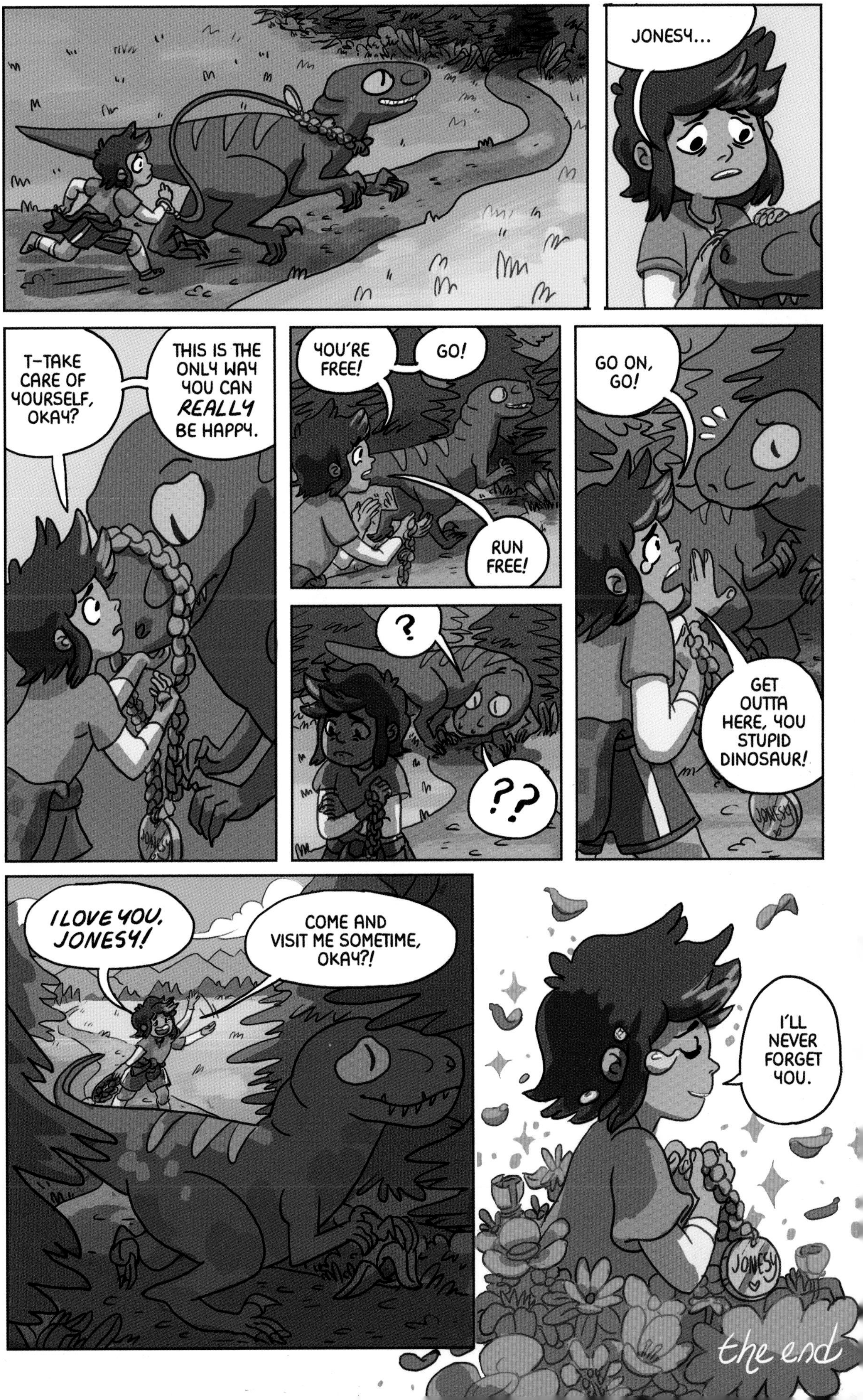
JONESY...
T-TAKE CARE OF YOURSELF, OKAY?
THIS IS THE ONLY WAY YOU CAN REALLY BE HAPPY.
YOU'RE FREE!
GO!
RUN FREE!
?
??
GO ON, GO!
GET OUTTA HERE, YOU STUPID DINOSAUR!
JONESY
I LOVE YOU, JONESY!
COME AND VISIT ME SOMETIME, OKAY?!
I'LL NEVER FORGET YOU.
JONESY
the end

LUMBERJANES FIELD MANUAL

CHAPTER SIX

Lumberjanes "Sports and Games" Program Field

JAIL BREAK BADGE

"Run as fast as you can."

Everyone experiences troubles, it is not something that is unique to one individual and it is something everyone must acknowledge. Some things can be planned for, some things require much luck, and some things require a bit of both and a lot of chaos. Incarceration will happen in some form or another, whether it's because she finds herself at a party that is terribly dull with only the window as a valid escape or she wasn't fast enough to escape the authorities after a good street race. Lumberjanes are considered to be girls who can find their way into and out of any situation.

The *Jail Break* badge is a badge that is only earned on the battlefield. It is something that every scout will get a chance to earn whether they are taken by their captors against their will or because they let it happen. One of the many fun opportunities with this badge is the chance for a scout to get the better of her enemies while freeing

her fellow soldiers so that they can return to their base and start again. Capture the flag is and will always be the biggest battle of the summer, but the real challenge to the game actually isn't getting the flag. It's breaking out of your enemies' prison.

To obtain the *Jail Break* badge a Lumberjane must be participating in one of the battle royales that summer. She will have to find herself captured by her enemy and taken into their holding cells. A Lumberjane must be able to adapt to her surroundings, she must be able to predict the movement of the other team and above all else, she must save as many fellow prisoners as possible. She will know the importance of teamwork, and she will be able to step down if she doubts in her abilities to free everyone safely just as she will be able to stand up to help a fellow scout in this challenge. She will never doubt her enemy, never underestimate their knowledge

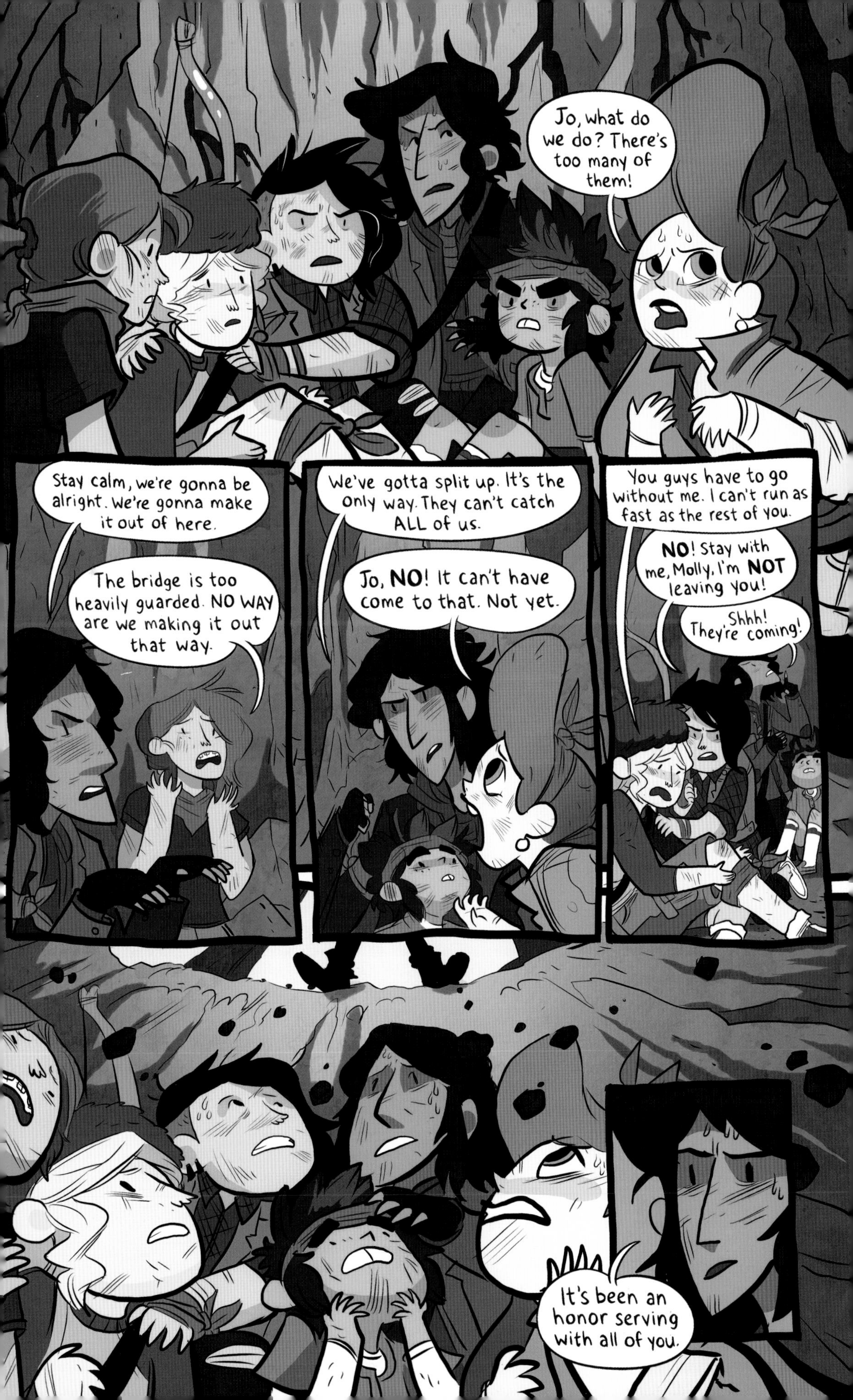
Jo, what do we do? There's too many of them!
Stay calm, we're gonna be alright. We're gonna make it out of here.
The bridge is too heavily guarded. NO WAY are we making it out that way.
We've gotta split up. It's the only way. They can't catch ALL of us.
Jo, NO! It can't have come to that. Not yet.
You guys have to go without me. I can't run as fast as the rest of you.
NO! Stay with me, Molly, I'm NOT leaving you!
Shhh! They're coming!
It's been an honor serving with all of you.

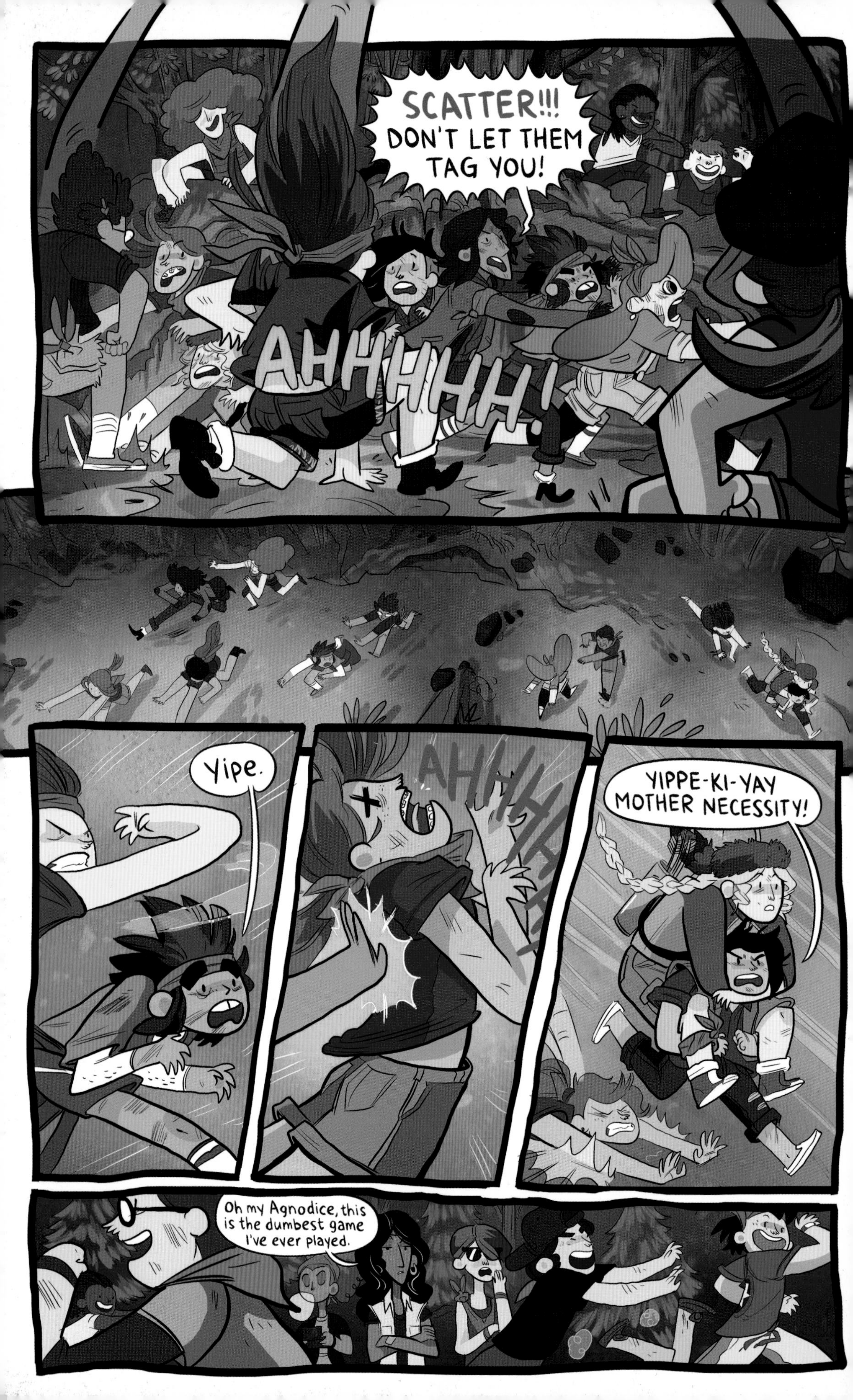
SCATTER!!!
DON'T LET THEM TAG YOU!
AHHHHHH!
Yipe.
AHHHHH
YIPPE-KI-YAY MOTHER NECESSITY!
Oh my Agnodice, this is the dumbest game I've ever played.

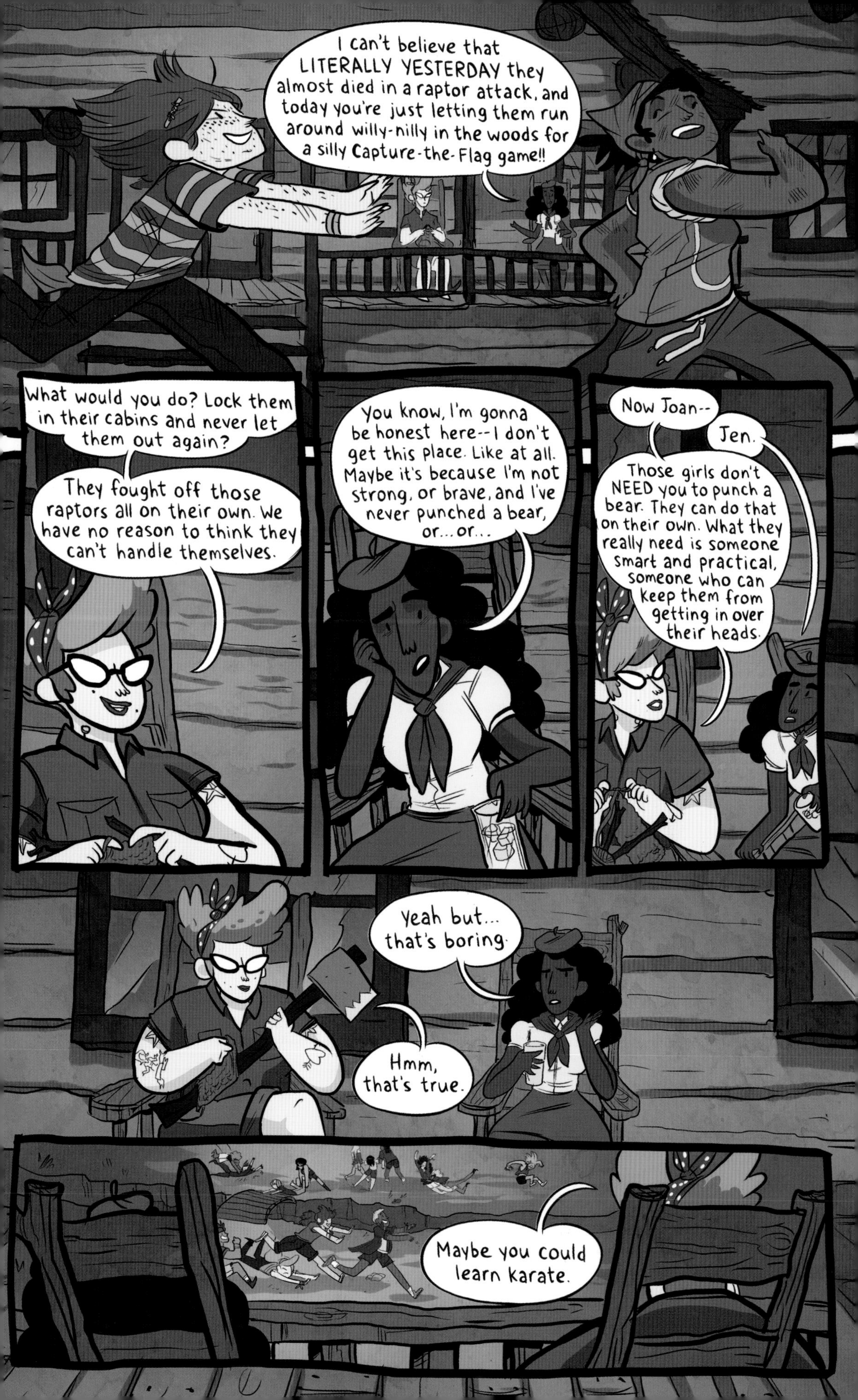
I can't believe that LITERALLY YESTERDAY they almost died in a raptor attack, and today you're just letting them run around willy-nilly in the woods for a silly Capture-the-Flag game!!
What would you do? Lock them in their cabins and never let them out again?
They fought off those raptors all on their own. We have no reason to think they can't handle themselves.
You know, I'm gonna be honest here--I don't get this place. Like at all. Maybe it's because I'm not strong, or brave, and I've never punched a bear, or... or...
Now Joan--
Jen.
Those girls don't NEED you to punch a bear. They can do that on their own. What they really need is someone smart and practical, someone who can keep them from getting in over their heads.
Yeah but... that's boring.
Hmm, that's true.
Maybe you could learn karate.

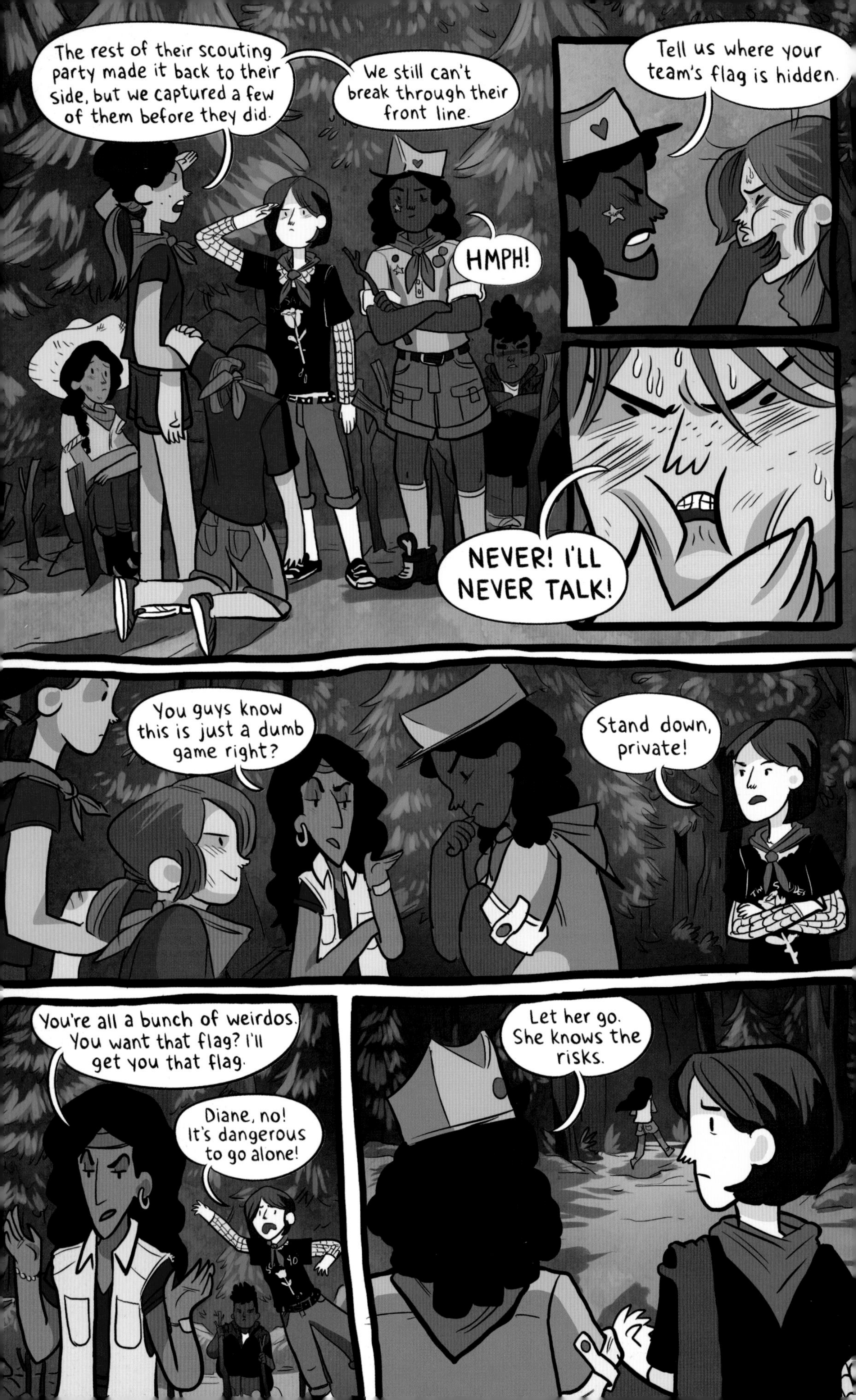
The rest of their scouting party made it back to their side, but we captured a few of them before they did.
We still can't break through their front line.
HMPH!
Tell us where your team's flag is hidden.
NEVER! I'LL NEVER TALK!
You guys know this is just a dumb game right?
Stand down, private!
You're all a bunch of weirdos. You want that flag? I'll get you that flag.
Diane, no! It's dangerous to go alone!
Let her go. She knows the risks.

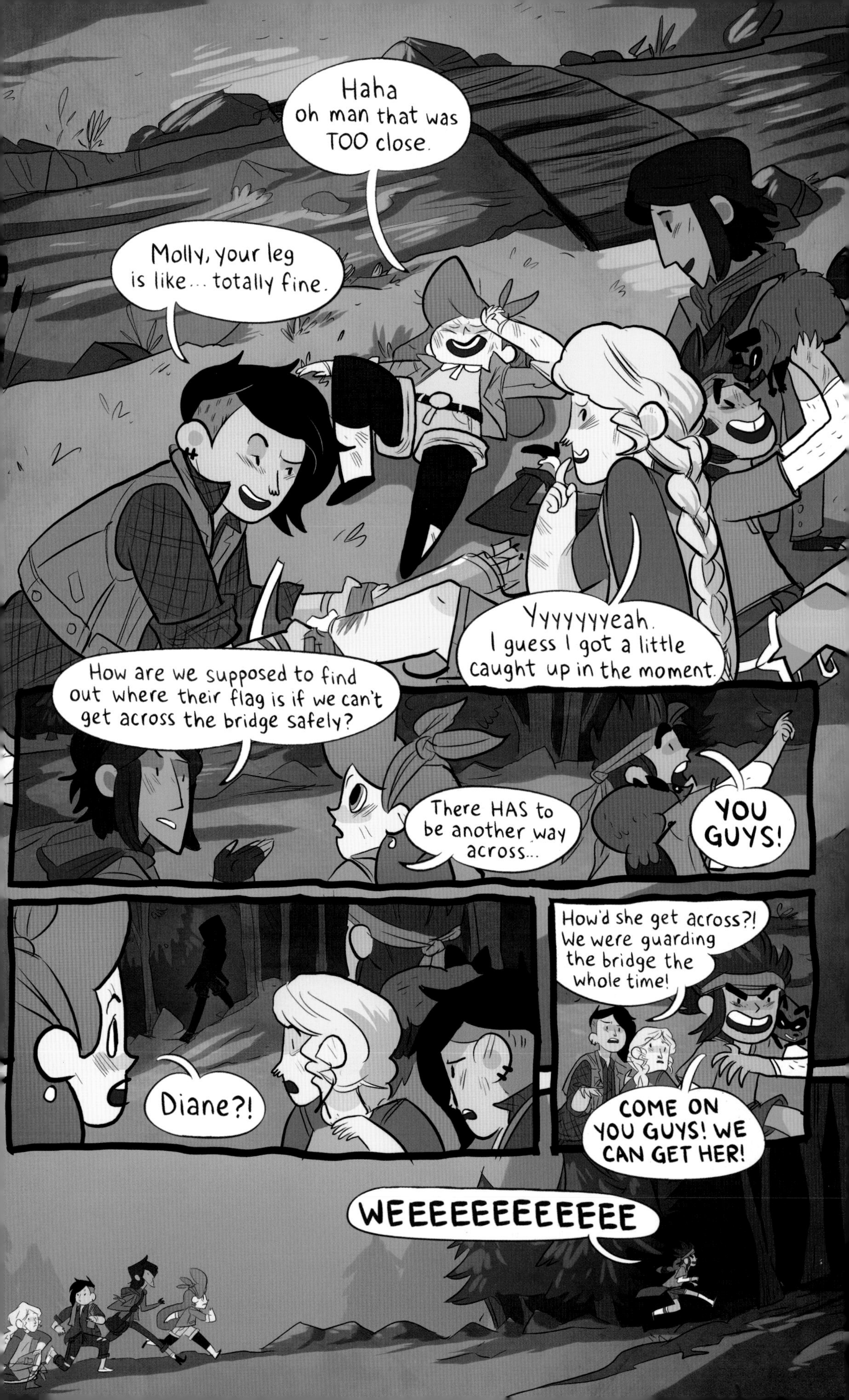
Haha
oh man that was
TOO close.
Molly, your leg
is like... totally fine.
Yyyyyyyeah.
I guess I got a little
caught up in the moment.
How are we supposed to find
out where their flag is if we can't
get across the bridge safely?
There HAS to
be another way
across...
YOU
GUYS!
Diane?!
How'd she get across?!
We were guarding
the bridge the
whole time!
COME ON
YOU GUYS! WE
CAN GET HER!
WEEEEEEEEEEEE

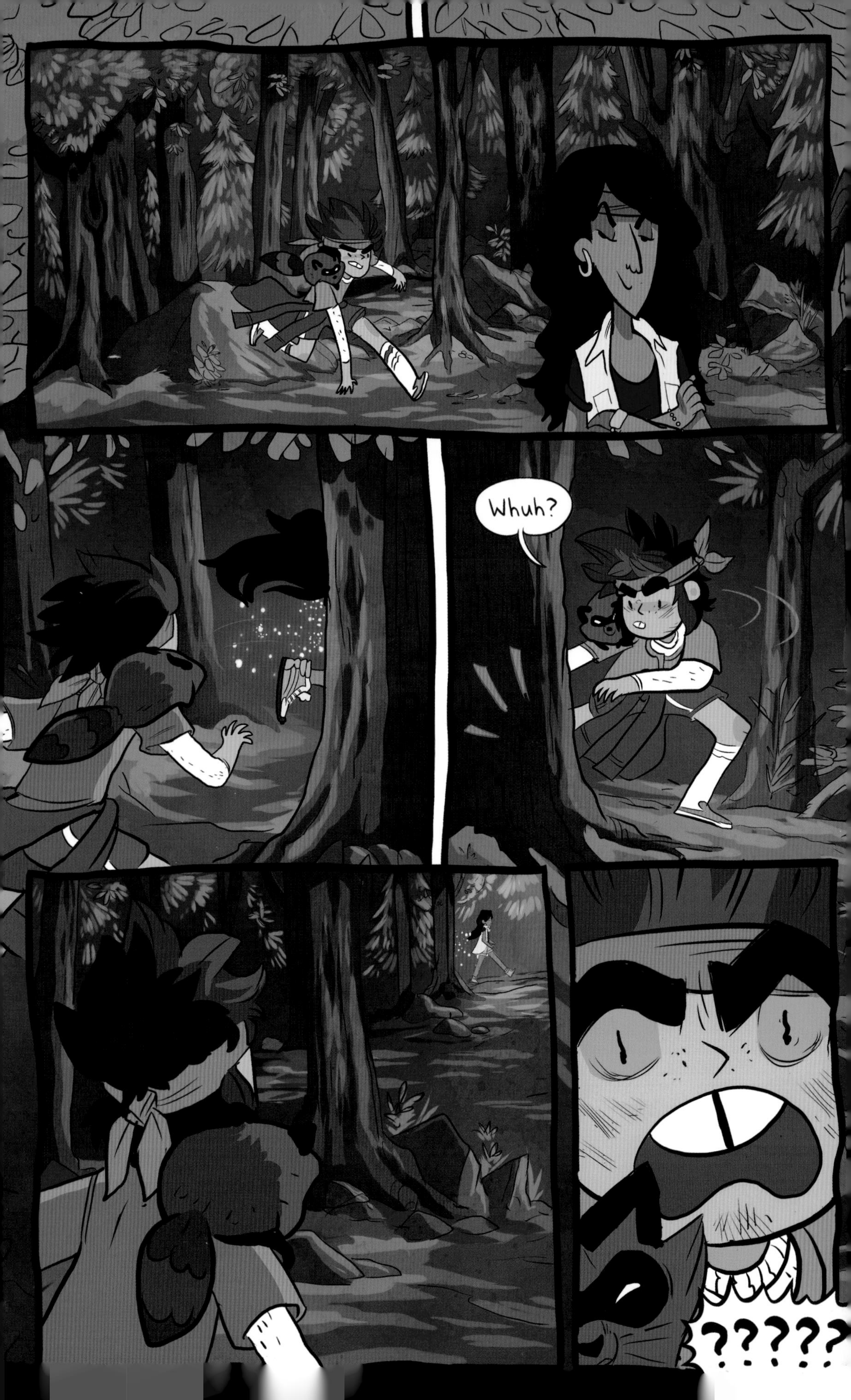
Whuh?
?????

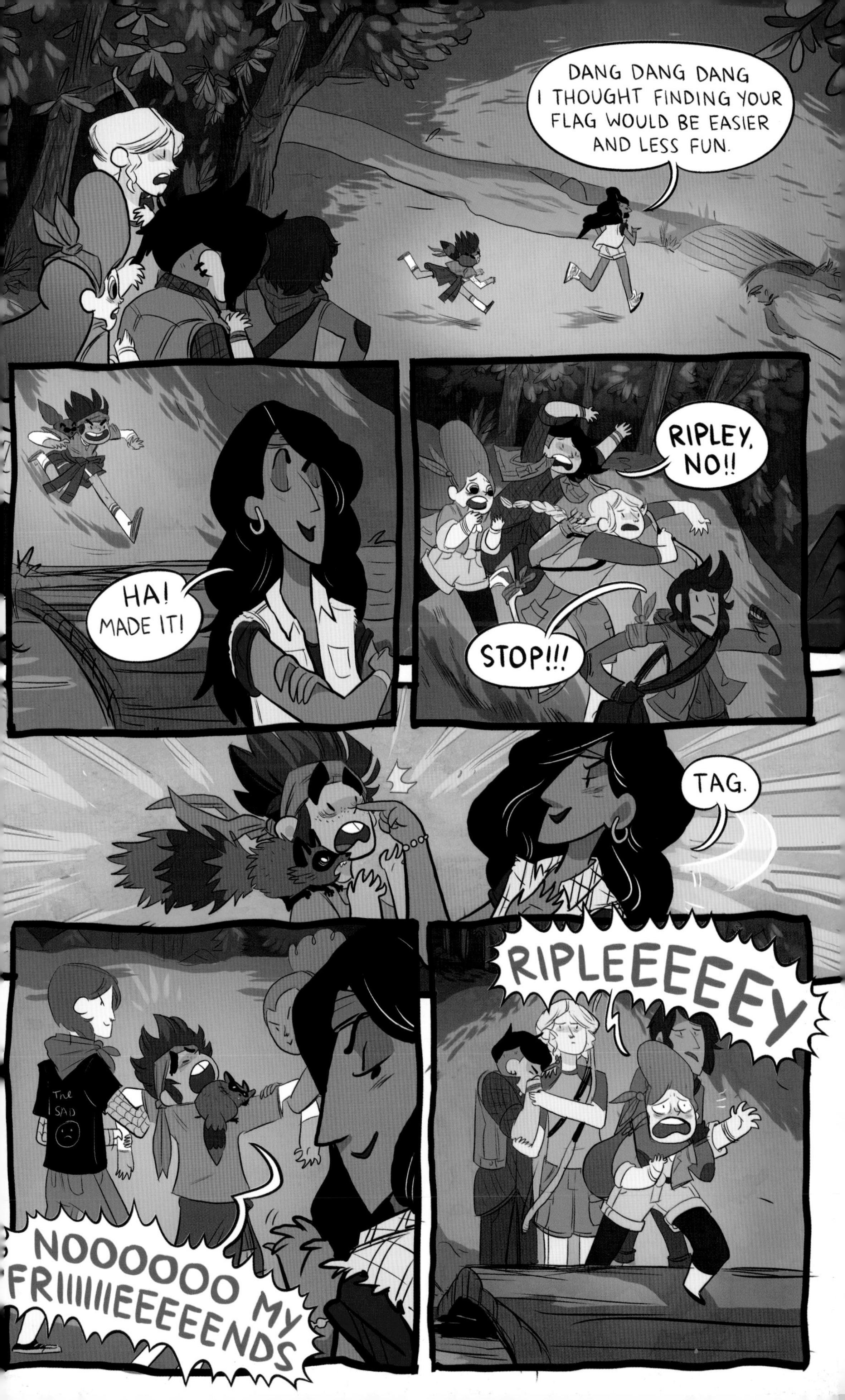
DANG DANG DANG I THOUGHT FINDING YOUR FLAG WOULD BE EASIER AND LESS FUN.
HA! MADE IT!
RIPLEY, NO!!
STOP!!!
TAG.
NOOOOOO MY FRIIIIIIEEEEEENDS
RIPLEEEEEEY

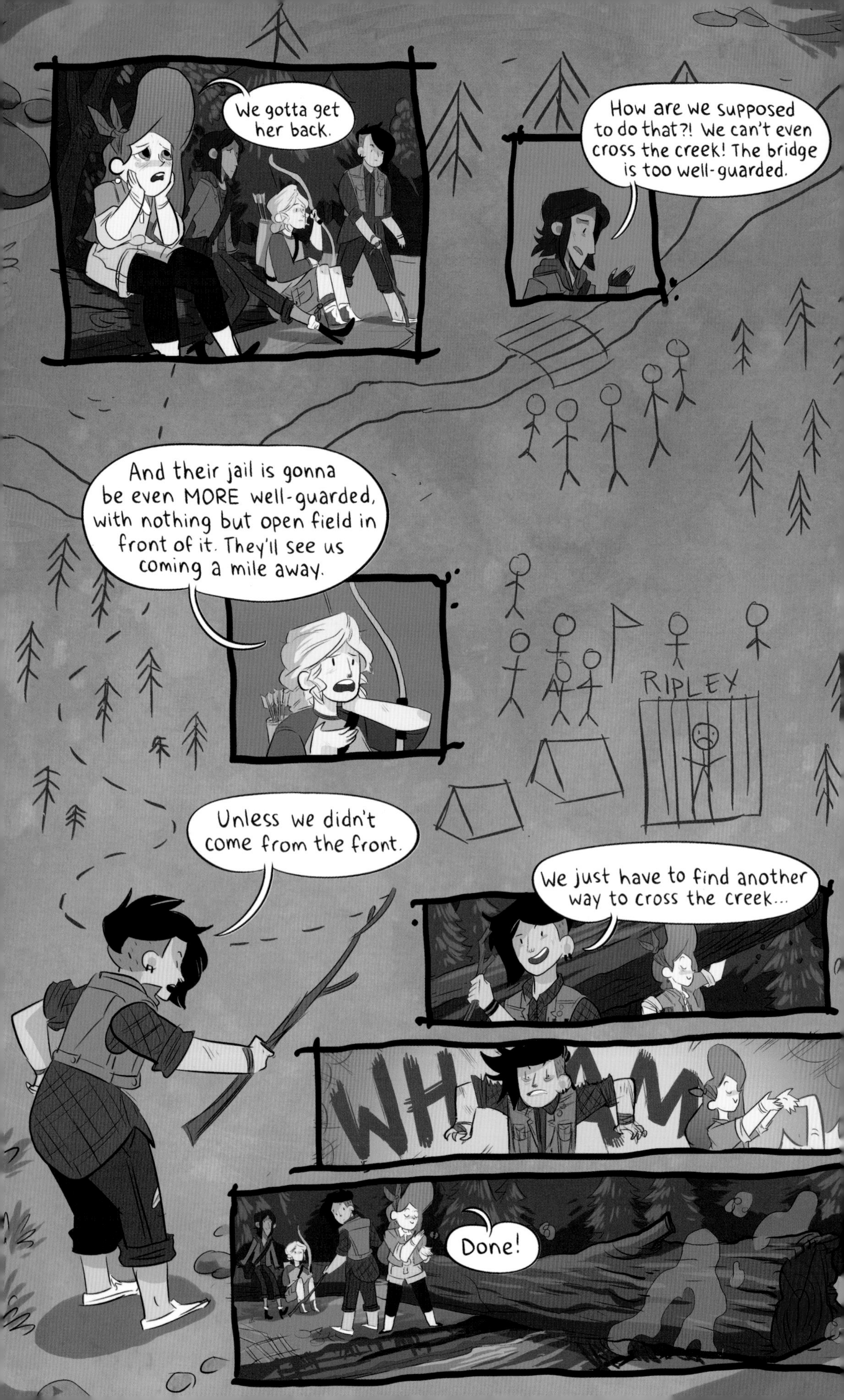
We gotta get her back.
How are we supposed to do that?! We can't even cross the creek! The bridge is too well-guarded.
And their jail is gonna be even MORE well-guarded, with nothing but open field in front of it. They'll see us coming a mile away.
RIPLEY
Unless we didn't come from the front.
We just have to find another way to cross the creek...
WHAM
Done!

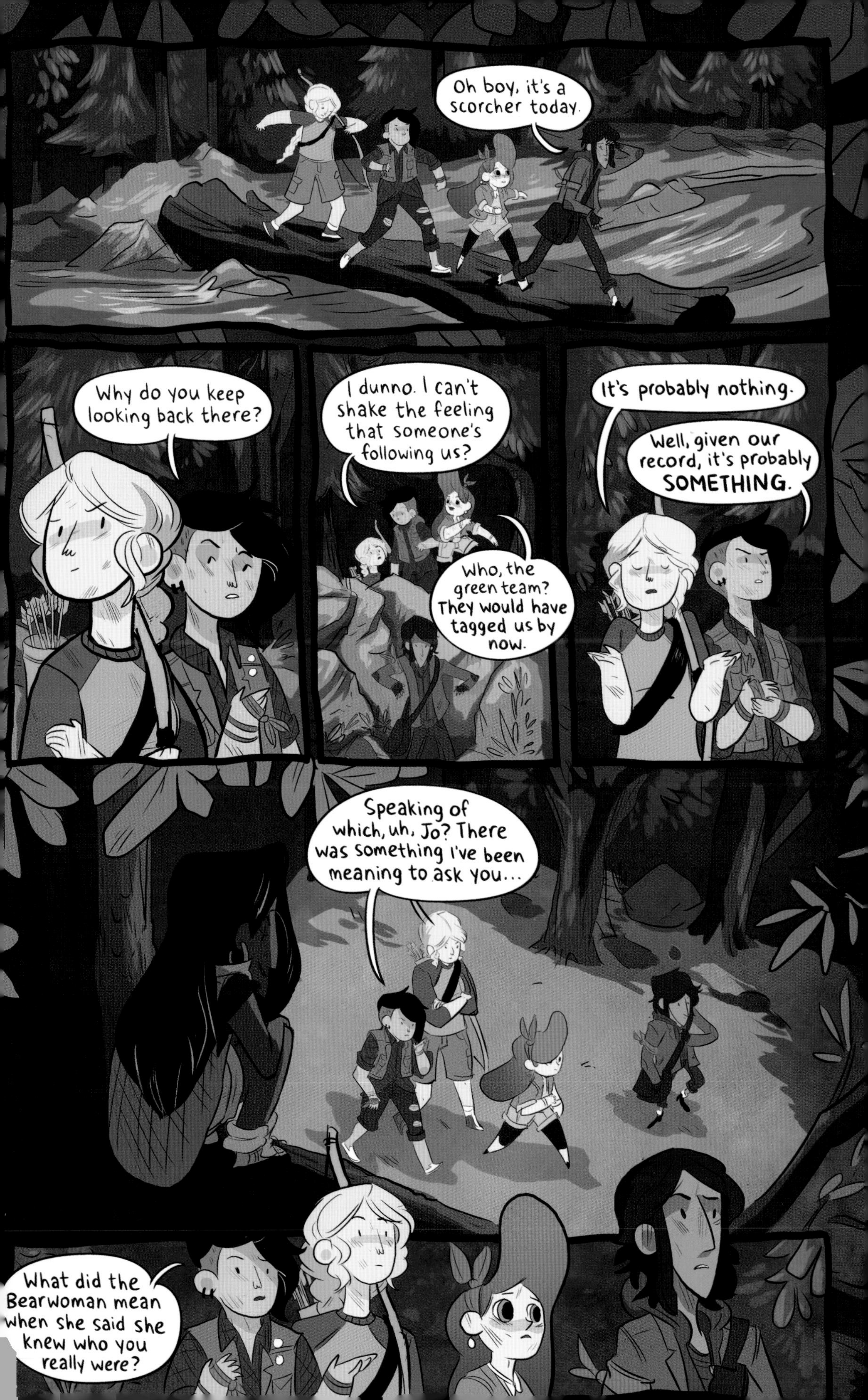
Oh boy, it's a scorcher today.
Why do you keep looking back there?
I dunno. I can't shake the feeling that someone's following us?
Who, the green team? They would have tagged us by now.
It's probably nothing.
Well, given our record, it's probably SOMETHING.
Speaking of which, uh, Jo? There was something I've been meaning to ask you...
What did the Bearwoman mean when she said she knew who you really were?

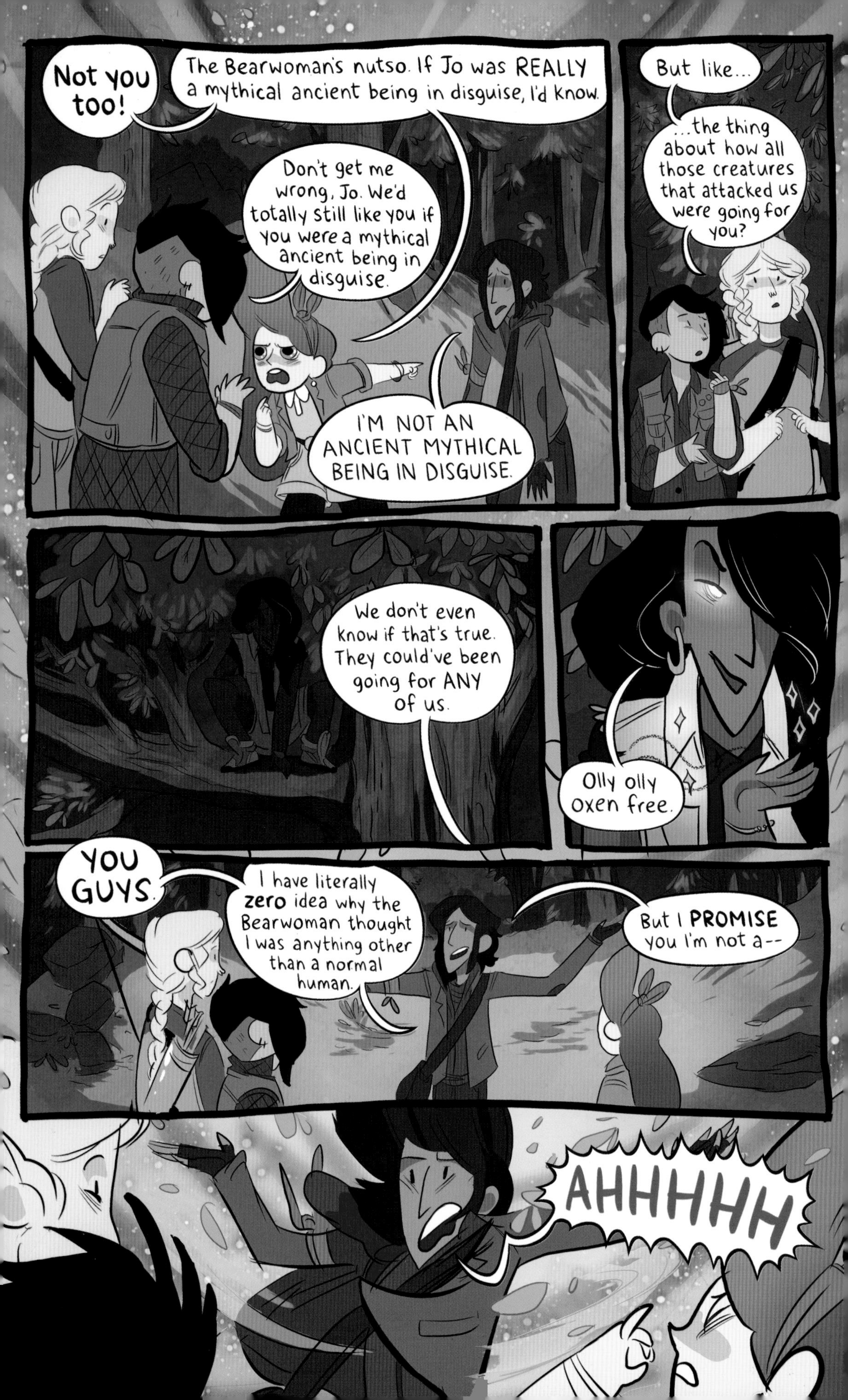
Not you too!
The Bearwoman's nutso. If Jo was REALLY a mythical ancient being in disguise, I'd know.
Don't get me wrong, Jo. We'd totally still like you if you were a mythical ancient being in disguise.
I'M NOT AN ANCIENT MYTHICAL BEING IN DISGUISE.
But like...
...the thing about how all those creatures that attacked us were going for you?
We don't even know if that's true. They could've been going for ANY of us.
Olly olly oxen free.
YOU GUYS.
I have literally **zero** idea why the Bearwoman thought I was anything other than a normal human.
But I **PROMISE** you I'm not a--
AHHHHH

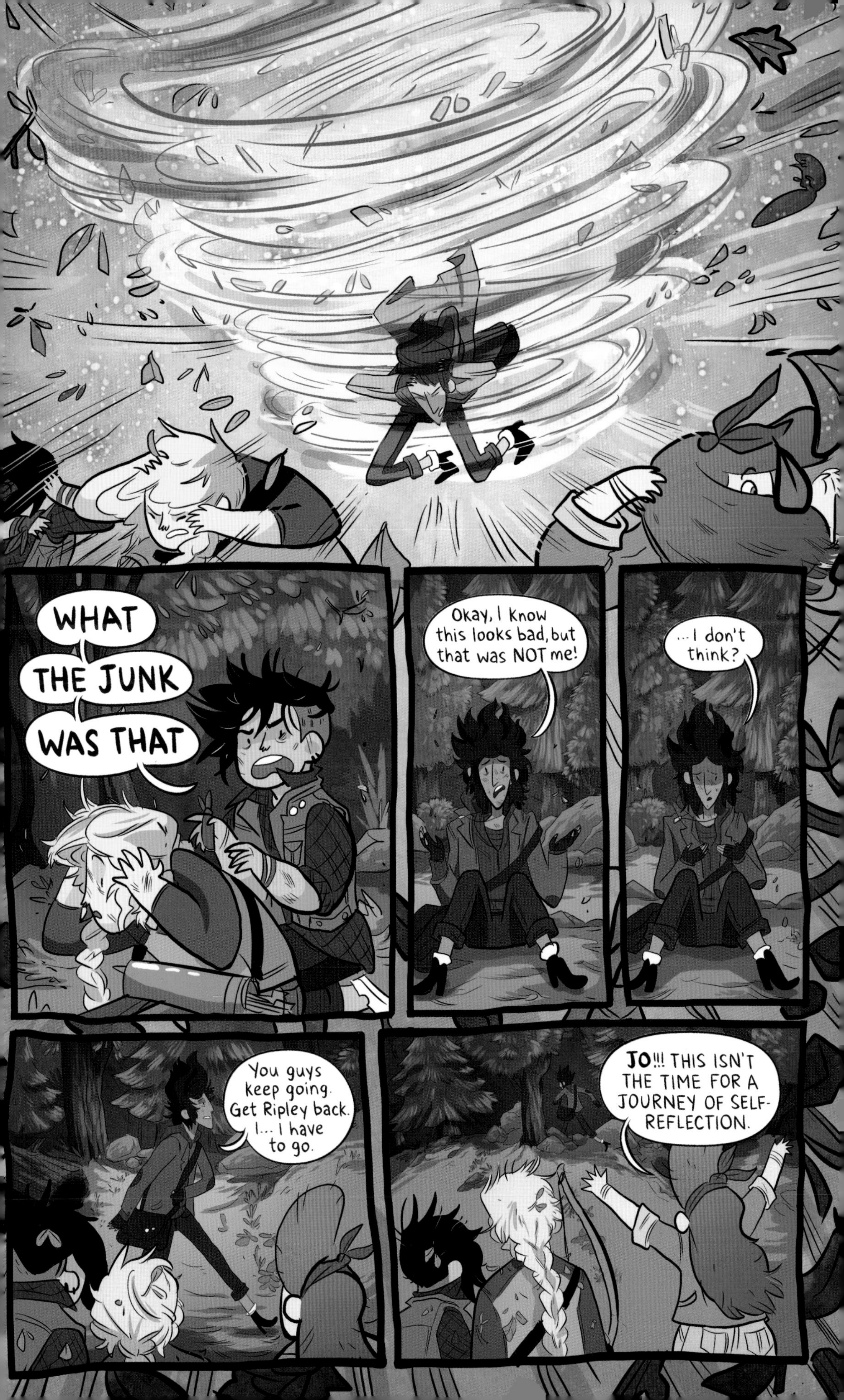
WHAT
THE JUNK
WAS THAT
Okay, I know this looks bad, but that was NOT me!
...I don't think?
You guys keep going. Get Ripley back. I... I have to go.
JO!!! THIS ISN'T THE TIME FOR A JOURNEY OF SELF-REFLECTION.

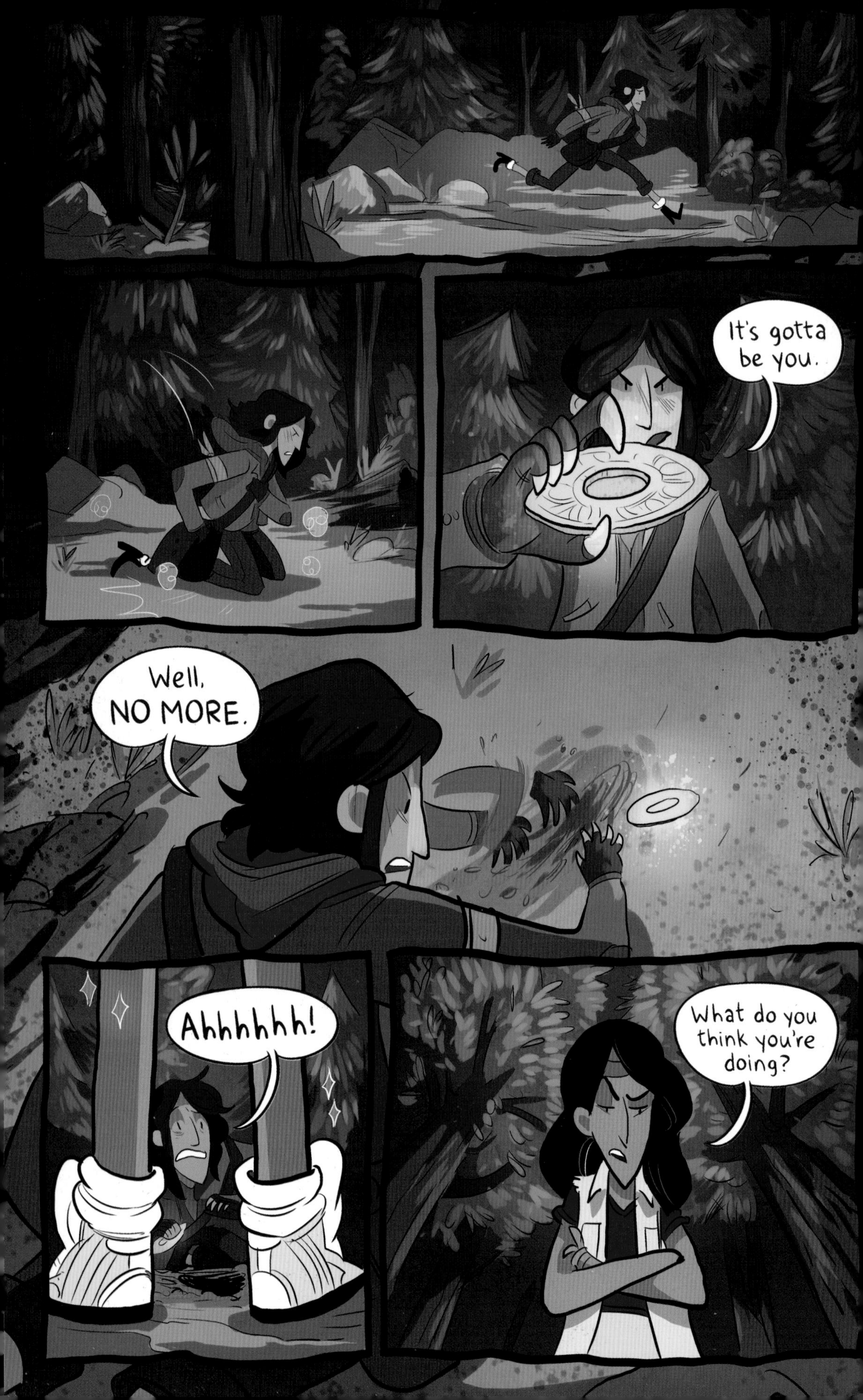
It's gotta be you.
Well, NO MORE.
Ahhhhhh!
What do you think you're doing?

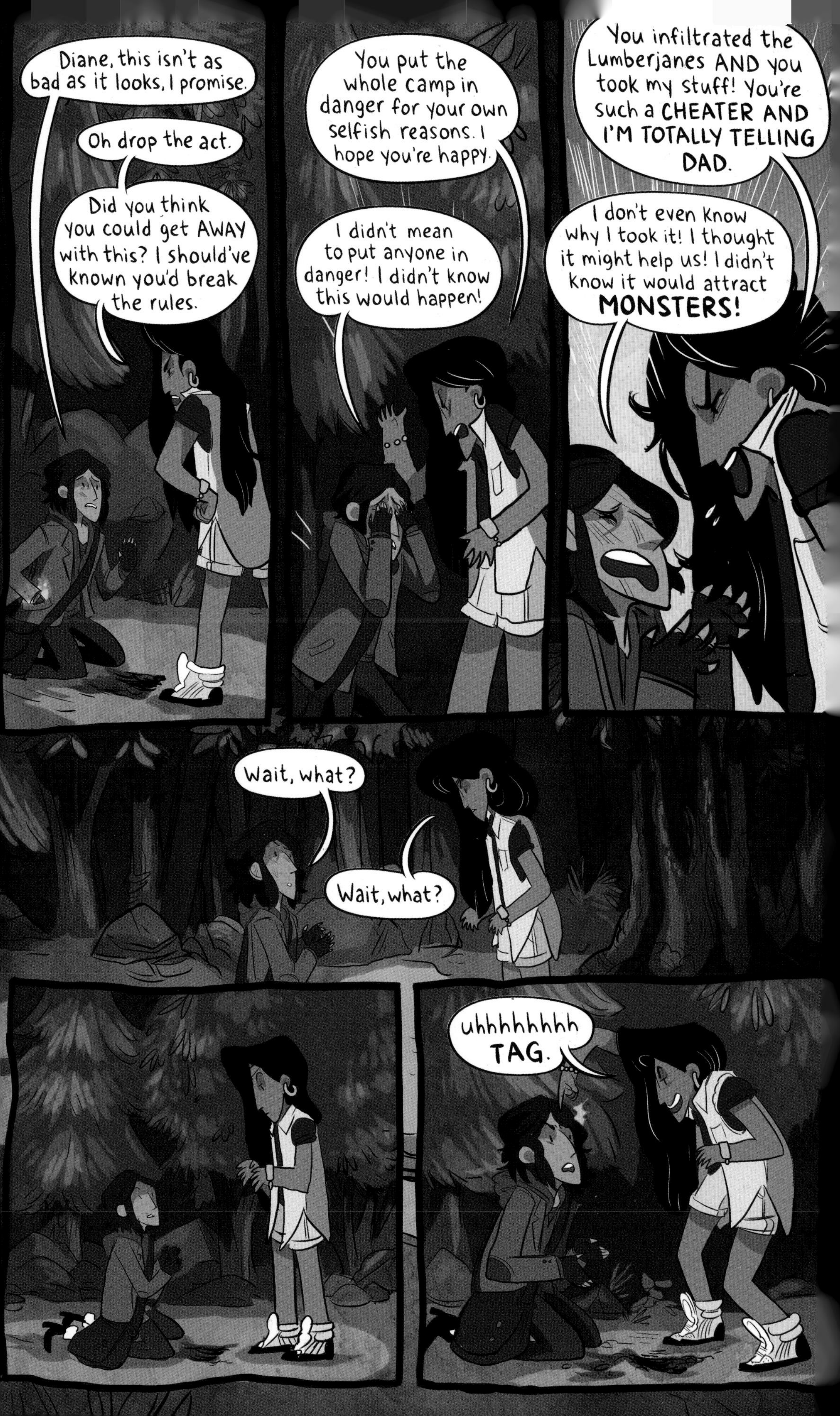
Diane, this isn't as bad as it looks, I promise.
Oh drop the act.
Did you think you could get AWAY with this? I should've known you'd break the rules.
You put the whole camp in danger for your own selfish reasons. I hope you're happy.
I didn't mean to put anyone in danger! I didn't know this would happen!
You infiltrated the Lumberjanes AND you took my stuff! You're such a CHEATER AND I'M TOTALLY TELLING DAD.
I don't even know why I took it! I thought it might help us! I didn't know it would attract MONSTERS!
Wait, what?
Wait, what?
uhhhhhhhh TAG.

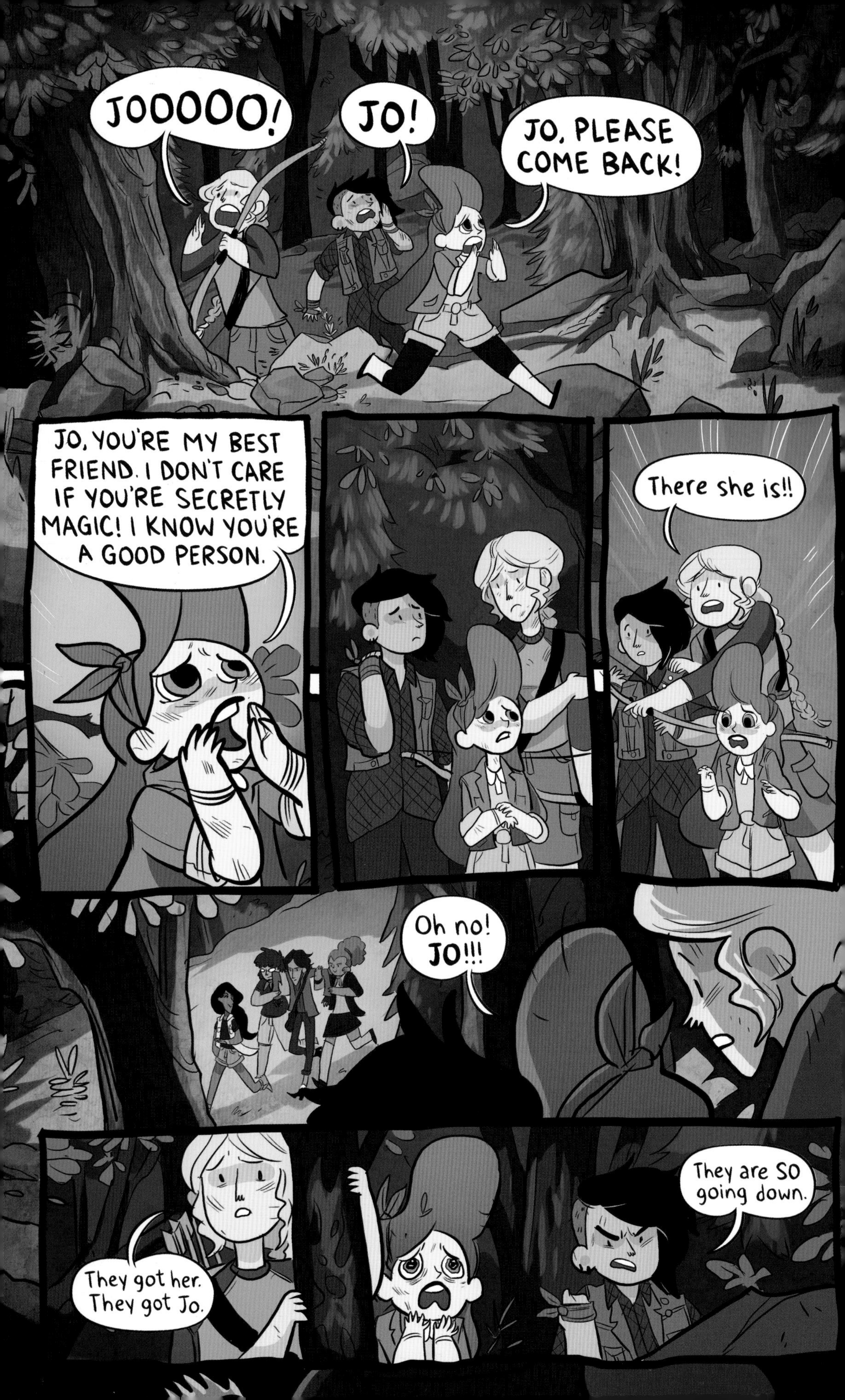
JOOOOO!
JO!
JO, PLEASE COME BACK!
JO, YOU'RE MY BEST FRIEND. I DON'T CARE IF YOU'RE SECRETLY MAGIC! I KNOW YOU'RE A GOOD PERSON.
There she is!!
Oh no! JO!!!
They got her. They got Jo.
They are SO going down.

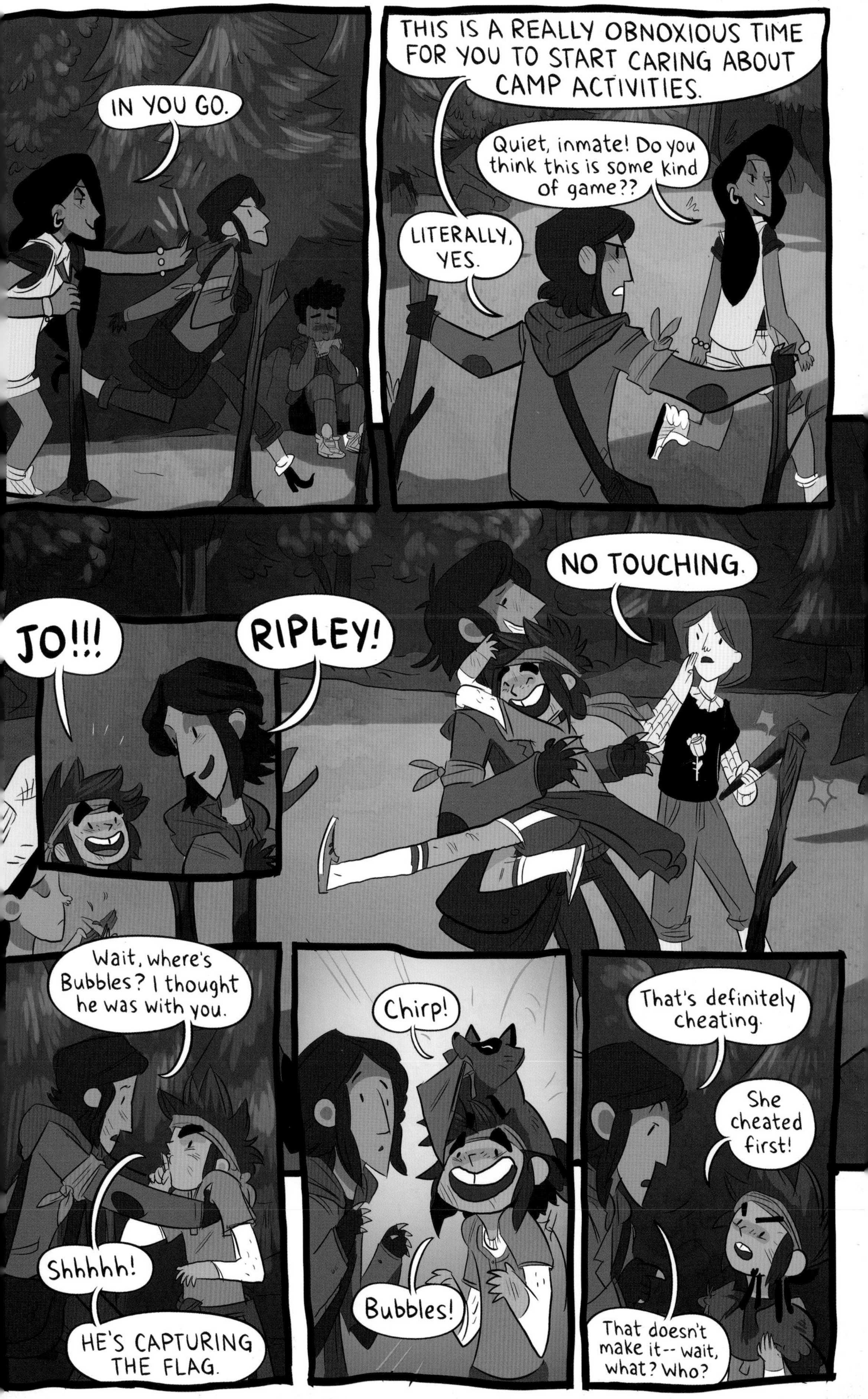
IN YOU GO.
THIS IS A REALLY OBNOXIOUS TIME FOR YOU TO START CARING ABOUT CAMP ACTIVITIES.
Quiet, inmate! Do you think this is some kind of game??
LITERALLY, YES.
JO!!!
RIPLEY!
NO TOUCHING.
Wait, where's Bubbles? I thought he was with you.
Shhhhh!
HE'S CAPTURING THE FLAG.
Chirp!
Bubbles!
That's definitely cheating.
She cheated first!
That doesn't make it-- wait, what? Who?

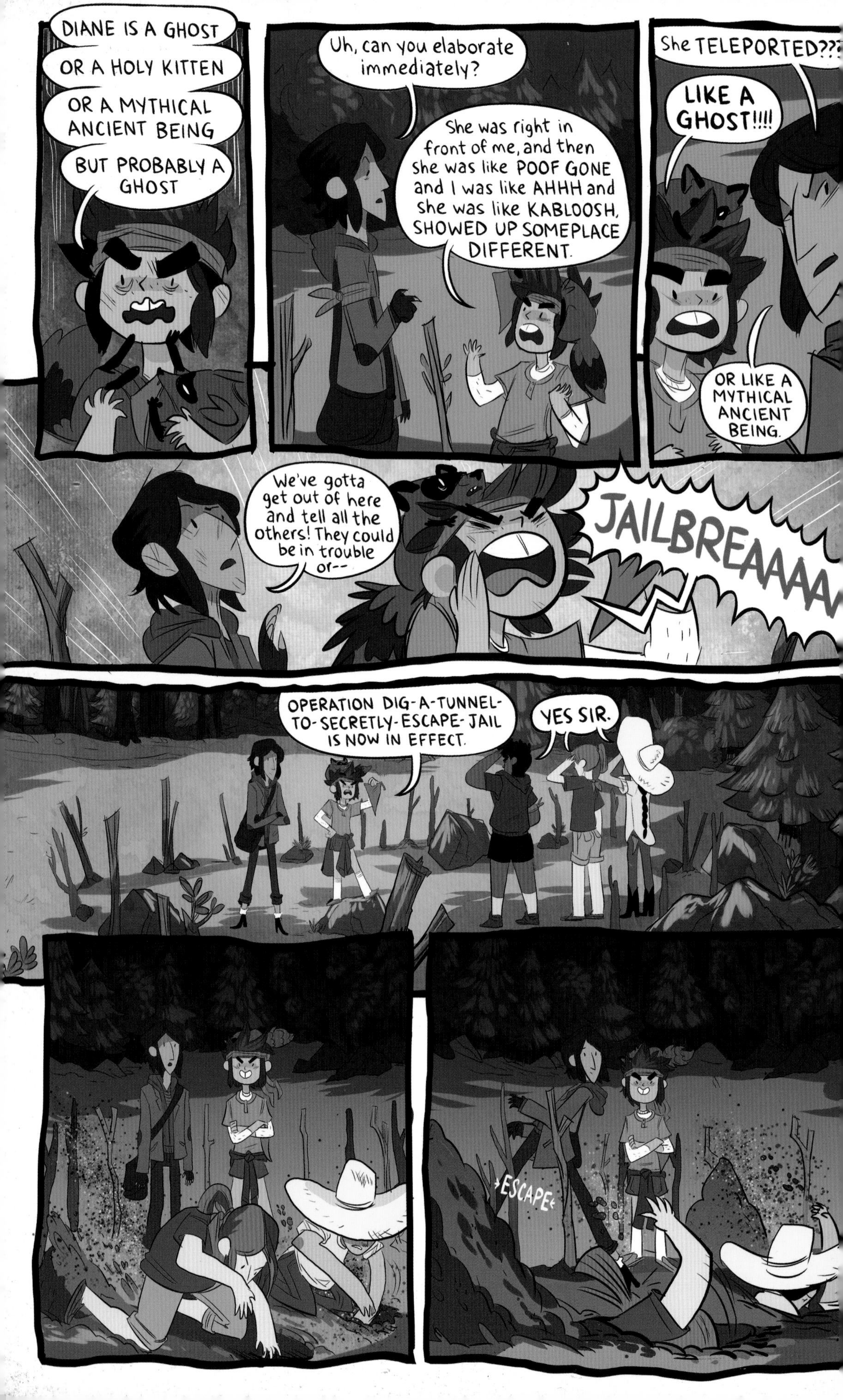
DIANE IS A GHOST
OR A HOLY KITTEN
OR A MYTHICAL ANCIENT BEING
BUT PROBABLY A GHOST
Uh, can you elaborate immediately?
She was right in front of me, and then she was like POOF GONE and I was like AHHH and she was like KABLOOSH, SHOWED UP SOMEPLACE DIFFERENT.
She TELEPORTED???
LIKE A GHOST!!!!
OR LIKE A MYTHICAL ANCIENT BEING.
We've gotta get out of here and tell all the others! They could be in trouble or--
JAILBREAAAAA
OPERATION DIG-A-TUNNEL-TO-SECRETLY-ESCAPE-JAIL IS NOW IN EFFECT.
YES SIR.
ESCAPE

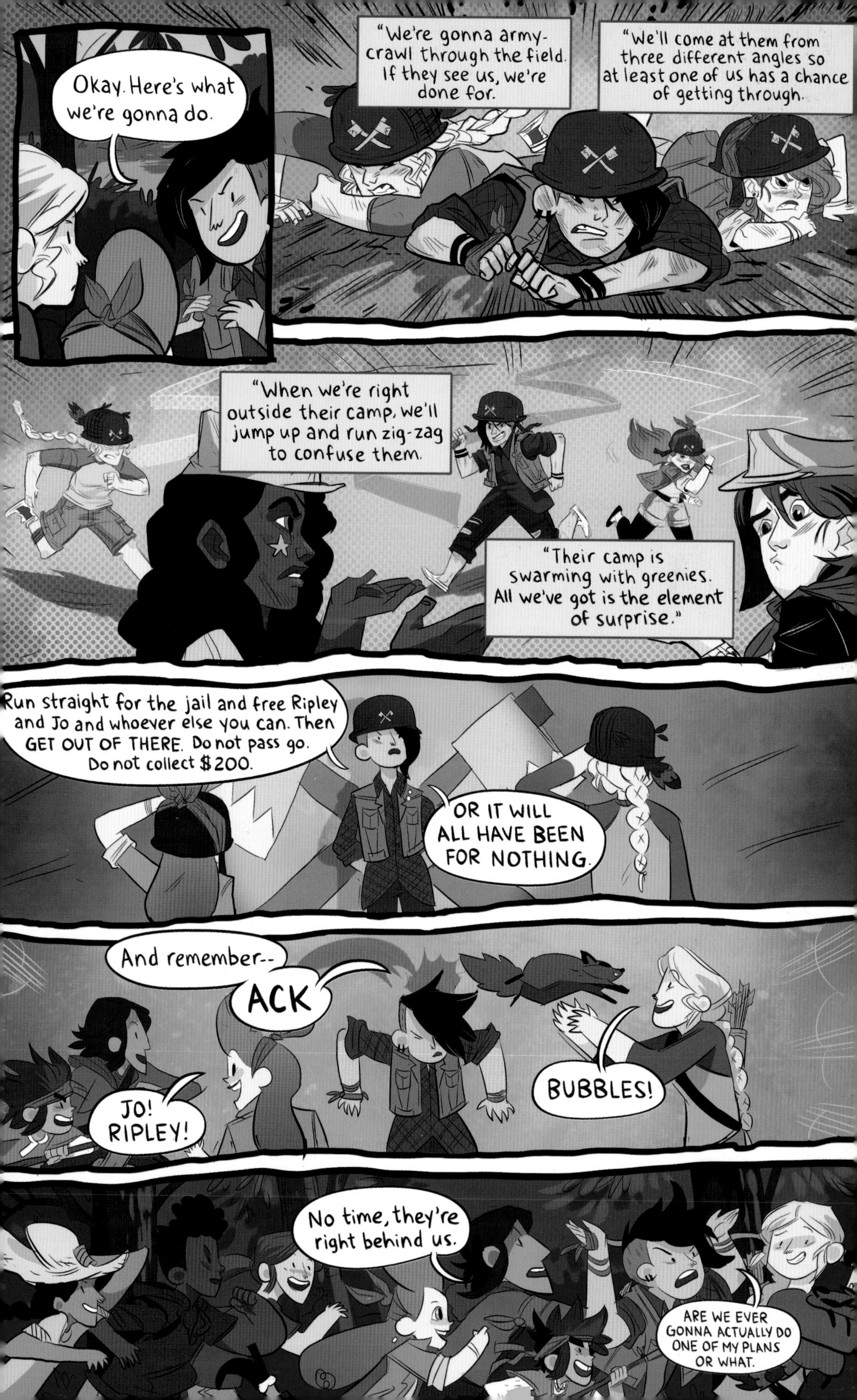
Okay. Here's what we're gonna do.
"We're gonna army-crawl through the field. If they see us, we're done for.
"We'll come at them from three different angles so at least one of us has a chance of getting through.
"When we're right outside their camp, we'll jump up and run zig-zag to confuse them.
"Their camp is swarming with greenies. All we've got is the element of surprise."
Run straight for the jail and free Ripley and Jo and whoever else you can. Then GET OUT OF THERE. Do not pass go. Do not collect $200.
OR IT WILL ALL HAVE BEEN FOR NOTHING.
And remember--
ACK
JO! RIPLEY!
BUBBLES!
No time, they're right behind us.
ARE WE EVER GONNA ACTUALLY DO ONE OF MY PLANS OR WHAT.

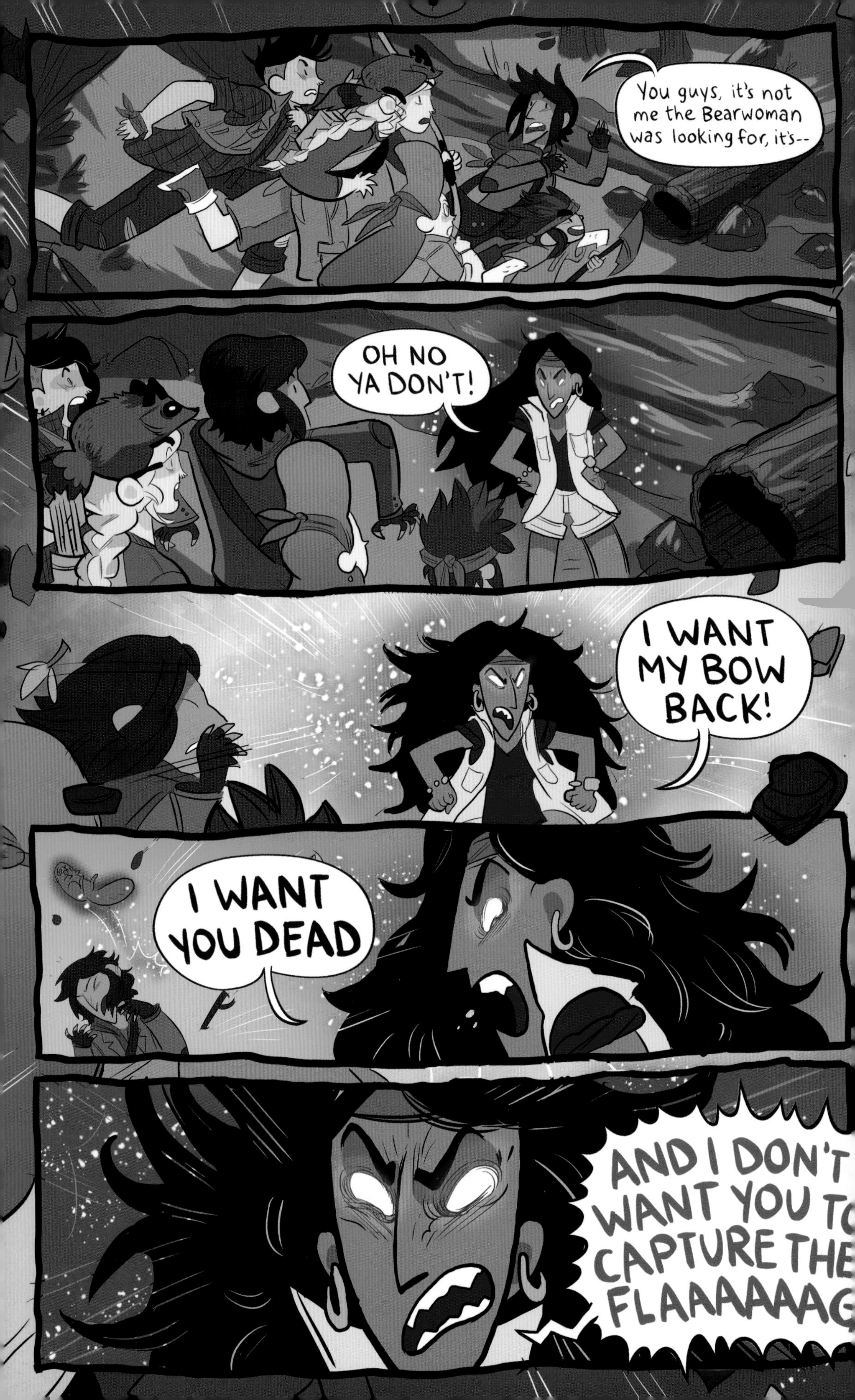

You guys, it's not me the Bearwoman was looking for, it's--
OH NO YA DON'T!
I WANT MY BOW BACK!
I WANT YOU DEAD
AND I DON'T WANT YOU TO CAPTURE THE FLAAAAAAG

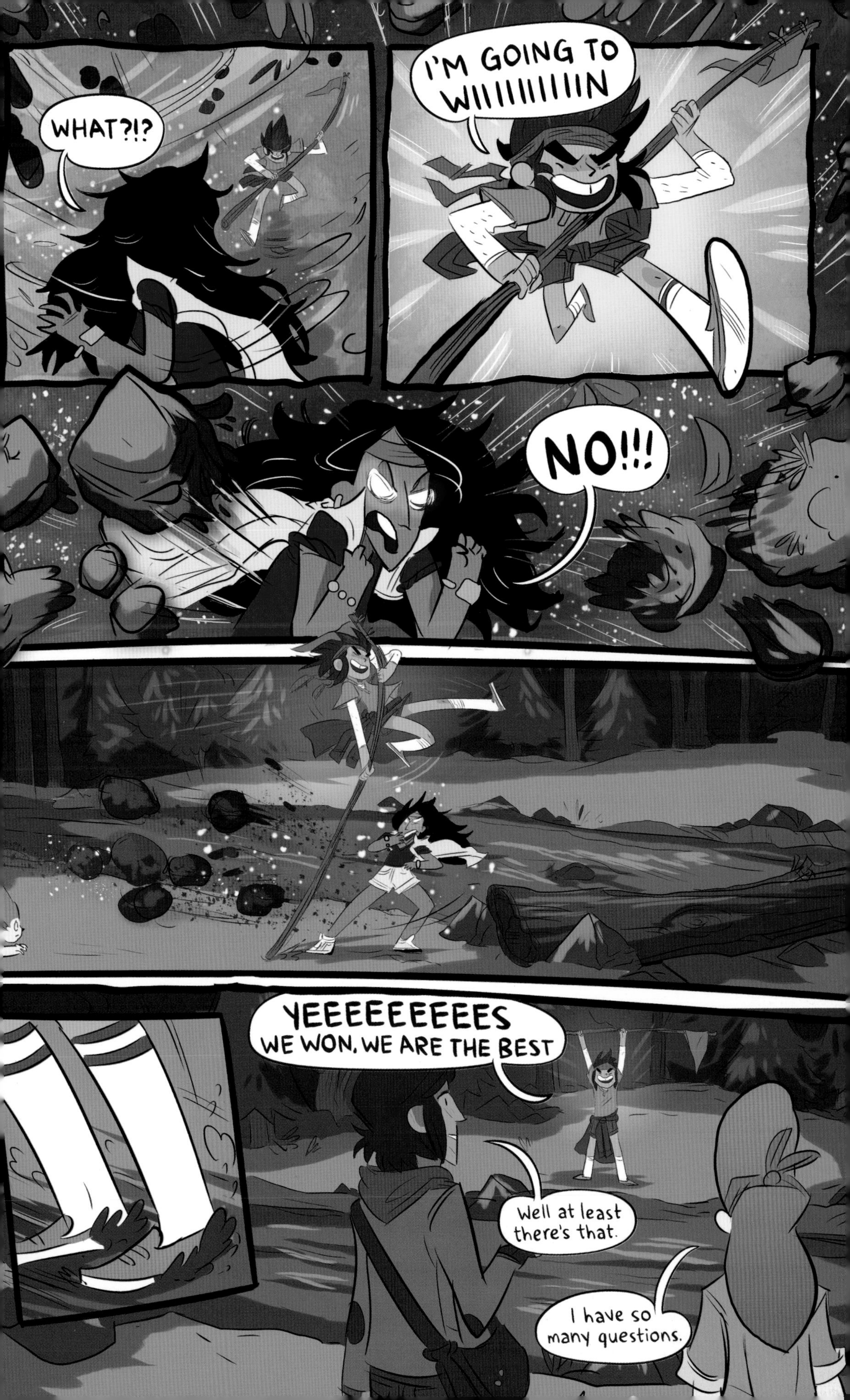
WHAT?!?
I'M GOING TO WIIIIIIIIIN
NO!!!
YEEEEEEEEES
WE WON, WE ARE THE BEST
Well at least there's that.
I have so many questions.

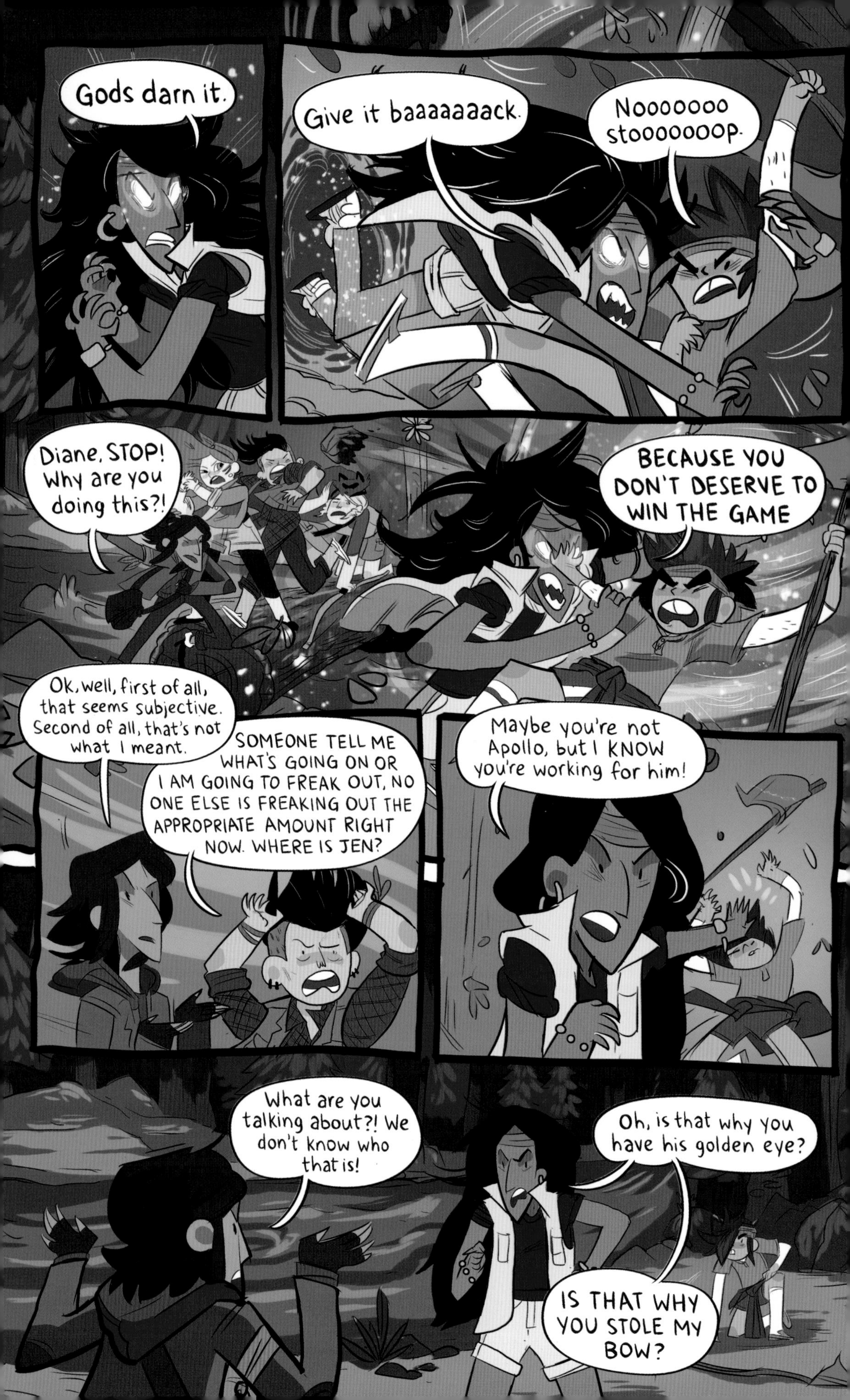
Gods darn it.
Give it baaaaaaack.
Noooooo stoooooOOP.
Diane, STOP! Why are you doing this?!
BECAUSE YOU DON'T DESERVE TO WIN THE GAME
Ok, well, first of all, that seems subjective. Second of all, that's not what I meant.
SOMEONE TELL ME WHAT'S GOING ON OR I AM GOING TO FREAK OUT, NO ONE ELSE IS FREAKING OUT THE APPROPRIATE AMOUNT RIGHT NOW. WHERE IS JEN?
Maybe you're not Apollo, but I KNOW you're working for him!
What are you talking about?! We don't know who that is!
Oh, is that why you have his golden eye?
IS THAT WHY YOU STOLE MY BOW?

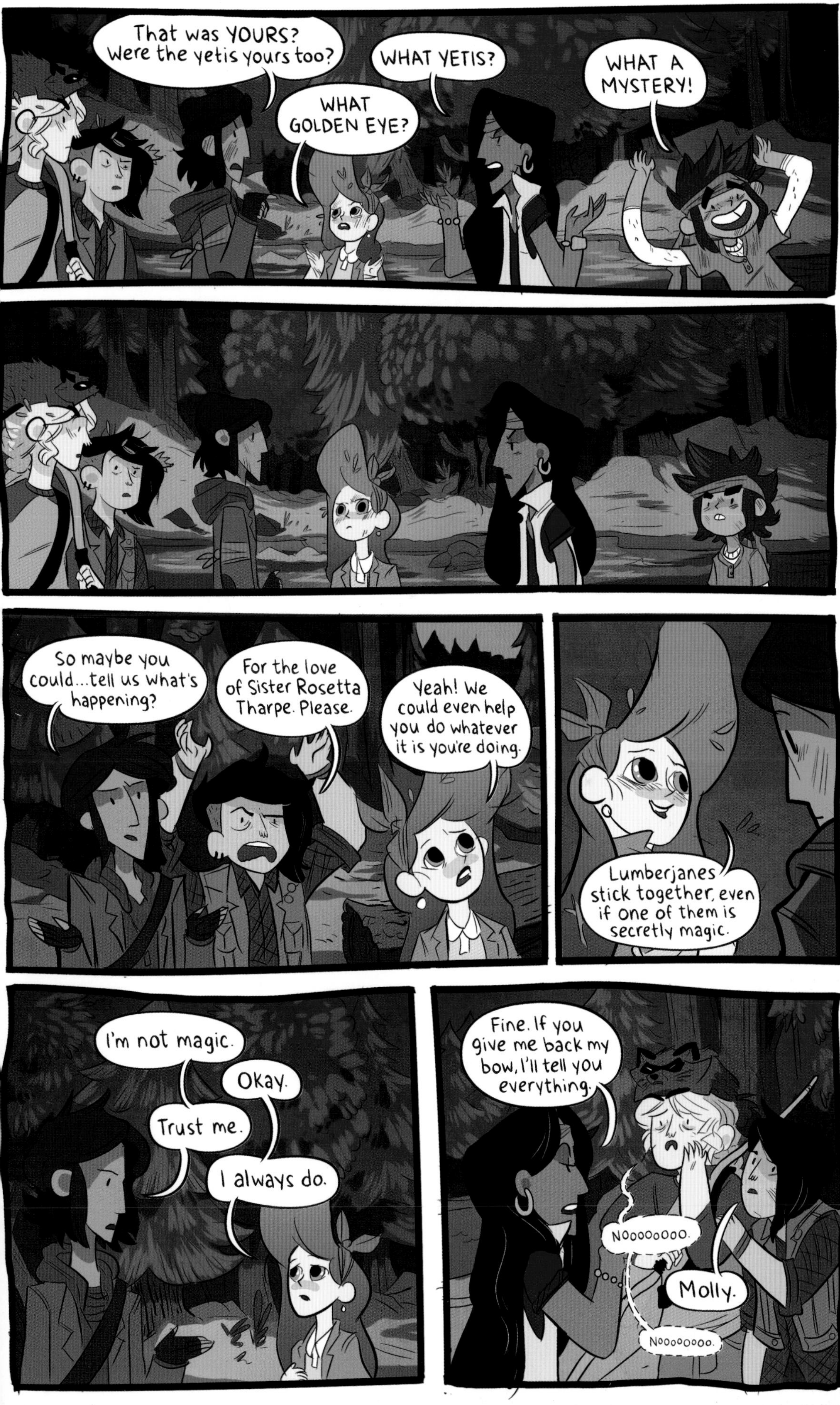
That was YOURS? Were the yetis yours too?
WHAT GOLDEN EYE?
WHAT YETIS?
WHAT A MYSTERY!
So maybe you could...tell us what's happening?
For the love of Sister Rosetta Tharpe. Please.
Yeah! We could even help you do whatever it is you're doing.
Lumberjanes stick together, even if one of them is secretly magic.
I'm not magic.
Okay.
Trust me.
I always do.
Fine. If you give me back my bow, I'll tell you everything.
Nooooooo.
Molly.
Nooooooo.

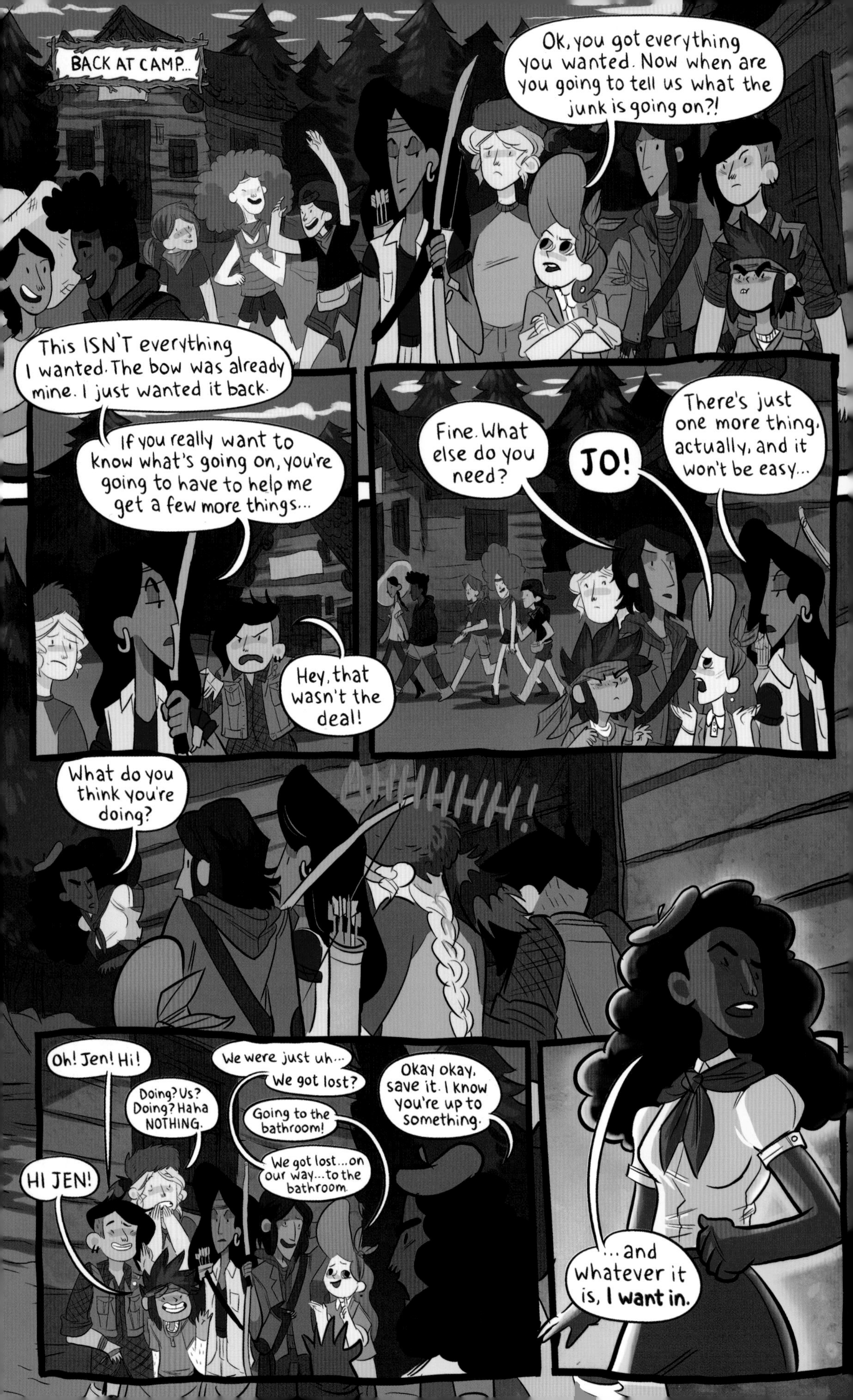
BACK AT CAMP...
Ok, you got everything you wanted. Now when are you going to tell us what the junk is going on?!
This ISN'T everything I wanted. The bow was already mine. I just wanted it back.
If you really want to know what's going on, you're going to have to help me get a few more things...
Hey, that wasn't the deal!
Fine. What else do you need?
JO!
There's just one more thing, actually, and it won't be easy...
What do you think you're doing?
AHHHHH!
Oh! Jen! Hi!
HI JEN!
Doing? Us? Doing? Haha NOTHING.
We were just uh...
We got lost?
Going to the bathroom!
We got lost... on our way... to the bathroom.
Okay okay, save it. I know you're up to something.
...and whatever it is, I want in.

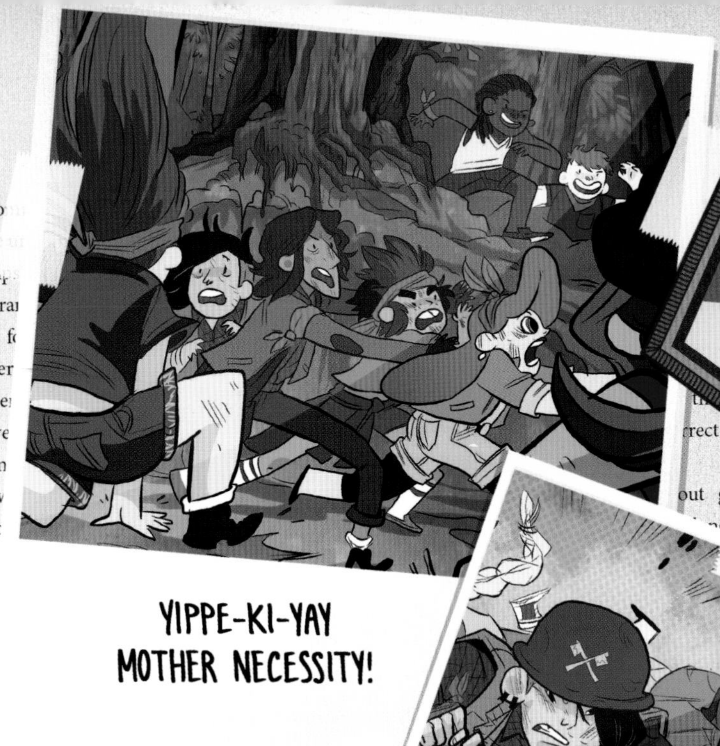
YIPPE-KI-YAY
MOTHER NECESSITY!

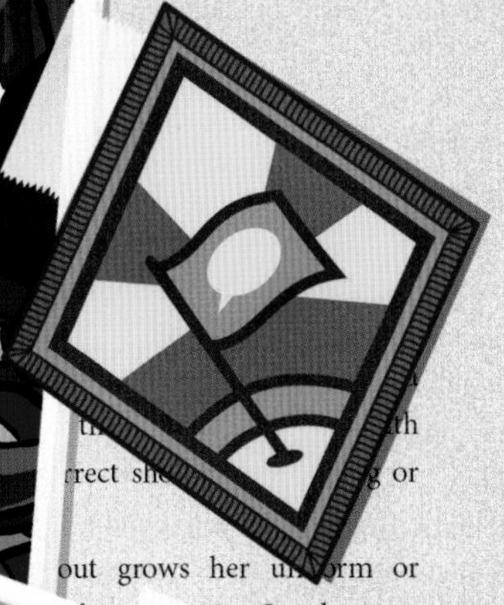

will co

The

It he

appear

dress f

Further

Lumbe

to have

part in

Thiskv

Hardc

have

them

th

rrect sh g or

out grows her u orm or

ter Lumberjane.

a she has

her

her

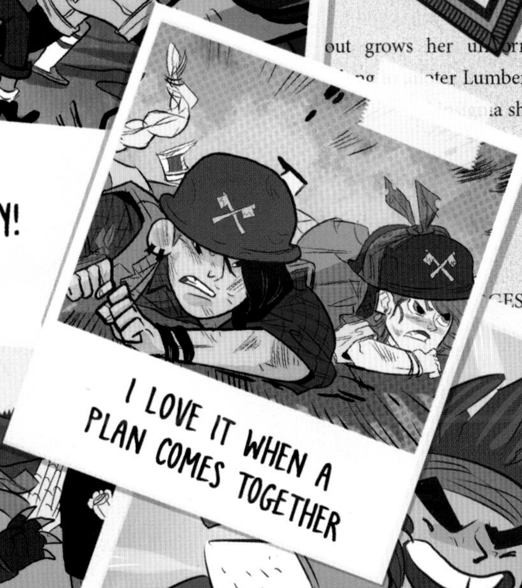
I LOVE IT WHEN A
PLAN COMES TOGETHER

GES

The

yellow, short sl

emb

the w

choose

slacks,

made o

out-of-dc

green bere

the colla

Shoes ma

heels, rou ngs or

socks shou ith the shoes or wi

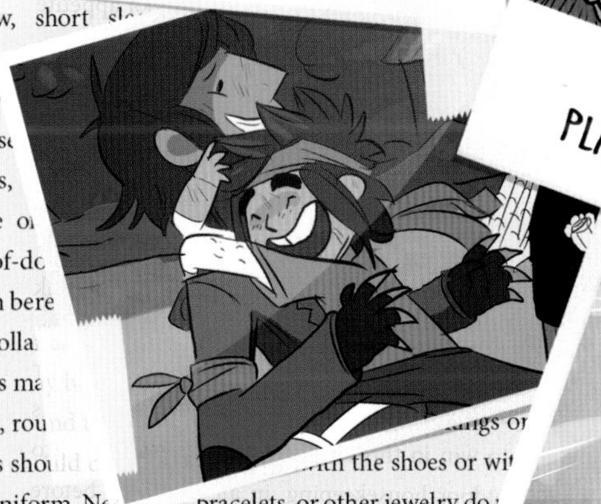

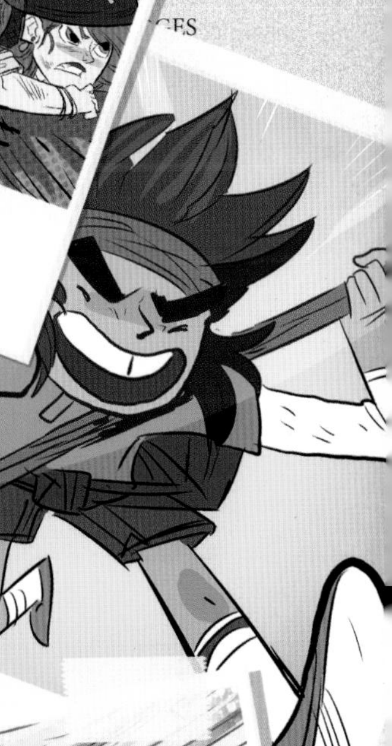

the uniform. Ne es, bracelets, or other jewelry do

belong with a Lumberjane uniform.

HOW TO WEAR THE UNIFORM

To look well in a uniform demands first of uniform be kept in good condition—clean pressed. See that the skirt is the right length height and build, that the belt is adjusted to that your shoes and stockings are in keeping uniform, that you watch your posture and carry with dignity and grace. If the beret is removed in be sure that your hair is neat and kept in place wit insonspicuous clip or ribbon. When you wear Lumberjane uniform you are identified as a member this organization and you should be doubly careful to conduct yourself in a way that will show everyone that courtesy and thoughtfullness are part of being a Lumberjane. People are likely to judge a whole nation by the selfishness of a few individuals, to criticize a whole family because of the misconduct of one member, and to feel unkindly toward and organization because of the

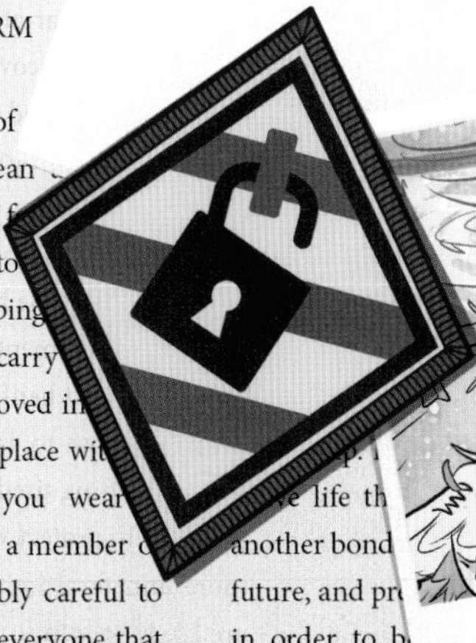

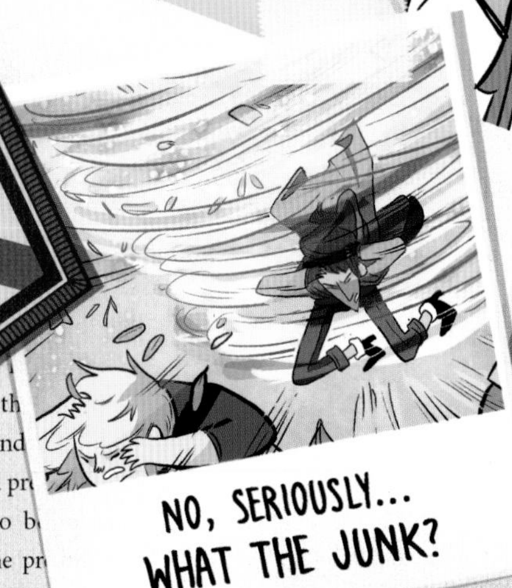
NO, SERIOUSLY...
WHAT THE JUNK?

ve life th

another bond

future, and pr

in order to b

Lumberjane pr

Penniquiql Thi ore Lady

Types, but m es will wish to have one. They

can either bu uniform, or make it themselves from

materials available at the trading post.

LUMBERJANES FIELD MANUAL

CHAPTER SEVEN

Lumberjanes "Community" Program Field

FRIENDSHIP TO THE MAX BADGE

"Together forever."

There are many things that a Lumberjane will learn while at camp, she will learn how to care for the wildlife available to her and how to use it to better her life and those around her. She will learn the importance of social customs and manners, while at the same time enjoying the chance to break the boundaries that society might place upon her. A Lumberjane will learn how to start a fire, she will learn how to survive in the harsh climates, and learn basic healing necessities to ensure good health for herself and her companions. Above all else, a Lumberjane will learn what it means to be a friend.

The *Friendship to the Max* badge is not just another step for a Lumberjane on her personal journey in camp but something much more. 'Friendship to the Max!' is the camp slogan and it has stood the test of time as the most valuable lesson a Lumberjane will ever learn in her time here. She will be taught everything she needs to

know how to survive on her own in nature and she will be taught how to stand on her own two feet when she returns home. But, no matter what she might face there will always be friendship and friendship is something a Lumberjane will teach herself.

To obtain the *Friendship to the Max* badge, a Lumberjane must be able to prove that she not only values the faith and friendship that others have given her but that she truly understands what it means to be a friend. She will put her friends before her without neglecting herself, she will not take advantage of her friends and she will be able to show her loyalty and dedication to them not only through her words but her actions. Her fellow Lumberjanes will understand what it means to be a true friend by following her example. The lesson from this badge is something a Lumberjane will take with her for the rest of her life as she learns to understand the

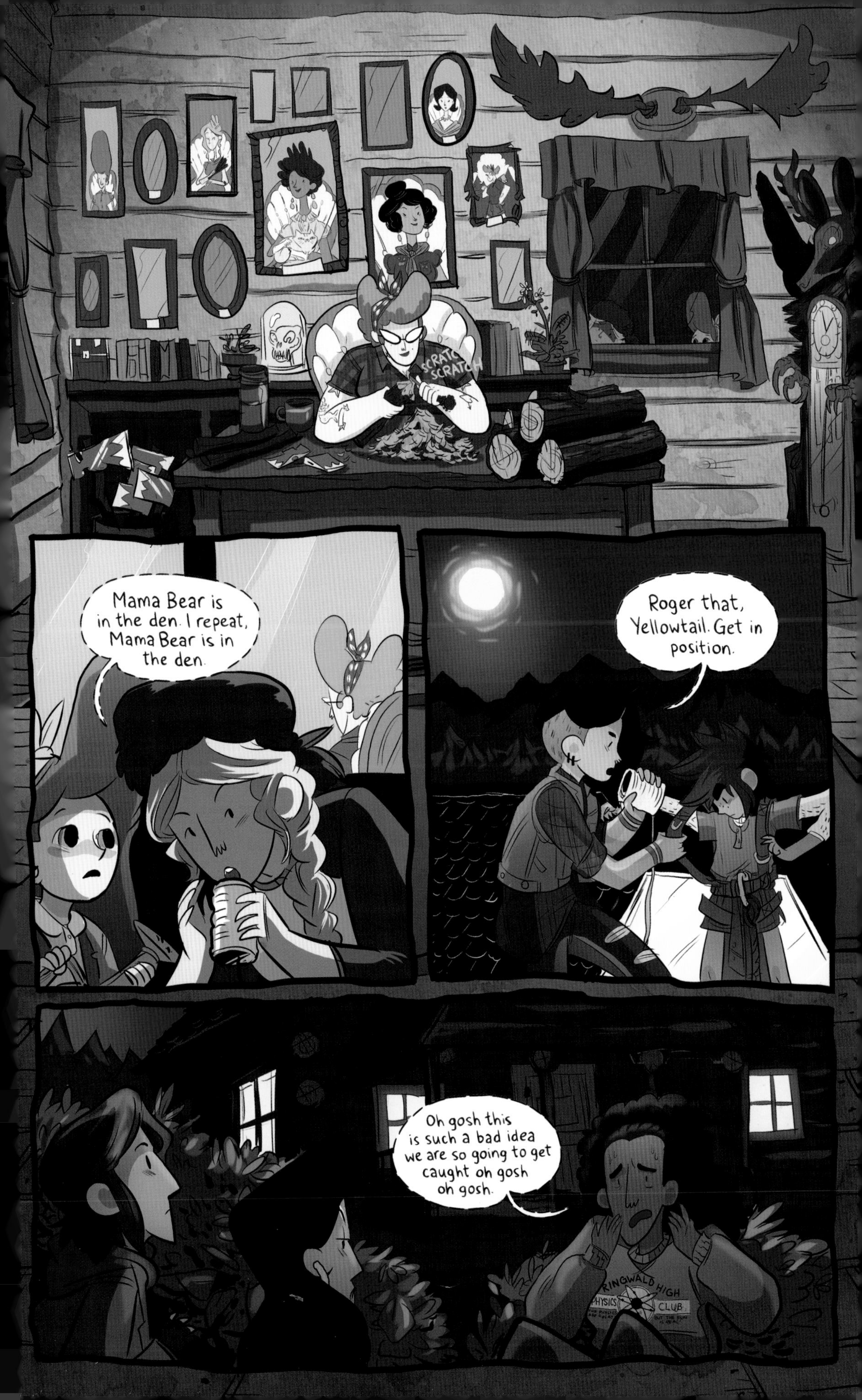
SCRATCH
Mama Bear is in the den. I repeat, Mama Bear is in the den.
Roger that, Yellowtail. Get in position.
Oh gosh this is such a bad idea we are so going to get caught oh gosh oh gosh.
RINGWALD HIGH PHYSICS CLUB

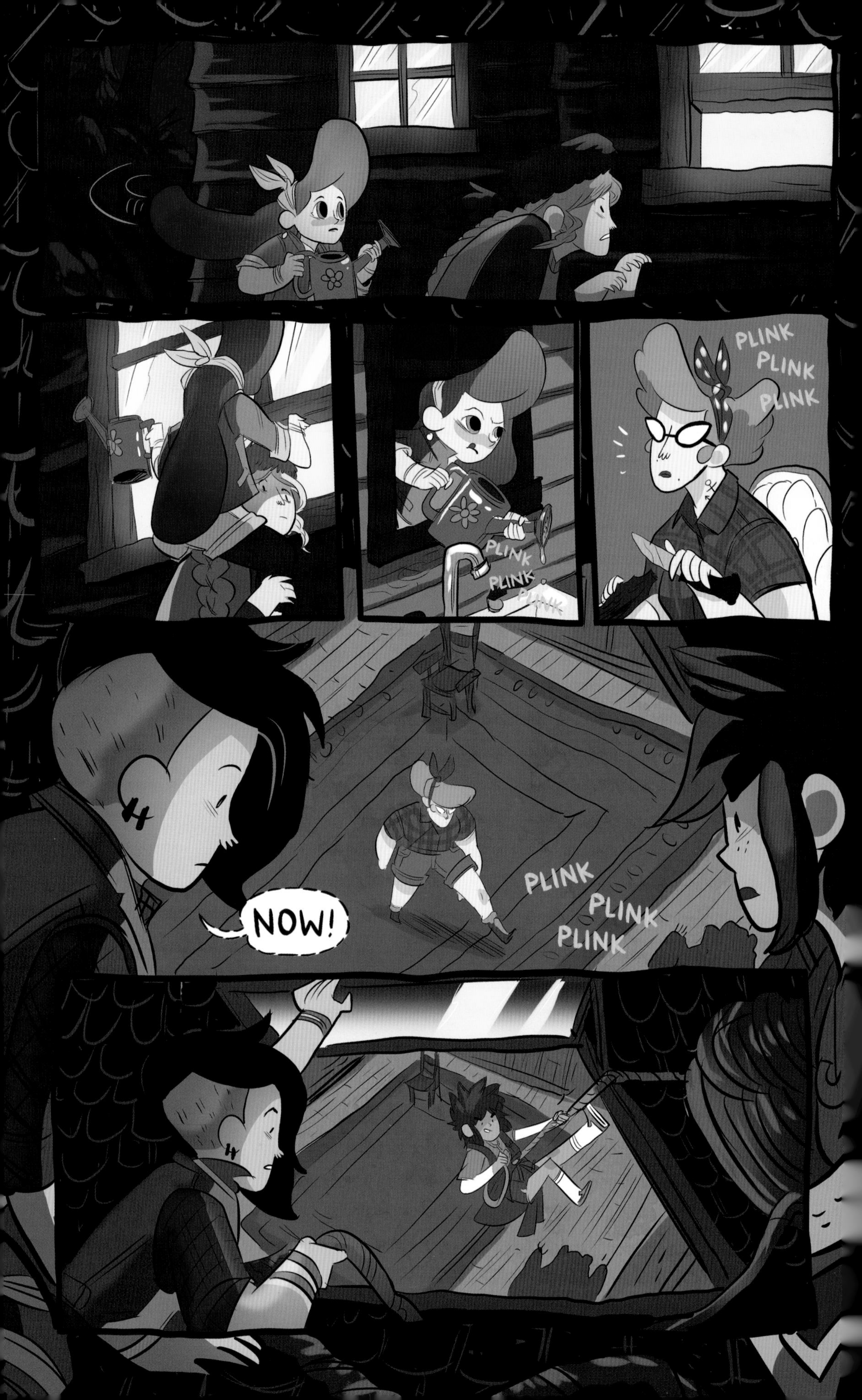
PLINK
PLINK
PLINK
PLINK
PLINK
PLINK
NOW!
PLINK
PLINK
PLINK

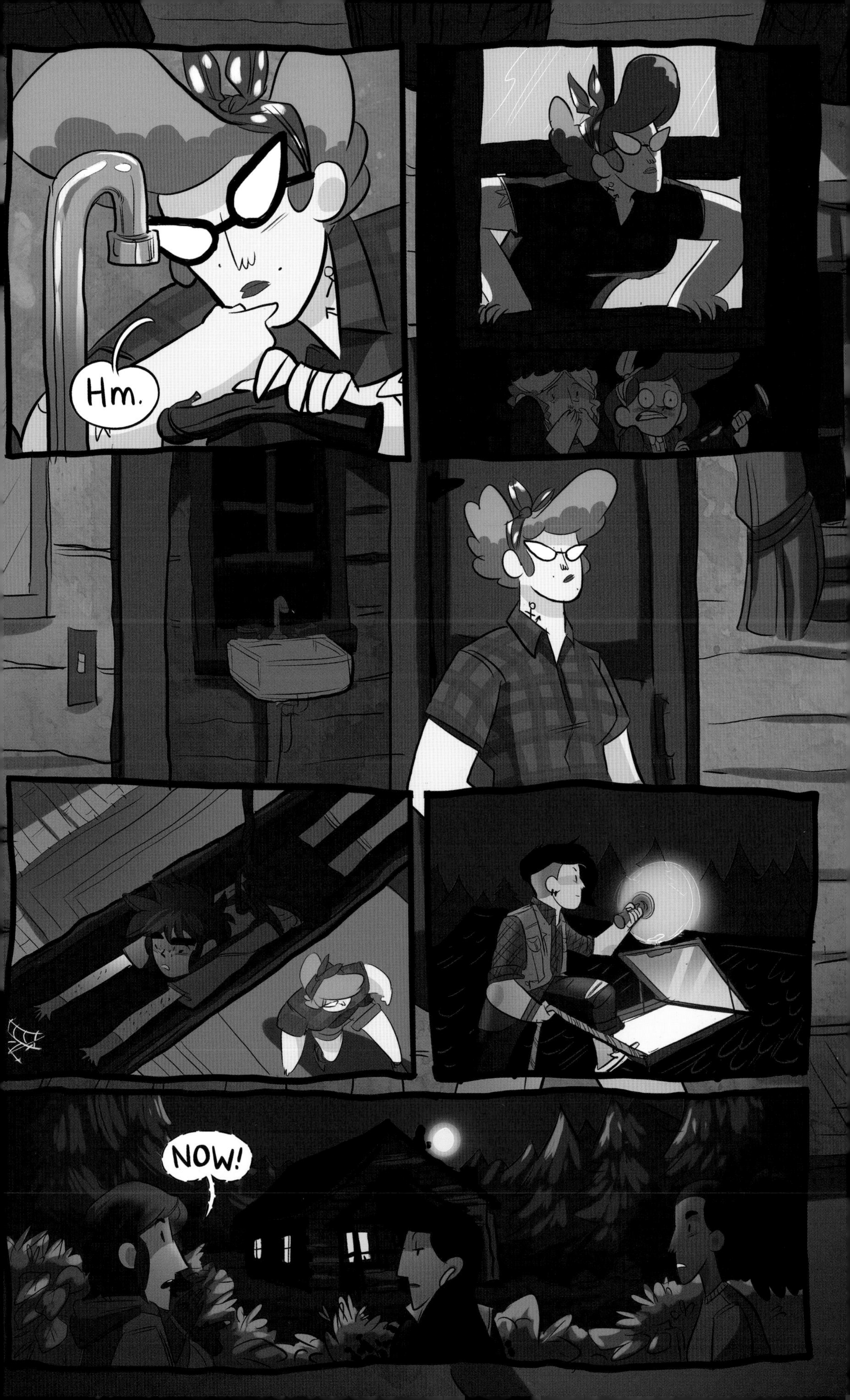
Hm.
NOW!

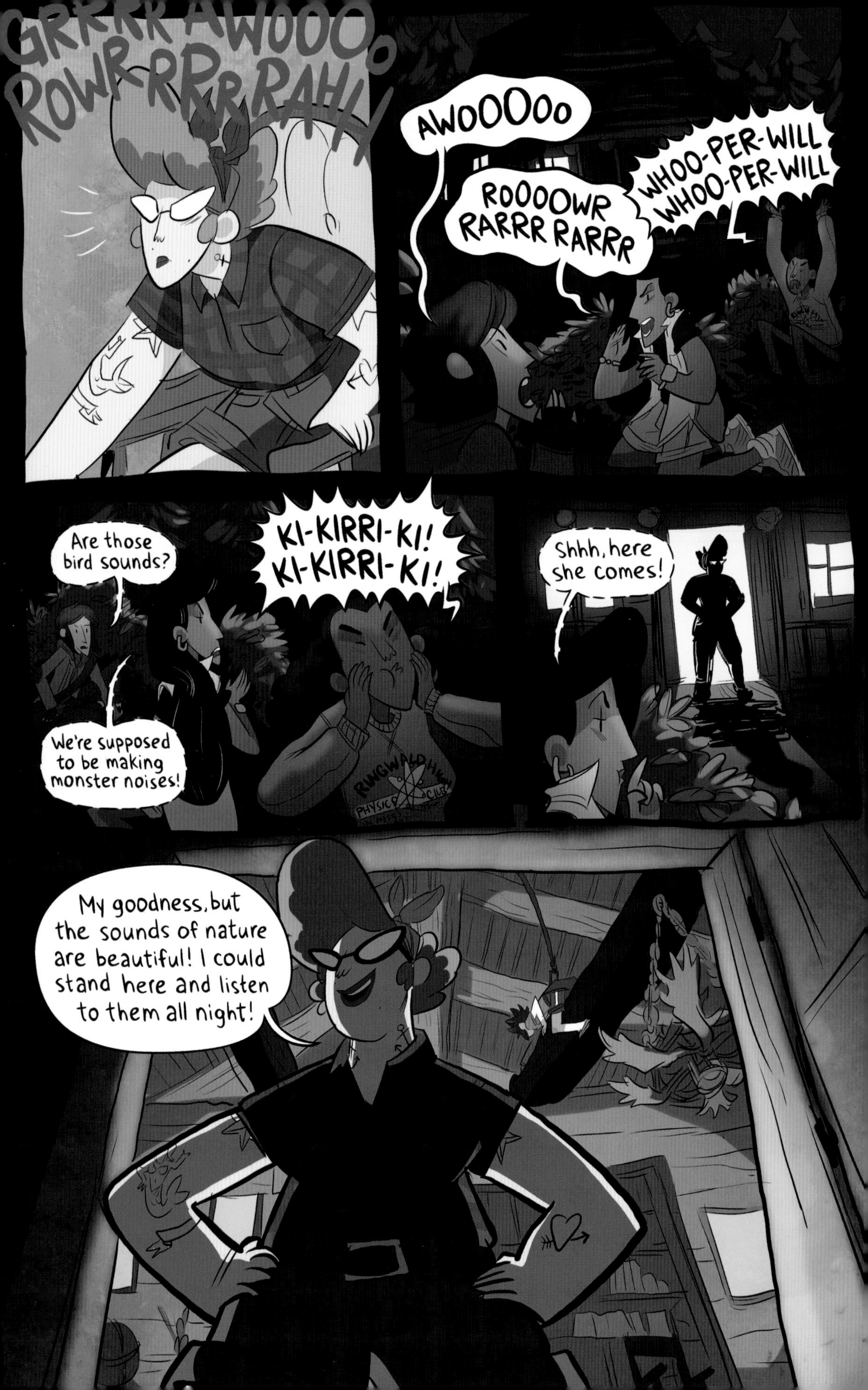
GRRRR AWOOOo
ROWRRRRRAH!
AWOOOOo
ROOOOWR RARRR RARRR
WHOO-PER-WILL WHOO-PER-WILL
Are those bird sounds?
KI-KIRRI-KI! KI-KIRRI-KI!
We're supposed to be making monster noises!
RINGWALD HIGH PHYSICS CLUB
Shhh, here she comes!
My goodness, but the sounds of nature are beautiful! I could stand here and listen to them all night!

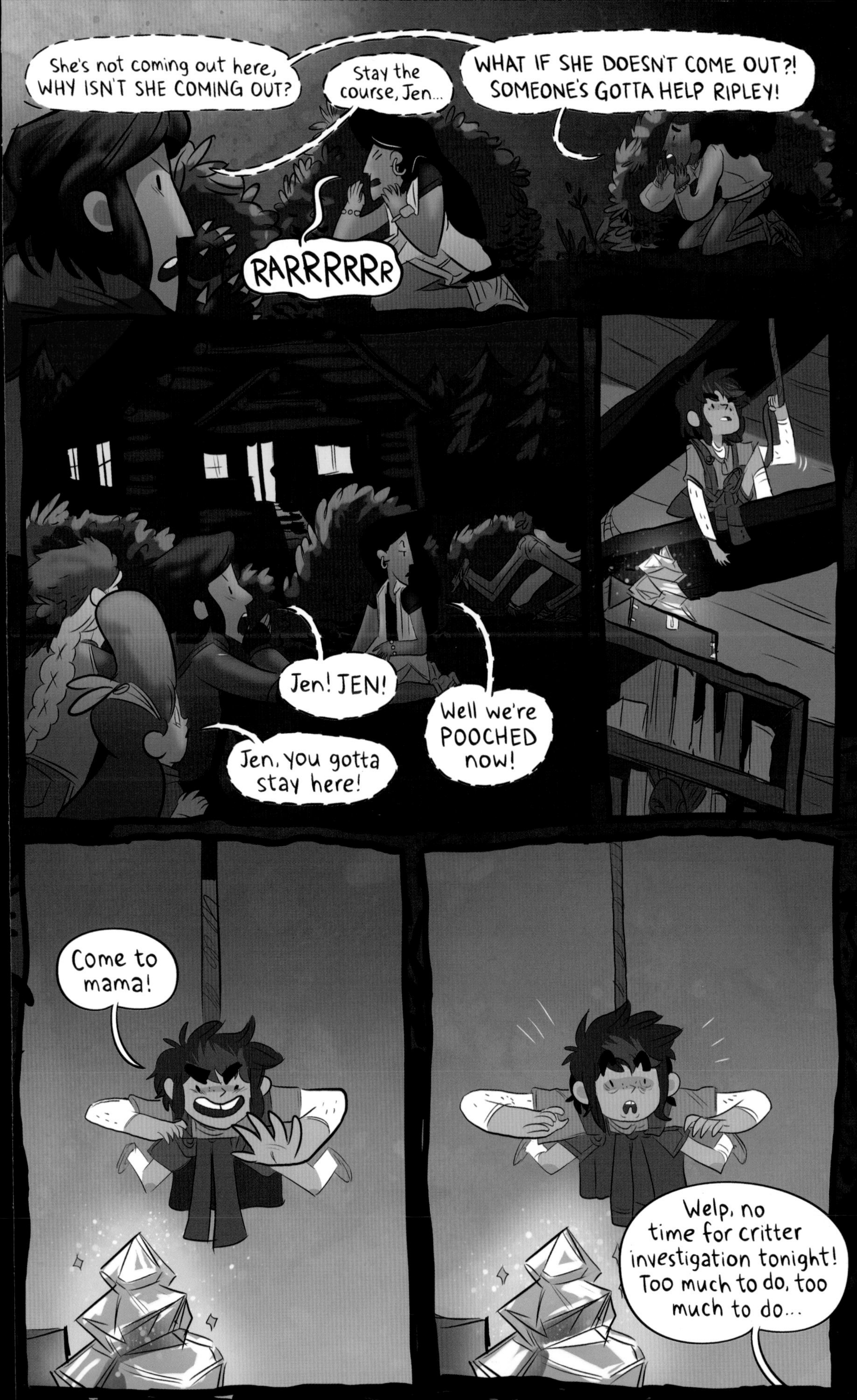
She's not coming out here, WHY ISN'T SHE COMING OUT?
Stay the course, Jen...
WHAT IF SHE DOESN'T COME OUT?! SOMEONE'S GOTTA HELP RIPLEY!
RARRRRRR
Jen! JEN!
Well we're POOCHED now!
Jen, you gotta stay here!
Come to mama!
Welp, no time for critter investigation tonight! Too much to do, too much to do...

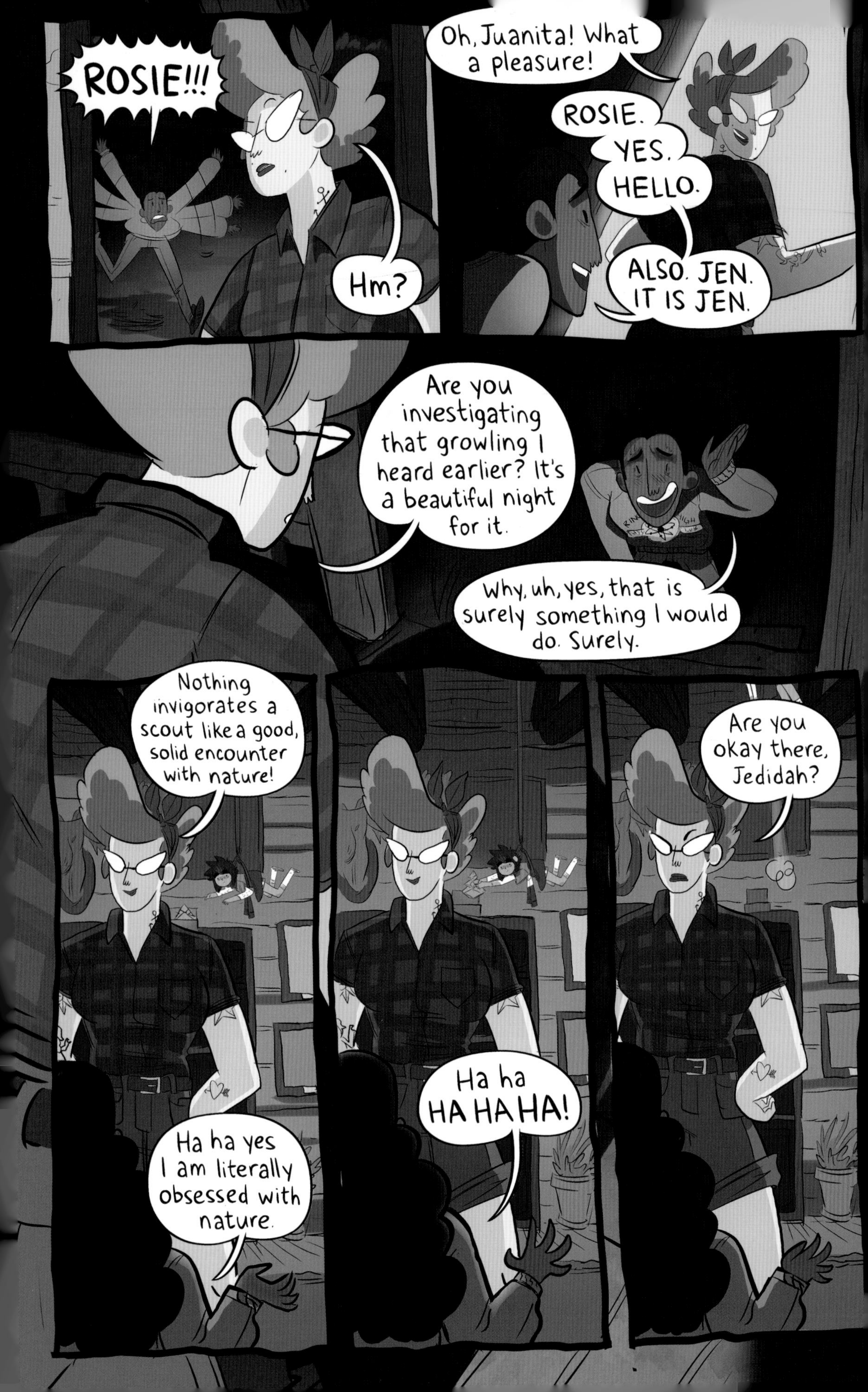
ROSIE!!!
Hm?
Oh, Juanita! What a pleasure!
ROSIE.
YES.
HELLO.
ALSO. JEN. IT IS JEN.
Are you investigating that growling I heard earlier? It's a beautiful night for it.
Why, uh, yes, that is surely something I would do. Surely.
Nothing invigorates a scout like a good, solid encounter with nature!
Ha ha yes I am literally obsessed with nature.
Ha ha HA HA HA!
Are you okay there, Jedidah?

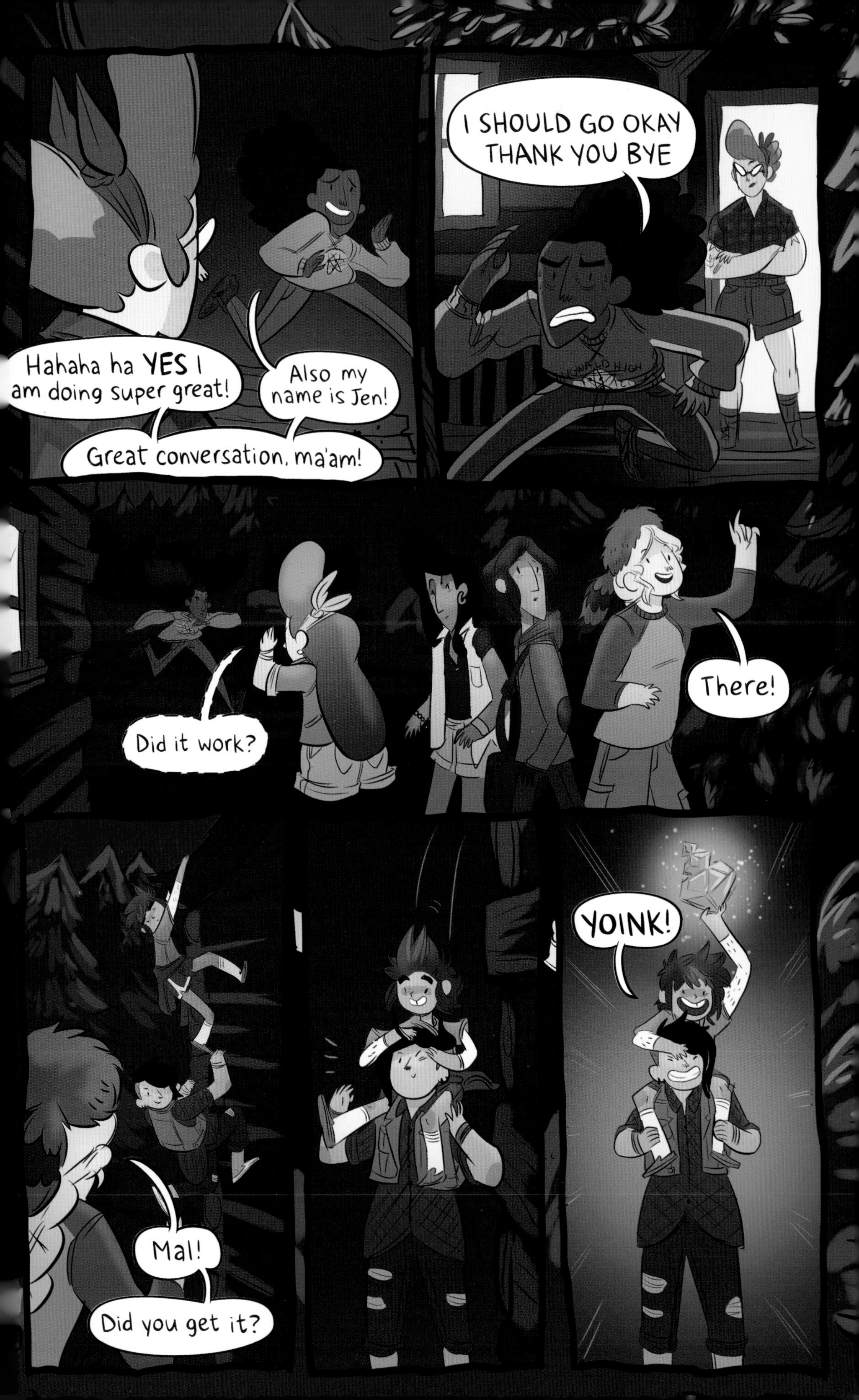
Hahaha ha YES I am doing super great!
Also my name is Jen!
Great conversation, ma'am!
I SHOULD GO OKAY THANK YOU BYE
Did it work?
There!
Mal!
Did you get it?
YOINK!

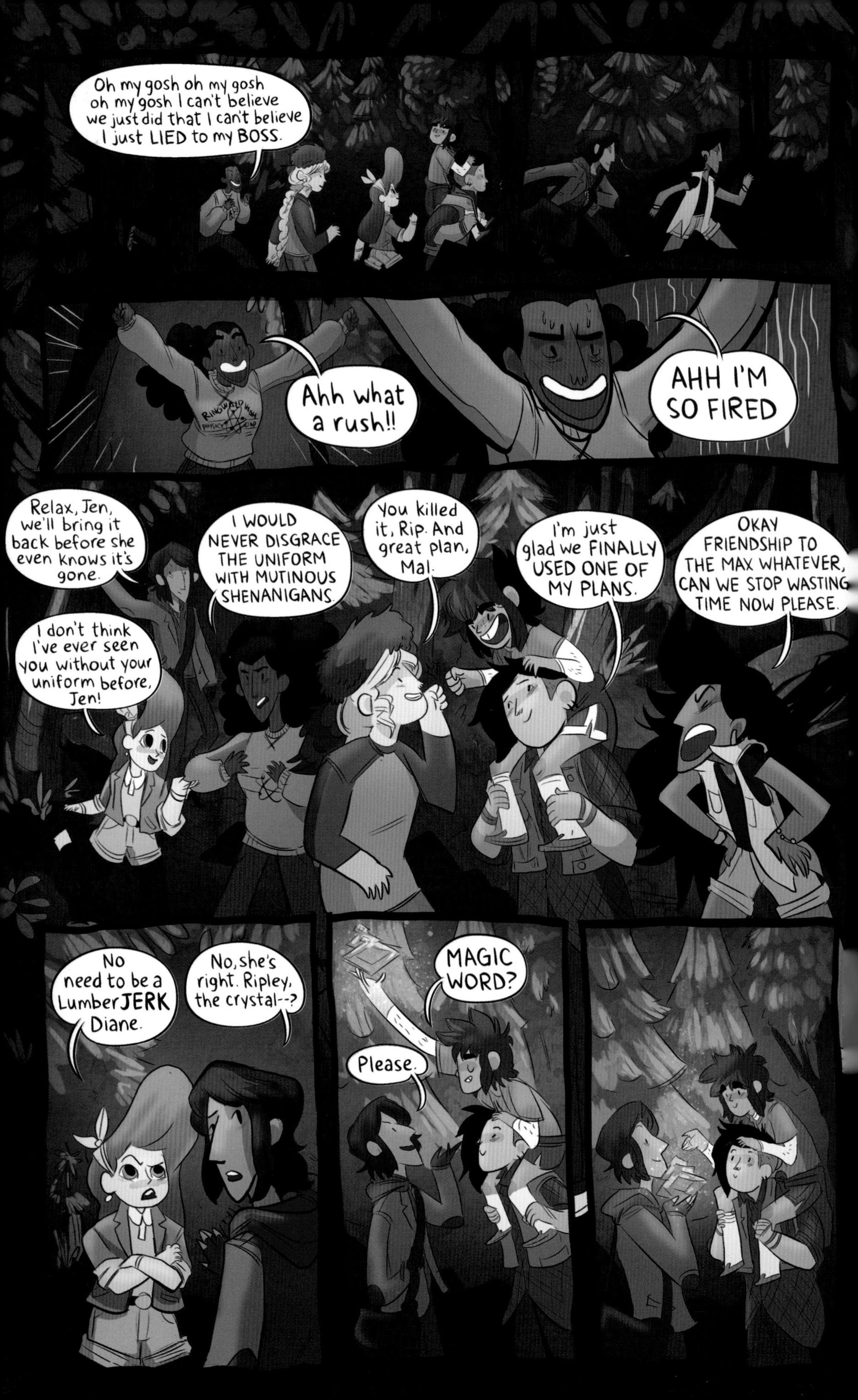
Oh my gosh oh my gosh oh my gosh I can't believe we just did that I can't believe I just LIED to my BOSS.
Ahh what a rush!!
AHH I'M SO FIRED
Relax, Jen, we'll bring it back before she even knows it's gone.
I WOULD NEVER DISGRACE THE UNIFORM WITH MUTINOUS SHENANIGANS.
I don't think I've ever seen you without your uniform before, Jen!
You killed it, Rip. And great plan, Mal.
I'm just glad we FINALLY USED ONE OF MY PLANS.
OKAY FRIENDSHIP TO THE MAX WHATEVER, CAN WE STOP WASTING TIME NOW PLEASE.
No need to be a LumberJERK Diane.
No, she's right. Ripley, the crystal--?
MAGIC WORD?
Please.

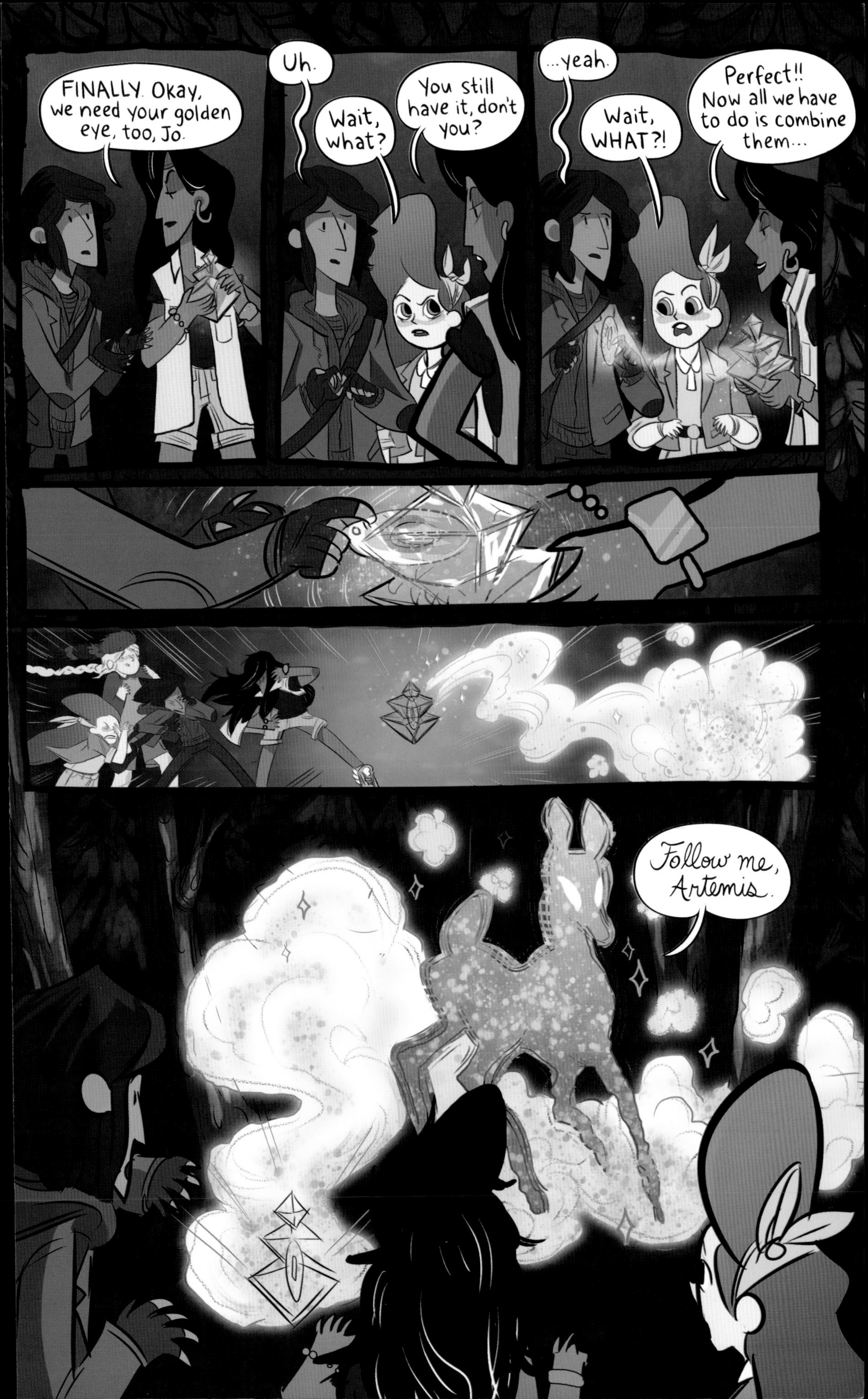
FINALLY. Okay, we need your golden eye, too, Jo.
Uh.
Wait, what?
You still have it, don't you?
...yeah.
Wait, WHAT?!
Perfect!! Now all we have to do is combine them...
Follow me, Artemis.

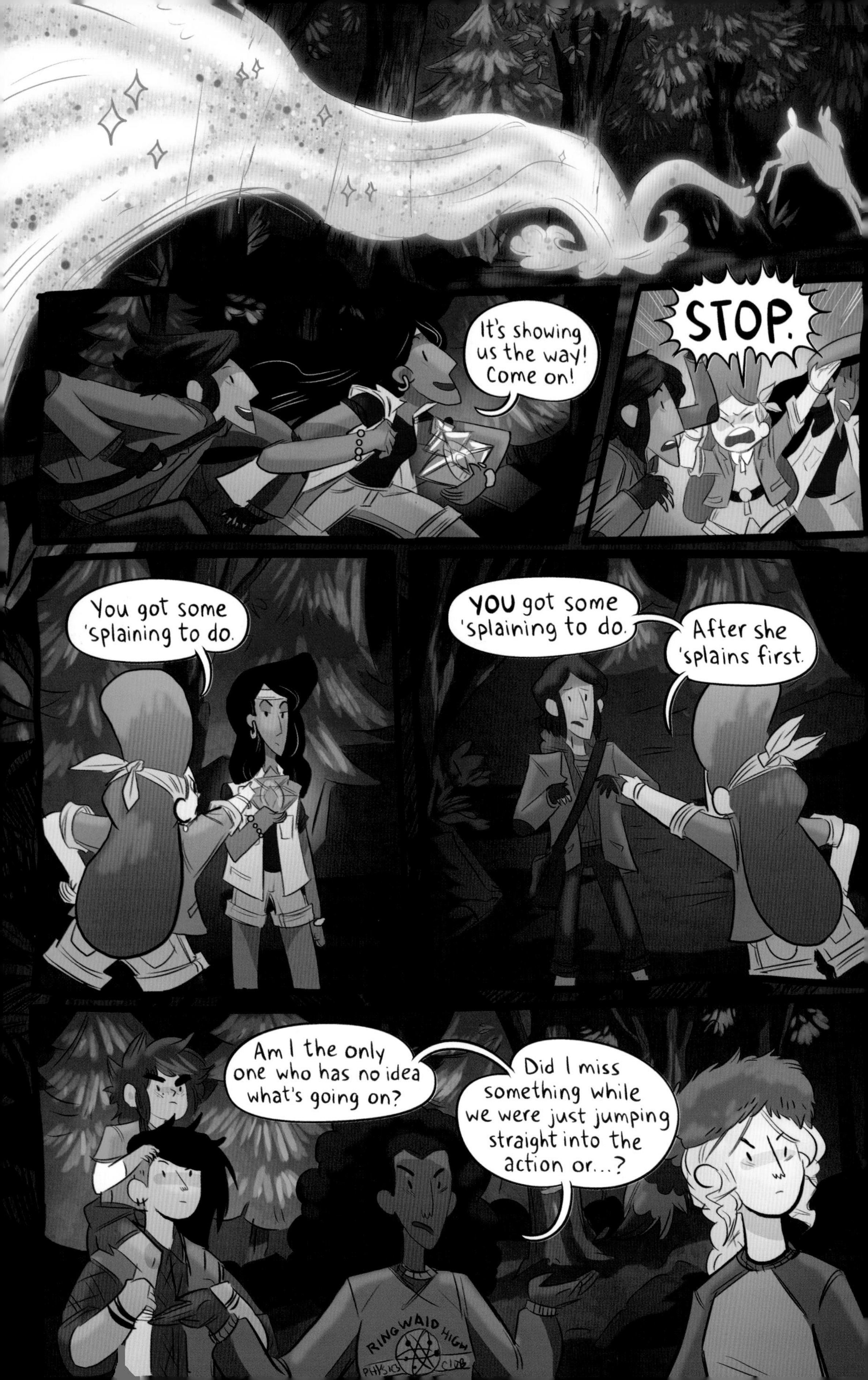
It's showing us the way! Come on!
STOP.
You got some 'splaining to do.
YOU got some 'splaining to do.
After she 'splains first.
Am I the only one who has no idea what's going on?
Did I miss something while we were just jumping straight into the action or...?
RINGWAID HIGH
PHYSICS CLUB

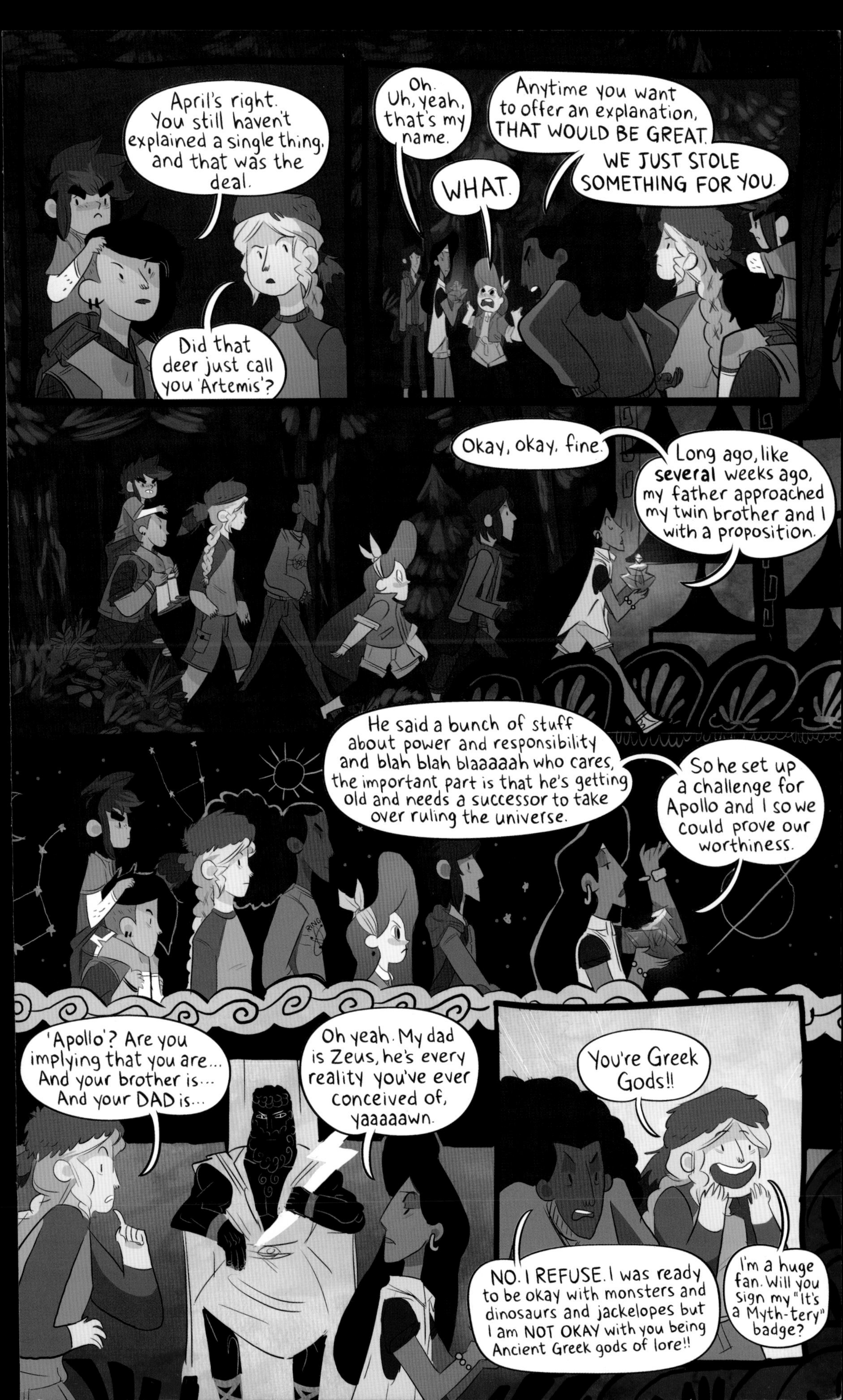

April's right. You still haven't explained a single thing, and that was the deal.
Did that deer just call you 'Artemis'?
Oh. Uh, yeah, that's my name.
WHAT.
Anytime you want to offer an explanation, THAT WOULD BE GREAT.
WE JUST STOLE SOMETHING FOR YOU.
Okay, okay, fine.
Long ago, like **several** weeks ago, my father approached my twin brother and I with a proposition.
He said a bunch of stuff about power and responsibility and blah blah blaaaaah who cares, the important part is that he's getting old and needs a successor to take over ruling the universe.
So he set up a challenge for Apollo and I so we could prove our worthiness.
'Apollo'? Are you implying that you are... And your brother is... And your DAD is...
Oh yeah. My dad is Zeus, he's every reality you've ever conceived of, yaaaaawn.
You're Greek Gods!!
NO. I REFUSE. I was ready to be okay with monsters and dinosaurs and jackelopes but I am NOT OKAY with you being Ancient Greek gods of lore!!
I'm a huge fan. Will you sign my "It's a Myth-tery" badge?

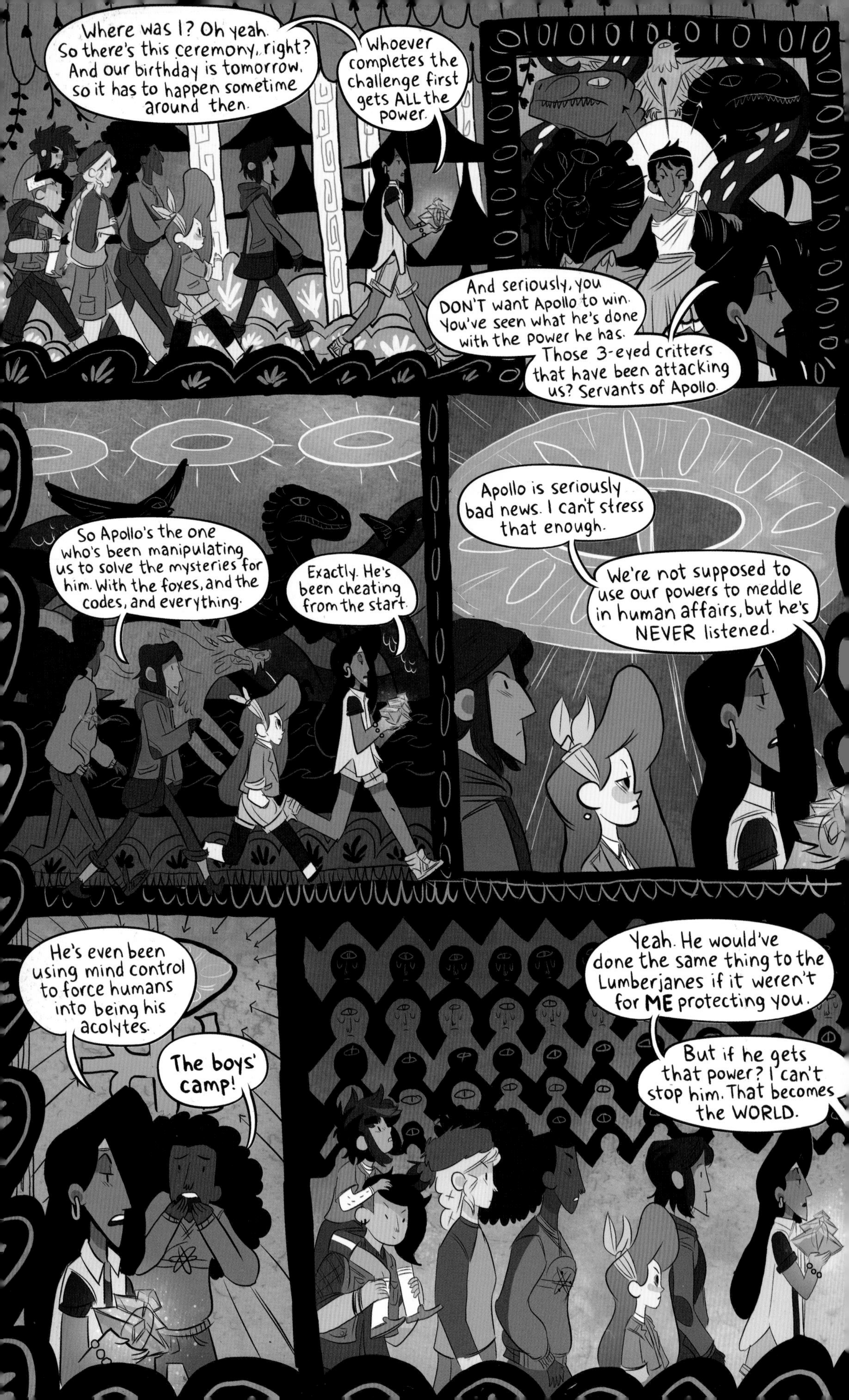
Where was I? Oh yeah. So there's this ceremony, right? And our birthday is tomorrow, so it has to happen sometime around then.
Whoever completes the challenge first gets ALL the power.
And seriously, you DON'T want Apollo to win. You've seen what he's done with the power he has.
Those 3-eyed critters that have been attacking us? Servants of Apollo.
So Apollo's the one who's been manipulating us to solve the mysteries for him. With the foxes, and the codes, and everything.
Exactly. He's been cheating from the start.
Apollo is seriously bad news. I can't stress that enough.
We're not supposed to use our powers to meddle in human affairs, but he's NEVER listened.
He's even been using mind control to force humans into being his acolytes.
The boys' camp!
Yeah. He would've done the same thing to the Lumberjanes if it weren't for ME protecting you.
But if he gets that power? I can't stop him. That becomes the WORLD.

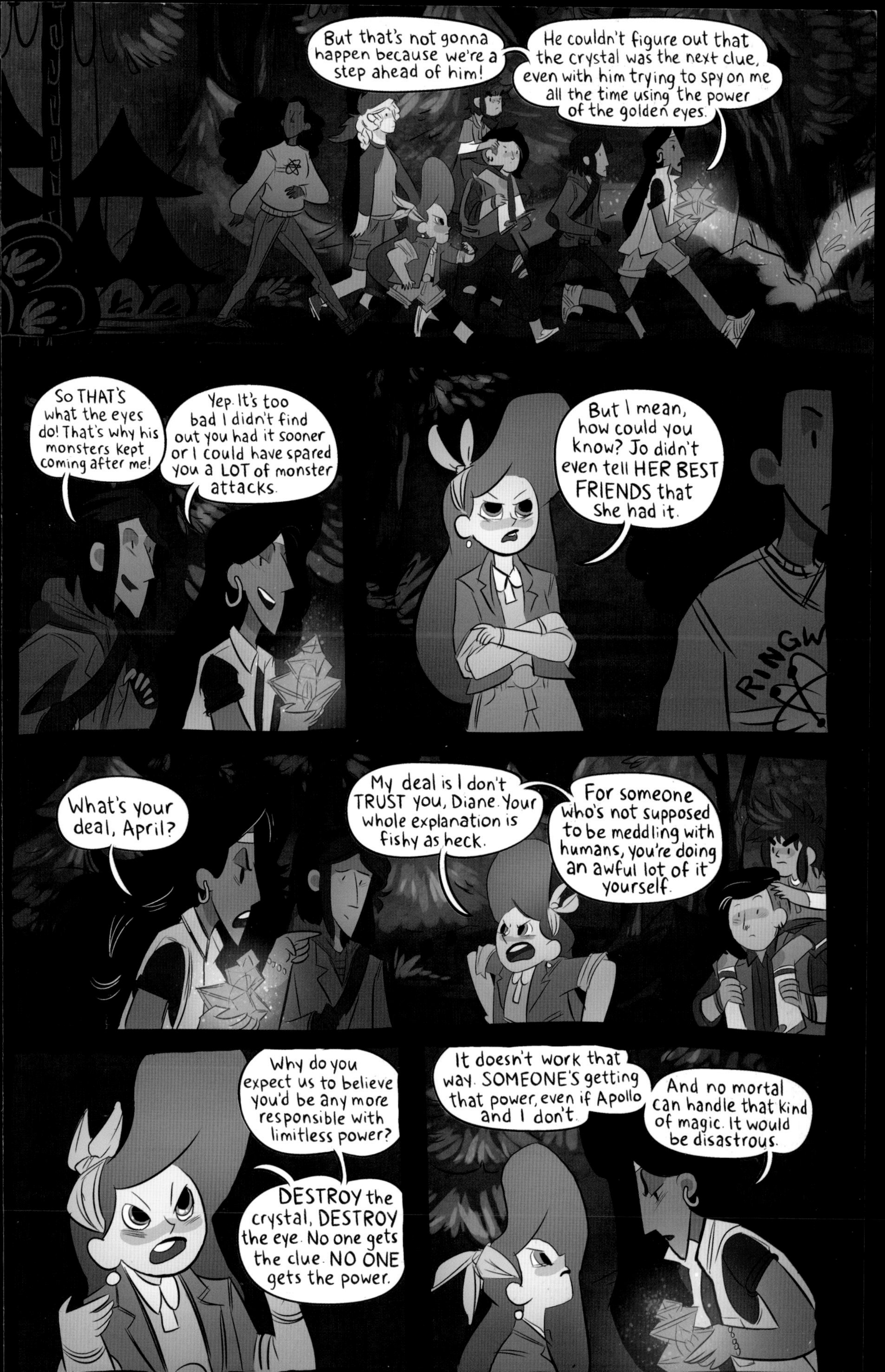
But that's not gonna happen because we're a step ahead of him!
He couldn't figure out that the crystal was the next clue, even with him trying to spy on me all the time using the power of the golden eyes.
So THAT'S what the eyes do! That's why his monsters kept coming after me!
Yep. It's too bad I didn't find out you had it sooner or I could have spared you a LOT of monster attacks.
But I mean, how could you know? Jo didn't even tell HER BEST FRIENDS that she had it.
RINGW
What's your deal, April?
My deal is I don't TRUST you, Diane. Your whole explanation is fishy as heck.
For someone who's not supposed to be meddling with humans, you're doing an awful lot of it yourself.
Why do you expect us to believe you'd be any more responsible with limitless power?
DESTROY the crystal, DESTROY the eye. No one gets the clue. NO ONE gets the power.
It doesn't work that way. SOMEONE'S getting that power, even if Apollo and I don't.
And no mortal can handle that kind of magic. It would be disastrous.

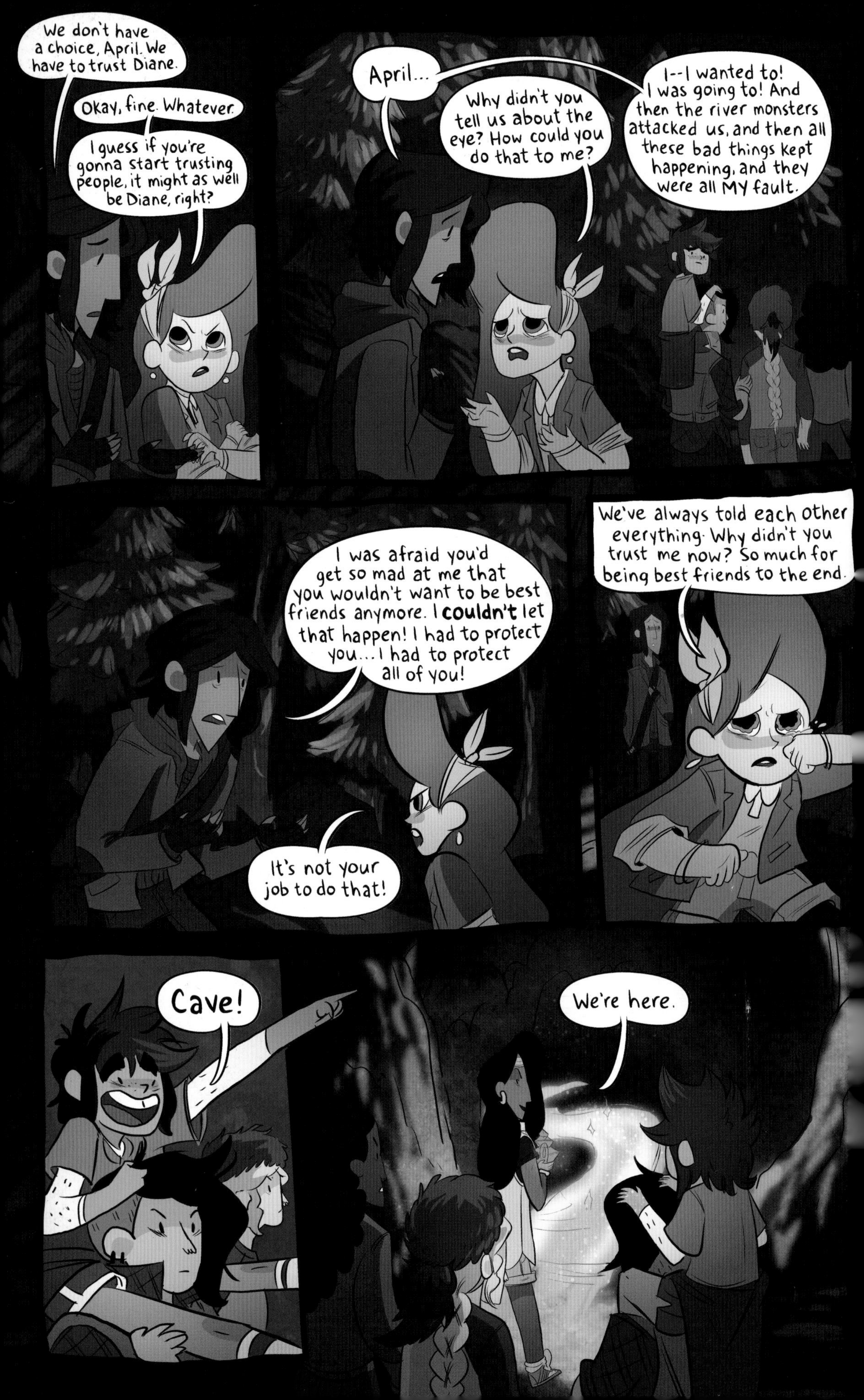

We don't have a choice, April. We have to trust Diane.
Okay, fine. Whatever.
I guess if you're gonna start trusting people, it might as well be Diane, right?
April...
Why didn't you tell us about the eye? How could you do that to me?
I--I wanted to! I was going to! And then the river monsters attacked us, and then all these bad things kept happening, and they were all MY fault.
I was afraid you'd get so mad at me that you wouldn't want to be best friends anymore. I **couldn't** let that happen! I had to protect you... I had to protect all of you!
It's not your job to do that!
We've always told each other everything. Why didn't you trust me now? So much for being best friends to the end.
Cave!
We're here.

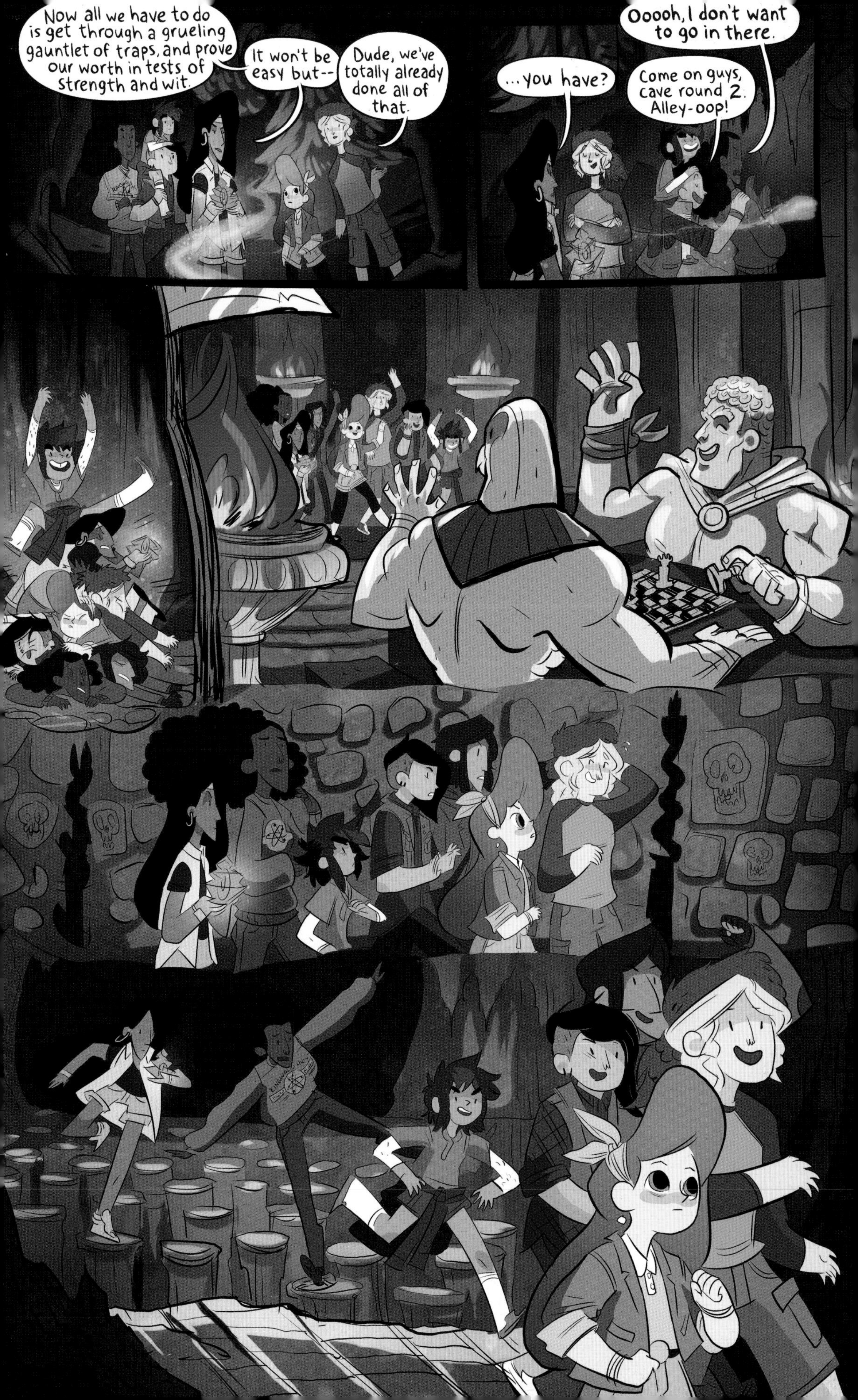
Now all we have to do is get through a grueling gauntlet of traps, and prove our worth in tests of strength and wit.
It won't be easy but--
Dude, we've totally already done all of that.
...you have?
Come on guys, cave round 2. Alley-oop!
Ooooh, I don't want to go in there.

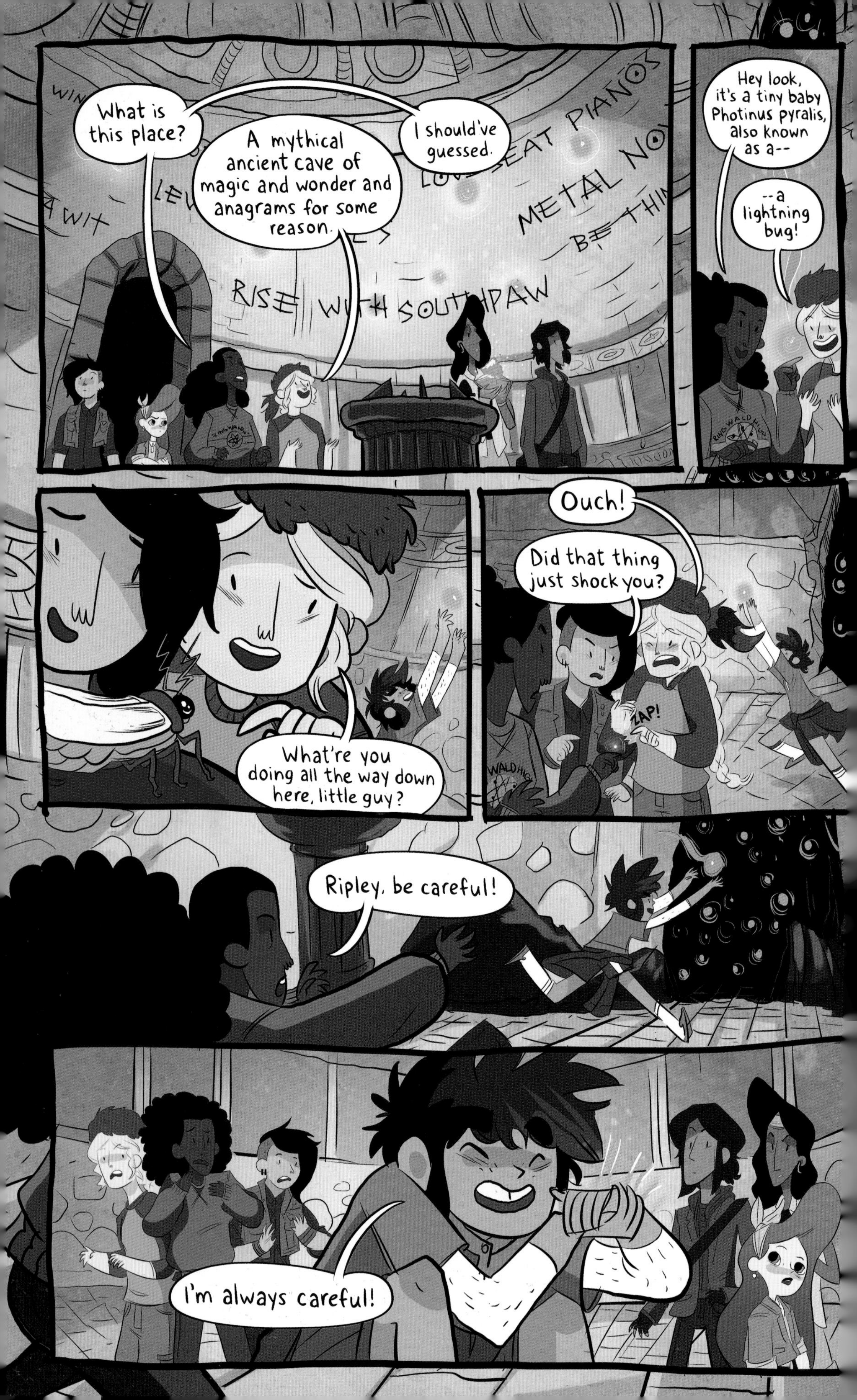

What is this place?
A mythical ancient cave of magic and wonder and anagrams for some reason.
I should've guessed.
RISE WITH SOUTHPAW
Hey look, it's a tiny baby Photinus pyralis, also known as a--
--a lightning bug!
What're you doing all the way down here, little guy?
Ouch!
Did that thing just shock you?
ZAP!
Ripley, be careful!
I'm always careful!

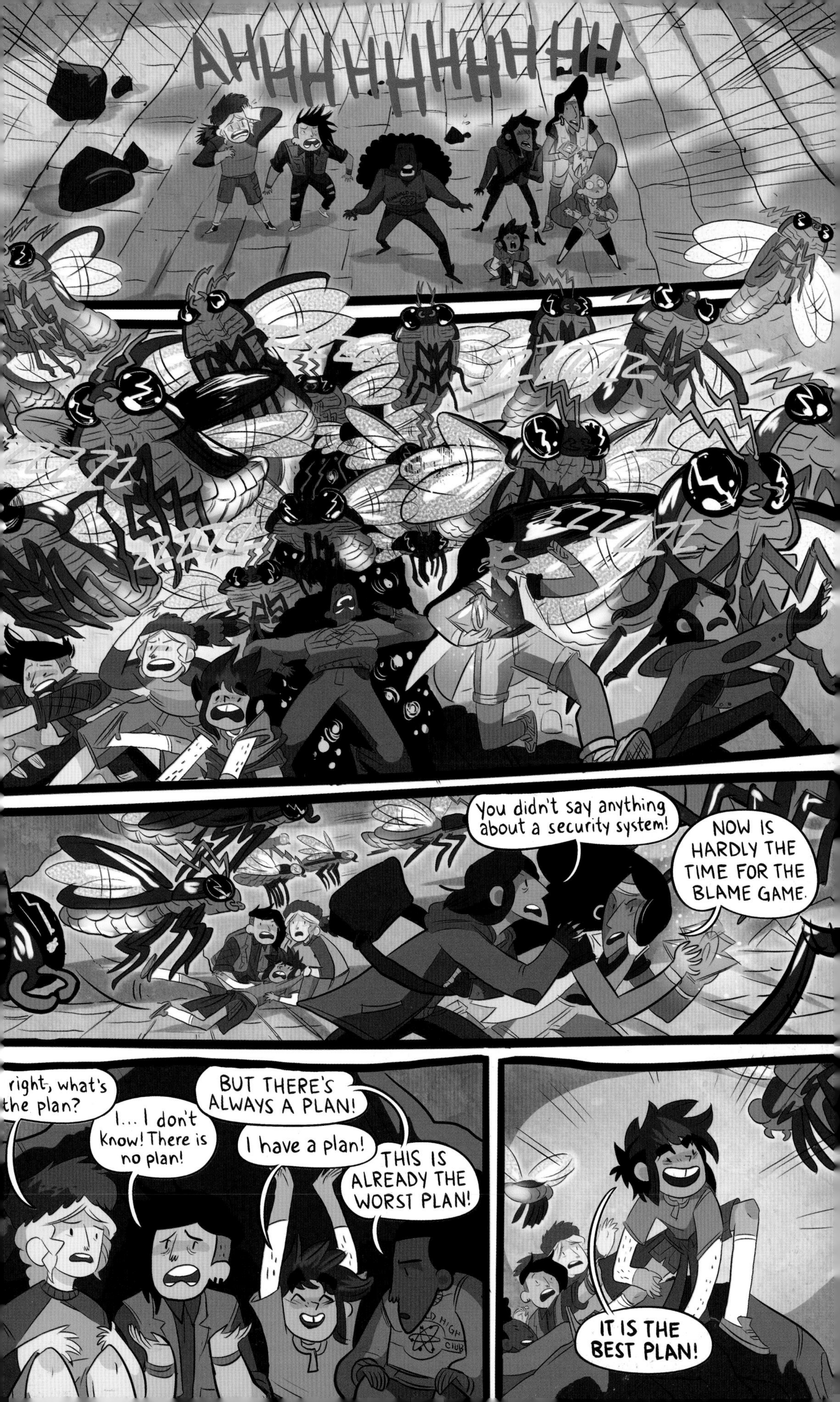
AHHHHHHHHHHH
ZZZZZZ
ZZZZZ
ZZZZZ
ZZZZZ
ZZZZZZ
You didn't say anything about a security system!
NOW IS HARDLY THE TIME FOR THE BLAME GAME.
right, what's the plan?
I... I don't know! There is no plan!
BUT THERE'S ALWAYS A PLAN!
I have a plan!
THIS IS ALREADY THE WORST PLAN!
IT IS THE BEST PLAN!

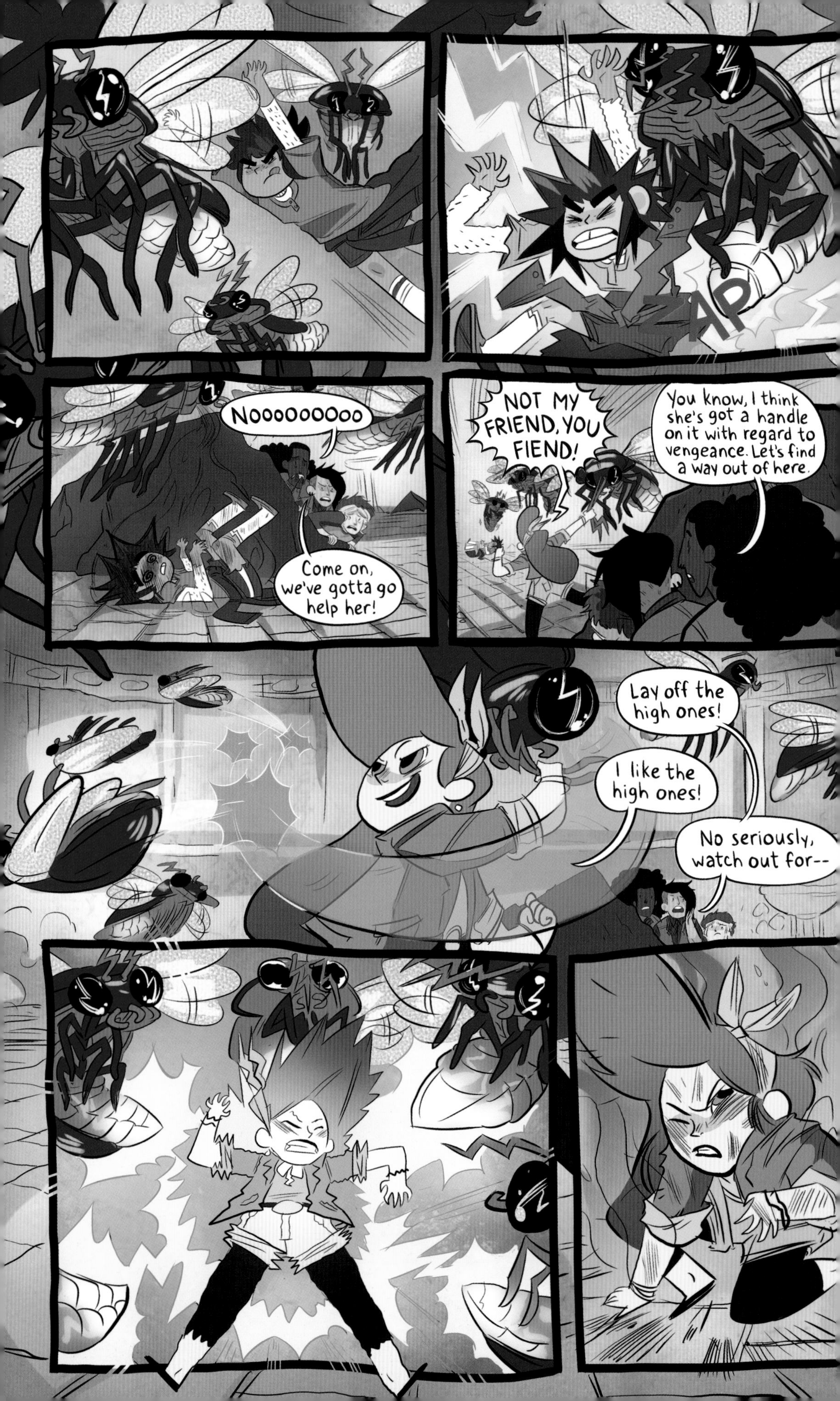

ZAP
Nooooooooo
Come on, we've gotta go help her!
NOT MY FRIEND, YOU FIEND!
You know, I think she's got a handle on it with regard to vengeance. Let's find a way out of here.
Lay off the high ones!
I like the high ones!
No seriously, watch out for--

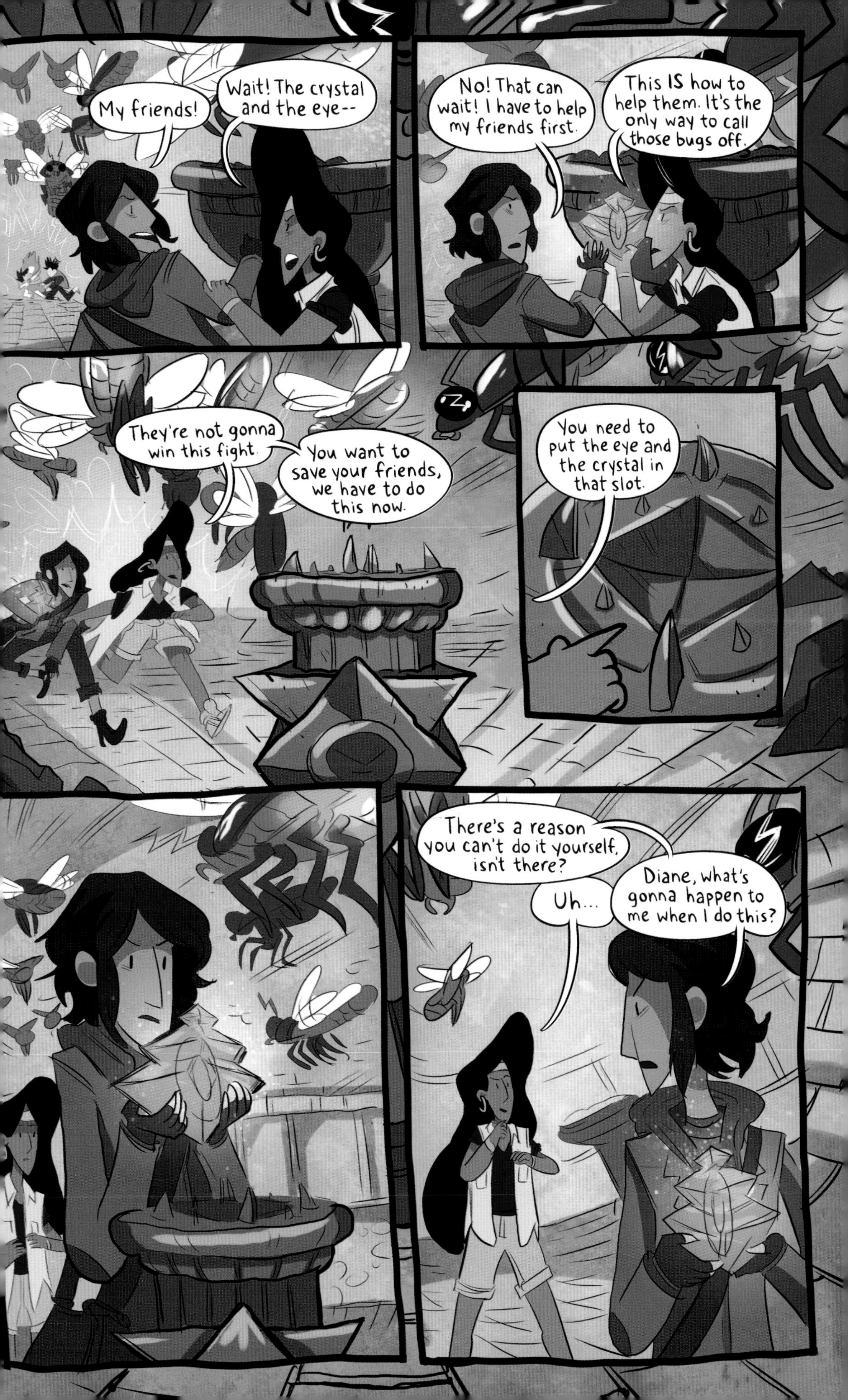
My friends!
Wait! The crystal and the eye--
No! That can wait! I have to help my friends first.
This IS how to help them. It's the only way to call those bugs off.
They're not gonna win this fight.
You want to save your friends, we have to do this now.
You need to put the eye and the crystal in that slot.
There's a reason you can't do it yourself, isn't there?
Uh...
Diane, what's gonna happen to me when I do this?

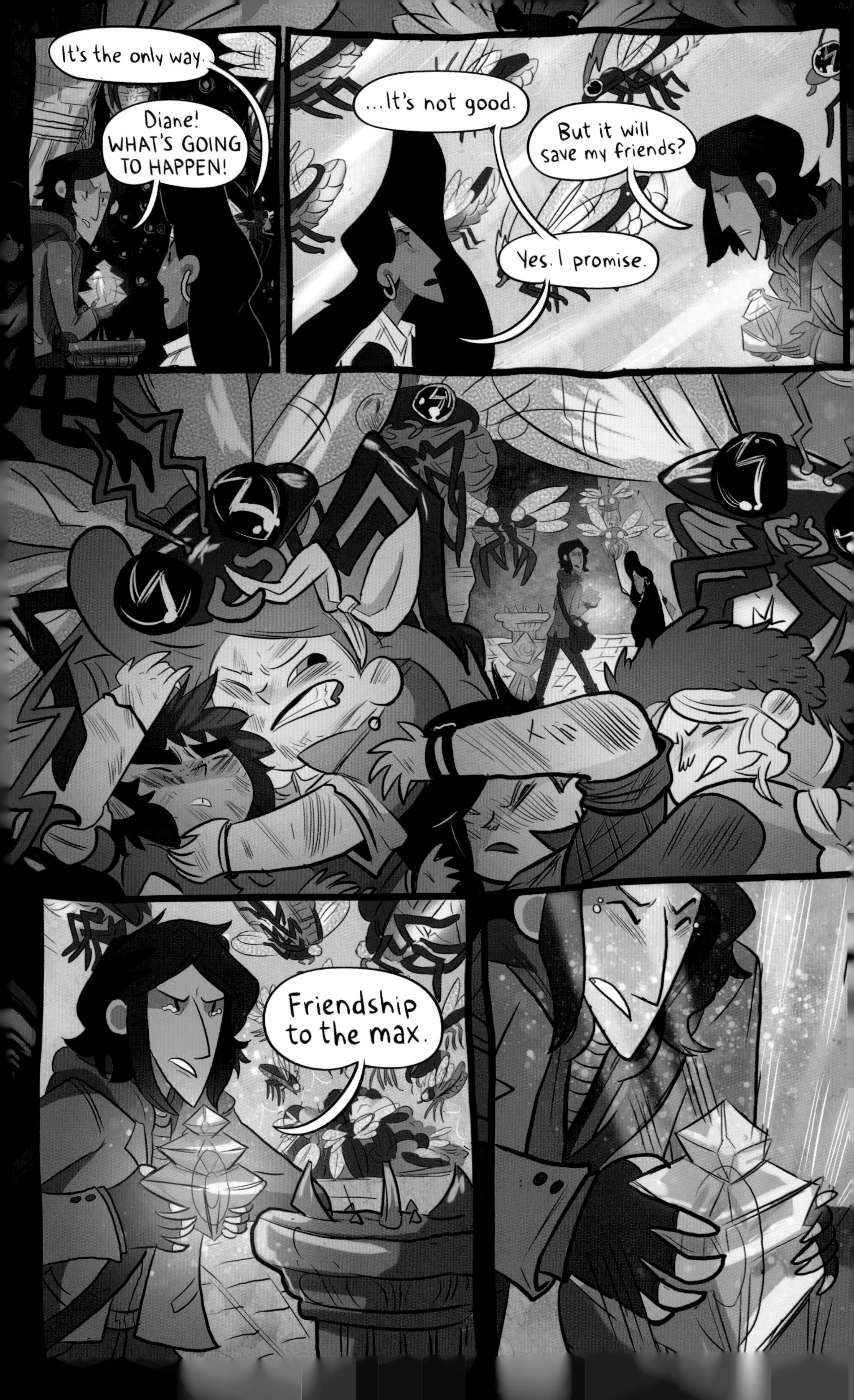
It's the only way.
Diane! WHAT'S GOING TO HAPPEN!
...It's not good.
But it will save my friends?
Yes. I promise.
Friendship to the max.

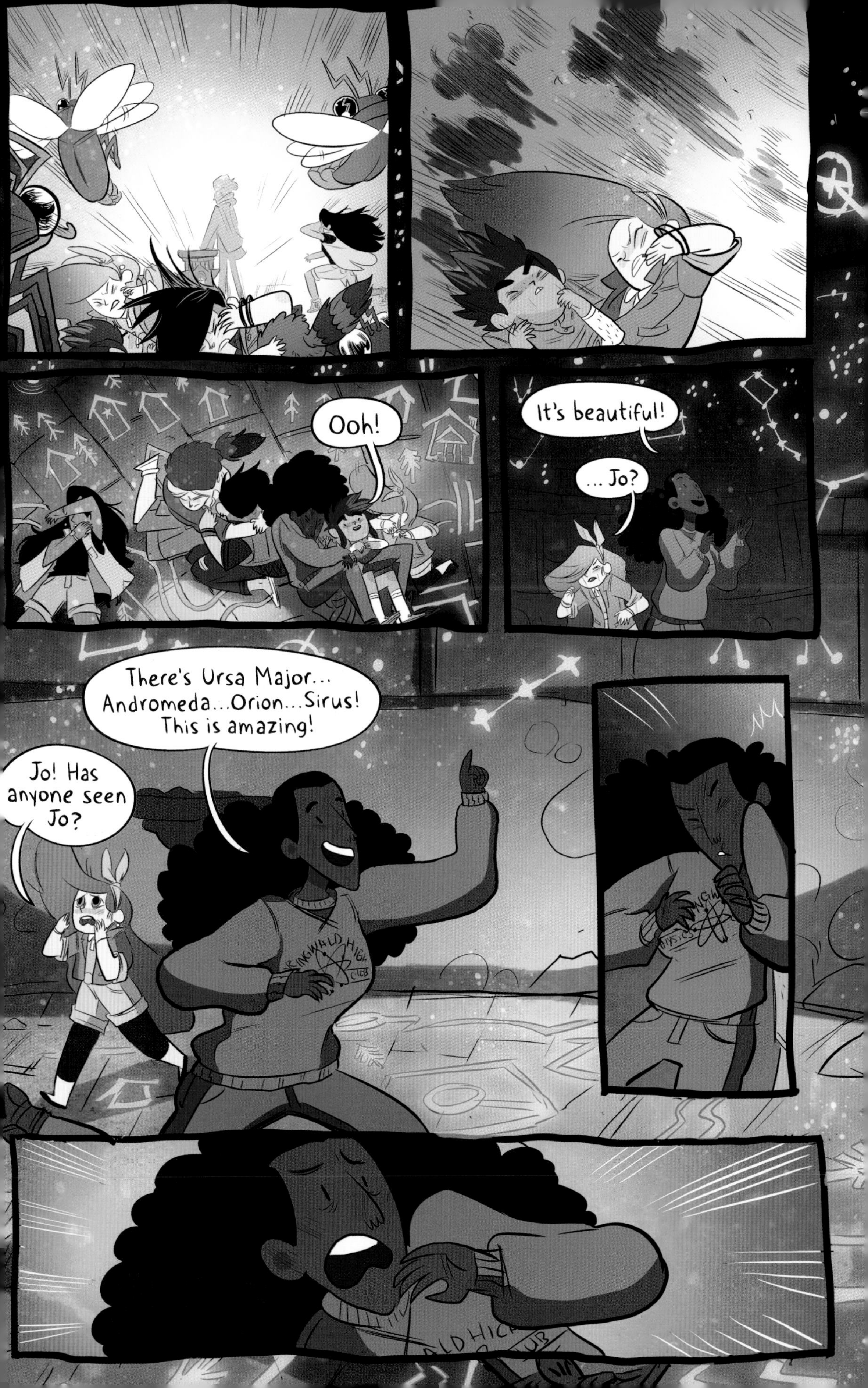
Ooh!
It's beautiful!
...Jo?
There's Ursa Major... Andromeda...Orion...Sirus! This is amazing!
Jo! Has anyone seen Jo?

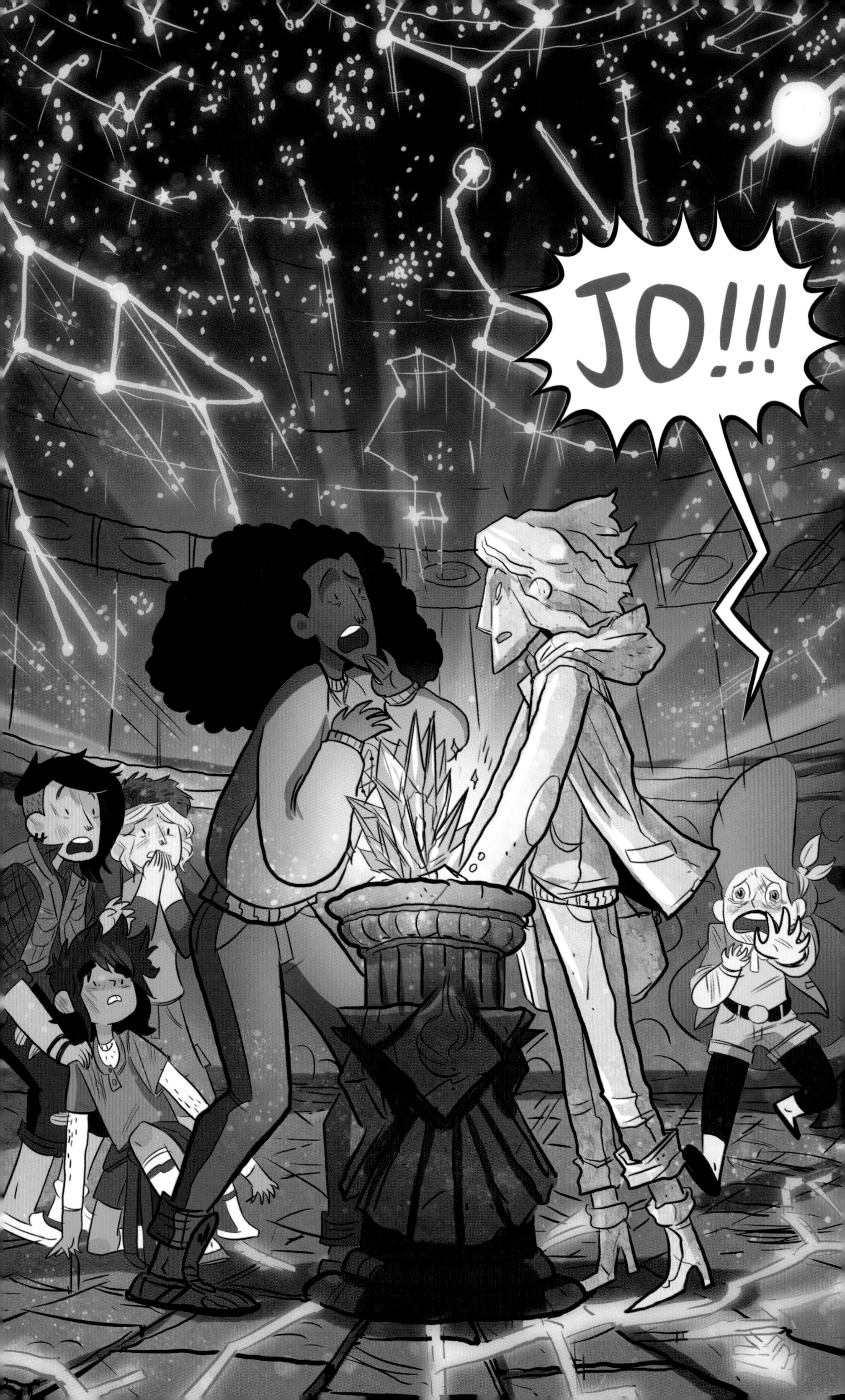
JO!!!

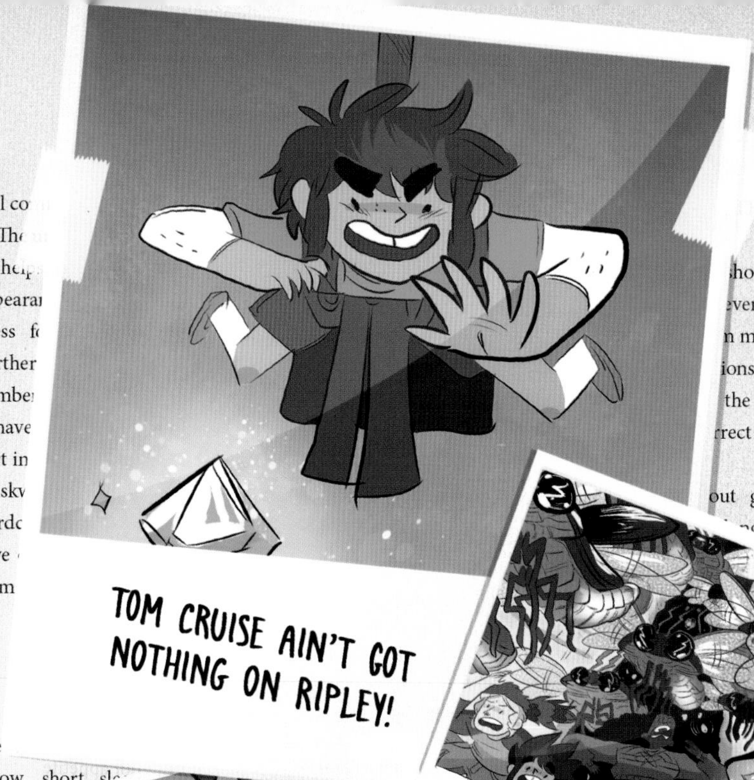
TOM CRUISE AIN'T GOT NOTHING ON RIPLEY!

will co

The

It he

appeara

dress f

Further

Lumbe

to have

part in

Thisk

Hardc

have

them

HE UNIFORM

hould be worn at camp events when Lumberjanes n may also be worn at other ions. It should be worn as a the uniform dress with rrect shoes, and stocking or

out grows her uniform or ter Lumberjane. a she has her her

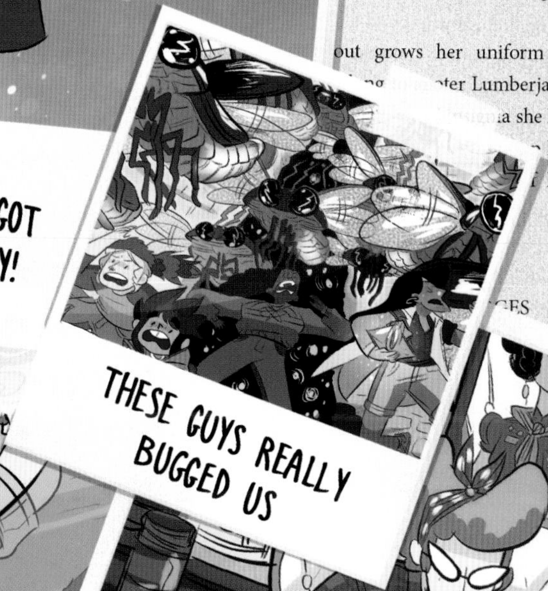
THESE GUYS REALLY BUGGED US

GES

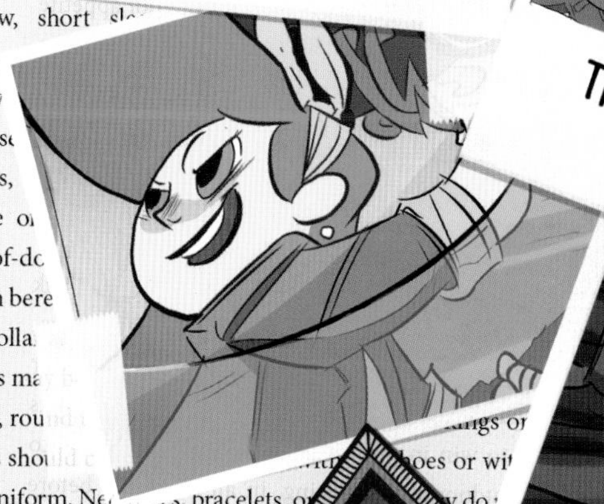

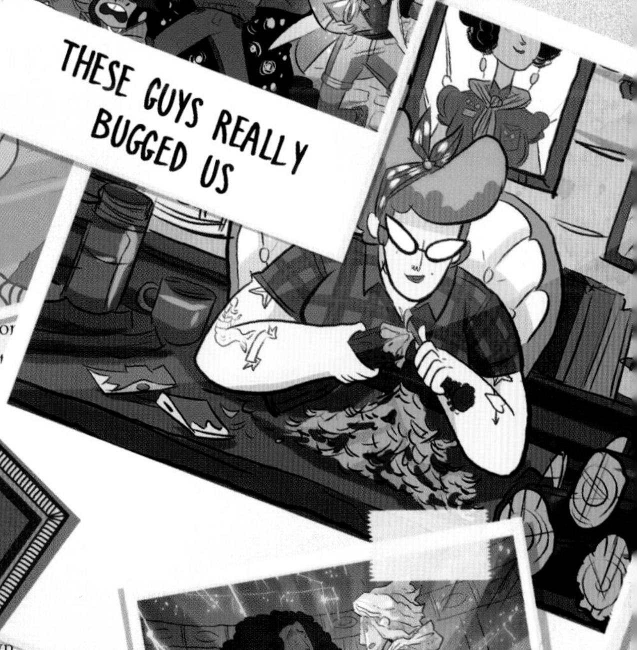

The

yellow, short

emb

the w

choose

slacks,

made o

out-of-do

green bere

the colla

Shoes ma

heels, rou ngs or

socks shou with oes or wi

the uniform. Ne es, bracelets, o do

belong with a Lumberjane unifor

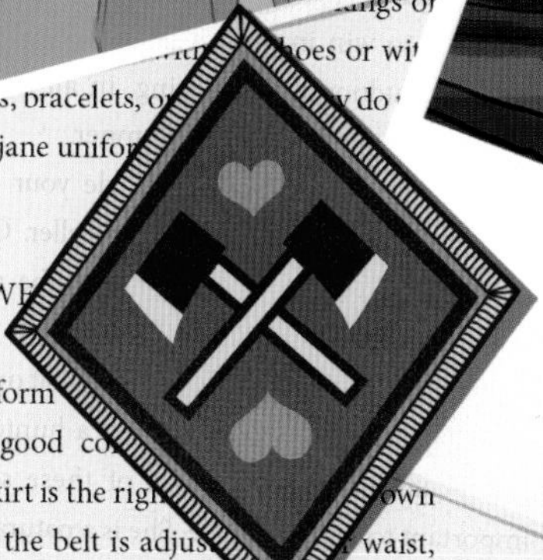

HOW TO WE

To look well in a uniform uniform be kept in good co pressed. See that the skirt is the righ own height and build, that the belt is adjus waist, that your shoes and stockings are in kee with the uniform, that you watch your posture and carry yourself with dignity and grace. If the beret is removed indoors, be sure that your hair is neat and kept in place with an insonspicuous clip or ribbon. When you wear a Lumberjane uniform you are identified as a member of this organization and you should be doubly careful to conduct yourself in a way that will show everyone that courtesy and thoughtfullness are part of being a Lumberjane. People are likely to judge a whole nation by the selfishness of a few individuals, to criticize a whole family because of the misconduct of one member, and to feel unkindly toward and organization because of the

The unifor helps to cre in a group. active life th another bond future, and pr in order to b Lumberjane pr Penniquiqul Thi re Lady Types, but m s will wish to have one. They can either bu the uniform, or make it themselves from materials available at the trading post.

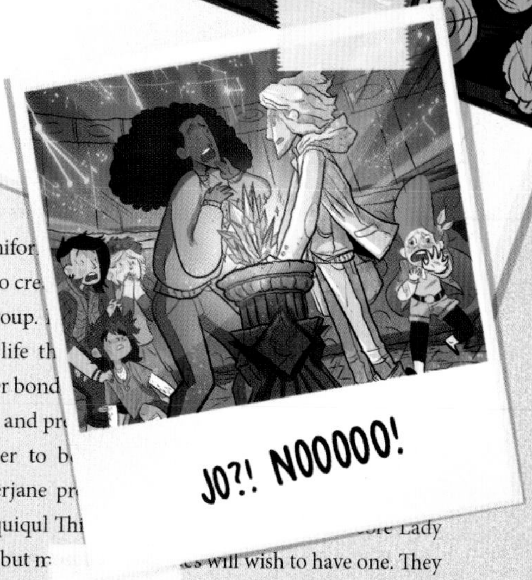
JO?! NOOOOO!

LUMBERJANES FIELD MANUAL

CHAPTER EIGHT

Lumberjanes "Out-of-Doors" Program Field

SPACE JAMBORIE BADGE

"This jam breaks the laws of physics."

Like any well rounded young woman, a Lumberjane will understand the importance of music and will do her best to remain educated enough in all music venues to ensure the possibility of polite conversation. Being a Lumberjane is more than learning skills for the great outdoors but also coming to terms on how to be a well rounded individual. She will explore the keys and notes that come with a variety of music, will be able to have a basic understanding of how to read a music sheet, and will at the very least be able to understand the importance of a steady beat even if she is not as musically inclined as her fellow scouts.

Music brings joy to everyone in life, from the earth as we understand it to beyond the stars that are impossible to know. The importance of the *Space Jamborie* badge is that it teaches poise under pressure as well as creative thinking. This badge is not earned by a well written

sonnet that hits every note that a text book would recommend but it is earned by the creative thinking that the scout puts into her work. The piece that she writes is meant to be something personal yet able to share, it will be judged by her cabin leader who will know if the scout is pushing herself.

To obtain the *Space Jamborie* badge a Lumberjane must compose and perform her own original piece. In this performance they will be able to judged on their understanding of music and on their stage presence. They are not required to perform on their own as to be a Lumberjane means to be constantly surrounded by friends, but only the main performer can earn badge at a time. While music can be considered subjective by society this badge is not judged by the standard of others but instead it is judged by the standard that a Lumberjane holds herself to. Her music will be honest

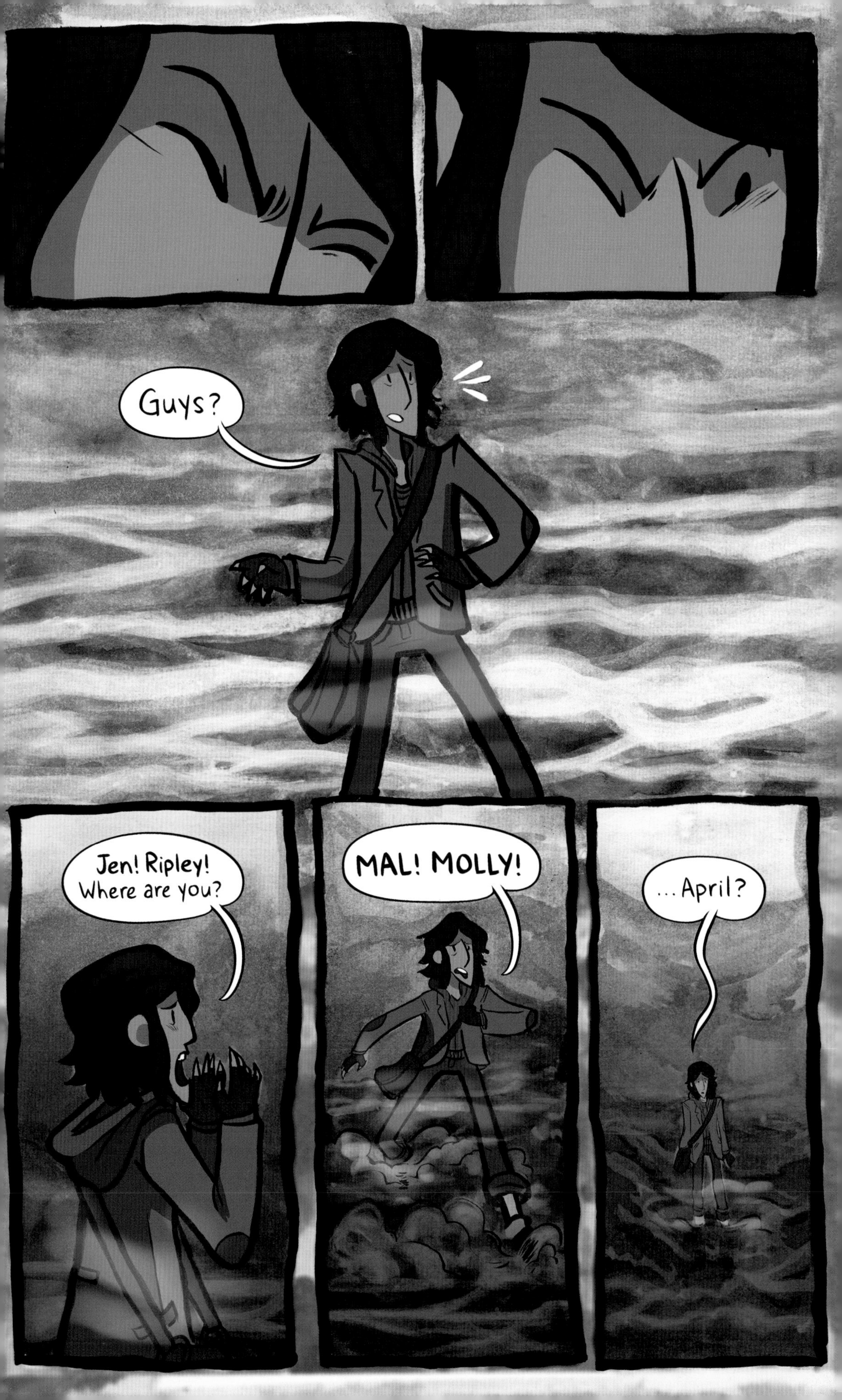
Guys?
Jen! Ripley! Where are you?
MAL! MOLLY!
...April?

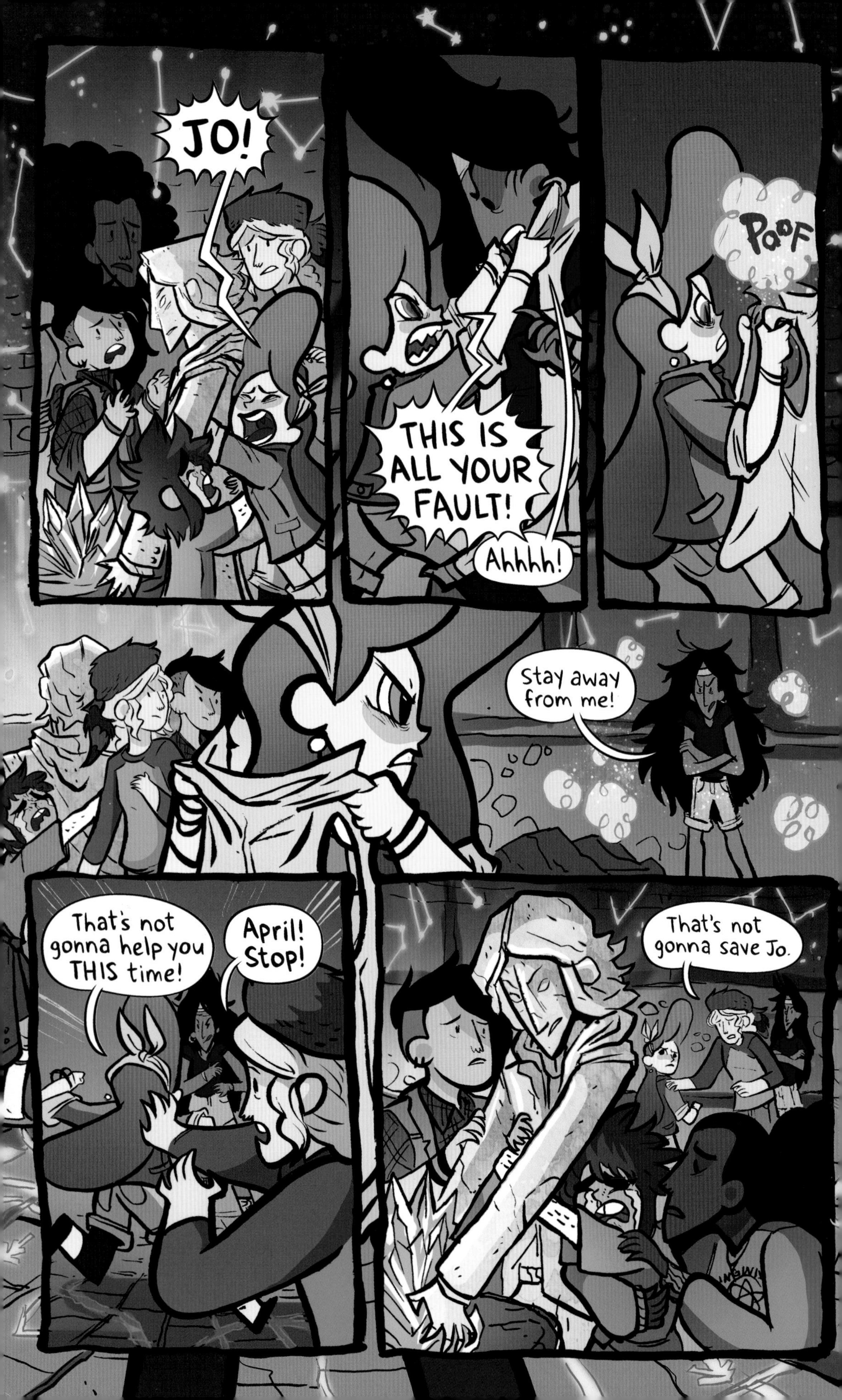
JO!
THIS IS ALL YOUR FAULT!
Ahhhh!
POOF
Stay away from me!
That's not gonna help you THIS time!
April! Stop!
That's not gonna save Jo.

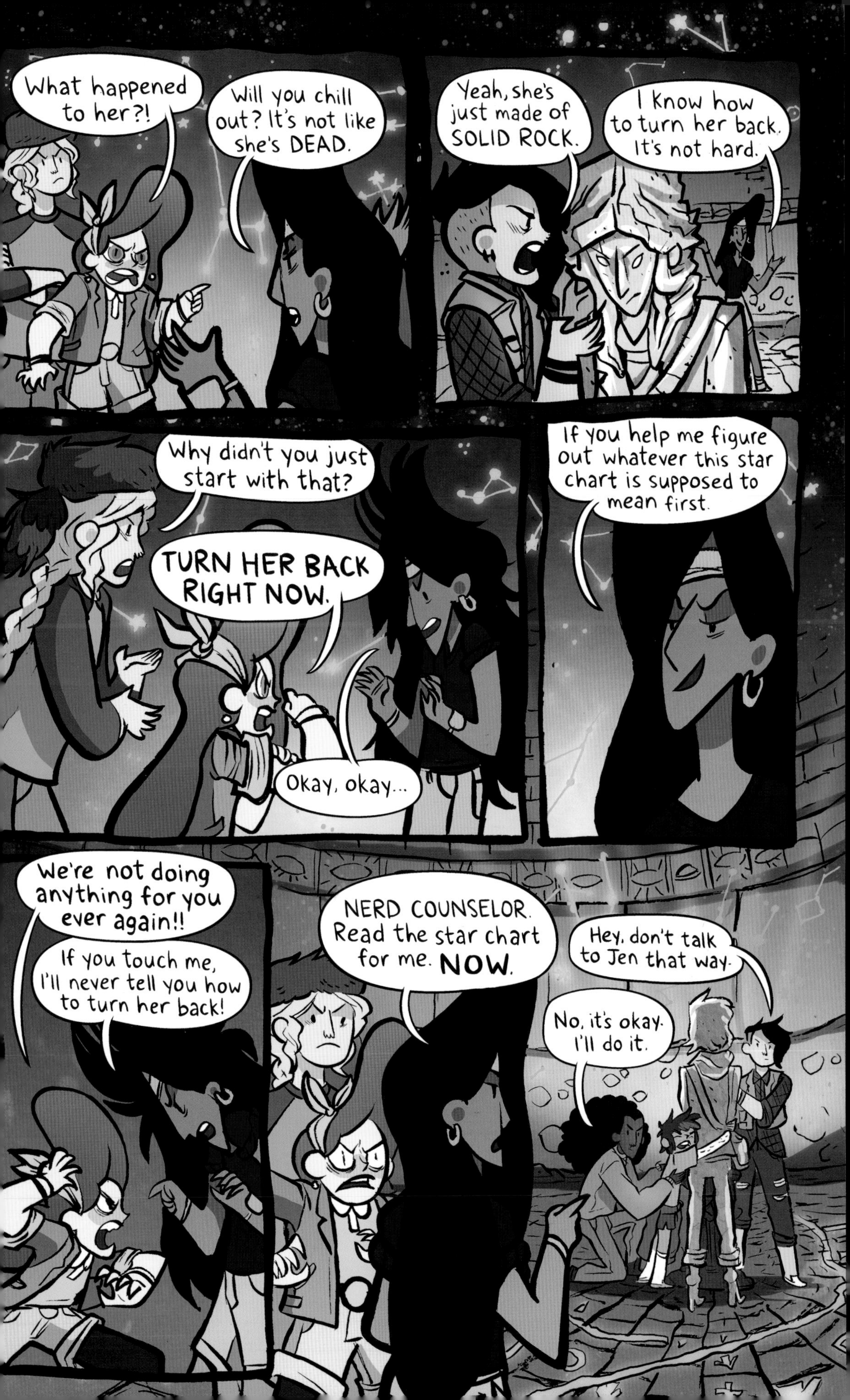
What happened to her?!
Will you chill out? It's not like she's DEAD.
Yeah, she's just made of SOLID ROCK.
I know how to turn her back. It's not hard.
Why didn't you just start with that?
TURN HER BACK RIGHT NOW.
Okay, okay...
If you help me figure out whatever this star chart is supposed to mean first.
We're not doing anything for you ever again!!
If you touch me, I'll never tell you how to turn her back!
NERD COUNSELOR. Read the star chart for me. NOW.
Hey, don't talk to Jen that way.
No, it's okay. I'll do it.

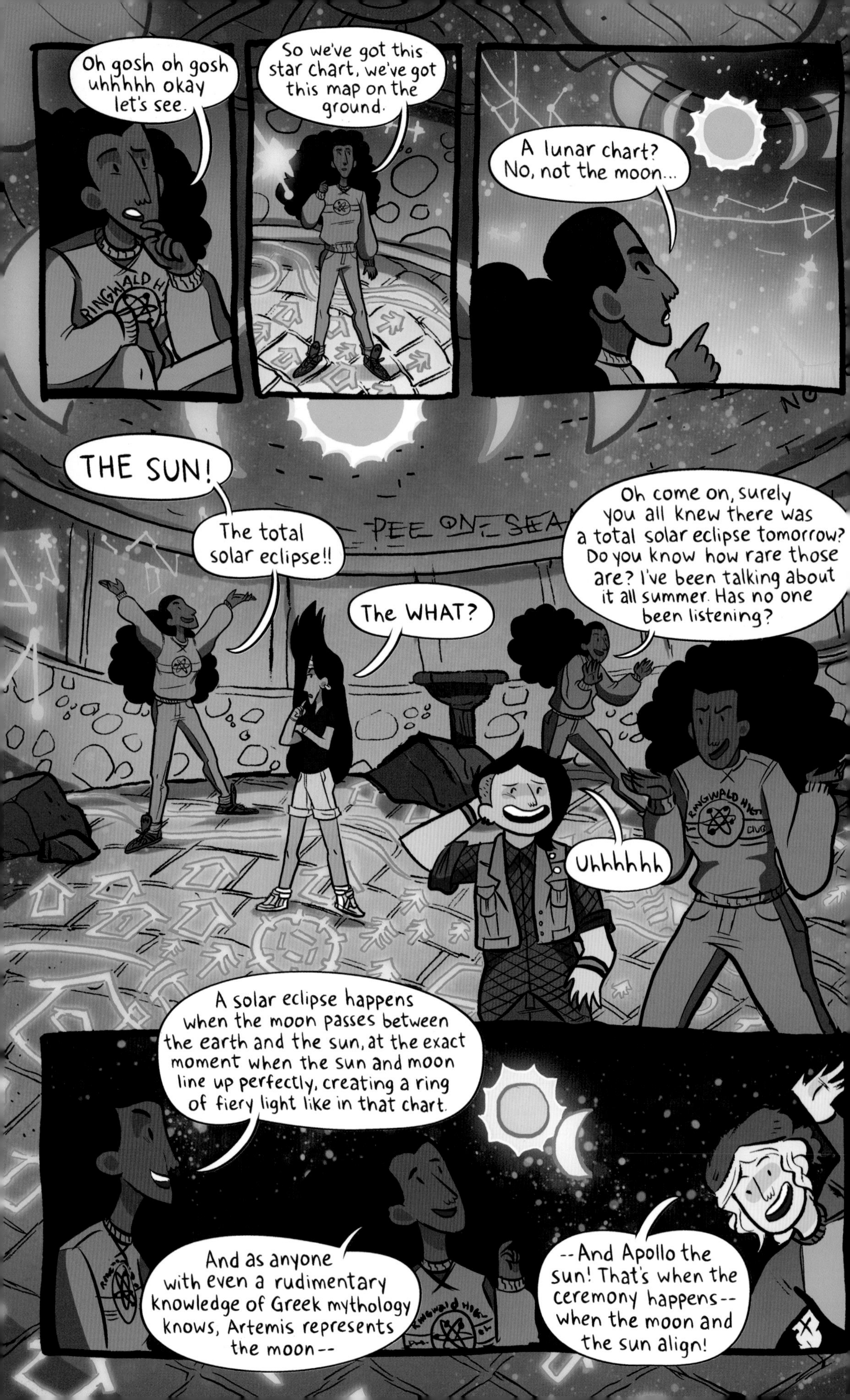
Oh gosh oh gosh uhhhhh okay let's see.
So we've got this star chart, we've got this map on the ground.
A lunar chart? No, not the moon...
THE SUN!
The total solar eclipse!!
PEE ON SEA
The WHAT?
Oh come on, surely you all knew there was a total solar eclipse tomorrow? Do you know how rare those are? I've been talking about it all summer. Has no one been listening?
Uhhhhhh
A solar eclipse happens when the moon passes between the earth and the sun, at the exact moment when the sun and moon line up perfectly, creating a ring of fiery light like in that chart.
And as anyone with even a rudimentary knowledge of Greek mythology knows, Artemis represents the moon--
--And Apollo the sun! That's when the ceremony happens--when the moon and the sun align!

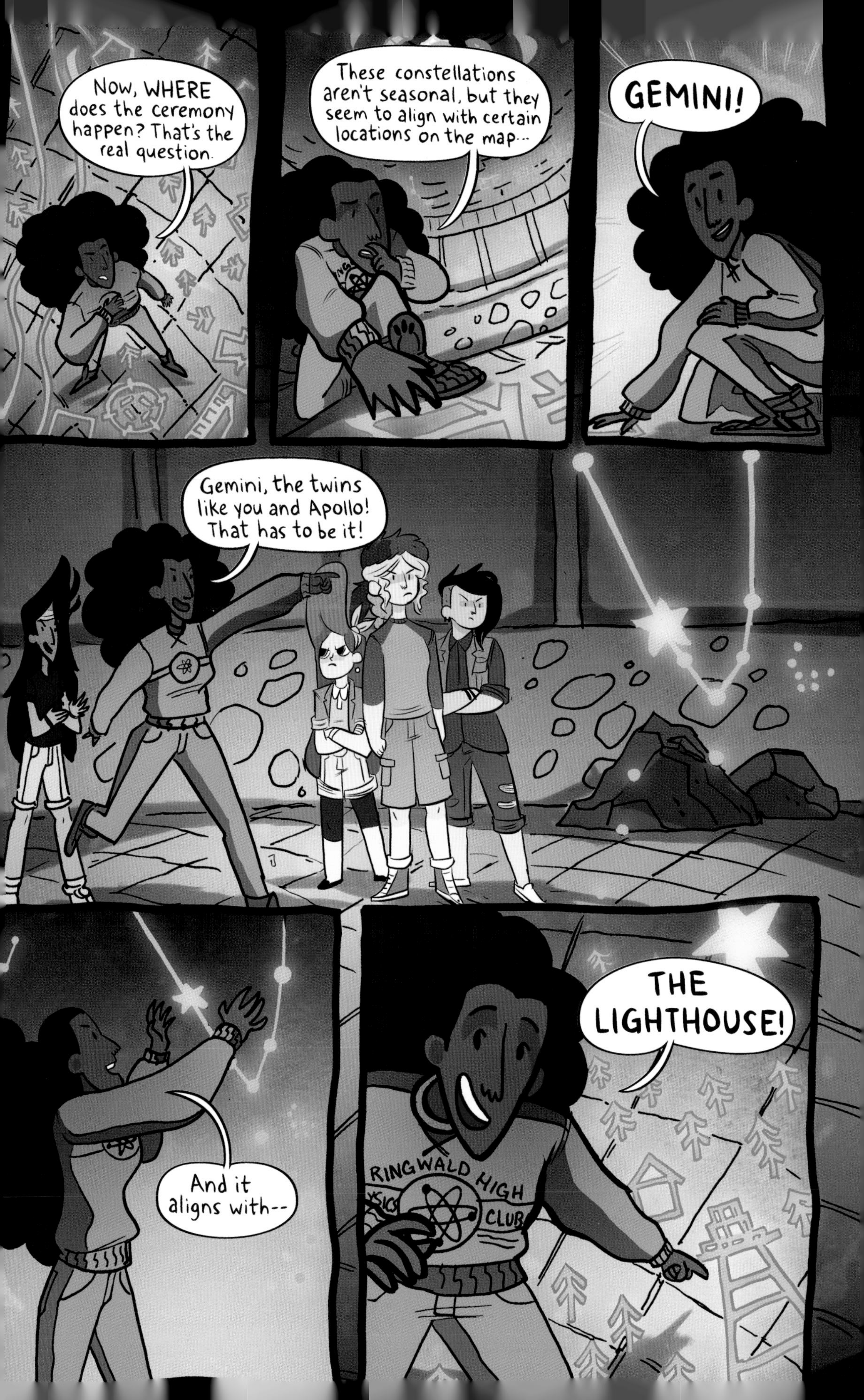
Now, WHERE does the ceremony happen? That's the real question.
These constellations aren't seasonal, but they seem to align with certain locations on the map...
GEMINI!
Gemini, the twins like you and Apollo! That has to be it!
And it aligns with--
THE LIGHTHOUSE!
RINGWALD HIGH
CLUB

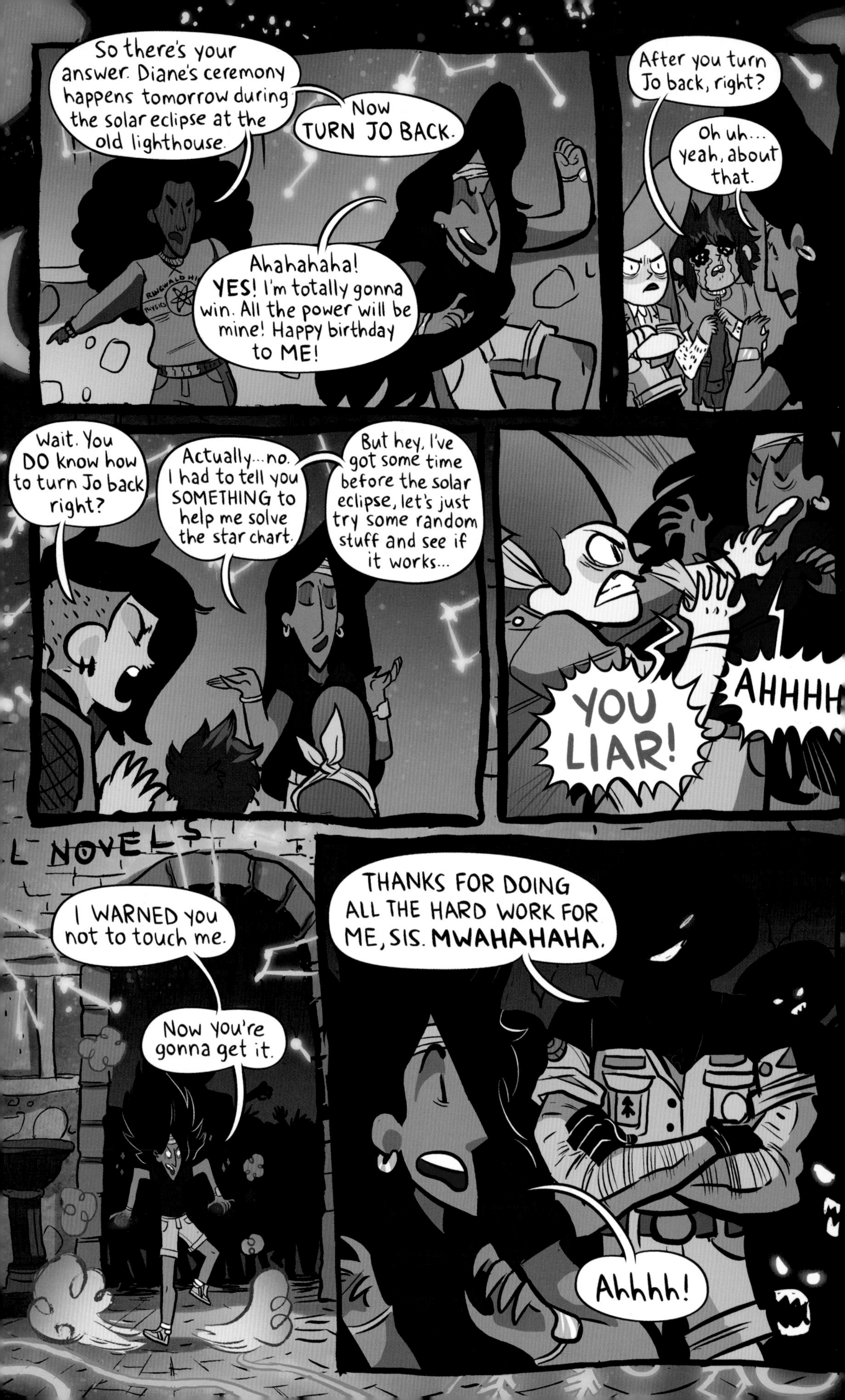

So there's your answer. Diane's ceremony happens tomorrow during the solar eclipse at the old lighthouse.
Now TURN JO BACK.
Ahahahaha! YES! I'm totally gonna win. All the power will be mine! Happy birthday to ME!
RINGWALD HI PHYSICS
After you turn Jo back, right?
Oh uh... yeah, about that.
Wait. You DO know how to turn Jo back right?
Actually... no. I had to tell you SOMETHING to help me solve the star chart.
But hey, I've got some time before the solar eclipse, let's just try some random stuff and see if it works...
YOU LIAR!
AHHHH
L NOVELS
I WARNED you not to touch me.
Now you're gonna get it.
THANKS FOR DOING ALL THE HARD WORK FOR ME, SIS. MWAHAHAHA.
Ahhhh!

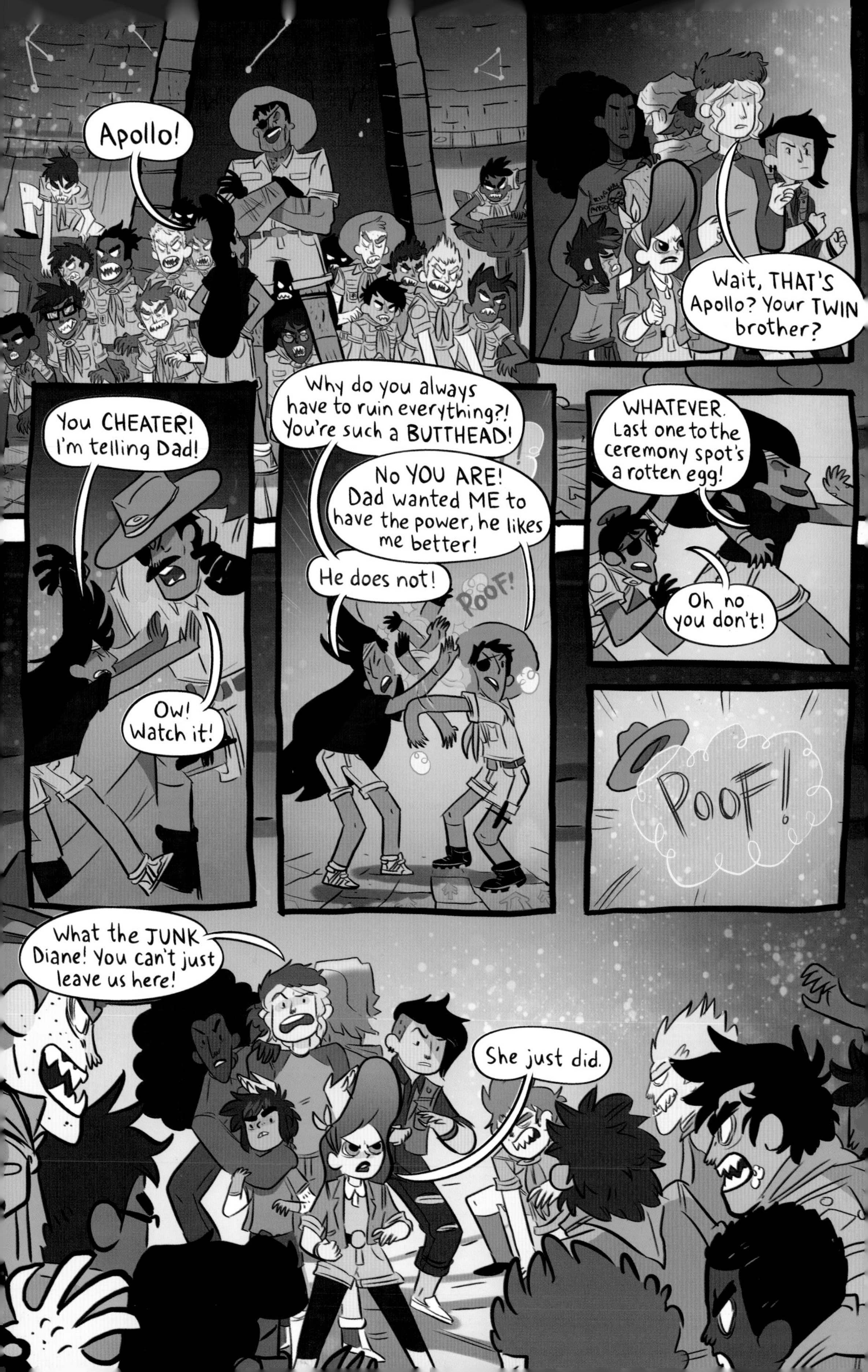
Apollo!
Wait, THAT'S Apollo? Your TWIN brother?
You CHEATER! I'm telling Dad!
Ow! Watch it!
Why do you always have to ruin everything?! You're such a BUTTHEAD!
No YOU ARE! Dad wanted ME to have the power, he likes me better!
He does not!
POOF!
WHATEVER. Last one to the ceremony spot's a rotten egg!
Oh no you don't!
POOF!
What the JUNK Diane! You can't just leave us here!
She just did.

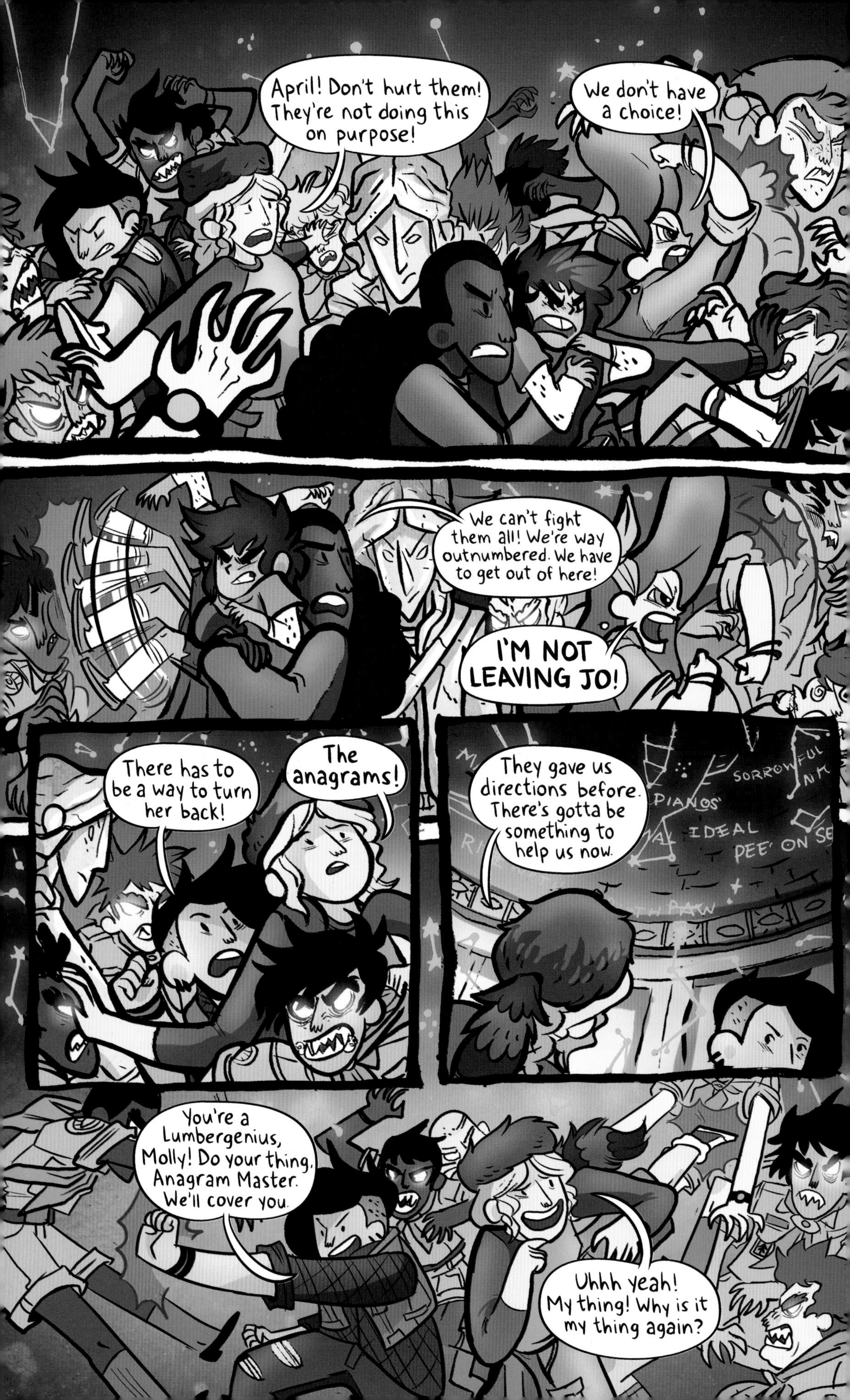
April! Don't hurt them! They're not doing this on purpose!
We don't have a choice!
We can't fight them all! We're way outnumbered. We have to get out of here!
I'M NOT LEAVING JO!
There has to be a way to turn her back!
The anagrams!
They gave us directions before. There's gotta be something to help us now.
SORROWFUL
PIANOS'
IDEAL
You're a Lumbergenius, Molly! Do your thing, Anagram Master. We'll cover you.
Uhhh yeah! My thing! Why is it my thing again?

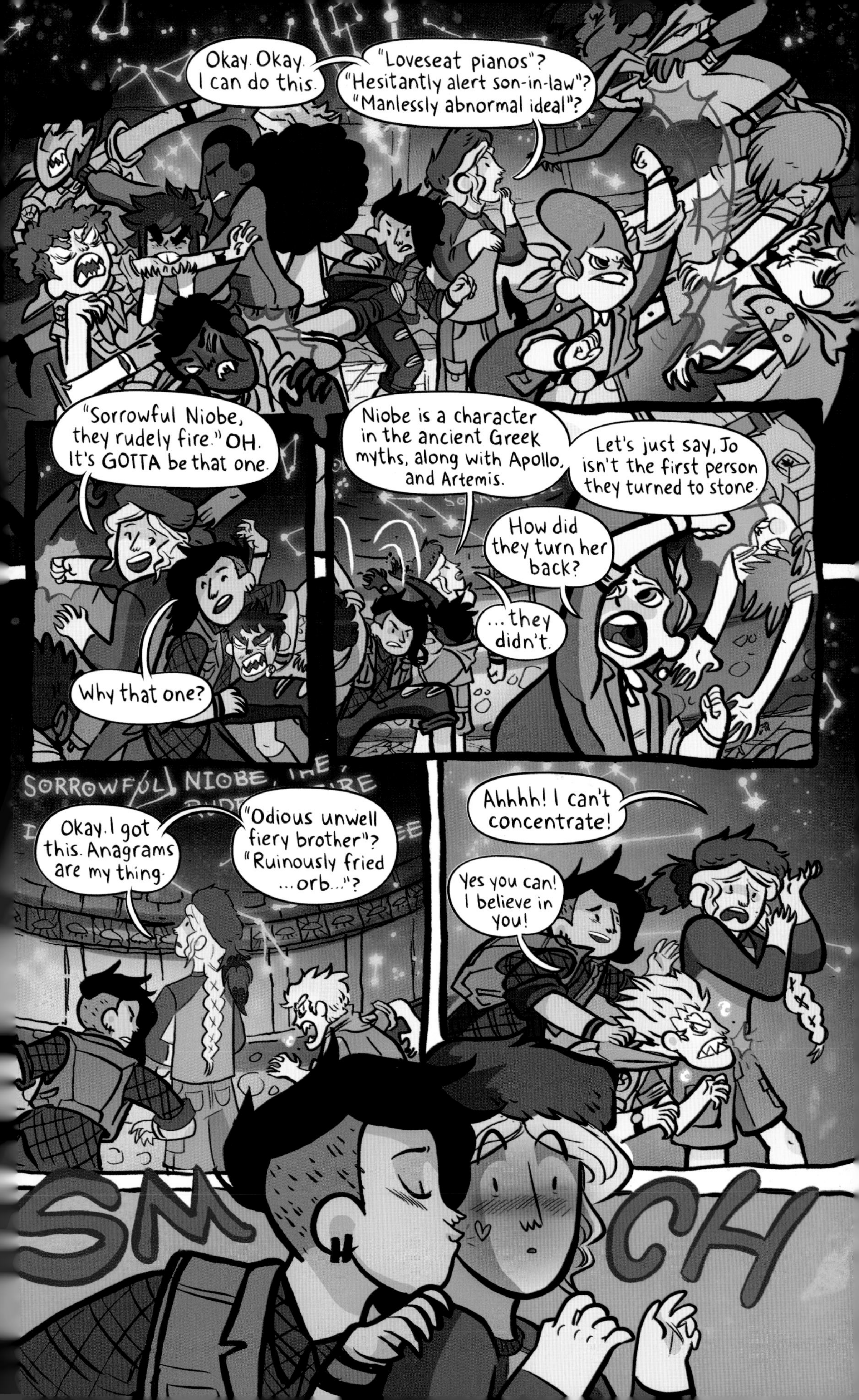
Okay. Okay. I can do this.
"Loveseat pianos"? "Hesitantly alert son-in-law"? "Manlessly abnormal ideal"?
"Sorrowful Niobe, they rudely fire." OH. It's GOTTA be that one.
Why that one?
Niobe is a character in the ancient Greek myths, along with Apollo, and Artemis.
Let's just say, Jo isn't the first person they turned to stone.
How did they turn her back?
...they didn't.
SORROWFUL NIOBE, THEY RUDELY FIRE
Okay. I got this. Anagrams are my thing.
"Odious unwell fiery brother"? "Ruinously fried ...orb..."?
Ahhhh! I can't concentrate!
Yes you can! I believe in you!
SMOOCH

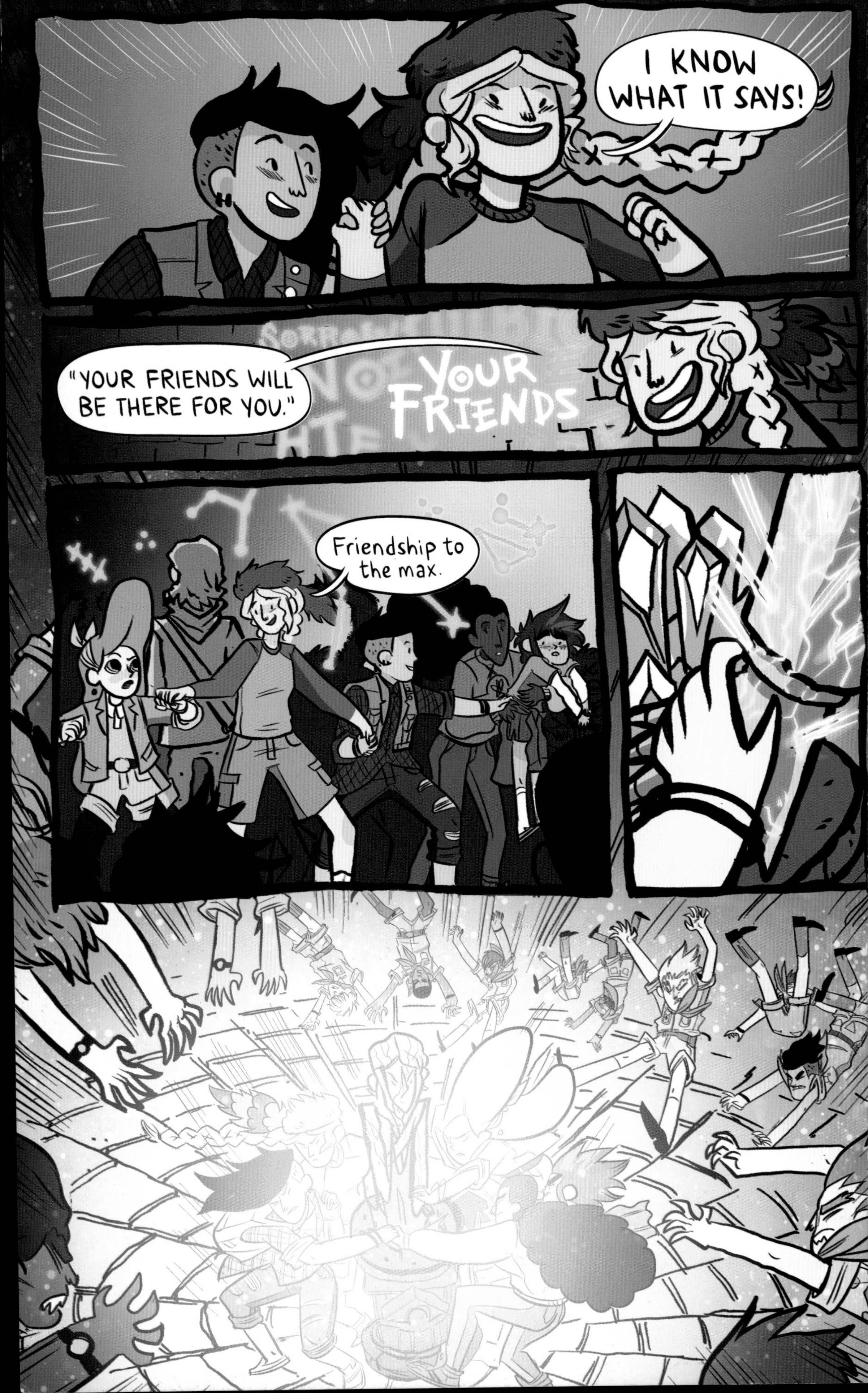
I KNOW WHAT IT SAYS!
"YOUR FRIENDS WILL BE THERE FOR YOU."
YOUR FRIENDS
Friendship to the max.

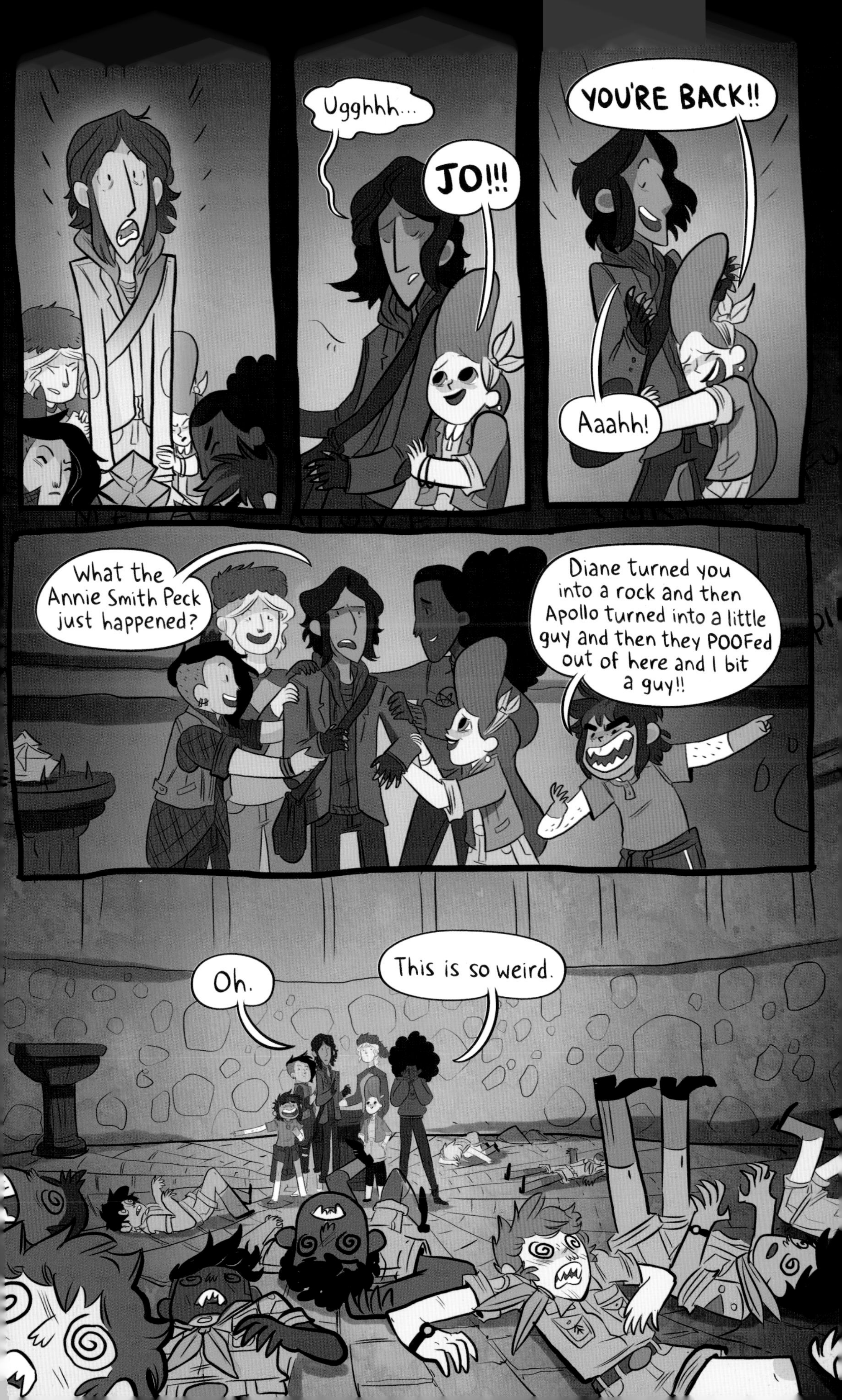
Ugghhh...
JO!!!
YOU'RE BACK!!
Aaahh!
What the Annie Smith Peck just happened?
Diane turned you into a rock and then Apollo turned into a little guy and then they POOFed out of here and I bit a guy!!
Oh.
This is so weird.

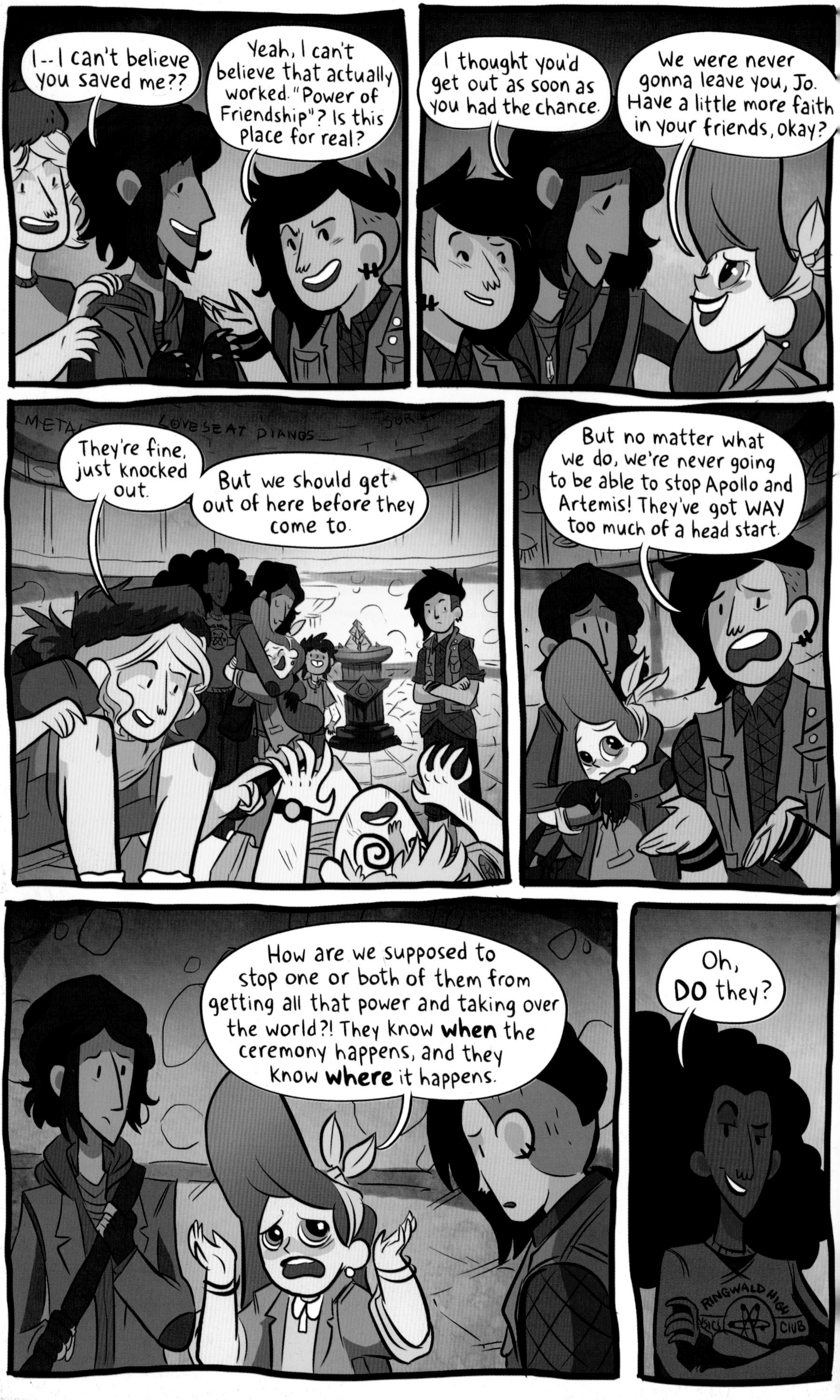

I--I can't believe you saved me??
Yeah, I can't believe that actually worked. "Power of Friendship"? Is this place for real?
I thought you'd get out as soon as you had the chance.
We were never gonna leave you, Jo. Have a little more faith in your friends, okay?
METAL
LOVESEAT PIANOS
They're fine, just knocked out.
But we should get out of here before they come to.
But no matter what we do, we're never going to be able to stop Apollo and Artemis! They've got WAY too much of a head start.
How are we supposed to stop one or both of them from getting all that power and taking over the world?! They know **when** the ceremony happens, and they know **where** it happens.
Oh, **DO** they?
RINGWALD HIGH
CLUB

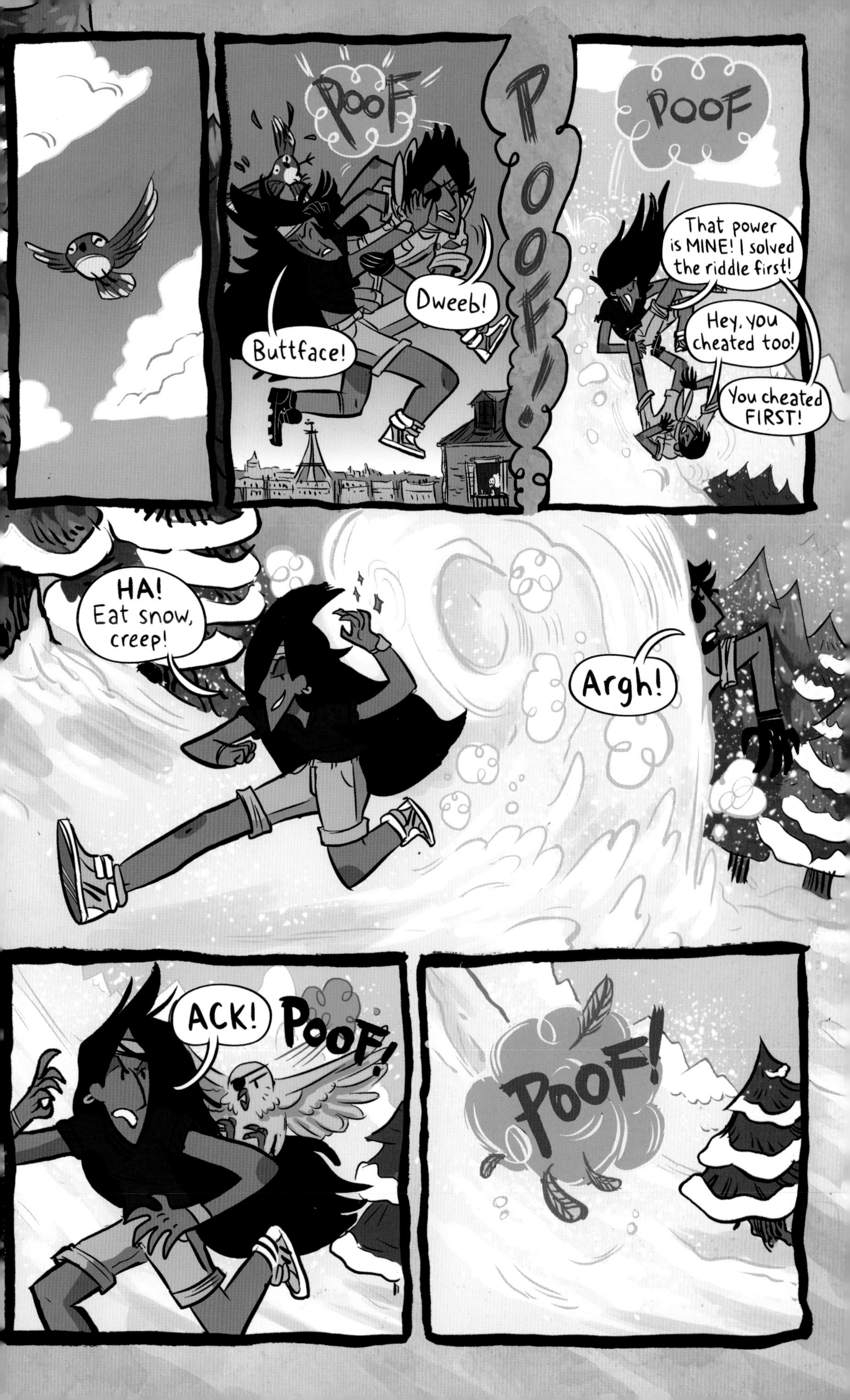
POOF
Dweeb!
Buttface!
POOF!
POOF
That power is MINE! I solved the riddle first!
Hey, you cheated too!
You cheated FIRST!
HA! Eat snow, creep!
Argh!
ACK!
POOF!
POOF!

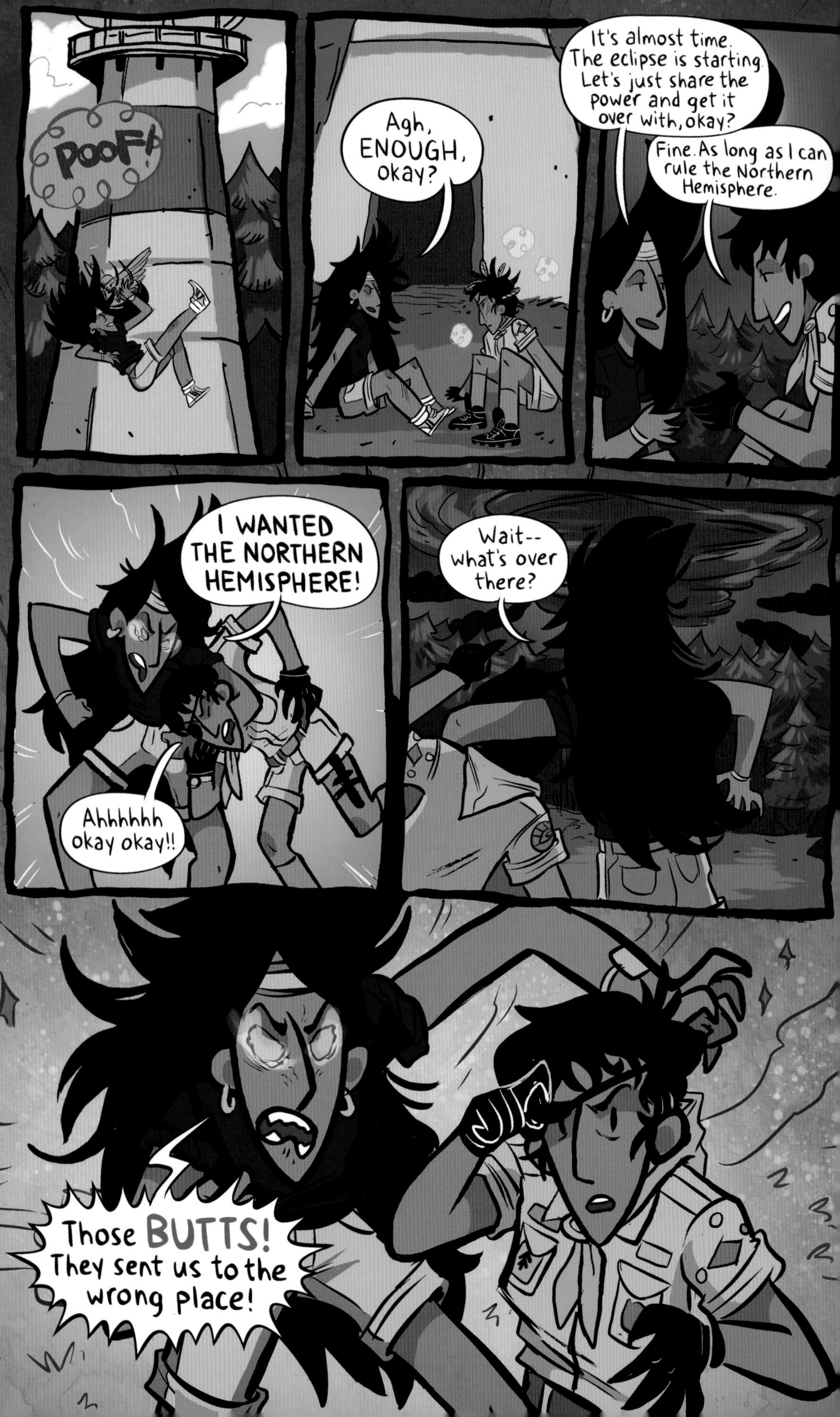
POOF!
Agh, ENOUGH, okay?
It's almost time. The eclipse is starting. Let's just share the power and get it over with, okay?
Fine. As long as I can rule the Northern Hemisphere.
I WANTED THE NORTHERN HEMISPHERE!
Ahhhhhh okay okay!!
Wait-- what's over there?
Those BUTTS! They sent us to the wrong place!

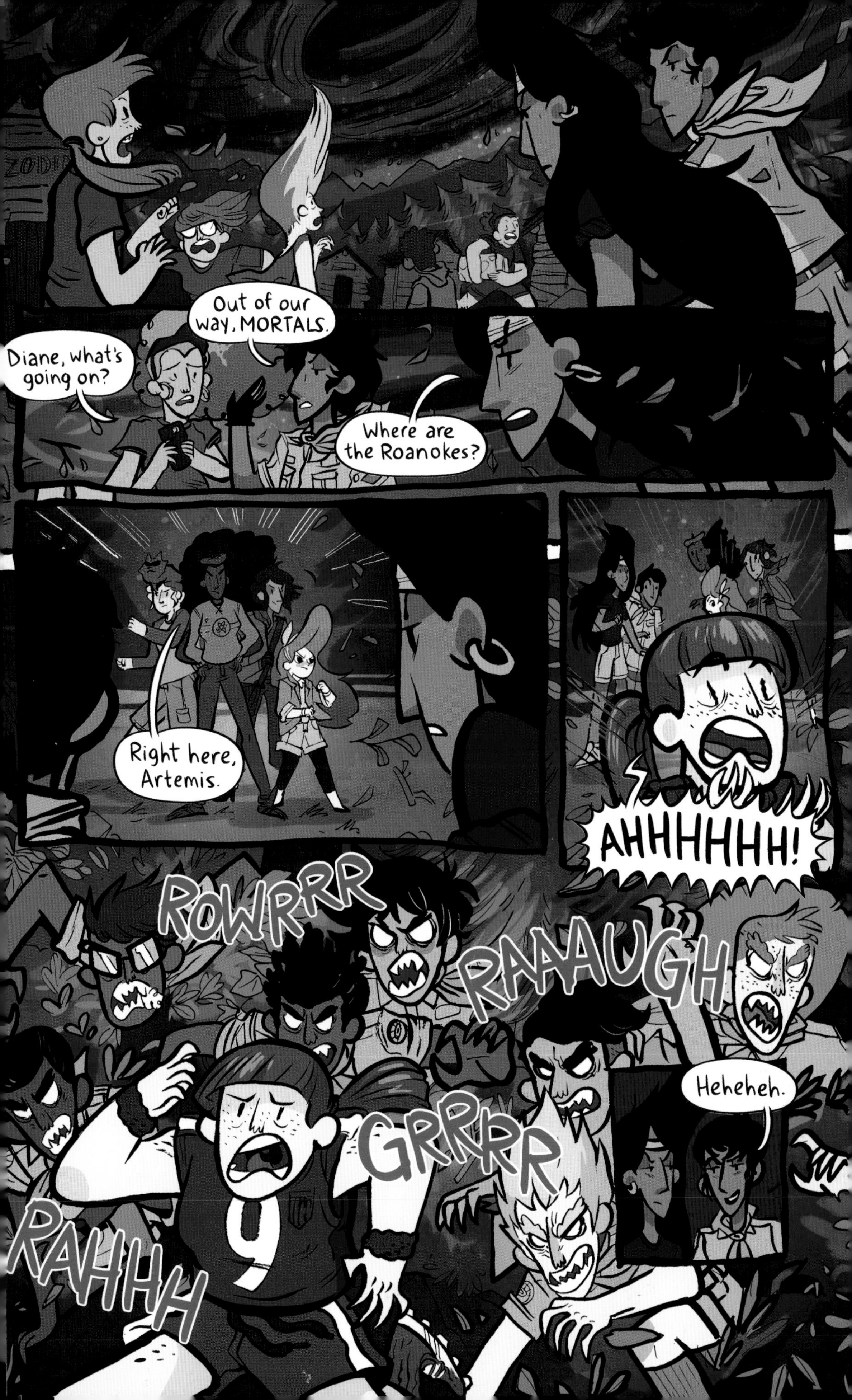
ZODI
Out of our way, MORTALS.
Diane, what's going on?
Where are the Roanokes?
Right here, Artemis.
AHHHHHH!
ROWRRR
RAAAUGH
Heheheh.
GRRRR
RAHHH

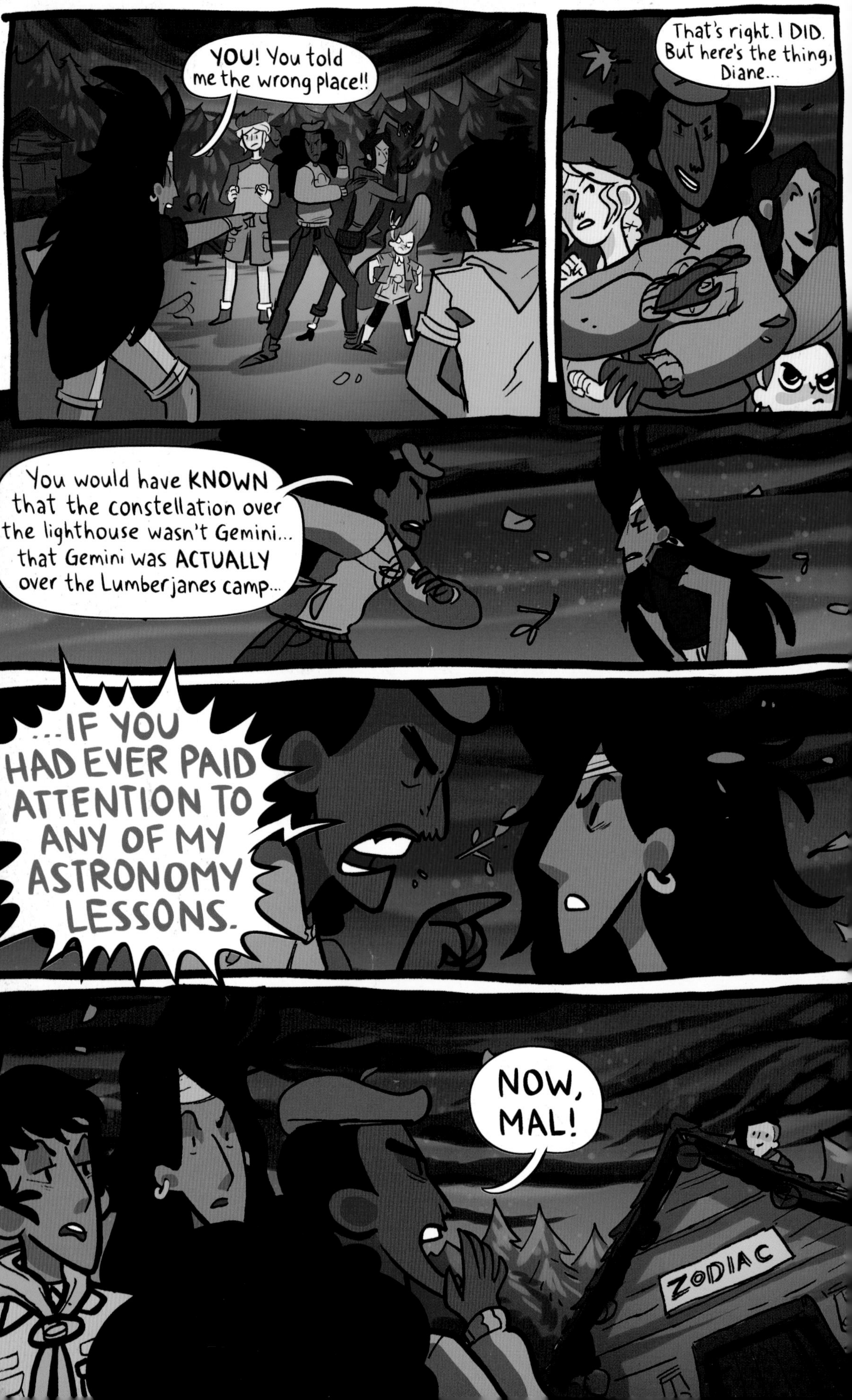
YOU! You told me the wrong place!!
That's right. I DID. But here's the thing, Diane...
You would have KNOWN that the constellation over the lighthouse wasn't Gemini... that Gemini was ACTUALLY over the Lumberjanes camp...
...IF YOU HAD EVER PAID ATTENTION TO ANY OF MY ASTRONOMY LESSONS.
NOW, MAL!
ZODIAC

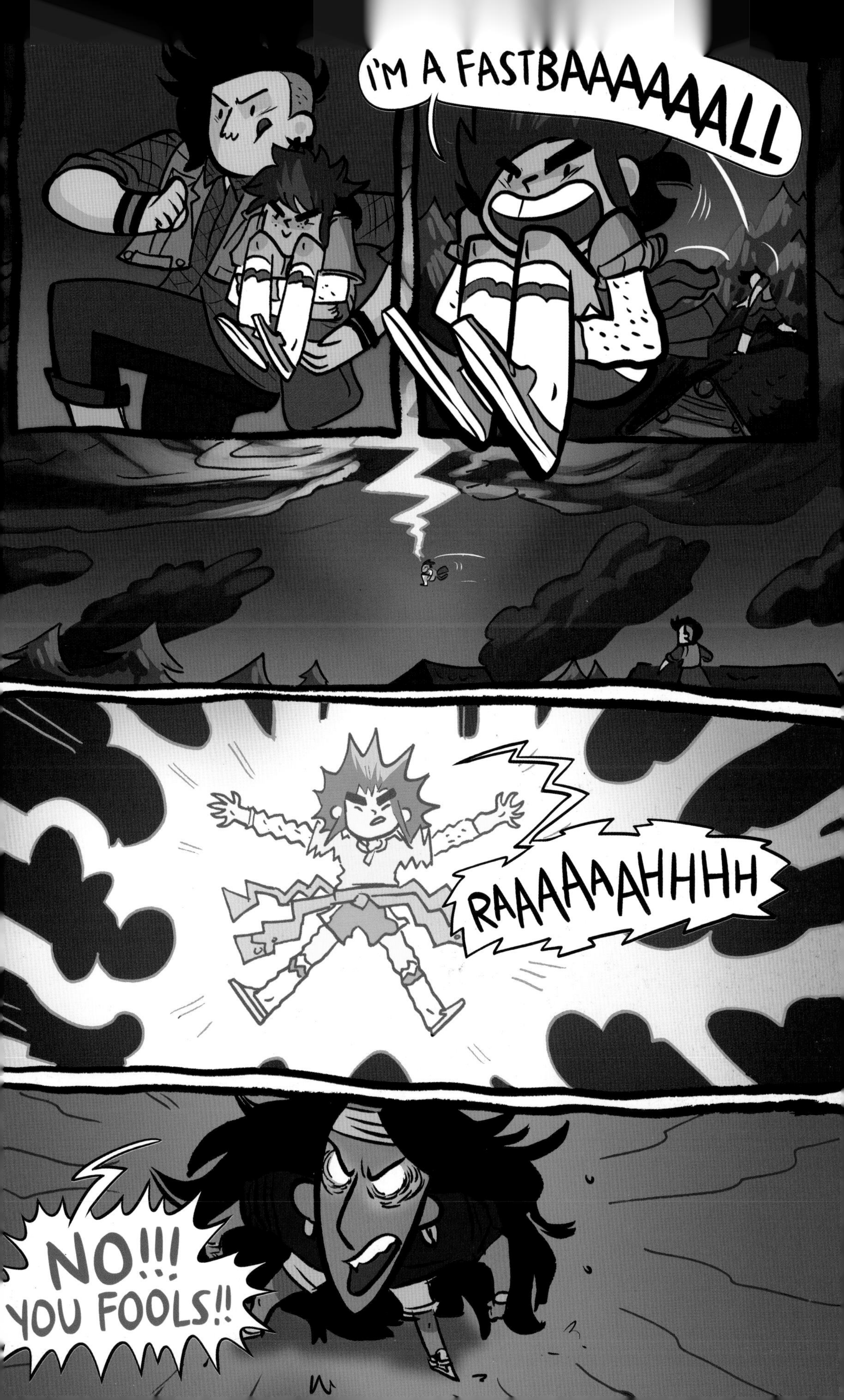
I'M A FASTBAAAAAAALL
RAAAAAAHHHH
NO!!! YOU FOOLS!!

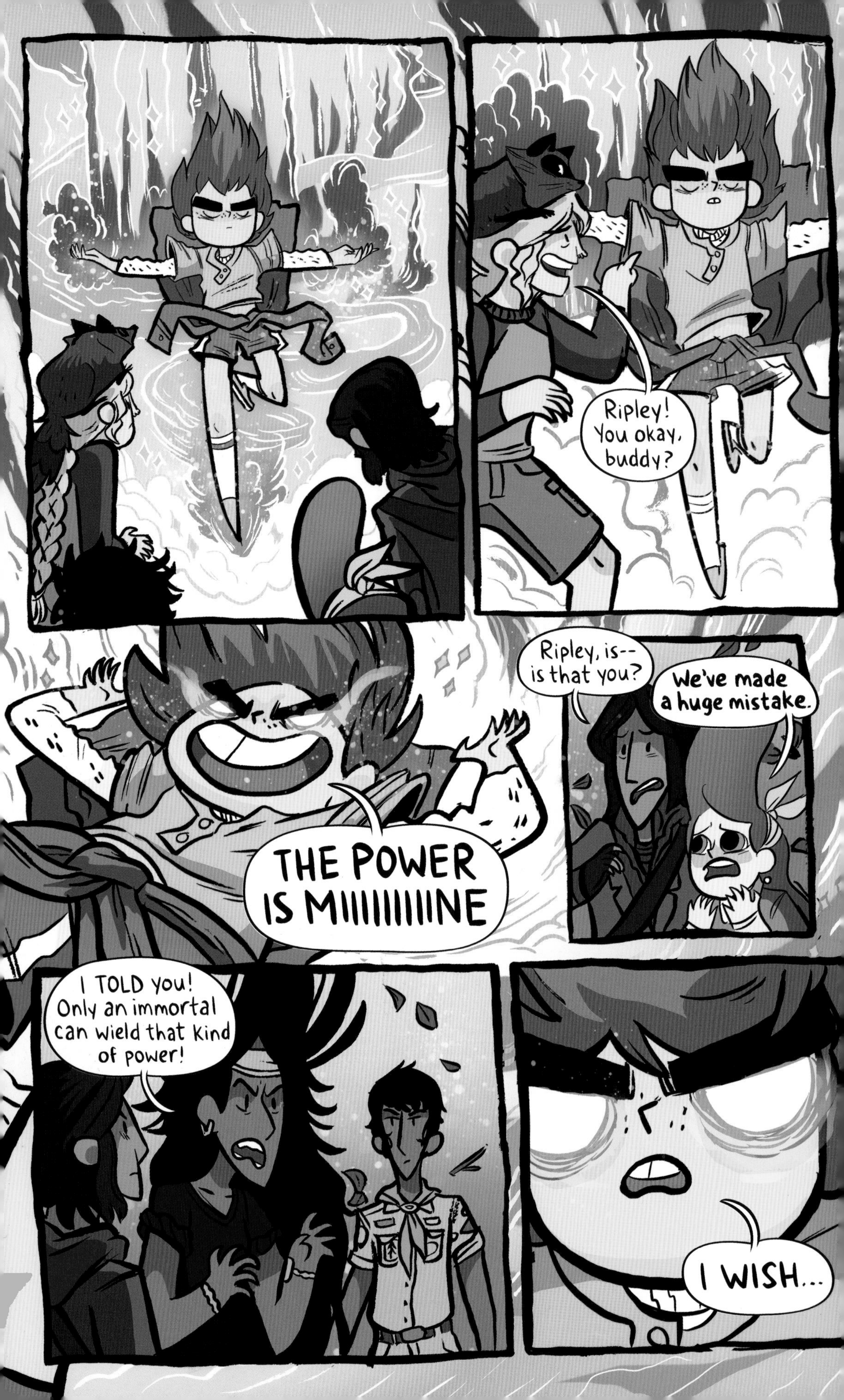
Ripley! You okay, buddy?
THE POWER IS MIIIIIIIIINE
Ripley, is-- is that you?
We've made a huge mistake.
I TOLD you! Only an immortal can wield that kind of power!
I WISH...

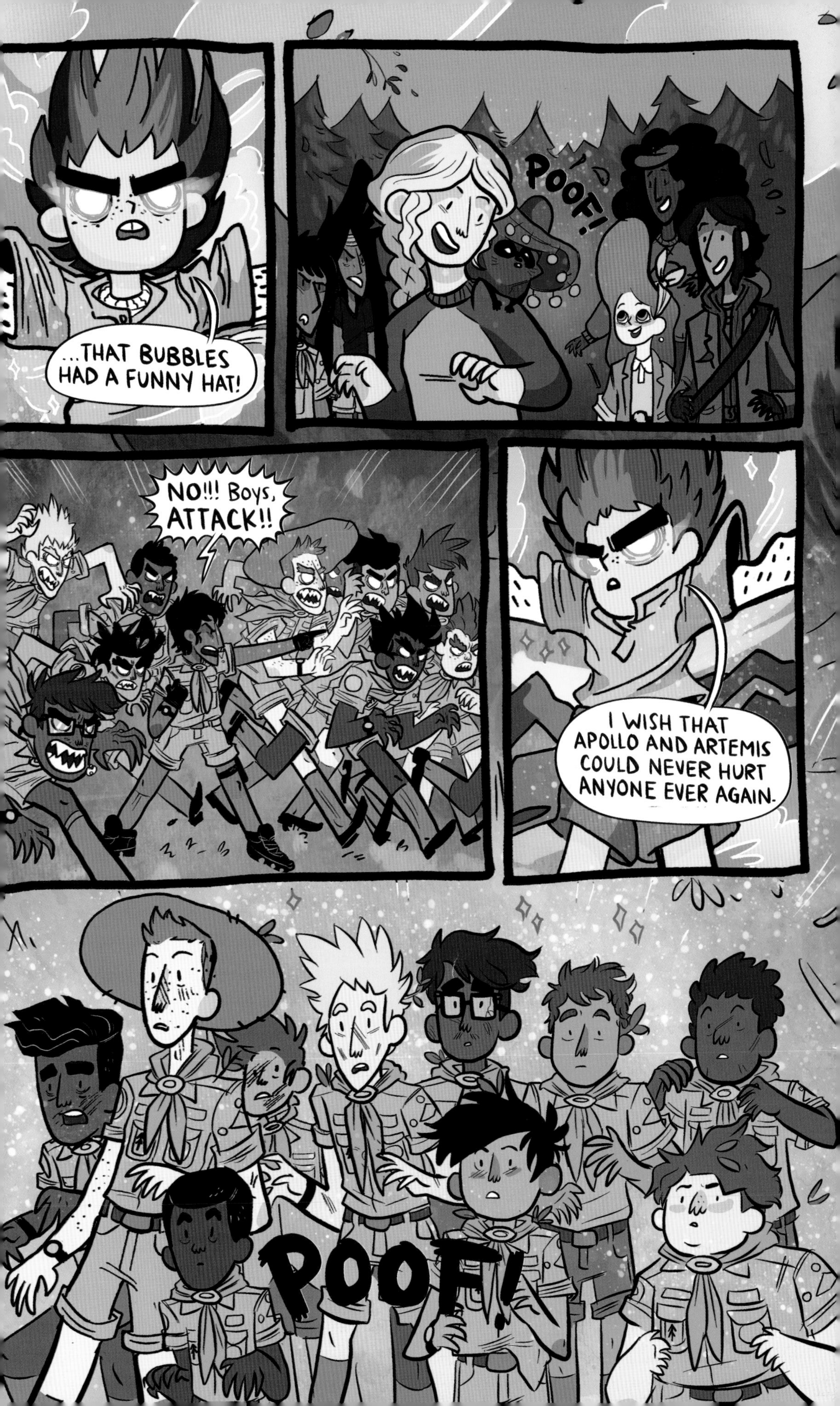
...THAT BUBBLES HAD A FUNNY HAT!
POOF!
NO!!! Boys, ATTACK!!
I WISH THAT APOLLO AND ARTEMIS COULD NEVER HURT ANYONE EVER AGAIN.
POOF!

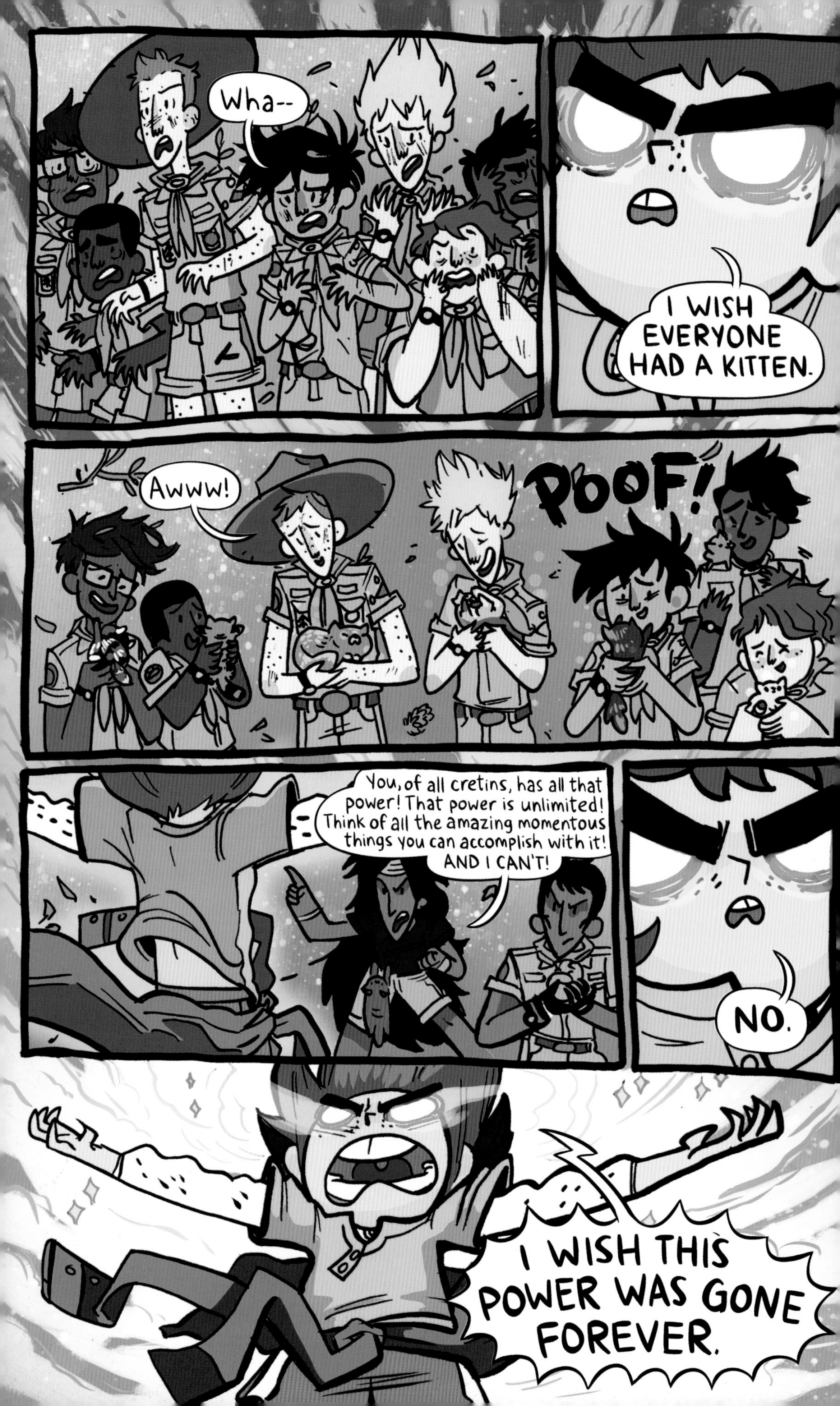
Wha--
I WISH EVERYONE HAD A KITTEN.
Awww!
POOF!
You, of all cretins, has all that power! That power is unlimited! Think of all the amazing momentous things you can accomplish with it! AND I CAN'T!
NO.
I WISH THIS POWER WAS GONE FOREVER.

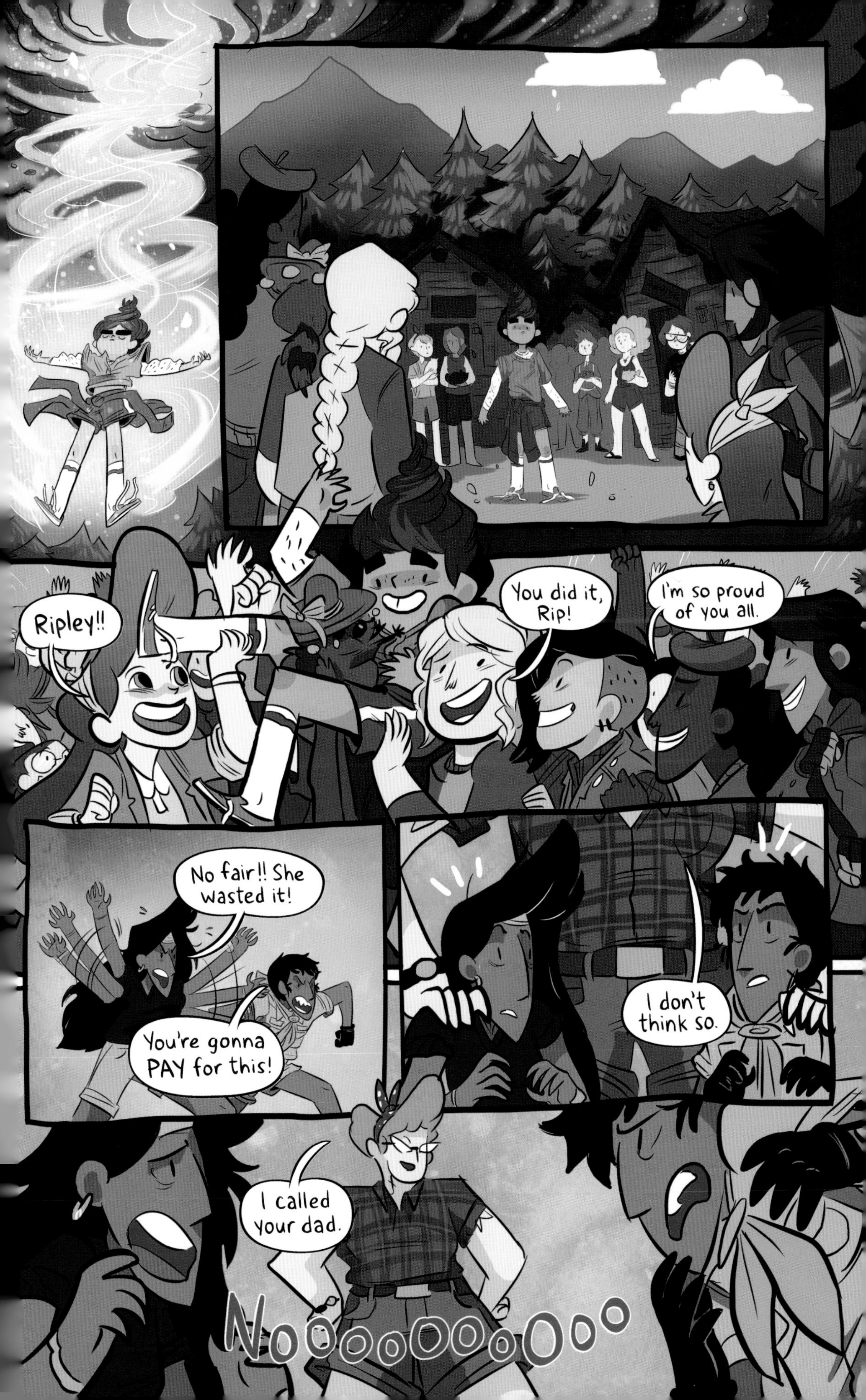
Ripley!!
You did it, Rip!
I'm so proud of you all.
No fair!! She wasted it!
You're gonna PAY for this!
I don't think so.
I called your dad.
NOooooOOooOoo

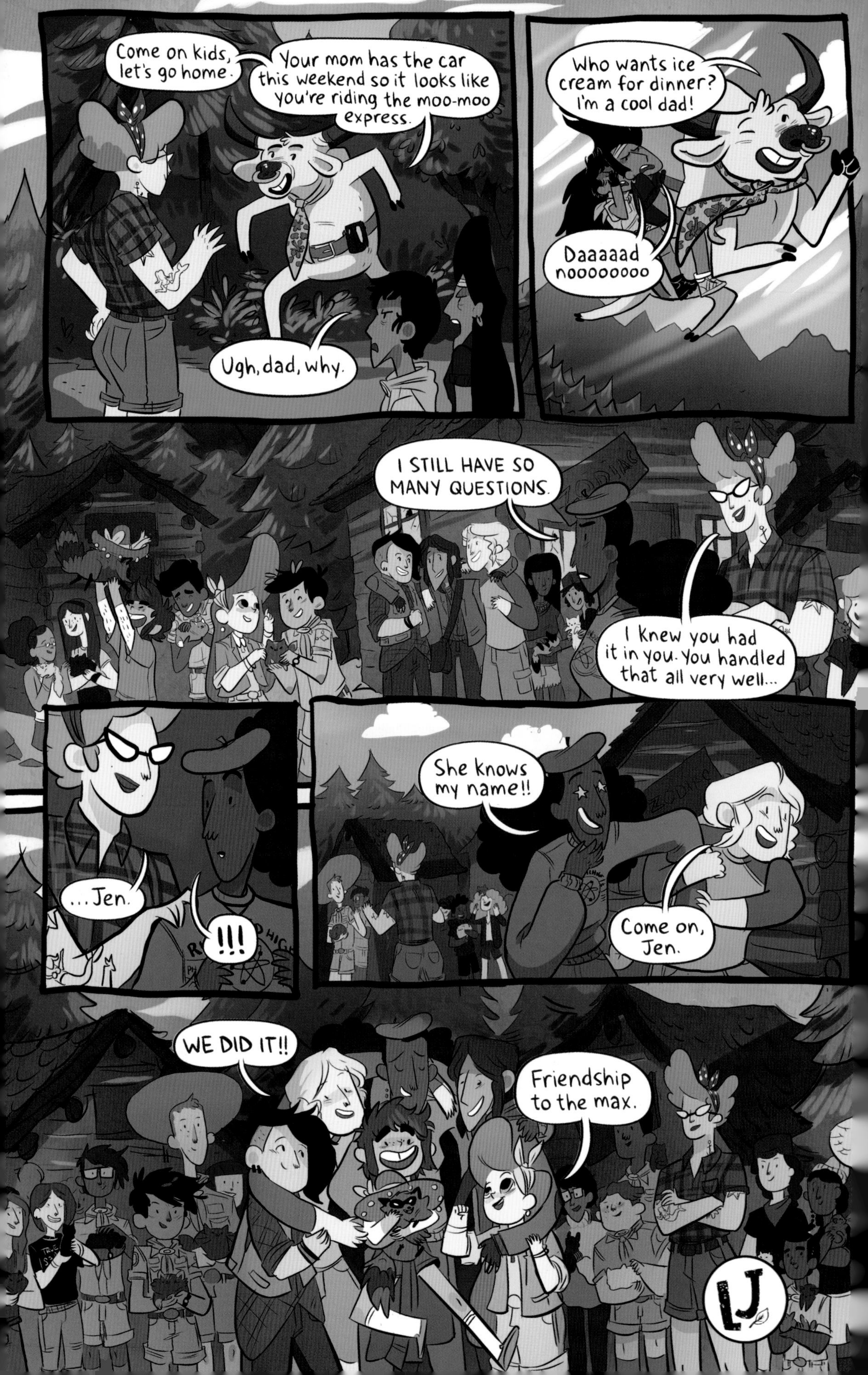
Come on kids, let's go home.
Your mom has the car this weekend so it looks like you're riding the moo-moo express.
Ugh, dad, why.
Who wants ice cream for dinner? I'm a cool dad!
Daaaaad noooooooo
I STILL HAVE SO MANY QUESTIONS.
I knew you had it in you. You handled that all very well...
...Jen.
!!!
She knows my name!!
Come on, Jen.
WE DID IT!!
Friendship to the max.

will co...

The...

It help...
appearan...
dress f...
Further...
Lumber...
to have...
part in...
Thiskv...
Hardo...
have...
them...

The...
yellow, short sl...
emb...
the w...
choose...
slacks,...
made o...
out-of-do...
green bere...
the colla...
Shoes ma...
heels, rou...
socks shou...
the uniform. Ne...es, bracelets, or other jewelry do...
belong with a Lumberjane uniform.

HOW TO WEAR...

To look well in a unifor...
uniform be kept in g...
pressed. See that the ski...
height and build, that the...
that your shoes and stock...
uniform, that you watch your p...
with dignity and grace. If the beret is...
be sure that your hair is neat and kept in place with an
insinspicuous clip or ribbon. When you wear a
Lumberjane uniform you are identified as a member of
this organization and you should be doubly careful to
conduct yourself in a way that will show everyone that
courtesy and thoughtfullness are part of being a
Lumberjane. People are likely to judge a whole nation by
the selfishness of a few individuals, to criticize a whole
family because of the misconduct of one member, and to
feel unkindly toward and organization because of the

...E UNIFORM

...should be worn at camp
...events when Lumberjanes
...may also be worn at other
...ions. It should be worn as a
...the uniform dress with
...rect shoes, and stocking or

...out grows her uniform or
...r Lumberjane.
...a she has
...her
...her

...ES

The unifor...
helps to cre...
in a group...
active life th...
another bond...
future, and pr...
in order to b...
Lumberjane pr...
Penniquiqul Thi... ...re Lady
Types, but m... ...s will wish to have one. They
can either b... ...niform, or make it themselves from
materials available at the trading post.

BROOKLYN ALLEN

LUMBERJANES FIELD MANUAL

AFTERWORD

I mean it when I say that none of us expected *Lumberjanes* to turn into what it is. It was a lark, an eight-issue comic book series that we ambitiously structured like a multi-season Saturday morning cartoon show, with everything in it we wished had been around when we were kids. As a comic book editor, I rely frequently on my "feelings" for figuring out creative biz; and I had a feeling, very early on, that *Lumberjanes* was special. There is an old joke that Grace and I have, where we think of something semi-ludicrous like an all-girl Broadway version of *Guys & Dolls* and we carry this to the nth brainstorming extreme, finally lamenting the punchline, "GOSH WHY DOESN'T SOMEONE GIVE US A MILLION DOLLARS" because we fancy ourselves creative geniuses that the entire entertainment industry should support early and often, even though none of these ever comes to fruition.

Lumberjanes was a situation where an idea was so special, someone gave it a figurative cool mil, which we leapt all over.

We put together the first pitch document in a week, that's how fast our minds tried to wrap around this thing. Brooklyn did our original character designs, and it was clear after falling hard and fast for them and their work that there would be no substitute for *Lumberjanes*.

Only a few weeks after, I had brunch with Noelle and told her I was looking for another writer and a character designer for this thing I was putting together, "and it's like Girl Scouts but there are monsters and it's like *Scooby Doo*—" and she cut me off before I could finished with YES YES OH MY GOSH YES. Then we finished our fancy pancakes and everything changed forever and *Lumberjanes* got its last essential missing piece.

I realized soon after that the entire team's alternative lifestyle haircuts swooped to the same side, which seemed like a sign.

It's a testament to everyone's talent and devotion to this book that you don't see how intense it is for us to put it together every month. It's grinding, taxing work. It's a group of people with other jobs and disparate personalities and myriad insecurities trying desperately to work through a story together month after month. It's exhausting, and if it were any other book, we'd have moved on a long time ago.

But *Lumberjanes* is important. To us, but most of all, to you. You're the reason we're all still here, that we continue to tell Jo, April, Molly, Mal and Ripley's story month after month. Because some of you are little kids seeing yourselves in comic books for the first time (HI!), and some of you are adults searching for exactly what we were…kids who are all their own person and whose friendship with each other is positive, joyful, and valuable. Whoever you are, whatever you're looking for…I'm so grateful to all of you who have been with us from the beginning, and those of you who are just joining us now.

Lumberjanes is special. And so are you.

Thank you for going on this journey with us. You lumber-rock.

SHANNON WATTERS
Co-creator & Co-writer of *Lumberjanes*

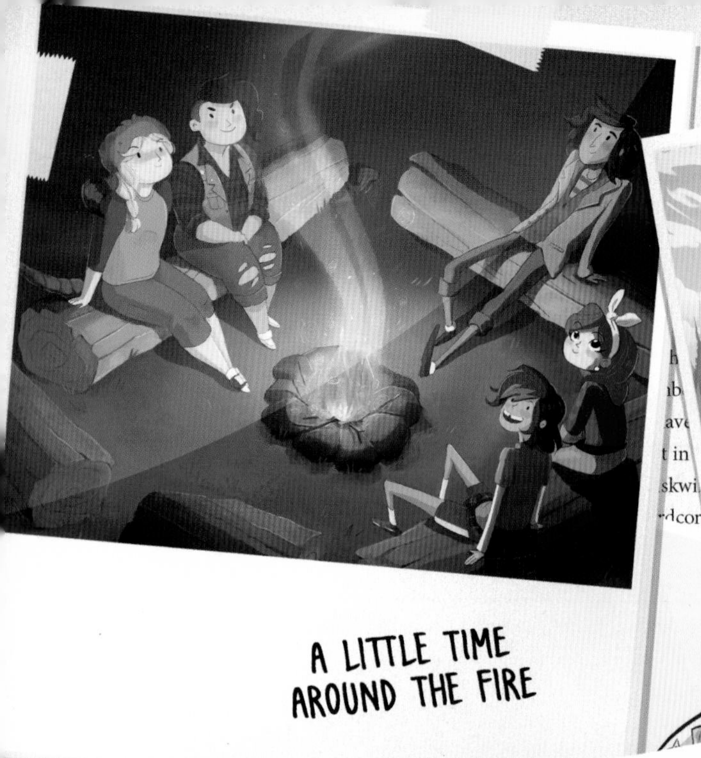
A LITTLE TIME
AROUND THE FIRE

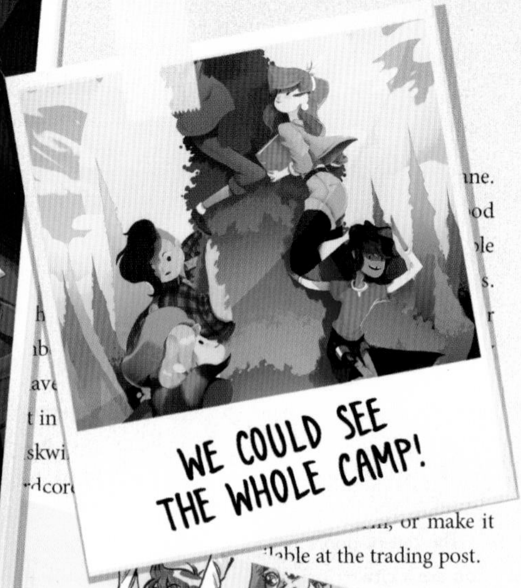
WE COULD SEE
THE WHOLE CAMP!

ne.
od
ple
s.
r

... or make it
...ilable at the trading post.

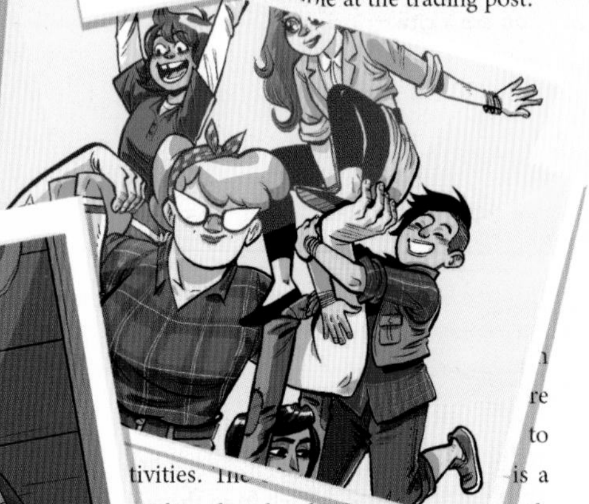

The Lumberjane uniform ...
meetings ...

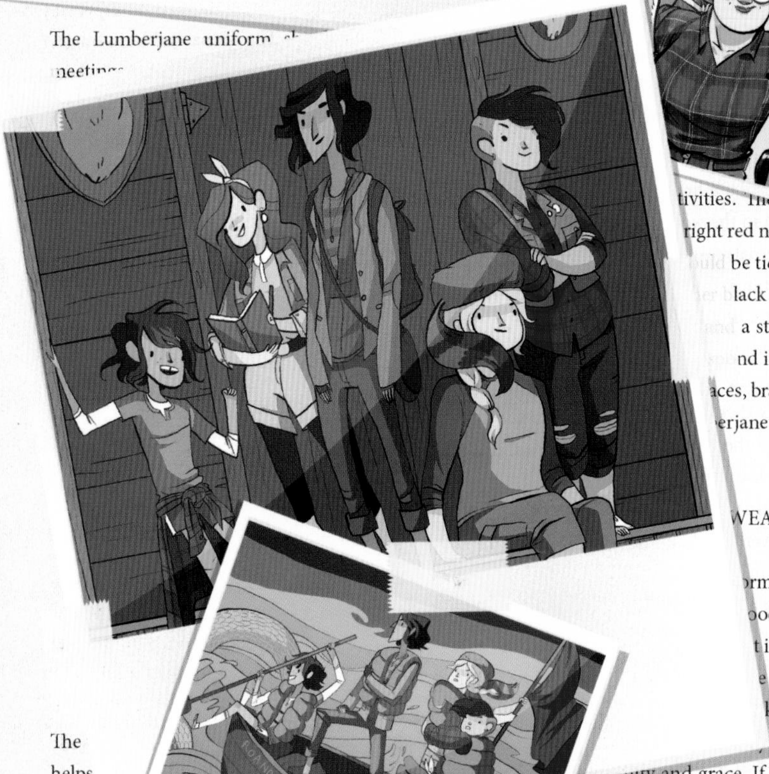

... re
... to
...tivities. The ... —is a
...right red neckerchief is wo... ...neath
...uld be tied in a simple friendship knot.
... lack or brown and should have flat
... a straight inner line. Stockings or
... nd in color with the shoes or with
...aces, bracelets, or other jewelry do not
...erjane uniform.

...WEAR THE UNIFORM

...orm demands first of all that the ...ood condition—clean and well ...t is the right length for your own ...e belt is adjusted to your waist, ...kings are in keeping with the ...our posture and carry yourself ...dignity and grace. If the beret is removed indoors, ...e sure that your hair is neat and kept in place with an insonspicuous clip or ribbon. When you wear a Lumberjane uniform you are identified as a member of this organization and you should be doubly careful to conduct yourself in a way that will show everyone that courtesy and thoughtfullness are part of being a Lumberjane. People are likely to judge a whole nation by the selfishness of a few individuals, to criticize a whole family because of the misconduct of one member, and to feel unkindly toward and organization because of the

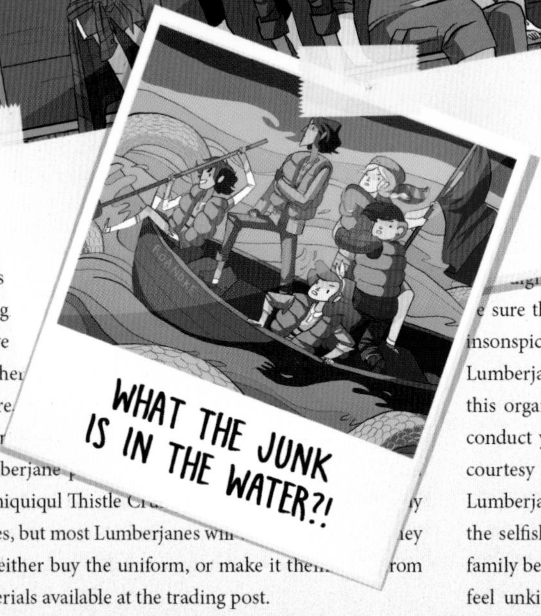
WHAT THE JUNK
IS IN THE WATER?!

The ...
helps ...
in a g...
active ...
another ...
future. ...
in or ...
Lumberjane p...
Penniquiqul Thistle Cr... ...y
Types, but most Lumberjanes wi... ...ney
can either buy the uniform, or make it them... ...rom
materials available at the trading post.

COVER GALLERY

Lumberjanes "Out-of-Doors" Program Field

PUNGEON MASTER BADGE

"The best kind of punishment."

The pun conundrum is that most view it as the lowest form of word-play, but we Lumberjanes say, if it was good enough for Shakespeare and Plautus, then it is definitely good enough of our camp literary masters. The original purpose of puns seems to be as diverse as the circumstances of how they first appeared in modern culture, and can be seen as more than a mere linguistic fillip. Lumberjanes recognize the value of a good pun and its cleverly worded effect on those around us and the future of civilization. A Lumberjane not only enjoys the creativity behind a pun but the importance of how it can bring a group together.

Wordplay is a great technique that Lumberjanes will continue to pursue with the fervor of every other skill they will learn at camp, and while this badge is the most popular, a Lumberjane knows the importance of not rushing headfirst into this lesson. A pun is meant for a perfect moment in time and the *Pungeon Master* badge teaches all Lumberjanes the importance of not only playing close attention to their current situation and their surroundings, but how to stay on their toes with their wit so as to always be available to improve the conversation around them.

To obtain the *Pungeon Master* badge, a Lumberjane must have a knowledge of the game laws of the state in which she lives. Great care must be taken to determine if it is the appropriate time or place for clever wordplay as a Lumberjane may also risk her pun being misconstrued. It is important to find not only the the right audience, but time and place in order to ensure that a pun will not be missed. She must preserve the importance of the pun and truly understand the strength of the words she is using. A Lumberjane understands the importance of a pun and the power that comes with it.

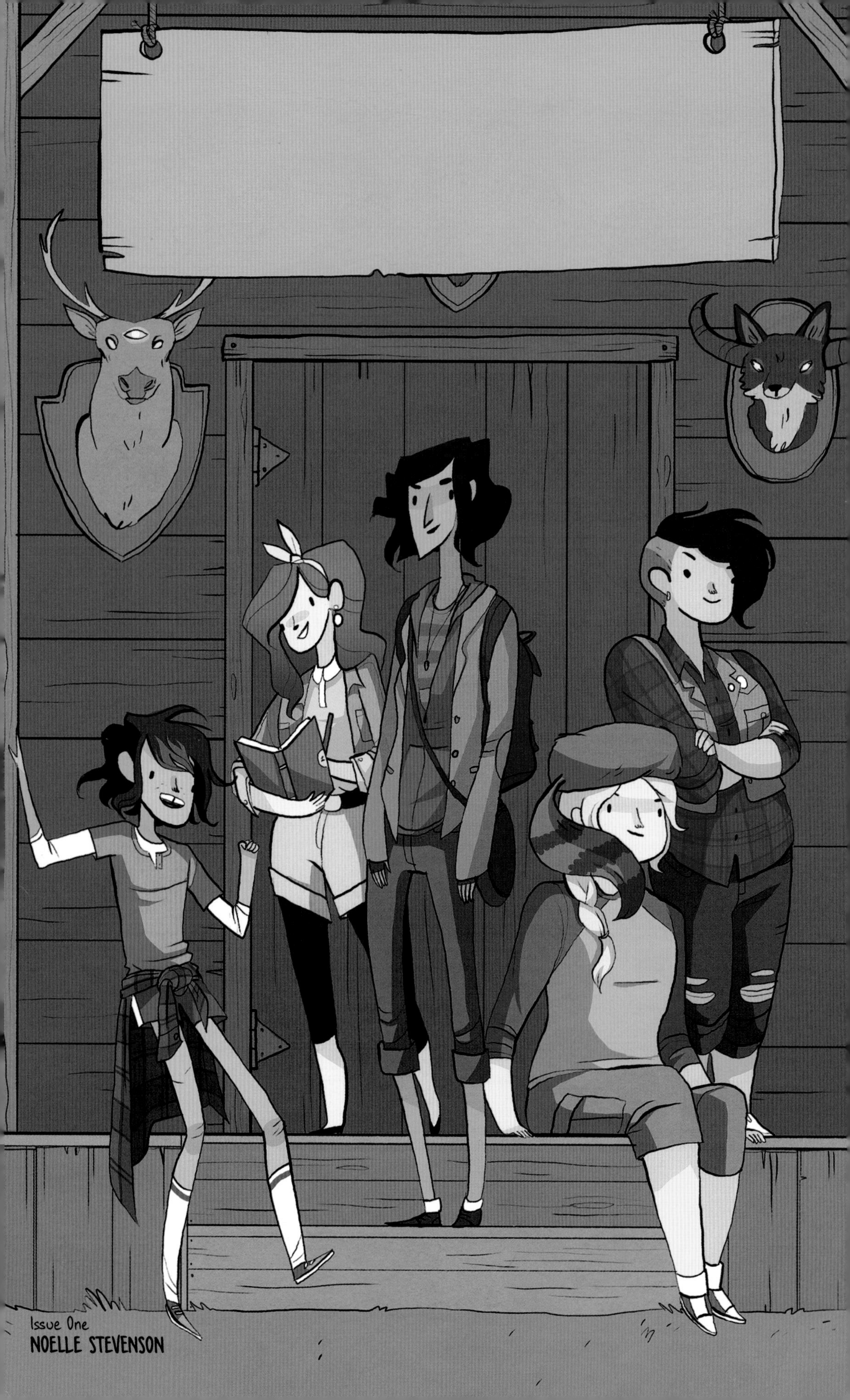
Issue One
NOELLE STEVENSON

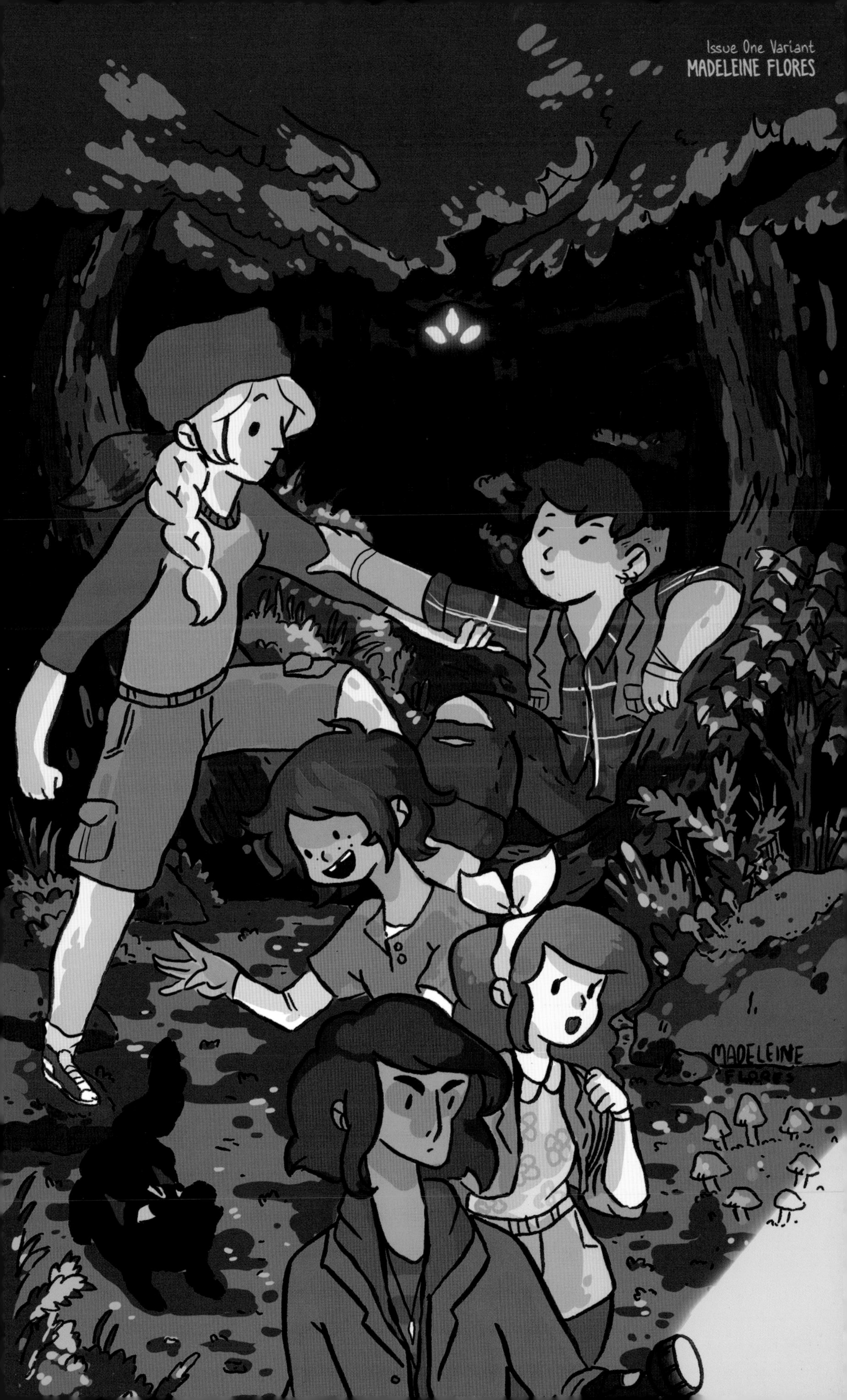
Issue One Variant
MADELEINE FLORES
MADELEINE FLORES

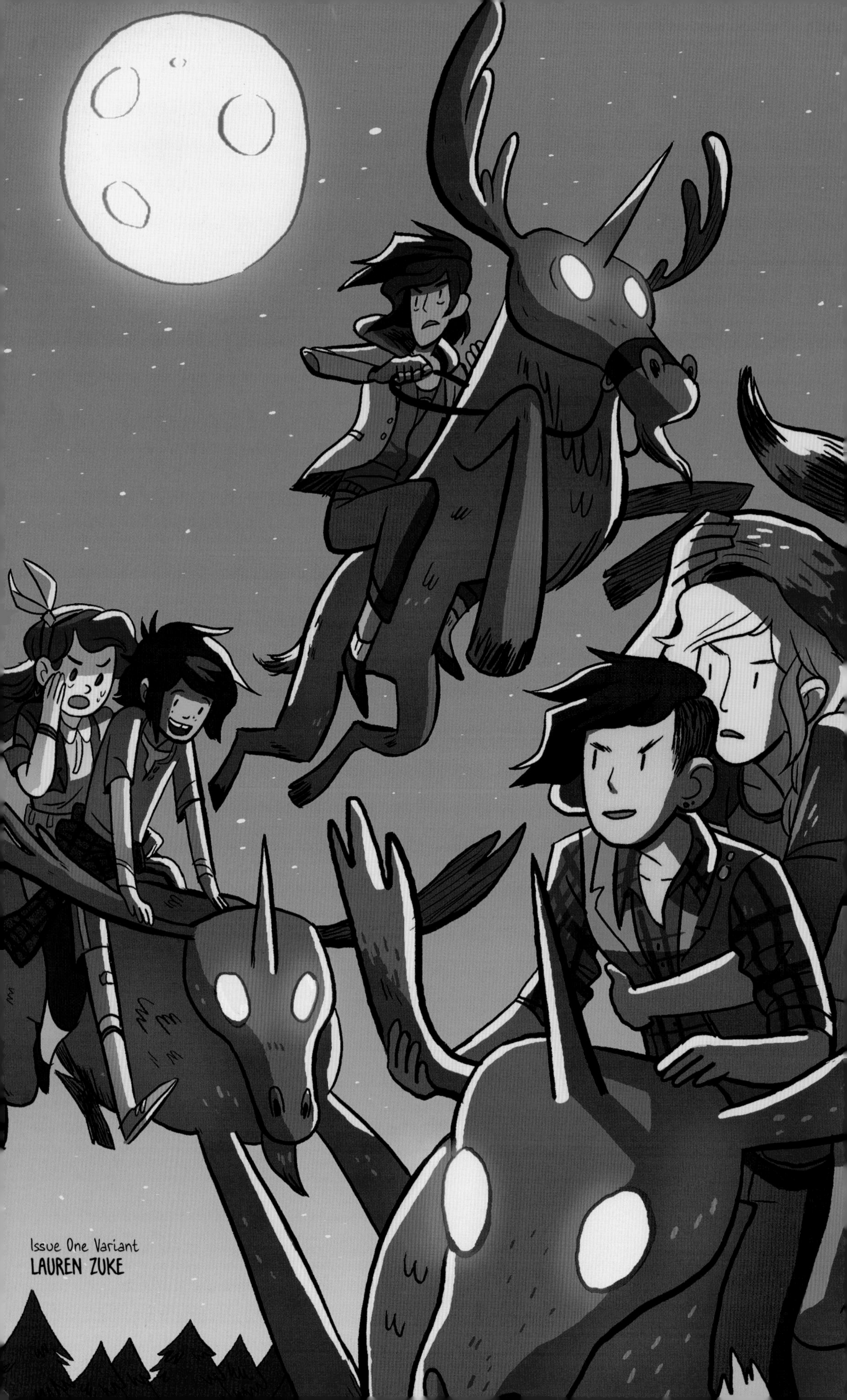

Issue One Variant
LAUREN ZUKE

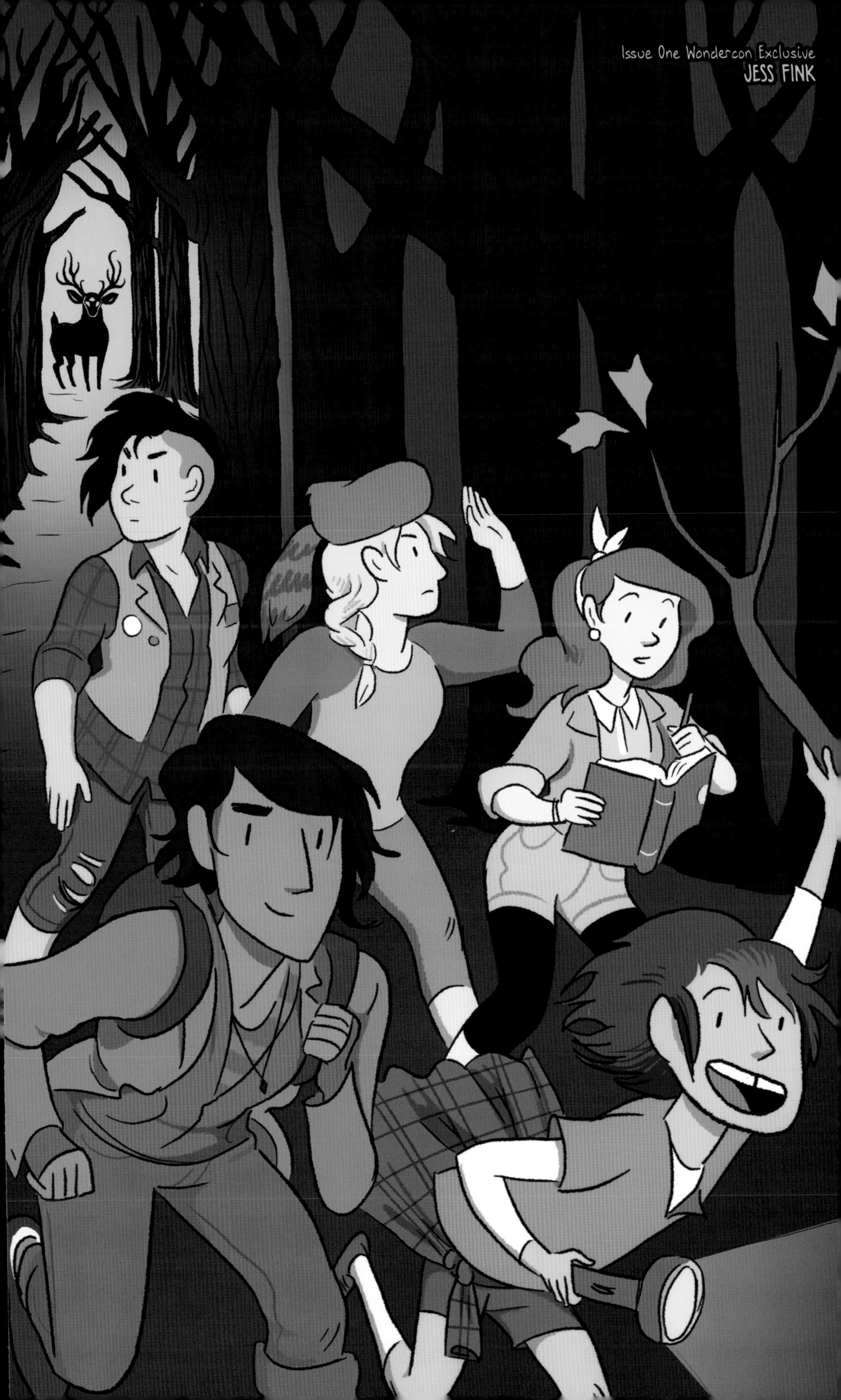
Issue One Wondercon Exclusive
JESS FINK

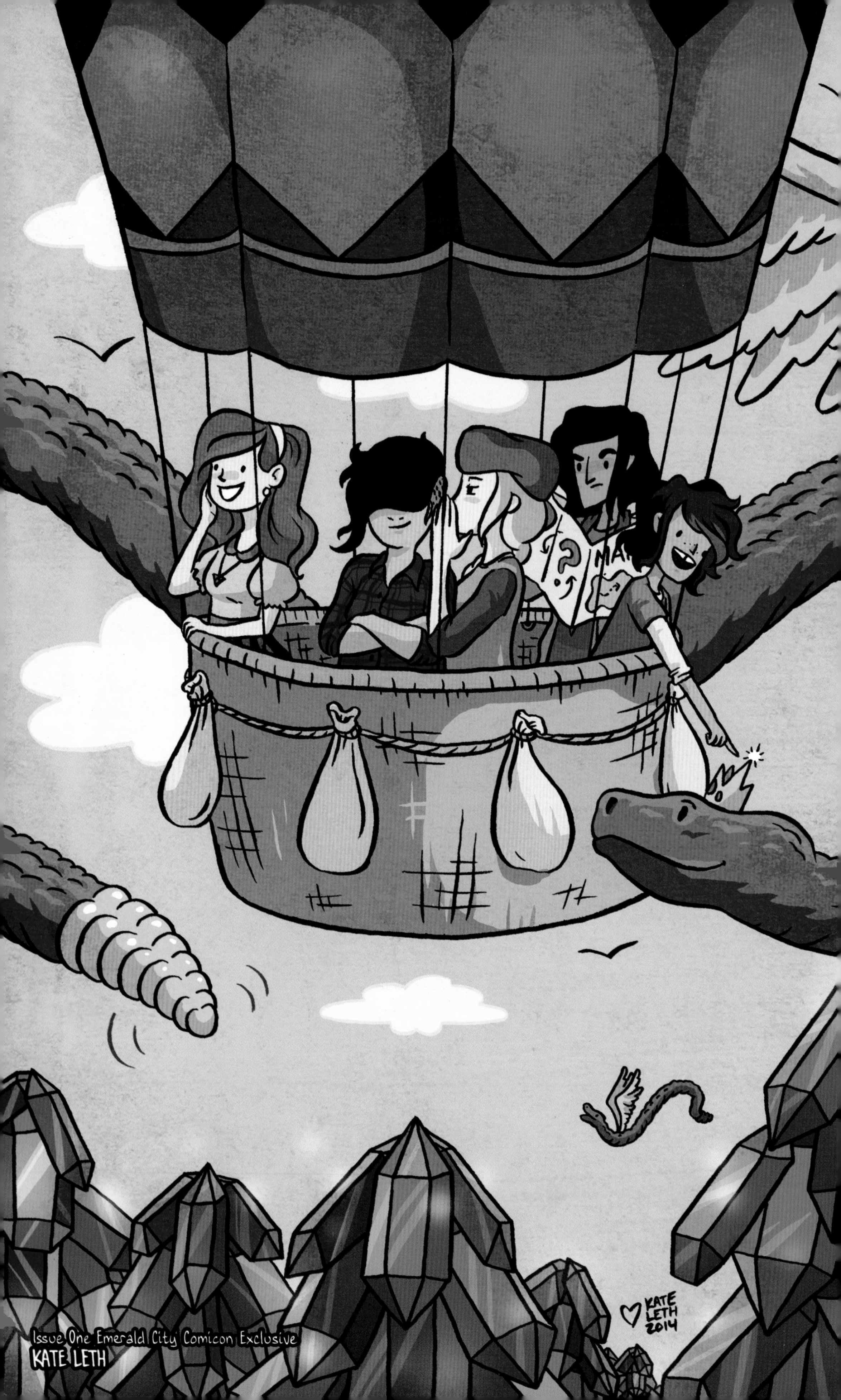

MA
KATE LETH 2014
Issue One Emerald City Comicon Exclusive
KATE LETH

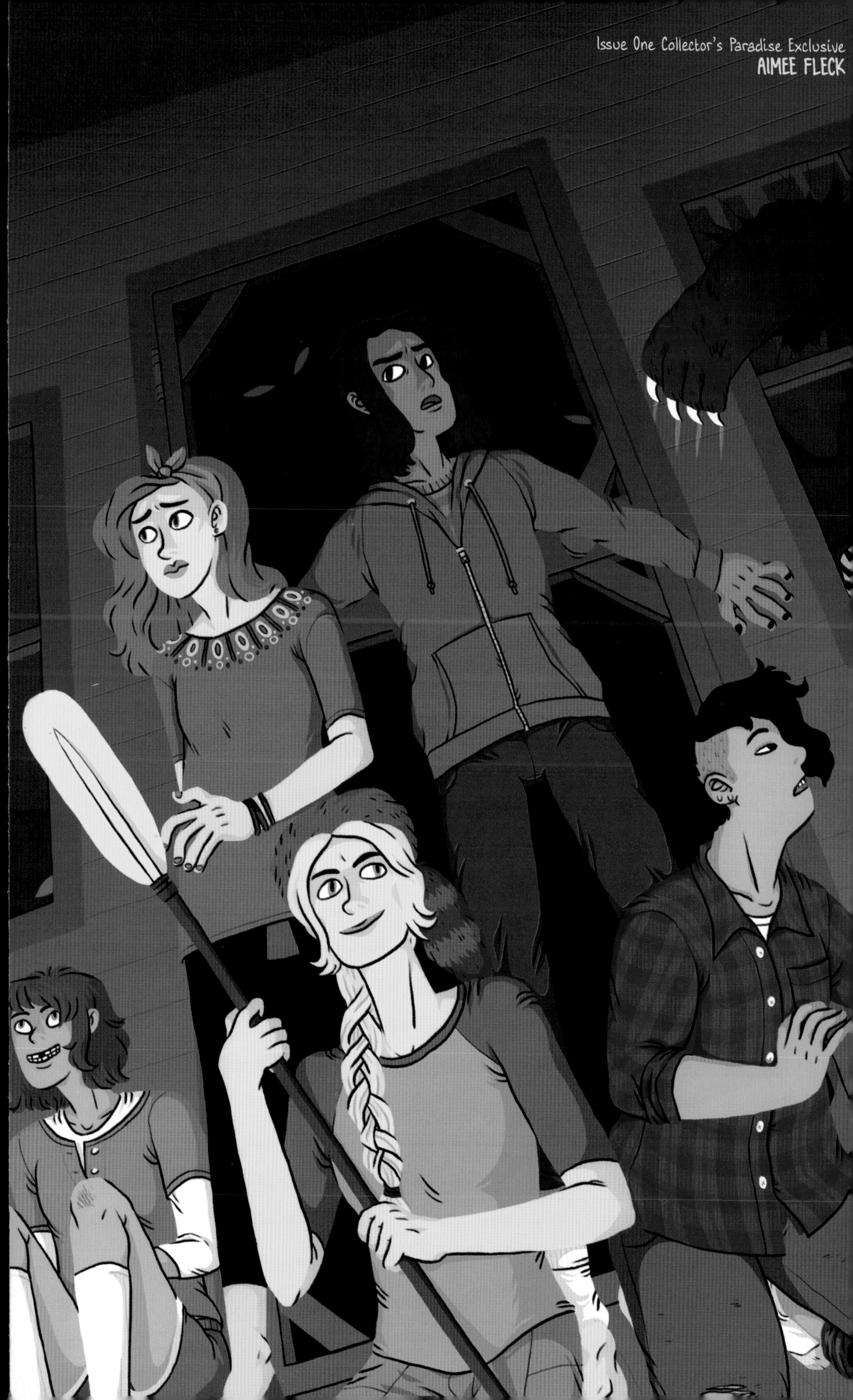
Issue One Collector's Paradise Exclusive
AIMEE FLECK

Original LumberJanes designs by Brooklyn A.

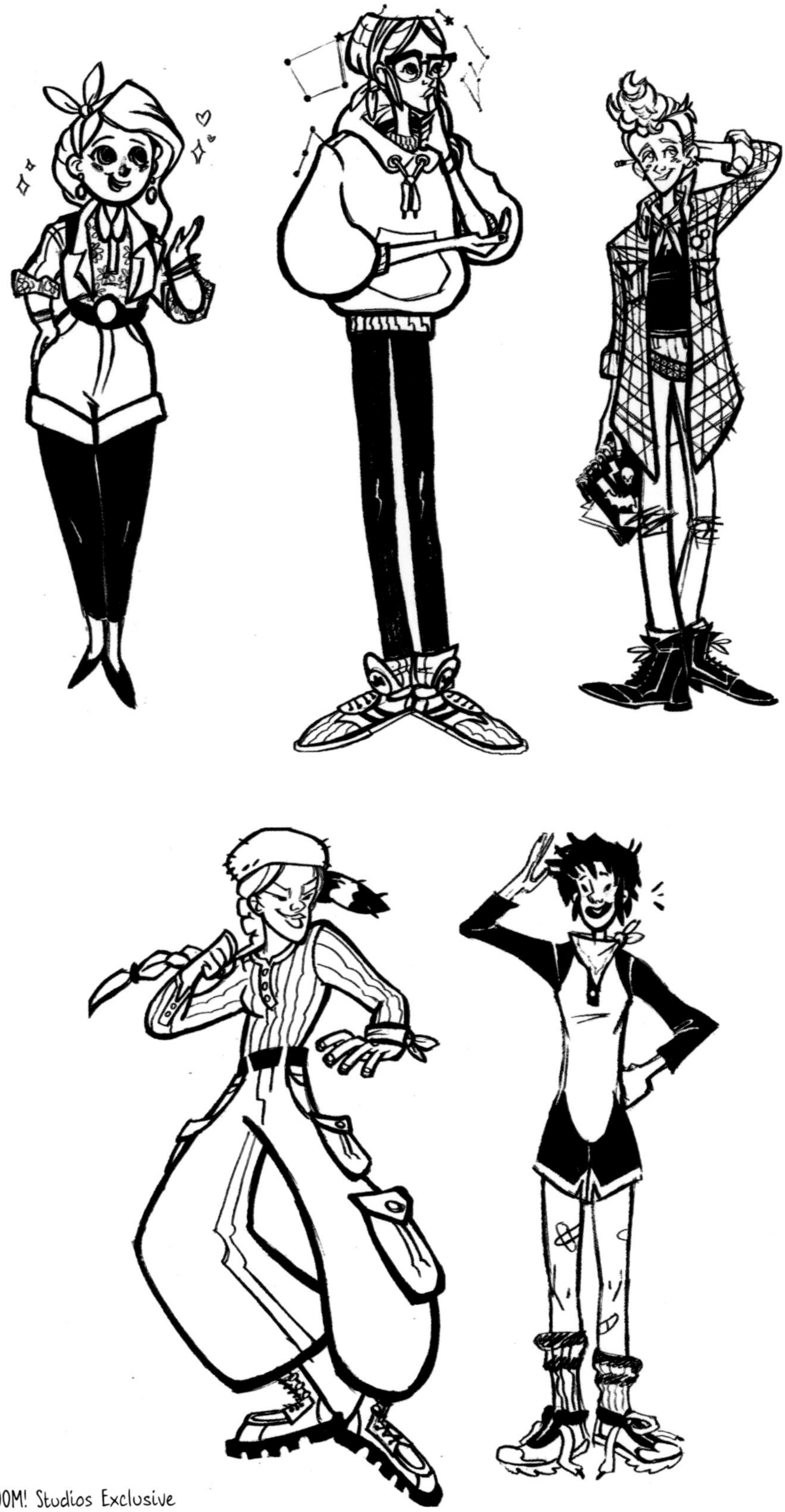

Issue One BOOM! Studios Exclusive
BROOKLYN ALLEN

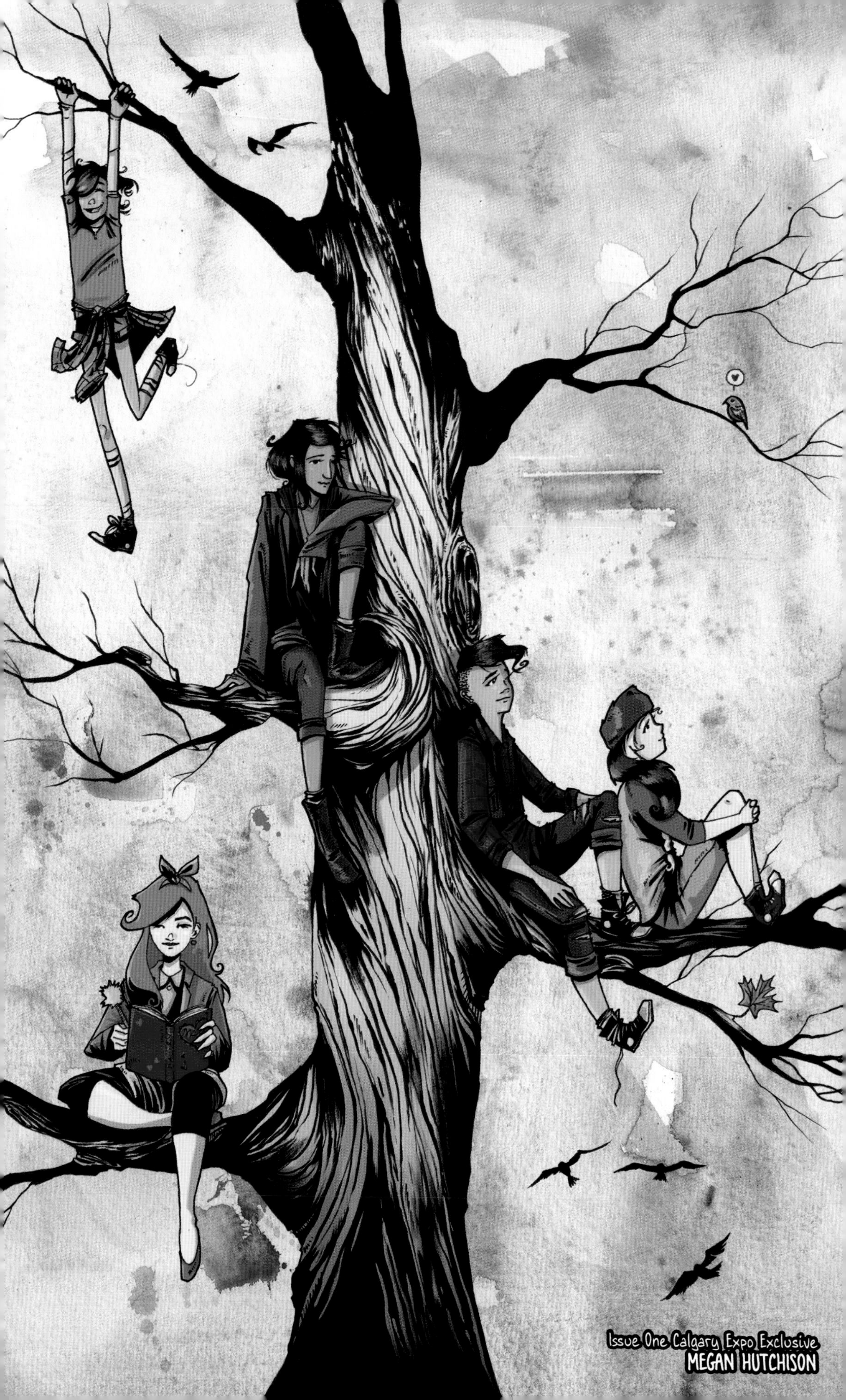
Issue One Calgary Expo Exclusive
MEGAN HUTCHISON

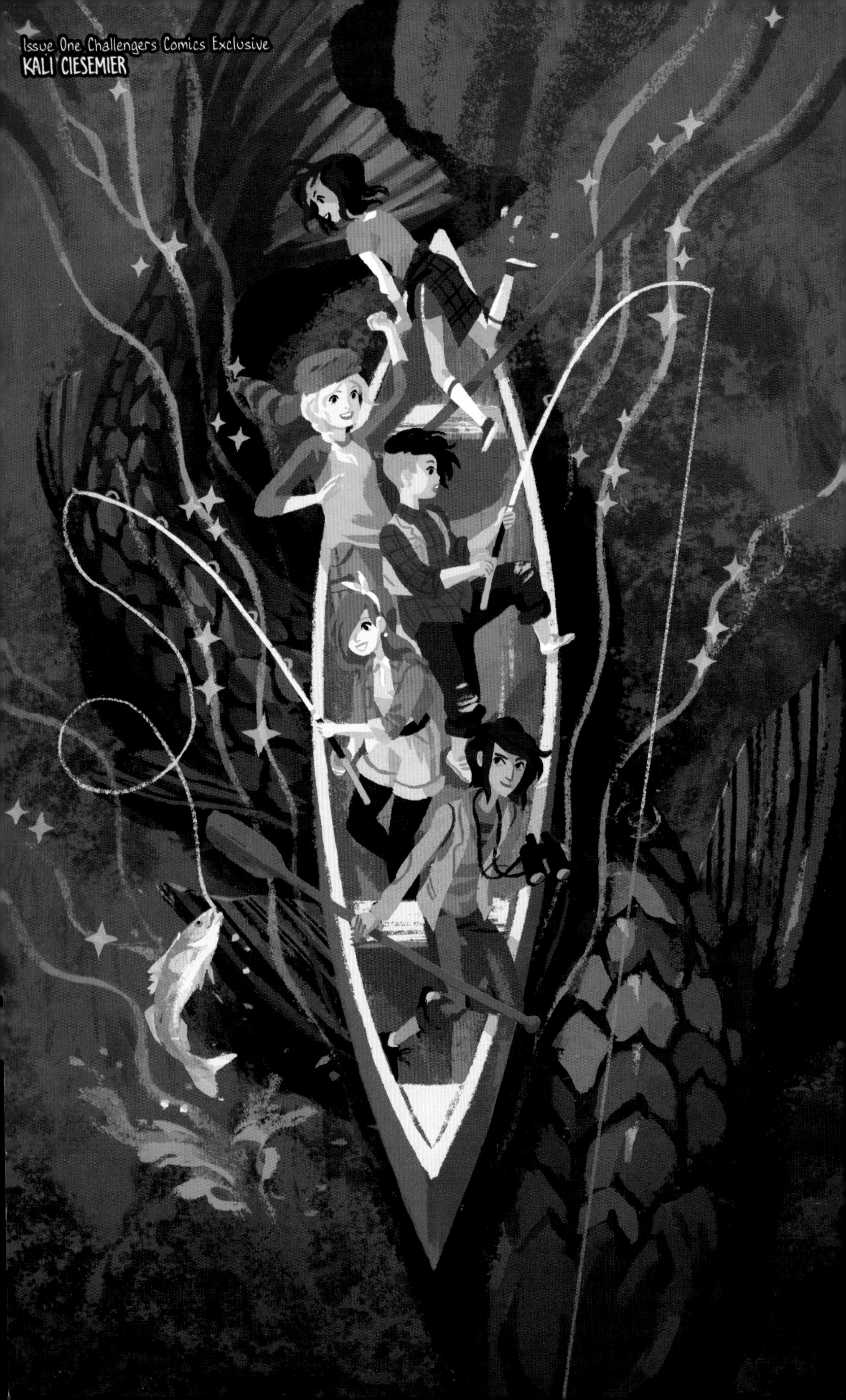
Issue One Challengers Comics Exclusive
KALI CIESEMIER

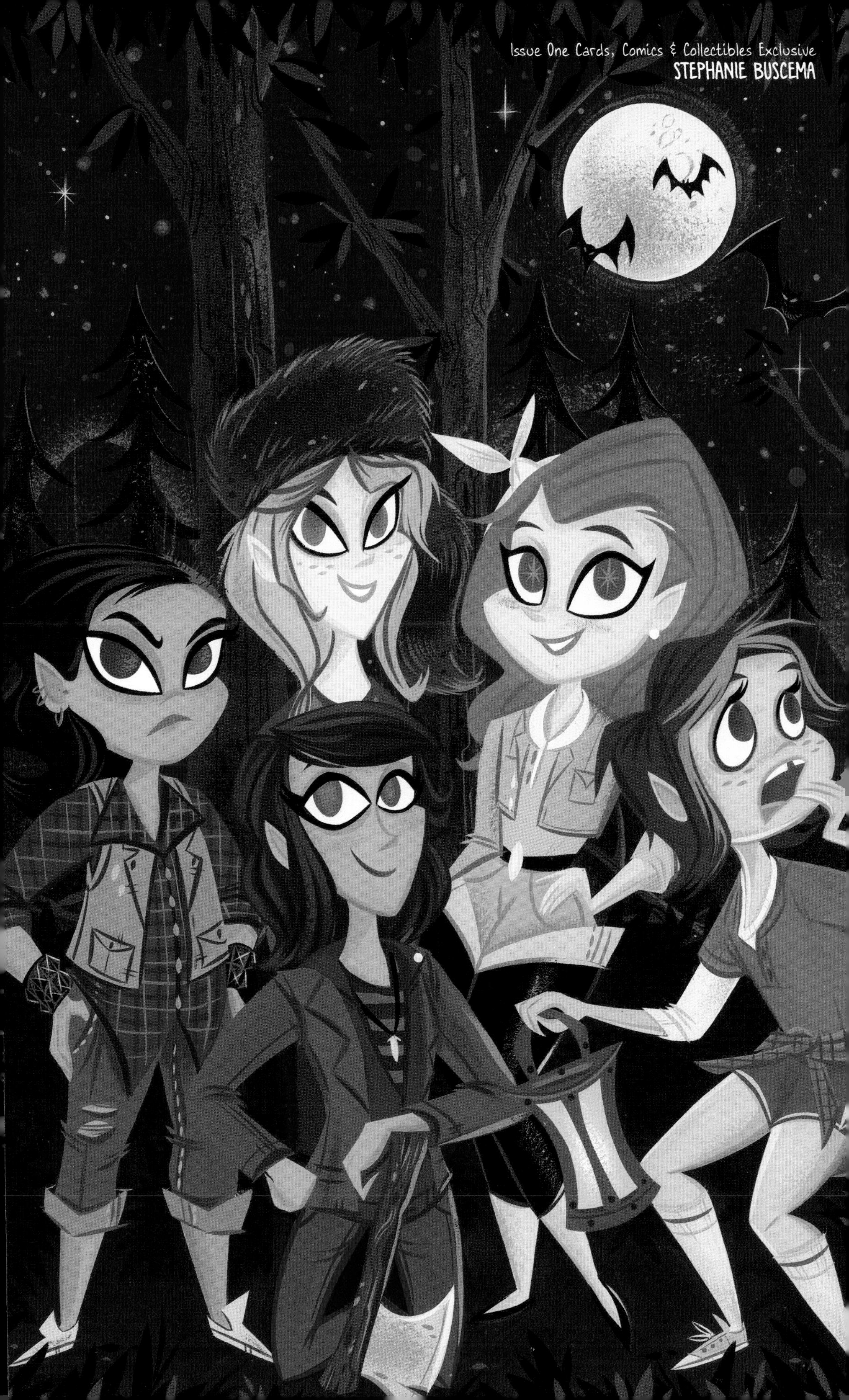
Issue One Cards, Comics & Collectibles Exclusive
STEPHANIE BUSCEMA

Issue One Laughing Ogre/Big Planet Exclusive
DANIELLE CORSETTO

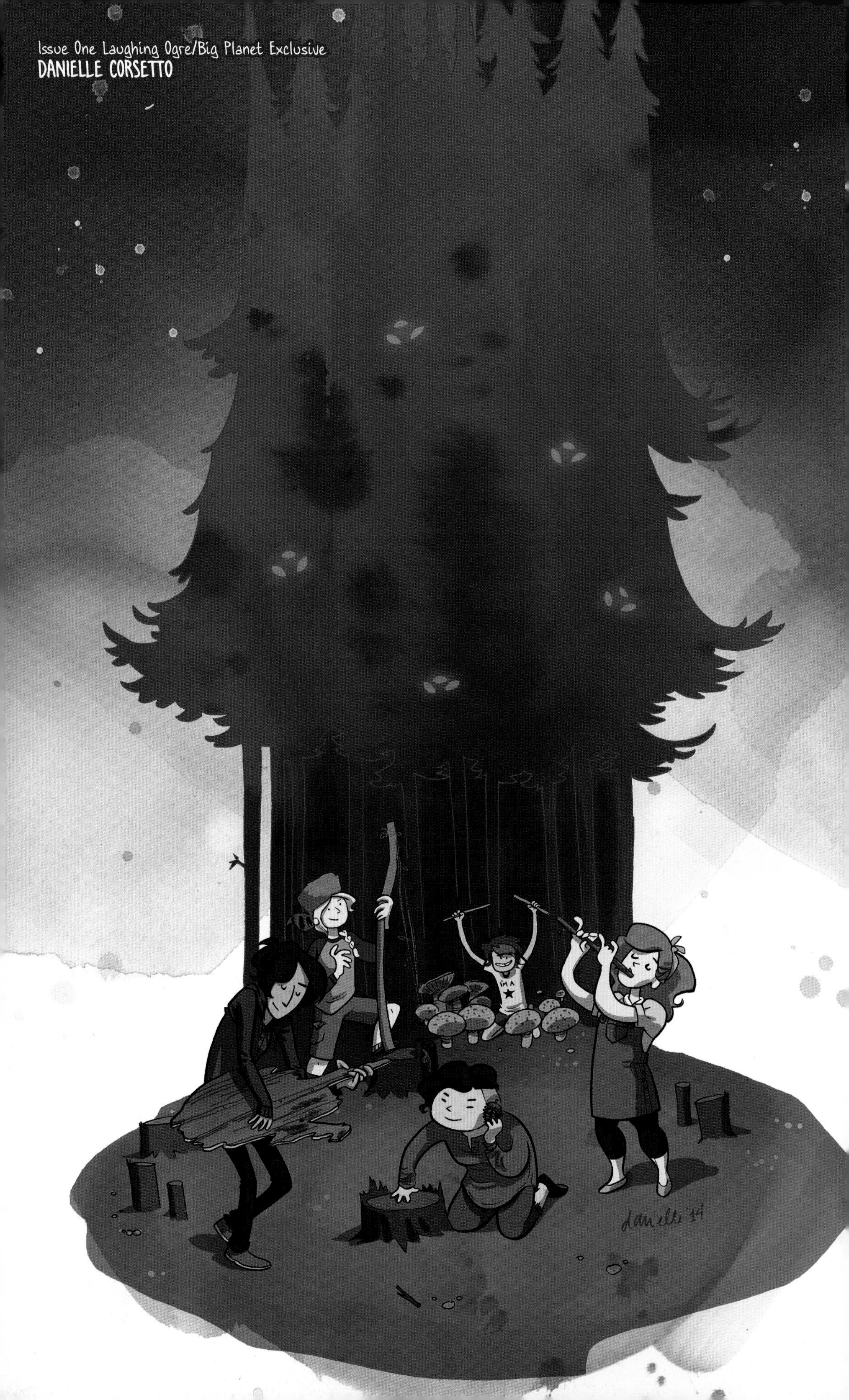
IM A ★
danielle '14

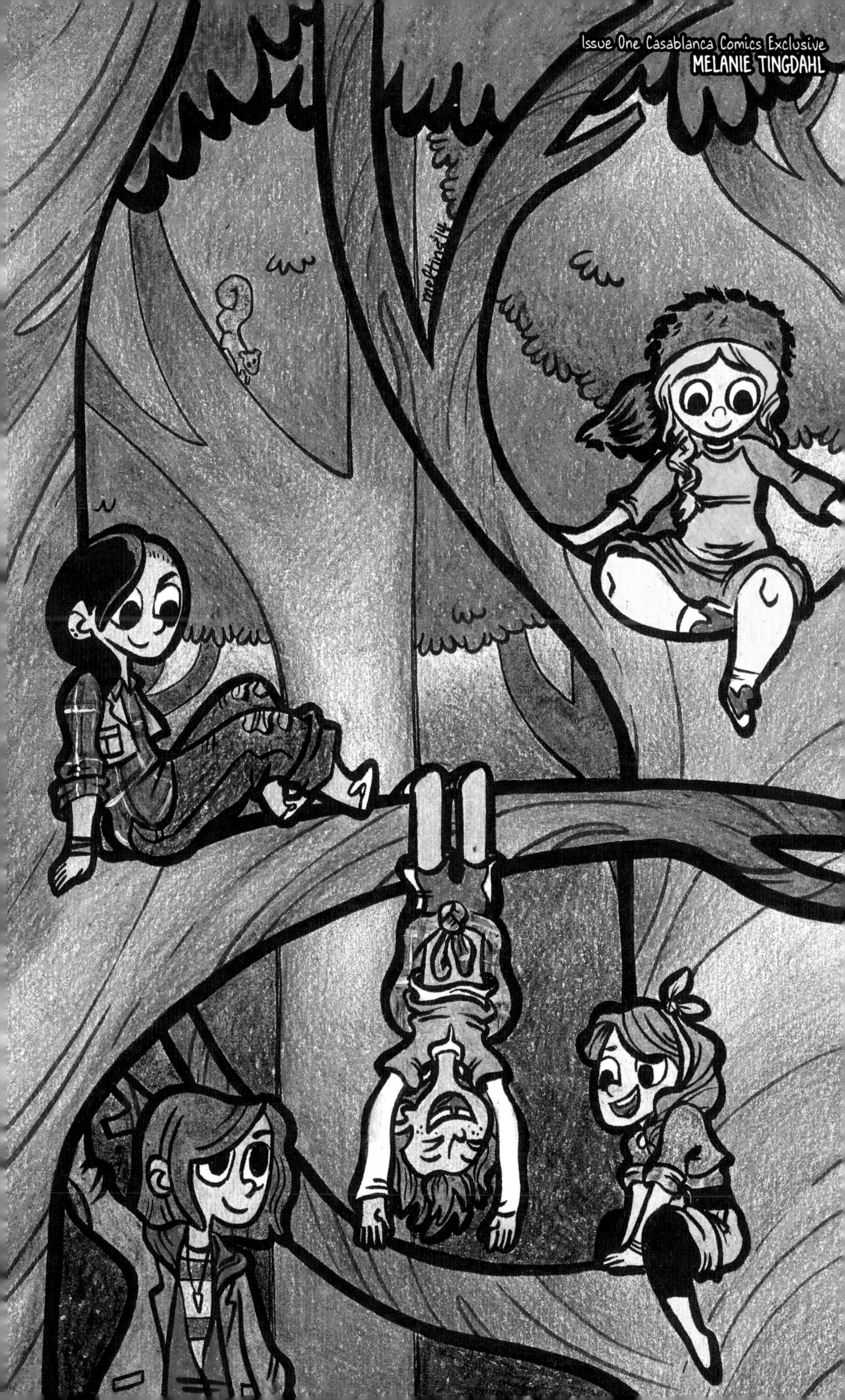
Issue One Casablanca Comics Exclusive
MELANIE TINGDAHL

Issue One Second Print
CHRYSTIN GARLAND

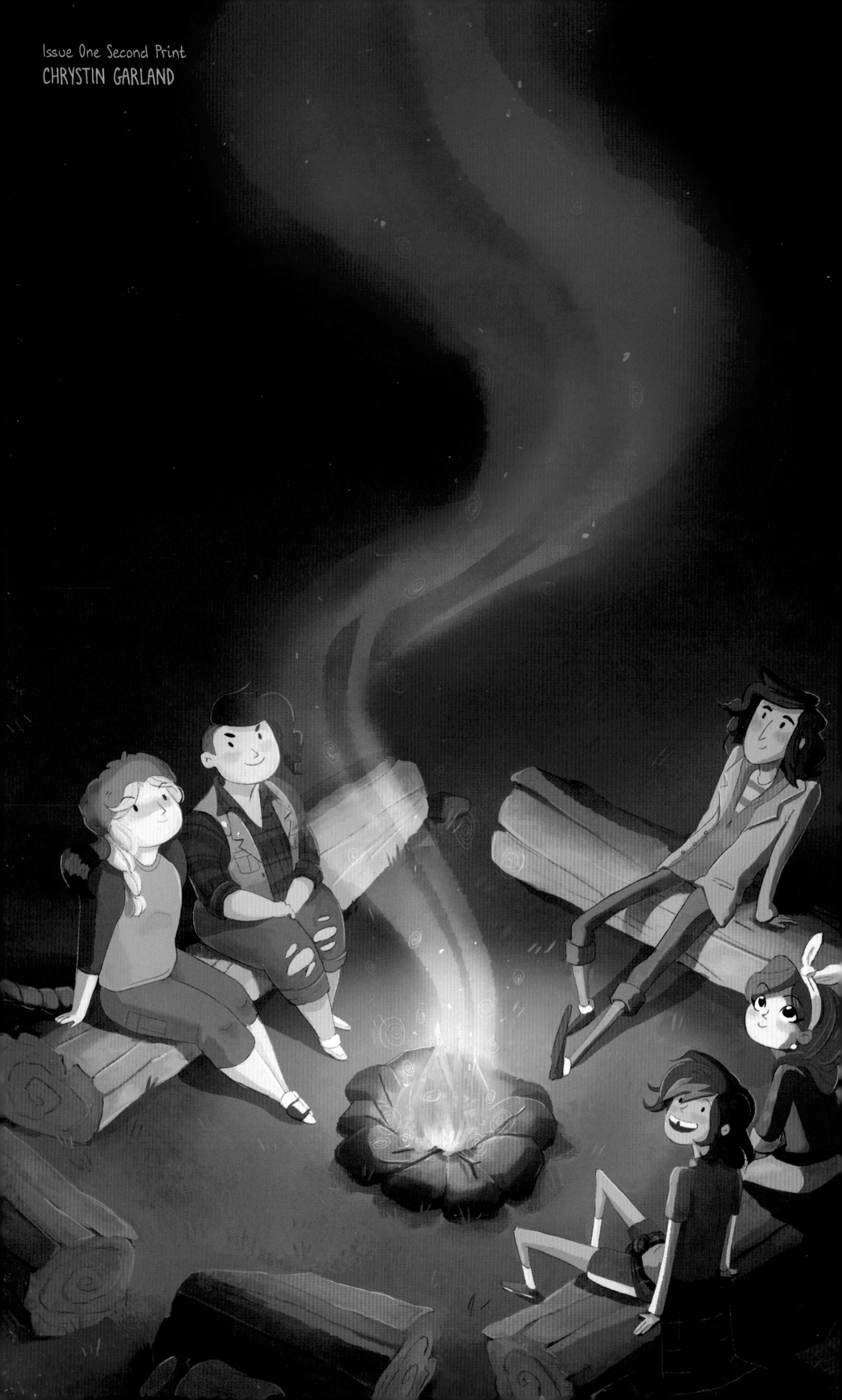

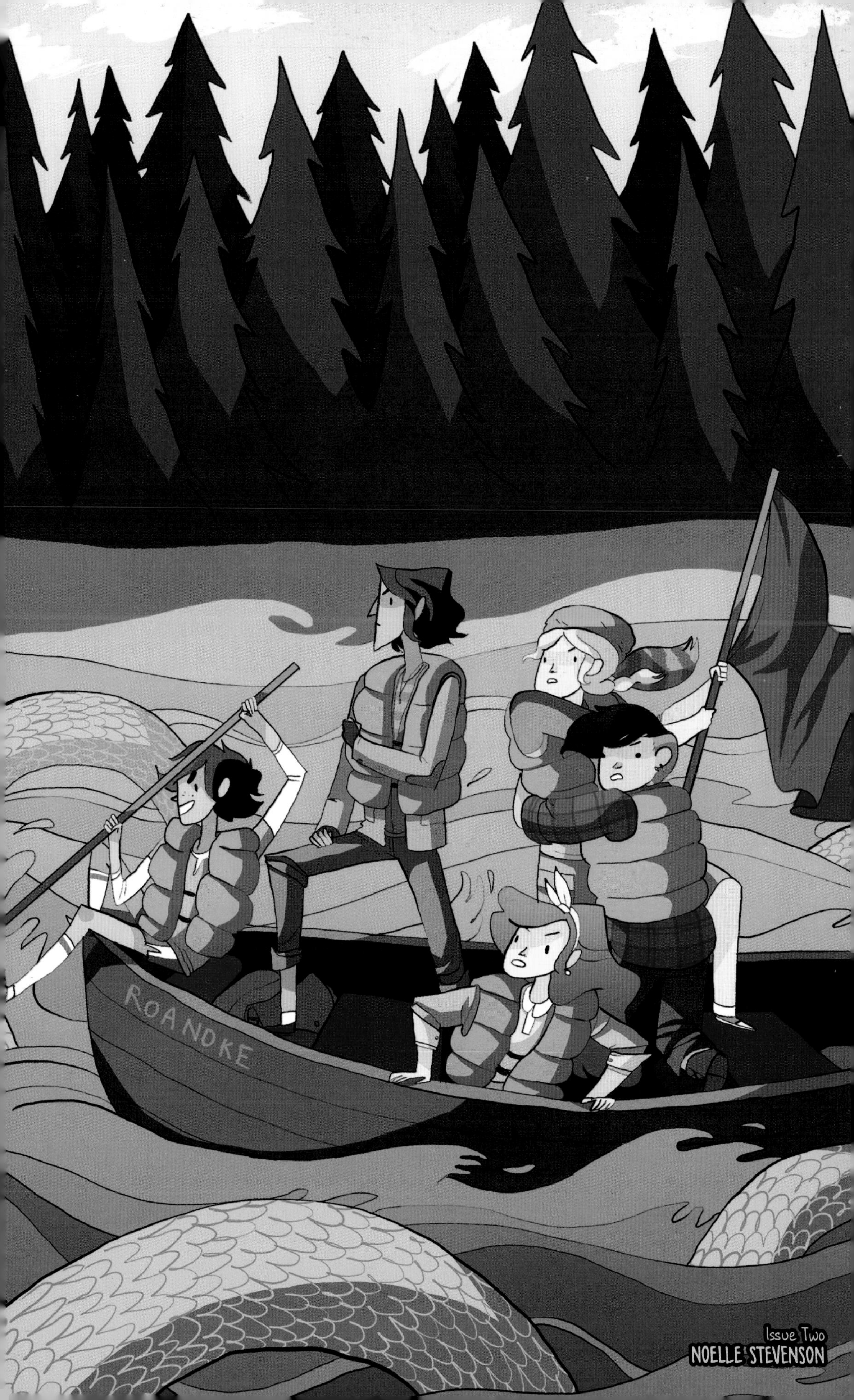
ROANOKE
Issue Two
NOELLE STEVENSON

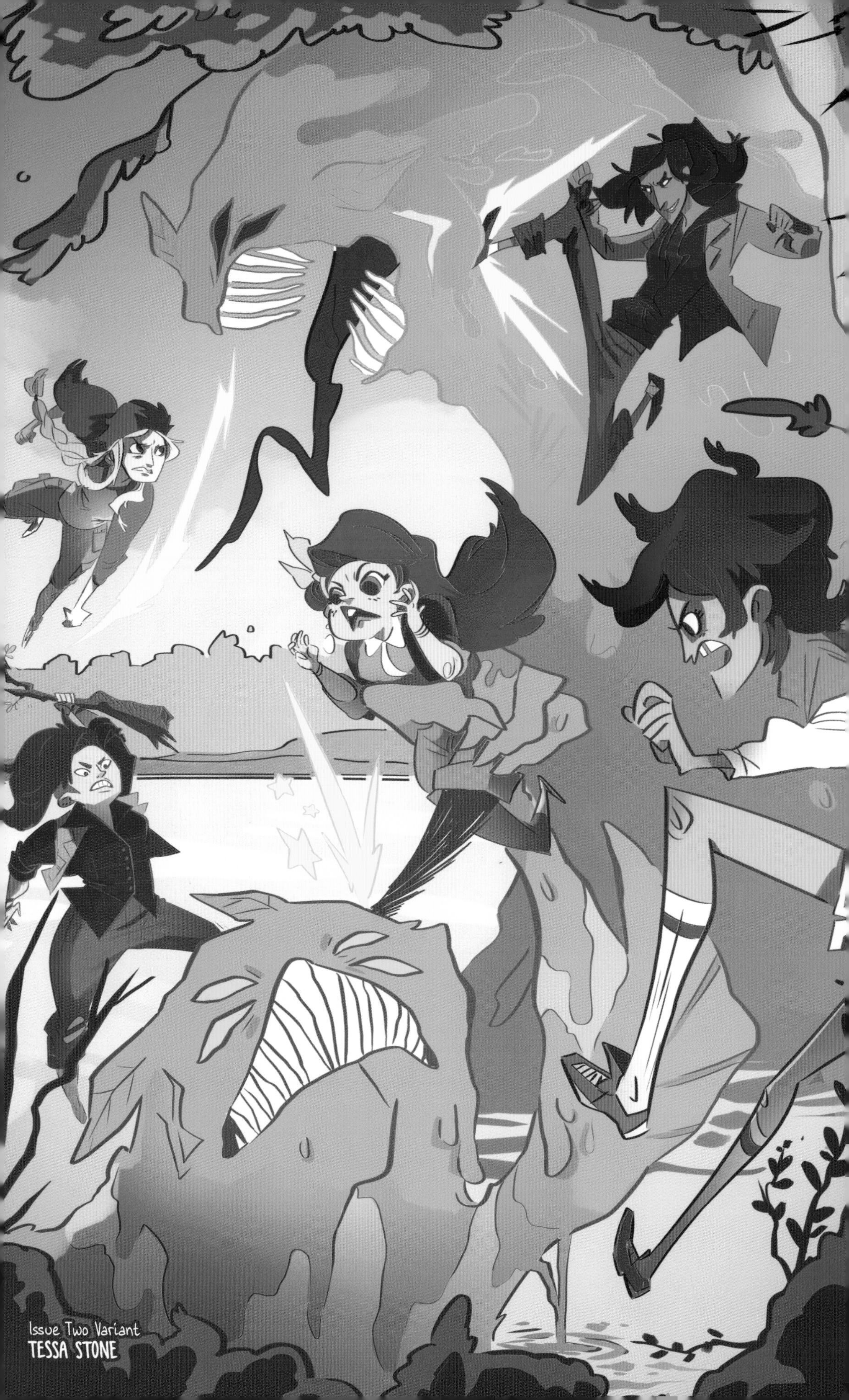

Issue Two Variant
TESSA STONE

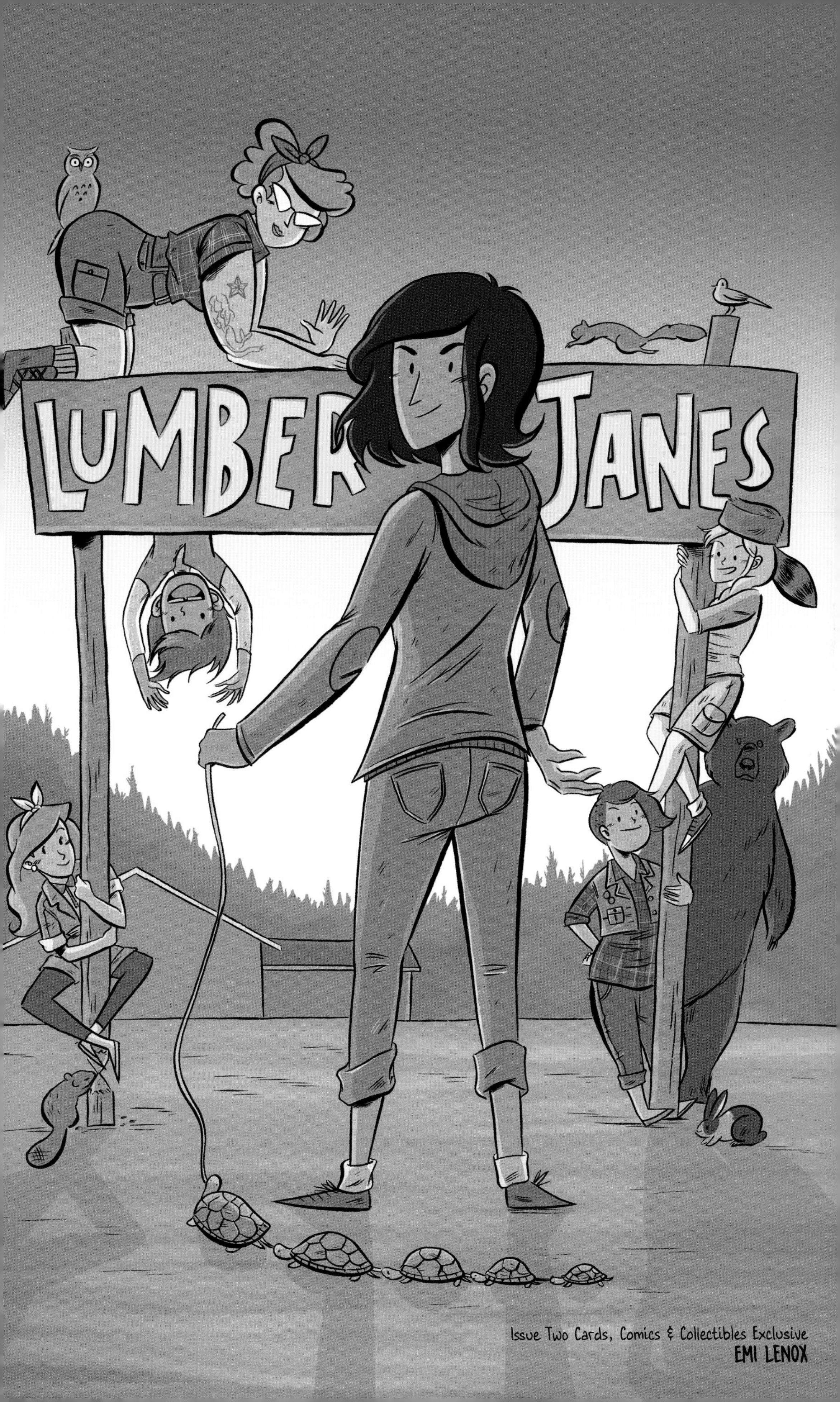
LUMBER JANES
Issue Two Cards, Comics & Collectibles Exclusive
EMI LENOX

Issue Two Second Print
PERRY MAPLE

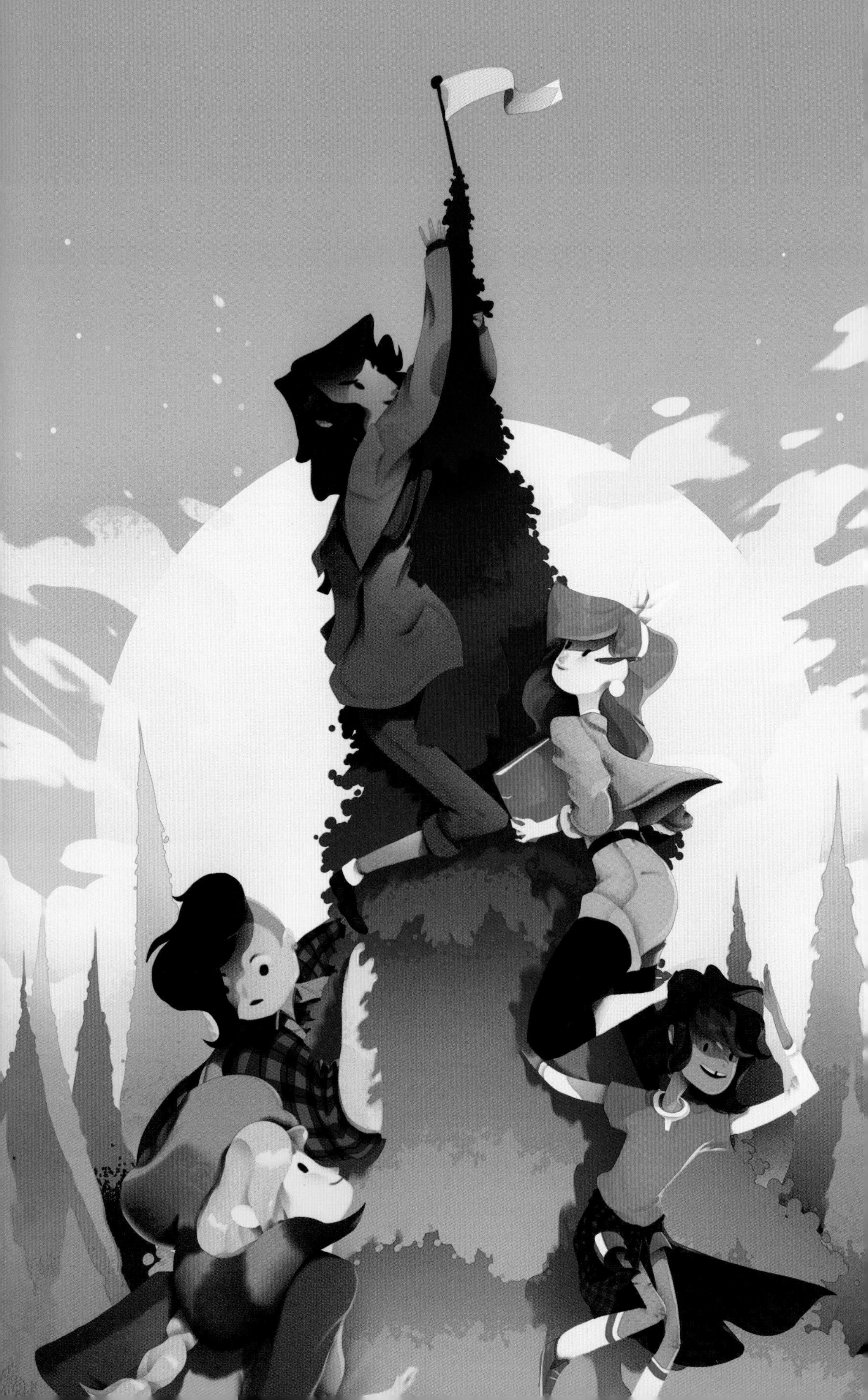

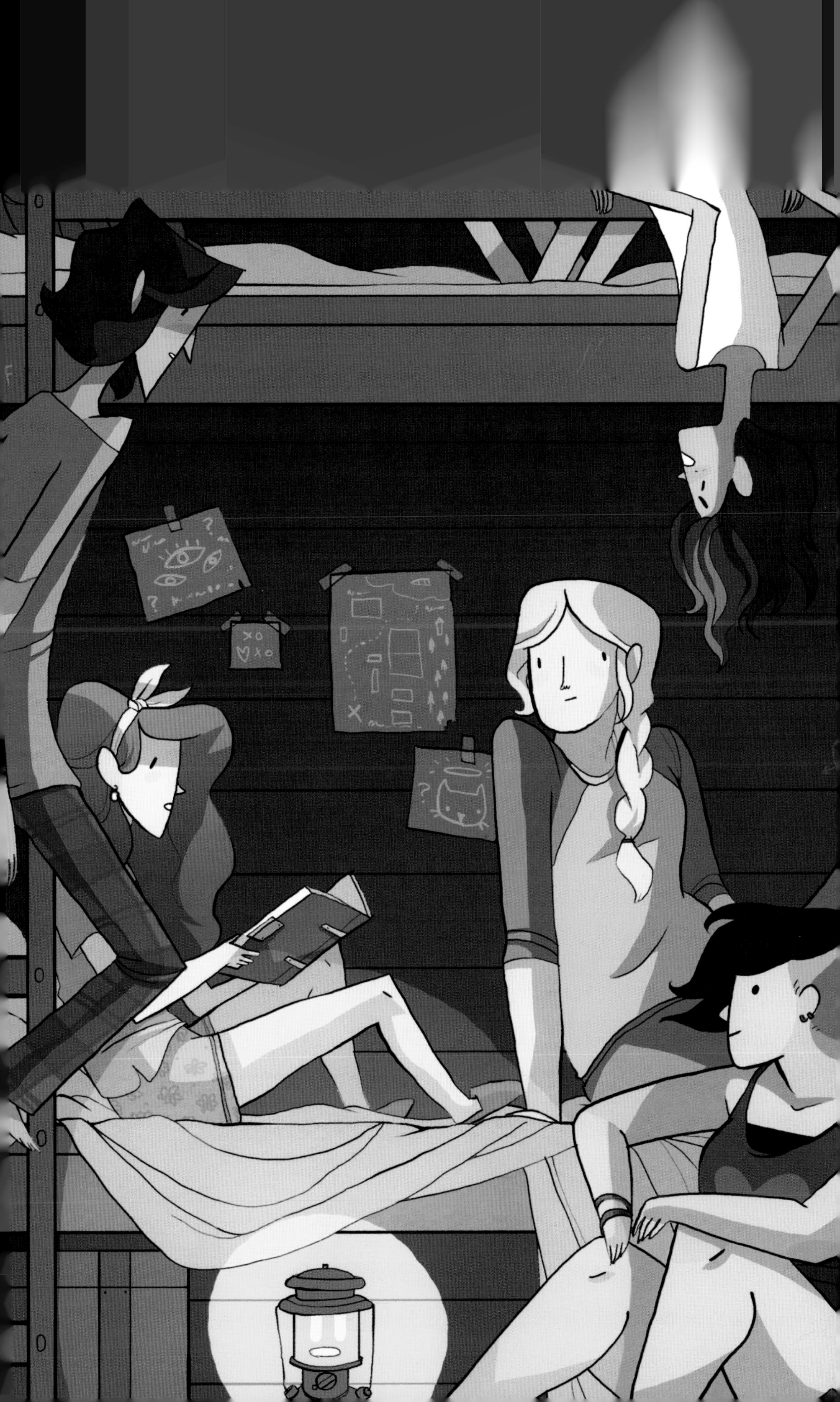
XO
XO

Issue Three Variant
FAITH ERIN HICKS

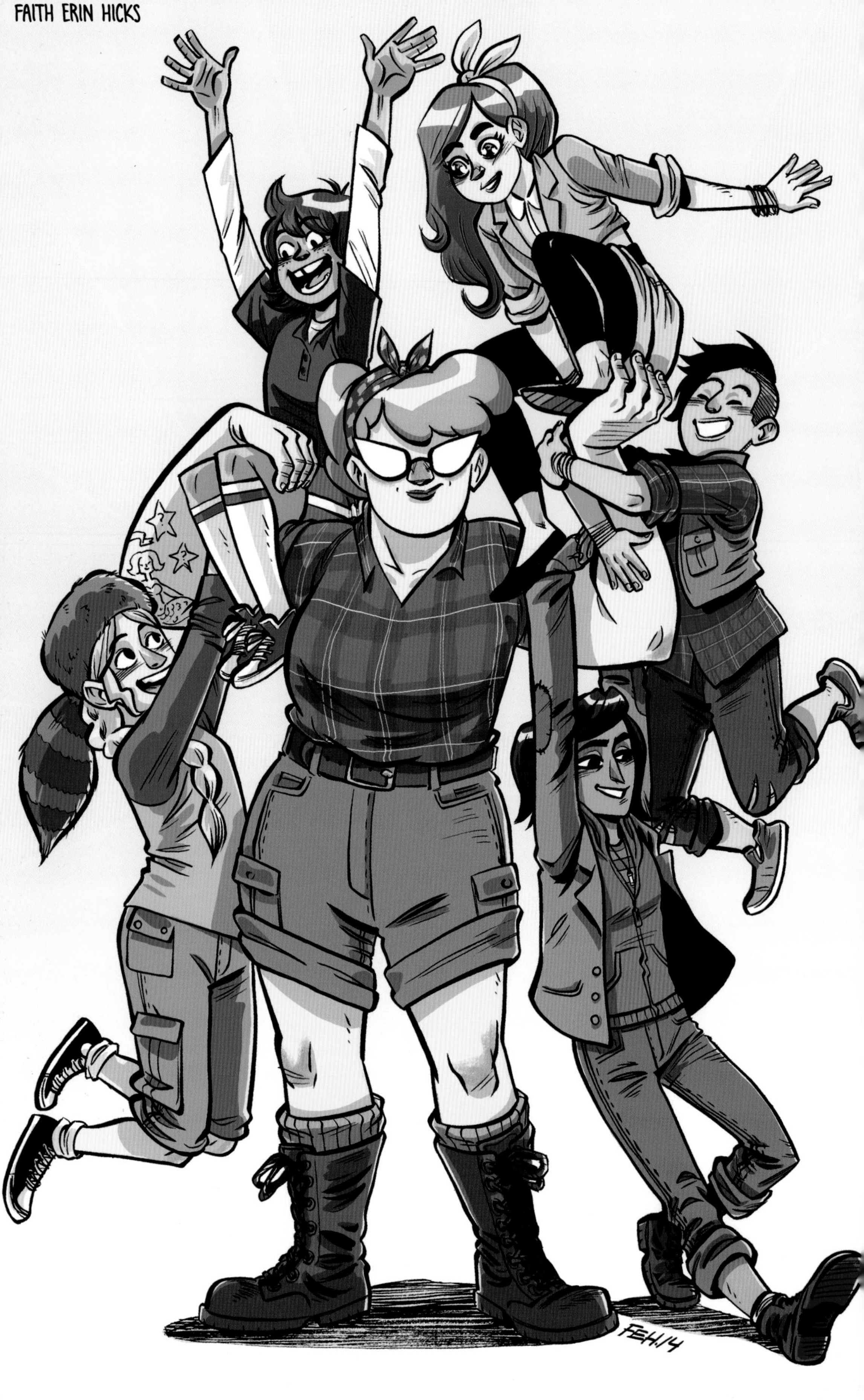
FEH/14

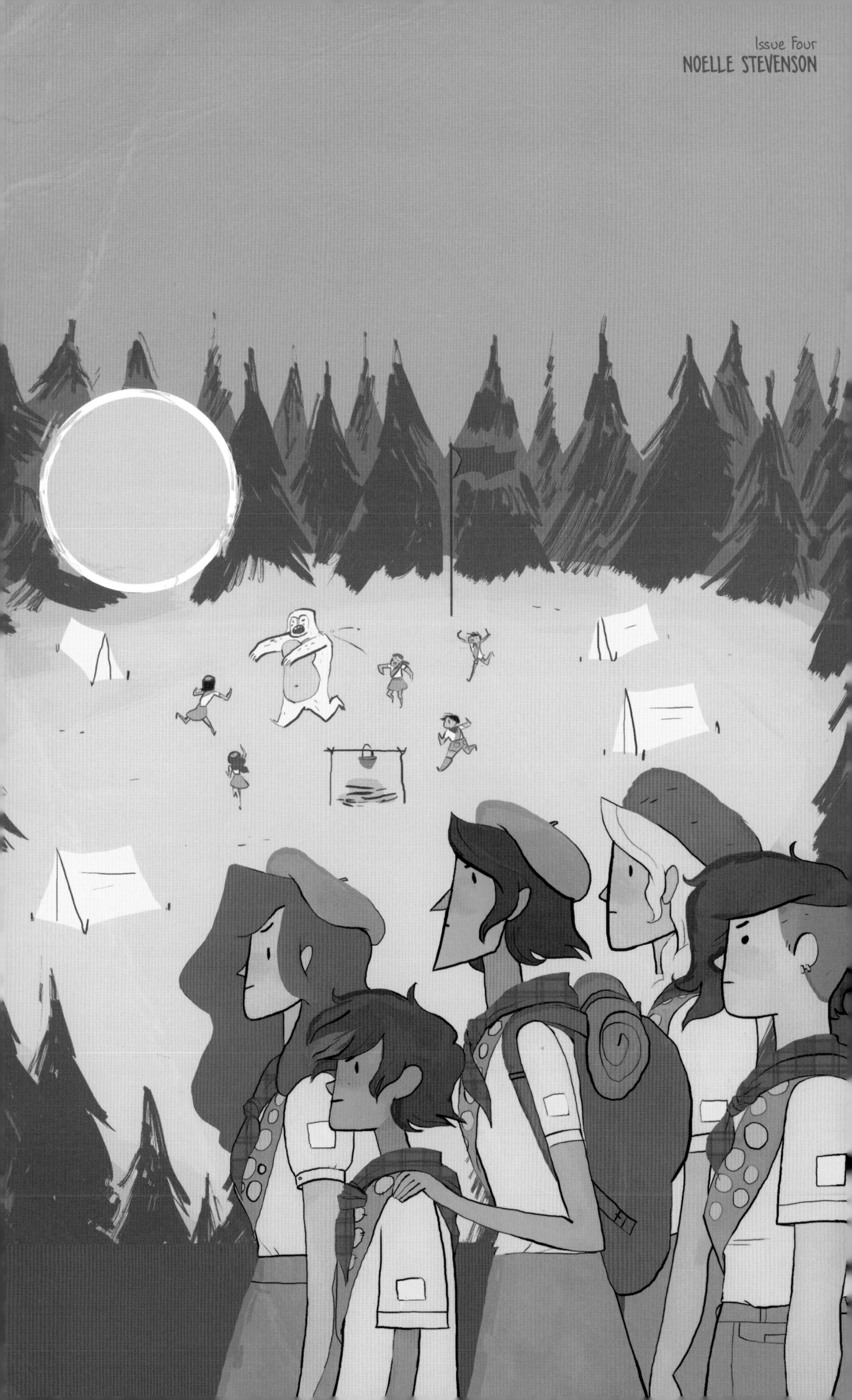

Issue Four
NOELLE STEVENSON

Issue Four Variant
KRIS ANKA

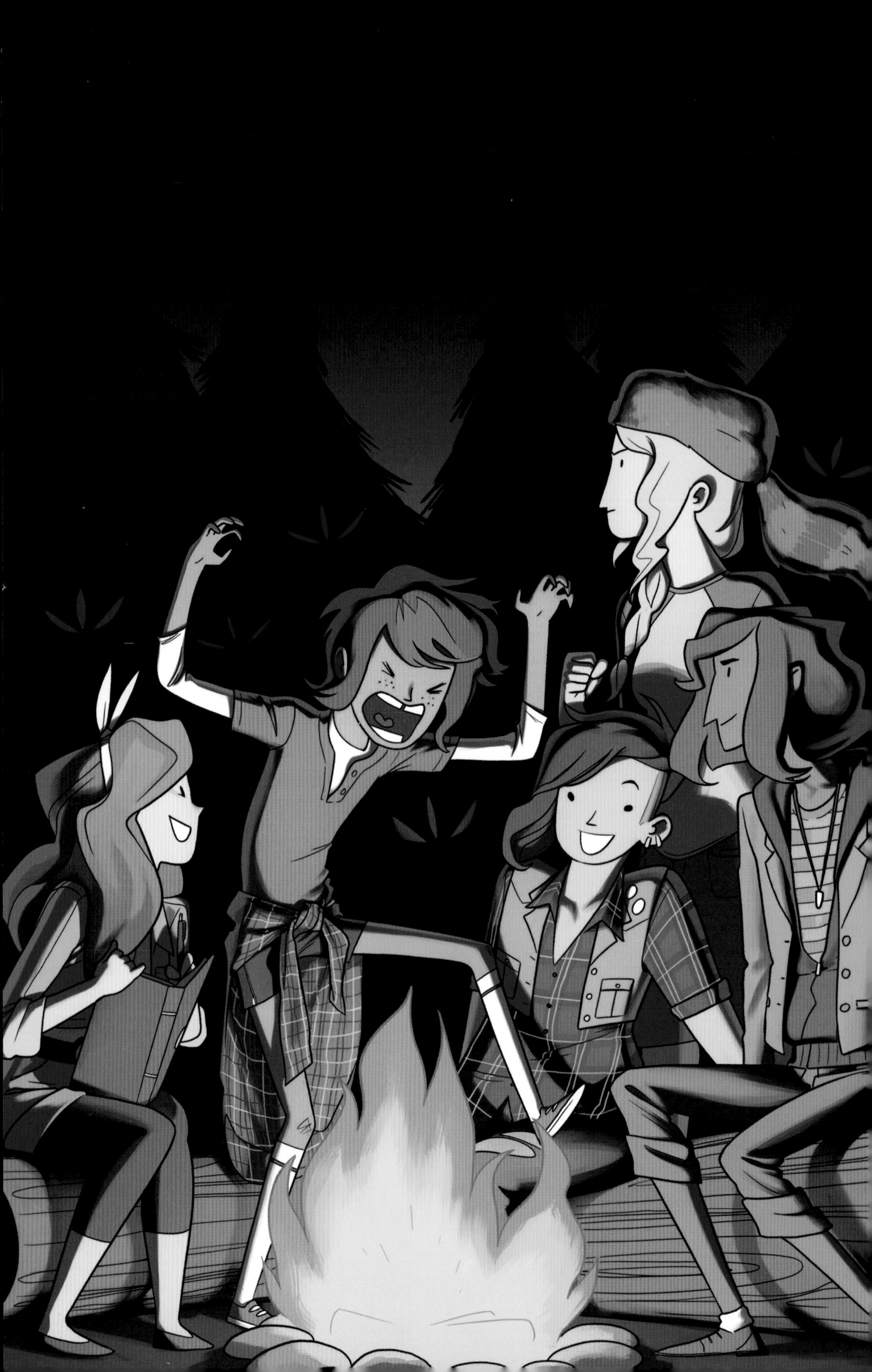

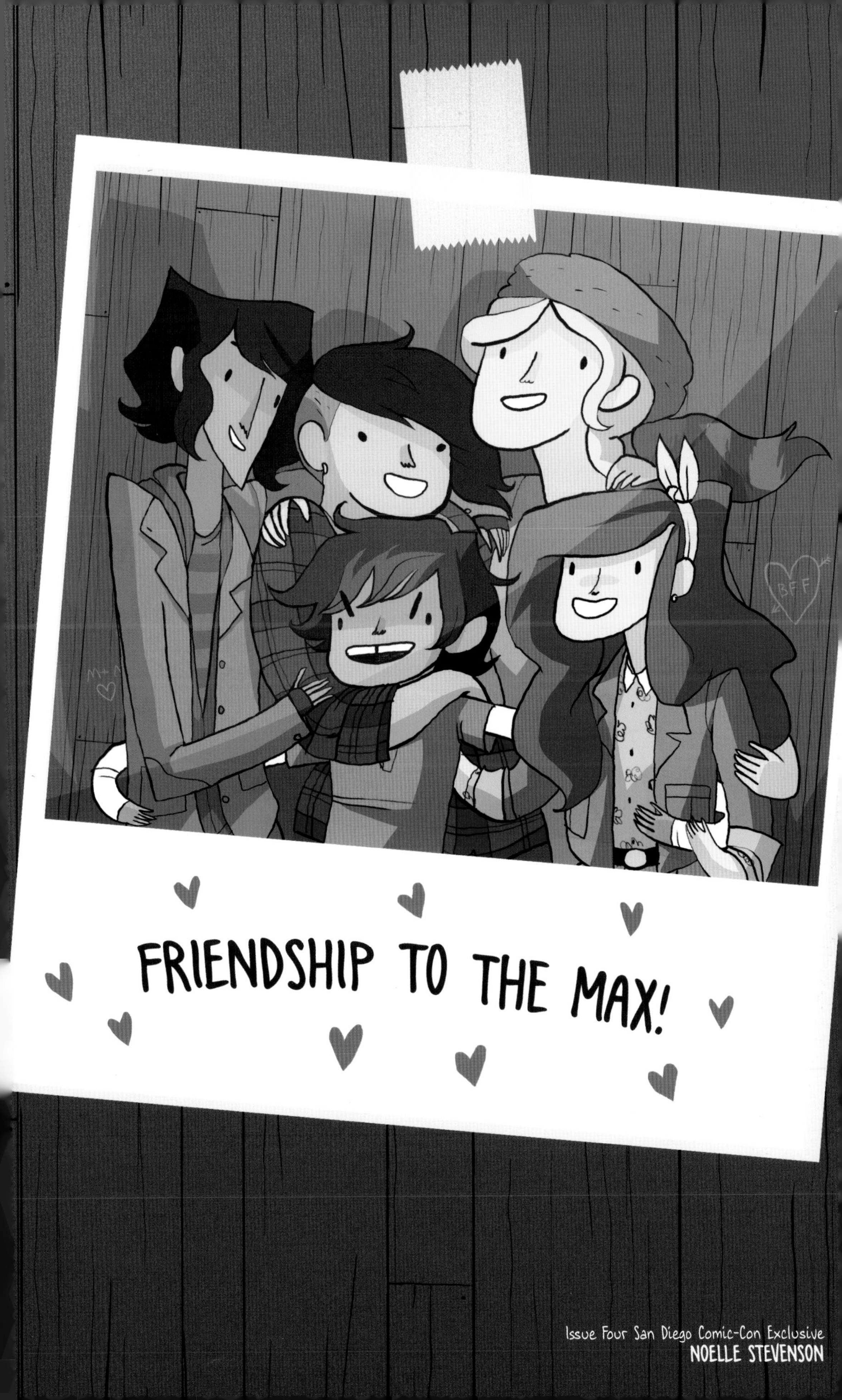
BFF
FRIENDSHIP TO THE MAX!

Issue Four San Diego Comic-Con Exclusive
NOELLE STEVENSON

Issue Five
NOELLE STEVENSON

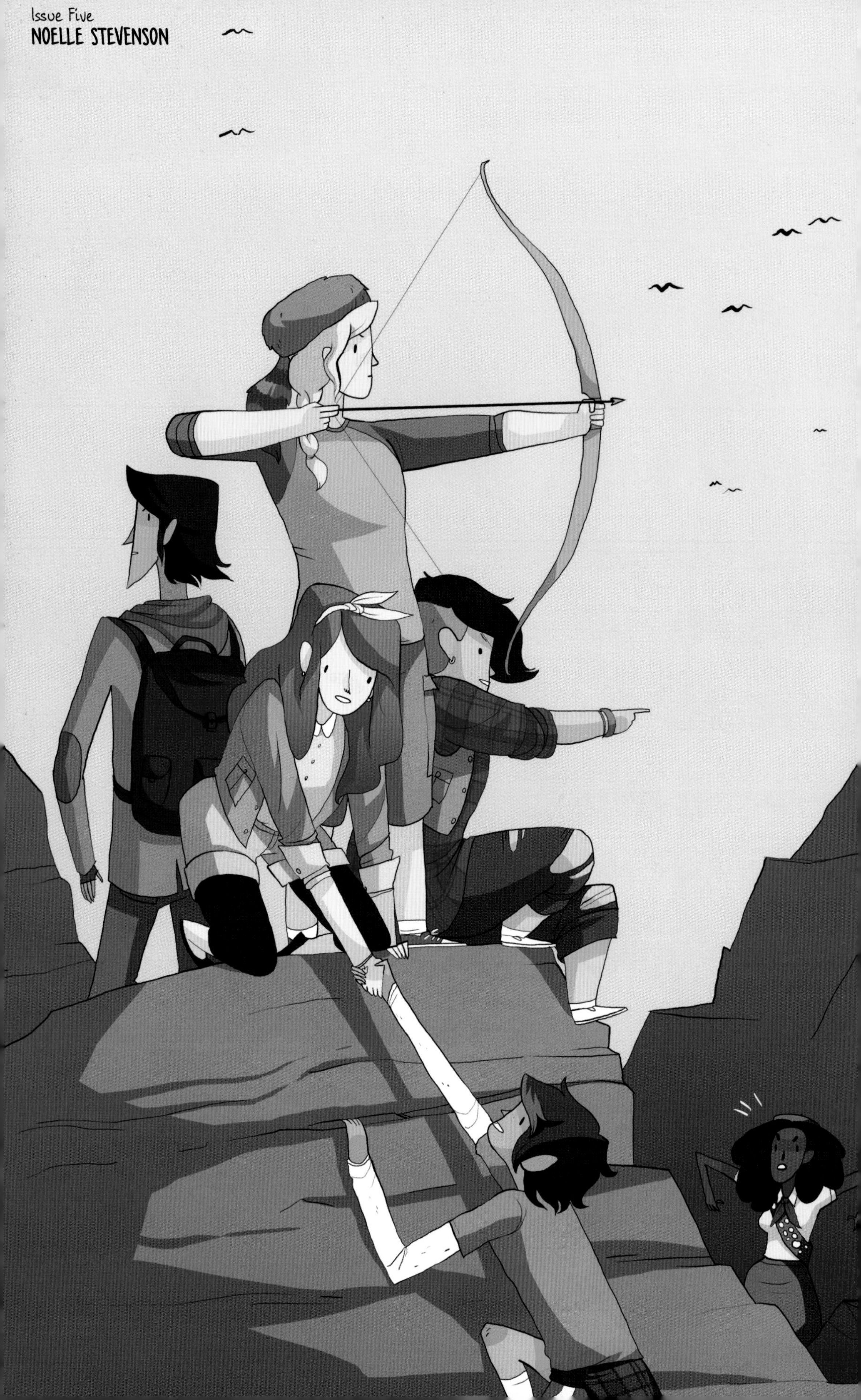

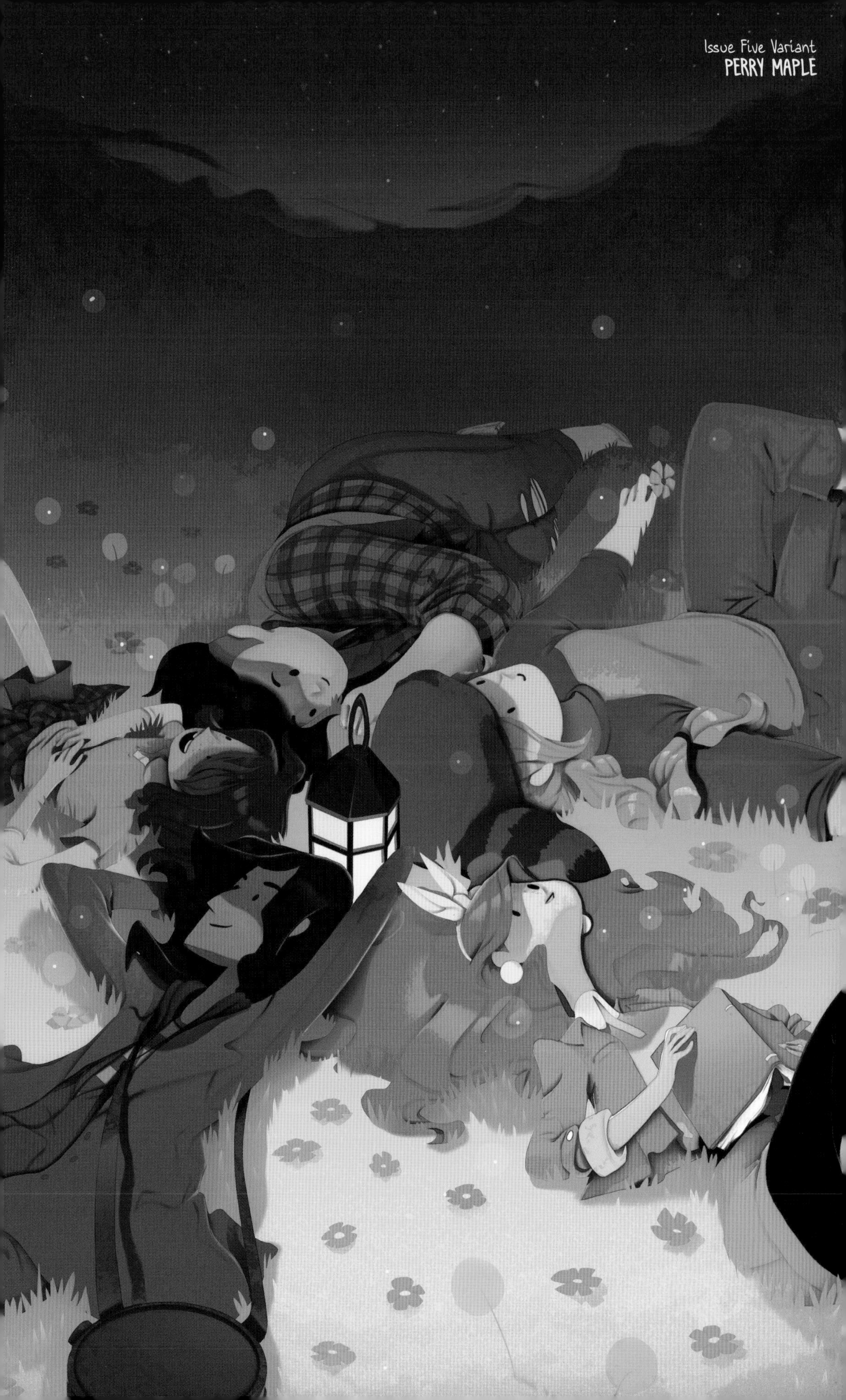
Issue Five Variant
PERRY MAPLE

Issue Six
NOELLE STEVENSON

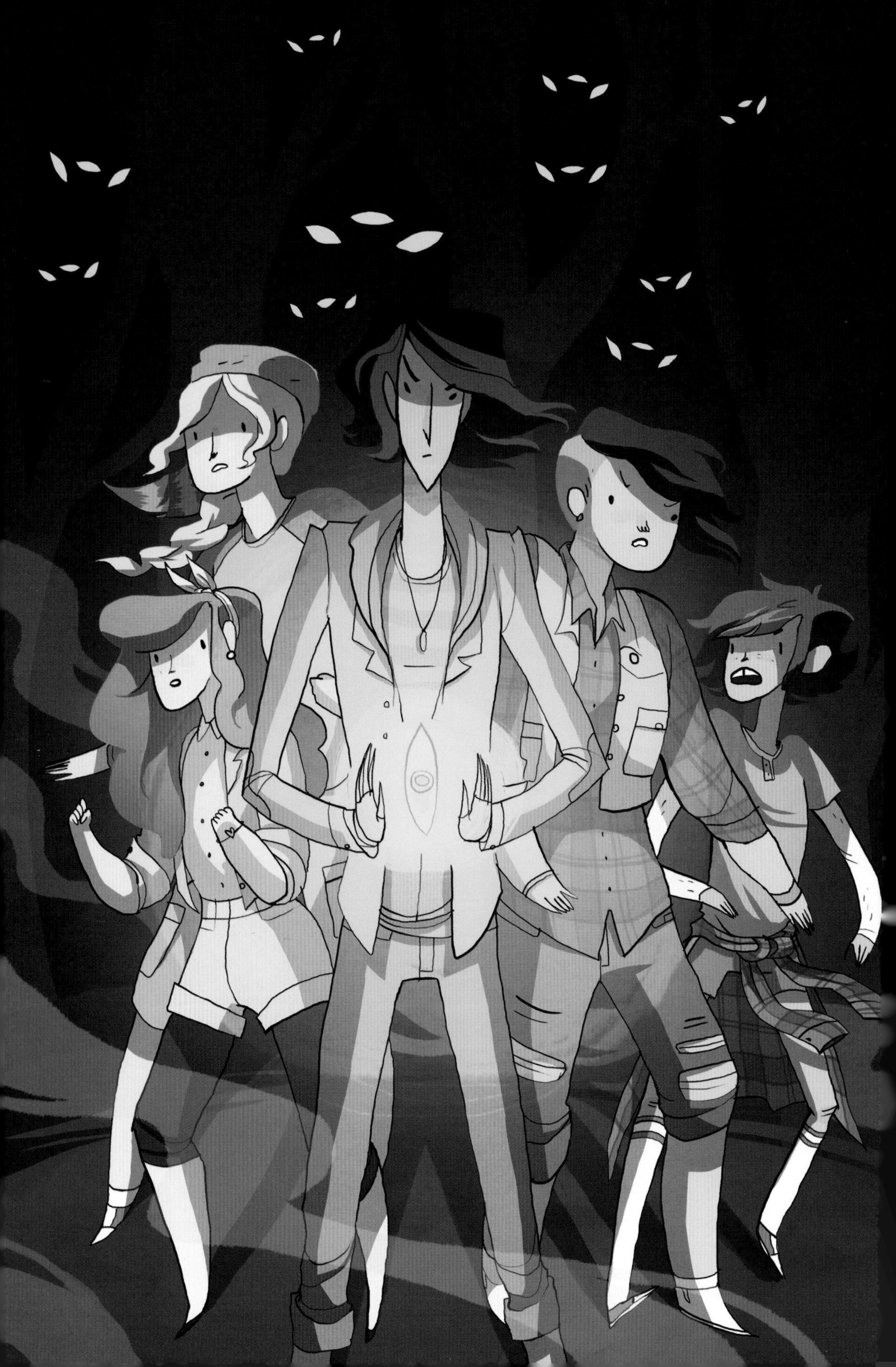

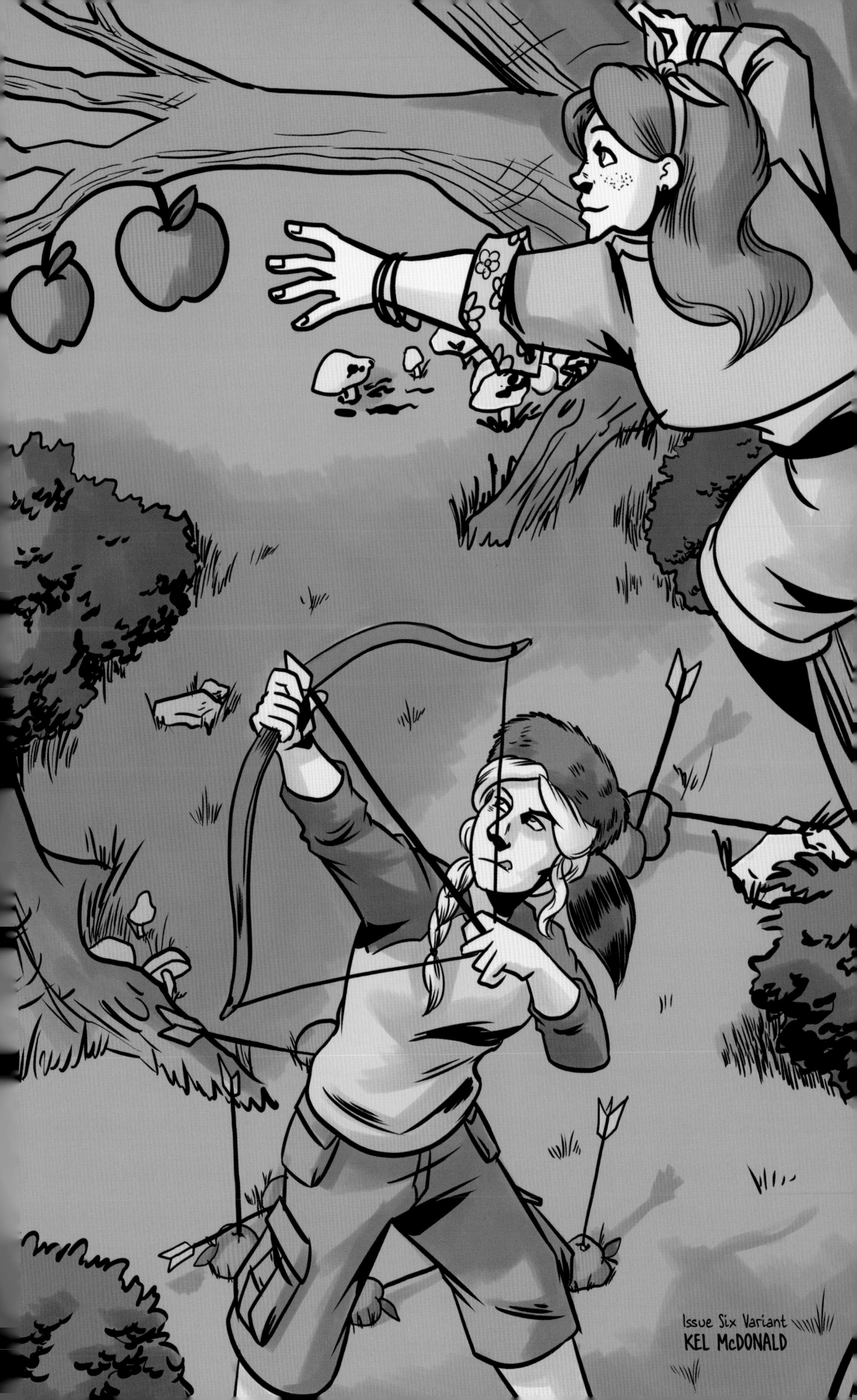
Issue Six Variant
KEL McDONALD

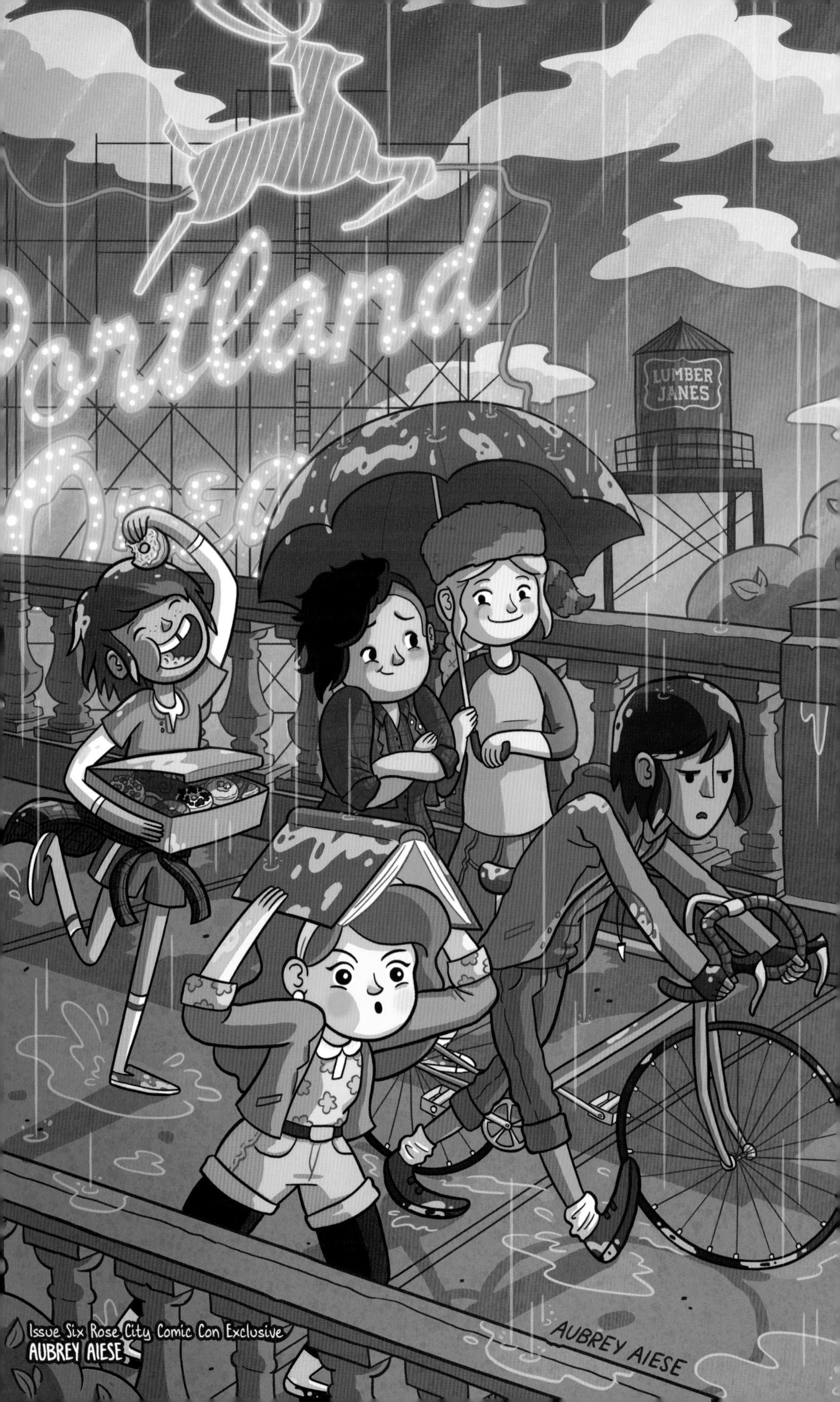
Portland Oregon
LUMBER JANES
AUBREY AIESE
Issue Six Rose City Comic Con Exclusive
AUBREY AIESE

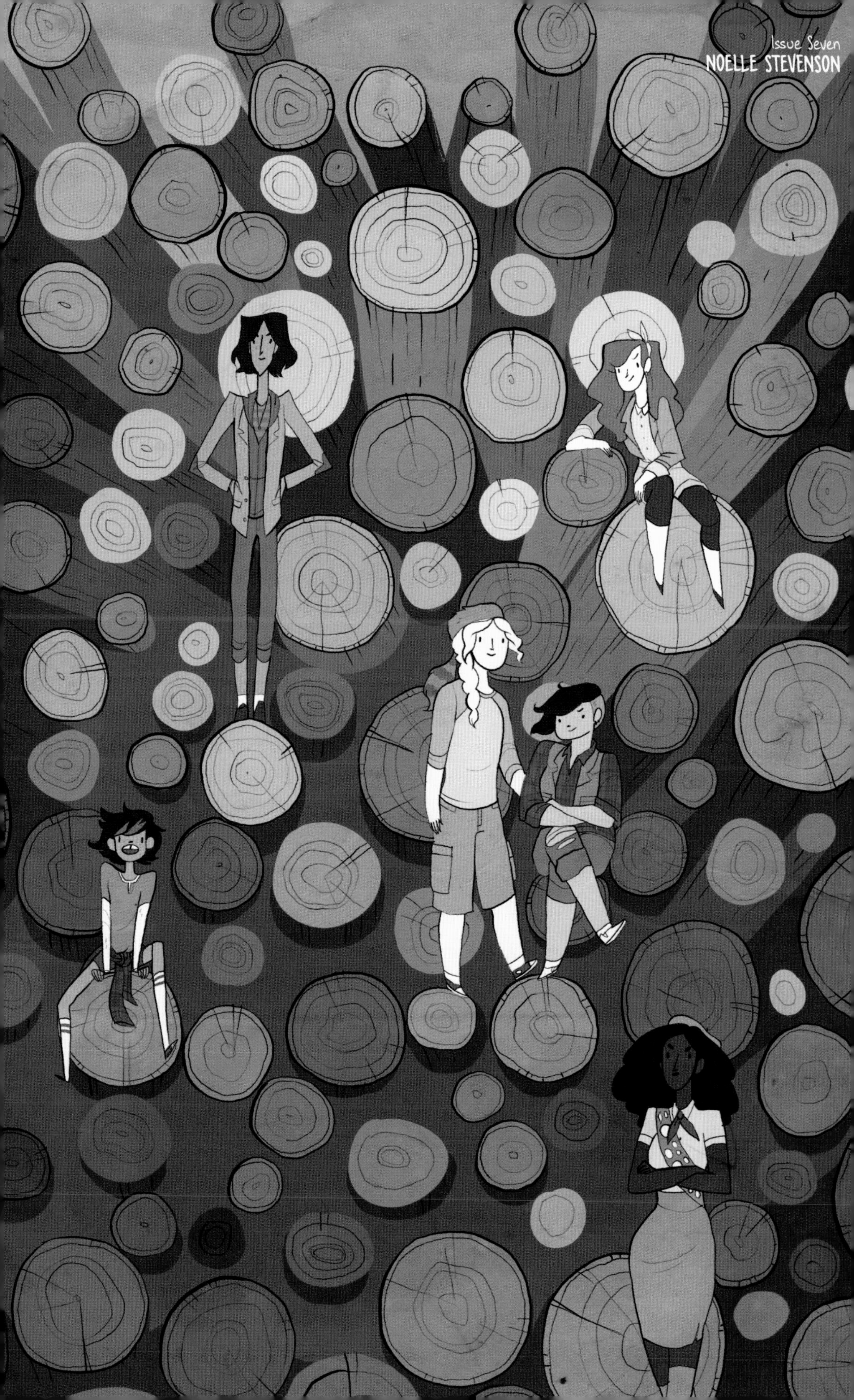
Issue Seven
NOELLE STEVENSON

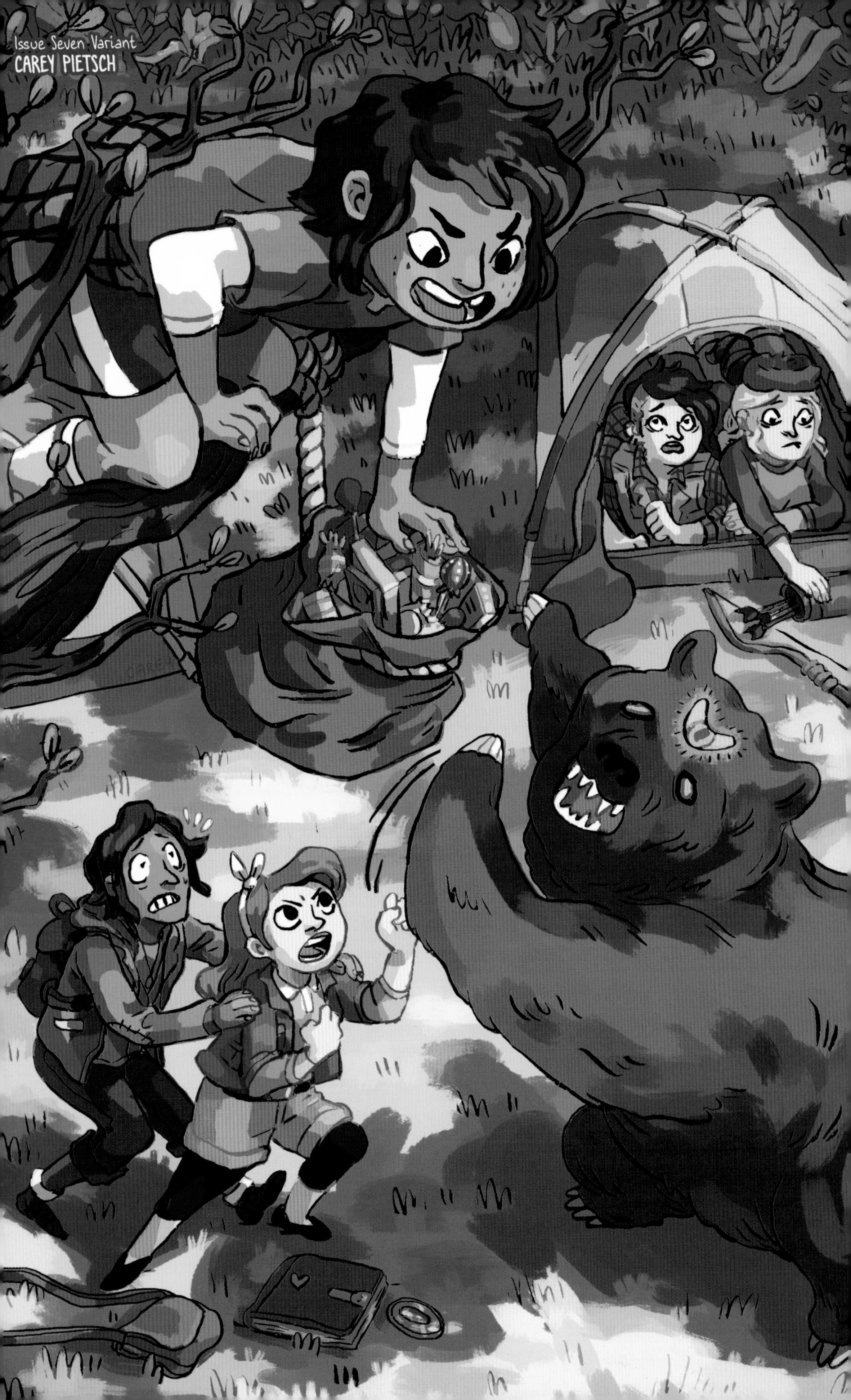
Issue Seven Variant
CAREY PIETSCH

Issue Eight
NOELLE STEVENSON

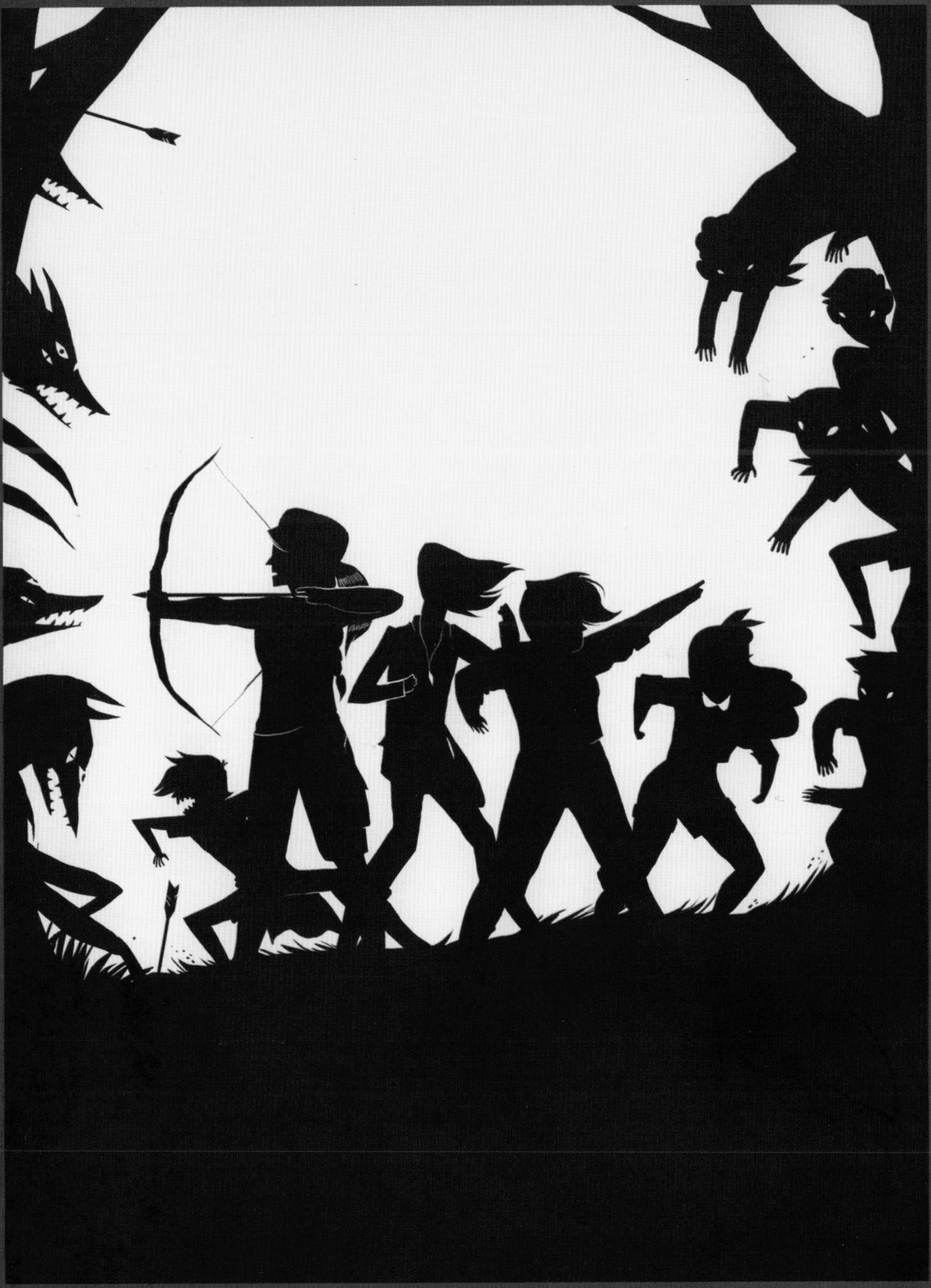

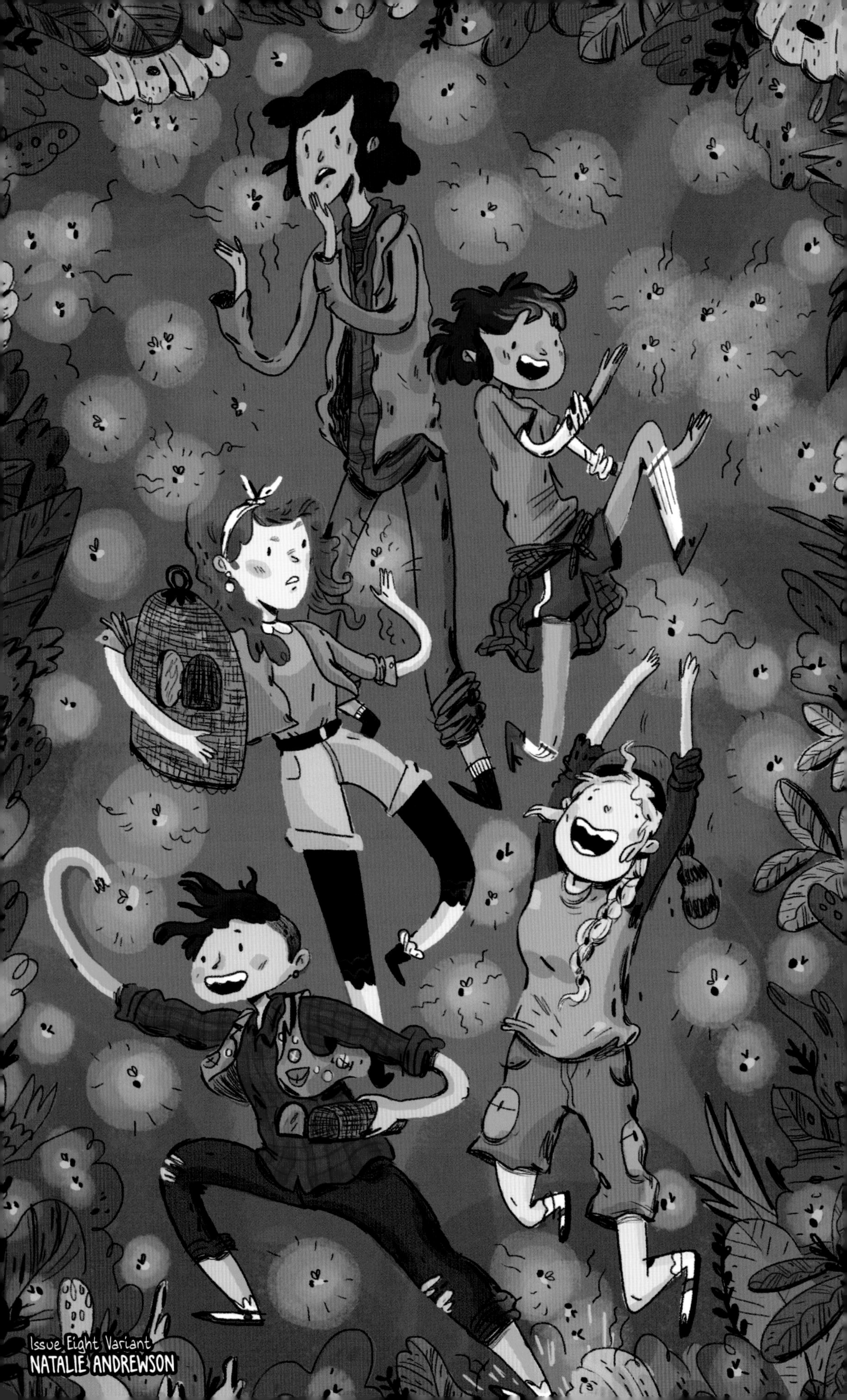
Issue Eight Variant
NATALIE ANDREWSON

will co

The

It he

appearan

dress fo

Further

Lumbe

to have

part in

Thiskv

Hardc

have

them

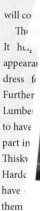

.E UNIFORM

hould be worn at camp

vents when Lumberjanes

n may also be worn at other

ions. It should be worn as a

the uniform dress with

rect shoes, and stocking or

out grows her uniform or

ng ster Lumberjane.

a she has

her

f her

The

yellow, short sle

emb

the w

choose

slacks,

made o

out-of-do

green bere

the colla

Shoes ma

heels, roun

socks sho

the uniform. Ne

belong with a Lumberjane uniform.

GES

HOW TO WEAR THE UNIFORM

To look well in a uniform demands first of

uniform be kept in good condition—clean

pressed. See that the skirt is the right length for your own

height and build, that the belt is adjusted to your waist,

that your shoes and stockings are in keeping with the

uniform, that you watch your posture and carry yourself

with dignity and grace. If the beret is removed indoors,

be sure that your hair is neat and kept in place with an

insconspicuous clip or ribbon. When you wear a

Lumberjane uniform you are identified as a member of

this organization and you should be doubly careful to

conduct yourself in a way that will show everyone that

courtesy and thoughtfullness are part of being a

Lumberjane. People are likely to judge a whole nation by

the selfishness of a few individuals, to criticize a whole

family because of the misconduct of one member, and to

feel unkindly toward and organization because of the

The unifor

helps to cre

in a group.

active life th

another bond

future, and pr

in order to b

Lumberjane pr

Penniquiqul Thi

Types, but m

Lady

s will wish to have one. They

can either bu   , or make it themselves from

materials available at the trading post.

MUSIC MIXES

Lumberjanes "Arts and Crafts" Program Field

TREBLE MAKER BADGE

"Some risks are worth the reward."

Music fuels the mind and thus fuels creativity. A creative mind has the ability to make discoveries and create innovations. The greatest minds and thinkers like Hildegard von Bingen, Barbara Strozzi, and Florence Mary Taylor all had something in common in that they were constantly exploring their imagination and creativity. As a Lumberjane it will be vital that we not only enrich our minds, but enrich those around us. Music is just one of the many mediums that can create an empowering environment, it is one of the few mediums that can be enjoyed at any time.

Listening to instrumental music challenges one to listen and tell a story about what one hears. In the same sense, playing a musical instrument gives a Lumberjane the ability to tell a story without words. This will become handy should words escape her, and every Lumberjane understands the importance of not being limited to just words. Listening and telling a story require maximum right brain usage which not only exercises one's creativity but also one's intellect. The strength of all the arts including writing, painting, dance, and theater have the ability to create a similar effect. It is the understanding of that strength that will help the Lumberjane earn her *Treble Maker* badge. This badge is considered a favorite at most camps, and will most likely continue to be one of the most anticipated badges a scout can earn.

To obtain the *Treble Maker* badge a Lumberjane must show off her knowledge in not only musical theory and understanding, but be able to prove that she exemplifies creativity in her problem solving. While it is just as important to think inside the box as it is to think outside of it a Lumberjane will need to know not only how to think outside the box, but how to create a new box altogether. It's through the many classes and trials that a Lumberjane will gain these skills as she continues on her path to the amazing future that undoubtedly waits for her.

EDGE OF SEVENTEEN - STEVIE NICKS · BAD REPUTATION - JOAN JETT · RUN THE WORLD (GIRLS) - BEYONCE · NORTHSHORE - TEGAN & SARA · WOO HOO - THE 5 6 7 8S · WILDERNESS - SLEATER-KINNEY · WOLF - NOW, NOW · SPIN AROUND - JOSIE AND THE PUSSYCATS · BUFFY THE VAMPIRE SLAYER THEME · JET PACK - DOG PARTY · PIRATES - JENNY OWEN YOUNGS · DANCE APOCALYPTIC - JANELLE MONAE · BAMBOO BONES - AGAINST ME! · PUSH IT - SALT-N-PEPA · I KNEW YOU WERE TROUBLE - TAYLOR SWIFT · UP ALL NIGHT - ONE DIRECTION · ROAR - KATY PERRY · EYE OF THE TIGER - SURVIVOR · SAY YOU'LL BE THERE - SPICE GIRLS · RIBS - LORDE · EDGE OF SEVENTEEN (THE BEST SONG EVER) - STEVIE NICKS

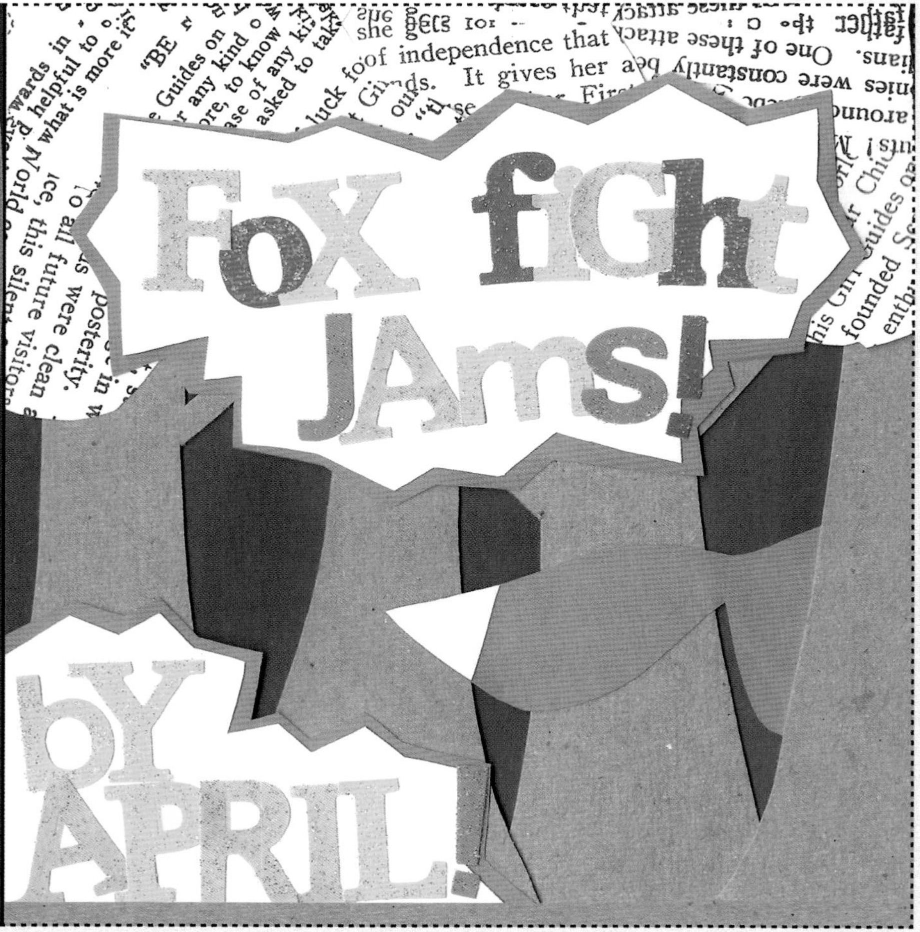
Fox fiGht JAms!
bY APRIL!

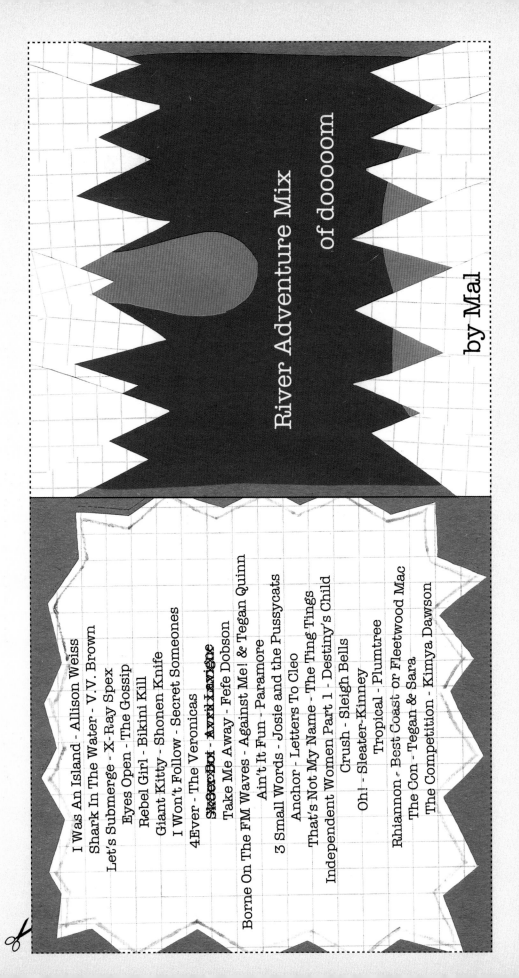

River Adventure Mix
of dooooom

by Mal

I Was An Island - Allison Weiss
Shark In The Water - V.V. Brown
Let's Submerge - X-Ray Spex
Eyes Open - The Gossip
Rebel Girl - Bikini Kill
Giant Kitty - Shonen Knife
I Won't Follow - Secret Someones
4Ever - The Veronicas
~~Sk8er Boi - Avril Lavigne~~
Take Me Away - Fefe Dobson
Borne On The FM Waves - Against Me! & Tegan Quinn
Ain't It Fun - Paramore
3 Small Words - Josie and the Pussycats
Anchor - Letters To Cleo
That's Not My Name - The Ting Tings
Independent Women Part 1 - Destiny's Child
Crush - Sleigh Bells
Oh! - Sleater-Kinney
Tropical - Plumtree
Rhiannon - Best Coast or Fleetwood Mac
The Con - Tegan & Sara
The Competition - Kimya Dawson

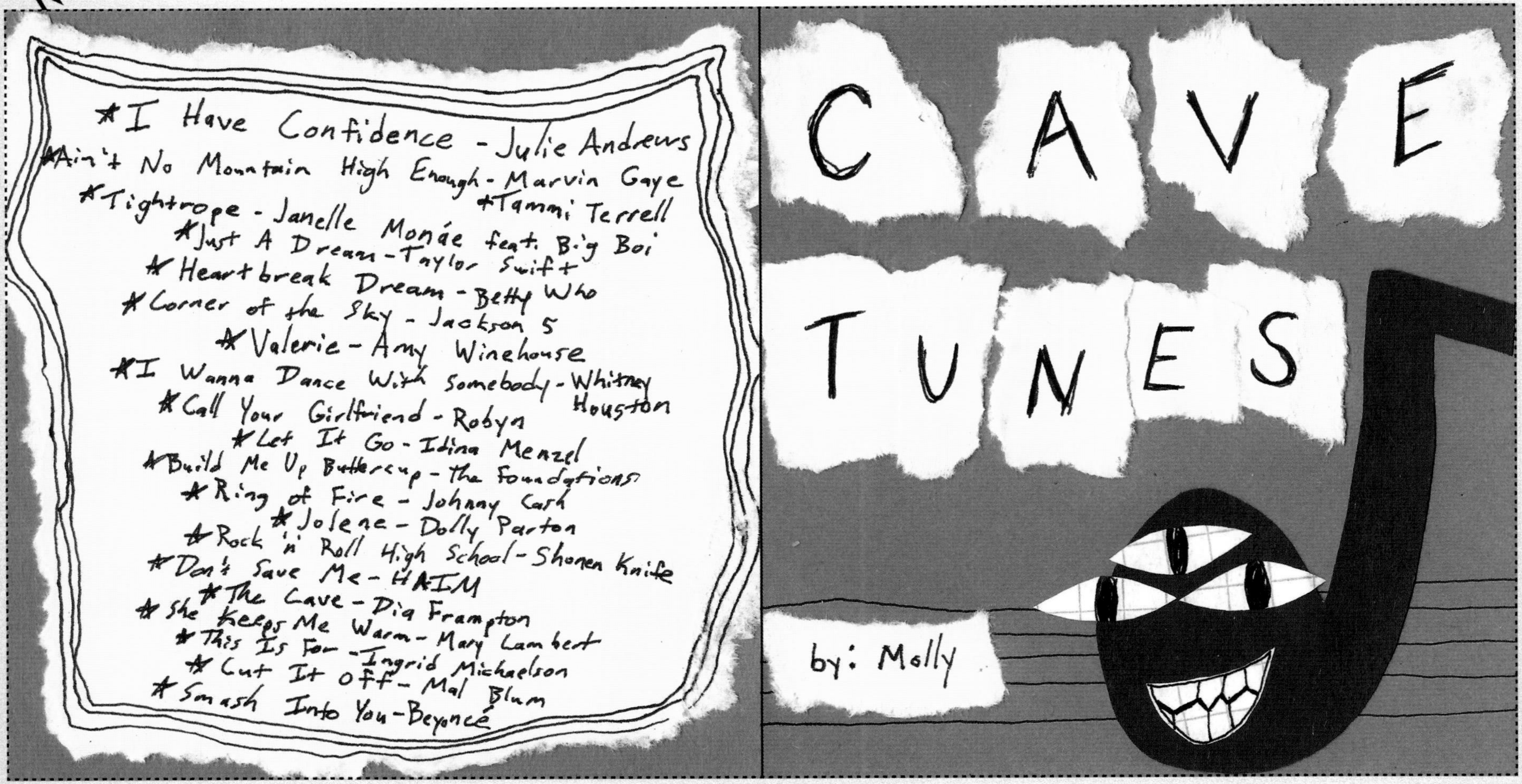

★I Have Confidence - Julie Andrews
★Ain't No Mountain High Enough - Marvin Gaye ★Tammi Terrell
★Tightrope - Janelle Monáe feat. Big Boi
★Just A Dream - Taylor Swift
★Heartbreak Dream - Betty Who
★Corner of the Sky - Jackson 5
★Valerie - Amy Winehouse
★I Wanna Dance With Somebody - Whitney Houston
★Call Your Girlfriend - Robyn
★Let It Go - Idina Menzel
★Build Me Up Buttercup - The Foundations
★Ring of Fire - Johnny Cash
★Jolene - Dolly Parton
★Rock 'n' Roll High School - Shonen Knife
★Don't Save Me - HAIM
★The Cave - Dia Frampton
★She Keeps Me Warm - Mary Lambert
★This Is For - Ingrid Michaelson
★Cut It Off - Mal Blum
★Smash Into You - Beyoncé
CAVE TUNES
by: Molly

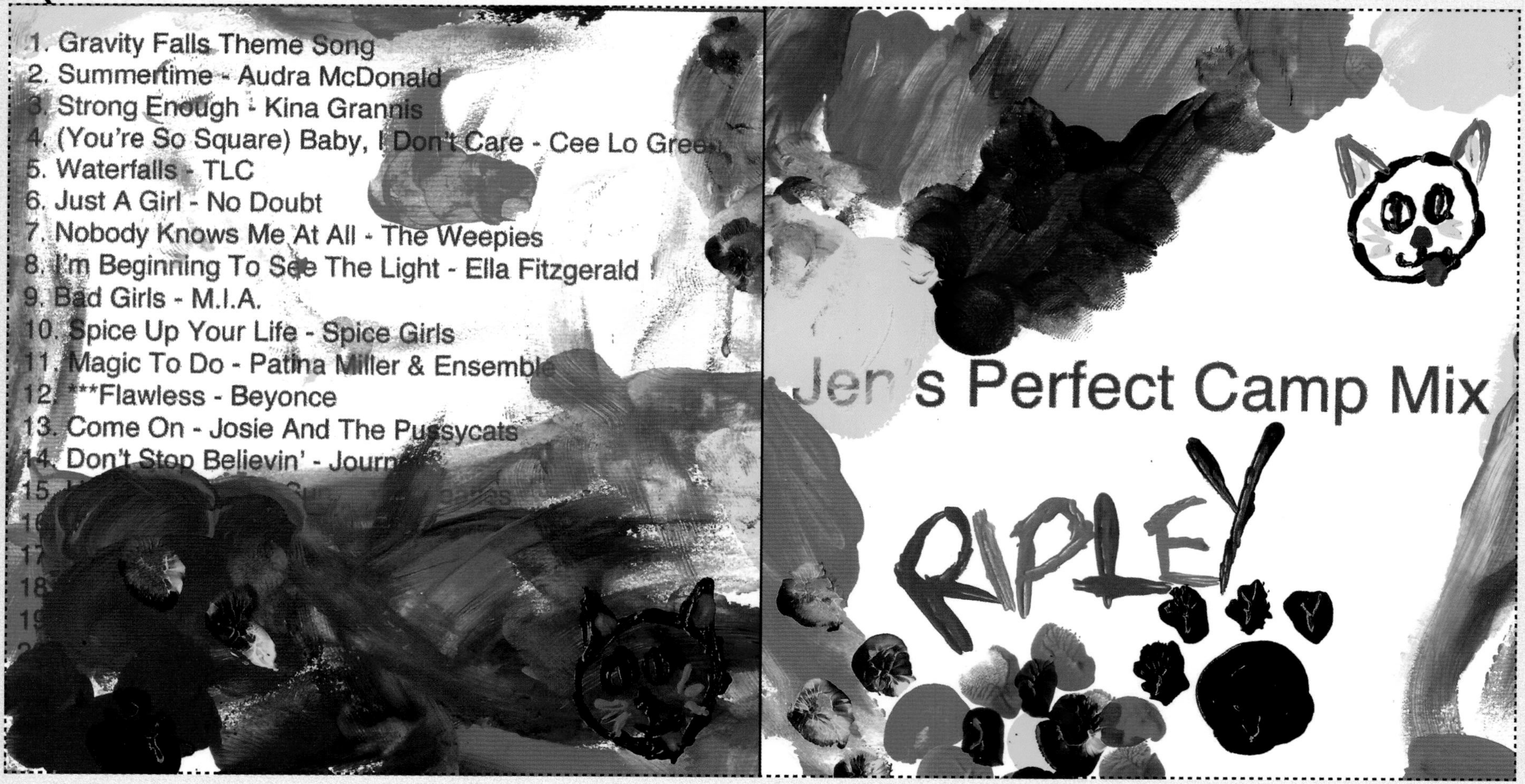
1. Gravity Falls Theme Song
2. Summertime - Audra McDonald
3. Strong Enough - Kina Grannis
4. (You're So Square) Baby, I Don't Care - Cee Lo Gree
5. Waterfalls - TLC
6. Just A Girl - No Doubt
7. Nobody Knows Me At All - The Weepies
8. I'm Beginning To See The Light - Ella Fitzgerald
9. Bad Girls - M.I.A.
10. Spice Up Your Life - Spice Girls
11. Magic To Do - Patina Miller & Ensemble
12. ***Flawless - Beyonce
13. Come On - Josie And The Pussycats
14. Don't Stop Believin' - Journ
Jen s Perfect Camp Mix
RIPLEY

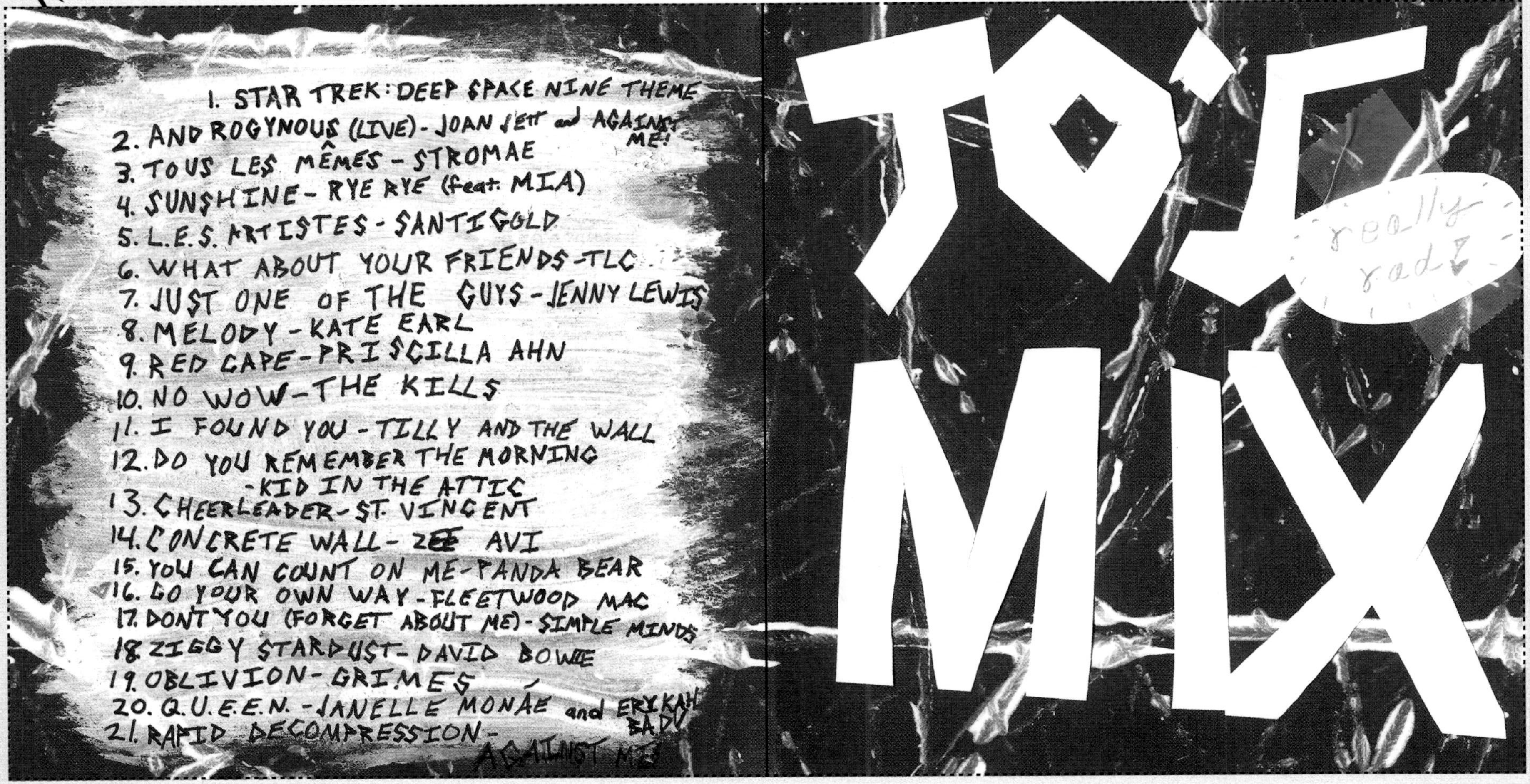

1. STAR TREK: DEEP SPACE NINE THEME
2. ANDROGYNOUS (LIVE) - JOAN JETT and AGAINST ME!
3. TOUS LES MÊMES - STROMAE
4. SUNSHINE - RYE RYE (feat. MIA)
5. L.E.S. ARTISTES - SANTIGOLD
6. WHAT ABOUT YOUR FRIENDS - TLC
7. JUST ONE OF THE GUYS - JENNY LEWIS
8. MELODY - KATE EARL
9. RED CAPE - PRISCILLA AHN
10. NO WOW - THE KILLS
11. I FOUND YOU - TILLY AND THE WALL
12. DO YOU REMEMBER THE MORNING - KID IN THE ATTIC
13. CHEERLEADER - ST. VINCENT
14. CONCRETE WALL - ZEE AVI
15. YOU CAN COUNT ON ME - PANDA BEAR
16. GO YOUR OWN WAY - FLEETWOOD MAC
17. DONT YOU (FORGET ABOUT ME) - SIMPLE MINDS
18. ZIGGY STARDUST - DAVID BOWIE
19. OBLIVION - GRIMES
20. Q.U.E.E.N. - JANELLE MONÁE and ERYKAH BADU
21. RAPID DECOMPRESSION - AGAINST ME!
TO'J
MIX
really rad!

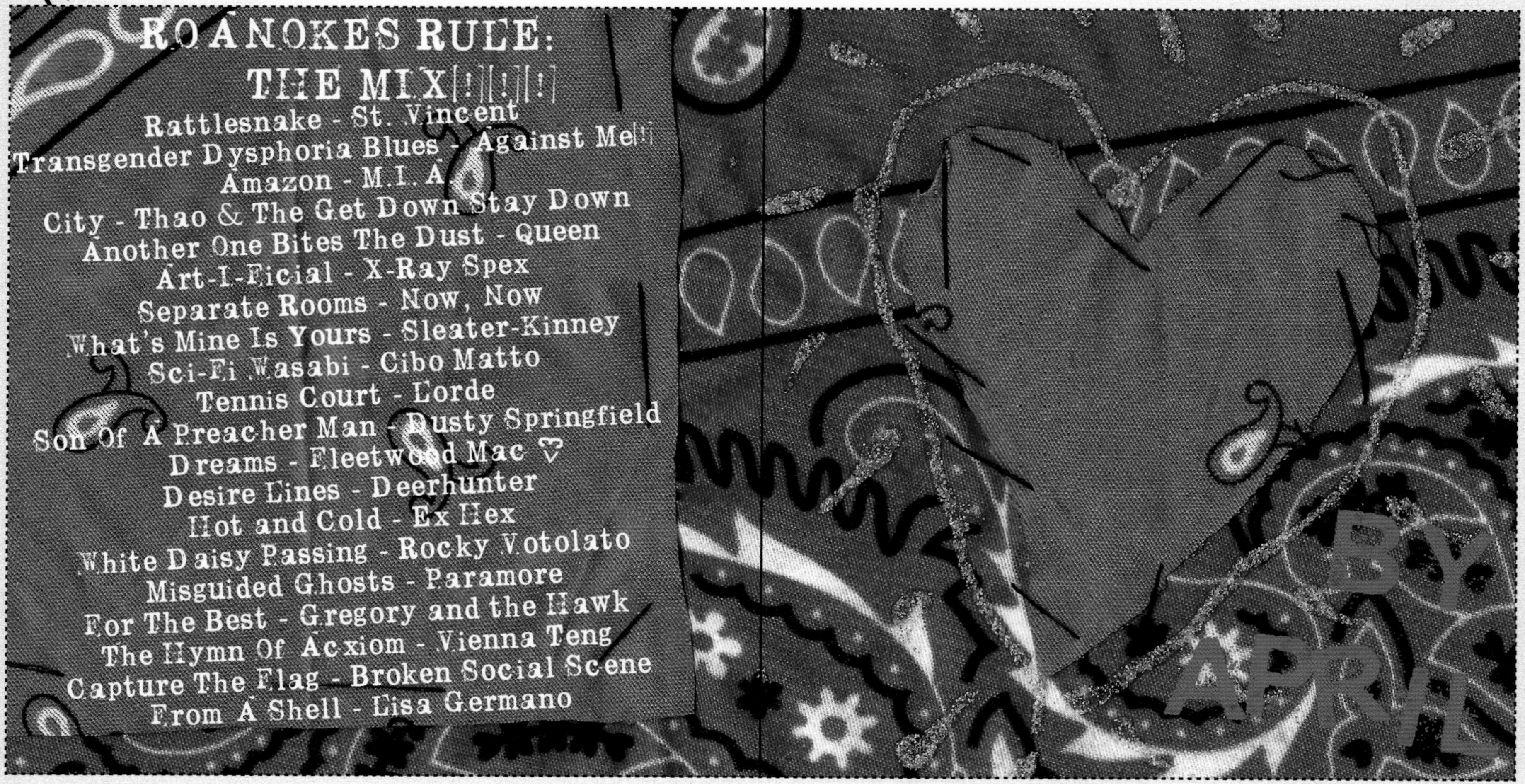
ROANOKES RULE:
THE MIX[!][!][!]
Rattlesnake - St. Vincent
Transgender Dysphoria Blues - Against Me[!]
Amazon - M.I.A.
City - Thao & The Get Down Stay Down
Another One Bites The Dust - Queen
Art-I-Ficial - X-Ray Spex
Separate Rooms - Now, Now
What's Mine Is Yours - Sleater-Kinney
Sci-Fi Wasabi - Cibo Matto
Tennis Court - Lorde
Son Of A Preacher Man - Dusty Springfield
Dreams - Fleetwood Mac
Desire Lines - Deerhunter
Hot and Cold - Ex Hex
White Daisy Passing - Rocky Votolato
Misguided Ghosts - Paramore
For The Best - Gregory and the Hawk
The Hymn Of Acxiom - Vienna Teng
Capture The Flag - Broken Social Scene
From A Shell - Lisa Germano
BY
APRIL

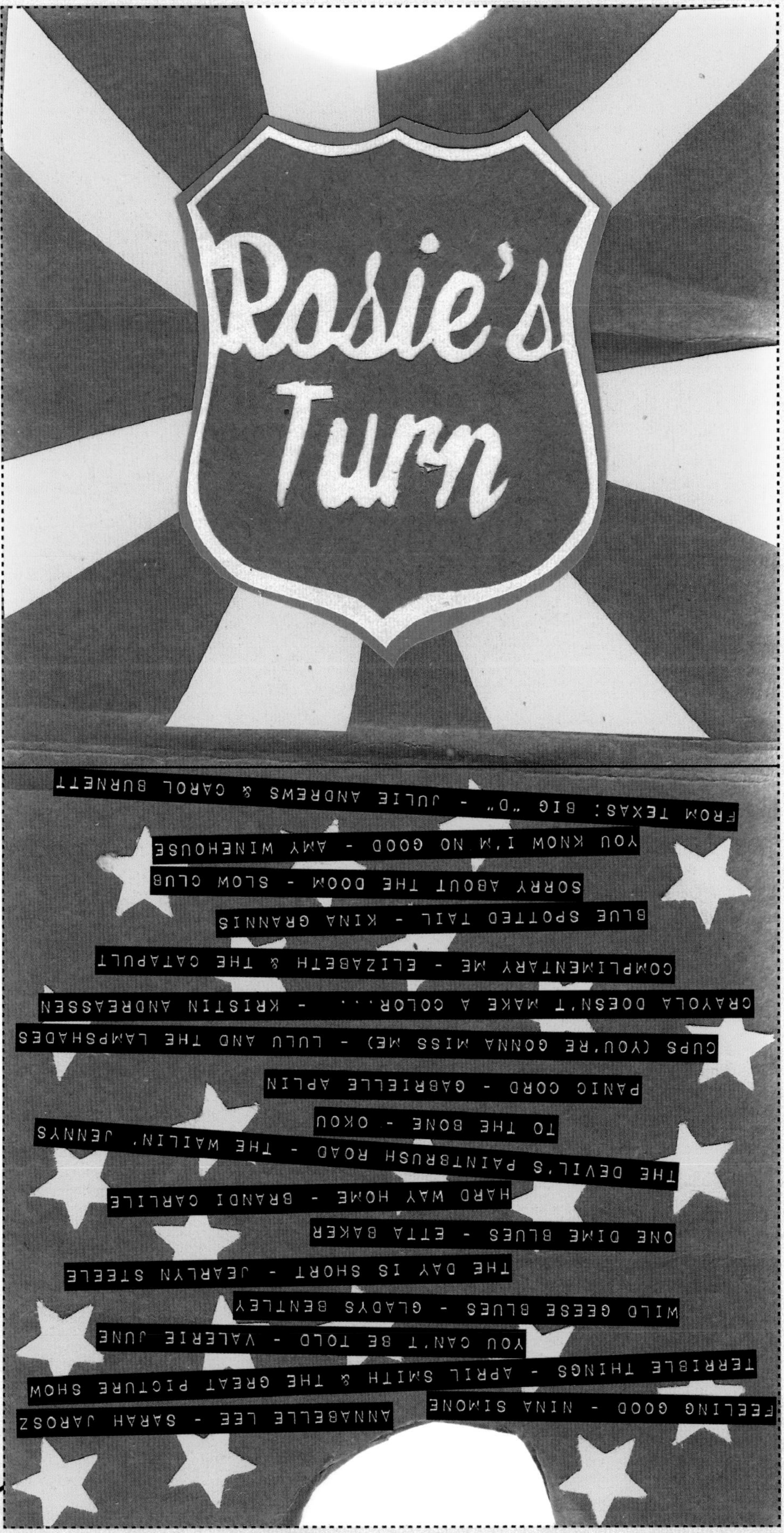
Rosie's Turn
FEELING GOOD - NINA SIMONE
ANNABELLE LEE - SARAH JAROSZ
TERRIBLE THINGS - APRIL SMITH & THE GREAT PICTURE SHOW
YOU CAN'T BE TOLD - VALERIE JUNE
WILD GEESE BLUES - GLADYS BENTLEY
THE DAY IS SHORT - JEARLYN STEELE
ONE DIME BLUES - ETTA BAKER
HARD WAY HOME - BRANDI CARLILE
THE DEVIL'S PAINTBRUSH ROAD - THE WAILIN' JENNYS
TO THE BONE - OKOU
PANIC CORD - GABRIELLE APLIN
CUPS (YOU'RE GONNA MISS ME) - LULU AND THE LAMPSHADES
CRAYOLA DOESN'T MAKE A COLOR... - KRISTIN ANDREASSEN
COMPLIMENTARY ME - ELIZABETH & THE CATAPULT
BLUE SPOTTED TAIL - KINA GRANNIS
SORRY ABOUT THE DOOM - SLOW CLUB
YOU KNOW I'M NO GOOD - AMY WINEHOUSE
FROM TEXAS: BIG "D" - JULIE ANDREWS & CAROL BURNETT

SKETCHBOOK

Lumberjanes "Literature" Program Field

CON-QUEST BADGE

"Divide and conquer, it actually works."

A Lumberjane will face many trials during her time at camp. It is through these trials that she grows and learns what kind of Lumberjane she truly is, but not all trials are meant for just one person. At camp there will be many obstacles and challenges that the Lumberjanes will face as a team. The teams could be divided by cabins or they may be divided by the counselor in charge of the group. In these groups the Lumberjane scout will learn what it means to work in a team, what it means to take charge and what it means to step back to let the best equipped person lead them to success. It is their grace under pressure that will get the Lumberjane scout through any of these trials.

These competitions will challenge Lumberjanes against their peers. In practice for the *Con-Quest* badge, a Lumberjane will understand what it means to win and lose. She will learn from her mistakes and gain experience

to better ensure her team's success. She will bring out the best of everyone she works with. She will be cordial and work with grace as she continues this challenge. If she wins then she will not belittle the efforts of the other team, she will understand that keeping a level head after success can be more challenging than keeping it during the competition.

To obtain the *Con-Quest* badge, the Lumberjanes must display their knowledge in the art of war. They must be able to look at their challenge and understand what it takes to win. They must be able to understand what they are capable of and the capabilities of their fellow scouts. The team that earns the *Con-Quest* is not necessarily the winner of the challenge but the team that was able to utilize its members and the tools at their disposal to the best of their abilities.

During the first summer that the Lumberjane attends

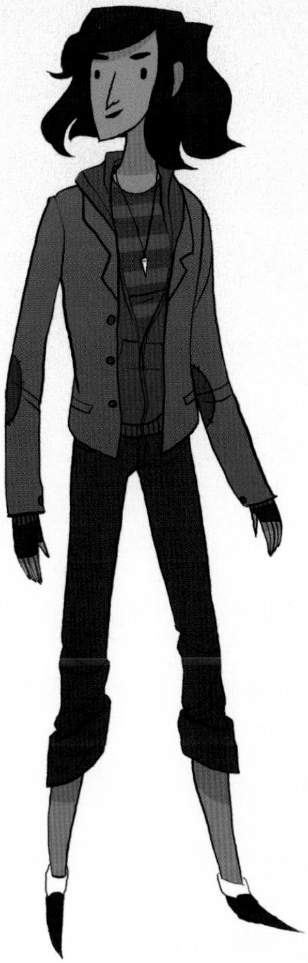

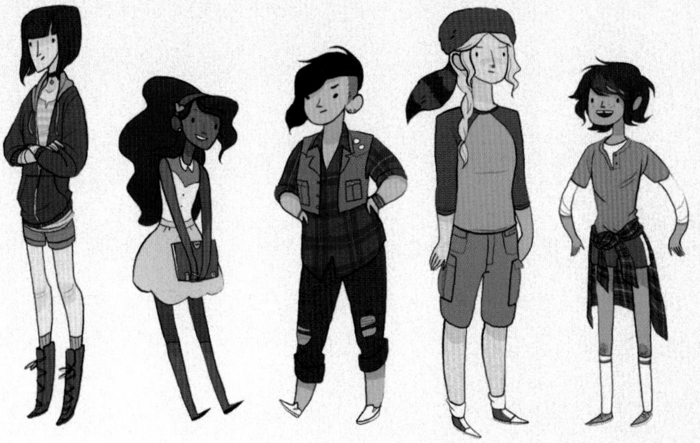

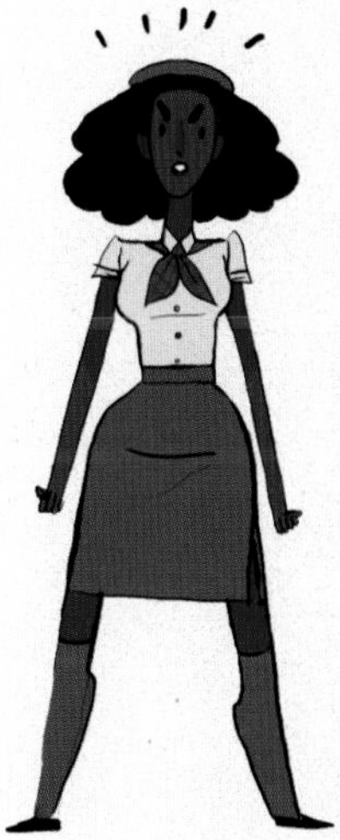

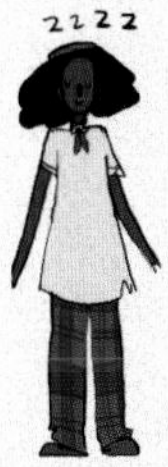
zzzz

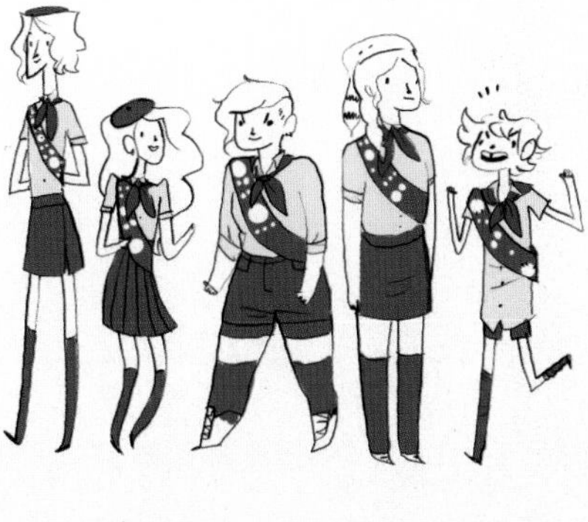

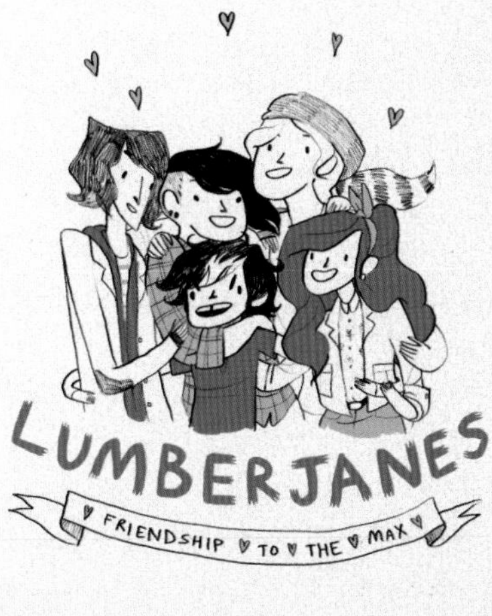
LUMBERJANES
FRIENDSHIP TO THE MAX

ILLUSTRATIONS BY NOELLE STEVENSON

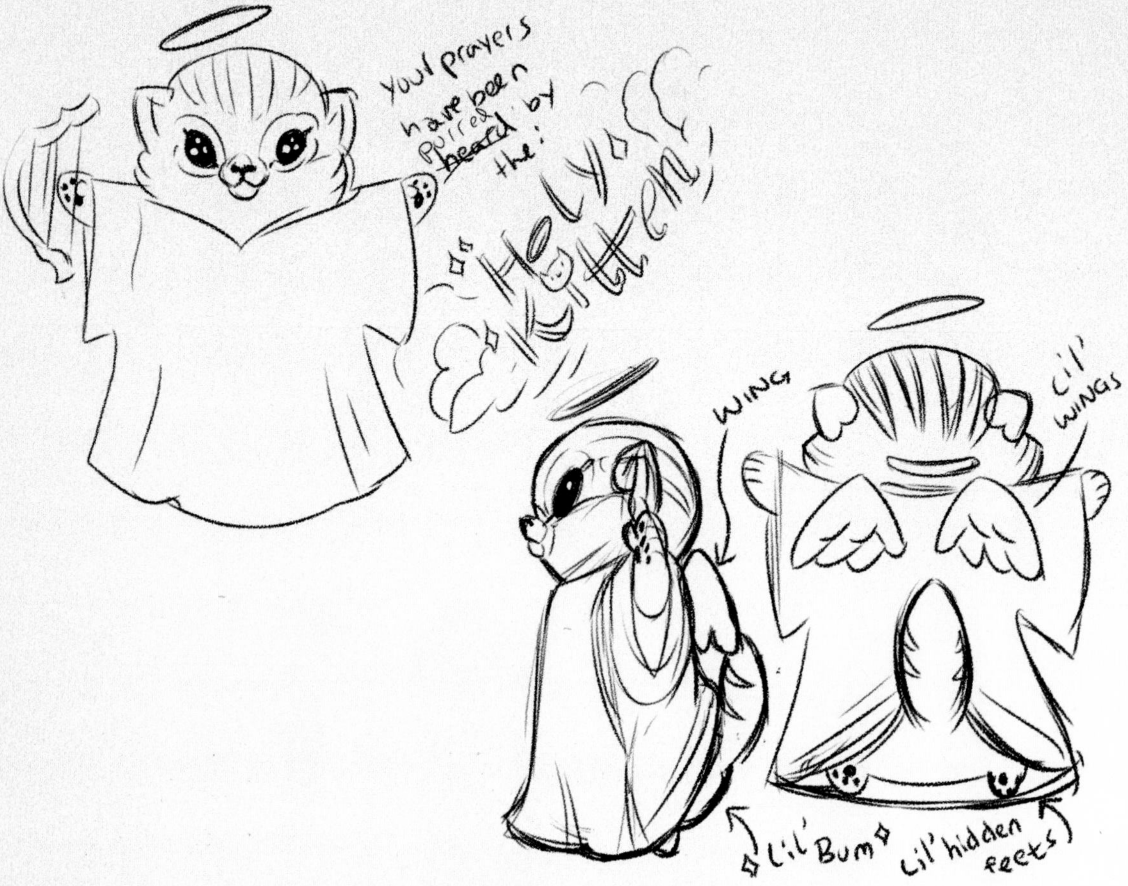

your prayers have been purred ~~heard~~ by the:
Holy Kitten!
WING
Lil' WINGS
Lil' Bum
Lil' hidden feets

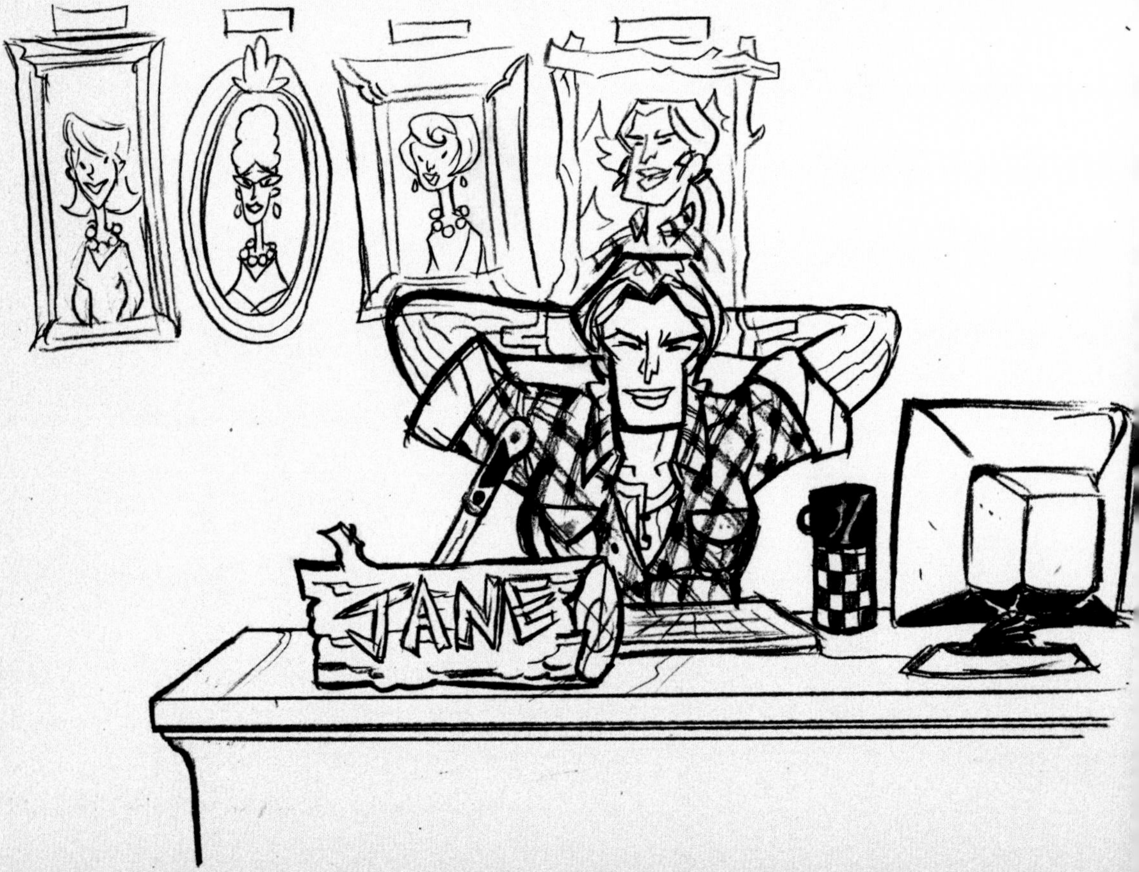

JANE

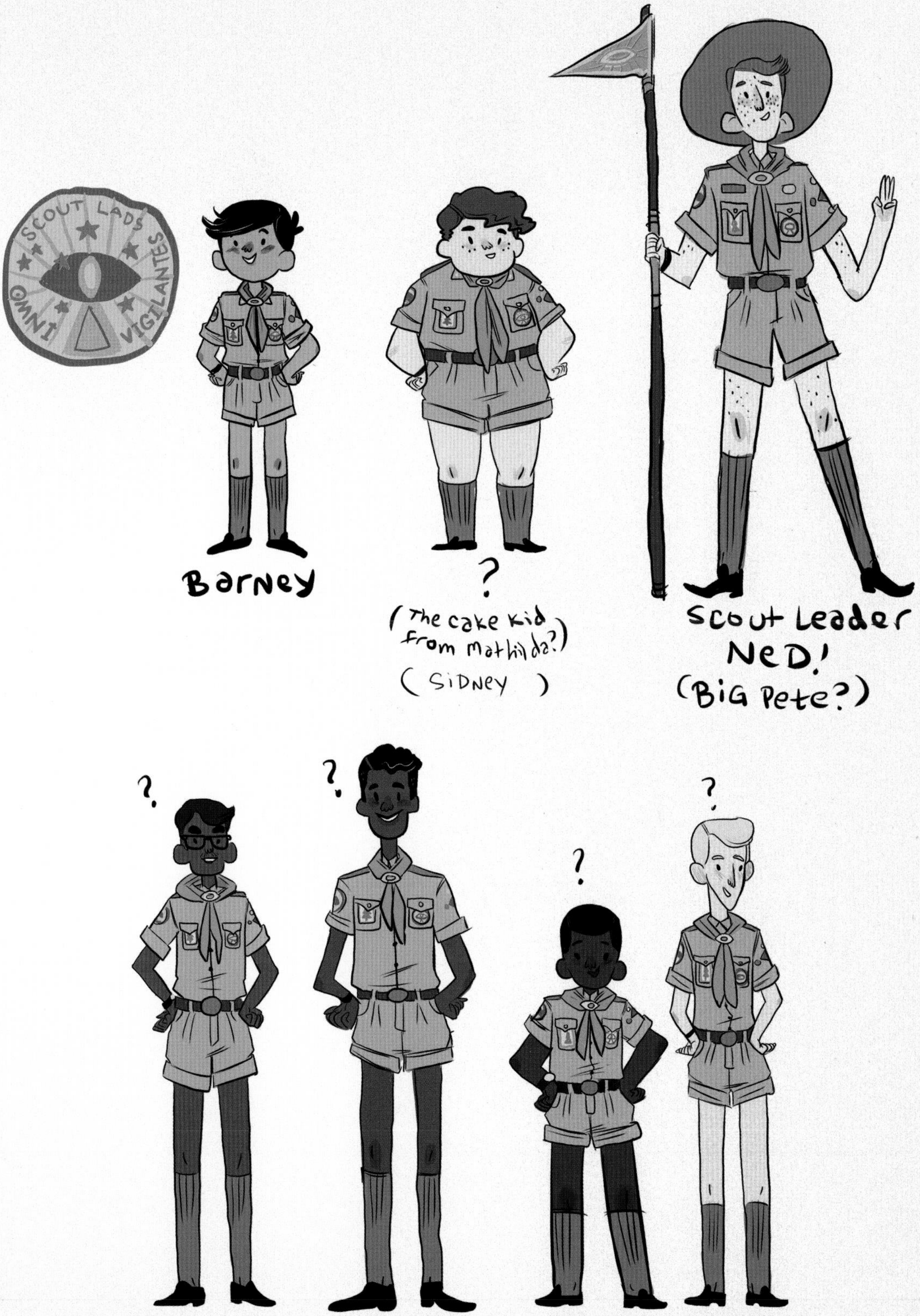
SCOUT LADS
OMNI VIGILANTES
Barney
?
(The cake kid from mathilda?)
(SIDNEY)
Scout Leader NED!
(BIG Pete?)
?
?
?
?
(Vic)
(Gus)
(Dale)
(Shawn)

ILLUSTRATIONS BY BROOKLYN ALLEN

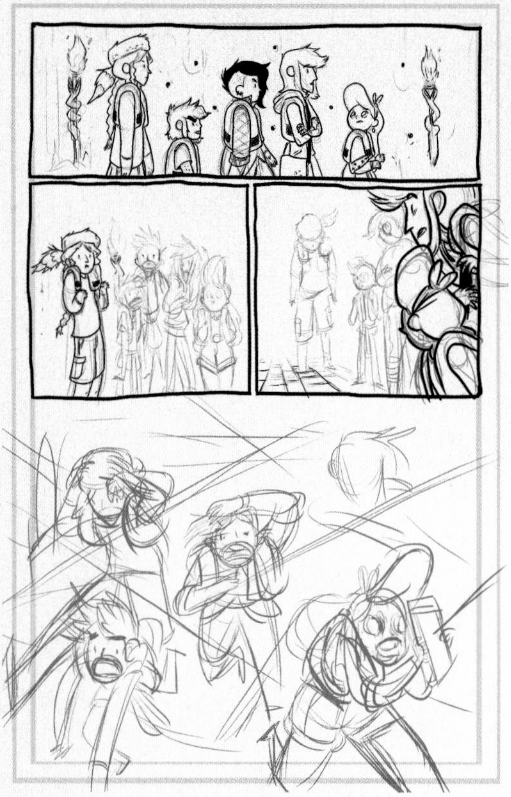

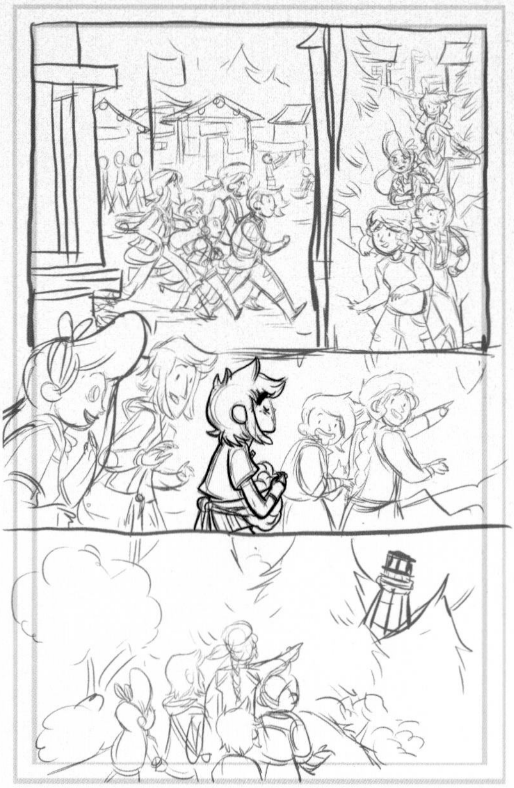

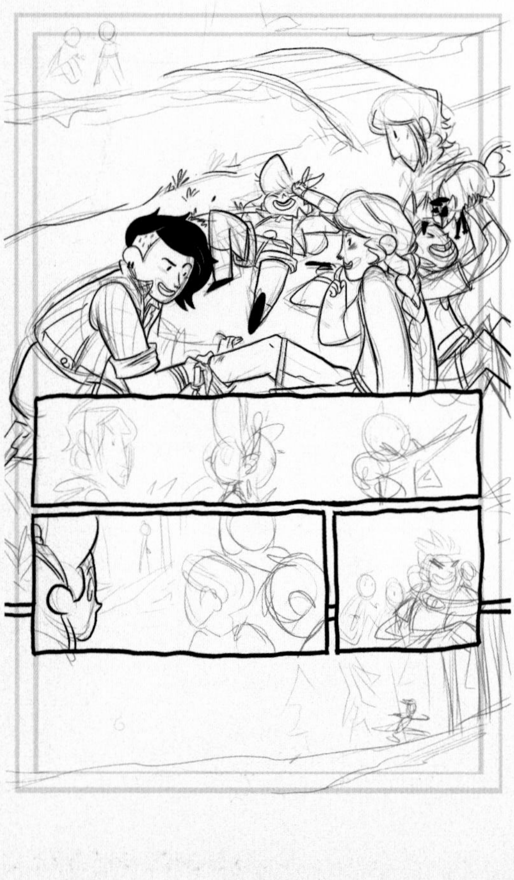

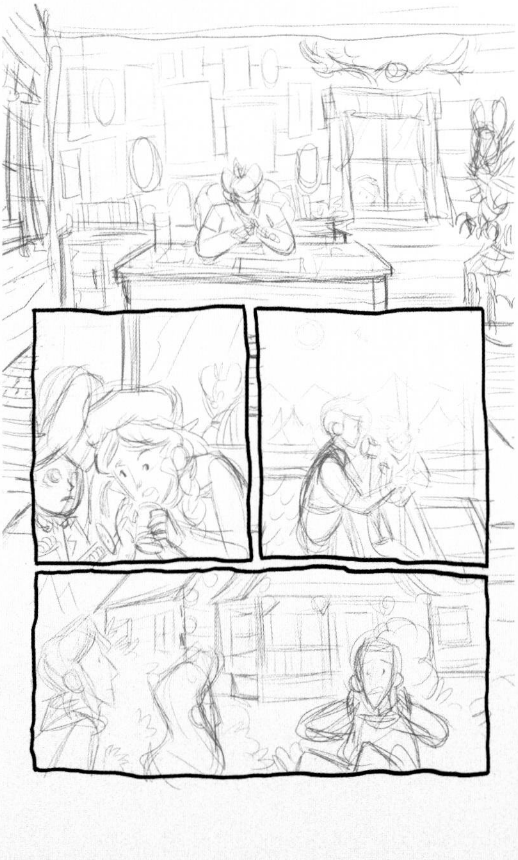

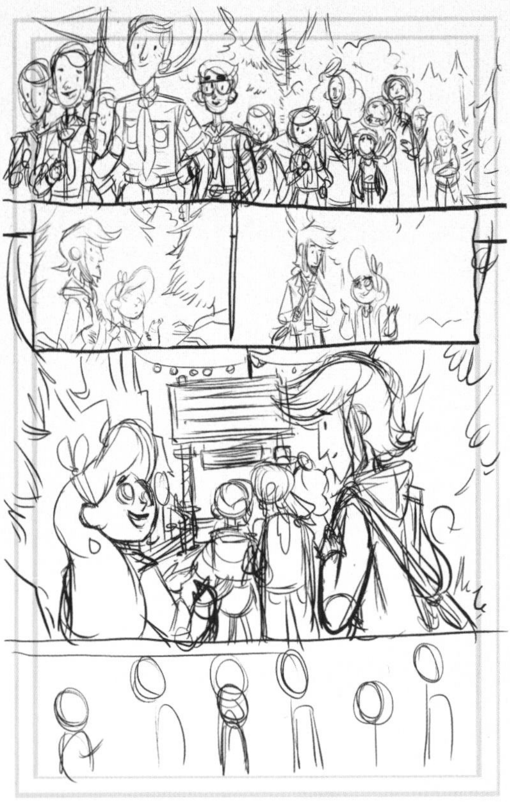

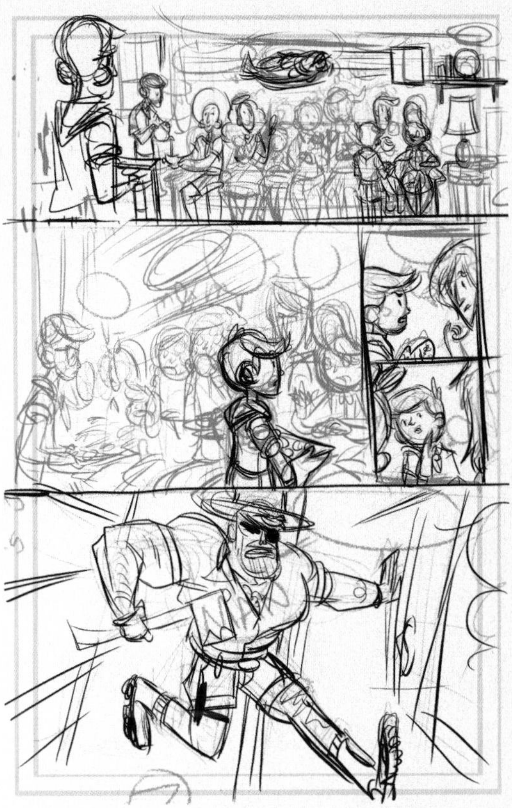

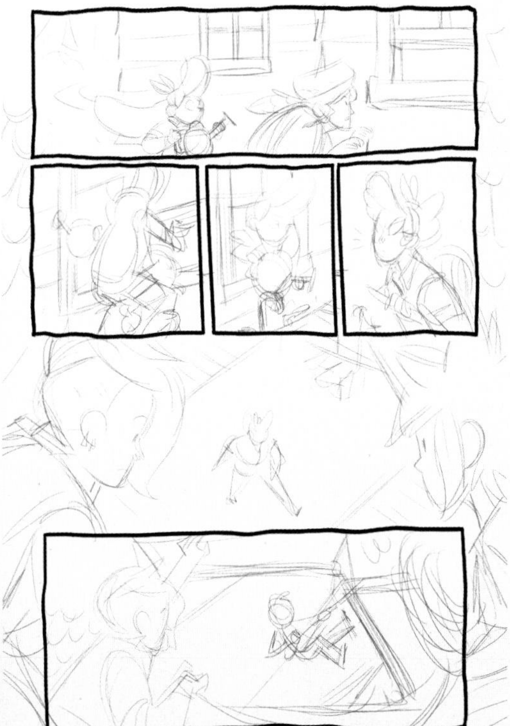

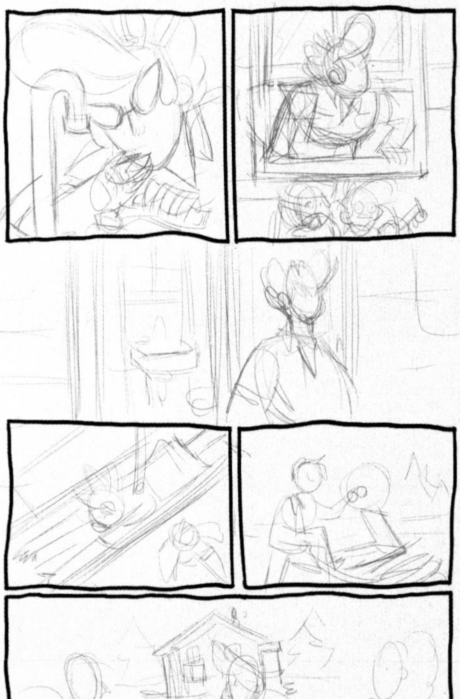

PENCILS BY **BROOKLYN ALLEN**

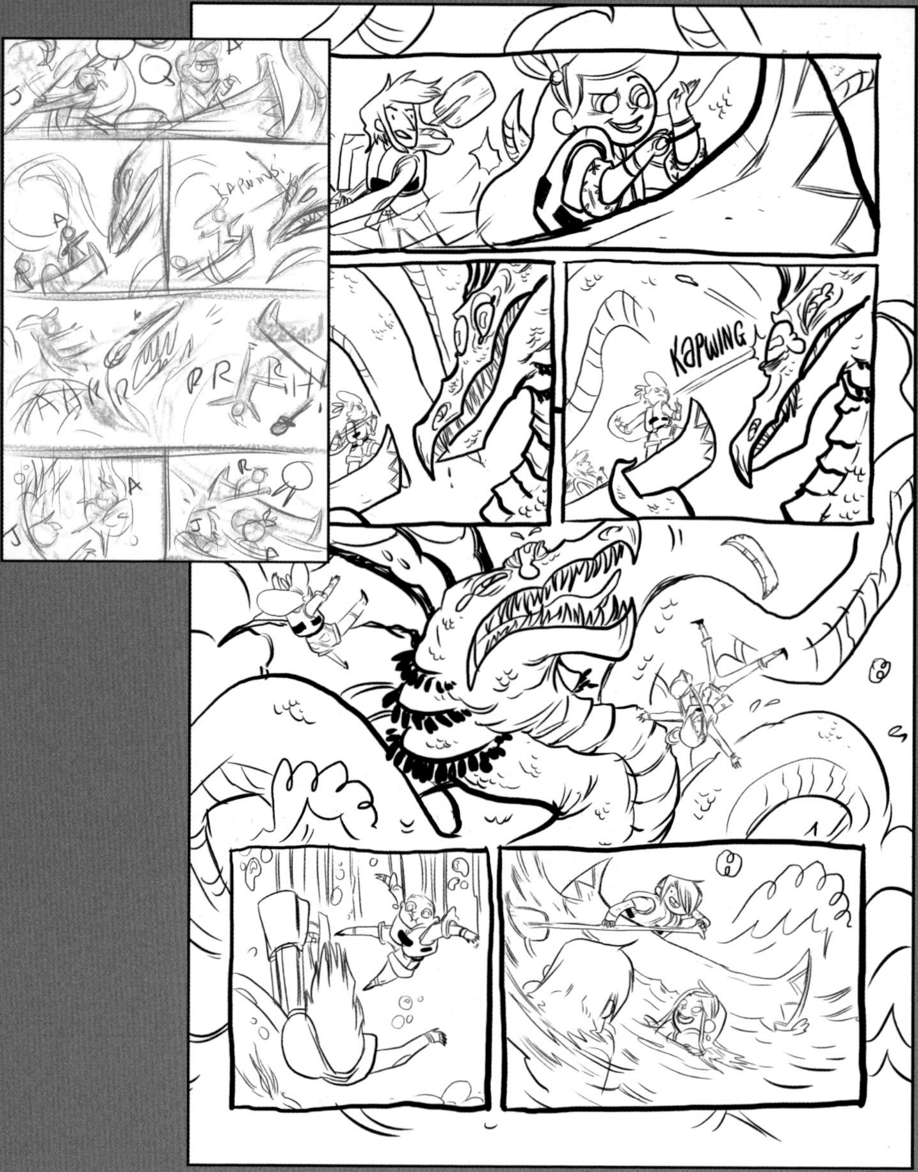
KAPWING

Issue Two, Page Twelve

PANEL ONE: Jo bravely wields her paddle, but April pulls one of her hairbands off her wrist.

APRIL: It's scrunchie time!

JO: This isn't the time for a new hairdo, April!

PANEL TWO: April stands up in the boat with one foot perched on the bow, directly in front of the monster's giant eyeball (one of the non-golden ones), and pulls back the scrunchie like a slingshot. All the action seems to freeze except for this movement. (Think Captain Jack Sparrow's "hello beastie" moment, http://www.youtube.com/watch?v=hDdSvpGNtWk)

PANEL THREE: Almost the exact same panel as the last one, April ka-pwings the scrunchie directly into the beast's eyeball.

SFX: KA-PWING

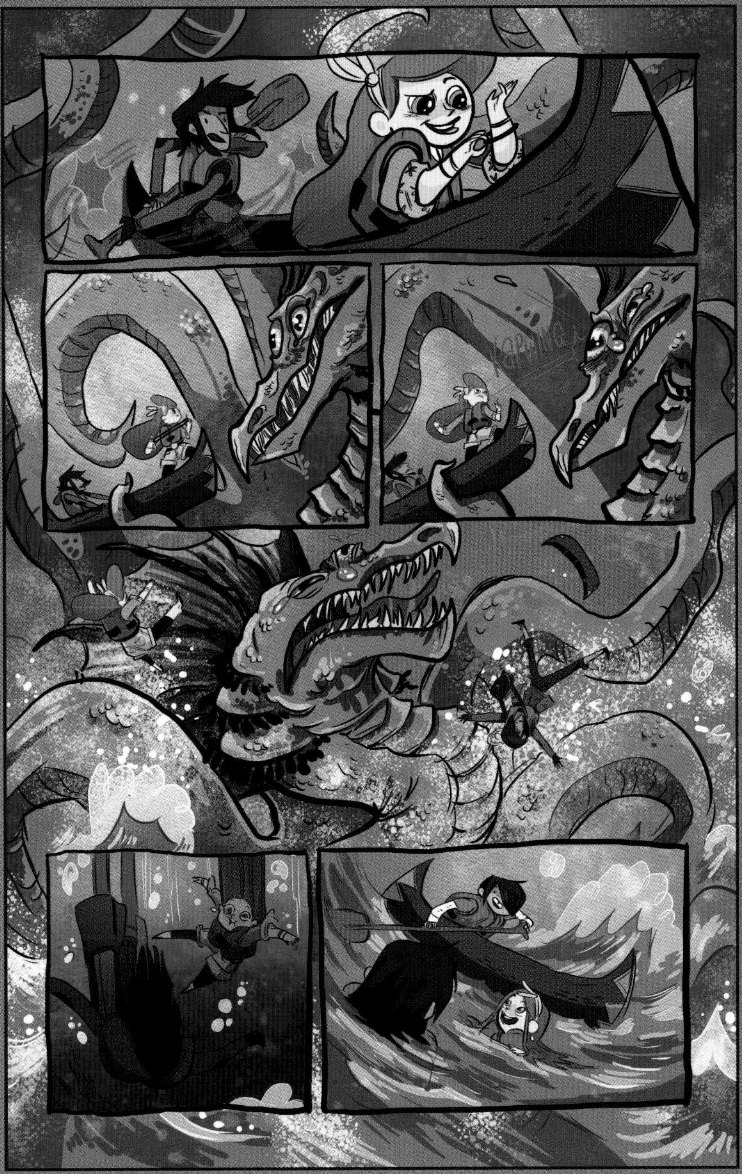

PANEL FOUR: Howling in pain, the beast waves the canoe around, spilling Jo and April out of it. They fall, screaming.

BEASTIE: GRRRAAAAAAAUGH

JO and APRIL: YIPE

PANEL FIVE: Jo and April splash into the water below.

PANEL SIX: Ripley paddles up in the other canoe as Jo and April surface again.

RIPLEY: You guys!

JO and APRIL: RIPLEY!

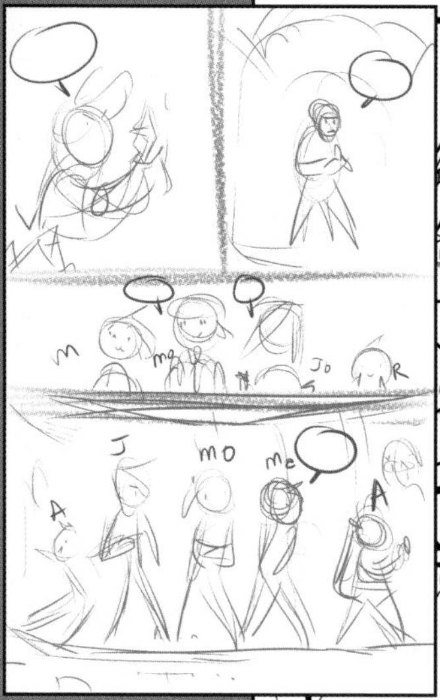

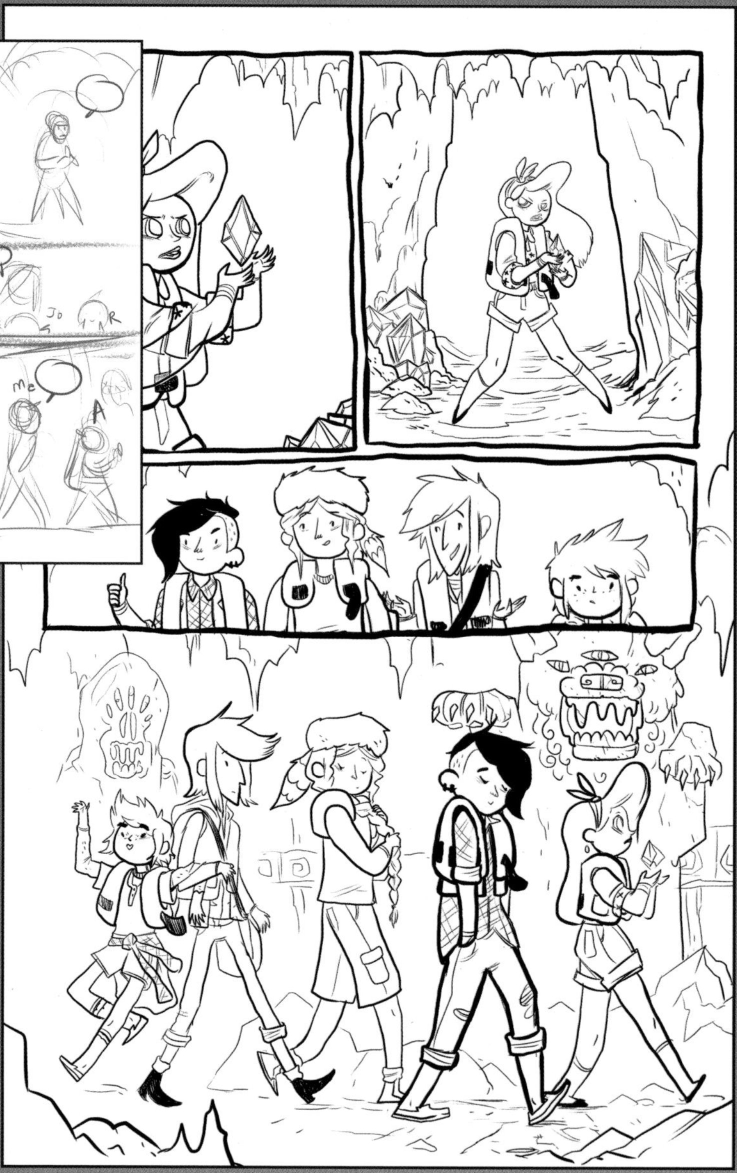

Issue Three, Page Two

PANEL ONE: April breaks of a chunk of crystal and holds it all mystical-like.

APRIL: Then there's only one thing to do!

PANEL TWO: The crystal lights her face up all weird from below like a kid telling a ghost story. She stands illuminated in front of the black mouth of the tunnel, turning back to look at the other girls.

APRIL: We must go…FURTHER IN TO THE TUNNEL!!

PANEL THREE: Reaction shot of the other girls, largely unperturbed and unimpressed by April's bravery - none of them are afraid of the dark.

JO: Yeah, okay.

MOLLY: Works for me.

PANEL FOUR: Long, in profile - they troop down the tunnel, following the light of April's crystal. The light just barely catches the frightening details of ominous-looking statues. Ripley is trying to wander off to examine them more closely, but Jo pulls her along by her arm. Mal and Molly are sort of pointedly avoiding contact out of shyness.

MAL: I'm pretty sure there wasn't a chapter in the Lumberjanes handbook about stuff like this.

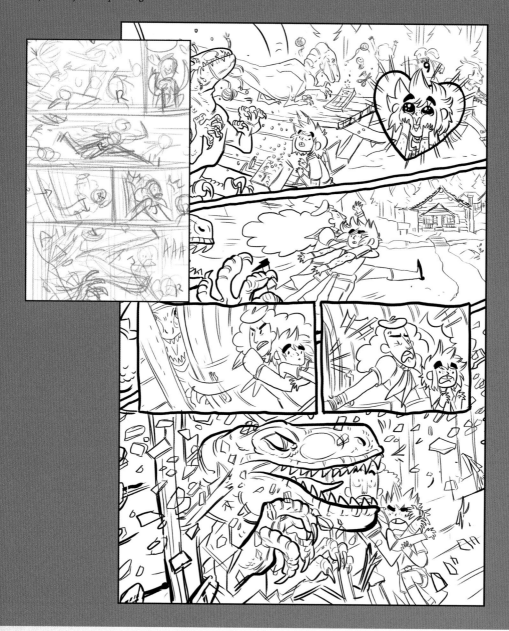

Issue Five Page Ten

PANEL ONE: The girls scatter as the dinosaurs descend on the picnic tables.

PANEL TWO: Ripley looks delighted.

    RIPLEY: DINOSAURS!

PANEL THREE: Jen runs past, scooping Ripley up and taking her with her as she goes.

PANEL FOUR: Jen and Ripley duck into a nearby cabin, slamming the door in the raptor's faces.

PANEL FIVE: Jen braces the door as the raptors batter it from outside.

PANEL SIX: CRASH. The window right next to the door is smashed as a raptor forces his its head in.

    SFX: KSSSSHHHH

    JEN AND RIPLEY: AHHHHHHHHH!

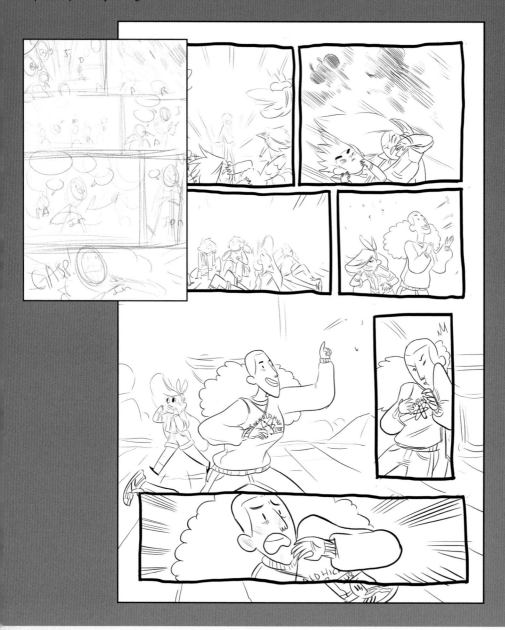

Issue Seven, Page Twenty One

PANLE ONE: A blinding light fills the room glows from the pedestal, so bright that all that's visible is Jo's very very vague silhouette in its center. The other girls turn to see what's going on - the bugs pause their attack.

PANEL TWO: The light washes over them - the girls shield their eyes and each other. The bugs dissolve in the light, turning to ash.

PANEL THREE: The light fades, leaving the room WAY dimmer than before. The only light source is an odd greenish glow. The girls are still shielding their eyes, huddling together. Ripley, who is being shielded by Jen, is the first to peek.

     RIPLEY: Ooh!

PANEL FOUR: They stand up and find themselves in the middle of a floating holographic star chart. Think the map from Treasure Planet. The glowing stars supply the only light - the floor has also lit up with a giant map of the Lumberjanes camp and the surrounding woods (including the boys camp, the lighthouse, the fishing shack, etc)

JEN: It's beautiful!

APRIL: (dazed, getting slowly to her feet) …Jo?

PANEL FIVE: Jen is getting super excited by the star chart. She starts running around identifying the different constellations in the foreground - she's looking up and pointing at the stars so she's not looking where she's going. Behind her, April is still looking for Jo.

JEN: There's Ursa Major…Andromeda…Orion…Sirus! This is amazing!!

APRIL: Jo! Has anyone seen Jo?

PANEL SIX: OOF. Jen runs into a slab of rock.

PANEL SEVEN: She steps back to see what she bumped into - and gasps. We see only her face - her expression is one of pure horror.

EPIC!

WHO DOES THEIR HAIR?

The Lumberjane uniform sh... meeting...

...ne.
...od
...ble
...s.

...or make it ...able at the trading post.

...tivities. The ... is a right red neckerchief is w... neath ...uld be tied in a simple friendship knot. ...lack or brown and should have flat ...a straight inner line. Stockings or ...nd in color with the shoes or with ...aces, bracelets, or other jewelry do not ...erjane uniform.

...WEAR THE UNIFORM

...rm demands first of all that the ...ood condition—clean and well ...t is the right length for your own ...e belt is adjusted to your waist, ...kings are in keeping with the ...ur posture and carry yourself ...gnity and grace. If the beret is removed indoors, ...e sure that your hair is neat and kept in place with an insonspicuous clip or ribbon. When you wear a Lumberjane uniform you are identified as a member of this organization and you should be doubly careful to conduct yourself in a way that will show everyone that courtesy and thoughtfullness are part of being a Lumberjane. People are likely to judge a whole nation by the selfishness of a few individuals, to criticize a whole family because of the misconduct of one member, and to feel unkindly toward and organization because of the

TRIUMPH!

The ...
helps ...
in a g...
active ...
another...
future...
in or...
Lumberjane p...
Penniquiqul Thistle Cr...
Types, but most Lumberjanes w... ...ey can either buy the uniform, or make it the... ...rom materials available at the trading post.

ORIGINAL PITCH

Lumberjanes "Literature" Program Field

DO THE WRITE THING BADGE

"The is pen might be mightier than the sword, but steel still hurts."

Words are a powerful tool that every Lumberjane scout will have to familiarize herself with. They carry weight, they explain things that actions can barely surmise and they open communication even during the hardest of times. Tone, nuance, and specific wording are all important no matter what language is being used. Lumberjanes will earn their *Do the Write Thing* badge as they fulfill several tasks during their time at camp. These projects will be supervised by the resident wordsmith and it will be up to that counselor to determine if a task is truly finished.

Writing is something for which, while it has its basic rules, everyone will have their own personal style. Some Lumberjanes embrace the world of fantasy, building detailed worlds that have their own words and understanding of what it means to be have a role in the world. Others stick to facts, they have the information that they've collected in their years and will put those facts to the page. There will be Lumberjane scouts who will be a little bit of both, and others who will push the envelope and discover that they are something else altogether.

To obtain the *Do the Write Thing* badge a Lumberjane must use her words, and her passion for the world around her to create something new. It has to be something that will challenge her fellow scouts as well as push the reader in a positive direction. They need to find the words that inspire. The importance of this badge is to recognize the power that words can carry, to know the feelings they can cause and the actions that will occur because of them. Words are not meant to be hidden, they are meant to be read, spoken, and shouted across the camp but every young lady at this camp will be prepared for the consequences if the words are used incorrectly.

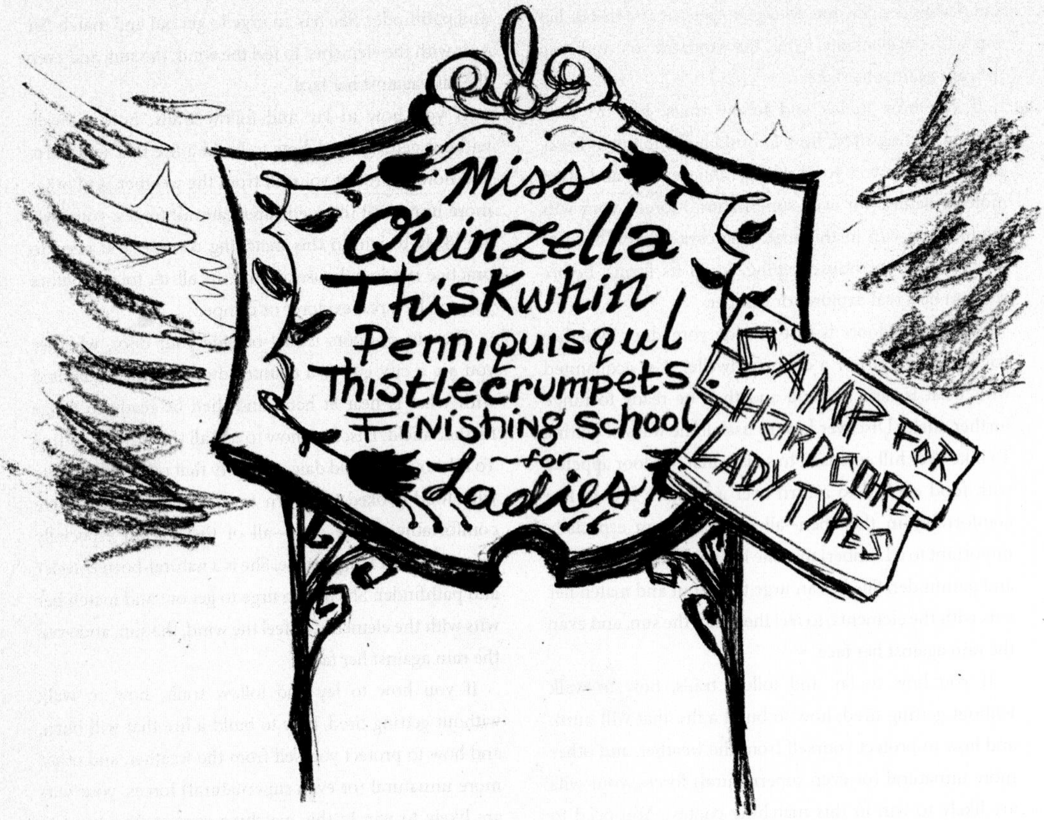
Miss
Quinzella
Thiskwhin
Penniquisqul
Thistlecrumpets
Finishing School
~for~
Ladies!
CAMP FOR
HARDCORE
LADYTYPES

THE CAMP

When Lumberjane Scouts Jo, April, Mal, Molly, and Ripley arrived at Miss Quinzella Thistlecrumpet's Camp for Hardcore Ladytypes, the girls expected a summer full of camping, hiking, and other rugged, outdoorsy activities that would improve the heck outta their character. What they didn't expect was a never-ending supply of supernatural forest critters, a troubled yeti, a genteel camp for gentle young boys, a mysterious Canadian on a moose, and a cosmic secret that could put the whole world in danger!

Their fear of the camp being shutdown (and consequently being separated from one another) forces them to keep their misadventures a secret from Lumbermaster Rosie, who not only secretly knows about the surrounding woods' dangers, but is also surreptitiously training her camp full of promising young ladies to defeat the "Big Bad" once and for all. Through friendship, bravery, creativity, and a never-ending supply of snappy dialogue, the girls learn to work together to beat up and outsmart every threat as they try to live out the camp motto: FRIENDSHIP TO THE MAX!

Buffy the Vampire Slayer meets *Twin Peaks* in this character-driven adventure series for girls of all ages (but especially 9-14).

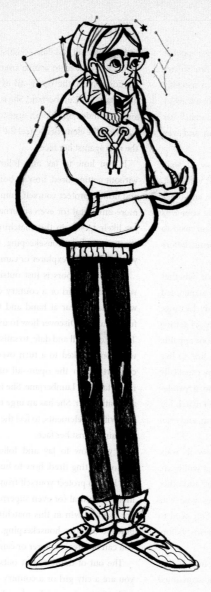

JO

If the group had a leader, it would be Jo, a clever world-class cynic with a strong sense of right and wrong. She would object to being called "bookish" because it's not hardcore enough, but she reads a lot and seems to innately know things, especially concerning her hobby of stargazing. Her encyclopedic knowledge of the Lumberjane Handbook would make Hermione jealous, which is a skill that frequently comes in handy, especially when the gang needs a clever loophole to get themselves out of trouble or in identifying a new mysterious creature. She is also the first person to seriously question the larger purpose of the Lumberjanes. Steadfast and unflappable, the girls never have to doubt her conviction and confidence. That being said, Jo is certainly the most stubborn of the group, and her loyalty to her convictions sometimes come in conflict with her loyalty to her friends. She is very self-aware.

Jo is tall and lanky but naturally graceful in the way that middle schoolers who grow too fast adapt to be. She wears a lot of hoodies because her overbearing father wanted to make sure his daughter would have the means to stay warm on cold camp nights. Right before camp, she cut her hair to about chin-length, which annoys her to no end because she can't tie it back in a ponytail so it is constantly in her face. Her nails have been painted black since third grade, and she chews them when she's thinking, much to the annoyance of her best friend April.

ART BY BROOKLYN ALLEN

APRIL

On the face of it, April seems like the least likely of the group to attend a camp for hardcore lady-types because she is the most traditionally feminine: She keeps her hair long, she puts a substantial amount of effort into her appearance, and she spends a lot of time thinking about boys. However, April's femininity is part of what her friends love about her. She experiences emotions very deeply and has no trouble empathizing with anyone. She is willing to put others' interests before her own, writes "roses are red"-style poetry, keeps a diary (which is important), and has a shameless and unironic love of teen pop music and a borderline obsession with a particular magazine in the vein of Rookie. Her girlishness is not seen as impractical or as a nuisance; it's just who she is. She also has a reputation for being melodramatic and a little self-serving, and over time, she learns to be more daring in dangerous situations.

Because she is the youngest (by six months), April hasn't quite hit her growth spurt yet. The embodiment of "small but mighty," she is by far the most physically strong of the group, even though she doesn't look it. While she prefers to keep her long hair down, she keeps two or three brightly colored hair ties around her wrist at all times to tie it back. If she had her way, April would always dress like the floral-pattern-loving hipster girls who run her favorite magazine. While she isn't very self-aware sometimes, April has a strong sense of self that is reflected in how she dresses. Strength in femininity. Word up. Next!

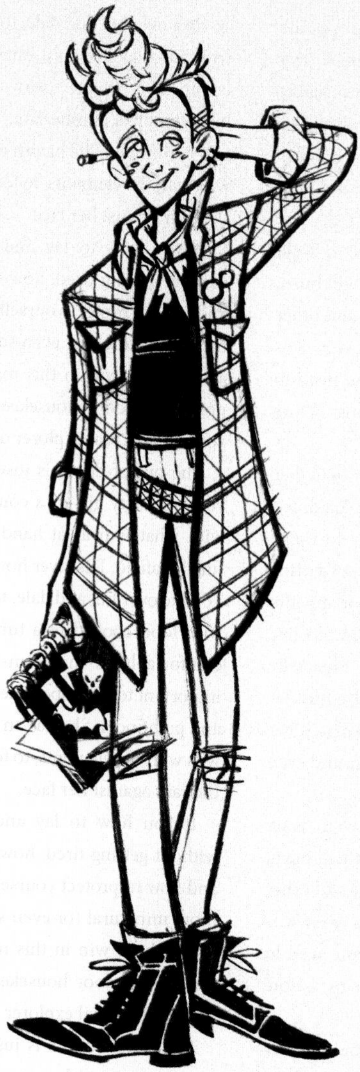

MAL

Mal is the definition of neutral-good. She takes her time to form opinions and is usually the first to notice how small details contribute to the larger picture. She gets excited by good ideas and feeds off of Ripley's high energy, although she would much rather direct her energy into forming a well-thought-out idea than jumping into action. She is the group's planner; her even-handedness and broad thinking allow her to be the most innovative and creative. Because she puts a lot of thought into her decisions, she can be short-tempered when she is frustrated or contradicted. She works really well with Jo most of the time, but the friends often disagree about methodology because of Mal's ends-justifying-the-means mentality.

After getting a straight-up alternative lifestyle haircut (buzzed sides with a tangle of curly hair on top of her head), she came out as a lesbian to her parents, who freaked out and shipped her off to camp until they could figure out how to deal with their daughter's budding lesbianism. Mal is most comfortable in her favorite, threadbare plaid shirts and holey jeans. She imagines herself as the most punk person she has ever met in her life. She likes to draw. Her fear of spiders is matched only by her giant, obvious, mutual crush on Molly.

ART BY **BROOKLYN ALLEN**

MOLLY

The bravest and most competitive, Molly is less concerned with planning and more concerned with executing plans. It is very important to her that she prove herself to be the most hardcore, and the gang knows that they can count on her to be a positive, forward-moving force on the team. She is the best at dealing with animals, and almost by extension, adults. Molly is skeptical of the motives of anyone who isn't in her trustworthy inner circle, probably because she understands the world to be a wicked, every-Lumberjane-for-herself place. Her parents think she's at musical theater camp. They don't really understand her. Despite her sometimes frosty and abrasive exterior, Molly is actually really soft and caring when she feels the situation allows for it. She has an obvious sweet spot for Mal, and when she's relaxed and with her friends, she's a goofy weirdo.

When it comes down to it, she's just a fighter, and it can takes a lot of effort for her to let her guard down.

Molly's hair is always pulled back in a neat, Hunger Games-style braid. Her cargo pants have Mary Poppins-style pockets; she is constantly pulling important items from their infinite depths. She wears a coonskin cap that is revealed to be an actual, possibly rabid raccoon named Bubbles who lives on her head full-time. Her friends accept this without question. She is Mal's perfect match. She's also best friends with April, sidenote.

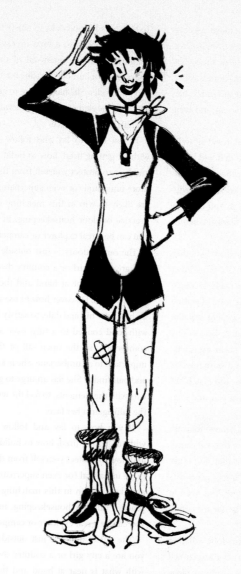

RIPLEY

Ripley is everybody's best friend. Extremely high-energy and passionate about everything, Ripley is the kind of person who does things and is, as a result, always the first one to attack a problem head-on, usually without thinking about the consequences of her actions. She is ferociously loyal to her friends, almost to the point of blindness. She likes to keep the mood light and believes that the happiness of her friends is more important than anything else. Unfortunately, she seems to have the worst luck out of everyone. When things don't go well, she can be moody and impulsive. She has a sense of who she is that is unusually strong for a twelve year old, and she thinks she's pretty awesome. (She is right.) She likes to dance and is really good at playing the drums for a twelve year old. She would never admit it, but horror movies scare the crap out of her. She is Jo's next-door neighbor outside of camp.

On the first day of camp, she snuck into the craft cabin and used a pair of safety scissors to cut her own hair, resulting in a choppy, adorably uneven mess of dark hair. She prefers t-shirts and things she can move around in over any other style of clothing. She is generally unkempt but not unhygienic. (I am thinking a t-shirt over a long-sleeved shirt for her? Because that's what I wore when I was 12. Or possibly a Henley because she's so flippin' rad.)

ART BY **BROOKLYN ALLEN**

LUMBERJANES FIELD MANUAL

ABOUT THE AUTHORS

SHANNON WATTERS

GRACE ELLIS

Shannon Watters is an editor lady by day and the co-creator of *Lumberjanes*...also by day. She helped guide KaBOOM!—BOOM! Studios' all-ages imprint—to commercial and critical success, and oversees BOOM! Box, an experimental imprint created "for the love of it." She has a great love for all things indie and comics, which is something she's been passionate about since growing up in the wilds of Arizona. When she's not working on comics she can be found watching classic films and enjoying the local cuisine.

Grace Ellis is a writer most well-known for co-creating *Lumberjanes* and her work on the site *Autostraddle*. She is from Ohio and when she's not coming up with amazing mix-tapes, she's most likely enjoying camp stories, the zoo and The Great American Musical, of which she's sure to write a hit one someday.

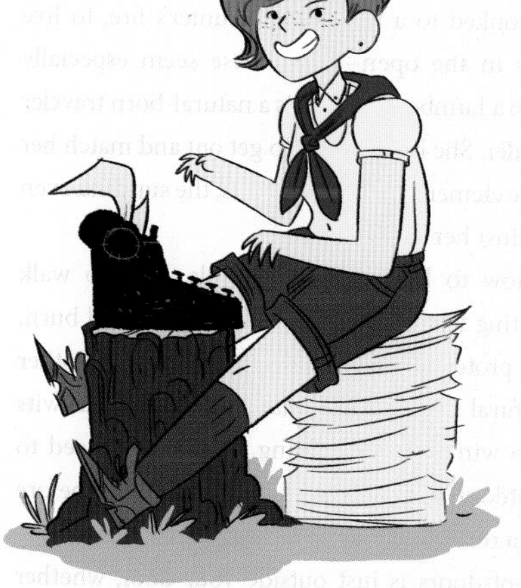

NOELLE STEVENSON

Noelle Stevenson is the *New York Times* bestselling author of *Nimona*, has won two Eisner Awards for the series she co-created; *Lumberjanes*. She's been nominated for Harvey Awards, and was awarded the Slate Cartoonist Studio Prize for Best Web Comic in 2012 for *Nimona*. A graduate of the Maryland Institute College of Art, Noelle is a writer on Disney's *Wander Over Yonder*, she has written for Marvel and DC Comics. She lives in Los Angeles. In her spare time she can be found drawing superheroes and talking about bad TV. **www.gingerhaze.com**

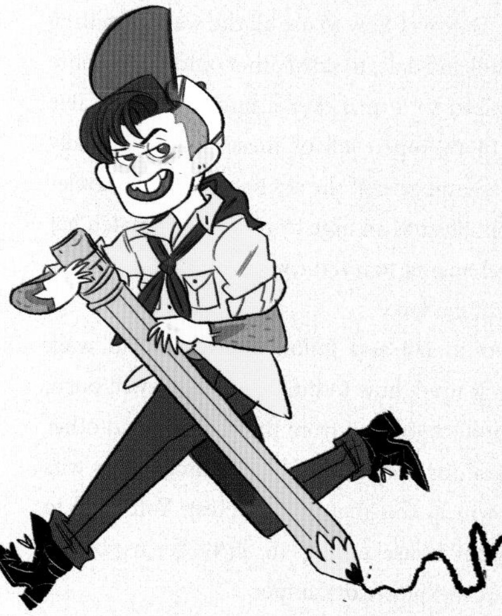

BROOKLYN ALLEN

Brooklyn Allen is the co-creator and the artist for *Lumberjanes* and when they are not drawing then they will most likely be found with a saw in their hand making something rad. Currently residing in the "for lovers" state of Virginia, they spend most of their time working on comics with their not-so-helpful assistant Linus...their dog.

ART BY BROOKLYN ALLEN

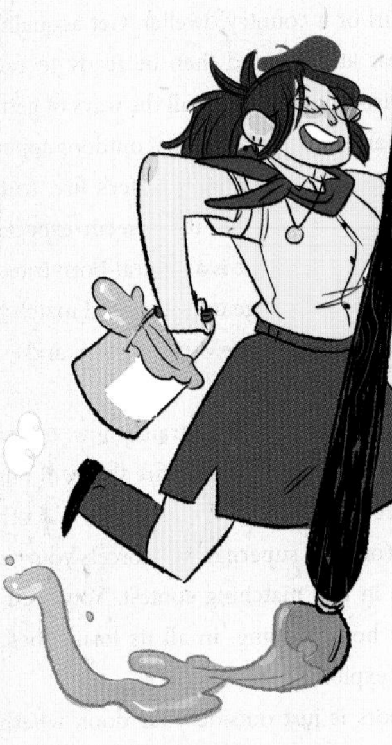

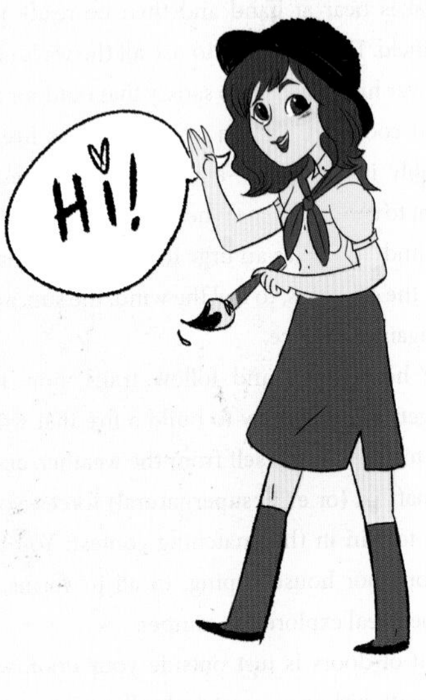
Hi!

MAARTA LAIHO

Maarta Laiho is a freelance illustrator, who was somehow tricked into becoming a successful comics colorist. She is a graduate from the Savannah College of Art and Design with a BFA in Sequential Art. She, with her chinchilla sidekick, currently resides in the woods of midcoast Maine. In her spare time she draws her webcomic *Madwillow*, hoards houseplants, and complains about the snow.
www.PencilCat.net

AUBREY AIESE

Aubrey Aiese is an illustrator and hand letterer from Brooklyn, New York currently living in Portland, Oregon. She loves eating ice cream, making comics, and playing with her super cute corgi pups, Ace and Penny. She's been nominated for a Harvey Award for her outstanding lettering on *Lumberjanes* and continues to find new ways to challenge herself in her field. She also puts an absurd amount of ketchup on her french fries.
www.lettersfromaubrey.com

ART BY BROOKLYN ALLEN

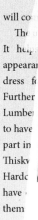

will co...

The ...

It hel...
appearan...
dress f...
Further...
Lumber...
to have...
part in...
Thiskv...
Hardc...
have ...
them ...

ALRIGHT!

...THE UNIFORM

...should be worn at camp
...events when Lumberjanes
...n may also be worn at other
...ions. It should be worn as a
...the uniform dress with
...rrect shoes, and stocking or

...out grows her uniform or
...ter Lumberjane.
...a she has
...her
...her

The ...
yellow, short sl...
emb...
the w...
choose...
slacks, ...
made o...
out-of-d...
green bere...
the colla...
Shoes ma...
heels, roun...
socks shou...
the uniform. Ne...es, bracelets, or other jewelry do ...
belong with a Lumberjane uniform.

WHY DO I ALWAYS DROP THE FLASHLIGHT?

HOW TO WEAR THE UNIFORM

To look well in a uniform demands first of ...
uniform be kept in good condition—clean ...
pressed. See that the skirt is the right length for your own
height and build, that the belt is adjusted to your waist,
that your shoes and stockings are in keeping with the
uniform, that you watch your posture and carry yourself
with dignity and grace. If the beret is removed indoors,
be sure that your hair is neat and kept in place with an
insconspicuous clip or ribbon. When you wear a
Lumberjane uniform you are identified as a member of
this organization and you should be doubly careful to
conduct yourself in a way that will show everyone that
courtesy and thoughtfullness are part of being a
Lumberjane. People are likely to judge a whole nation by
the selfishness of a few individuals, to criticize a whole
family because of the misconduct of one member, and to
feel unkindly toward and organization because of the

DUCKFACE PRACTICE

The unifor...
helps to cre...
in a group. ...
active life th...
another bond...
future, and pr...
in order to b...
Lumberjane pr...
Penniquiqul Thi... ...ore Lady
Types, but m... ...es will wish to have one. They
can either b...e uniform, or make it themselves from
materials available at the trading post.

LJ

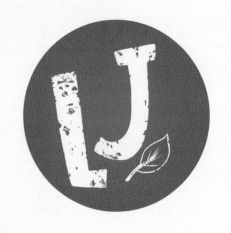